EVERYMAN'S LIBRARY

EVERYMAN,
I WILL GO WITH THEE,
AND BE THY GUIDE,
IN THY MOST NEED
TO GO BY THY SIDE

LEO TOLSTOY

Collected Shorter Fiction

Translated from the Russian by Louise and Aylmer Maude
and Nigel J. Cooper
with an Introduction by John Bayley

VOLUME 2

EVERYMAN'S LIBRARY

243

First included in Everyman's Library, 2001
Translations in the Appendix © Nigel J. Cooper, 2001
Introduction, Bibliography and Chronology © Everyman
Publishers plc, 2001
Typography by Peter B. Willberg

ISBN 1-85715-758-3

A CIP catalogue record for this book is available from the
British Library

Published by Everyman Publishers plc,
Gloucester Mansions, 140A Shaftesbury Avenue,
London WC2H 8HD

Distributed by Random House (UK) Ltd.,
20 Vauxhall Bridge Road, London SW1V 2SA

CONTENTS OF VOLUME 2

John Bayley's introduction and Tolstoy's shorter fiction 1852–84 appear in Volume 1.

A SPARK NEGLECTED
BURNS THE HOUSE

'THEN came Peter, and said to him, Lord, how oft shall my brother sin against me, and I forgive him? until seven times? Jesus saith unto him, I say not unto thee, Until seven times; but, Until seventy times seven. Therefore is the kingdom of heaven likened unto a certain king, which would make a reckoning with his servants. And when he had begun to reckon, one was brought unto him, which owed him ten thousand talents. But forasmuch as he had not wherewith to pay, his lord commanded him to be sold, and his wife, and children, and all that he had, and payment to be made. The servant therefore fell down and worshipped him, saying, Lord, have patience with me, and I will pay thee all. And the lord of that servant, being moved with compassion, released him, and forgave him the debt. But that servant went out, and found one of his fellow-servants, which owed him a hundred pence; and he laid hold on him, and took him by the throat, saying, Pay what thou owest. So his fellow-servant fell down and besought him, saying, Have patience with me, and I will pay thee. And he would not: but went and cast him into prison, till he should pay that which was due. So when his fellow-servants saw what was done, they were exceeding sorry, and came and told unto their lord all that was done. Then his lord called him unto him, and saith to him, Thou wicked servant, I forgave thee all that debt, because thou besoughtest me: shouldest not thou also have had mercy on thy fellow-servant, even as I had mercy on thee? And his lord was wroth, and delivered him to the tormentors, till he should pay all that was due. So shall also my heavenly Father do unto you, if ye forgive not every one his brother from your hearts.' – *Matt.* xviii. 21–35.

THERE once lived in a village a peasant named Iván Stcher-bakóf. He was comfortably off, in the prime of life, the best worker in the village, and had three sons all able to work. The eldest was married, the second about to marry, and the third was a big lad who could mind the horses and was already beginning to plough. Iván's wife was an able and thrifty woman, and they were fortunate in having a quiet, hard-working daughter-in-law. There was nothing to prevent Iván and his family from living happily. They had only one idle mouth to feed; that was Iván's old father, who suffered from asthma and had been lying ill on the top of the brick oven for seven years. Iván had all he needed: three horses and a colt, a cow with a calf, and fifteen sheep. The women made all the clothing for the family, besides helping in the fields, and the men tilled the land. They always had grain enough of their own to last over beyond the next harvest, and sold enough oats to pay the taxes and meet their other needs. So Iván and his children might have lived quite comfortably had it not been for a feud between him and his next-door neighbour, Limping Gabriel, the son of Gordéy Ivánof.

As long as old Gordéy was alive and Iván's father was still able to manage the household, the peasants lived as neighbours should. If the women of either house happened to want a sieve or a tub, or the men required a sack, or if a cart-wheel got broken and could not be mended at once, they used to send to the other house, and helped each other in neighbourly fashion. When a calf strayed into the neighbour's threshing-ground they would just drive it out, and only say, 'Don't let it get in again; our grain is lying there.' And such things as locking up

5

the barns and outhouses, hiding things from one another, or backbiting were never thought of in those days.

That was in the fathers' time. When the sons came to be at the head of the families, everything changed.

It all began about a trifle.

Iván's daughter-in-law had a hen that began laying rather early in the season, and she started collecting its eggs for Easter. Every day she went to the cart-shed, and found an egg in the cart; but one day the hen, probably frightened by the children, flew across the fence into the neighbour's yard and laid its egg there. The woman heard the cackling, but said to herself: 'I have no time now; I must tidy up for Sunday. I'll fetch the egg later on.' In the evening she went to the cart, but found no egg there. She went and asked her mother-in-law and brother-in-law whether they had taken the egg. 'No,' they had not; but her youngest brother-in-law, Tarás, said: 'Your Biddy laid its egg in the neighbour's yard. It was there she was cackling, and she flew back across the fence from there.'

The woman went and looked at the hen. There she was on the perch with the other birds, her eyes just closing ready to go to sleep. The woman wished she could have asked the hen and got an answer from her.

Then she went to the neighbour's, and Gabriel's mother came out to meet her.

'What do you want, young woman?'

'Why, Granny, you see, my hen flew across this morning. Did she not lay an egg here?'

'We never saw anything of it. The Lord be thanked, our own hens started laying long ago. We collect our own eggs and have no need of other people's! And we don't go looking for eggs in other people's yards, lass!'

The young woman was offended, and said more than she should have done. Her neighbour answered back with interest, and the women began abusing each other. Iván's wife, who had been to fetch water, happening to pass just then, joined in too. Gabriel's wife rushed out, and began reproaching the young woman with things that had really happened and with other things that never had happened at all. Then a general uproar commenced, all shouting at once, trying to get out two words at a time, and not choice words either.

'You're this!' and 'You're that!' 'You're a thief!' and 'You're a slut!' and 'You're starving your old father-in-law to death!' and 'You're a good-for-nothing!' and so on.

'And you've made a hole in the sieve I lent you, you jade! And it's our yoke you're carrying your pails on – you just give back our yoke!'

Then they caught hold of the yoke, and spilt the water, snatched off one another's shawls, and began fighting. Gabriel, returning from the fields, stopped to take his wife's part. Out rushed Iván and his son, and joined in with the rest. Iván was a strong fellow; he scattered the whole lot of them, and pulled a handful of hair out of Gabriel's beard. People came to see what was the matter, and the fighters were separated with difficulty.

That was how it all began.

Gabriel wrapped the hair torn from his beard in a paper, and went to the District Court to have the law on Iván. 'I didn't grow my beard,' said he, 'for pockmarked Iván to pull it out!' And his wife went bragging to the neighbours, saying they'd have Iván condemned and sent to Siberia. And so the feud grew.

The old man, from where he lay on the top of the oven, tried from the very first to persuade them to make peace, but they would not listen. He told them, 'It's a stupid thing you are after, children, picking quarrels about such a paltry matter. Just think! The whole thing began about an egg. The children may have taken it – well, what matter? What's the value of one egg? God sends enough for all! And suppose your neighbour did say an unkind word – put it right; show her how to say a better one! If there *has* been a fight – well, such things will happen; we're all sinners, but make it up, and let there be an end of it! If you nurse your anger it will be worse for you yourselves.'

But the younger folk would not listen to the old man. They thought his words were mere senseless dotage. Iván would not humble himself before his neighbour.

'I never pulled his beard,' he said, 'he pulled the hair out himself. But his son has burst all the fastenings on my shirt, and torn it. . . . Look at it!'

And Iván also went to law. They were tried by the Justice of the Peace and by the District Court. While all this was going on, the coupling-pin of Gabriel's cart disappeared. Gabriel's womenfolk accused Iván's son of having taken it. They said: 'We saw him in the night go past our window, towards the cart; and a neighbour says he saw him at the pub, offering the pin to the landlord.'

So they went to law about that. And at home not a day passed without a quarrel or even a fight. The children, too, abused one another, having learnt to do so from their elders; and when the women happened to meet by the river-side, where they went to rinse the clothes, their arms did not do as much wringing as their tongues did nagging, and every word was a bad one.

At first the peasants only slandered one another; but afterwards they began in real earnest to snatch anything that lay handy, and the children followed their example. Life became harder and harder for them. Iván Stcherbakóf and Limping Gabriel kept suing one another at the Village Assembly, and at the District Court, and before the Justice of the Peace, until all the judges were tired of them. Now Gabriel got Iván fined or imprisoned; then Iván did as much to Gabriel; and the more they spited each other the angrier they grew – like dogs that attack one another and get more and more furious the longer they fight. You strike one dog from behind, and it thinks it's the other dog biting him, and gets still fiercer. So these peasants: they went to law, and one or other of them was fined or locked up, but that only made them more and more angry with each other. 'Wait a bit,' they said, 'and I'll make you pay for it.' And so it went on for six years. Only the old man lying on the top of the oven kept telling them again and again: 'Children, what are you doing? Stop all this paying back; keep to your work, and don't bear malice – it will be better for you. The more you bear malice, the worse it will be.'

But they would not listen to him.

In the seventh year, at a wedding, Iván's daughter-in-law held Gabriel up to shame, accusing him of having been caught horse-stealing. Gabriel was tipsy, and, unable to contain his anger, gave the woman such a blow that she was laid up for a week; and she was pregnant at the time. Iván was delighted. He went to the magistrate to lodge a complaint. 'Now I'll get rid of my neighbour! He won't escape imprisonment, or exile to Siberia.' But Iván's wish was not fulfilled. The magistrate dismissed the case. The woman was examined, but she was up and about and showed no sign of any injury. Then Iván went to the Justice of the Peace, but he referred the business to the District Court. Iván bestirred himself: treated the clerk and the Elder of the District Court to a gallon of liquor, and got Gabriel condemned to be flogged. The sentence was read out to Gabriel by the clerk: 'The Court decrees that the peasant Gabriel Gordéyef shall receive twenty lashes with a birch rod at the District Court.'

Iván too heard the sentence read, and looked at Gabriel to see how he would take it. Gabriel grew as pale as a sheet, and turned round and went out into the passage. Iván followed him, meaning to see to the horse, and he overheard Gabriel say, 'Very well! He will have my back flogged: that will make it burn; but something of his may burn worse than that!'

Hearing these words, Iván at once went back into the Court, and said: 'Upright judges! He threatens to set my house on fire! Listen: he said it in the presence of witnesses!'

Gabriel was recalled. 'Is it true that you said this?'

'I haven't said anything. Flog me, since you have the power. It seems that I alone am to suffer, and all for being in the right, while he is allowed to do as he likes.'

Gabriel wished to say something more, but his lips and his cheeks quivered, and he turned towards the wall. Even the officials were frightened by his looks. 'He may do some mischief to himself or to his neighbour,' thought they.

Then the old Judge said: 'Look here, my men; you'd better be reasonable and make it up. Was it right of you, friend Gabriel, to strike a pregnant woman? It was lucky it passed off so well, but think what might have happened! Was it right? You had better confess and beg his pardon, and he will forgive you, and we will alter the sentence.'

The clerk heard these words, and remarked: 'That's impossible under Statute 117. An agreement between the parties not having been arrived at, a decision of the Court has been pronounced and must be executed.'

But the Judge would not listen to the clerk.

'Keep your tongue still, my friend,' said he. 'The first of all laws is to obey God, Who loves peace.' And the Judge began again to persuade the peasants, but could not succeed. Gabriel would not listen to him.

'I shall be fifty next year,' said he, 'and have a married son, and have never been flogged in my life, and now that pockmarked Iván has had me condemned to be flogged, and am I to go and ask his forgiveness? No; I've borne enough. . . . Iván shall have cause to remember me!'

Again Gabriel's voice quivered, and he could say no more, but turned round and went out.

It was seven miles from the Court to the village, and it was getting late when Iván reached home. He unharnessed his horse, put it up for the night, and entered the cottage. No one was there. The women had already gone to drive the cattle in, and the young fellows were not yet back from the fields. Iván went in, and sat down, thinking. He remembered how Gabriel had listened to the sentence, and how pale he had become, and how he had turned to the wall; and Iván's heart grew heavy. He thought how he himself would feel if he were sentenced, and he pitied Gabriel. Then he heard his old father up on the oven cough, and saw him sit up, lower his legs, and scramble down. The old man dragged himself slowly to a seat, and sat down. He was quite tired out with the exertion, and coughed a long time till he had cleared his throat. Then, leaning against the table, he said: 'Well, has he been condemned?'

'Yes, to twenty strokes with the rods,' answered Iván.

The old man shook his head.

'A bad business,' said he. 'You are doing wrong, Iván! Ah!

it's very bad – not for him so much as for yourself!... Well, they'll flog him: but will that do you any good?'

'He'll not do it again,' said Iván.

'What is it he'll not do again? What has he done worse than you?'

'Why, think of the harm he has done me!' said Iván. 'He nearly killed my wife, and now he's threatening to burn us up. Am I to thank him for it?'

The old man sighed, and said: 'You go about the wide world, Iván, while I am lying on the oven all these years, so you think you see everything, and that I see nothing.... Ah, lad! It's you that don't see; malice blinds you. Others' sins are before your eyes, but your own are behind your back. "He's acted badly!" What a thing to say! If he were the only one to act badly, how could strife exist? Is strife among men ever bred by one alone? Strife is always between two. His badness you see, but your own you don't. If he were bad, but you were good, there would be no strife. Who pulled the hair out of his beard? Who spoilt his haystack? Who dragged him to the law court? Yet you put it all on him! You live a bad life yourself, that's what is wrong! It's not the way I used to live, lad, and it's not the way I taught you. Is that the way his old father and I used to live? How did we live? Why, as neighbours should! If he happened to run out of flour, one of the women would come across: "Uncle Trol, we want some flour." "Go to the barn, dear," I'd say: "take what you need." If he'd no one to take his horses to pasture, "Go, Iván," I'd say, "and look after his horses." And if I was short of anything, I'd go to him. "Uncle Gordéy," I'd say, "I want so-and-so!" "Take it, Uncle Trol!" That's how it was between us, and we had an easy time of it. But now?... That soldier the other day was telling us about the fight at Plevna.[1] Why, there's war between you worse than at Plevna! Is that living?... What a sin it is! You are a man, and master of the house; it's you who will have to answer. What are you teaching the women and the children?

1 A town in Bulgaria, the scene of fierce and prolonged fighting between the Turks and the Russians in the war of 1877.

To snarl and snap? Why, the other day your Taráska – that greenhorn – was swearing at neighbour Irena, calling her names; and his mother listened and laughed. Is that right? It is you will have to answer. Think of your soul. Is this all as it should be? You throw a word at me, and I give you two in return; you give me a blow, and I give you two. No, lad! Christ, when He walked on earth, taught us fools something very different. . . . If you get a hard word from anyone, keep silent, and his own conscience will accuse him. That is what our Lord taught. If you get a slap, turn the other cheek. "Here, beat me, if that's what I deserve!" And his own conscience will rebuke him. He will soften, and will listen to you. That's the way He taught us, not to be proud! . . . Why don't you speak? Isn't it as I say?'

Iván sat silent and listened.

The old man coughed, and having with difficulty cleared his throat, began again: 'You think Christ taught us wrong? Why, it's all for our own good. Just think of your earthly life; are you better off, or worse, since this Plevna began among you? Just reckon up what you've spent on all this law business – what the driving backwards and forwards and your food on the way have cost you! What fine fellows your sons have grown; you might live and get on well; but now your means are lessening. And why? All because of this folly; because of your pride. You ought to be ploughing with your lads, and do the sowing yourself; but the fiend carries you off to the judge, or to some pettifogger or other. The ploughing is not done in time, nor the sowing, and mother earth can't bear properly. Why did the oats fail this year? When did you sow them? When you came back from town! And what did you gain? A burden for your own shoulders. . . . Eh, lad, think of your own business! Work with your boys in the field and at home, and if someone offends you, forgive him, as God wishes you to. Then life will be easy, and your heart will always be light.'

Iván remained silent.

'Iván, my boy, hear your old father! Go and harness the roan, and go at once to the Government office; put an end to all this affair there; and in the morning go and make it up with

Gabriel in God's name, and invite him to your house for to-morrow's holiday' (it was the eve of the Virgin's Nativity). 'Have tea ready, and get a bottle of vodka and put an end to this wicked business, so that there should not be any more of it in future, and tell the women and children to do the same.'

Iván sighed, and thought, 'What he says is true,' and his heart grew lighter. Only he did not know how, now, to begin to put matters right.

But again the old man began, as if he had guessed what was in Iván's mind.

'Go, Iván, don't put it off! Put out the fire before it spreads, or it will be too late.'

The old man was going to say more, but before he could do so the women came in, chattering like magpies. The news that Gabriel was sentenced to be flogged, and of his threat to set fire to the house, had already reached them. They had heard all about it and added to it something of their own, and had again had a row, in the pasture, with the women of Gabriel's household. They began telling how Gabriel's daughter-in-law threatened a fresh action: Gabriel had got the right side of the examining magistrate, who would now turn the whole affair upside down; and the schoolmaster was writing out another petition, to the Tsar himself this time, about Iván; and everything was in the petition – all about the coupling-pin and the kitchen-garden – so that half of Iván's homestead would be theirs soon. Iván heard what they were saying, and his heart grew cold again, and he gave up the thought of making peace with Gabriel.

In a farmstead there is always plenty for the master to do. Iván did not stop to talk to the women, but went out to the threshing-floor and to the barn. By the time he had tidied up there, the sun had set and the young fellows had returned from the field. They had been ploughing the field for the winter crops with two horses. Iván met them, questioned them about their work, helped to put everything in its place, set a torn horse-collar aside to be mended, and was going to put away some stakes under the barn, but it had grown quite dusk, so he decided to leave them where they were till next day. Then he gave the cattle their food, opened the gate, let out the horses Tarás was to take to pasture for the night, and again closed the gate and barred it. 'Now,' thought he, 'I'll have my supper, and then to bed.' He took the horse-collar and entered the hut. By this time he had forgotten about Gabriel and about what his old father had been saying to him. But, just as he took hold of the door-handle to enter the passage, he heard his neighbour on the other side of the fence cursing somebody in a hoarse voice: 'What the devil is he good for?' Gabriel was saying. 'He's only fit to be killed!' At these words all Iván's former bitterness towards his neighbour reawoke. He stood listening while Gabriel scolded, and, when he stopped, Iván went into the hut.

There was a light inside; his daughter-in-law sat spinning, his wife was getting supper ready, his eldest son was making straps for bark shoes, his second sat near the table with a book, and Tarás was getting ready to go out to pasture the horses for the night. Everything in the hut would have been pleasant and bright, but for that plague – a bad neighbour!

Iván entered, sullen and cross; threw the cat down from the bench, and scolded the women for putting the slop-pail in the wrong place. He felt despondent, and sat down, frowning, to mend the horse-collar. Gabriel's words kept ringing in his ears: his threat at the law court, and what he had just been shouting in a hoarse voice about someone who was 'only fit to be killed'.

His wife gave Tarás his supper, and, having eaten it, Tarás put on an old sheepskin and another coat, tied a sash round his waist, took some bread with him, and went out to the horses. His eldest brother was going to see him off, but Iván himself rose instead, and went out into the porch. It had grown quite dark outside, clouds had gathered, and the wind had risen. Iván went down the steps, helped his boy to mount, started the foal after him, and stood listening while Tarás rode down the village and was there joined by other lads with their horses. Iván waited until they were all out of hearing. As he stood there by the gate he could not get Gabriel's words out of his head: 'Mind that something of yours does not burn worse!'

'He is desperate,' thought Iván. 'Everything is dry, and it's windy weather besides. He'll come up at the back somewhere, set fire to something, and be off. He'll burn the place and escape scot free, the villain! . . . There now, if one could but catch him in the act, he'd not get off then!' And the thought fixed itself so firmly in his mind that he did not go up the steps, but went out into the street and round the corner. 'I'll just walk round the buildings; who can tell what he's after?' And Iván, stepping softly, passed out of the gate. As soon as he reached the corner, he looked round along the fence, and seemed to see something suddenly move at the opposite corner, as if someone had come out and disappeared again. Iván stopped, and stood quietly, listening and looking. Everything was still; only the leaves of the willows fluttered in the wind, and the straws of the thatch rustled. At first it seemed pitch dark, but, when his eyes had grown used to the darkness, he could see the far corner, and a plough that lay there, and the eaves. He looked a while, but saw no one.

'I suppose it was a mistake,' thought Iván; 'but still I will go round,' and Iván went stealthily along by the shed. Iván stepped so softly in his bark shoes that he did not hear his own footsteps. As he reached the far corner, something seemed to flare up for a moment near the plough and to vanish again. Iván felt as if struck to the heart; and he stopped. Hardly had he stopped, when something flared up more brightly in the same place, and he clearly saw a man with a cap on his head, crouching down, with his back towards him, lighting a bunch of straw he held in his hand. Iván's heart fluttered within him like a bird. Straining every nerve, he approached with great strides, hardly feeling his legs under him. 'Ah,' thought Iván, 'now he won't escape! I'll catch him in the act!'

Iván was still some distance off, when suddenly he saw a bright light, but not in the same place as before, and not a small flame. The thatch had flared up at the eaves, the flames were reaching up to the roof, and, standing beneath it, Gabriel's whole figure was clearly visible.

Like a hawk swooping down on a lark, Iván rushed at Limping Gabriel. 'Now I'll have him; he shan't escape me!'

thought Iván. But Gabriel must have heard his steps, and (however he managed it) glancing round, he scuttled away past the barn like a hare.

'You shan't escape!' shouted Iván, darting after him.

Just as he was going to seize Gabriel, the latter dodged him; but Iván managed to catch the skirt of Gabriel's coat. It tore right off, and Iván fell down. He recovered his feet, and shouting, 'Help! Seize him! Thieves! Murder!' ran on again. But meanwhile Gabriel had reached his own gate. There Iván overtook him and was about to seize him, when something struck Iván a stunning blow, as though a stone had hit his temple, quite deafening him. It was Gabriel who, seizing an oak wedge that lay near the gate, had struck out with all his might.

Iván was stunned; sparks flew before his eyes, then all grew dark and he staggered. When he came to his senses Gabriel was no longer there: it was as light as day, and from the side where his homestead was, something roared and crackled like an engine at work. Iván turned round and saw that his back shed was all ablaze, and the side shed had also caught fire, and flames and smoke and bits of burning straw mixed with the smoke were being driven towards his hut.

'What is this, friends?...' cried Iván, lifting his arms and striking his thighs. 'Why, all I had to do was just to snatch it out from under the eaves and trample on it! What is this, friends?...' he kept repeating. He wished to shout, but his breath failed him; his voice was gone. He wanted to run, but his legs would not obey him, and got in each other's way. He moved slowly, but again staggered and again his breath failed. He stood still till he had regained breath, and then went on. Before he had got round the back shed to reach the fire, the side shed was also all ablaze; and the corner of the hut and the covered gateway had caught fire as well. The flames were leaping out of the hut, and it was impossible to get into the yard. A large crowd had collected, but nothing could be done. The neighbours were carrying their belongings out of their own houses, and driving the cattle out of their own sheds. After Iván's house, Gabriel's also caught fire, then, the wind rising, the flames spread to the other side of the street and half the village was burnt down.

At Iván's house they barely managed to save his old father; and the family escaped in what they had on; everything else, except the horses that had been driven out to pasture for the night, was lost; all the cattle, the fowls on their perches, the carts, ploughs, and harrows, the women's trunks with their clothes, and the grain in the granaries – all were burnt up!

At Gabriel's, the cattle were driven out, and a few things saved from his house.

The fire lasted all night. Iván stood in front of his homestead and kept repeating, 'What is this?... Friends!... One need only have pulled it out and trampled on it!' But when the roof fell in, Iván rushed into the burning place, and seizing a charred beam, tried to drag it out. The women saw him, and called him back; but he pulled out the beam, and was going in again for another when he lost his footing and fell among the flames. Then his son made his way in after him and dragged him out. Iván had singed his hair and beard and burnt his clothes and scorched his hands, but he felt nothing. 'His grief has stupefied him,' said the people. The fire was burning itself out, but Iván still stood repeating: 'Friends!... What is this?... One need only have pulled it out!'

In the morning the village Elder's son came to fetch Iván.

'Daddy Iván, your father is dying! He has sent for you to say good-bye.'

Iván had forgotten about his father, and did not understand what was being said to him.

'What father?' he said. 'Whom has he sent for?'

'He sent for you, to say good-bye; he is dying in our cottage! Come along, daddy Iván,' said the Elder's son, pulling him by the arm; and Iván followed the lad.

When he was being carried out of the hut, some burning straw had fallen on to the old man and burnt him, and he had been taken to the village Elder's in the farther part of the village, which the fire did not reach.

When Iván came to his father, there was only the Elder's wife in the hut, besides some little children on the top of the oven. All the rest were still at the fire. The old man, who was lying on a bench holding a wax candle[1] in his hand, kept turning his eyes towards the door. When his son entered, he moved a little. The old woman went up to him and told him that his son had come. He asked to have him brought nearer. Iván came closer.

'What did I tell you, Iván?' began the old man. 'Who has burnt down the village?'

'It was he, father!' Iván answered. 'I caught him in the act. I saw him shove the firebrand into the thatch. I might have pulled away the burning straw and stamped it out, and then nothing would have happened.'

'Iván,' said the old man, 'I am dying, and you in your turn will have to face death. Whose is the sin?'

Iván gazed at his father in silence, unable to utter a word.

'Now, before God, say whose is the sin? What did I tell you?'

Only then Iván came to his senses and understood it all. He sniffed and said, 'Mine, father!' And he fell on his knees before his father, saying, 'Forgive me, father; I am guilty before you and before God.'

The old man moved his hands, changed the candle from his right hand to his left, and tried to lift his right hand to his forehead to cross himself, but could not do it, and stopped.

'Praise the Lord! Praise the Lord!' said he, and again he turned his eyes towards his son.

'Iván! I say, Iván!'

'What, father?'

'What must you do now?'

Iván was weeping.

'I don't know how we are to live now, father!' he said.

The old man closed his eyes, moved his lips as if to gather strength, and opening his eyes again, said: 'You'll manage. If you obey God's will, you'll manage!' He paused, then smiled,

---

1 Wax candles are much used in the services of the Russian Church, and it is usual to place one in the hand of a dying man, especially when he receives unction.

and said: 'Mind, Iván! Don't tell who started the fire! Hide another man's sin, and God will forgive two of yours!' And the old man took the candle in both hands and, folding them on his breast, sighed, stretched out, and died.

Iván did not say anything against Gabriel, and no one knew what had caused the fire.

And Iván's anger against Gabriel passed away, and Gabriel wondered that Iván did not tell anybody. At first Gabriel felt afraid, but after a while he got used to it. The men left off quarrelling, and then their families left off also. While rebuilding their huts, both families lived in one house; and when the village was rebuilt and they might have moved farther apart, Iván and Gabriel built next to each other, and remained neighbours as before.

They lived as good neighbours should. Iván Stcherbakóf remembered his old father's command to obey God's law, and quench a fire at the first spark; and if anyone does him an injury he now tries not to revenge himself, but rather to set matters right again; and if anyone gives him a bad word, instead of giving a worse in return, he tries to teach the other not to use evil words; and so he teaches his womenfolk and children. And Iván Stcherbakóf has got on his feet again, and now lives better even than he did before.

TWO OLD MEN

'THE woman saith unto him, Sir, I perceive that thou art a prophet.
Our fathers worshipped in this mountain: and ye say, that in Jerusalem is the place where men ought to worship. Jesus saith unto her,
Woman, believe me, the hour cometh when neither in this mountain, nor in Jerusalem, shall ye worship the Father. . . . But the hour
cometh, and now is, when the true worshippers shall worship the
Father in spirit and truth: for such doth the Father seek to be his
worshippers.' – *John* iv. 19–21, 23.

I

THERE were once two old men who decided to go on a pilgrimage to worship God at Jerusalem. One of them was a well-to-do peasant named Efím Tarásitch Shevélef. The other, Elisha Bódrof, was not so well off.

Efím was a staid man, serious and firm. He neither drank nor smoked nor took snuff, and had never used bad language in his life. He had twice served as village Elder, and when he left office his accounts were in good order. He had a large family: two sons and a married grandson, all living with him. He was hale, long-bearded and erect, and it was only when he was past sixty that a little grey began to show itself in his beard.

Elisha was neither rich nor poor. He had formerly gone out carpentering, but now that he was growing old he stayed at home and kept bees. One of his sons had gone away to find work, the other was living at home. Elisha was a kindly and cheerful old man. It is true he drank sometimes, and he took snuff, and was fond of singing; but he was a peaceable man, and lived on good terms with his family and with his neighbours. He was short and dark, with a curly beard, and, like his patron saint Elisha, he was quite bald-headed.

The two old men had taken a vow long since and had arranged to go on a pilgrimage to Jerusalem together: but Efím could never spare the time; he always had so much business on hand; as soon as one thing was finished he started another. First he had to arrange his grandson's marriage; then to wait for his youngest son's return from the army, and after that he began building a new hut.

One holiday the two old men met outside the hut and, sitting down on some timber, began to talk.

'Well,' asked Elisha, 'when are we to fulfil our vow?'

Efím made a wry face.

'We must wait,' he said. 'This year has turned out a hard one for me. I started building this hut thinking it would cost me something over a hundred rubles, but now it's getting on for three hundred and it's still not finished. We shall have to wait till the summer. In summer, God willing, we will go without fail.'

'It seems to me we ought not to put it off, but should go at once,' said Elisha. 'Spring is the best time.'

'The time's right enough, but what about my building? How can I leave that?'

'As if you had no one to leave in charge! Your son can look after it.'

'But how? My eldest son is not trustworthy – he sometimes takes a glass too much.'

'Ah, neighbour, when we die they'll get on without us. Let your son begin now to get some experience.'

'That's true enough; but somehow when one begins a thing one likes to see it done.'

'Eh, friend, we can never get through all we have to do. The other day the women-folk at home were washing and house-cleaning for Easter. Here something needed doing, there something else, and they could not get everything done. So my eldest daughter-in-law, who's a sensible woman, says: "We may be thankful the holiday comes without waiting for us, or however hard we worked we should never be ready for it."'

Efím became thoughtful.

'I've spent a lot of money on this building,' he said, 'and one can't start on the journey with empty pockets. We shall want a hundred rubles apiece – and it's no small sum.'

Elisha laughed.

'Now, come, come, old friend!' he said, 'you have ten times as much as I, and yet you talk about money. Only say when we are to start, and though I have nothing now I shall have enough by then.'

Efím also smiled.

'Dear me, I did not know you were so rich!' said he. 'Why, where will you get it from?'

'I can scrape some together at home, and if that's not enough, I'll sell half a score of hives to my neighbour. He's long been wanting to buy them.'

'If they swarm well this year, you'll regret it.'

'Regret it! Not I, neighbour! I never regretted anything in my life, except my sins. There's nothing more precious than the soul.'

'That's so; still it's not right to neglect things at home.'

'But what if our souls are neglected? That's worse. We took the vow, so let us go! Now, seriously, let us go!'

II

ELISHA succeeded in persuading his comrade. In the morning, after thinking it well over, Efím came to Elisha.

'You are right,' said he, 'let us go. Life and death are in God's hands. We must go now, while we are still alive and have the strength.'

A week later the old men were ready to start. Efím had money enough at hand. He took a hundred rubles himself, and left two hundred with his wife.

Elisha, too, got ready. He sold ten hives to his neighbour, with any new swarms that might come from them before the summer. He took seventy rubles for the lot. The rest of the hundred rubles he scraped together from the other members of his household, fairly clearing them all out. His wife gave him all she had been saving up for her funeral; and his daughter-in-law also gave him what she had.

Efím gave his eldest son definite orders about everything: when and how much grass to mow, where to cart the manure, and how to finish off and roof the cottage. He thought out everything, and gave his orders accordingly. Elisha, on the other hand, only explained to his wife that she was to keep separate the swarms from the hives he had sold, and to be sure to let the neighbour have them all, without any tricks. As to household affairs, he did not even mention them.

'You will see what to do and how to do it, as the needs arise,' he said. 'You are the masters, and will know how to do what's best for yourselves.'

So the old men got ready. Their people baked them cakes, and made bags for them, and cut them linen for leg-bands.[1] They put on new leather shoes, and took with them spare shoes of plaited bark. Their families went with them to the end of the village and there took leave of them, and the old men started on their pilgrimage.

Elisha left home in a cheerful mood, and as soon as he was out of the village forgot all his home affairs. His only care was how to please his comrade, how to avoid saying a rude word to anyone, how to get to his destination and home again in peace and love. Walking along the road, Elisha would either whisper some prayer to himself or go over in his mind such of the lives of the saints as he was able to remember. When he came across anyone on the road, or turned in anywhere for the night, he tried to behave as gently as possible and to say a godly word. So he journeyed on, rejoicing. One thing only he could not do, he could not give up taking snuff. Though he had left his snuff-box behind, he hankered after it. Then a man he met on the road gave him some snuff; and every now and then he would lag behind (not to lead his comrade into temptation) and would take a pinch of snuff.

Efím too walked well and firmly; doing no wrong and speaking no vain words, but his heart was not so light. Household cares weighed on his mind. He kept worrying about what was going on at home. Had he not forgotten to give his son this or that order? Would his son do things properly? If he happened to see potatoes being planted or manure carted, as he went along, he wondered if his son was doing as he had been told. And he almost wanted to turn back and show him how to do things, or even do them himself.

---

1 Worn by Russian peasants instead of stockings.

III

THE old men had been walking for five weeks, they had worn out their home-made bark shoes, and had to begin buying new ones when they reached Little Russia.[1] From the time they left home they had had to pay for their food and for their night's lodging, but when they reached Little Russia the people vied with one another in asking them into their huts. They took them in and fed them, and would accept no payment; and, more than that, they put bread or even cakes into their bags for them to eat on the road.

The old men travelled some five hundred miles in this manner free of expense, but after they had crossed the next province, they came to a district where the harvest had failed. The peasants still gave them free lodging at night, but no longer fed them for nothing. Sometimes, even, they could get no bread: they offered to pay for it, but there was none to be had. The people said the harvest had completely failed the year before. Those who had been rich were ruined and had had to sell all they possessed; those of moderate means were left destitute, and those of the poor who had not left those parts, wandered about begging, or starved at home in utter want. In the winter they had had to eat husks and goosefoot.

One night the old men stopped in a small village; they bought fifteen pounds of bread, slept there, and started before sunrise, to get well on their way before the heat of the day. When they had gone some eight miles, on coming to a stream they sat down, and, filling a bowl with water, they steeped some bread in it, and ate it. Then they changed their leg-bands, and rested for a while. Elisha took out his snuff-box. Efím shook his head at him.

'How is it you don't give up that nasty habit?' said he.

Elisha waved his hand. 'The evil habit is stronger than I,' he said.

---

1 Little Russia is situated in the south-western part of Russia, and consists of the Governments of Kief, Poltava, Tchernigof, and part of Kharkof and Kherson.

Presently they got up and went on. After walking for nearly another eight miles, they came to a large village and passed right through it. It had now grown hot. Elisha was tired out and wanted to rest and have a drink, but Efím did not stop. Efím was the better walker of the two, and Elisha found it hard to keep up with him.

'If I could only have a drink,' said he.

'Well, have a drink,' said Efím. 'I don't want any.'

Elisha stopped.

'You go on,' he said, 'but I'll just run in to the little hut there. I will catch you up in a moment.'

'All right,' said Efím, and he went on along the high road alone, while Elisha turned back to the hut.

It was a small hut plastered with clay, the bottom a dark colour, the top whitewashed; but the clay had crumbled away. Evidently it was long since it had been re-plastered, and the thatch was off the roof on one side. The entrance to the hut was through the yard. Elisha entered the yard, and saw, lying close to a bank of earth that ran round the hut, a gaunt, beardless man with his shirt tucked into his trousers, as is the custom in Little Russia.[1] The man must have lain down in the shade, but the sun had come round and now shone full on him. Though not asleep, he still lay there. Elisha called to him, and asked for a drink, but the man gave no answer.

'He is either ill or unfriendly,' thought Elisha; and going to the door he heard a child crying in the hut. He took hold of the ring that served as a door-handle, and knocked with it.

'Hey, masters!' he called. No answer. He knocked again with his staff.

'Hey, Christians!' Nothing stirred.

'Hey, servants of God!' Still no reply.

Elisha was about to turn away, when he thought he heard a groan the other side of the door.

'Dear me, some misfortune must have happened to the people? I had better have a look.'

And Elisha entered the hut.

---

1 In Great Russia the peasants let their shirt hang outside their trousers.

IV

ELISHA turned the ring; the door was not fastened. He opened it and went along up the narrow passage. The door into the dwelling-room was open. To the left was a brick oven; in front against the wall was an icon-stand and a table before it; by the table was a bench on which sat an old woman, bareheaded and wearing only a single garment. There she sat with her head resting on the table, and near her was a thin, wax-coloured boy, with a protruding stomach. He was asking for something, pulling at her sleeve, and crying bitterly. Elisha entered. The air in the hut was very foul. He looked round, and saw a woman lying on the floor behind the oven: she lay flat on the ground with her eyes closed and her throat rattling, now stretching out a leg, now dragging it in, tossing from side to side; and the foul smell came from her. Evidently she could do nothing for herself and no one had been attending to her needs. The old woman lifted her head, and saw the stranger.

'What do you want?' said she. 'What do you want, man? We have nothing.'

Elisha understood her, though she spoke in the Little-Russian dialect.

'I came in for a drink of water, servant of God,' he said.

'There's no one – no one – we have nothing to fetch it in. Go your way.'

Then Elisha asked:

'Is there no one among you, then, well enough to attend to that woman?'

'No, we have no one. My son is dying outside, and we are dying in here.'

The little boy had ceased crying when he saw the stranger, but when the old woman began to speak, he began again, and clutching hold of her sleeve cried:

'Bread, Granny, bread.'

Elisha was about to question the old woman, when the man staggered into the hut. He came along the passage, clinging to the wall, but as he was entering the dwelling-room he fell in the corner near the threshold, and without trying to get up again to reach the bench, he began to speak in broken words. He brought out a word at a time, stopping to draw breath, and gasping.

'Illness has seized us...' said he, 'and famine. He is dying ... of hunger.'

And he motioned towards the boy, and began to sob.

Elisha jerked up the sack behind his shoulder and, pulling the straps off his arms, put it on the floor. Then he lifted it on to the bench, and untied the strings. Having opened the sack, he took out a loaf of bread, and, cutting off a piece with his knife, handed it to the man. The man would not take it, but pointed to the little boy and to a little girl crouching behind the oven, as if to say:

'Give it to them.'

Elisha held it out to the boy. When the boy smelt bread, he stretched out his arms, and seizing the slice with both his little hands, bit into it so that his nose disappeared in the chunk. The little girl came out from behind the oven and fixed her eyes on the bread. Elisha gave her also a slice. Then he cut off another piece and gave it to the old woman, and she too began munching it.

'If only some water could be brought,' she said, 'their mouths are parched. I tried to fetch some water yesterday – or was it to-day – I can't remember, but I fell down and could go no further, and the pail has remained there, unless someone has taken it.'

Elisha asked where the well was. The old woman told him. Elisha went out, found the pail, brought some water, and gave the people a drink. The children and the old woman ate some more bread with the water, but the man would not eat.

'I cannot eat,' he said.

All this time the younger woman did not show any consciousness, but continued to toss from side to side. Presently Elisha went to the village shop and bought some millet, salt, flour, and oil. He found an axe, chopped some wood, and made a fire. The little girl came and helped him. Then he boiled some soup, and gave the starving people a meal.

V

THE man ate a little, the old woman had some too, and the little girl and boy licked the bowl clean, and then curled up and fell fast asleep in one another's arms.

The man and the old woman then began telling Elisha how they had sunk to their present state.

'We were poor enough before,' said they, 'but when the crops failed, what we gathered hardly lasted us through the autumn. We had nothing left by the time winter came, and had to beg from the neighbours and from anyone we could. At first they gave, then they began to refuse. Some would have been glad enough to help us, but had nothing to give. And we were ashamed of asking: we were in debt all round, and owed money, and flour, and bread.'

'I went to look for work,' the man said, 'but could find none. Everywhere people were offering to work merely for their own keep. One day you'd get a short job, and then you might spend two days looking for work. Then the old woman and the girl went begging, further away. But they got very little; bread was so scarce. Still we scraped food together somehow, and hoped to struggle through till next harvest, but towards spring people ceased to give anything. And then this illness seized us. Things became worse and worse. One day we might have something to eat, and then nothing for two days. We began eating grass. Whether it was the grass, or what, made my wife ill, I don't know. She could not keep on her legs, and I had no strength left, and there was nothing to help us to recovery.'

'I struggled on alone for a while,' said the old woman, 'but at last I broke down too for want of food, and grew quite weak. The girl also grew weak and timid. I told her to go to the neighbours – she would not leave the hut, but crept into a corner and sat there. The day before yesterday a neighbour looked in, but seeing that we were ill and hungry she turned away and left us. Her husband has had to go away, and she has nothing for her own little ones to eat. And so we lay, waiting for death.'

Having heard their story, Elisha gave up the thought of overtaking his comrade that day, and remained with them all night. In the morning he got up and began doing the housework, just as if it were his own home. He kneaded the bread with the old woman's help, and lit the fire. Then he went with the little girl to the neighbours to get the most necessary things; for there was nothing in the hut: everything had been sold for bread – cooking utensils, clothing, and all. So Elisha began replacing what was necessary, making some things himself, and buying some. He remained there one day, then another, and then a third. The little boy picked up strength and, whenever Elisha sat down, crept along the bench and nestled up to him. The little girl brightened up and helped in all the work, running after Elisha and calling,

'Daddy, daddy.'

The old woman grew stronger, and managed to go out to see a neighbour. The man too improved, and was able to get about, holding on to the wall. Only the wife could not get up, but even she regained consciousness on the third day, and asked for food.

'Well,' thought Elisha, 'I never expected to waste so much time on the way. Now I must be getting on.'

VI

THE fourth day was the feast day after the summer fast, and Elisha thought:

'I will stay and break the fast with these people. I'll go and buy them something, and keep the feast with them, and to-morrow evening I will start.'

So Elisha went into the village, bought milk, wheat-flour and dripping, and helped the old woman to boil and bake for the morrow. On the feast day Elisha went to church, and then broke the fast with his friends at the hut. That day the wife got up, and managed to move about a bit. The husband had shaved and put on a clean shirt, which the old woman had washed for him; and he went to beg for mercy of a rich peasant in the village to whom his plough-land and meadow were mort-

gaged. He went to beg the rich peasant to grant him the use of
the meadow and field till after the harvest; but in the evening
he came back very sad, and began to weep. The rich peasant
had shown no mercy, but had said: 'Bring me the money.'

Elisha again grew thoughtful. 'How are they to live now?'
thought he to himself. 'Other people will go haymaking,
but there will be nothing for these to mow, their grass land
is mortgaged. The rye will ripen. Others will reap (and what
a fine crop mother earth is giving this year), but they have
nothing to look forward to. Their three acres are pledged to
the rich peasant. When I am gone, they'll drift back into the
state I found them in.'

Elisha was in two minds, but finally decided not to leave
that evening, but to wait until the morrow. He went out into
the yard to sleep. He said his prayers, and lay down; but he
could not sleep. On the one hand he felt he ought to be going,
for he had spent too much time and money as it was; on the
other hand he felt sorry for the people.

'There seems to be no end to it,' he said. 'First I only meant
to bring them a little water and give them each a slice of bread:
and just see where it has landed me. It's a case of redeeming the
meadow and the cornfield. And when I have done that, I shall
have to buy a cow for them, and a horse for the man to cart his
sheaves. A nice coil you've got yourself into, brother Elisha!
You've slipped your cables and lost your reckoning!'

Elisha got up, lifted his coat which he had been using for
a pillow, unfolded it, got out his snuff-box and took a pinch,
thinking that it might perhaps clear his thoughts.

But no! He thought and thought, and came to no
conclusion. He ought to be going; and yet pity held him
back. He did not know what to do. He re-folded his coat
and put it under his head again. He lay thus for a long time,
till the cocks had already crowed once: then he was quite
drowsy. And suddenly it seemed as if someone had roused
him. He saw that he was dressed for the journey, with the sack
on his back and the staff in his hand, and the gate stood ajar
so that he could just squeeze through. He was about to pass
out, when his sack caught against the fence on one side: he

tried to free it, but then his leg-band caught on the other side and came undone. He pulled at the sack, and saw that it had not caught on the fence, but that the little girl was holding it and crying,

'Bread, daddy, bread!'

He looked at his foot, and there was the tiny boy holding him by the leg-band, while the master of the hut and the old woman were looking at him through the window.

Elisha awoke, and said to himself in an audible voice:

'To-morrow I will redeem their cornfield, and will buy them a horse, and flour to last till the harvest, and a cow for the little ones; or else while I go to seek the Lord beyond the sea, I may lose Him in myself.'

Then Elisha fell asleep, and slept till morning. He awoke early, and going to the rich peasant, redeemed both the cornfield and the meadow land. He bought a scythe (for that also had been sold) and brought it back with him. Then he sent the man to mow, and himself went into the village. He heard that there was a horse and cart for sale at the public-house, and he struck a bargain with the owner, and bought them. Then he bought a sack of flour, put it in the cart, and went to see about a cow. As he was going along he overtook two women talking as they went. Though they spoke the Little-Russian dialect, he understood what they were saying.

'At first, it seems, they did not know him; they thought he was just an ordinary man. He came in to ask for a drink of water, and then he remained. Just think of the things he has bought for them! Why they say he bought a horse and cart for them at the publican's, only this morning! There are not many such men in the world. It's worth while going to have a look at him.'

Elisha heard and understood that he was being praised, and he did not go to buy the cow, but returned to the inn, paid for the horse, harnessed it, drove up to the hut, and got out. The people in the hut were astonished when they saw the horse. They thought it might be for them, but dared not ask. The man came out to open the gate.

'Where did you get a horse from, grandfather?' he asked.

'Why, I bought it,' said Elisha. 'It was going cheap. Go and cut some grass and put it in the manger for it to eat during the night. And take in the sack.'

The man unharnessed the horse, and carried the sack into the barn. Then he mowed some grass and put it in the manger. Everybody lay down to sleep. Elisha went outside and lay by the roadside. That evening he took his bag out with him. When everyone was asleep, he got up, packed and fastened his bag, wrapped the linen bands round his legs, put on his shoes and coat, and set off to follow Efím.

VII

WHEN Elisha had walked rather more than three miles it began to grow light. He sat down under a tree, opened his bag, counted his money, and found he had only seventeen rubles and twenty kopeks left.

'Well,' thought he, 'it is no use trying to cross the sea with this. If I beg my way it may be worse than not going at all. Friend Efím will get to Jerusalem without me, and will place a candle at the shrines in my name. As for me, I'm afraid I shall never fulfil my vow in this life. I must be thankful it was made to a merciful Master, and to one who pardons sinners.'

Elisha rose, jerked his bag well up on his shoulders, and turned back. Not wishing to be recognized by anyone, he made a circuit to avoid the village, and walked briskly home-ward. Coming from home the way had seemed difficult to him, and he had found it hard to keep up with Efím, but now on his return journey, God helped him to get over the ground so that he hardly felt fatigue. Walking seemed like child's play. He went along swinging his staff, and did his forty to fifty miles a day.

When Elisha reached home the harvest was over. His family were delighted to see him again, and all wanted to know what had happened: Why and how he had been left behind? And why he had returned without reaching Jerusalem? But Elisha did not tell them.

'It was not God's will that I should get there,' said he. 'I lost my money on the way, and lagged behind my companion. Forgive me, for the Lord's sake!'

Elisha gave his old wife what money he had left. Then he questioned them about home affairs. Everything was going on well; all the work had been done, nothing neglected, and all were living in peace and concord.

Efím's family heard of his return the same day, and came for news of their old man; and to them Elisha gave the same answers.

'Efím is a fast walker. We parted three days before St Peter's day, and I meant to catch him up again, but all sorts of things happened. I lost my money, and had no means to get any further, so I turned back.'

The folks were astonished that so sensible a man should have acted so foolishly: should have started and not got to his destination, and should have squandered all his money. They wondered at it for a while, and then forgot all about it; and Elisha forgot it too. He set to work again on his homestead. With his son's help he cut wood for fuel for the winter. He and the women threshed the corn. Then he mended the thatch on the outhouses, put the bees under cover, and handed over to his neighbour the ten hives he had sold him in spring, and all the swarms that had come from them. His wife tried not to tell how many swarms there had been from these hives, but Elisha knew well enough from which there had been swarms and from which not. And instead of ten, he handed over seventeen swarms to his neighbour. Having got everything ready for the winter, Elisha sent his son away to find work, while he himself took to plaiting shoes of bark, and hollowing out logs for hives.

VIII

ALL that day while Elisha stopped behind in the hut with the sick people, Efím waited for him. He only went on a little way before he sat down. He waited and waited, had a nap, woke up again, and again sat waiting; but his comrade did not come.

He gazed till his eyes ached. The sun was already sinking behind a tree, and still no Elisha was to be seen.

'Perhaps he has passed me,' thought Efím, 'or perhaps someone gave him a lift and he drove by while I slept, and did not see me. But how could he help seeing me? One can see so far here in the steppe. Shall I go back? Suppose he is on in front, we shall then miss each other completely and it will be still worse. I had better go on, and we shall be sure to meet where we put up for the night.'

He came to a village, and told the watchman, if an old man of a certain description came along, to bring him to the hut where Efím stopped. But Elisha did not turn up that night. Efím went on, asking all he met whether they had not seen a little, bald-headed, old man? No one had seen such a travel-ler. Efím wondered, but went on alone, saying:

'We shall be sure to meet in Odessa, or on board the ship,' and he did not trouble more about it.

On the way, he came across a pilgrim wearing a priest's coat, with long hair and a skull-cap such as priests wear. This pilgrim had been to Mount Athos, and was now going to Jerusalem for the second time. They both stopped at the same place one night, and, having met, they travelled on together.

They got safely to Odessa, and there had to wait three days for a ship. Many pilgrims from many different parts were in the same case. Again Efím asked about Elisha, but no one had seen him.

Efím got himself a foreign passport, which cost him five rubles. He paid forty rubles for a return ticket to Jerusalem, and bought a supply of bread and herrings for the voyage.

The pilgrim began explaining to Efím how he might get on to the ship without paying his fare; but Efím would not listen. 'No, I came prepared to pay, and I shall pay,' said he.

The ship was freighted, and the pilgrims went on board, Efím and his new comrade among them. The anchors were weighed, and the ship put out to sea.

All day they sailed smoothly, but towards night a wind arose, rain came on, and the vessel tossed about and shipped water. The people were frightened: the women wailed and screamed, and some of the weaker men ran about the ship looking for shelter. Efím too was frightened, but he would not show it, and remained at the place on deck where he had settled down when first he came on board, beside some old men from Tambóf. There they sat silent, all night and all next day, holding on to their sacks. On the third day it grew calm, and on the fifth day they anchored at Constantinople. Some of the pilgrims went on shore to visit the Church of St Sophia, now held by the Turks. Efím remained on the ship, and only bought some white bread. They lay there for twenty-four hours, and then put to sea again. At Smyrna they stopped again; and at Alexandria; but at last they arrived safely at Jaffa, where all the pilgrims had to disembark. From there still it was more than forty miles by road to Jerusalem. When disembarking the people were again much frightened. The ship was high, and the people were dropped into boats, which rocked so much that it was easy to miss them and fall into the water. A couple of men did get a wetting, but at last all were safely landed.

They went on on foot, and at noon on the third day reached Jerusalem. They stopped outside the town, at the Russian inn, where their passports were endorsed. Then, after dinner, Efím visited the Holy Places with his companion, the pilgrim. It was not the time when they could be admitted to the Holy Sepulchre, but they went to the Patriarchate. All the pilgrims assembled there. The women were separated from the men, who were all told to sit in a circle, barefoot. Then a monk came in with a towel to wash their feet. He washed, wiped, and then kissed their feet, and did this to everyone in the circle. Efím's feet were washed and kissed, with the rest. He stood through vespers and matins, prayed, placed candles at the shrines, handed in booklets inscribed with his parents' names, that they might be mentioned in the church prayers. Here at the Patriarchate food and wine were given them. Next morning they went to the cell of Mary of Egypt, where she had lived doing penance. Here too they placed candles and had prayers read. From there they went to Abraham's Monastery, and saw the place where Abraham intended to slay his son as an offering to God. Then they visited the spot where Christ appeared to Mary Magdalene, and the Church of James, the Lord's brother. The pilgrim showed Efím all these places, and told him how much money to give at each place. At mid-day they returned to the inn and had dinner. As they were preparing to lie down and rest, the pilgrim cried out, and began to search his clothes, feeling them all over.

'My purse has been stolen, there were twenty-three rubles in it,' said he, 'two ten-ruble notes and the rest in change.'

He sighed and lamented a great deal, but as there was no help for it, they lay down to sleep.

IX

As Efím lay there, he was assailed by temptation.

'No one has stolen any money from this pilgrim,' thought he, 'I do not believe he had any. He gave none away anywhere, though he made me give, and even borrowed a ruble off me.'

This thought had no sooner crossed his mind, than Efím rebuked himself, saying: 'What right have I to judge a man? It is a sin. I will think no more about it.' But as soon as his thoughts began to wander, they turned again to the pilgrim: how interested he seemed to be in money, and how unlikely it sounded when he declared that his purse had been stolen.

'He never had any money,' thought Efím. 'It's all an invention.'

Towards evening they got up, and went to midnight Mass at the great Church of the Resurrection, where the Lord's Sepulchre is. The pilgrim kept close to Efím and went with him everywhere. They came to the church; a great many pilgrims were there; some Russians and some of other nationalities: Greeks, Armenians, Turks, and Syrians. Efím entered the Holy Gates with the crowd. A monk led them past the Turkish sentinels, to the place where the Saviour was taken down from the cross and anointed, and where candles were burning in nine great candlesticks. The monk showed and explained everything. Efím offered a candle there. Then the monk led Efím to the right, up the steps to Golgotha, to the place where the cross had stood. Efím prayed there. Then they showed him the cleft where the ground had been rent asunder to its nethermost depths; then the place where Christ's hands and feet were nailed to the cross; then Adam's tomb, where the blood of Christ had dripped on to Adam's bones. Then they showed him the stone on which Christ sat when the crown of thorns was placed on His head; then the post to which Christ was bound when He was scourged. Then Efím saw the stone with two holes for Christ's feet. They were going to show him something else, but there was a stir in the crowd, and the people all hurried to the church of the Lord's Sepulchre itself. The Latin Mass had just finished there, and the Russian Mass was beginning. And Efím went with the crowd to the tomb cut in the rock.

He tried to get rid of the pilgrim, against whom he was still sinning in his mind, but the pilgrim would not leave him, but went with him to the Mass at the Holy Sepulchre. They tried to get to the front, but were too late. There was such a crowd that it was impossible to move either backwards or forwards. Efím stood looking in front of him, praying, and every now and then feeling for his purse. He was in two minds: sometimes he thought that the pilgrim was deceiving him, and then again he thought that if the pilgrim spoke the truth and his purse had really been stolen, the same thing might happen to himself.

X

Efím stood there gazing into the little chapel in which was the Holy Sepulchre itself with thirty-six lamps burning above it. As he stood looking over the people's heads, he saw something that surprised him. Just beneath the lamps in which the sacred fire burns, and in front of everyone, Efím saw an old man in a grey coat, whose bald, shining head was just like Elisha Bódrof.

'It is like him,' thought Efím, 'but it cannot be Elisha. He could not have got ahead of me. The ship before ours started a week sooner. He could not have caught that; and he was not on ours, for I saw every pilgrim on board.'

Hardly had Efím thought this, when the little old man began to pray, and bowed three times: once forwards to God, then once on each side – to the brethren. And as he turned his head to the right, Efím recognized him. It was Elisha Bódrof himself, with his dark, curly beard turning grey at the cheeks, with his brows, his eyes and nose, and his expression of face. Yes, it was he!

Efím was very pleased to have found his comrade again, and wondered how Elisha had got ahead of him.

'Well done, Elisha!' thought he. 'See how he has pushed ahead. He must have come across someone who showed him the way. When we get out, I will find him, get rid of this fellow in the skull-cap, and keep to Elisha. Perhaps he will show me how to get to the front also.'

Efím kept looking out, so as not to lose sight of Elisha. But when the Mass was over, the crowd began to sway, pushing forward to kiss the tomb, and pushed Efím aside. He was again seized with fear lest his purse should be stolen. Pressing it with his hand, he began elbowing through the crowd, anxious only to get out. When he reached the open, he went about for a long time searching for Elisha both outside and in the church itself. In the cells of the church he saw many people of all kinds, eating, and drinking wine, and reading and sleeping there. But Elisha was nowhere to be seen. So Efím returned to the inn without having found his comrade. That evening the pilgrim in the skull-cap did not turn up. He had gone off without repaying the ruble, and Efím was left alone.

The next day Efím went to the Holy Sepulchre again, with an old man from Tambóf, whom he had met on the ship. He tried to get to the front, but was again pressed back; so he stood by a pillar and prayed. He looked before him, and there in the foremost place under the lamps, close to the very Sepulchre of the Lord, stood Elisha, with his arms spread out like a priest at the altar, and with his bald head all shining.

'Well, now,' thought Efím, 'I won't lose him!'

He pushed forward to the front, but when he got there, there was no Elisha: he had evidently gone away.

Again on the third day Efím looked, and saw at the Sepulchre, in the holiest place, Elisha standing in the sight of all men, his arms outspread, and his eyes gazing upwards as if he saw something above. And his bald head was all shining.

'Well, this time,' thought Efím, 'he shall not escape me! I will go and stand at the door, then we can't miss one another!'

Efím went out and stood by the door till past noon. Every-one had passed out, but still Elisha did not appear.

Efím remained six weeks in Jerusalem, and went every-where: to Bethlehem, and to Bethany, and to the Jordan. He had a new shirt sealed at the Holy Sepulchre for his burial, and he took a bottle of water from the Jordan, and some holy earth, and bought candles that had been lit at the sacred flame. In eight places he inscribed names to be prayed for, and he spent all his money, except just enough to get home with. Then he started homeward. He walked to Jaffa, sailed thence to Odessa, and walked home from there on foot.

XI

EFÍM travelled the same road he had come by; and as he drew nearer home his former anxiety returned, as to how affairs were getting on in his absence. 'Much water flows away in a year,' the proverb says. It takes a lifetime to build up a homestead, but not long to ruin it, thought he. And he wondered how his son had managed without him, what sort of spring they were having, how the cattle had wintered, and whether the cottage was well finished. When Efím came to the district where he had parted from Elisha the summer before, he could hardly believe that the people living there were the same. The year before they had been starving, but now they were living in comfort. The harvest had been good, and the people had recovered, and had forgotten their former misery.

One evening Efím reached the very place where Elisha had remained behind; and as he entered the village, a little girl in a white smock ran out of a hut.

'Daddy, daddy, come to our house!'

Efím meant to pass on, but the little girl would not let him. She took hold of his coat, laughing, and pulled him towards the hut, where a woman with a small boy came out into the porch and beckoned to him.

'Come in, grandfather,' she said. 'Have supper and spend the night with us.'

So Efím went in.

'I may as well ask about Elisha,' he thought. 'I fancy this is the very hut he went to for a drink of water.'

The woman helped him off with the bag he carried, and gave him water to wash his face. Then she made him sit down to table, and set milk, curd-cakes and porridge before him. Efím thanked her, and praised her for her kindness to a pilgrim. The woman shook her head.

'We have good reason to welcome pilgrims,' she said. 'It was a pilgrim who showed us what life is. We were living forgetful of God, and God punished us almost to death. We reached such a pass last summer, that we all lay ill and helpless with nothing to eat. And we should have died, but that God sent an old man to help us – just such a one as you. He came in one day to ask for a drink of water, saw the state we were in, took pity on us, and remained with us. He gave us food and drink, and set us on our feet again; and he redeemed our land, and bought a cart and horse and gave them to us.'

Here the old woman entering the hut, interrupted the younger one and said:

'We don't know whether it was a man, or an angel from God. He loved us all, pitied us all, and went away without telling us his name, so that we don't even know whom to pray for. I can see it all before me now! There I lay waiting for death, when in comes a bald-headed old man. He was not anything much to look at, and he asked for a drink of water. I, sinner that I am, thought to myself: "What does he come prowling about here for?" And just think what he did! As soon as he saw us, he let down his bag, on this very spot, and untied it.'

Here the little girl joined in.

'No, Granny,' said she, 'first he put it down here in the middle of the hut, and then he lifted it on to the bench.'

And they began discussing and recalling all he had said and done, where he sat and slept, and what he had said to each of them.

At night the peasant himself came home on his horse, and he too began to tell about Elisha and how he had lived with them.

'Had he not come we should all have died in our sins. We were dying in despair, murmuring against God and man. But he set us on our feet again; and through him we learned to know God, and to believe that there is good in man. May the Lord bless him! We used to live like animals; he made human beings of us.'

After giving Efím food and drink, they showed him where he was to sleep; and lay down to sleep themselves.

But though Efím lay down, he could not sleep. He could not get Elisha out of his mind, but remembered how he had seen him three times at Jerusalem, standing in the foremost place.

'So that is how he got ahead of me,' thought Efím. 'God may or may not have accepted my pilgrimage, but He has certainly accepted his!'

Next morning Efím bade farewell to the people, who put some patties in his sack before they went to their work, and he continued his journey.

XII

EFÍM had been away just a year, and it was spring again when he reached home one evening. His son was not at home, but had gone to the public-house, and when he came back, he had had a drop too much. Efím began questioning him. Everything showed that the young fellow had been unsteady during his father's absence. The money had all been wrongly spent, and the work had been neglected. The father began to upbraid the son; and the son answered rudely.

'Why didn't you stay and look after it yourself?' he said. 'You go off, taking the money with you, and now you demand it of me!'

The old man grew angry, and struck his son.

In the morning Efím went to the village Elder to complain of his son's conduct. As he was passing Elisha's house, his friend's wife greeted him from the porch.

'How do you do, neighbour,' she said. 'How do you do, dear friend? Did you get to Jerusalem safely?'

Efím stopped.

'Yes, thank God,' he said. 'I have been there. I lost sight of your old man, but I hear he got home safely.'

The old woman was fond of talking:

'Yes, neighbour, he has come back,' said she. 'He's been back a long time. Soon after Assumption, I think it was, he returned. And we were glad the Lord had sent him back to us! We were dull without him. We can't expect much work from him any more, his years for work are past; but still he is the head of the household and it's more cheerful when he's at home. And how glad our lad was! He said, "It's like being without sunlight, when father's away!" It was dull without him, dear friend. We're fond of him, and take good care of him.'

'Is he at home now?'

'He is, dear friend. He is with his bees. He is hiving the swarms. He says they are swarming well this year. The Lord has given such strength to the bees that my husband doesn't remember the like. "The Lord is not rewarding us according to our sins," he says. Come in, dear neighbour, he will be so glad to see you again.'

Efím passed through the passage into the yard and to the apiary, to see Elisha. There was Elisha in his grey coat, without any face-net or gloves, standing under the birch trees, looking upwards, his arms stretched out and his bald head shining, as Efím had seen him at the Holy Sepulchre in Jerusalem: and above him the sunlight shone through the birches as the flames of fire had done in the holy place, and the golden bees flew round his head like a halo, and did not sting him.

Efím stopped. The old woman called to her husband.

'Here's your friend come,' she cried.

Elisha looked round with a pleased face, and came towards Efím, gently picking bees out of his own beard.

'Good-day, neighbour, good-day, dear friend. Did you get there safely?'

'My feet walked there, and I have brought you some water from the river Jordan. You must come to my house for it. But whether the Lord accepted my efforts. . . .'

'Well the Lord be thanked! May Christ bless you!' said Elisha.

Efím was silent for a while, and then added:

'My feet have been there, but whether my soul, or another's, has been there more truly. . . .'

'That's God's business, neighbour, God's business,' interrupted Elisha.

'On my return journey I stopped at the hut where you remained behind. . . .'

Elisha was alarmed, and said hurriedly:

'God's business, neighbour, God's business! Come into the cottage, I'll give you some of our honey.' And Elisha changed the conversation, and talked of home affairs.

Efím sighed, and did not speak to Elisha of the people in the hut, nor of how he had seen him in Jerusalem. But he now understood that the best way to keep one's vows to God and to do His will, is for each man while he lives to show love and do good to others.

WHERE LOVE IS, GOD IS

IN a certain town there lived a cobbler, Martin Avdéitch by name. He had a tiny room in a basement, the one window of which looked out on to the street. Through it one could only see the feet of those who passed by, but Martin recognized the people by their boots. He had lived long in the place and had many acquaintances. There was hardly a pair of boots in the neighbourhood that had not been once or twice through his hands, so he often saw his own handiwork through the window. Some he had re-soled, some patched, some stitched up, and to some he had even put fresh uppers. He had plenty to do, for he worked well, used good material, did not charge too much, and could be relied on. If he could do a job by the day required, he undertook it; if not, he told the truth and gave no false promises; so he was well known and never short of work.

Martin had always been a good man; but in his old age he began to think more about his soul and to draw nearer to God. While he still worked for a master, before he set up on his own account, his wife had died, leaving him with a three-year-old son. None of his elder children had lived, they had all died in infancy. At first Martin thought of sending his little son to his sister's in the country, but then he felt sorry to part with the boy, thinking: 'It would be hard for my little Kapitón to have to grow up in a strange family; I will keep him with me.'

Martin left his master and went into lodgings with his little son. But he had no luck with his children. No sooner had the boy reached an age when he could help his father and be a support as well as a joy to him, than he fell ill and, after being laid up for a week with a burning fever, died. Martin buried his son, and gave way to despair so great and overwhelming that

49

he murmured against God. In his sorrow he prayed again and again that he too might die, reproaching God for having taken the son he loved, his only son, while he, old as he was, remained alive. After that Martin left off going to church.

One day an old man from Martin's native village, who had been a pilgrim for the last eight years, called in on his way from Tróitsa Monastery. Martin opened his heart to him, and told him of his sorrow.

'I no longer even wish to live, holy man,' he said. 'All I ask of God is that I soon may die. I am now quite without hope in the world.'

The old man replied: 'You have no right to say such things, Martin. We cannot judge God's ways. Not our reasoning, but God's will, decides. If God willed that your son should die and you should live, it must be best so. As to your despair – that comes because you wish to live for your own happiness.'

'What else should one live for?' asked Martin.

'For God, Martin,' said the old man. 'He gives you life, and you must live for Him. When you have learnt to live for Him, you will grieve no more, and all will seem easy to you.'

Martin was silent awhile, and then asked: 'But how is one to live for God?'

The old man answered: 'How one may live for God has been shown us by Christ. Can you read? Then buy the Gospels, and read them: there you will see how God would have you live. You have it all there.'

These words sank deep into Martin's heart, and that same day he went and bought himself a Testament in large print, and began to read.

At first he meant only to read on holidays, but having once begun he found it made his heart so light that he read every day. Sometimes he was so absorbed in his reading that the oil in his lamp burnt out before he could tear himself away from the book. He continued to read every night, and the more he read the more clearly he understood what God required of him, and how he might live for God. And his heart grew lighter and lighter. Before, when he went to bed he used to lie with a heavy heart, moaning as he thought of his little Kapitón;

but now he only repeated again and again: 'Glory to Thee, glory to Thee, O Lord! Thy will be done!'

From that time Martin's whole life changed. Formerly, on holidays he used to go and have tea at the public-house, and did not even refuse a glass or two of vodka. Sometimes, after having had a drop with a friend, he left the public-house not drunk, but rather merry, and would say foolish things: shout at a man, or abuse him. Now, all that sort of thing passed away from him. His life became peaceful and joyful. He sat down to his work in the morning, and when he had finished his day's work he took the lamp down from the wall, stood it on the table, fetched his book from the shelf, opened it, and sat down to read. The more he read the better he understood, and the clearer and happier he felt in his mind.

It happened once that Martin sat up late, absorbed in his book. He was reading Luke's Gospel; and in the sixth chapter he came upon the verses:

'To him that smiteth thee on the one cheek offer also the other; and from him that taketh away thy cloke withhold not thy coat also. Give to every man that asketh thee; and of him that taketh away thy goods ask them not again. And as ye would that men should do to you, do ye also to them likewise.'

He also read the verses where our Lord says:

'And why call ye me, Lord, Lord, and do not the things which I say? Whosoever cometh to me, and heareth my sayings, and doeth them, I will shew you to whom he is like: He is like a man which built an house, and digged deep, and laid the foundation on a rock: and when the flood arose, the stream beat vehemently upon that house, and could not shake it: for it was founded upon a rock. But he that heareth, and doeth not, is like a man that without a foundation built an house upon the earth, against which the stream did beat vehemently, and immediately it fell; and the ruin of that house was great.'

When Martin read these words his soul was glad within him. He took off his spectacles and laid them on the book, and leaning his elbows on the table pondered over what he had read. He tried his own life by the standard of those words, asking himself:

'Is my house built on the rock, or on sand? If it stands on the rock, it is well. It seems easy enough while one sits here alone, and one thinks one has done all that God commands; but as soon as I cease to be on my guard, I sin again. Still I will persevere. It brings such joy. Help me, O Lord!'

He thought all this, and was about to go to bed, but was loth to leave his book. So he went on reading the seventh chapter – about the centurion, the widow's son, and the answer to John's disciples – and he came to the part where a rich Pharisee invited the Lord to his house; and he read how the woman who was a sinner, anointed his feet and washed them with her tears, and how he justified her. Coming to the forty-fourth verse, he read:

'And turning to the woman, he said unto Simon, Seest thou this woman? I entered into thine house, thou gavest me no water for my feet: but she hath wetted my feet with her tears, and wiped them with her hair. Thou gavest me no kiss; but she, since the time I came in, hath not ceased to kiss my feet. My head with oil thou didst not anoint: but she hath anointed my feet with ointment.'

He read these verses and thought: 'He gave no water for his feet, gave no kiss, his head with oil he did not anoint. . . . ' And Martin took off his spectacles once more, laid them on his book, and pondered.

'He must have been like me, that Pharisee. He too thought only of himself – how to get a cup of tea, how to keep warm and comfortable; never a thought of his guest. He took care of himself, but for his guest he cared nothing at all. Yet who was the guest? The Lord himself! If he came to me, should I behave like that?'

Then Martin laid his head upon both his arms and, before he was aware of it, he fell asleep.

'Martin!' he suddenly heard a voice, as if someone had breathed the word above his ear.

He started from his sleep. 'Who's there?' he asked.

He turned round and looked at the door; no one was there. He called again. Then he heard quite distinctly: 'Martin, Martin! Look out into the street to-morrow, for I shall come.'

Martin roused himself, rose from his chair and rubbed his eyes, but did not know whether he had heard these words in a dream or awake. He put out the lamp and lay down to sleep.

Next morning he rose before daylight, and after saying his prayers he lit the fire and prepared his cabbage soup and buckwheat porridge. Then he lit the samovar, put on his apron, and sat down by the window to his work. As he sat working Martin thought over what had happened the night before. At times it seemed to him like a dream, and at times he thought that he had really heard the voice. 'Such things have happened before now,' thought he.

So he sat by the window, looking out into the street more than he worked, and whenever anyone passed in unfamiliar boots he would stoop and look up, so as to see not the feet only but the face of the passer-by as well. A house-porter passed in new felt boots; then a water-carrier. Presently an old soldier of Nicholas's reign came near the window spade in hand. Martin knew him by his boots, which were shabby old felt ones, goloshed with leather. The old man was called Stepánitch: a neighbouring tradesman kept him in his house for charity, and his duty was to help the house-porter. He began to clear away the snow before Martin's window. Martin glanced at him and then went on with his work.

'I must be growing crazy with age,' said Martin, laughing at his fancy. 'Stepánitch comes to clear away the snow, and I must needs imagine it's Christ coming to visit me. Old dotard that I am!'

Yet after he had made a dozen stitches he felt drawn to look out of the window again. He saw that Stepánitch had leaned his spade against the wall, and was either resting himself or trying to get warm. The man was old and broken down, and had evidently not enough strength even to clear away the snow.

'What if I called him in and gave him some tea?' thought Martin. 'The samovar is just on the boil.'

He stuck his awl in its place, and rose; and putting the samovar on the table, made tea. Then he tapped the window with his fingers. Stepánitch turned and came to the window.

Martin beckoned to him to come in, and went himself to open the door.

'Come in,' he said, 'and warm yourself a bit. I'm sure you must be cold.'

'May God bless you!' Stepánitch answered. 'My bones do ache to be sure.' He came in, first shaking off the snow, and lest he should leave marks on the floor he began wiping his feet; but as he did so he tottered and nearly fell.

'Don't trouble to wipe your feet,' said Martin; 'I'll wipe up the floor – it's all in the day's work. Come, friend, sit down and have some tea.'

Filling two tumblers, he passed one to his visitor, and pouring his own out into the saucer, began to blow on it.

Stepánitch emptied his glass, and, turning it upside down, put the remains of his piece of sugar on the top. He began to express his thanks, but it was plain that he would be glad of some more.

'Have another glass,' said Martin, refilling the visitor's tumbler and his own. But while he drank his tea Martin kept looking out into the street.

'Are you expecting anyone?' asked the visitor.

'Am I expecting anyone? Well, now, I'm ashamed to tell you. It isn't that I really expect anyone; but I heard something last night which I can't get out of my mind. Whether it was a vision, or only a fancy, I can't tell. You see, friend, last night I was reading the Gospel, about Christ the Lord, how he suffered, and how he walked on earth. You have heard tell of it, I dare say.'

'I have heard tell of it,' answered Stepánitch; 'but I'm an ignorant man and not able to read.'

'Well, you see, I was reading of how he walked on earth. I came to that part, you know, where he went to a Pharisee who did not receive him well. Well, friend, as I read about it, I thought how that man did not receive Christ the Lord with proper honour. Suppose such a thing could happen to such a man as myself, I thought, what would I not do to receive him! But that man gave him no reception at all. Well, friend, as I was thinking of this, I began to doze, and as I dozed I heard someone call me by name. I got up, and thought I heard someone whispering, "Expect me; I will come to-morrow." This happened twice over. And to tell you the truth, it sank so into my mind that, though I am ashamed of it myself, I keep on expecting him, the dear Lord!'

Stepánitch shook his head in silence, finished his tumbler and laid it on its side; but Martin stood it up again and refilled it for him.

'Here, drink another glass, bless you! And I was thinking, too, how he walked on earth and despised no one, but went mostly among common folk. He went with plain people, and chose his disciples from among the likes of us, from workmen like us, sinners that we are. "He who raises himself," he said, "shall be humbled; and he who humbles himself shall be raised." "You call me Lord," he said, "and I will wash your feet." "He who would be first," he said, "let him be the servant of all; because," he said, "blessed are the poor, the humble, the meek, and the merciful."'

Stepánitch forgot his tea. He was an old man, easily moved to tears, and as he sat and listened the tears ran down his cheeks.

'Come, drink some more,' said Martin. But Stepánitch crossed himself, thanked him, moved away his tumbler, and rose.

'Thank you, Martin Avdéitch,' he said, 'you have given me food and comfort both for soul and body.'

'You're very welcome. Come again another time. I am glad to have a guest,' said Martin.

Stepánitch went away; and Martin poured out the last of the tea and drank it up. Then he put away the tea things and sat down to his work, stitching the back seam of a boot. And as he stitched he kept looking out of the window, waiting for Christ, and thinking about him and his doings. And his head was full of Christ's sayings.

Two soldiers went by: one in Government boots, the other in boots of his own; then the master of a neighbouring house, in shining goloshes; then a baker carrying a basket. All these passed on. Then a woman came up in worsted stockings and peasant-made shoes. She passed the window, but stopped by the wall. Martin glanced up at her through the window, and saw that she was a stranger, poorly dressed, and with a baby in her arms. She stopped by the wall with her back to the wind, trying to wrap the baby up though she had hardly anything to wrap it in. The woman had only summer clothes on, and even they were shabby and worn. Through the window Martin heard the baby crying, and the woman trying to soothe it, but unable to do so. Martin rose, and going out of the door and up the steps he called to her.

'My dear, I say, my dear!'

The woman heard, and turned round.

'Why do you stand out there with the baby in the cold? Come inside. You can wrap him up better in a warm place. Come this way!'

The woman was surprised to see an old man in an apron, with spectacles on his nose, calling to her, but she followed him in.

They went down the steps, entered the little room, and the old man led her to the bed.

'There, sit down, my dear, near the stove. Warm yourself, and feed the baby.'

'Haven't any milk. I have eaten nothing myself since early morning,' said the woman, but still she took the baby to her breast.

Martin shook his head. He brought out a basin and some bread. Then he opened the oven door and poured some cabbage soup into the basin. He took out the porridge pot also, but the porridge was not yet ready, so he spread a cloth on the table and served only the soup and bread.

'Sit down and eat, my dear, and I'll mind the baby. Why, bless me, I've had children of my own; I know how to manage them.'

The woman crossed herself, and sitting down at the table began to eat, while Martin put the baby on the bed and sat down by it. He chucked and chucked, but having no teeth he could not do it well and the baby continued to cry. Then Martin tried poking at him with his finger; he drove his finger straight at the baby's mouth and then quickly drew it back, and did this again and again. He did not let the baby take his finger in its mouth, because it was all black with cobbler's wax. But the baby first grew quiet watching the finger, and then began to laugh. And Martin felt quite pleased.

The woman sat eating and talking, and told him who she was, and where she had been.

'I'm a soldier's wife,' said she. 'They sent my husband somewhere, far away, eight months ago, and I have heard nothing of him since. I had a place as cook till my baby was born, but then they would not keep me with a child. For three months now I have been struggling, unable to find a place, and I've had to sell all I had for food. I tried to go as a wet-nurse, but no one would have me; they said I was too starved-looking and thin. Now I have just been to see a tradesman's wife (a woman from our village is in service with her) and she has promised to take me. I thought it was all settled at last, but she tells me not to come till next week. It is far to her place, and I am fagged out, and baby is quite starved, poor mite. Fortunately our landlady has pity on us, and lets us lodge free, else I don't know what we should do.'

Martin sighed. 'Haven't you any warmer clothing?' he asked.

'How could I get warm clothing?' said she. 'Why, I pawned my last shawl for sixpence yesterday.'

Then the woman came and took the child, and Martin got up. He went and looked among some things that were hanging on the wall, and brought back an old cloak.

'Here,' he said, 'though it's a worn-out old thing, it will do to wrap him up in.'

The woman looked at the cloak, then at the old man, and taking it, burst into tears. Martin turned away, and groping under the bed brought out a small trunk. He fumbled about in it, and again sat down opposite the woman. And the woman said:

'The Lord bless you, friend. Surely Christ must have sent me to your window, else the child would have frozen. It was mild when I started, but now see how cold it has turned.

Surely it must have been Christ who made you look out of your window and take pity on me, poor wretch!'

Martin smiled and said, 'It is quite true; it was he made me do it. It was no mere chance made me look out.'

And he told the woman his dream, and how he had heard the Lord's voice promising to visit him that day.

'Who knows? All things are possible,' said the woman. And she got up and threw the cloak over her shoulders, wrapping it round herself and round the baby. Then she bowed, and thanked Martin once more.

'Take this for Christ's sake,' said Martin, and gave her sixpence to get her shawl out of pawn. The woman crossed herself, and Martin did the same, and then he saw her out.

After the woman had gone, Martin ate some cabbage soup, cleared the things away, and sat down to work again. He sat and worked, but did not forget the window, and every time a shadow fell on it he looked up at once to see who was passing. People he knew and strangers passed by, but no one remarkable.

After a while Martin saw an apple-woman stop just in front of his window. She had a large basket, but there did not seem to be many apples left in it; she had evidently sold most of her stock. On her back she had a sack full of chips, which she was taking home. No doubt she had gathered them at some place where building was going on. The sack evidently hurt her, and she wanted to shift it from one shoulder to the other, so she put it down on the footpath and, placing her basket on a post, began to shake down the chips in the sack. While she was doing this a boy in a tattered cap ran up, snatched an apple out of the basket, and tried to slip away; but the old woman noticed it, and turning, caught the boy by his sleeve. He began to struggle, trying to free himself, but the old woman held on with both hands, knocked his cap off his head, and seized hold of his hair. The boy screamed and the old woman scolded. Martin dropped his awl, not waiting to stick it in its place, and rushed out of the door. Stumbling up the steps, and dropping his spectacles in his hurry, he ran out into the street.

The old woman was pulling the boy's hair and scolding him, and threatening to take him to the police. The lad was struggling and protesting, saying, 'I did not take it. What are you beating me for? Let me go!'

Martin separated them. He took the boy by the hand and said, 'Let him go, Granny. Forgive him for Christ's sake.'

'I'll pay him out, so that he won't forget it for a year! I'll take the rascal to the police!'

Martin began entreating the old woman.

'Let him go, Granny. He won't do it again. Let him go for Christ's sake!'

The old woman let go, and the boy wished to run away, but Martin stopped him

'Ask the Granny's forgiveness!' said he. 'And don't do it another time. I saw you take the apple.'

The boy began to cry and to beg pardon.

'That's right. And now here's an apple for you,' and Martin took an apple from the basket and gave it to the boy, saying, 'I will pay you, Granny.'

'You will spoil them that way, the young rascals,' said the old woman. 'He ought to be whipped so that he should remember it for a week.'

'Oh, Granny, Granny,' said Martin, 'that's our way – but it's not God's way. If he should be whipped for stealing an apple, what should be done to us for our sins?'

The old woman was silent.

And Martin told her the parable of the lord who forgave his servant a large debt, and how the servant went out and seized his debtor by the throat. The old woman listened to it all, and the boy, too, stood by and listened.

'God bids us forgive,' said Martin, 'or else we shall not be forgiven. Forgive everyone; and a thoughtless youngster most of all.'

The old woman wagged her head and sighed.

'It's true enough,' said she, 'but they are getting terribly spoilt.'

'Then we old ones must show them better ways,' Martin replied.

'That's just what I say,' said the old woman. 'I have had seven of them myself, and only one daughter is left.' And the old woman began to tell how and where she was living with her daughter, and how many grandchildren she had. 'There now,' she said, 'I have but little strength left, yet I work hard for the sake of my grandchildren; and nice children they are, too. No one comes out to meet me but the children. Little Annie, now, won't leave me for anyone. "It's grandmother, dear grandmother, darling grandmother."' And the old woman completely softened at the thought.

'Of course, it was only his childishness, God help him,' said she, referring to the boy.

As the old woman was about to hoist her sack on her back, the lad sprang forward to her, saying, 'Let me carry it for you, Granny. I'm going that way.'

The old woman nodded her head, and put the sack on the boy's back, and they went down the street together, the old woman quite forgetting to ask Martin to pay for the apple. Martin stood and watched them as they went along talking to each other.

When they were out of sight Martin went back to the house. Having found his spectacles unbroken on the steps, he picked up his awl and sat down again to work. He worked a little, but could soon not see to pass the bristle through the holes in the leather; and presently he noticed the lamplighter passing on his way to light the street lamps.

'Seems it's time to light up,' thought he. So he trimmed his lamp, hung it up, and sat down again to work. He finished off one boot and, turning it about, examined it. It was all right. Then he gathered his tools together, swept up the cuttings, put away the bristles and the thread and the awls, and, taking down the lamp, placed it on the table. Then he took the Gospels from the shelf. He meant to open them at the place he had marked the day before with a bit of morocco, but the book opened at another place. As Martin opened it, his yesterday's dream came back to his mind, and no sooner had he thought of it than he seemed to hear footsteps, as though someone were moving behind him. Martin turned round, and it seemed to him as if people were standing in the dark corner, but he could not make out who they were. And a voice whispered in his ear: 'Martin, Martin, don't you know me?'

'Who is it?' muttered Martin.

'It is I,' said the voice. And out of the dark corner stepped Stepánitch, who smiled and vanishing like a cloud was seen no more.

'It is I,' said the voice again. And out of the darkness stepped the woman with the baby in her arms, and the woman smiled and the baby laughed, and they too vanished.

'It is I,' said the voice once more. And the old woman and the boy with the apple stepped out and both smiled, and then they too vanished.

And Martin's soul grew glad. He crossed himself, put on his spectacles, and began reading the Gospel just where it had opened; and at the top of the page he read:

'I was an hungred, and ye gave me meat: I was thirsty, and ye gave me drink: I was a stranger, and ye took me in.'

And at the bottom of the page he read:

'Inasmuch as ye did it unto one of these my brethren, even these least, ye did it unto me' (*Matt.* xxv).

And Martin understood that his dream had come true; and that the Saviour had really come to him that day, and he had welcomed him.

THE STORY OF IVÁN
THE FOOL

AND OF HIS TWO BROTHERS, SIMON THE SOLDIER AND TARÁS THE STOUT; AND OF HIS DUMB SISTER MARTHA, AND OF THE OLD DEVIL AND THE THREE LITTLE IMPS.

ONCE upon a time, in a certain province of a certain country, there lived a rich peasant, who had three sons: Simon the Soldier, Tarás the Stout, and Iván the Fool, besides an unmarried daughter, Martha, who was deaf and dumb. Simon the Soldier went to the wars to serve the king; Tarás the Stout went to a merchant's in town to trade, and Iván the Fool stayed at home with the lass, to till the ground till his back bent.

Simon the Soldier obtained high rank and an estate, and married a nobleman's daughter. His pay was large and his estate was large, but yet he could not make ends meet. What the husband earned his lady wife squandered, and they never had money enough.

So Simon the Soldier went to his estate to collect the income, but his steward said, 'Where is any income to come from? We have neither cattle, nor tools, nor horse, nor plough, nor harrow. We must first get all these, and then the money will come.'

Then Simon the Soldier went to his father and said: 'You, father, are rich, but have given me nothing. Divide what you have, and give me a third part, that I may improve my estate.'

But the old man said: 'You brought nothing into my house; why should I give you a third part? It would be unfair to Iván and to the girl.'

But Simon answered, 'He is a fool; and she is an old maid, and deaf and dumb besides; what's the good of property to them?'

The old man said, 'We will see what Iván says about it.'

And Iván said, 'Let him take what he wants.'

So Simon the Soldier took his share of his father's goods and removed them to his estate, and went off again to serve the king.

Tarás the Stout also gathered much money, and married into a merchant's family, but still he wanted more. So he, also, came to his father and said, 'Give me my portion.'

But the old man did not wish to give Tarás a share either, and said, 'You brought nothing here. Iván has earned all we have in the house, and why should we wrong him and the girl?'

But Tarás said, 'What does he need? He is a fool! He cannot marry, no one would have him; and the dumb lass does not need anything either. Look here, Iván!' said he, 'give me half the corn; I don't want the tools, and of the live stock I will take only the grey stallion, which is of no use to you for the plough.'

Iván laughed and said, 'Take what you want. I will work to earn some more.'

So they gave a share to Tarás also; and he carted the corn away to town, and took the grey stallion. And Iván was left with one old mare, to lead his peasant life as before, and to support his father and mother.

II

Now the old Devil was vexed that the brothers had not quarrelled over the division, but had parted peacefully; and he summoned three imps.

'Look here,' said he, 'there are three brothers: Simon the Soldier, Tarás the Stout, and Iván the Fool. They should have quarrelled, but are living peaceably and meet on friendly terms. The fool Iván has spoilt the whole business for me. Now you three go and tackle those three brothers, and worry them till they scratch each other's eyes out! Do you think you can do it?'

'Yes, we'll do it,' said they.

'How will you set about it?'

'Why,' said they, 'first we'll ruin them. And when they

haven't a crust to eat we'll tie them up together, and then they'll fight each other, sure enough!'

'That's capital; I see you understand your business. Go, and don't come back till you've set them by the ears, or I'll skin you alive!'

The imps went off into a swamp, and began to consider how they should set to work. They disputed and disputed, each wanting the lightest job; but at last they decided to cast lots which of the brothers each imp should tackle. If one imp finished his task before the others, he was to come and help them. So the imps cast lots, and appointed a time to meet again in the swamp to learn who had succeeded and who needed help.

The appointed time came round, and the imps met again in the swamp as agreed. And each began to tell how matters stood. The first, who had undertaken Simon the Soldier, began: 'My business is going on well. To-morrow Simon will return to his father's house.'

His comrades asked, 'How did you manage it?'

'First,' says he, 'I made Simon so bold that he offered to conquer the whole world for his king; and the king made him his general and sent him to fight the King of India. They met for battle, but the night before, I damped all the powder in Simon's camp, and made more straw soldiers for the Indian King than you could count. And when Simon's soldiers saw the straw soldiers surrounding them, they grew frightened. Simon ordered them to fire; but their cannons and guns would not go off. Then Simon's soldiers were quite frightened, and ran like sheep, and the Indian King slaughtered them. Simon was disgraced. He has been deprived of his estate, and to-morrow they intend to execute him. There is only one day's work left for me to do; I have just to let him out of prison that he may escape home. To-morrow I shall be ready to help whichever of you needs me.'

Then the second imp, who had Tarás in hand, began to tell how he had fared. 'I don't want any help,' said he; 'my job is going all right. Tarás can't hold out for more than a week. First I caused him to grow greedy and fat. His covetousness became so great that whatever he saw he wanted to buy. He has spent all his money in buying immense lots of goods, and still continues to buy. Already he has begun to use borrowed money. His debts hang like a weight round his neck, and he is so involved that he can never get clear. In a week his bills come due, and before then I will spoil all his stock. He will be unable to pay and will have to go home to his father.'

Then they asked the third imp (Iván's), 'And how are you getting on?'

'Well,' said he, 'my affair goes badly. First I spat into his drink to make his stomach ache, and then I went into his field and hammered the ground hard as a stone that he should not be able to till it. I thought he wouldn't plough it, but like the fool that he is, he came with his plough and began to make a furrow. He groaned with the pain in his stomach, but went on ploughing. I broke his plough for him, but he went home, got out another, and again started ploughing. I crept under the earth and caught hold of the ploughshares, but there was no holding them; he leant heavily upon the plough, and the ploughshare was sharp and cut my hands. He has all but finished ploughing the field, only one little strip is left. Come, brothers, and help me; for if we don't get the better of him, all our labour is lost. If the fool holds out and keeps on working the land, his brothers will never know want, for he will feed them both.'

Simon the Soldier's imp promised to come next day to help, and so they parted.

III

I v Á N had ploughed up the whole fallow, all but one little strip. He came to finish it. Though his stomach ached, the ploughing must be done. He freed the harness ropes, turned the plough, and began to work. He drove one furrow, but coming back the plough began to drag as if it had caught in a root. It was the imp, who had twisted his legs round the ploughshare and was holding it back.

'What a strange thing!' thought Iván. 'There were no roots here at all, and yet here's a root.'

Iván pushed his hand deep into the furrow, groped about, and, feeling something soft, seized hold of it and pulled it out. It was black like a root, but it wriggled. Why, it was a live imp!

'What a nasty thing!' said Iván, and he lifted his hand to dash it against the plough, but the imp squealed out:

'Don't hurt me, and I'll do anything you tell me to.'

'What can you do?'

'Anything you tell me to.'

Iván scratched his head.

'My stomach aches,' said he; 'can you cure that?'

'Certainly I can.'

'Well then, do so.'

The imp went down into the furrow, searched about, scratched with his claws, and pulled out a bunch of three little roots, which he handed to Iván.

'Here,' says he, 'whoever swallows one of these will be cured of any illness.'

Iván took the roots, separated them, and swallowed one. The pain in his stomach was cured at once. The imp again begged to be let off; 'I will jump right into the earth, and never come back,' said he.

'All right,' said Iván; 'begone, and God be with you!'

And as soon as Iván mentioned God, the imp plunged into the earth like a stone thrown into the water. Only a hole was left.

Iván put the other two pieces of root into his cap and went on with his ploughing. He ploughed the strip to the end, turned his plough over, and went home. He unharnessed the horse, entered the hut, and there he saw his elder brother, Simon the Soldier and his wife, sitting at supper. Simon's estate had been confiscated, he himself had barely managed to escape from prison, and he had come back to live in his father's house.

Simon saw Iván, and said: 'I have come to live with you. Feed me and my wife till I get another appointment.'

'All right,' said Iván, 'you can stay with us.'

But when Iván was about to sit down on the bench, the lady

disliked the smell, and said to her husband: 'I cannot sup with a dirty peasant.'

So Simon the Soldier said, 'My lady says you don't smell nice. You'd better go and eat outside.'

'All right,' said Iván; 'anyway I must spend the night outside, for I have to pasture the mare.'

So he took some bread, and his coat, and went with the mare into the fields.

IV

HAVING finished his work that night, Simon's imp came, as agreed, to find Iván's imp and help him to subdue the fool. He came to the field and searched and searched; but instead of his comrade he found only a hole.

'Clearly,' thought he, 'some evil has befallen my comrade. I must take his place. The field is ploughed up, so the fool must be tackled in the meadow.'

So the imp went to the meadows and flooded Iván's hay-field with water, which left the grass all covered with mud.

Iván returned from the pasture at dawn, sharpened his scythe, and went to mow the hayfield. He began to mow but had only swung the scythe once or twice when the edge turned so that it would not cut at all, but needed resharpening. Iván struggled on for awhile, and then said: 'It's no good. I must go home and bring a tool to straighten the scythe, and I'll get a chunk of bread at the same time. If I have to spend a week here, I won't leave till the mowing's done.'

The imp heard this and thought to himself, 'This fool is a tough 'un; I can't get round him this way. I must try some other dodge.'

Iván returned, sharpened his scythe, and began to mow. The imp crept into the grass and began to catch the scythe by the heel, sending the point into the earth. Iván found the work very hard, but he mowed the whole meadow, except one little bit which was in the swamp. The imp crept into the swamp and, thought he to himself, 'Though I cut my paws I will not let him mow.'

Iván reached the swamp. The grass didn't seem thick, but yet it resisted the scythe. Iván grew angry and began to swing the scythe with all his might. The imp had to give in; he could not keep up with the scythe, and, seeing it was a bad business, he scrambled into a bush. Iván swung the scythe, caught the bush, and cut off half the imp's tail. Then he finished mowing the grass, told his sister to rake it up, and went himself to mow the rye. He went with the scythe, but the dock-tailed imp was there first, and entangled the rye so that the scythe was of no use. But Iván went home and got his sickle, and began to reap with that, and he reaped the whole of the rye.

'Now it's time,' said he, 'to start on the oats.'

The dock-tailed imp heard this, and thought, 'I couldn't get the better of him on the rye, but I shall on the oats. Only wait till the morning.'

In the morning the imp hurried to the oat field, but the oats were already mowed down! Iván had mowed them by night, in order that less grain should shake out. The imp grew angry.

'He has cut me all over and tired me out – the fool. It is worse than war. The accursed fool never sleeps; one can't keep up with him. I will get into his stacks now and rot them.'

So the imp entered the rye, and crept among the sheaves, and they began to rot. He heated them, grew warm himself, and fell asleep.

Iván harnessed the mare, and went with the lass to cart the rye. He came to the heaps, and began to pitch the rye into the cart. He tossed two sheaves, and again thrust his fork – right into the imp's back. He lifts the fork and sees on the prongs a live imp, dock-tailed, struggling, wriggling, and trying to jump off.

'What, you nasty thing, are you here again?'

'I'm another,' said the imp. 'The first was my brother. I've been with your brother Simon.'

'Well,' said Iván, 'whoever you are, you've met the same fate!'

He was about to dash him against the cart, but the imp cried out: 'Let me off, and I will not only let you alone, but I'll do anything you tell me to do.'

'What can you do?'

'I can make soldiers out of anything you like.'

'But what use are they?'

'You can turn them to any use; they can do anything you please.'

'Can they sing?'

'Yes, if you want them to.'

'All right; you may make me some.'

And the imp said, 'Here, take a sheaf of rye, then bump it upright on the ground, and simply say:

> '"O sheaf! my slave
> This order gave:
> Where a straw has been
> Let a soldier be seen!"'

Iván took the sheaf, struck it on the ground, and said what the imp had told him to. The sheaf fell asunder, and all the straws changed into soldiers, with a trumpeter and a drummer playing in front, so that there was a whole regiment.

Iván laughed.

'How clever!' said he. 'This is fine! How pleased the girls will be!'

'Now let me go,' said the imp.

'No,' said Iván, 'I must make my soldiers of threshed straw, otherwise good grain will be wasted. Teach me how to change them back again into the sheaf. I want to thresh it.'

And the imp said, 'Repeat:

> '"Let each be a straw
> Who was soldier before,
> For my true slave
> This order gave!"'

Iván said this, and the sheaf reappeared.

Again the imp began to beg, 'Now let me go!'

'All right.' And Iván pressed him against the side of the cart, held him down with his hand, and pulled him off the fork.

'God be with you,' said he.

And as soon as he mentioned God, the imp plunged into the earth like a stone into water. Only a hole was left.

Iván returned home, and there was his other brother, Tarás, with his wife, sitting at supper.

Tarás the Stout had failed to pay his debts, had run away from his creditors, and had come home to his father's house. When he saw Iván, 'Look here,' said he, 'till I can start in business again, I want you to keep me and my wife.'

'All right,' said Iván, 'you can live here, if you like.'

Iván took off his coat and sat down to table, but the merchant's wife said: 'I cannot sit at table with this clown, he smells of perspiration.'

Then Tarás the Stout said, 'Iván, you smell too strong. Go and eat outside.'

'All right,' said Iván, taking some bread and going into the yard. 'It is time, anyhow, for me to go and pasture the mare.'

V

TARÁS's imp, being also free that night, came, as agreed, to help his comrades subdue Iván the Fool. He came to the cornfield, looked and looked for his comrades – no one was there. He only found a hole. He went to the meadow, and there he found an imp's tail in the swamp, and another hole in the rye stubble.

'Evidently, some ill-luck has befallen my comrades,' thought he. 'I must take their place and tackle the fool.'

So the imp went to look for Iván, who had already stacked the corn and was cutting trees in the wood. The two brothers had begun to feel crowded, living together, and had told Iván to cut down trees to build new houses for them.

The imp ran to the wood, climbed among the branches, and began to hinder Iván from felling the trees. Iván undercut one tree so that it should fall clear, but in falling it turned askew and caught among some branches. Iván cut a pole with which to lever it aside, and with difficulty contrived to bring it to the ground. He set to work to fell another tree – again the same thing occurred; and with all his efforts he could hardly get the tree clear. He began on a third tree, and again the same thing happened.

Iván had hoped to cut down half a hundred small trees, but had not felled even half a score, and now the night was come and he was tired out. The steam from him spread like a mist through the wood, but still he stuck to his work. He undercut another tree, but his back began to ache so that he could not stand. He drove his axe into the tree and sat down to rest.

The imp, noticing that Iván had stopped work, grew cheerful.

'At last,' thought he, 'he is tired out! He will give it up. Now I can take a rest myself.'

He seated himself astride a branch and chuckled. But soon Iván got up, pulled the axe out, swung it, and smote the tree from the opposite side with such force that the tree gave way at once and came crashing down. The imp had not expected this, and had no time to get his feet clear, and the tree in breaking, gripped his paw. Iván began to lop off the branches, when he noticed a live imp hanging in the tree! Iván was surprised.

'What, you nasty thing,' says he, 'so you are here again!'

'I am another one,' says the imp. 'I have been with your brother Tarás.'

'Whoever you are, you have met your fate,' said Iván, and swinging his axe he was about to strike him with the haft, but the imp begged for mercy: 'Don't strike me,' said he, 'and I will do anything you tell me to.'

'What can you do?'

'I can make money for you, as much as you want.'

'All right, make some.' So the imp showed him how to do it.

'Take', said he, 'some leaves from this oak and rub them in your hands, and gold will fall out on the ground.'

Iván took some leaves and rubbed them, and gold ran down from his hands.

'This stuff will do fine', said he, 'for the fellows to play with on their holidays.'

'Now let me go,' said the imp.

'All right,' said Iván, and taking a lever he set the imp free. 'Now begone! And God be with you,' says he.

And as soon as he mentioned God, the imp plunged into the earth, like a stone into water. Only a hole was left.

VI

So the brothers built houses, and began to live apart; and Iván finished the harvest work, brewed beer, and invited his brothers to spend the next holiday with him. His brothers would not come.

'We don't care about peasant feasts,' said they.

So Iván entertained the peasants and their wives, and drank until he was rather tipsy. Then he went into the street to a ring of dancers; and going up to them he told the women to sing a song in his honour; 'for', said he, 'I will give you something you never saw in your lives before!'

The women laughed and sang his praises, and when they had finished they said, 'Now let us have your gift.'

'I will bring it directly,' said he.

He took a seed-basket and ran into the woods. The women laughed. 'He is a fool!' said they, and they began to talk of something else.

But soon Iván came running back, carrying the basket full of something heavy.

'Shall I give it you?'

'Yes! give it to us.'

Iván took a handful of gold and threw it to the women. You should have seen them throw themselves upon it to pick it up! And the men around scrambled for it, and snatched it from one another. One old woman was nearly crushed to death. Iván laughed.

'Oh, you fools!' says he. 'Why did you crush the old grand-mother? Be quiet, and I will give you some more,' and he threw them some more. The people all crowded round, and Iván threw them all the gold he had. They asked for more, but Iván said, 'I have no more just now. Another time I'll give you some more. Now let us dance, and you can sing me your songs.'

The women began to sing.

'Your songs are no good,' says he.

'Where will you find better ones?' say they.

'I'll soon show you,' says he.

He went to the barn, took a sheaf, threshed it, stood it up, and bumped it on the ground.

'Now,' said he:

> 'O sheaf! my slave
> This order gave:
> Where a straw has been
> Let a soldier be seen!'

And the sheaf fell asunder and became so many soldiers. The drums and trumpets began to play. Iván ordered the soldiers to play and sing. He led them out into the street, and the people were amazed. The soldiers played and sang, and then Iván (forbidding anyone to follow him) led them back to the threshing ground, changed them into a sheaf again, and threw it in its place.

He then went home and lay down in the stables to sleep.

VII

SIMON the Soldier heard of all these things next morning, and went to his brother.

'Tell me', says he, 'where you got those soldiers from, and where you have taken them to?'

'What does it matter to you?' said Iván.

'What does it matter? Why, with soldiers one can do anything. One can win a kingdom.'

Iván wondered.

'Really!' said he; 'why didn't you say so before? I'll make you as many as you like. It's well the lass and I have threshed so much straw.'

Iván took his brother to the barn and said:

'Look here; if I make you some soldiers, you must take them away at once, for if we have to feed them, they will eat up the whole village in a day.'

Simon the Soldier promised to lead the soldiers away; and Iván began to make them. He bumped a sheaf on the threshing floor – a company appeared. He bumped another sheaf, and there was a second company. He made so many that they covered the field.

'Will that do?' he asked.

Simon was overjoyed, and said: 'That will do! Thank you, Iván!'

'All right,' said Iván. 'If you want more, come back, and I'll make them. There is plenty of straw this season.'

Simon the Soldier at once took command of his army, collected and organized it, and went off to make war.

Hardly had Simon the Soldier gone, when Tarás the Stout came along. He, too, had heard of yesterday's affair, and he said to his brother:

'Show me where you get gold money! If I only had some to start with, I could make it bring me in money from all over the world.'

Iván was astonished.

'Really!' said he. 'You should have told me sooner. I will make you as much as you like.'

His brother was delighted.

'Give me three baskets-full to begin with.'

'All right,' said Iván. 'Come into the forest; or, better still, let us harness the mare, for you won't be able to carry it all.'

They drove to the forest, and Iván began to rub the oak leaves. He made a great heap of gold.

'Will that do?'

Tarás was overjoyed.

'It will do for the present,' said he. 'Thank you, Iván!'

'All right,' says Iván, 'if you want more, come back for it. There are plenty of leaves left.'

Tarás the Stout gathered up a whole cartload of money, and went off to trade.

So the two brothers went away: Simon to fight, and Tarás to buy and sell. And Simon the Soldier conquered a kingdom for himself; and Tarás the Stout made much money in trade.

When the two brothers met, each told the other: Simon

how he got the soldiers, and Tarás how he got the money. And Simon the Soldier said to his brother, 'I have conquered a kingdom and live in grand style, but I have not money enough to keep my soldiers.'

And Tarás the Stout said, 'And I have made much money, but the trouble is, I have no one to guard it.'

Then said Simon the Soldier, 'Let us go to our brother. I will tell him to make more soldiers, and will give them to you to guard your money, and you can tell him to make money for me to feed my men.'

And they drove away to Iván; and Simon said, 'Dear brother, I have not enough soldiers; make me another couple of ricks or so.'

Iván shook his head.

'No!' says he, 'I will not make any more soldiers.'

'But you promised you would.'

'I know I promised, but I won't make any more.'

'But why not, fool?'

'Because your soldiers killed a man. I was ploughing the other day near the road, and I saw a woman taking a coffin along in a cart, and crying. I asked her who was dead. She said, "Simon's soldiers have killed my husband in the war." I thought the soldiers would only play tunes, but they have killed a man. I won't give you any more.'

And he stuck to it, and would not make any more soldiers.

Tarás the Stout, too, began to beg Iván to make him more gold money. But Iván shook his head.

'No, I won't make any more,' said he.

'Didn't you promise?'

'I did, but I'll make no more,' said he.

'Why not, fool?'

'Because your gold coins took away the cow from Michael's daughter.'

'How?'

'Simply took it away! Michael's daughter had a cow. Her children used to drink the milk. But the other day her children came to me to ask for milk. I said, "Where's your cow?" They answered, "The steward of Tarás the Stout came and gave mother three bits of gold, and she gave him the cow, so we have nothing to drink." I thought you were only going to play with the gold pieces, but you have taken the children's cow away. I will not give you any more.'

And Iván stuck to it and would not give him any more. So the brothers went away. And as they went they discussed how they could meet their difficulties. And Simon said:

'Look here, I tell you what to do. You give me money to feed my soldiers, and I will give you half my kingdom with soldiers enough to guard your money.' Tarás agreed. So the brothers divided what they possessed, and both became kings, and both were rich.

VIII

IVÁN lived at home, supporting his father and mother and working in the fields with his dumb sister. Now it happened that Iván's yard-dog fell sick, grew mangy, and was near dying. Iván, pitying it, got some bread from his sister, put it in his cap, carried it out, and threw it to the dog. But the cap was torn, and together with the bread one of the little roots fell to the ground. The old dog ate it up with the bread, and as soon as she had swallowed it she jumped up and began to play, bark, and wag her tail – in short became quite well again.

The father and mother saw it and were amazed.

'How did you cure the dog?' asked they.

Iván answered: 'I had two little roots to cure any pain, and she swallowed one.'

Now about that time it happened that the King's daughter fell ill, and the King proclaimed in every town and village, that he would reward anyone who could heal her, and if any unmarried man could heal the King's daughter he should have her for his wife. This was proclaimed in Iván's village as well as everywhere else.

His father and mother called Iván, and said to him: 'Have you heard what the King has proclaimed? You said you had a root that would cure any sickness. Go and heal the King's daughter, and you will be made happy for life.'

'All right,' said he.

And Iván prepared to go, and they dressed him in his best. But as he went out of the door he met a beggar woman with a crippled hand.

'I have heard', said she, 'that you can heal people. I pray you cure my arm, for I cannot even put on my boots myself.'

'All right,' said Iván, and giving the little root to the beggar woman he told her to swallow it. She swallowed it, and was cured. She was at once able to move her arm freely.

His father and mother came out to accompany Iván to the King, but when they heard that he had given away the root, and that he had nothing left to cure the King's daughter with, they began to scold him.

'You pity a beggar woman, but are not sorry for the King's daughter!' said they. But Iván felt sorry for the King's daughter also. So he harnessed the horse, put straw in the cart to sit on, and sat down to drive away.

'Where are you going, fool?'

'To cure the King's daughter.'

'But you've nothing left to cure her with!'

'Never mind,' said he, and drove off.

He drove to the King's palace, and as soon as he stepped on the threshold the King's daughter got well.

The King was delighted, and had Iván brought to him, and had him dressed in fine robes.

'Be my son-in-law,' said he.

'All right,' said Iván.

And Iván married the Princess. Her father died soon after, and Iván became King. So all three brothers were now kings.

IX

THE three brothers lived and reigned. The eldest brother, Simon the Soldier, prospered. With his straw soldiers he levied real soldiers. He ordered throughout his whole kingdom a levy of one soldier from every ten houses, and each soldier had to be tall, and clean in body and in face. He gathered many such soldiers and trained them; and when anyone opposed him, he sent these soldiers at once, and got his own way, so that everyone began to fear him, and his life was a comfortable one. Whatever he cast his eyes on and wished for, was his. He sent soldiers, and they brought him all he desired.

Tarás the Stout also lived comfortably. He did not waste the money he got from Iván, but increased it largely. He introduced law and order into his kingdom. He kept his money in coffers, and taxed the people. He instituted a poll-tax, tolls for walking and driving, and a tax on shoes and stockings and dress trimmings. And whatever he wished for he got. For the sake of money, people brought him everything, and they offered to work for him – for everyone wanted money.

Iván the Fool, also, did not live badly. As soon as he had buried his father-in-law, he took off all his royal robes and gave them to his wife to put away in a chest; and he again donned his hempen shirt, his breeches and peasant shoes, and started again to work.

'It's dull for me,' said he. 'I'm getting fat and have lost my appetite and my sleep.' So he brought his father and mother and his dumb sister to live with him, and worked as before.

People said, 'But you are a king!'

'Yes,' said he, 'but even a king must eat.'

One of his ministers came to him and said, 'We have no money to pay salaries.'

'All right,' says he, 'then don't pay them.'

'Then no one will serve.'

'All right; let them not serve. They will have more time to work; let them cart manure. There is plenty of scavenging to be done.'

And people came to Iván to be tried. One said, 'He stole my money.' And Iván said, 'All right, that shows that he wanted it.'

And they all got to know that Iván was a fool. And his wife said to him, 'People say that you are a fool.'

'All right,' said Iván.

His wife thought and thought about it, but she also was a fool.

'Shall I go against my husband? Where the needle goes the thread follows,' said she.

So she took off her royal dress, put it away in a chest, and went to the dumb girl to learn to work. And she learned to work and began to help her husband.

And all the wise men left Iván's kingdom; only the fools remained.

Nobody had money. They lived and worked. They fed themselves; and they fed others.

X

THE old Devil waited and waited for news from the imps of their having ruined the three brothers. But no news came. So he went himself to inquire about it. He searched and searched, but instead of finding the three imps he found only the three holes.

'Evidently they have failed,' thought he. 'I shall have to tackle it myself.'

So he went to look for the brothers, but they were no longer in their old places. He found them in three different kingdoms. All three were living and reigning. This annoyed the old Devil very much.

'Well,' said he, 'I must try my own hand at the job.'

First he went to King Simon. He did not go to him in his own shape, but disguised himself as a general, and drove to Simon's palace.

'I hear, King Simon,' said he, 'that you are a great warrior, and as I know that business well, I desire to serve you.'

King Simon questioned him, and seeing that he was a wise man, took him into his service.

The new commander began to teach King Simon how to form a strong army.

'First,' said he, 'we must levy more soldiers, for there are in your kingdom many people unemployed. We must recruit all the young men without exception. Then you will have five times as many soldiers as formerly. Secondly, we must get new rifles and cannons. I will introduce rifles that will fire a hundred balls at once; they will fly out like peas. And I will get cannons that will consume with fire either man, or horse, or wall. They will burn up everything!'

Simon the King listened to the new commander, ordered all young men without exception to be enrolled as soldiers, and had new factories built in which he manufactured large quantities of improved rifles and cannons. Then he made haste to declare war against a neighbouring king. As soon as he met the other army, King Simon ordered his soldiers to rain balls against it and shoot fire from the cannons, and at one blow he burned and crippled half the enemy's army. The neighbouring king was so thoroughly frightened that he gave way and surrendered his kingdom. King Simon was delighted.

'Now,' said he, 'I will conquer the King of India.'

But the Indian King had heard about King Simon, and had adopted all his inventions, and added more of his own. The Indian King enlisted not only all the young men, but all the single women also, and got together a greater army even than King Simon's. And he copied all King Simon's rifles and cannons, and invented a way of flying through the air to throw explosive bombs from above.

King Simon set out to fight the Indian King, expecting to beat him as he had beaten the other king; but the scythe that had cut so well had lost its edge. The King of India did not let Simon's army come within gunshot, but sent his women through the air to hurl down explosive bombs on to Simon's army. The women began to rain down bombs on to the army like borax upon cockroaches. The army ran away, and Simon the King was left alone. So the Indian King took Simon's kingdom, and Simon the Soldier fled as best he might.

Having finished with his brother, the old Devil went to King Tarás. Changing himself into a merchant, he settled in Tarás's kingdom, started a house of business, and began spending money. He paid high prices for everything, and everybody hurried to the new merchant's to get money. And so much money spread among the people that they began to pay all their taxes promptly, and paid up all their arrears, and King Tarás rejoiced.

'Thanks to the new merchant,' thought he, 'I shall have more money than ever; and my life will be yet more comfortable.'

And Tarás the King began to form fresh plans, and began to build a new palace. He gave notice that people should bring him wood and stone, and come to work, and he fixed high prices for everything. King Tarás thought people would come in crowds to work as before, but to his surprise all the wood and stone was taken to the merchant's, and all the workmen went there too. King Tarás increased his price, but the merchant bid yet more. King Tarás had much money, but the merchant had still more, and outbid the King at every point.

The King's palace was at a standstill; the building did not get on.

King Tarás planned a garden, and when autumn came he called for the people to come and plant the garden, but nobody came. All the people were engaged digging a pond for the merchant. Winter came, and King Taras wanted to buy sable furs for a new overcoat. He sent to buy them, but the messengers returned and said, 'There are no sables left. The merchant has all the furs. He gave the best price, and made carpets of the skins.'

King Tarás wanted to buy some stallions. He sent to buy them, but the messengers returned saying, 'The merchant has all the good stallions; they are carrying water to fill his pond.'

All the King's affairs came to a standstill. Nobody would work for him, for everyone was busy working for the merchant; and they only brought King Tarás the merchant's money to pay their taxes.

And the King collected so much money that he had nowhere to store it, and his life became wretched. He ceased to form plans, and would have been glad enough simply to live, but he was hardly able even to do that. He ran short of everything. One after another his cooks, coachmen, and servants left him to go to the merchant. Soon he lacked even food. When he sent to the market to buy anything, there was nothing to be got – the merchant had bought up everything, and people only brought the King money to pay their taxes.

Tarás the King got angry, and banished the merchant from the country. But the merchant settled just across the frontier, and went on as before. For the sake of the merchant's money, people took everything to him instead of to the King.

Things went badly with King Tarás. For days together he had nothing to eat, and a rumour even got about that the merchant was boasting that he would buy up the King himself! King Tarás got frightened, and did not know what to do.

At this time Simon the Soldier came to him, saying, 'Help me, for the King of India has conquered me.'

But King Tarás himself was over head and ears in difficulties. 'I myself', said he, 'have had nothing to eat for two days.'

XI

HAVING done with the two brothers, the old Devil went to Iván. He changed himself into a General, and coming to Iván began to persuade him that he ought to have an army.

'It does not become a king,' said he, 'to be without an army. Only give me the order, and I will collect soldiers from among your people, and form one.'

Iván listened to him. 'All right,' said Iván, 'form an army, and teach them to sing songs well. I like to hear them do that.'

So the old Devil went through Iván's kingdom to enlist men. He told them to go and be entered as soldiers, and each should have a quart of spirits and a fine red cap.

The people laughed.

'We have plenty of spirits,' said they. 'We make it ourselves; and as for caps, the women make all kinds of them, even striped ones with tassels.'

So nobody would enlist.

The old Devil came to Iván and said: 'Your fools won't enlist of their own free will. We shall have to make them.'

'All right,' said Iván, 'you can try.'

So the old Devil gave notice that all the people were to enlist, and that Iván would put to death anyone who refused.

The people came to the General and said, 'You say that if we do not go as soldiers the King will put us to death, but you don't say what will happen if we do enlist. We have heard say that soldiers get killed!'

'Yes, that happens sometimes.'

When the people heard this they became obstinate.

'We won't go,' said they. 'Better meet death at home. Either way we must die.'

'Fools! You are fools!' said the old Devil. 'A soldier may be killed or he may not, but if you don't go, King Iván will have you killed for certain.'

The people were puzzled, and went to Iván the Fool to consult him.

'A General has come,' said they, 'who says we must all become soldiers. "If you go as soldiers," says he, "you may be killed or you may not, but if you don't go, King Iván will certainly kill you." Is this true?'

Iván laughed and said, 'How can I, alone, put all you to death? If I were not a fool I would explain it to you, but as it is, I don't understand it myself.'

'Then,' said they, 'we will not serve.'

'All right,' says he, 'don't.'

So the people went to the General and refused to enlist. And the old Devil saw that this game was up, and he went off and ingratiated himself with the King of Tarakán.

'Let us make war,' says he, 'and conquer King Iván's country. It is true there is no money, but there is plenty of corn and cattle and everything else.'

So the King of Tarakán prepared to make war. He mustered a great army, provided rifles and cannons, marched to the frontier, and entered Iván's kingdom.

And people came to Iván and said, 'The King of Tarakán is coming to make war on us.'

'All right,' said Iván, 'let him come.'

Having crossed the frontier, the King of Tarakán sent scouts to look for Iván's army. They looked and looked, but there was no army! They waited and waited for one to appear somewhere, but there were no signs of an army, and nobody to fight with. The King of Tarakán then sent to seize the villages. The soldiers came to a village, and the people, both men and women, rushed out in astonishment to stare at the soldiers. The soldiers began to take their corn and cattle; the people let them have it, and did not resist. The soldiers went on to another village; the same thing happened again. The soldiers went on for one day, and for two days, and everywhere the same thing happened. The people let them have everything, and no one resisted, but only invited the soldiers to live with them.

'Poor fellows,' said they, 'if you have a hard life in your own land, why don't you come and stay with us altogether?'

The soldiers marched and marched: still no army, only people living and feeding themselves and others, and not resisting, but inviting the soldiers to stay and live with them. The soldiers found it dull work, and they came to the King of Tarakán and said, 'We cannot fight here, lead us elsewhere. War is all right, but what is this? It is like cutting pea-soup! We will not make war here any more.'

The King of Tarakán grew angry, and ordered his soldiers to over-run the whole kingdom, to destroy the villages, to burn the grain and the houses, and to slaughter the cattle. 'And if you do not obey my orders,' said he, 'I will execute you all.'

The soldiers were frightened, and began to act according to the King's orders. They began to burn houses and corn, and to kill cattle. But the fools still offered no resistance, and only wept. The old men wept, and the old women wept, and the young people wept.

'Why do you harm us?' they said. 'Why do you waste good things? If you need them, why do you not take them for yourselves?'

At last the soldiers could stand it no longer. They refused to go any further, and the army disbanded and fled.

XII

THE old Devil had to give it up. He could not get the better of Iván with soldiers. So he changed himself into a fine gentleman, and settled down in Iván's kingdom. He meant to overcome him by means of money, as he had overcome Tarás the Stout.

'I wish', says he, 'to do you a good turn, to teach you sense and reason. I will build a house among you and organize a trade.'

'All right,' said Iván, 'come and live among us if you like.'

Next morning the fine gentleman went out into the public square with a big sack of gold and a sheet of paper, and said, 'You all live like swine. I wish to teach you how to live properly. Build me a house according to this plan. You shall work, I will tell you how, and I will pay you with gold coins.' And he showed them the gold.

The fools were astonished; there was no money in use among them; they bartered their goods, and paid one another with labour. They looked at the gold coins with surprise.

'What nice little things they are!' said they.

And they began to exchange their goods and labour for the gentleman's gold pieces. And the old Devil began, as in Tarás's kingdom, to be free with his gold, and the people began to exchange everything for gold and to do all sorts of work for it.

The old Devil was delighted, and thought he to himself, 'Things are going right this time. Now I shall ruin the Fool as I did Tarás, and I shall buy him up body and soul.'

But as soon as the fools had provided themselves with gold pieces they gave them to the women for necklaces. The lasses plaited them into their tresses, and at last the children in the street began to play with the little pieces. Everybody had plenty of them, and they stopped taking them. But the fine gentleman's mansion was not yet half-built, and the grain and cattle for the year were not yet provided. So he gave notice that he wished people to come and work for him, and that he wanted cattle and grain; for each thing, and for each service, he was ready to give many more pieces of gold.

But nobody came to work, and nothing was brought. Only sometimes a boy or a little girl would run up to exchange an egg for a gold coin, but nobody else came, and he had nothing to eat. And being hungry, the fine gentleman went through the village to try and buy something for dinner. He tried at one house, and offered a gold piece for a fowl, but the housewife wouldn't take it.

'I have a lot already,' said she.

He tried at a widow's house to buy a herring, and offered a gold piece.

'I don't want it, my good sir,' said she. 'I have no children to play with it, and I myself already have three coins as curiosities.'

He tried at a peasant's house to get bread, but neither would the peasant take money.

'I don't need it,' said he, 'but if you are begging "for Christ's sake",[1] wait a bit and I'll tell the housewife to cut you a piece of bread.'

At that the Devil spat, and ran away. To hear Christ's name mentioned, let alone receiving anything for Christ's sake, hurt him more than sticking a knife into him.

And so he got no bread. Everyone had gold, and no matter where the old Devil went, nobody would give anything for money, but everyone said, 'Either bring something else, or come and work, or receive what you want in charity for Christ's sake.'

But the old Devil had nothing but money; for work he had no liking, and as for taking anything 'for Christ's sake' he could not do that. The old Devil grew very angry.

'What more do you want, when I give you money?' said he. 'You can buy everything with gold, and hire any kind of labourer.' But the fools did not heed him.

'No, we do not want money,' said they. 'We have no payments to make, and no taxes, so what should we do with it?'

The old Devil lay down to sleep – supperless.

The affair was told to Iván the Fool. People came and asked him, 'What are we to do? A fine gentleman has turned up, who likes to eat and drink and dress well, but he does not like to work, does not beg in "Christ's name", but only offers gold pieces to everyone. At first people gave him all he wanted,

1 'For Christ's sake' is the usual appeal of Russian beggars or poor pilgrims.

until they had plenty of gold pieces, but now no one gives him anything. What's to be done with him? He will die of hunger before long.'

Iván listened.

'All right,' says he, 'we must feed him. Let him live by turn at each house as a shepherd[1] does.'

There was no help for it. The old Devil had to begin making the round.

In due course the turn came for him to go to Iván's house. The old Devil came in to dinner, and the dumb girl was getting it ready.

She had often been deceived by lazy folk who came early to dinner – without having done their share of work – and ate up all the porridge, so it had occurred to her to find out the sluggards by their hands. Those who had horny hands, she put at the table, but the others got only the scraps that were left over.

The old Devil sat down at the table, but the dumb girl seized him by the hands and looked at them – there were no hard places there: the hands were clean and smooth, with long nails. The dumb girl gave a grunt and pulled the Devil away from the table. And Iván's wife said to him, 'Don't be offended, fine gentleman. My sister-in-law does not allow anyone to come to table who hasn't horny hands. But wait awhile, after the folk have eaten you shall have what is left.'

The old Devil was offended that in the King's house they wished him to feed like a pig. He said to Iván, 'It is a foolish law you have in your kingdom that everyone must work with his hands. It's your stupidity that invented it. Do people work only with their hands? What do you think wise men work with?'

And Iván said, 'How are we fools to know? We do most of our work with our hands and our backs.'

'That is because you are fools! But I will teach you how to work with the head. Then you will know that it is more profitable to work with the head than with the hands.'

1 It is often arranged that the shepherd who looks after the cattle of a Russian village Commune should get his board and lodging at the houses of the villagers, passing from one to another in turn.

Iván was surprised.

'If that is so,' said he, 'then there is some sense in calling us fools!'

And the old Devil went on. 'Only it is not easy to work with one's head. You give me nothing to eat, because I have no hard places on my hands, but you do not know that it is a hundred times more difficult to work with the head. Sometimes one's head quite splits.'

Iván became thoughtful.

'Why, then, friend, do you torture yourself so? Is it pleasant when the head splits? Would it not be better to do easier work with your hands and your back?'

But the Devil said, 'I do it all out of pity for you fools. If I didn't torture myself you would remain fools for ever. But, having worked with my head, I can now teach you.'

Iván was surprised.

'Do teach us!' said he, 'so that when our hands get cramped we may use our heads for a change.'

And the Devil promised to teach the people. So Iván gave notice throughout the kingdom that a fine gentleman had come who would teach everybody how to work with their heads; that with the head more could be done than with the hands; and that the people ought all to come and learn.

Now there was in Iván's kingdom a high tower, with many steps leading up to a lantern on the top. And Iván took the gentleman up there that everyone might see him.

So the gentleman took his place on the top of the tower and began to speak, and the people came together to see him. They thought the gentleman would really show them how to work with the head without using the hands. But the old Devil only taught them in many words how they might live without working. The people could make nothing of it. They looked and considered, and at last went off to attend to their affairs.

The old Devil stood on the tower a whole day, and after that a second day, talking all the time. But standing there so long he grew hungry, and the fools never thought of taking food to him up in the tower. They thought that if he could work with his head better than with his hands, he could at any rate easily provide himself with bread.

The old Devil stood on the top of the tower yet another day, talking away. People came near, looked on for awhile, and then went away.

And Iván asked, 'Well, has the gentleman begun to work with his head yet?'

'Not yet,' said the people; 'he's still spouting away.'

The old Devil stood on the tower one day more, but he began to grow weak, so that he staggered and hit his head against one of the pillars of the lantern. One of the people noticed it and told Iván's wife, and she ran to her husband, who was in the field.

'Come and look,' said she. 'They say the gentleman is beginning to work with his head.'

Iván was surprised.

'Really?' says he, and he turned his horse round, and went to the tower. And by the time he reached the tower the old Devil was quite exhausted with hunger, and was staggering and knocking his head against the pillars. And just as Iván arrived at the tower, the Devil stumbled, fell, and came bump, bump, bump, straight down the stairs to the bottom, counting each step with a knock of his head!

'Well!' says Iván, 'the fine gentleman told the truth when he said that "sometimes one's head quite splits". This is worse than blisters; after such work there will be swellings on the head.'

The old Devil tumbled out at the foot of the stairs, and struck his head against the ground. Iván was about to go up to him to see how much work he had done – when suddenly the earth opened and the old Devil fell through. Only a hole was left.

Iván scratched his head.

'What a nasty thing,' says he. 'It's one of those devils again! What a whopper! He must be the father of them all.'

Iván is still living, and people crowd to his kingdom. His own brothers have come to live with him, and he feeds them, too. To everyone who comes and says, 'Give me food!' Iván says, 'All right. You can stay with us; we have plenty of everything.'

Only there is one special custom in his kingdom: whoever has horny hands comes to table, but whoever has not, must eat what the others leave.

STORIES WRITTEN TO PICTURES

EVIL ALLURES, BUT GOOD ENDURES

THERE lived in olden times a good and kindly man. He had this world's goods in abundance, and many slaves to serve him. And the slaves prided themselves on their master, saying:

'There is no better lord than ours under the sun. He feeds and clothes us well, and gives us work suited to our strength. He bears no malice, and never speaks a harsh word to anyone. He is not like other masters, who treat their slaves worse than cattle: punishing them whether they deserve it or not, and never giving them a friendly word. He wishes us well, does good, and speaks kindly to us. We do not wish for a better life.'

Thus the slaves praised their lord, and the Devil, seeing it, was vexed that slaves should live in such love and harmony with their master. So getting one of them, whose name was Aleb, into his power, the Devil ordered him to tempt the other slaves. And one day, when they were all sitting together resting and talking of their master's goodness, Aleb raised his voice, and said:

'It is stupid to make so much of our master's goodness. The Devil himself would be kind to you, if you did what he wanted. We serve our master well, and humour him in all things. As soon as he thinks of anything, we do it: foreseeing all his wishes. What can he do but be kind to us? Just try how it will be if, instead of humouring him, we do him some harm instead. He will act like anyone else, and will repay evil for evil, as the worst of masters do.'

The other slaves began denying what Aleb had said, and at last bet with him. Aleb undertook to make their master angry. If he failed, he was to lose his holiday garment; but if he succeeded, the other slaves were to give him theirs. Moreover,

97

they promised to defend him against the master, and to set him free if he should be put in chains or imprisoned. Having arranged this bet, Aleb agreed to make his master angry next morning.

Aleb was a shepherd, and had in his charge a number of valuable, pure-bred sheep, of which his master was very fond. Next morning, when the master brought some visitors into the enclosure to show them the valuable sheep, Aleb winked at his companions, as if to say:

'See, now, how angry I will make him.'

All the other slaves assembled, looking in at the gates or over the fence, and the Devil climbed a tree near by to see how his servant would do his work. The master walked about the enclosure, showing his guests the ewes and lambs, and presently he wished to show them his finest ram.

'All the rams are valuable,' said he, 'but I have one with closely twisted horns, which is priceless. I prize him as the apple of my eye.'

Startled by the strangers, the sheep rushed about the enclosure, so that the visitors could not get a good look at the ram. As soon as it stood still, Aleb startled the sheep as if by accident, and they all got mixed up again. The visitors could not make out which was the priceless ram. At last the master got tired of it.

'Aleb, dear friend,' he said, 'pray catch our best ram for me, the one with the tightly twisted horns. Catch him very carefully, and hold him still for a moment.'

Scarcely had the master said this, when Aleb rushed in among the sheep like a lion, and clutched the priceless ram. Holding him fast by the wool, he seized the left hind leg with one hand, and, before his master's eyes, lifted it and jerked it so that it snapped like a dry branch. He had broken the ram's leg, and it fell bleating on to its knees. Then Aleb seized the right hind leg, while the left twisted round and hung quite limp. The visitors and the slaves exclaimed in dismay, and the Devil, sitting up in the tree, rejoiced that Aleb had done his task so cleverly. The master looked as black as thunder, frowned, bent his head, and did not say a word. The visitors and the slaves were silent, too, waiting to see what would follow. After remaining silent for a while, the master shook himself as if to throw off some burden. Then he lifted his head, and raising his eyes heavenward, remained so for a short time. Presently the wrinkles passed from his face, and he looked down at Aleb with a smile, saying:

'Oh, Aleb, Aleb! Your master bade you anger me; but my master is stronger than yours. I am not angry with you, but I will make your master angry. You are afraid that I shall punish you, and you have been wishing for your freedom. Know, then, Aleb, that I shall not punish you; but, as you wish to be free, here, before my guests, I set you free. Go where you like, and take your holiday garment with you!'

And the kind master returned with his guests to the house; but the Devil, grinding his teeth, fell down from the tree, and sank through the ground.

LITTLE GIRLS WISER THAN MEN

IT was an early Easter. Sledging was only just over; snow still lay in the yards; and water ran in streams down the village street.

Two little girls from different houses happened to meet in a lane between two homesteads, where the dirty water after running through the farm-yards had formed a large puddle. One girl was very small, the other a little bigger. Their mothers had dressed them both in new frocks. The little one wore a blue frock, the other a yellow print, and both had red kerchiefs on their heads. They had just come from church when they met, and first they showed each other their finery, and then they began to play. Soon the fancy took them to splash about in the water, and the smaller one was going to step into the puddle, shoes and all, when the elder checked her:

'Don't go in so, Malásha,' said she, 'your mother will scold you. I will take off my shoes and stockings, and you take off yours.'

They did so; and then, picking up their skirts, began walking towards each other through the puddle. The water came up to Malásha's ankles, and she said:

'It is deep, Akoúlya, I'm afraid!'

'Come on,' replied the other. 'Don't be frightened. It won't get any deeper.'

When they got near one another, Akoúlya said:

'Mind, Malásha, don't splash. Walk carefully!'

She had hardly said this, when Malásha plumped down her foot so that the water splashed right on to Akoúlya's frock. The frock was splashed, and so were Akoúlya's eyes and nose. When she saw the stains on her frock, she was angry and ran after Malásha to strike her. Malásha was frightened, and seeing that she had got herself into trouble, she scrambled out of the puddle, and prepared to run home. Just then Akoúlya's mother happened to be passing, and seeing that her daughter's skirt was splashed, and her sleeves dirty, she said:

'You naughty, dirty girl, what have you been doing?'

'Malásha did it on purpose,' replied the girl.

At this Akoúlya's mother seized Malásha, and struck her on the back of her neck. Malásha began to howl so that she could be heard all down the street. Her mother came out.

'What are you beating my girl for?' said she; and began scolding her neighbour. One word led to another and they had an angry quarrel. The men came out, and a crowd collected in the street, everyone shouting and no one listening. They all went on quarrelling, till one gave another a push, and the affair had very nearly come to blows, when Akoúlya's old grandmother, stepping in among them, tried to calm them.

'What are you thinking of, friends? Is it right to behave so? On a day like this, too! It is a time for rejoicing, and not for such folly as this.'

They would not listen to the old woman, and nearly knocked her off her feet. And she would not have been able to quiet the crowd, if it had not been for Akoúlya and Malásha themselves. While the women were abusing each other, Akoúlya had wiped the mud off her frock, and gone back to the puddle. She took a stone and began scraping away the earth in front of the puddle to make a channel through which the water could run out into the street. Presently Malásha joined her, and with a chip of wood helped her dig the channel. Just as the men were beginning to fight, the water from the little girls' channel ran streaming into the street towards the very place where the old woman was trying to pacify the men. The girls followed it; one running each side of the little stream.

'Catch it, Malásha! Catch it!' shouted Akoúlya; while Malásha could not speak for laughing.

Highly delighted, and watching the chip float along on their stream, the little girls ran straight into the group of men; and the old woman, seeing them, said to the men:

'Are you not ashamed of yourselves? To go fighting on account of these lassies, when they themselves have forgotten all about it, and are playing happily together. Dear little souls! They are wiser than you!'

The men looked at the little girls, and were ashamed, and, laughing at themselves, went back each to his own home.

'Except ye turn, and become as little children, ye shall in no wise enter into the kingdom of heaven.'

ILYÁS

THERE once lived, in the Government of Oufá, a Bashkír named Ilyás. His father, who died a year after he had found his son a wife, did not leave him much property. Ilyás then had only seven mares, two cows, and about a score of sheep. He was a good manager, however, and soon began to acquire more. He and his wife worked from morn till night; rising earlier than others and going later to bed; and his possessions increased year by year. Living in this way, Ilyás little by little acquired great wealth. At the end of thirty-five years he had 200 horses, 150 head of cattle, and 1,200 sheep. Hired labourers tended his flocks and herds, and hired women milked his mares and cows, and made kumiss,[1] butter and cheese. Ilyás had abundance of everything, and everyone in the district envied him. They said of him:

'Ilyás is a fortunate man: he has plenty of everything. This world must be a pleasant place for him.'

People of position heard of Ilyás and sought his acquaintance. Visitors came to him from afar; and he welcomed everyone, and gave them food and drink. Whoever might come, there was always kumiss, tea, sherbet, and mutton to set before them. Whenever visitors arrived a sheep would be killed, or sometimes two; and if many guests came he would even slaughter a mare for them.

Ilyás had three children: two sons and a daughter; and he married them all off. While he was poor, his sons worked with him, and looked after the flocks and herds themselves; but

---

1 Kumiss (or more properly *koumýs*) is a fermented drink prepared from mare's milk.

when he grew rich they got spoiled, and one of them took to drink. The eldest was killed in a brawl; and the younger, who had married a self-willed woman, ceased to obey his father, and they could not live together any more.

So they parted, and Ilyás gave his son a house and some of the cattle; and this diminished his wealth. Soon after that, a disease broke out among Ilyás's sheep, and many died. Then followed a bad harvest, and the hay crop failed; and many cattle died that winter. Then the Kirghíz captured his best herd of horses; and Ilyás's property dwindled away. It became smaller and smaller, while at the same time his strength grew less; till, by the time he was seventy years old, he had begun to sell his furs, carpets, saddles, and tents. At last he had to part with his remaining cattle, and found himself face to face with want. Before he knew how it had happened, he had lost everything, and in their old age he and his wife had to go into service. Ilyás had nothing left, except the clothes on his back, a fur cloak, a cup, his indoor shoes and overshoes, and his wife, Sham-Shemagi, who also was old by this time. The son who had parted from him had gone into a far country, and his daughter was dead, so that there was no one to help the old couple.

Their neighbour, Muhammad-Shah, took pity on them. Muhammad-Shah was neither rich nor poor, but lived comfortably, and was a good man. He remembered Ilyás's hospitality, and pitying him, said:

'Come and live with me, Ilyás, you and your old woman. In summer you can work in my melon-garden as much as your strength allows, and in winter feed my cattle; and Sham-Shemagi shall milk my mares and make kumiss. I will feed and clothe you both. When you need anything, tell me, and you shall have it.'

Ilyás thanked his neighbour, and he and his wife took service with Muhammad-Shah as labourers. At first the position seemed hard to them, but they got used to it, and lived on, working as much as their strength allowed.

Muhammad-Shah found it was to his advantage to keep such people, because, having been masters themselves, they knew how to manage and were not lazy, but did all the work they could. Yet it grieved Muhammad-Shah to see people brought so low who had been of such high standing.

It happened once that some of Muhammad-Shah's relatives came from a great distance to visit him, and a Mullah came too. Muhammad-Shah told Ilyás to catch a sheep and kill it. Ilyás skinned the sheep, and boiled it, and sent it in to the guests. The guests ate the mutton, had some tea, and then began drinking kumiss. As they were sitting with their host on down cushions on a carpet, conversing and sipping kumiss from their cups, Ilyás, having finished his work, passed by the open door. Muhammad-Shah, seeing him pass, said to one of the guests:

'Did you notice that old man who passed just now?'

'Yes,' said the visitor, 'what is there remarkable about him?'

'Only this – that he was once the richest man among us,' replied the host. 'His name is Ilyás. You may have heard of him.'

'Of course I have heard of him,' the guest answered. 'I never saw him before, but his fame has spread far and wide.'

'Yes, and now he has nothing left,' said Muhammad-Shah, 'and he lives with me as my labourer, and his old woman is here too – she milks the mares.'

The guest was astonished: he clicked with his tongue, shook his head, and said:

'Fortune turns like a wheel. One man it lifts, another it sets down! Does not the old man grieve over all he has lost?'

'Who can tell? He lives quietly and peacefully, and works well.'

'May I speak to him?' asked the guest. 'I should like to ask him about his life.'

'Why not?' replied the master, and he called from the *kibítka*[1] in which they were sitting:

'Babay'; (which in the Bashkír tongue means 'Grandfather') 'come in and have a cup of kumiss with us, and call your wife here also.'

---

1 A *kibítka* is a movable dwelling, made up of detachable wooden frames, forming a round, and covered over with felt.

Ilyás entered with his wife; and after exchanging greetings with his master and the guests, he repeated a prayer, and seated himself near the door. His wife passed in behind the curtain and sat down with her mistress.

A cup of kumiss was handed to Ilyás; he wished the guests and his master good health, bowed, drank a little, and put down the cup.

'Well, Daddy,' said the guest who had wished to speak to him, 'I suppose you feel rather sad at the sight of us. It must remind you of your former prosperity, and of your present sorrows.'

Ilyás smiled, and said:

'If I were to tell you what is happiness and what is misfortune, you would not believe me. You had better ask my wife. She is a woman, and what is in her heart is on her tongue. She will tell you the whole truth.'

The guest turned towards the curtain.

'Well, Granny,' he cried, 'tell me how your former happiness compares with your present misfortune.'

And Sham-Shemagi answered from behind the curtain:

'This is what I think about it: My old man and I lived for fifty years seeking happiness and not finding it; and it is only now, these last two years, since we had nothing left and have lived as labourers, that we have found real happiness, and we wish for nothing better than our present lot.'

The guests were astonished, and so was the master; he even rose and drew the curtain back, so as to see the old woman's face. There she stood with her arms folded, looking at her old husband, and smiling; and he smiled back at her. The old woman went on:

'I speak the truth and do not jest. For half a century we sought for happiness, and as long as we were rich we never found it. Now that we have nothing left, and have taken service as labourers, we have found such happiness that we want nothing better.'

'But in what does your happiness consist?' asked the guest.

'Why, in this,' she replied, 'when we were rich, my husband and I had so many cares that we had no time to talk to one another, or to think of our souls, or to pray to God. Now we had visitors, and had to consider what food to set before them, and what presents to give them, lest they should speak ill of us. When they left, we had to look after our labourers, who were always trying to shirk work and get the best food, while we wanted to get all we could out of them. So we sinned. Then we were in fear lest a wolf should kill a foal or a calf, or thieves steal our horses. We lay awake at night, worrying lest the ewes should overlie their lambs, and we got up again and again to see that all was well. One thing attended to, another care would spring up: how, for instance, to get enough fodder for the winter. And besides that, my old man and I used to disagree. He would say we must do so and so, and I would differ from him; and then we disputed – sinning again. So we passed from one trouble to another, from one sin to another, and found no happiness.'

'Well, and now?'

'Now, when my husband and I wake in the morning, we always have a loving word for one another, and we live peacefully, having nothing to quarrel about. We have no care but how best to serve our master. We work as much as our strength allows, and do it with a will, that our master may not lose, but profit by us. When we come in, dinner or supper is ready and there is kumiss to drink. We have fuel to burn when it is cold, and we have our fur cloak. And we have time to talk, time to think of our souls, and time to pray. For fifty years we sought happiness, but only now at last have we found it.'

The guests laughed.

But Ilyás said:

'Do not laugh, friends. It is not a matter for jesting – it is the truth of life. We also were foolish at first, and wept at the loss of our wealth; but now God has shown us the truth, and we tell it, not for our own consolation, but for your good.'

And the Mullah said:

'That is a wise speech. Ilyás has spoken the exact truth. The same is said in Holy Writ.'

And the guests ceased laughing and became thoughtful.

THE DEATH OF IVÁN ILÝCH

I

During an interval in the Melvínski trial in the large building of the Law Courts the members and public prosecutor met
in Iván Egórovich Shébek's private room, where the conversation turned on the celebrated Krasóvski case. Fëdor Vasílievich warmly maintained that it was not subject to their
jurisdiction, Iván Egórovich maintained the contrary, while
Peter Ivánovich, not having entered into the discussion at the
start, took no part in it but looked through the *Gazette* which
had just been handed in.

'Gentlemen,' he said, 'Iván Ilých has died!'

'You don't say so!'

'Here, read it yourself,' replied Peter Ivánovich, handing
Fëdor Vasílievich the paper still damp from the press. Surrounded by a black border were the words: 'Praskóvya Fëdorovna Goloviná, with profound sorrow, informs relatives and
friends of the demise of her beloved husband Iván Ilých
Golovín, Member of the Court of Justice, which occurred
on February the 4th of this year 1882. The funeral will take
place on Friday at one o'clock in the afternoon.'

Iván Ilých had been a colleague of the gentlemen present
and was liked by them all. He had been ill for some weeks with
an illness said to be incurable. His post had been kept open for
him, but there had been conjectures that in case of his death
Alexéev might receive his appointment, and that either Vínnikov or Shtábel would succeed Alexéev. So on receiving the
news of Iván Ilých's death the first thought of each of the
gentlemen in that private room was of the changes and
promotions it might occasion among themselves or their
acquaintances.

'I shall be sure to get Shtábel's place or Vínnikov's,' thought Fëdor Vasílievich. 'I was promised that long ago, and the promotion means an extra eight hundred rubles a year for me besides the allowance.'

'Now I must apply for my brother-in-law's transfer from Kalúga,' thought Peter Ivánovich. 'My wife will be very glad, and then she won't be able to say that I never do anything for her relations.'

'I thought he would never leave his bed again,' said Peter Ivánovich aloud. 'It's very sad.'

'But what really was the matter with him?'

'The doctors couldn't say – at least they could, but each of them said something different. When last I saw him I thought he was getting better.'

'And I haven't been to see him since the holidays. I always meant to go.'

'Had he any property?'

'I think his wife had a little – but something quite trifling.'

'We shall have to go to see her, but they live so terribly far away.'

'Far away from you, you mean. Everything's far away from your place.'

'You see, he never can forgive my living on the other side of the river,' said Peter Ivánovich, smiling at Shébek. Then, still talking of the distances between different parts of the city, they returned to the Court.

Besides considerations as to the possible transfers and pro-motions likely to result from Iván Ilých's death, the mere fact of the death of a near acquaintance aroused, as usual, in all who heard of it the complacent feeling that, 'it is he who is dead and not I'.

Each one thought or felt, 'Well, he's dead but I'm alive!' But the more intimate of Iván Ilých's acquaintances, his so-called friends, could not help thinking also that they would now have to fulfil the very tiresome demands of propriety by attending the funeral service and paying a visit of condolence to the widow.

Fëdor Vasílievich and Peter Ivánovich had been his nearest acquaintances. Peter Ivánovich had studied law with Iván Ilých and had considered himself to be under obligations to him.

Having told his wife at dinner-time of Iván Ilých's death, and of his conjecture that it might be possible to get her brother transferred to their circuit, Peter Ivánovich sacrificed his usual nap, put on his evening clothes, and drove to Iván Ilých's house.

At the entrance stood a carriage and two cabs. Leaning against the wall in the hall downstairs near the cloak-stand was a coffin-lid covered with cloth of gold, ornamented with gold cord and tassels, that had been polished up with metal powder. Two ladies in black were taking off their fur cloaks. Peter Ivánovich recognized one of them as Iván Ilých's sister, but the other was a stranger to him. His colleague Schwartz was just coming downstairs, but on seeing Peter Ivánovich enter he stopped and winked at him, as if to say: 'Iván Ilých has made a mess of things – not like you and me.'

Schwartz's face with his Piccadilly whiskers, and his slim figure in evening dress, had as usual an air of elegant solemnity which contrasted with the playfulness of his character and had a special piquancy here, or so it seemed to Peter Ivánovich.

Peter Ivánovich allowed the ladies to precede him and slowly followed them upstairs. Schwartz did not come down but remained where he was, and Peter Ivánovich understood that he wanted to arrange where they should play bridge that evening. The ladies went upstairs to the widow's room, and Schwartz with seriously compressed lips but a playful look in his eyes, indicated by a twist of his eyebrows the room to the right where the body lay.

Peter Ivánovich, like everyone else on such occasions, entered feeling uncertain what he would have to do. All he knew was that at such times it is always safe to cross oneself. But he was not quite sure whether one should make obeisances while doing so. He therefore adopted a middle course. On entering the room he began crossing himself and made a slight movement resembling a bow. At the same time, as far as the motion of his head and arm allowed, he surveyed the room. Two young men – apparently nephews, one of whom was a high-school pupil – were leaving the room, crossing themselves as they did so. An old woman was standing motionless, and a lady with strangely arched eyebrows was saying something to her in a whisper. A vigorous, resolute Church Reader, in a frock-coat, was reading something in a loud voice with an expression that precluded any contradiction. The butler's assistant, Gerásim, stepping lightly in front of Peter Ivánovich, was strewing something on the floor. Noticing this, Peter Ivánovich was immediately aware of a faint odour of a decomposing body.

The last time he had called on Iván Ilých, Peter Ivánovich had seen Gerásim in the study. Iván Ilých had been particularly fond of him and he was performing the duty of a sick-nurse.

Peter Ivánovich continued to make the sign of the cross slightly inclining his head in an intermediate direction between the coffin, the Reader, and the icons on the table in a corner of the room. Afterwards, when it seemed to him that this movement of his arm in crossing himself had gone on too long, he stopped and began to look at the corpse.

The dead man lay, as dead men always lie, in a specially heavy way, his rigid limbs sunk in the soft cushions of the coffin, with the head forever bowed on the pillow. His yellow waxen brow with bald patches over his sunken temples was thrust up in the way peculiar to the dead, the protruding nose seeming to press on the upper lip. He was much changed and had grown even thinner since Peter Ivánovich had last seen him, but, as is always the case with the dead, his face was handsomer and above all more dignified than when he was alive. The expression on the face said that what was necessary had been accomplished, and accomplished rightly. Besides this there was in that expression a reproach and a warning to the living. This warning seemed to Peter Ivánovich out of place, or at least not applicable to him. He felt a certain discomfort and so he hurriedly crossed himself once more and turned and went out of the door – too hurriedly and too regardless of propriety, as he himself was aware.

Schwartz was waiting for him in the adjoining room with legs spread wide apart and both hands toying with his top-hat behind his back. The mere sight of that playful, well-groomed, and elegant figure refreshed Peter Ivánovich. He felt that Schwartz was above all these happenings and would not surrender to any depressing influences. His very look said that this incident of a church service for Iván Ilých could not be a sufficient reason for infringing the order of the session – in other words, that it would certainly not prevent his unwrapping a new pack of cards and shuffling them that evening while a footman placed four fresh candles on the table: in fact, that there was no reason for supposing that this incident would hinder their spending the evening agreeably. Indeed he said this in a whisper as Peter Ivánovich passed him, proposing that they should meet for a game at Fëdor Vasílievich's. But apparently Peter Ivánovich was not destined to play bridge that evening. Praskóvya Fëdorovna (a short, fat woman who despite all efforts to the contrary had continued to broaden steadily from her shoulders downwards and who had the same extraordinarily arched eyebrows as the lady who had been standing by the coffin), dressed all in black, her head covered with lace, came out of her own room with some other ladies, conducted them to the room where the dead body lay, and said: 'The service will begin immediately. Please go in.'

Schwartz, making an indefinite bow, stood still, evidently neither accepting nor declining this invitation. Praskóvya Fëdorovna recognizing Peter Ivánovich, sighed, went close up to him, took his hand, and said: 'I know you were a true friend to Iván Ilých . . .' and looked at him awaiting some suitable response. And Peter Ivánovich knew that, just as it had been the right thing to cross himself in that room, so what he had to do here was to press her hand, sigh, and say, 'Believe me . . .'. So he did all this and as he did it felt that the desired result had been achieved: that both he and she were touched.

'Come with me. I want to speak to you before it begins,' said the widow. 'Give me your arm.'

Peter Ivánovich gave her his arm and they went to the inner rooms, passing Schwartz who winked at Peter Ivánovich compassionately.

'That does for our bridge! Don't object if we find another player. Perhaps you can cut in when you do escape,' said his playful look.

Peter Ivánovich sighed still more deeply and despondently, and Praskóvya Fëdorovna pressed his arm gratefully. When they reached the drawing-room, upholstered in pink cretonne and lighted by a dim lamp, they sat down at the table – she on a sofa and Peter Ivánovich on a low pouffe, the springs of which yielded spasmodically under his weight. Praskóvya Fëdorovna had been on the point of warning him to take another seat, but felt that such a warning was out of keeping with her present condition and so changed her mind. As he sat down on the pouffe Peter Ivánovich recalled how Iván Ilých had arranged this room and had consulted him regarding this pink cretonne with green leaves. The whole room was full of furniture and knick-knacks, and on her way to the sofa the lace of the widow's black shawl caught on the carved edge of the table. Peter Ivánovich rose to detach it, and the springs of the pouffe, relieved of his weight, rose also and gave him a push. The widow began detaching her shawl herself, and Peter Ivánovich again sat down, suppressing the rebellious springs of the pouffe under him. But the widow had not quite freed herself and Peter Ivánovich got up again, and again the pouffe rebelled and even creaked. When this was all over she took out a clean cambric handkerchief and began to weep. The episode with the shawl and the struggle with the pouffe had cooled Peter Ivánovich's emotions and he sat there with a sullen look on his face. This awkward situation was interrupted by Sokolóv, Iván Ilých's butler, who came to report that the plot in the cemetery that Praskóvya Fëdorovna had chosen would cost two hundred rubles. She stopped weeping and, looking at Peter Ivánovich with the air of a victim, remarked in French that it was very hard for her. Peter Ivánovich made a silent gesture signifying his full conviction that it must indeed be so.

'Please smoke,' she said in a magnanimous yet crushed voice, and turned to discuss with Sokolóv the price of the plot for the grave.

Peter Ivánovich while lighting his cigarette heard her inquiring very circumstantially into the prices of different plots in the cemetery and finally decide which she would take. When that was done she gave instructions about engaging the choir. Sokolóv then left the room.

'I look after everything myself,' she told Peter Ivánovich, shifting the albums that lay on the table; and noticing that the table was endangered by his cigarette-ash, she immediately passed him an ashtray, saying as she did so: 'I consider it an affectation to say that my grief prevents my attending to practical affairs. On the contrary, if anything can – I won't say console me, but – distract me, it is seeing to everything concerning him.' She again took out her handkerchief as if preparing to cry, but suddenly, as if mastering her feeling, she shook herself and began to speak calmly. 'But there is something I want to talk to you about.'

Peter Ivánovich bowed, keeping control of the springs of the pouffe, which immediately began quivering under him.

'He suffered terribly the last few days.'

'Did he?' said Peter Ivánovich.

'Oh, terribly! He screamed unceasingly, not for minutes but for hours. For the last three days he screamed incessantly. It was unendurable. I cannot understand how I bore it; you could hear him three rooms off. Oh, what I have suffered!'

'Is it possible that he was conscious all that time?' asked Peter Ivánovich.

'Yes,' she whispered. 'To the last moment. He took leave of us a quarter of an hour before he died, and asked us to take Volódya away.'

The thought of the sufferings of this man he had known so intimately, first as a merry little boy, then as a school-mate, and later as a grown-up colleague, suddenly struck Peter Ivánovich with horror, despite an unpleasant consciousness of his own and this woman's dissimulation. He again saw that brow, and that nose pressing down on the lip, and felt afraid for himself.

'Three days of frightful suffering and then death! Why, that might suddenly, at any time, happen to me,' he thought, and for a moment felt terrified. But – he did not himself know how – the customary reflection at once occurred to him that this had happened to Iván Ilých and not to him, and that it should not and could not happen to him, and that to think that it could would be yielding to depression which he ought not to do, as Schwartz's expression plainly showed. After which reflection Peter Ivánovich felt reassured, and began to ask with interest about the details of Iván Ilých's death, as though death was an accident natural to Iván Ilých but certainly not to himself.

After many details of the really dreadful physical sufferings Iván Ilých had endured (which details he learnt only from the effect those sufferings had produced on Praskóvya Fëdorovna's nerves) the widow apparently found it necessary to get to business.

'Oh, Peter Ivánovich, how hard it is! How terribly, terribly hard!' and she again began to weep.

Peter Ivánovich sighed and waited for her to finish blowing her nose. When she had done so he said, 'Believe me . . .', and she again began talking and brought out what was evidently her chief concern with him – namely, to question him as to how she could obtain a grant of money from the government on the occasion of her husband's death. She made it appear that she was asking Peter Ivánovich's advice about her pension, but he soon saw that she already knew about that to the minutest detail, more even than he did himself. She knew how much could be got out of the government in consequence of her husband's death, but wanted to find out whether she could not possibly extract something more. Peter Ivánovich tried to think of some means of doing so, but after reflecting for a while and, out of propriety, condemning the government for its niggardliness, he said he thought that nothing more could be got. Then she sighed and evidently began to devise means of getting rid of her visitor. Noticing this, he put out his cigarette, rose, pressed her hand, and went out into the ante-room.

In the dining-room where the clock stood that Iván Ilých had liked so much and had bought at an antique shop, Peter Ivánovich met a priest and a few acquaintances who had come to attend the service, and he recognized Iván Ilých's daughter, a handsome young woman. She was in black and her slim figure appeared slimmer than ever. She had a gloomy, determined, almost angry expression, and bowed to Peter Ivánovich as though he were in some way to blame. Behind her, with the same offended look, stood a wealthy young man, an examining magistrate, whom Peter Ivánovich also knew and who was her fiancé, as he had heard. He bowed mournfully to them and was about to pass into the death-chamber, when from under the stairs appeared the figure of Iván Ilých's schoolboy son, who was extremely like his father. He seemed a little Iván Ilých, such as Peter Ivánovich remembered when they studied law together. His tear-stained eyes had in them the look that is seen in the eyes of boys of thirteen or fourteen who are not pure-minded. When he saw Peter Ivánovich he scowled morosely and shamefacedly. Peter Ivánovich nodded to him and entered the death-chamber. The service began: candles, groans, incense, tears, and sobs. Peter Ivánovich stood looking gloomily down at his feet. He did not look once at the dead man, did not yield to any depressing influence, and was one of the first to leave the room. There was no one in the ante-room, but Gerásim darted out of the dead man's room, rummaged with his strong hands among the fur coats to find Peter Ivánovich's and helped him on with it.

'Well, friend Gerásim,' said Peter Ivánovich, so as to say something. 'It's a sad affair, isn't it?'

'It's God's will. We shall all come to it some day,' said Gerásim, displaying his teeth – the even, white teeth of a healthy peasant – and, like a man in the thick of urgent work, he briskly opened the front door, called the coachman, helped Peter Ivánovich into the sledge, and sprang back to the porch as if in readiness for what he had to do next.

Peter Ivánovich found the fresh air particularly pleasant after the smell of incense, the dead body, and carbolic acid.

'Where to, sir?' asked the coachman.

'It's not too late even now.... I'll call round on Fëdor Vasílievich.'

He accordingly drove there and found them just finishing the first rubber, so that it was quite convenient for him to cut in.

II

IVÁN Ilých's life had been most simple and most ordinary and therefore most terrible.

He had been a member of the Court of Justice, and died at the age of forty-five. His father had been an official who after serving in various ministries and departments in Petersburg had made the sort of career which brings men to positions from which by reason of their long service they cannot be dismissed, though they are obviously unfit to hold any responsible position, and for whom therefore posts are specially created, which though fictitious carry salaries of from six to ten thousand rubles that are not fictitious, and in receipt of which they live on to a great age.

Such was the Privy Councillor and superfluous member of various superfluous institutions, Ilyá Epímovich Golovín.

He had three sons, of whom Iván Ilých was the second. The eldest son was following in his father's footsteps only in another department, and was already approaching that stage in the service at which a similar sinecure would be reached. The third son was a failure. He had ruined his prospects in a number of positions and was now serving in the railway department. His father and brothers, and still more their wives, not merely disliked meeting him, but avoided remembering his existence unless compelled to do so. His sister had married Baron Greff, a Petersburg official of her father's type. Iván Ilých was *le phénix de la famille* as people said. He was neither as cold and formal as his elder brother nor as wild as the younger, but was a happy mean between them – an intelligent, polished, lively and agreeable man. He had studied with his younger brother at the School of Law, but the latter had failed to complete the course and was expelled when he was in the fifth class. Iván Ilých finished the course well. Even when he was at the School of Law he was just what he remained for the rest of his life: a capable, cheerful, good-natured, and sociable man, though strict in the fulfilment of what he considered to be his duty: and he considered his duty to be what was so considered by those in authority. Neither as a boy nor as a man was he a toady, but from early youth was by nature attracted to people of high station as a fly is drawn to the light, assimilating their ways and views of life and establishing friendly relations with them. All the enthusiasms of childhood and youth passed without leaving much trace on him; he succumbed to sensuality, to vanity, and latterly among the highest classes to liberalism, but always within limits which his instinct unfailingly indicated to him as correct.

At school he had done things which had formerly seemed to him very horrid and made him feel disgusted with himself when he did them; but when later on he saw that such actions were done by people of good position and that they did not regard them as wrong, he was able not exactly to regard them as right, but to forget about them entirely or not be at all troubled at remembering them.

Having graduated from the School of Law and qualified for the tenth rank of the civil service, and having received money from his father for his equipment, Iván Ilých ordered himself clothes at Scharmer's, the fashionable tailor, hung a medallion inscribed *respice finem* on his watch-chain, took leave of his professor and the prince who was patron of the school, had a farewell dinner with his comrades at Donon's first-class restaurant, and with his new and fashionable portmanteau, linen, clothes, shaving and other toilet appliances, and a travelling rug, all purchased at the best shops, he set off for one of the provinces where, through his father's influence, he had been attached to the Governor as an official for special service.

In the province Iván Ilých soon arranged as easy and agreeable a position for himself as he had had at the School of Law. He performed his official tasks, made his career, and at the same time amused himself pleasantly and decorously. Occasionally he paid official visits to country districts, where he behaved with dignity both to his superiors and inferiors, and performed the duties entrusted to him, which related chiefly to the sectarians, with an exactness and incorruptible honesty of which he could not but feel proud.

In official matters, despite his youth and taste for frivolous gaiety, he was exceedingly reserved, punctilious, and even severe; but in society he was often amusing and witty, and always good-natured, correct in his manner, and *bon enfant*, as the Governor and his wife – with whom he was like one of the family – used to say of him.

In the province he had an affair with a lady who made advances to the elegant young lawyer, and there was also a milliner; and there were carousals with aides-de-camp who visited the district, and after-supper visits to a certain outlying street of doubtful reputation; and there was too some obsequiousness to his chief and even to his chief's wife, but all this was done with such a tone of good breeding that no hard names could be applied to it. It all came under the heading of the French saying: '*Il faut que jeunesse se passe*.'[1] It was all done with clean hands, in clean linen, with French phrases, and above all among people of the best society and consequently with the approval of people of rank.

So Iván Ilých served for five years and then came a change in his official life. The new and reformed judicial institutions were introduced, and new men were needed. Iván Ilých became such a new man. He was offered the post of examining magistrate, and he accepted it though the post was in another province and obliged him to give up the connexions he had formed and to make new ones. His friends met to give him a send-off; they had a group-photograph taken and presented him with a silver cigarette-case, and he set off to his new post.

As examining magistrate Iván Ilých was just as *comme il faut* and decorous a man, inspiring general respect and capable of separating his official duties from his private life, as he had been when acting as an official on special service. His duties now as

1 Youth must have its fling.

examining magistrate were far more interesting and attractive than before. In his former position it had been pleasant to wear an undress uniform made by Scharmer, and to pass through the crowd of petitioners and officials who were timorously awaiting an audience with the Governor, and who envied him as with free and easy gait he went straight into his chief's private room to have a cup of tea and a cigarette with him. But not many people had then been directly dependent on him – only police officials and the sectarians when he went on special missions – and he liked to treat them politely, almost as comrades, as if he were letting them feel that he who had the power to crush them was treating them in this simple, friendly way. There were then but few such people. But now, as an examining magistrate, Iván Ilých felt that everyone without exception, even the most important and self-satisfied, was in his power, and that he need only write a few words on a sheet of paper with a certain heading, and this or that important, self-satisfied person would be brought before him in the role of an accused person or a witness, and if he did not choose to allow him to sit down, would have to stand before him and answer his questions. Iván Ilých never abused his power; he tried on the contrary to soften its expression, but the consciousness of it and of the possibility of softening its effect, supplied the chief interest and attraction of his office. In his work itself, especially in his examinations, he very soon acquired a method of eliminating all considerations irrelevant to the legal aspect of the case, and reducing even the most complicated case to a form in which it would be presented on paper only in its externals, completely excluding his personal opinion of the matter, while above all observing every prescribed formality. The work was new and Iván Ilých was one of the first men to apply the new Code of 1864.[1]

On taking up the post of examining magistrate in a new town, he made new acquaintances and connexions, placed himself on a new footing, and assumed a somewhat different

1 The emancipation of the serfs in 1861 was followed by a thorough all-round reform of judicial proceedings.

tone. He took up an attitude of rather dignified aloofness towards the provincial authorities, but picked out the best circle of legal gentlemen and wealthy gentry living in the town and assumed a tone of slight dissatisfaction with the government, of moderate liberalism, and of enlightened citizenship. At the same time, without at all altering the elegance of his toilet, he ceased shaving his chin and allowed his beard to grow as it pleased.

Iván Ilých settled down very pleasantly in this new town. The society there, which inclined towards opposition to the Governor, was friendly, his salary was larger, and he began to play *vint* [a form of bridge], which he found added not a little to the pleasure of life, for he had a capacity for cards, played good-humouredly, and calculated rapidly and astutely, so that he usually won.

After living there for two years he met his future wife, Praskóvya Fëdorovna Míkhel, who was the most attractive, clever, and brilliant girl of the set in which he moved, and among other amusements and relaxations from his labours as examining magistrate, Iván Ilých established light and playful relations with her.

While he had been an official on special service he had been accustomed to dance, but now as an examining magistrate it was exceptional for him to do so. If he danced now, he did it as if to show that though he served under the reformed order of things, and had reached the fifth official rank, yet when it came to dancing he could do it better than most people. So at the end of an evening he sometimes danced with Praskóvya Fëdorovna, and it was chiefly during these dances that he captivated her. She fell in love with him. Iván Ilých had at first no definite intention of marrying, but when the girl fell in love with him he said to himself: 'Really, why shouldn't I marry?'

Praskóvya Fëdorovna came of a good family, was not bad looking, and had some little property. Iván Ilých might have aspired to a more brilliant match, but even this was good. He had his salary, and she, he hoped, would have an equal income. She was well connected, and was a sweet, pretty, and thoroughly correct young woman. To say that Iván Ilých married because he fell in love with Praskóvya Fëdorovna and found that she sympathized with his views of life would be as incorrect as to say that he married because his social circle approved of the match. He was swayed by both these considerations: the marriage gave him personal satisfaction, and at the same time it was considered the right thing by the most highly placed of his associates.

So Iván Ilých got married.

The preparations for marriage and the beginning of married life, with its conjugal caresses, the new furniture, new crockery, and new linen, were very pleasant until his wife became pregnant – so that Iván Ilých had begun to think that marriage would not impair the easy, agreeable, gay and always decorous character of his life, approved of by society and regarded by himself as natural, but would even improve it. But from the first months of his wife's pregnancy, something new, unpleasant, depressing, and unseemly, and from which there was no way of escape, unexpectedly showed itself.

His wife, without any reason – *de gaieté de cœur* as Iván Ilých expressed it to himself – began to disturb the pleasure and propriety of their life. She began to be jealous without any cause, expected him to devote his whole attention to her, found fault with everything, and made coarse and ill-mannered scenes.

At first Iván Ilých hoped to escape from the unpleasantness of this state of affairs by the same easy and decorous relation to life that had served him heretofore: he tried to ignore his wife's disagreeable moods, continued to live in his usual easy and pleasant way, invited friends to his house for a game of cards, and also tried going out to his club or spending his evenings with friends. But one day his wife began upbraiding him so vigorously, using such coarse words, and continued to abuse him every time he did not fulfil her demands, so resolutely and with such evident determination not to give way till he submitted – that is, till he stayed at home and was bored just as she was – that he became alarmed. He now realized that matrimony – at any rate with Praskóvya Fëdorovna – was not always conducive to the pleasures and amenities of life, but on the contrary often infringed both comfort and propriety, and that he must therefore entrench himself against such infringement. And Iván Ilých began to seek for means of doing so. His official duties were the one thing that imposed upon Praskóvya Fëdorovna, and by means of his official work and the duties attached to it he began struggling with his wife to secure his own independence.

With the birth of their child, the attempts to feed it and the various failures in doing so, and with the real and imaginary illnesses of mother and child, in which Iván Ilých's sympathy was demanded but about which he understood nothing, the need of securing for himself an existence outside his family life became still more imperative.

As his wife grew more irritable and exacting and Iván Ilých transferred the centre of gravity of his life more and more to his official work, so did he grow to like his work better and became more ambitious than before.

Very soon, within a year of his wedding, Iván Ilých had realized that marriage, though it may add some comforts to life, is in fact a very intricate and difficult affair towards which in order to perform one's duty, that is, to lead a decorous life approved of by society, one must adopt a definite attitude just as towards one's official duties.

And Iván Ilých evolved such an attitude towards married life. He only required of it those conveniences – dinner at home, housewife, and bed – which it could give him, and above all that propriety of external forms required by public opinion. For the rest he looked for light-hearted pleasure and propriety, and was very thankful when he found them, but if he met with antagonism and querulousness he at once retired into his separate fenced-off world of official duties, where he found satisfaction.

Iván Ilých was esteemed a good official, and after three years was made Assistant Public Prosecutor. His new duties, their importance, the possibility of indicting and imprisoning anyone he chose, the publicity his speeches received, and the success he had in all these things, made his work still more attractive.

More children came. His wife became more and more querulous and ill-tempered, but the attitude Iván Ilých had adopted towards his home life rendered him almost impervious to her grumbling.

After seven years' service in that town he was transferred to another province as Public Prosecutor. They moved, but were short of money and his wife did not like the place they moved to. Though the salary was higher the cost of living was greater, besides which two of their children died and family life became still more unpleasant for him.

Praskóvya Fëdorovna blamed her husband for every inconvenience they encountered in their new home. Most of the conversations between husband and wife, especially as to the children's education, led to topics which recalled former disputes, and those disputes were apt to flare up again at any moment. There remained only those rare periods of amorousness which still came to them at times but did not last long. These were islets at which they anchored for a while and then again set out upon that ocean of veiled hostility which showed itself in their aloofness from one another. This aloofness might have grieved Iván Ilých had he considered that it ought not to exist, but he now regarded the position as normal, and even made it the goal at which he aimed in family life. His aim was to free himself more and more from those unpleasantnesses and to give them a semblance of harmlessness and propriety. He attained this by spending less and less time with his family, and when obliged to be at home he tried to safeguard his position by the presence of outsiders. The chief thing however was that he had his official duties. The whole interest of his life now centred in the official world and that interest absorbed him. The consciousness of his power, being able to ruin anybody he wished to ruin, the importance, even the external dignity of his entry into court, or meetings with his subordinates, his success with superiors and inferiors, and above all his masterly handling of cases, of which he was conscious – all this gave him pleasure and filled his life, together with chats with his colleagues, dinners, and bridge. So that on the whole Iván Ilých's life continued to flow as he considered it should do – pleasantly and properly.

So things continued for another seven years. His eldest daughter was already sixteen, another child had died, and only one son was left, a schoolboy and a subject of dissension. Iván Ilých wanted to put him in the School of Law, but to spite him Praskóvya Fëdorovna entered him at the High School. The daughter had been educated at home and had turned out well: the boy did not learn badly either.

III

So Iván Ilých lived for seventeen years after his marriage. He was already a Public Prosecutor of long standing, and had declined several proposed transfers while awaiting a more desirable post, when an unanticipated and unpleasant occurrence quite upset the peaceful course of his life. He was expecting to be offered the post of presiding judge in a University town, but Happe somehow came to the front and obtained the appointment instead. Iván Ilých became irritable, reproached Happe, and quarrelled both with him and with his immediate superiors – who became colder to him and again passed him over when other appointments were made.

This was in 1880, the hardest year of Iván Ilých's life. It was then that it became evident on the one hand that his salary was insufficient for them to live on, and on the other that he had been forgotten, and not only this, but that what was for him the greatest and most cruel injustice appeared to others a quite ordinary occurrence. Even his father did not consider it his duty to help him. Iván Ilých felt himself abandoned by every-one, and that they regarded his position with a salary of 3,500 rubles [about £350] as quite normal and even fortunate. He alone knew that with the consciousness of the injustices done him, with his wife's incessant nagging, and with the debts he had contracted by living beyond his means, his position was far from normal.

In order to save money that summer he obtained leave of absence and went with his wife to live in the country at her brother's place.

In the country, without his work, he experienced *ennui* for the first time in his life, and not only *ennui* but intolerable depression, and he decided that it was impossible to go on living like that, and that it was necessary to take energetic measures.

Having passed a sleepless night pacing up and down the veranda, he decided to go to Petersburg and bestir himself, in order to punish those who had failed to appreciate him and to get transferred to another ministry.

Next day, despite many protests from his wife and her brother, he started for Petersburg with the sole object of obtaining a post with a salary of five thousand rubles a year. He was no longer bent on any particular department, or tendency, or kind of activity. All he now wanted was an appointment to another post with a salary of five thousand rubles, either in the administration, in the banks, with the railways, in one of the Empress Márya's Institutions, or even in the customs – but it had to carry with it a salary of five thousand rubles and be in a ministry other than that in which they had failed to appreciate him.

And this quest of Iván Ilých's was crowned with remarkable and unexpected success. At Kursk an acquaintance of his, F. I. Ilyín, got into the first-class carriage, sat down beside Iván Ilých, and told him of a telegram just received by the Governor of Kursk announcing that a change was about to take place in the ministry: Peter Ivánovich was to be superseded by Iván Semënovich.

The proposed change, apart from its significance for Russia, had a special significance for Iván Ilých, because by bringing forward a new man, Peter Petróvich, and consequently his friend Zachár Ivánovich, it was highly favourable for Iván Ilých, since Zachár Ivánovich was a friend and colleague of his.

In Moscow this news was confirmed, and on reaching Petersburg Iván Ilých found Zachár Ivánovich and received a definite promise of an appointment in his former department of Justice.

A week later he telegraphed to his wife: 'Zachár in Miller's place. I shall receive appointment on presentation of report.'

Thanks to this change of personnel, Iván Ilých had unexpectedly obtained an appointment in his former ministry which placed him two stages above his former colleagues besides giving him five thousand rubles salary and three thousand five hundred rubles for expenses connected with his removal. All his ill humour towards his former enemies and the whole department vanished, and Iván Ilých was completely happy.

He returned to the country more cheerful and contented than he had been for a long time. Praskóvya Fëdorovna also cheered up and a truce was arranged between them. Iván Ilých told of how he had been fêted by everybody in Petersburg, how all those who had been his enemies were put to shame and now fawned on him, how envious they were of his appointment, and how much everybody in Petersburg had liked him.

Praskóvya Fëdorovna listened to all this and appeared to believe it. She did not contradict anything, but only made plans for their life in the town to which they were going. Iván Ilých saw with delight that these plans were his plans, that he and his wife agreed, and that, after a stumble, his life was regaining its due and natural character of pleasant light-heartedness and decorum.

Iván Ilých had come back for a short time only, for he had to take up his new duties on the 10th of September. Moreover, he needed time to settle into the new place, to move all his belongings from the province, and to buy and order many additional things: in a word, to make such arrangements as he had resolved on, which were almost exactly what Praskóvya Fëdorovna too had decided on.

Now that everything had happened so fortunately, and that he and his wife were at one in their aims and moreover saw so little of one another, they got on together better than they had done since the first years of marriage. Iván Ilých had thought of taking his family away with him at once, but the insistence of his wife's brother and her sister-in-law, who had suddenly become particularly amiable and friendly to him and his family, induced him to depart alone.

THE DEATH OF IVÁN ILÝCH

So he departed, and the cheerful state of mind induced by his success and by the harmony between his wife and himself, the one intensifying the other, did not leave him. He found a delightful house, just the thing both he and his wife had dreamt of. Spacious, lofty reception-rooms in the old style, a convenient and dignified study, rooms for his wife and daughter, a study for his son – it might have been specially built for them. Iván Ilých himself superintended the arrangements, chose the wall-papers, supplemented the furniture (preferably with antiques which he considered particularly *comme il faut*), and supervised the upholstering. Everything progressed and progressed and approached the ideal he had set himself: even when things were only half completed they exceeded his expectations. He saw what a refined and elegant character, free from vulgarity, it would all have when it was ready. On falling asleep he pictured to himself how the reception-room would look. Looking at the yet unfinished drawing-room he could see the fireplace, the screen, the what-not, the little chairs dotted here and there, the dishes and plates on the walls, and the bronzes, as they would be when everything was in place. He was pleased by the thought of how his wife and daughter, who shared his taste in this matter, would be impressed by it. They were certainly not expecting as much. He had been particularly successful in finding, and buying cheaply, antiques which gave a particularly aristocratic character to the whole place. But in his letters he intentionally understated everything in order to be able to surprise them. All this so absorbed him that his new duties – though he liked his official work – interested him less than he had expected. Sometimes he even had moments of absent-mindedness during the Court Sessions, and would consider whether he should have straight or curved cornices for his curtains. He was so interested in it all that he often did things himself, rearranging the furniture, or rehanging the curtains. Once when mounting a step-ladder to show the upholsterer, who did not understand, how he wanted the hangings draped, he made a false step and slipped, but being a strong and agile man he clung on and only knocked his side against the knob of the window-frame. The bruised place was painful but the pain soon passed, and he felt particularly bright and well just then. He wrote: 'I feel fifteen years younger.' He thought he would have everything ready by September, but it dragged on till mid-October. But the result was charming not only in his eyes but to everyone who saw it.

In reality it was just what is usually seen in the houses of people of moderate means who want to appear rich, and therefore succeed only in resembling others like themselves: there were damasks, dark wood, plants, rugs, and dull and polished bronzes – all the things people of a certain class have in order to resemble other people of that class. His house was so like the others that it would never have been noticed, but to him it all seemed to be quite exceptional. He was very happy when he met his family at the station and brought them to the newly furnished house all lit up, where a footman in a white tie opened the door into the hall decorated with plants, and when they went on into the drawing-room and the study uttering exclamations of delight. He conducted them everywhere, drank in their praises eagerly, and beamed with pleasure. At tea that evening, when Praskóvya Fëdorovna among other things asked him about his fall, he laughed, and showed them how he had gone flying and had frightened the upholsterer.

'It's a good thing I'm a bit of an athlete. Another man might have been killed, but I merely knocked myself, just here; it hurts when it's touched, but it's passing off already – it's only a bruise.'

So they began living in their new home – in which, as always happens, when they got thoroughly settled in they found they were just one room short – and with the increased income, which as always was just a little (some five hundred rubles) too little, but it was all very nice.

Things went particularly well at first, before everything was finally arranged and while something had still to be done: this thing bought, that thing ordered, another thing moved, and something else adjusted. Though there were some disputes between husband and wife, they were both so well satisfied and had so much to do that it all passed off without any serious quarrels. When nothing was left to arrange it became rather dull and something seemed to be lacking, but they were then making acquaintances, forming habits, and life was growing fuller.

Iván Ilých spent his mornings at the law court and came home to dinner, and at first he was generally in a good humour, though he occasionally became irritable just on account of his house. (Every spot on the table-cloth or the upholstery, and every broken window-blind string, irritated him. He had devoted so much trouble to arranging it all that every disturbance of it distressed him.) But on the whole his life ran its course as he believed life should do: easily, pleasantly, and decorously.

He got up at nine, drank his coffee, read the paper, and then put on his undress uniform and went to the law courts. There the harness in which he worked had already been stretched to fit him and he donned it without a hitch: petitioners, inquiries at the chancery, the chancery itself, and the sittings public and administrative. In all this the thing was to exclude everything fresh and vital, which always disturbs the regular course of official business, and to admit only official relations with people, and then only on official grounds. A man would come, for instance, wanting some information. Iván Ilých, as one in whose sphere the matter did not lie, would have nothing to do with him: but if the man had some business with him in his official capacity, something that could be expressed on officially stamped paper, he would do everything, positively everything he could within the limits of such relations, and in doing so would maintain the semblance of friendly human relations, that is, would observe the courtesies of life. As soon as the official relations ended, so did everything else. Iván Ilých possessed this capacity to separate his real life from the official side of affairs and not mix the two, in the highest degree, and by long practice and natural aptitude had brought it to such a pitch that sometimes, in the manner of a virtuoso, he would even allow himself to let the human and official relations mingle. He let himself do this just because he felt that he could at any time he chose resume the strictly official attitude again and drop the human relation. And he did it all easily, pleasantly, correctly, and even artistically. In the intervals between the sessions he smoked, drank tea, chatted a little about politics, a little about general topics, a little about cards, but most of all about official appointments. Tired, but with the feelings of a virtuoso – one of the first violins who has played his part in an orchestra with precision – he would return home to find that his wife and daughter had been out paying calls, or had a visitor, and that his son had been to school, had done his homework with his tutor, and was duly learning what is taught at High Schools. Everything was as it should be. After dinner, if they had no visitors, Iván Ilých sometimes read a book that was being much discussed at the time, and in the evening settled down to work, that is, read official papers, compared the depositions of witnesses, and noted paragraphs of the Code applying to them. This was neither dull nor amusing. It was dull when he might have been playing bridge, but if no bridge was available it was at any rate better than doing nothing or sitting with his wife. Iván Ilých's chief pleasure was giving little dinners to which he invited men and women of good social position, and just as his drawing-room resembled all other drawing-rooms so did his enjoyable little parties resemble all other such parties.

Once they even gave a dance. Iván Ilých enjoyed it and everything went off well, except that it led to a violent quarrel with his wife about the cakes and sweets. Praskóvya Fëdorovna had made her own plans, but Iván Ilých insisted on getting everything from an expensive confectioner and ordered too many cakes, and the quarrel occurred because some of those cakes were left over and the confectioner's bill came to forty-five rubles. It was a great and disagreeable quarrel. Praskóvya Fëdorovna called him 'a fool and an imbecile', and he clutched at his head and made angry allusions to divorce.

But the dance itself had been enjoyable. The best people were there, and Iván Ilých had danced with Princess Trúfo-nova, a sister of the distinguished founder of the Society 'Bear my Burden'.

The pleasures connected with his work were pleasures of ambition; his social pleasures were those of vanity; but Iván Ilých's greatest pleasure was playing bridge. He acknowledged that whatever disagreeable incident happened in his life, the pleasure that beamed like a ray of light above everything else was to sit down to bridge with good players, not noisy partners, and of course to four-handed bridge (with five players it was annoying to have to stand out, though one pretended not to mind), to play a clever and serious game (when the cards allowed it) and then to have supper and drink a glass of wine. After a game of bridge, especially if he had won a little (to win a large sum was unpleasant), Iván Ilých went to bed in specially good humour.

So they lived. They formed a circle of acquaintances among the best people and were visited by people of importance and by young folk. In their views as to their acquaintances, husband, wife and daughter were entirely agreed, and tacitly and unanimously kept at arm's length and shook off the various shabby friends and relations who, with much show of affection, gushed into the drawing-room with its Japanese plates on the walls. Soon these shabby friends ceased to obtrude themselves and only the best people remained in the Golovíns' set.

Young men made up to Lisa, and Petríshchev, an examining magistrate and Dmítri Ivánovich Petríshchev's son and sole heir, began to be so attentive to her that Iván Ilých had already spoken to Praskóvya Fëdorovna about it, and considered whether they should not arrange a party for them, or get up some private theatricals.

So they lived, and all went well, without change, and life flowed pleasantly.

IV

THEY were all in good health. It could not be called ill health if Iván Ilých sometimes said that he had a queer taste in his mouth and felt some discomfort in his left side.

But this discomfort increased and, though not exactly painful, grew into a sense of pressure in his side accompanied by ill humour. And his irritability became worse and worse and began to mar the agreeable, easy, and correct life that had established itself in the Golovín family. Quarrels between husband and wife became more and more frequent, and soon the ease and amenity disappeared and even the decorum was barely maintained. Scenes again became frequent, and very few of those islets remained on which husband and wife could meet without an explosion. Praskóvya Fëdorovna now had good reason to say that her husband's temper was trying. With characteristic exaggeration she said he had always had a dreadful temper, and that it had needed all her good nature to put up with it for twenty years. It was true that now the quarrels were started by him. His bursts of temper always came just before dinner, often just as he began to eat his soup. Sometimes he noticed that a plate or dish was chipped, or the food was not right, or his son put his elbow on the table, or his daughter's hair was not done as he liked it, and for all this he blamed Praskóvya Fëdorovna. At first she retorted and said disagreeable things to him, but once or twice he fell into such a rage at the beginning of dinner that she realized it was due to some physical derangement brought on by taking food, and so she restrained herself and did not answer, but only hurried to get the dinner over. She regarded this self-restraint as highly praiseworthy. Having come to the conclusion that her husband had a dreadful temper and made her life miserable, she began to feel sorry for herself, and the more she pitied herself the more she hated her husband. She began to wish he would die; yet she did not want him to die because then his salary would cease. And this irritated her against him still more. She considered herself dreadfully unhappy just because not even his death could save her, and though she concealed her exasperation, that hidden exasperation of hers increased his irritation also.

After one scene in which Iván Ilých had been particularly unfair and after which he had said in explanation that he certainly was irritable but that it was due to his not being well, she said that if he was ill it should be attended to, and insisted on his going to see a celebrated doctor.

He went. Everything took place as he had expected and as it always does. There was the usual waiting and the important air assumed by the doctor, with which he was so familiar (resembling that which he himself assumed in court), and the sounding and listening, and the questions which called for answers that were foregone conclusions and were evidently unnecessary, and the look of importance which implied that 'if only you put yourself in our hands we will arrange everything – we know indubitably how it has to be done, always in the same way for everybody alike'. It was all just as it was in the law courts. The doctor put on just the same air towards him as he himself put on towards an accused person.

The doctor said that so-and-so indicated that there was so-and-so inside the patient, but if the investigation of so-and-so did not confirm this, then he must assume that and that. If he assumed that and that, then ... and so on. To Iván Ilých only one question was important: was his case serious or not? But the doctor ignored that inappropriate question. From his point of view it was not the one under consideration, the real question was to decide between a floating kidney, chronic catarrh, or appendicitis. It was not a question of Iván Ilých's life or death, but one between a floating kidney and appendicitis. And that question the doctor solved brilliantly, as it seemed to Iván Ilých, in favour of the appendix, with the reservation that should an examination of the urine give fresh indications the matter would be reconsidered. All this was just what Iván Ilých had himself brilliantly accomplished a thousand times in dealing with men on trial. The doctor summed up just as brilliantly, looking over his spectacles triumphantly and even gaily at the accused. From the doctor's summing up Iván Ilých concluded that things were bad, but that for the doctor, and perhaps for everybody else, it was a matter of indifference, though for him it was bad. And this conclusion struck him painfully, arousing in him a great feeling of pity for himself and of bitterness towards the doctor's indifference to a matter of such importance.

He said nothing of this, but rose, placed the doctor's fee on the table, and remarked with a sigh: 'We sick people probably often put inappropriate questions. But tell me, in general, is this complaint dangerous, or not?...'

The doctor looked at him sternly over his spectacles with one eye, as if to say: 'Prisoner, if you will not keep to the questions put to you, I shall be obliged to have you removed from the court.'

'I have already told you what I consider necessary and proper. The analysis may show something more.' And the doctor bowed.

Iván Ilých went out slowly, seated himself disconsolately in his sledge, and drove home. All the way home he was going over what the doctor had said, trying to translate those complicated, obscure, scientific phrases into plain language and find in them an answer to the question: 'Is my condition bad? Is it very bad? Or is there as yet nothing much wrong?' And it seemed to him that the meaning of what the doctor had said was that it was very bad. Everything in the streets seemed depressing. The cabmen, the houses, the passers-by, and the shops, were dismal. His ache, this dull gnawing ache that never ceased for a moment, seemed to have acquired a new and more serious significance from the doctor's dubious remarks. Iván Ilých now watched it with a new and oppressive feeling.

He reached home and began to tell his wife about it. She listened, but in the middle of his account his daughter came in with her hat on, ready to go out with her mother. She sat down reluctantly to listen to this tedious story, but could not stand it long, and her mother too did not hear him to the end.

'Well, I am very glad,' she said. 'Mind now to take your medicine regularly. Give me the prescription and I'll send Gerásim to the chemist's.' And she went to get ready to go out.

While she was in the room Iván Ilých had hardly taken time to breathe, but he sighed deeply when she left it.

'Well,' he thought, 'perhaps it isn't so bad after all.'

He began taking his medicine and following the doctor's directions, which had been altered after the examination of the urine. But then it happened that there was a contradiction between the indications drawn from the examination of the urine and the symptoms that showed themselves. It turned out that what was happening differed from what the doctor had told him, and that he had either forgotten, or blundered, or hidden something from him. He could not, however, be blamed for that, and Iván Ilých still obeyed his orders implicitly and at first derived some comfort from doing so.

From the time of his visit to the doctor, Iván Ilých's chief occupation was the exact fulfilment of the doctor's instructions regarding hygiene and the taking of medicine, and the observation of his pain and his excretions. His chief interests came to be people's ailments and people's health. When sickness, deaths, or recoveries were mentioned in his presence, especially when the illness resembled his own, he listened with agitation which he tried to hide, asked questions, and applied what he heard to his own case.

The pain did not grow less, but Iván Ilých made efforts to force himself to think that he was better. And he could do this so long as nothing agitated him. But as soon as he had any unpleasantness with his wife, any lack of success in his official work, or held bad cards at bridge, he was at once acutely sensible of his disease. He had formerly borne such mischances, hoping soon to adjust what was wrong, to master it and attain success, or make a grand slam. But now every mischance upset him and plunged him into despair. He would say to himself: 'There now, just as I was beginning to get better and the medicine had begun to take effect, comes this accursed misfortune, or unpleasantness...' And he was furious with the mishap, or with the people who were causing the unpleasantness and killing him, for he felt that this fury was killing him but could not restrain it. One would have thought that it should have been clear to him that this exasperation with circumstances and people aggravated his illness, and that he ought therefore to ignore unpleasant occurrences. But he drew the very opposite conclusion: he said that he needed peace, and he watched for everything that might disturb it and became irritable at the slightest infringement of it. His condition was rendered worse by the fact that he read medical books and consulted doctors. The progress of his disease was so gradual that he could deceive himself when comparing one day with another – the difference was so slight. But when he consulted the doctors it seemed to him that he was getting worse, and even very rapidly. Yet despite this he was continually consulting them.

That month he went to see another celebrity, who told him almost the same as the first had done but put his questions rather differently, and the interview with this celebrity only increased Iván Ilých's doubts and fears. A friend of a friend of his, a very good doctor, diagnosed his illness again quite differently from the others, and though he predicted recovery, his questions and suppositions bewildered Iván Ilých still more and increased his doubts. A homoeopathist diagnosed the disease in yet another way, and prescribed medicine which Iván Ilých took secretly for a week. But after a week, not feeling any improvement and having lost confidence both in the former doctor's treatment and in this one's, he became still more despondent. One day a lady acquaintance mentioned a cure effected by a wonder-working icon. Iván Ilých caught himself listening attentively and beginning to believe that it had occurred. This incident alarmed him. 'Has my mind really weakened to such an extent?' he asked himself. 'Nonsense! It's all rubbish. I mustn't give way to nervous fears but having chosen a doctor must keep strictly to his treatment. That is what I will do. Now it's all settled. I won't think about it, but will follow the treatment seriously till summer, and then we shall see. From now there must be no more of this wavering!' This was easy to say but impossible to carry out. The pain in his side oppressed him and seemed to grow worse and more incessant, while the taste in his mouth grew stranger and stranger. It seemed to him that his breath had a disgusting smell, and he was conscious of a loss of appetite and strength. There was no deceiving himself: something terrible, new, and more important than anything before in his life, was taking place within him of which he alone was aware. Those about him did not understand or would not understand it, but thought everything in the world was going on as usual. That tormented Iván Ilých more than anything. He saw that his household, especially his wife and daughter who were in a perfect whirl of visiting, did not understand anything of it and were annoyed that he was so depressed and so exacting, as if he were to blame for it. Though they tried to disguise it he saw that he was an obstacle in their path, and that his wife had adopted a definite line in regard to his illness and kept to it regardless of anything he said or did. Her attitude was this: 'You know,' she would say to her friends, 'Iván Ilých can't do as other people do, and keep to the treatment prescribed for him. One day he'll take his drops and keep strictly to his diet and go to bed in good time, but the next day unless I watch him he'll suddenly forget his medicine, eat sturgeon – which is forbidden – and sit up playing cards till one o'clock in the morning.'

'Oh, come, when was that?' Iván Ilých would ask in vexation. 'Only once at Peter Ivánovich's.'

'And yesterday with Shébek.'

'Well, even if I hadn't stayed up, this pain would have kept me awake.'

'Be that as it may you'll never get well like that, but will always make us wretched.'

Praskóvya Fëdorovna's attitude to Iván Ilých's illness, as she expressed it both to others and to him, was that it was his own fault and was another of the annoyances he caused her. Iván Ilých felt that this opinion escaped her involuntarily – but that did not make it easier for him.

At the law courts too, Iván Ilých noticed, or thought he noticed, a strange attitude towards himself. It sometimes seemed to him that people were watching him inquisitively as a man whose place might soon be vacant. Then again, his friends would suddenly begin to chaff him in a friendly way about his low spirits, as if the awful, horrible, and unheard-of thing that was going on within him, incessantly gnawing at him and irresistibly drawing him away, was a very agreeable subject for jests. Schwartz in particular irritated him by his jocularity, vivacity, and *savoir-faire*, which reminded him of what he himself had been ten years ago.

Friends came to make up a set and they sat down to cards. They dealt, bending the new cards to soften them, and he sorted the diamonds in his hand and found he had seven. His partner said 'No trumps' and supported him with two diamonds. What more could be wished for? It ought to be jolly and lively. They would make a grand slam. But suddenly Iván Ilých was conscious of that gnawing pain, that taste in his mouth, and it seemed ridiculous that in such circumstances he should be pleased to make a grand slam.

He looked at his partner Mikháil Mikháylovich, who rapped the table with his strong hand and instead of snatching up the tricks pushed the cards courteously and indulgently towards Iván Ilých that he might have the pleasure of gathering them up without the trouble of stretching out his hand for them. 'Does he think I am too weak to stretch out my arm?' thought Iván Ilých, and forgetting what he was doing he over-trumped his partner, missing the grand slam by three tricks. And what was most awful of all was that he saw how upset Mikháil Mikháylovich was about it but did not himself care. And it was dreadful to realize why he did not care.

They all saw that he was suffering, and said: 'We can stop if you are tired. Take a rest.' Lie down? No, he was not at all tired, and he finished the rubber. All were gloomy and silent. Iván Ilých felt that he had diffused this gloom over them and could not dispel it. They had supper and went away, and Iván Ilých was left alone with the consciousness that his life was poisoned and was poisoning the lives of others, and that this poison did not weaken but penetrated more and more deeply into his whole being.

With this consciousness, and with physical pain besides the terror, he must go to bed, often to lie awake the greater part of the night. Next morning he had to get up again, dress, go to the law courts, speak, and write; or if he did not go out, spend at home those twenty-four hours a day each of which was a torture. And he had to live thus all alone on the brink of an abyss, with no one who understood or pitied him.

V

So one month passed and then another. Just before the New Year his brother-in-law came to town and stayed at their house. Iván Ilých was at the law courts and Praskóvya

Fëdorovna had gone shopping. When Iván Ilých came home and entered his study he found his brother-in-law there – a healthy, florid man – unpacking his portmanteau himself. He raised his head on hearing Iván Ilých's footsteps and looked up at him for a moment without a word. That stare told Iván Ilých everything. His brother-in-law opened his mouth to utter an exclamation of surprise but checked himself, and that action confirmed it all.

'I have changed, eh?'

'Yes, there is a change.'

And after that, try as he would to get his brother-in-law to return to the subject of his looks, the latter would say nothing about it. Praskóvya Fëdorovna came home and her brother went out to her. Iván Ilých locked the door and began to examine himself in the glass, first full face, then in profile. He took up a portrait of himself taken with his wife, and compared it with what he saw in the glass. The change in him was immense. Then he bared his arms to the elbow, looked at them, drew the sleeves down again, sat down on an ottoman, and grew blacker than night.

'No, no, this won't do!' he said to himself, and jumped up, went to the table, took up some law papers and began to read them, but could not continue. He unlocked the door and went into the reception-room. The door leading to the drawing-room was shut. He approached it on tiptoe and listened.

'No, you are exaggerating!' Praskóvya Fëdorovna was saying.

'Exaggerating! Don't you see it? Why, he's a dead man! Look at his eyes – there's no light in them. But what is it that is wrong with him?'

'No one knows. Nikoláevich [that was another doctor] said something, but I don't know what. And Leshchetítsky [this was the celebrated specialist] said quite the contrary...'

Iván Ilých walked away, went to his own room, lay down, and began musing: 'The kidney, a floating kidney.' He recalled all the doctors had told him of how it detached itself and swayed about. And by an effort of imagination he tried to catch that kidney and arrest it and support it. So little was needed for this, it seemed to him. 'No, I'll go to see Peter Ivánovich again.' [That was the friend whose friend was a doctor.] He rang, ordered the carriage, and got ready to go.

'Where are you going, Jean?' asked his wife, with a specially sad and exceptionally kind look.

This exceptionally kind look irritated him. He looked morosely at her.

'I must go to see Peter Ivánovich.'

He went to see Peter Ivánovich, and together they went to see his friend, the doctor. He was in, and Iván Ilých had a long talk with him.

Reviewing the anatomical and physiological details of what in the doctor's opinion was going on inside him, he understood it all.

There was something, a small thing, in the vermiform appendix. It might all come right. Only stimulate the energy of one organ and check the activity of another, then absorption would take place and everything would come right. He got home rather late for dinner, ate his dinner, and conversed cheerfully, but could not for a long time bring himself to go back to work in his room. At last, however, he went to his study and did what was necessary, but the consciousness that he had put something aside – an important, intimate matter which he would revert to when his work was done – never left him. When he had finished his work he remembered that this intimate matter was the thought of his vermiform appendix. But he did not give himself up to it, and went to the drawing-room for tea. There were callers there, including the examining magistrate who was a desirable match for his daughter, and they were conversing, playing the piano, and singing. Iván Ilých, as Praskóvya Fëdorovna remarked, spent that evening more cheerfully than usual, but he never for a moment forgot that he had postponed the important matter of the appendix. At eleven o'clock he said good-night and went to his bedroom. Since his illness he had slept alone in a small room next to his study. He undressed and took up a novel by Zola, but instead of reading it he fell into thought, and in his imagination that desired improvement in the vermiform appendix occurred.

There was the absorption and evacuation and the re-establishment of normal activity. 'Yes, that's it!' he said to himself. 'One need only assist nature, that's all.' He remembered his medicine, rose, took it, and lay down on his back watching for the beneficent action of the medicine and for it to lessen the pain. 'I need only take it regularly and avoid all injurious influences. I am already feeling better, much better.' He began touching his side: it was not painful to the touch. 'There, I really don't feel it. It's much better already.' He put out the light and turned on his side ... 'The appendix is getting better, absorption is occurring.' Suddenly he felt the old, familiar, dull, gnawing pain, stubborn and serious. There was the same familiar loathsome taste in his mouth. His heart sank and he felt dazed. 'My God! My God!' he muttered. 'Again, again! And it will never cease.' And suddenly the matter presented itself in a quite different aspect. 'Vermiform appendix! Kidney!' he said to himself. 'It's not a question of appendix or kidney, but of life and ... death. Yes, life was there and now it is going, going and I cannot stop it. Yes. Why deceive myself? Isn't it obvious to everyone but me that I'm dying, and that it's only a question of weeks, days ... it may happen this moment. There was light and now there is darkness. I was here and now I'm going there! Where?' A chill came over him, his breathing ceased, and he felt only the throbbing of his heart.

'When I am not, what will there be? There will be nothing. Then where shall I be when I am no more? Can this be dying? No, I don't want to!' He jumped up and tried to light the candle, felt for it with trembling hands, dropped candle and candlestick on the floor, and fell back on his pillow.

'What's the use? It makes no difference,' he said to himself, staring with wide-open eyes into the darkness. 'Death. Yes, death. And none of them know or wish to know it, and they have no pity for me. Now they are playing.' (He heard through the door the distant sound of a song and its accompaniment.) 'It's all the same to them, but they will die too! Fools! I first, and they later, but it will be the same for them. And now they are merry ... the beasts!'

Anger choked him and he was agonizingly, unbearably miserable. 'It is impossible that all men have been doomed to suffer this awful horror!' He raised himself.

'Something must be wrong. I must calm myself – must think it all over from the beginning.' And he again began thinking. 'Yes, the beginning of my illness: I knocked my side, but I was still quite well that day and the next. It hurt a little, then rather more. I saw the doctors, then followed despondency and anguish, more doctors, and I drew nearer to the abyss. My strength grew less and I kept coming nearer and nearer, and now I have wasted away and there is no light in my eyes. I think of the appendix – but this is death! I think of mending the appendix, and all the while here is death! Can it really be death?' Again terror seized him and he gasped for breath. He leant down and began feeling for the matches, pressing with his elbow on the stand beside the bed. It was in his way and hurt him, he grew furious with it, pressed on it still harder, and upset it. Breathless and in despair he fell on his back, expecting death to come immediately.

Meanwhile the visitors were leaving. Praskóvya Fëdorovna was seeing them off. She heard something fall and came in.

'What has happened?'

'Nothing. I knocked it over accidentally.'

She went out and returned with a candle. He lay there panting heavily, like a man who has run a thousand yards, and stared upwards at her with a fixed look.

'What is it, Jean?'

'No . . . o . . . thing. I upset it.' ('Why speak of it? She won't understand,' he thought.)

And in truth she did not understand. She picked up the stand, lit his candle, and hurried away to see another visitor off. When she came back he still lay on his back, looking upwards.

'What is it? Do you feel worse?'

'Yes.'

She shook her head and sat down.

'Do you know, Jean, I think we must ask Leshchetítsky to come and see you here.'

This meant calling in the famous specialist, regardless of expense. He smiled malignantly and said 'No'. She remained a little longer and then went up to him and kissed his forehead.

While she was kissing him he hated her from the bottom of his soul and with difficulty refrained from pushing her away.

'Good-night. Please God you'll sleep.'

'Yes.'

VI

IVÁN Ilých saw that he was dying, and he was in continual despair.

In the depth of his heart he knew he was dying, but not only was he not accustomed to the thought, he simply did not and could not grasp it.

The syllogism he had learnt from Kiezewetter's Logic: 'Caius is a man, men are mortal, therefore Caius is mortal', had always seemed to him correct as applied to Caius, but certainly not as applied to himself. That Caius – man in the abstract – was mortal, was perfectly correct, but he was not Caius, not an abstract man, but a creature quite, quite separate from all others. He had been little Ványa, with a mamma and a papa, with Mítya and Volódya, with the toys, a coachman and a nurse, afterwards with Kátenka and with all the joys, griefs, and delights of childhood, boyhood, and youth. What did Caius know of the smell of that striped leather ball Ványa had been so fond of? Had Caius kissed his mother's hand like that, and did the silk of her dress rustle so for Caius? Had he rioted like that at school when the pastry was bad? Had Caius been in love like that? Could Caius preside at a session as he did? 'Caius really was mortal, and it was right for him to die; but for me, little Ványa, Iván Ilých, with all my thoughts and emotions, it's altogether a different matter. It cannot be that I ought to die. That would be too terrible.'

Such was his feeling.

'If I had to die like Caius I should have known it was so. An inner voice would have told me so, but there was nothing of the sort in me and I and all my friends felt that our case was

quite different from that of Caius. And now here it is!' he said
to himself. 'It can't be. It's impossible! But here it is. How is
this? How is one to understand it?'

He could not understand it, and tried to drive this false,
incorrect, morbid thought away and to replace it by other proper
and healthy thoughts. But that thought, and not the thought
only but the reality itself, seemed to come and confront him.

And to replace that thought he called up a succession of
others, hoping to find in them some support. He tried to get
back into the former current of thoughts that had once
screened the thought of death from him. But strange to say,
all that had formerly shut off, hidden, and destroyed, his
consciousness of death, no longer had that effect. Iván Ilých
now spent most of his time in attempting to re-establish that
old current. He would say to himself: 'I will take up my duties
again – after all I used to live by them.' And banishing all
doubts he would go to the law courts, enter into conversation
with his colleagues, and sit carelessly as was his wont, scanning
the crowd with a thoughtful look and leaning both his emaciated arms on the arms of his oak chair; bending over as usual
to a colleague and drawing his papers nearer he would inter-
change whispers with him, and then suddenly raising his eyes
and sitting erect would pronounce certain words and open the
proceedings. But suddenly in the midst of those proceedings
the pain in his side, regardless of the stage the proceedings had
reached, would begin its own gnawing work. Iván Ilých
would turn his attention to it and try to drive the thought of
it away, but without success. *It* would come and stand before
him and look at him, and he would be petrified and the light
would die out of his eyes, and he would again begin asking
himself whether *It* alone was true. And his colleagues and
subordinates would see with surprise and distress that he, the
brilliant and subtle judge, was becoming confused and making
mistakes. He would shake himself, try to pull himself together,
manage somehow to bring the sitting to a close, and return
home with the sorrowful consciousness that his judicial labours
could not as formerly hide from him what he wanted them to
hide, and could not deliver him from *It*. And what was worst

of all was that *It* drew his attention to itself not in order to make him take some action but only that he should look at *It*, look it straight in the face: look at it and without doing anything, suffer inexpressibly.

And to save himself from this condition Iván Ilých looked for consolations – new screens – and new screens were found and for a while seemed to save him, but then they immediately fell to pieces or rather became transparent, as if *It* penetrated them and nothing could veil *It*.

In these latter days he would go into the drawing-room he had arranged – that drawing-room where he had fallen and for the sake of which (how bitterly ridiculous it seemed) he had sacrificed his life – for he knew that his illness originated with that knock. He would enter and see that something had scratched the polished table. He would look for the cause of this and find that it was the bronze ornamentation of an album, that had got bent. He would take up the expensive album which he had lovingly arranged, and feel vexed with his daughter and her friends for their untidiness – for the album was torn here and there and some of the photographs turned upside down. He would put it carefully in order and bend the ornamentation back into position. Then it would occur to him to place all those things in another corner of the room, near the plants. He would call the footman, but his daughter or wife would come to help him. They would not agree, and his wife would contradict him, and he would dispute and grow angry. But that was all right, for then he did not think about *It*. *It* was invisible.

But then, when he was moving something himself, his wife would say: 'Let the servants do it. You will hurt yourself again.' And suddenly *It* would flash through the screen and he would see it. It was just a flash, and he hoped it would disappear, but he would involuntarily pay attention to his side. 'It sits there as before, gnawing just the same!' And he could no longer forget *It*, but could distinctly see it looking at him from behind the flowers. 'What is it all for?'

'It really is so! I lost my life over that curtain as I might have done when storming a fort. Is that possible? How terrible and how stupid. It can't be true! It can't, but it is.'

He would go to his study, lie down, and again be alone with *It*: face to face with *It*. And nothing could be done with *It* except to look at it and shudder.

VII

How it happened it is impossible to say because it came about step by step, unnoticed, but in the third month of Iván Ilých's illness, his wife, his daughter, his son, his acquaintances, the doctors, the servants, and above all he himself, were aware that the whole interest he had for other people was whether he would soon vacate his place, and at last release the living from the discomfort caused by his presence and be himself released from his sufferings.

He slept less and less. He was given opium and hypodermic injections of morphine, but this did not relieve him. The dull depression he experienced in a somnolent condition at first gave him a little relief, but only as something new, afterwards it became as distressing as the pain itself or even more so.

Special foods were prepared for him by the doctors' orders, but all those foods became increasingly distasteful and disgusting to him.

For his excretions also special arrangements had to be made, and this was a torment to him every time – a torment from the uncleanliness, the unseemliness, and the smell, and from knowing that another person had to take part in it.

But just through this most unpleasant matter, Iván Ilých obtained comfort. Gerásim, the butler's young assistant, always came in to carry the things out. Gerásim was a clean, fresh peasant lad, grown stout on town food and always cheerful and bright. At first the sight of him, in his clean Russian peasant costume, engaged on that disgusting task embarrassed Iván Ilých.

Once when he got up from the commode too weak to draw up his trousers, he dropped into a soft armchair and looked with horror at his bare, enfeebled thighs with the muscles so sharply marked on them.

Gerásim with a firm light tread, his heavy boots emitting a pleasant smell of tar and fresh winter air, came in wearing a clean Hessian apron, the sleeves of his print shirt tucked up over his strong bare young arms; and refraining from looking at his sick master out of consideration for his feelings, and restraining the joy of life that beamed from his face, he went up to the commode.

'Gerásim!' said Iván Ilých in a weak voice.

Gerásim started, evidently afraid he might have committed some blunder, and with a rapid movement turned his fresh, kind, simple young face which just showed the first downy signs of a beard.

'Yes, sir?'

'That must be very unpleasant for you. You must forgive me. I am helpless.'

'Oh, why, sir,' and Gerásim's eyes beamed and he showed his glistening white teeth, 'what's a little trouble? It's a case of illness with you, sir.'

And his deft strong hands did their accustomed task, and he went out of the room stepping lightly. Five minutes later he as lightly returned.

Iván Ilých was still sitting in the same position in the arm-chair.

'Gerásim,' he said when the latter had replaced the freshly-washed utensil. 'Please come here and help me.' Gerásim went up to him. 'Lift me up. It is hard for me to get up, and I have sent Dmítri away.'

Gerásim went up to him, grasped his master with his strong arms deftly but gently, in the same way that he stepped – lifted him, supported him with one hand, and with the other drew up his trousers and would have set him down again, but Iván Ilých asked to be led to the sofa. Gerásim, without an effort and without apparent pressure, led him, almost lifting him, to the sofa and placed him on it.

'Thank you. How easily and well you do it all!'

Gerásim smiled again and turned to leave the room. But Iván Ilých felt his presence such a comfort that he did not want to let him go.

'One thing more, please move up that chair. No, the other one – under my feet. It is easier for me when my feet are raised.'

Gerásim brought the chair, set it down gently in place, and raised Iván Ilých's legs on to it. It seemed to Iván Ilých that he felt better while Gerásim was holding up his legs.

'It's better when my legs are higher,' he said. 'Place that cushion under them.'

Gerásim did so. He again lifted the legs and placed them, and again Iván Ilých felt better while Gerásim held his legs. When he set them down Iván Ilých fancied he felt worse.

'Gerásim,' he said. 'Are you busy now?'

'Not at all, sir,' said Gerásim, who had learnt from the townsfolk how to speak to gentlefolk.

'What have you still to do?'

'What have I to do? I've done everything except chopping the logs for to-morrow.'

'Then hold my legs up a bit higher, can you?'

'Of course I can. Why not?' And Gerásim raised his master's legs higher and Iván Ilých thought that in that position he did not feel any pain at all.

'And how about the logs?'

'Don't trouble about that, sir. There's plenty of time.'

Iván Ilých told Gerásim to sit down and hold his legs, and began to talk to him. And strange to say it seemed to him that he felt better while Gerásim held his legs up.

After that Iván Ilých would sometimes call Gerásim and get him to hold his legs on his shoulders, and he liked talking to him. Gerásim did it all easily, willingly, simply, and with a good nature that touched Iván Ilých. Health, strength, and vitality in other people were offensive to him, but Gerásim's strength and vitality did not mortify but soothed him.

What tormented Iván Ilých most was the deception, the lie, which for some reason they all accepted, that he was not dying but was simply ill, and that he only need keep quiet and undergo a treatment and then something very good would result. He however knew that do what they would nothing would come of it, only still more agonizing suffering and death. This deception tortured him – their not wishing to admit what they all knew and what he knew, but wanting to lie to him concerning his terrible condition, and wishing and forcing him to participate in that lie. Those lies – lies enacted over him on the eve of his death and destined to degrade this awful, solemn act to the level of their visitings, their curtains, their sturgeon for dinner – were a terrible agony for Iván Ilých. And strangely enough, many times when they were going through their antics over him he had been within a hairbreadth of calling out to them: 'Stop lying! You know and I know that I am dying. Then at least stop lying about it!' But he had never had the spirit to do it. The awful, terrible act of his dying was, he could see, reduced by those about him to the level of a casual, unpleasant, and almost indecorous incident (as if someone entered a drawing-room diffusing an unpleasant odour) and this was done by that very decorum which he had served all his life long. He saw that no one felt for him, because no one even wished to grasp his position. Only Gerásim recognized it and pitied him. And so Iván Ilých felt at ease only with him. He felt comforted when Gerásim supported his legs (sometimes all night long) and refused to go to bed, saying: 'Don't you worry, Iván Ilých. I'll get sleep enough later on,' or when he suddenly became familiar and exclaimed: 'If you weren't sick it would be another matter, but as it is, why should I grudge a little trouble?' Gerásim alone did not lie; everything showed that he alone understood the facts of the case and did not consider it necessary to disguise them, but simply felt sorry for his emaciated and enfeebled master. Once when Iván Ilých was sending him away he even said straight out: 'We shall all of us die, so why should I grudge a little trouble?' – expressing the fact that he did not think his work burdensome, because he was doing it for a dying man and hoped someone would do the same for him when his time came.

Apart from this lying, or because of it, what most tormented Iván Ilých was that no one pitied him as he wished to be pitied. At certain moments after prolonged suffering he wished most of all (though he would have been ashamed to confess it) for someone to pity him as a sick child is pitied. He longed to be petted and comforted. He knew he was an important functionary, that he had a beard turning grey, and that therefore what he longed for was impossible, but still he longed for it. And in Gerásim's attitude towards him there was something akin to what he wished for, and so that attitude comforted him. Iván Ilých wanted to weep, wanted to be petted and cried over, and then his colleague Shébek would come, and instead of weeping and being petted, Iván Ilých would assume a serious, severe, and profound air, and by force of habit would express his opinion on a decision of the Court of Cassation and would stubbornly insist on that view. This falsity around him and within him did more than anything else to poison his last days.

VIII

IT was morning. He knew it was morning because Gerásim had gone, and Peter the footman had come and put out the candles, drawn back one of the curtains, and begun quietly to tidy up. Whether it was morning or evening, Friday or Sunday, made no difference, it was all just the same: the gnawing, unmitigated, agonizing pain, never ceasing for an instant, the consciousness of life inexorably waning but not yet extinguished, the approach of that ever dreaded and hateful Death which was the only reality, and always the same falsity. What were days, weeks, hours, in such a case?

'Will you have some tea, sir?'

'He wants things to be regular, and wishes the gentlefolk to drink tea in the morning,' thought Iván Ilých, and only said 'No'.

'Wouldn't you like to move onto the sofa, sir?'

'He wants to tidy up the room, and I'm in the way. I am uncleanliness and disorder,' he thought, and said only:

'No, leave me alone.'

The man went on bustling about. Iván Ilých stretched out his hand. Peter came up, ready to help.

'What is it, sir?'

'My watch.'

Peter took the watch which was close at hand and gave it to his master.

'Half-past eight. Are they up?'

'No sir, except Vladímir Ivánich' (the son) 'who has gone to school. Praskóvya Fëdorovna ordered me to wake her if you asked for her. Shall I do so?'

'No, there's no need to.' 'Perhaps I'd better have some tea,' he thought, and added aloud: 'Yes, bring me some tea.'

Peter went to the door, but Iván Ilých dreaded being left alone. 'How can I keep him here? Oh yes, my medicine.' 'Peter, give me my medicine.' 'Why not? Perhaps it may still do me some good.' He took a spoonful and swallowed it. 'No, it won't help. It's all tomfoolery, all deception,' he decided as soon as he became aware of the familiar, sickly, hopeless taste. 'No, I can't believe in it any longer. But the pain, why this pain? If it would only cease just for a moment!' And he moaned. Peter turned towards him. 'It's all right. Go and fetch me some tea.'

Peter went out. Left alone Iván Ilých groaned not so much with pain, terrible though that was, as from mental anguish. Always and for ever the same, always these endless days and nights. If only it would come quicker! If only *what* would come quicker? Death, darkness? . . . No, no! Anything rather than death!

When Peter returned with the tea on a tray, Iván Ilých stared at him for a time in perplexity, not realizing who and what he was. Peter was disconcerted by that look and his embarrassment brought Iván Ilých to himself.

'Oh, tea! All right, put it down. Only help me to wash and put on a clean shirt.'

And Iván Ilých began to wash. With pauses for rest, he washed his hands and then his face, cleaned his teeth, brushed his hair, and looked in the glass. He was terrified by what he saw, especially by the limp way in which his hair clung to his pallid forehead.

While his shirt was being changed he knew that he would be still more frightened at the sight of his body, so he avoided looking at it. Finally he was ready. He drew on a dressing-gown, wrapped himself in a plaid, and sat down in the arm-chair to take his tea. For a moment he felt refreshed, but as soon as he began to drink the tea he was again aware of the same taste, and the pain also returned. He finished it with an effort, and then lay down stretching out his legs, and dismissed Peter.

Always the same. Now a spark of hope flashes up, then a sea of despair rages, and always pain; always pain, always despair, and always the same. When alone he had a dreadful and distressing desire to call someone, but he knew beforehand that with others present it would be still worse. 'Another dose of morphine – to lose consciousness. I will tell him, the doctor, that he must think of something else. It's impossible, imposs-ible, to go on like this.'

An hour and another pass like that. But now there is a ring at the door bell. Perhaps it's the doctor? It is. He comes in fresh, hearty, plump, and cheerful, with that look on his face that seems to say: 'There now, you're in a panic about something, but we'll arrange it all for you directly!' The doctor knows this expression is out of place here, but he has put it on once for all and can't take it off – like a man who has put on a frock-coat in the morning to pay a round of calls.

The doctor rubs his hands vigorously and reassuringly.

'Brr! How cold it is! There's such a sharp frost; just let me warm myself!' he says, as if it were only a matter of waiting till he was warm, and then he would put everything right.

'Well now, how are you?'

Iván Ilých feels that the doctor would like to say: 'Well, how are our affairs?' but that even he feels that this would not do, and says instead: 'What sort of a night have you had?'

Iván Ilých looks at him as much as to say: 'Are you really never ashamed of lying?' But the doctor does not wish to understand this question, and Iván Ilých says: 'Just as terrible as ever. The pain never leaves me and never subsides. If only something . . .'

'Yes, you sick people are always like that. . . . There, now I think I am warm enough. Even Praskóvya Fëdorovna, who is so particular, could find no fault with my temperature. Well, now I can say good-morning,' and the doctor presses his patient's hand.

Then, dropping his former playfulness, he begins with a most serious face to examine the patient, feeling his pulse and taking his temperature, and then begins the sounding and auscultation.

Iván Ilých knows quite well and definitely that all this is nonsense and pure deception, but when the doctor, getting down on his knee, leans over him, putting his ear first higher then lower, and performs various gymnastic movements over him with a significant expression on his face, Iván Ilých submits to it all as he used to submit to the speeches of the lawyers, though he knew very well that they were all lying and why they were lying.

The doctor, kneeling on the sofa, is still sounding him when Praskóvya Fëdorovna's silk dress rustles at the door and she is heard scolding Peter for not having let her know of the doctor's arrival.

She comes in, kisses her husband, and at once proceeds to prove that she has been up a long time already, and only owing to a misunderstanding failed to be there when the doctor arrived.

Iván Ilých looks at her, scans her all over, sets against her the whiteness and plumpness and cleanness of her hands and neck, the gloss of her hair, and the sparkle of her vivacious eyes. He hates her with his whole soul. And the thrill of hatred he feels for her makes him suffer from her touch.

Her attitude towards him and his disease is still the same. Just as the doctor had adopted a certain relation to his patient which he could not abandon, so had she formed one towards him – that he was not doing something he ought to do and was himself to blame, and that she reproached him lovingly for this – and she could not now change that attitude.

'You see he doesn't listen to me and doesn't take his medicine at the proper time. And above all he lies in a position that is no doubt bad for him – with his legs up.'

She described how he made Gerásim hold his legs up.

The doctor smiled with a contemptuous affability that said: 'What's to be done? These sick people do have foolish fancies of that kind, but we must forgive them.'

When the examination was over the doctor looked at his watch, and then Praskóvya Fëdorovna announced to Iván Ilých that it was of course as he pleased, but she had sent to-day for a celebrated specialist who would examine him and have a consultation with Michael Danílovich (their regular doctor).

'Please don't raise any objections. I am doing this for my own sake,' she said ironically, letting it be felt that she was doing it all for his sake and only said this to leave him no right to refuse. He remained silent, knitting his brows. He felt that he was so surrounded and involved in a mesh of falsity that it was hard to unravel anything.

Everything she did for him was entirely for her own sake, and she told him she was doing for herself what she actually was doing for herself, as if that was so incredible that he must understand the opposite.

At half-past eleven the celebrated specialist arrived. Again the sounding began and the significant conversations in his presence and in another room, about the kidneys and the appendix, and the questions and answers, with such an air of importance that again, instead of the real question of life and death which now alone confronted him, the question arose of the kidney and appendix which were not behaving as they ought to and would now be attacked by Michael Danílovich and the specialist and forced to amend their ways.

The celebrated specialist took leave of him with a serious though not hopeless look, and in reply to the timid question Iván Ilých, with eyes glistening with fear and hope, put to him as to whether there was a chance of recovery, said that he could not vouch for it but there was a possibility. The look of hope with which Iván Ilých watched the doctor out was so pathetic that Praskóvya Fëdorovna, seeing it, even wept as she left the room to hand the doctor his fee.

The gleam of hope kindled by the doctor's encouragement did not last long. The same room, the same pictures, curtains, wall-paper, medicine bottles, were all there, and the same aching suffering body, and Iván Ilých began to moan. They gave him a subcutaneous injection and he sank into oblivion.

It was twilight when he came to. They brought him his dinner and he swallowed some beef tea with difficulty, and then everything was the same again and night was coming on.

After dinner, at seven o'clock, Praskóvya Fëdorovna came into the room in evening dress, her full bosom pushed up by her corset, and with traces of powder on her face. She had reminded him in the morning that they were going to the theatre. Sarah Bernhardt was visiting the town and they had a box, which he had insisted on their taking. Now he had forgotten about it and her toilet offended him, but he concealed his vexation when he remembered that he had himself insisted on their securing a box and going because it would be an instructive and aesthetic pleasure for the children.

Praskóvya Fëdorovna came in, self-satisfied but yet with a rather guilty air. She sat down and asked how he was, but, as he saw, only for the sake of asking and not in order to learn about it, knowing that there was nothing to learn – and then went on to what she really wanted to say: that she would not on any account have gone but that the box had been taken and Helen and their daughter were going, as well as Petríshchev (the examining magistrate, their daughter's fiancé) and that it was out of the question to let them go alone; but that she would have much preferred to sit with him for a while; and he must be sure to follow the doctor's orders while she was away.

'Oh, and Fëdor Petróvich' (the fiancé) 'would like to come in. May he? And Lisa?'

'All right.'

Their daughter came in in full evening dress, her fresh young flesh exposed (making a show of that very flesh which in his own case caused so much suffering), strong, healthy, evidently in love, and impatient with illness, suffering, and death, because they interfered with her happiness.

Fëdor Petróvich came in too, in evening dress, his hair curled *à la Capoul*, a tight stiff collar round his long sinewy neck, an enormous white shirt-front and narrow black trousers tightly stretched over his strong thighs. He had one white glove tightly drawn on, and was holding his opera hat in his hand.

Following him the schoolboy crept in unnoticed, in a new uniform, poor little fellow, and wearing gloves. Terribly dark shadows showed under his eyes, the meaning of which Iván Ilých knew well.

His son had always seemed pathetic to him, and now it was dreadful to see the boy's frightened look of pity. It seemed to Iván Ilých that Vásya was the only one besides Gerásim who understood and pitied him.

They all sat down and again asked how he was. A silence followed. Lisa asked her mother about the opera-glasses, and there was an altercation between mother and daughter as to who had taken them and where they had been put. This occasioned some unpleasantness.

Fëdor Petróvich inquired of Iván Ilých whether he had ever seen Sarah Bernhardt. Iván Ilých did not at first catch the question, but then replied: 'No, have you seen her before?'

'Yes, in *Adrienne Lecouvreur*.'

Praskóvya Fëdorovna mentioned some rôles in which Sarah Bernhardt was particularly good. Her daughter disagreed. Conversation sprang up as to the elegance and realism of her acting – the sort of conversation that is always repeated and is always the same.

In the midst of the conversation Fëdor Petróvich glanced at Iván Ilých and became silent. The others also looked at him and grew silent. Iván Ilých was staring with glittering eyes straight before him, evidently indignant with them. This had to be rectified, but it was impossible to do so. The silence had to be broken, but for a time no one dared to break it and they all became afraid that the conventional deception would suddenly become obvious and the truth become plain to all. Lisa was the first to pluck up courage and break that silence, but by trying to hide what everybody was feeling, she betrayed it.

'Well, if we are going it's time to start,' she said, looking at her watch, a present from her father, and with a faint and significant smile at Fëdor Petróvich relating to something known only to them. She got up with a rustle of her dress.

They all rose, said good-night, and went away.

When they had gone it seemed to Iván Ilých that he felt better; the falsity had gone with them. But the pain remained – that same pain and that same fear that made everything monotonously alike, nothing harder and nothing easier. Everything was worse.

Again minute followed minute and hour followed hour. Everything remained the same and there was no cessation. And the inevitable end of it all became more and more terrible.

'Yes, send Gerásim here,' he replied to a question Peter asked.

IX

His wife returned late at night. She came in on tiptoe, but he heard her, opened his eyes, and made haste to close them again. She wished to send Gerásim away and to sit with him herself, but he opened his eyes and said: 'No, go away.'

'Are you in great pain?'

'Always the same.'

'Take some opium.'

He agreed and took some. She went away.

Till about three in the morning he was in a state of stupefied misery. It seemed to him that he and his pain were being thrust into a narrow, deep black sack, but though they were pushed further and further in they could not be pushed to the bottom. And this, terrible enough in itself, was accompanied by suffering. He was frightened yet wanted to fall through the sack, he struggled but yet co-operated. And suddenly he broke through, fell, and regained consciousness. Gerásim was sitting at the foot of the bed dozing quietly and patiently, while he himself lay with his emaciated stockinged legs resting on Gerásim's shoulders; the same shaded candle was there and the same unceasing pain.

'Go away, Gerásim,' he whispered.

'It's all right, sir. I'll stay a while.'

'No. Go away.'

He removed his legs from Gerásim's shoulders, turned sideways onto his arm, and felt sorry for himself. He only waited till Gerásim had gone into the next room and then restrained himself no longer but wept like a child. He wept on account of his helplessness, his terrible loneliness, the cruelty of man, the cruelty of God, and the absence of God.

'Why hast Thou done all this? Why hast Thou brought me here? Why, why dost Thou torment me so terribly?'

He did not expect an answer and yet wept because there was no answer and could be none. The pain again grew more acute, but he did not stir and did not call. He said to himself: 'Go on! Strike me! But what is it for? What have I done to Thee? What is it for?'

Then he grew quiet and not only ceased weeping but even held his breath and became all attention. It was as though he were listening not to an audible voice but to the voice of his soul, to the current of thoughts arising within him.

'What is it you want?' was the first clear conception capable of expression in words, that he heard.

'What do you want? What do you want?' he repeated to himself.

'What do I want? To live and not to suffer,' he answered.

And again he listened with such concentrated attention that even his pain did not distract him.

'To live? How?' asked his inner voice.

'Why, to live as I used to – well and pleasantly.'

'As you lived before, well and pleasantly?' the voice repeated.

And in imagination he began to recall the best moments of his pleasant life. But strange to say none of those best moments of his pleasant life now seemed at all what they had then seemed – none of them except the first recollections of childhood. There, in childhood, there had been something really pleasant with which it would be possible to live if it could return. But the child who had experienced that happiness existed no longer, it was like a reminiscence of somebody else.

As soon as the period began which had produced the present Iván Ilých, all that had then seemed joys now melted before his sight and turned into something trivial and often nasty.

And the further he departed from childhood and the nearer he came to the present the more worthless and doubtful were the joys. This began with the School of Law. A little that was really good was still found there – there was light-heartedness, friendship, and hope. But in the upper classes there had already been fewer of such good moments. Then during the first years of his official career, when he was in the service of the Governor, some pleasant moments again occurred: they were the memories of love for a woman. Then all became confused and there was still less of what was good; later on again there was still less that was good, and the further he went the less there was. His marriage, a mere accident, then the disenchantment that followed it, his wife's bad breath and the sensuality and hypocrisy: then that deadly official life and those preoccupations about money, a year of it, and two, and ten, and twenty, and always the same thing. And the longer it lasted the more deadly it became. 'It is as if I had been going downhill while I imagined I was going up. And that is really what it was. I was going up in public opinion, but to the same extent life was ebbing away from me. And now it is all done and there is only death.'

'Then what does it mean? Why? It can't be that life is so senseless and horrible. But if it really has been so horrible and senseless, why must I die and die in agony? There is something wrong!'

'Maybe I did not live as I ought to have done,' it suddenly occurred to him. 'But how could that be, when I did everything properly?' he replied, and immediately dismissed from his mind this, the sole solution of all the riddles of life and death, as something quite impossible.

'Then what do you want now? To live? Live how? Live as you lived in the law courts when the usher proclaimed "The judge is coming!" The judge is coming, the judge!' he repeated to himself. 'Here he is, the judge. But I am not guilty!' he exclaimed angrily. 'What is it for?' And he ceased crying, but turning his face to the wall continued to ponder on the same question: Why, and for what purpose, is there all this horror? But however much he pondered he found no answer. And whenever the thought occurred to him, as it often did, that it all resulted from his not having lived as he ought to have done, he at once recalled the correctness of his whole life and dismissed so strange an idea.

X

ANOTHER fortnight passed. Iván Ilých now no longer left his sofa. He would not lie in bed but lay on the sofa, facing the wall nearly all the time. He suffered ever the same unceasing agonies and in his loneliness pondered always on the same insoluble question: 'What is this? Can it be that it is Death?' And the inner voice answered: 'Yes, it is Death.'

'Why these sufferings?' And the voice answered, 'For no reason – they just are so.' Beyond and besides this there was nothing.

From the very beginning of his illness, ever since he had first been to see the doctor, Iván Ilých's life had been divided between two contrary and alternating moods: now it was despair and the expectation of this uncomprehended and terrible death, and now hope and an intently interested observation of the functioning of his organs. Now before his eyes there was only a kidney or an intestine that temporarily evaded its duty, and now only that incomprehensible and dreadful death from which it was impossible to escape.

These two states of mind had alternated from the very beginning of his illness, but the further it progressed the more doubtful and fantastic became the conception of the kidney, and the more real the sense of impending death.

He had but to call to mind what he had been three months before and what he was now, to call to mind with what regularity he had been going downhill, for every possibility of hope to be shattered.

Latterly during that loneliness in which he found himself as he lay facing the back of the sofa, a loneliness in the midst of a populous town and surrounded by numerous acquaintances and relations but that yet could not have been more complete anywhere – either at the bottom of the sea or under the earth – during that terrible loneliness Iván Ilých had lived only in memories of the past. Pictures of his past rose before him one after another. They always began with what was nearest in time and then went back to what was most remote – to his childhood – and rested there. If he thought of the stewed prunes that had been offered him that day, his mind went back to the raw shrivelled French plums of his childhood, their peculiar flavour and the flow of saliva when he sucked their stones, and along with the memory of that taste came a whole series of memories of those days: his nurse, his brother, and their toys. 'No, I mustn't think of that. . . . It is too painful,' Iván Ilých said to himself, and brought himself back to the present – to the button on the back of the sofa and the creases in its morocco. 'Morocco is expensive, but it does not wear well: there had been a quarrel about it. It was a different kind of quarrel and a different kind of morocco that time when we tore father's portfolio and were punished, and mamma brought us some tarts. . . . ' And again his thoughts dwelt on his childhood, and again it was painful and he tried to banish them and fix his mind on something else.

Then again together with that chain of memories another series passed through his mind – of how his illness had progressed and grown worse. There also the further back he looked the more life there had been. There had been more of what was good in life and more of life itself. The two merged together. 'Just as the pain went on getting worse and worse, so my life grew worse and worse,' he thought. 'There is one bright spot there at the back, at the beginning of life, and afterwards all becomes blacker and blacker and proceeds more and more rapidly – in inverse ratio to the square of the distance from death,' thought Iván Ilých. And the example of a stone falling downwards with increasing velocity entered his mind. Life, a series of increasing sufferings, flies further and further towards its end – the most terrible suffering. 'I am flying. . . . ' He shuddered, shifted himself, and tried to resist, but was already aware that resistance was impossible, and again with eyes weary of gazing but unable to cease seeing what was before them, he stared at the back of the sofa and waited – awaiting that dreadful fall and shock and destruction.

'Resistance is impossible!' he said to himself. 'If I could only understand what it is all for! But that too is impossible. An explanation would be possible if it could be said that I have not lived as I ought to. But it is impossible to say that,' and he remembered all the legality, correctitude, and propriety of his life. 'That at any rate can certainly not be admitted,' he thought, and his lips smiled ironically as if someone could see that smile and be taken in by it. 'There is no explanation! Agony, death. . . . What for?'

XI

ANOTHER two weeks went by in this way and during that fortnight an event occurred that Iván Ilých and his wife had desired. Petríshchev formally proposed. It happened in the evening. The next day Praskóvya Fëdorovna came into her husband's room considering how best to inform him of it, but that very night there had been a fresh change for the worse in his condition. She found him still lying on the sofa but in a different position. He lay on his back, groaning and staring fixedly straight in front of him.

She began to remind him of his medicines, but he turned his eyes towards her with such a look that she did not finish what she was saying; so great an animosity, to her in particular, did that look express.

'For Christ's sake let me die in peace!' he said.

She would have gone away, but just then their daughter came in and went up to say good morning. He looked at her as he had done at his wife, and in reply to her inquiry about his health said dryly that he would soon free them all of himself. They were both silent and after sitting with him for a while went away.

'Is it our fault?' Lisa said to her mother. 'It's as if we were to blame! I am sorry for papa, but why should we be tortured?'

The doctor came at his usual time. Iván Ilých answered 'Yes' and 'No', never taking his angry eyes from him, and at last said: 'You know you can do nothing for me, so leave me alone.'

'We can ease your sufferings.'

'You can't even do that. Let me be.'

The doctor went into the drawing-room and told Praskóvya Fëdorovna that the case was very serious and that the only resource left was opium to allay her husband's sufferings, which must be terrible.

It was true, as the doctor said, that Iván Ilých's physical sufferings were terrible, but worse than the physical sufferings were his mental sufferings which were his chief torture.

His mental sufferings were due to the fact that that night, as he looked at Gerásim's sleepy, good-natured face with its prominent cheek-bones, the question suddenly occurred to him: 'What if my whole life has really been wrong?'

It occurred to him that what had appeared perfectly impossible before, namely that he had not spent his life as he should have done, might after all be true. It occurred to him that his scarcely perceptible attempts to struggle against what was considered good by the most highly placed people, those scarcely noticeable impulses which he had immediately suppressed, might have been the real thing, and all the rest false. And his professional duties and the whole arrangement of his life and of his family, and all his social and official interests, might all have been false. He tried to defend all those things to himself and suddenly felt the weakness of what he was defending. There was nothing to defend.

'But if that is so,' he said to himself, 'and I am leaving this life with the consciousness that I have lost all that was given me and it is impossible to rectify it – what then?'

He lay on his back and began to pass his life in review in quite a new way. In the morning when he saw first his footman, then his wife, then his daughter, and then the doctor, their every word and movement confirmed to him the awful truth that had been revealed to him during the night. In them he saw himself – all that for which he had lived – and saw clearly that it was not real at all, but a terrible and huge deception which had hidden both life and death. This consciousness intensified his physical suffering tenfold. He groaned and tossed about, and pulled at his clothing which choked and stifled him. And he hated them on that account.

He was given a large dose of opium and became unconscious, but at noon his sufferings began again. He drove everybody away and tossed from side to side.

His wife came to him and said:

'Jean, my dear, do this for me. It can't do any harm and often helps. Healthy people often do it.'

He opened his eyes wide.

'What? Take Communion? Why? It's unnecessary! However. . . .'

She began to cry.

'Yes, do, my dear. I'll send for our priest. He is such a nice man.'

'All right. Very well,' he muttered.

When the priest came and heard his confession, Iván Ilých was softened and seemed to feel a relief from his doubts and consequently from his sufferings, and for a moment there came a ray of hope. He again began to think of the vermiform appendix and the possibility of correcting it. He received the sacrament with tears in his eyes.

When they laid him down again afterwards he felt a moment's ease, and the hope that he might live awoke in him again. He began to think of the operation that had been suggested to him. 'To live! I want to live!' he said to himself.

His wife came in to congratulate him after his Communion, and when uttering the usual conventional words she added:

'You feel better, don't you?'

Without looking at her he said 'Yes'.

Her dress, her figure, the expression of her face, the tone of her voice, all revealed the same thing. 'This is wrong, it is not as it should be. All you have lived for and still live for is falsehood and deception, hiding life and death from you.' And as soon as he admitted that thought, his hatred and his agonizing physical suffering again sprang up, and with that suffering a consciousness of the unavoidable, approaching end. And to this was added a new sensation of grinding shooting pain and a feeling of suffocation.

The expression of his face when he uttered that 'yes' was dreadful. Having uttered it, he looked her straight in the eyes, turned on his face with a rapidity extraordinary in his weak state and shouted:

'Go away! Go away and leave me alone!'

XII

FROM that moment the screaming began that continued for three days, and was so terrible that one could not hear it through two closed doors without horror. At the moment he answered his wife he realized that he was lost, that there was no return, that the end had come, the very end, and his doubts were still unsolved and remained doubts.

'Oh! Oh! Oh!' he cried in various intonations. He had begun by screaming 'I won't!' and continued screaming on the letter 'o'.

For three whole days, during which time did not exist for him, he struggled in that black sack into which he was being thrust by an invisible, resistless force. He struggled as a man condemned to death struggles in the hands of the executioner, knowing that he cannot save himself. And every moment he felt that despite all his efforts he was drawing nearer and nearer to what terrified him. He felt that his agony was due to his being thrust into that black hole and still more to his not being able to get right into it. He was hindered from getting into it by his conviction that his life had been a good one. That very justification of his life held him fast and prevented his moving forward, and it caused him most torment of all.

Suddenly some force struck him in the chest and side, making it still harder to breathe, and he fell through the hole and there at the bottom was a light. What had happened to him was like the sensation one sometimes experiences in a railway carriage when one thinks one is going backwards while one is really going forwards and suddenly becomes aware of the real direction.

'Yes, it was all not the right thing,' he said to himself, 'but that's no matter. It can be done. But what *is* the right thing?' he asked himself, and suddenly grew quiet.

This occurred at the end of the third day, two hours before his death. Just then his schoolboy son had crept softly in and gone up to the bedside. The dying man was still screaming desperately and waving his arms. His hand fell on the boy's head, and the boy caught it, pressed it to his lips, and began to cry.

At that very moment Iván Ilých fell through and caught sight of the light, and it was revealed to him that though his life had not been what it should have been, this could still be rectified. He asked himself, 'What *is* the right thing?' and grew still, listening. Then he felt that someone was kissing his hand. He opened his eyes, looked at his son, and felt sorry for him. His wife came up to him and he glanced at her. She was gazing at him open-mouthed, with undried tears on her nose and cheek and a despairing look on her face. He felt sorry for her too.

'Yes, I am making them wretched,' he thought. 'They are sorry, but it will be better for them when I die.' He wished to say this but had not the strength to utter it. 'Besides, why speak? I must act,' he thought. With a look at his wife he indicated his son and said: 'Take him away . . . sorry for him . . . sorry for you too. . . .' He tried to add, 'forgive me', but said 'forego' and waved his hand, knowing that He whose understanding mattered would understand.

And suddenly it grew clear to him that what had been oppressing him and would not leave him was all dropping away at once from two sides, from ten sides, and from all sides. He was sorry for them, he must act so as not to hurt them: release them and free himself from these sufferings. 'How good and how simple!' he thought. 'And the pain?' he asked himself. 'What has become of it? Where are you, pain?'

He turned his attention to it.

'Yes, here it is. Well, what of it? Let the pain be.'

'And death ... where is it?'

He sought his former accustomed fear of death and did not find it. 'Where is it? What death?' There was no fear because there was no death.

In place of death there was light.

'So that's what it is!' he suddenly exclaimed aloud. 'What joy!'

To him all this happened in a single instant, and the meaning of that instant did not change. For those present his agony continued for another two hours. Something rattled in his throat, his emaciated body twitched, then the gasping and rattle became less and less frequent.

'It is finished!' said someone near him.

He heard these words and repeated them in his soul.

'Death is finished,' he said to himself. 'It is no more!'

He drew in a breath, stopped in the midst of a sigh, stretched out, and died.

THE THREE HERMITS

AN OLD LEGEND CURRENT IN
THE VOLGA DISTRICT

'And in praying use not vain repetitions, as the Gentiles do: for they think that they shall be heard for their much speaking. Be not therefore like unto them: for your Father knoweth what things ye have need of, before ye ask Him.' – *Matt.* vi. 7, 8.

A BISHOP was sailing from Archangel to the Solovétsk Monastery; and on the same vessel were a number of pilgrims on their way to visit the shrines at that place. The voyage was a smooth one. The wind favourable, and the weather fair. The pilgrims lay on deck, eating, or sat in groups talking to one another. The Bishop, too, came on deck, and as he was pacing up and down, he noticed a group of men standing near the prow and listening to a fisherman, who was pointing to the sea and telling them something. The Bishop stopped, and looked in the direction in which the man was pointing. He could see nothing, however, but the sea glistening in the sunshine. He drew nearer to listen, but when the man saw him, he took off his cap and was silent. The rest of the people also took off their caps, and bowed.

'Do not let me disturb you, friends,' said the Bishop. 'I came to hear what this good man was saying.'

'The fisherman was telling us about the hermits,' replied one, a tradesman, rather bolder than the rest.

'What hermits?' asked the Bishop, going to the side of the vessel and seating himself on a box. 'Tell me about them. I should like to hear. What were you pointing at?'

'Why, that little island you can just see over there,' answered the man, pointing to a spot ahead and a little to the right. 'That is the island where the hermits live for the salvation of their souls.'

'Where is the island?' asked the Bishop. 'I see nothing.'

'There, in the distance, if you will please look along my hand. Do you see that little cloud? Below it, and a bit to the left, there is just a faint streak. That is the island.'

The Bishop looked carefully, but his unaccustomed eyes could make out nothing but the water shimmering in the sun.

'I cannot see it,' he said. 'But who are the hermits that live there?'

'They are holy men,' answered the fisherman. 'I had long heard tell of them, but never chanced to see them myself till the year before last.'

And the fisherman related how once, when he was out fishing, he had been stranded at night upon that island, not knowing where he was. In the morning, as he wandered about the island, he came across an earth hut, and met an old man standing near it. Presently two others came out, and after having fed him, and dried his things, they helped him mend his boat.

'And what are they like?' asked the Bishop.

'One is a small man and his back is bent. He wears a priest's cassock and is very old; he must be more than a hundred, I should say. He is so old that the white of his beard is taking a greenish tinge, but he is always smiling, and his face is as bright as an angel's from heaven. The second is taller, but he also is very old. He wears a tattered, peasant coat. His beard is broad, and of a yellowish grey colour. He is a strong man. Before I had time to help him, he turned my boat over as if it were only a pail. He too, is kindly and cheerful. The third is tall, and has a beard as white as snow and reaching to his knees. He is stern, with over-hanging eyebrows; and he wears nothing but a mat tied round his waist.'

'And did they speak to you?' asked the Bishop.

'For the most part they did everything in silence, and spoke but little even to one another. One of them would just give a glance, and the others would understand him. I asked the tallest whether they had lived there long. He frowned, and muttered something as if he were angry; but the oldest one took his hand and smiled, and then the tall one was quiet. The oldest one only said: "Have mercy upon us," and smiled.'

While the fisherman was talking, the ship had drawn nearer to the island.

'There, now you can see it plainly, if your Grace will please to look,' said the tradesman, pointing with his hand.

The Bishop looked, and now he really saw a dark streak – which was the island. Having looked at it a while, he left the prow of the vessel, and going to the stern, asked the helmsman:

'What island is that?'

'That one,' replied the man, 'has no name. There are many such in this sea.'

'Is it true that there are hermits who live there for the salvation of their souls?'

'So it is said, your Grace, but I don't know if it's true. Fishermen say they have seen them; but of course they may only be spinning yarns.'

'I should like to land on the island and see these men,' said the Bishop. 'How could I manage it?'

'The ship cannot get close to the island,' replied the helmsman, 'but you might be rowed there in a boat. You had better speak to the captain.'

The captain was sent for and came.

'I should like to see these hermits,' said the Bishop. 'Could I not be rowed ashore?'

The captain tried to dissuade him.

'Of course it could be done,' said he, 'but we should lose much time. And if I might venture to say so to your Grace, the old men are not worth your pains. I have heard say that they are foolish old fellows, who understand nothing, and never speak a word, any more than the fish in the sea.'

'I wish to see them,' said the Bishop, 'and I will pay you for your trouble and loss of time. Please let me have a boat.'

There was no help for it; so the order was given. The sailors trimmed the sails, the steersman put up the helm, and the ship's course was set for the island. A chair was placed at the prow for the Bishop, and he sat there, looking ahead. The passengers all collected at the prow, and gazed at the island. Those who had the sharpest eyes could presently make out the rocks on it, and then a mud hut was seen. At last one man saw the hermits themselves. The captain brought a telescope and, after looking through it, handed it to the Bishop.

'It's right enough. There are three men standing on the shore. There, a little to the right of that big rock.'

The Bishop took the telescope, got it into position, and he saw the three men: a tall one, a shorter one, and one very small and bent, standing on the shore and holding each other by the hand.

The captain turned to the Bishop.

'The vessel can get no nearer in than this, your Grace. If you wish to go ashore, we must ask you to go in the boat, while we anchor here.'

The cable was quickly let out, the anchor cast, and the sails furled. There was a jerk, and the vessel shook. Then, a boat having been lowered, the oarsmen jumped in, and the Bishop descended the ladder and took his seat. The men pulled at their oars, and the boat moved rapidly towards the island. When they came within a stone's throw, they saw three old men: a tall one with only a mat tied round his waist: a shorter one in a tattered peasant coat, and a very old one bent with age and wearing an old cassock – all three standing hand in hand.

The oarsmen pulled in to the shore, and held on with the boathook while the Bishop got out.

The old men bowed to him, and he gave them his benediction, at which they bowed still lower. Then the Bishop began to speak to them.

'I have heard,' he said, 'that you, godly men, live here saving your own souls, and praying to our Lord Christ for your fellow men. I, an unworthy servant of Christ, am called, by God's mercy, to keep and teach His flock. I wished to see you, servants of God, and to do what I can to teach you, also.'

The old men looked at each other smiling, but remained silent.

'Tell me,' said the Bishop, 'what you are doing to save your souls, and how you serve God on this island.'

The second hermit sighed, and looked at the oldest, the very ancient one. The latter smiled, and said:

'We do not know how to serve God. We only serve and support ourselves, servant of God.'

'But how do you pray to God?' asked the Bishop.

'We pray in this way,' replied the hermit. 'Three are ye, three are we, have mercy upon us.'

And when the old man said this, all three raised their eyes to heaven, and repeated:

'Three are ye, three are we, have mercy upon us!'

The Bishop smiled.

'You have evidently heard something about the Holy Trinity,' said he. 'But you do not pray aright. You have won my affection, godly men. I see you wish to please the Lord, but you do not know how to serve Him. That is not the way to pray; but listen to me, and I will teach you. I will teach you, not a way of my own, but the way in which God in the Holy Scriptures has commanded all men to pray to Him.'

And the Bishop began explaining to the hermits how God had revealed Himself to men; telling them of God the Father, and God the Son, and God the Holy Ghost.

'God the Son came down on earth,' said he, 'to save men, and this is how He taught us all to pray. Listen, and repeat after me: "Our Father".'

And the first old man repeated after him, 'Our Father', and the second said, 'Our Father', and the third said, 'Our Father'.

'Which art in heaven,' continued the Bishop.

The first hermit repeated, 'Which art in heaven,' but the second blundered over the words, and the tall hermit could not say them properly. His hair had grown over his mouth so that he could not speak plainly. The very old hermit, having no teeth, also mumbled indistinctly.

The Bishop repeated the words again, and the old men repeated them after him. The Bishop sat down on a stone, and the old men stood before him, watching his mouth, and repeating the words as he uttered them. And all day long the Bishop laboured, saying a word twenty, thirty, a hundred times over, and the old men repeated it after him. They blundered, and he corrected them, and made them begin again.

The Bishop did not leave off till he had taught them the whole of the Lord's prayer so that they could not only repeat it after him, but could say it by themselves. The middle one was the first to know it, and to repeat the whole of it alone. The

Bishop made him say it again and again, and at last the others could say it too.

It was getting dark, and the moon was appearing over the water, before the Bishop rose to return to the vessel. When he took leave of the old men, they all bowed down to the ground before him. He raised them, and kissed each of them, telling them to pray as he had taught them. Then he got into the boat and returned to the ship.

And as he sat in the boat and was rowed to the ship he could hear the three voices of the hermits loudly repeating the Lord's prayer. As the boat drew near the vessel their voices could no longer be heard, but they could still be seen in the moonlight, standing as he had left them on the shore, the shortest in the middle, the tallest on the right, the middle one on the left. As soon as the Bishop had reached the vessel and got on board, the anchor was weighed and the sails unfurled. The wind filled them, and the ship sailed away, and the Bishop took a seat in the stern and watched the island they had left. For a time he could still see the hermits, but presently they disappeared from sight, though the island was still visible. At last it too vanished, and only the sea was to be seen, rippling in the moonlight.

The pilgrims lay down to sleep, and all was quiet on deck. The Bishop did not wish to sleep, but sat alone at the stern, gazing at the sea where the island was no longer visible, and thinking of the good old men. He thought how pleased they had been to learn the Lord's prayer; and he thanked God for having sent him to teach and help such godly men.

So the Bishop sat, thinking, and gazing at the sea where the island had disappeared. And the moonlight flickered before his eyes, sparkling, now here, now there, upon the waves. Suddenly he saw something white and shining, on the bright path which the moon cast across the sea. Was it a seagull, or the little gleaming sail of some small boat? The Bishop fixed his eyes on it, wondering.

'It must be a boat sailing after us,' thought he, 'but it is overtaking us very rapidly. It was far, far away a minute ago, but now it is much nearer. It cannot be a boat, for I can see no sail; but whatever it may be, it is following us, and catching us up.'

And he could not make out what it was. Not a boat, nor a bird, nor a fish! It was too large for a man, and besides a man could not be out there in the midst of the sea. The Bishop rose, and said to the helmsman:

'Look there, what is that, my friend? What is it?' the Bishop repeated, though he could now see plainly what it was – the three hermits running upon the water, all gleaming white, their grey beards shining, and approaching the ship as quickly as though it were not moving.

The steersman looked, and let go the helm in terror.

'Oh Lord! The hermits are running after us on the water as though it were dry land!'

The passengers hearing him, jumped up, and crowded to the stern. They saw the hermits coming along hand in hand, and the two outer ones beckoning the ship to stop. All three were gliding along upon the water without moving their feet. Before the ship could be stopped, the hermits had reached it, and raising their heads, all three as with one voice, began to say:

'We have forgotten your teaching, servant of God. As long as we kept repeating it we remembered, but when we stopped saying it for a time, a word dropped out, and now it has all gone to pieces. We can remember nothing of it. Teach us again.'

The Bishop crossed himself, and leaning over the ship's side, said:

'Your own prayer will reach the Lord, men of God. It is not for me to teach you. Pray for us sinners.'

And the Bishop bowed low before the old men; and they turned and went back across the sea. And a light shone until daybreak on the spot where they were lost to sight.

THE IMP AND THE
CRUST

A POOR peasant set out early one morning to plough, taking with him for his breakfast a crust of bread. He got his plough ready, wrapped the bread in his coat, put it under a bush, and set to work. After a while, when his horse was tired and he was hungry, the peasant fixed the plough, let the horse loose to graze, and went to get his coat and his breakfast.

He lifted the coat, but the bread was gone! He looked and looked, turned the coat over, shook it out – but the bread was gone. The peasant could not make this out at all.

'That's strange,' thought he; 'I saw no one, but all the same someone has been here and has taken the bread!'

It was an imp who had stolen the bread while the peasant was ploughing, and at that moment he was sitting behind the bush, waiting to hear the peasant swear and call on the Devil.

The peasant was sorry to lose his breakfast, but 'It can't be helped,' said he. 'After all, I shan't die of hunger! No doubt whoever took the bread needed it. May it do him good!'

And he went to the well, had a drink of water, and rested a bit. Then he caught his horse, harnessed it, and began ploughing again.

The imp was crestfallen at not having made the peasant sin, and he went to report what had happened to the Devil, his master.

He came to the Devil and told how he had taken the peasant's bread, and how the peasant instead of cursing had said, 'May it do him good!'

The Devil was angry, and replied: 'If the man got the better of you, it was your own fault – you don't understand your business! If the peasants, and their wives after them, take to that

185

sort of thing, it will be all up with us. The matter can't be left like that! Go back at once,' said he, 'and put things right. If in three years you don't get the better of that peasant, I'll have you ducked in holy water!'

The imp was frightened. He scampered back to earth, thinking how he could redeem his fault. He thought and thought, and at last hit upon a good plan.

He turned himself into a labouring man, and went and took service with the poor peasant. The first year he advised the peasant to sow corn in a marshy place. The peasant took his advice, and sowed in the marsh. The year turned out a very dry one, and the crops of the other peasants were all scorched by the sun, but the poor peasant's corn grew thick and tall and full-eared. Not only had he grain enough to last him for the whole year, but he had much left over besides.

The next year the imp advised the peasant to sow on the hill; and it turned out a wet summer. Other people's corn was beaten down and rotted and the ears did not fill; but the peasant's crop, up on the hill, was a fine one. He had more grain left over than before, so that he did not know what to do with it all.

Then the imp showed the peasant how he could mash the grain and distil spirit from it; and the peasant made strong drink, and began to drink it himself and to give it to his friends.

So the imp went to the Devil, his master, and boasted that he had made up for his failure. The Devil said that he would come and see for himself how the case stood.

He came to the peasant's house, and saw that the peasant had invited his well-to-do neighbours and was treating them to drink. His wife was offering the drink to the guests, and as she handed it round she tumbled against the table and spilt a glassful.

The peasant was angry, and scolded his wife: 'What do you mean, you slut? Do you think it's ditch-water, you cripple, that you must go pouring good stuff like that over the floor?'

The imp nudged the Devil, his master, with his elbow: 'See,' said he, 'that's the man who did not grudge his last crust!'

The peasant, still railing at his wife, began to carry the drink round himself. Just then a poor peasant returning from work came in uninvited. He greeted the company, sat down, and saw that they were drinking. Tired with his day's work, he felt that he too would like a drop. He sat and sat, and his mouth kept watering, but the host instead of offering him any only muttered: 'I can't find drink for everyone who comes along.'

This pleased the Devil; but the imp chuckled and said, 'Wait a bit, there's more to come yet!'

The rich peasants drank, and their host drank too. And they began to make false, oily speeches to one another.

The Devil listened and listened, and praised the imp.

'If', said he, 'the drink makes them so foxy that they begin to cheat each other, they will soon all be in our hands.'

'Wait for what's coming,' said the imp. 'Let them have another glass all round. Now they are like foxes, wagging their tails and trying to get round one another; but presently you will see them like savage wolves.'

The peasants had another glass each, and their talk became wilder and rougher. Instead of oily speeches, they began to abuse and snarl at one another. Soon they took to fighting, and punched one another's noses. And the host joined in the fight, and he too got well beaten.

The Devil looked on and was much pleased at all this.

'This is first-rate!' said he.

But the imp replied: 'Wait a bit – the best is yet to come. Wait till they have had a third glass. Now they are raging like wolves, but let them have one more glass, and they will be like swine.'

The peasants had their third glass, and became quite like brutes. They muttered and shouted, not knowing why, and not listening to one another.

Then the party began to break up. Some went alone, some in twos, and some in threes, all staggering down the street. The host went out to speed his guests, but he fell on his nose into a puddle, smeared himself from top to toe, and lay there grunting like a hog.

This pleased the Devil still more.

'Well,' said he, 'you have hit on a first-rate drink, and have quite made up for your blunder about the bread. But now tell me how this drink is made. You must first have put in fox's blood: that was what made the peasants sly as foxes. Then, I suppose, you added wolf's blood: that is what made them fierce like wolves. And you must have finished off with swine's blood, to make them behave like swine.'

'No,' said the imp, 'that was not the way I did it. All I did was to see that the peasant had more corn than he needed. The blood of the beasts is always in man; but as long as he has only enough corn for his needs, it is kept in bounds. While that was the case, the peasant did not grudge his last crust. But when he had corn left over, he looked for ways of getting pleasure out of it. And I showed him a pleasure – drinking! And when he began to turn God's good gifts into spirits for his own pleasure – the fox's, wolf's and swine's blood in him all came out. If only he goes on drinking, he will always be a beast!'

The Devil praised the imp, forgave him for his former blunder, and advanced him to a post of high honour.

HOW MUCH LAND DOES A MAN NEED?

I

A N elder sister came to visit her younger sister in the country. The elder was married to a tradesman in town, the younger to a peasant in the village. As the sisters sat over their tea talking, the elder began to boast of the advantages of town life: saying how comfortably they lived there, how well they dressed, what fine clothes her children wore, what good things they ate and drank, and how she went to the theatre, promenades, and entertainments.

The younger sister was piqued, and in turn disparaged the life of a tradesman, and stood up for that of a peasant.

'I would not change my way of life for yours,' said she. 'We may live roughly, but at least we are free from anxiety. You live in better style than we do, but though you often earn more than you need, you are very likely to lose all you have. You know the proverb, "Loss and gain are brothers twain." It often happens that people who are wealthy one day are begging their bread the next. Our way is safer. Though a peasant's life is not a fat one, it is a long one. We shall never grow rich, but we shall always have enough to eat.'

The elder sister said sneeringly:

'Enough? Yes, if you like to share with the pigs and the calves! What do you know of elegance or manners! However much your goodman may slave, you will die as you are living – on a dung heap – and your children the same.'

'Well, what of that?' replied the younger. 'Of course our work is rough and coarse. But, on the other hand, it is sure; and we need not bow to anyone. But you, in your towns, are surrounded by temptations; to-day all may be right, but to-morrow the Evil One may tempt your husband with cards, wine, or women, and all will go to ruin. Don't such things happen often enough?'

Pahóm, the master of the house, was lying on the top of the oven, and he listened to the women's chatter.

'It is perfectly true,' thought he. 'Busy as we are from childhood tilling mother earth, we peasants have no time to let any nonsense settle in our heads. Our only trouble is that we haven't land enough. If I had plenty of land, I shouldn't fear the Devil himself!'

The women finished their tea, chatted a while about dress, and then cleared away the tea-things and lay down to sleep.

But the Devil had been sitting behind the oven, and had heard all that was said. He was pleased that the peasant's wife had led her husband into boasting, and that he had said that if he had plenty of land he would not fear the Devil himself.

'All right,' thought the Devil. 'We will have a tussle. I'll give you land enough; and by means of that land I will get you into my power.'

II

CLOSE to the village there lived a lady, a small landowner, who had an estate of about three hundred acres.[1] She had always lived on good terms with the peasants, until she engaged as her steward an old soldier, who took to burdening the people with fines. However careful Pahóm tried to be, it happened again and again that now a horse of his got among the lady's oats, now a cow strayed into her garden, now his calves found their way into her meadows – and he always had to pay a fine.

Pahóm paid up, but grumbled, and, going home in a temper, was rough with his family. All through that summer, Pahóm had much trouble because of this steward; and he was even glad when winter came and the cattle had to be stabled. Though he grudged the fodder when they could no

1 120 *desyatins*. The *desyatina* is properly 2.7 acres; but in this story round numbers are used.

longer graze on the pastureland, at least he was free from anxiety about them.

In the winter the news got about that the lady was going to sell her land, and that the keeper of the inn on the high road was bargaining for it. When the peasants heard this they were very much alarmed.

'Well,' thought they, 'if the inn-keeper gets the land, he will worry us with fines worse than the lady's steward. We all depend on that estate.'

So the peasants went on behalf of their Commune, and asked the lady not to sell the land to the inn-keeper; offering her a better price for it themselves. The lady agreed to let them have it. Then the peasants tried to arrange for the Commune to buy the whole estate, so that it might be held by them all in common. They met twice to discuss it, but could not settle the matter; the Evil One sowed discord among them, and they could not agree. So they decided to buy the land individually, each according to his means; and the lady agreed to this plan as she had to the other.

Presently Pahóm heard that a neighbour of his was buying fifty acres, and that the lady had consented to accept one half in cash and to wait a year for the other half. Pahóm felt envious.

'Look at that,' thought he, 'the land is all being sold, and I shall get none of it.' So he spoke to his wife.

'Other people are buying,' said he, 'and we must also buy twenty acres or so. Life is becoming impossible. That steward is simply crushing us with his fines.'

So they put their heads together and considered how they could manage to buy it. They had one hundred rubles laid by. They sold a colt, and one half of their bees; hired out one of their sons as a labourer, and took his wages in advance; borrowed the rest from a brother-in-law, and so scraped together half the purchase money.

Having done this, Pahóm chose out a farm of forty acres, some of it wooded, and went to the lady to bargain for it. They came to an agreement, and he shook hands with her upon it, and paid her a deposit in advance. Then they went to town and signed the deeds; he paying half the price down, and undertaking to pay the remainder within two years.

So now Pahóm had land of his own. He borrowed seed, and sowed it on the land he had bought. The harvest was a good one, and within a year he had managed to pay off his debts both to the lady and to his brother-in-law. So he became a landowner, ploughing and sowing his own land, making hay on his own land, cutting his own trees, and feeding his cattle on his own pasture. When he went out to plough his fields, or to look at his growing corn, or at his grass-meadows, his heart would fill with joy. The grass that grew and the flowers that bloomed there, seemed to him unlike any that grew elsewhere. Formerly, when he had passed by that land, it had appeared the same as any other land, but now it seemed quite different.

III

So Pahóm was well-contented, and everything would have been right if the neighbouring peasants would only not have trespassed on his corn-fields and meadows. He appealed to them most civilly, but they still went on: now the Communal herdsmen would let the village cows stray into his meadows; then horses from the night pasture would get among his corn. Pahóm turned them out again and again, and forgave their owners, and for a long time he forbore from prosecuting anyone. But at last he lost patience and complained to the District Court. He knew it was the peasants' want of land, and no evil intent on their part, that caused the trouble; but he thought:

'I cannot go on overlooking it, or they will destroy all I have. They must be taught a lesson.'

So he had them up, gave them one lesson, and then another, and two or three of the peasants were fined. After a time Pahóm's neighbours began to bear him a grudge for this, and would now and then let their cattle on to his land on purpose. One peasant even got into Pahóm's wood at night and cut down five young lime trees for their bark. Pahóm passing through the wood one day noticed something white. He came nearer, and saw the stripped trunks lying on the ground, and close by stood the stumps, where the trees had been. Pahóm was furious.

'If he had only cut one here and there it would have been bad enough,' thought Pahóm, 'but the rascal has actually cut down a whole clump. If I could only find out who did this, I would pay him out.'

He racked his brains as to who it could be. Finally he decided: 'It must be Simon – no one else could have done it.' So he went to Simon's homestead to have a look round, but he found nothing, and only had an angry scene. However, he now felt more certain than ever that Simon had done it, and he lodged a complaint. Simon was summoned. The case was tried, and re-tried, and at the end of it all Simon was acquitted, there being no evidence against him. Pahóm felt still more aggrieved, and let his anger loose upon the Elder and the Judges.

'You let thieves grease your palms,' said he. 'If you were honest folk yourselves, you would not let a thief go free.'

So Pahóm quarrelled with the Judges and with his neighbours. Threats to burn his building began to be uttered. So though Pahóm had more land, his place in the Commune was much worse than before.

About this time a rumour got about that many people were moving to new parts.

'There's no need for me to leave my land,' thought Pahóm. 'But some of the others might leave our village, and then there would be more room for us. I would take over their land myself, and make my estate a bit bigger. I could then live more at ease. As it is, I am still too cramped to be comfortable.'

One day Pahóm was sitting at home, when a peasant, passing through the village, happened to call in. He was allowed to stay the night, and supper was given him. Pahóm had a talk with this peasant and asked him where he came from. The stranger answered that he came from beyond the Volga, where he had been working. One word led to another, and the man went on to say that many people were settling in those parts. He told how some people from his village had settled there. They had joined the Commune, and had had twenty-five acres per man granted them. The land was so good, he said, that the rye sown on it grew as high as a horse, and so thick that five cuts of a sickle made a sheaf. One peasant, he said, had brought nothing with him but his bare hands, and now he had six horses and two cows of his own.

Pahóm's heart kindled with desire. He thought:

'Why should I suffer in this narrow hole, if one can live so well elsewhere? I will sell my land and my homestead here, and with the money I will start afresh over there and get everything new. In this crowded place one is always having trouble. But I must first go and find out all about it myself.'

Towards summer he got ready and started. He went down the Volga on a steamer to Samára, then walked another three hundred miles on foot, and at last reached the place. It was just as the stranger had said. The peasants had plenty of land: every man had twenty-five acres of Communal land given him for his use, and anyone who had money could buy, besides, at two shillings an acre[1] as much good freehold land as he wanted.

Having found out all he wished to know, Pahóm returned home as autumn came on, and began selling off his belongings. He sold his land at a profit, sold his homestead and all his cattle, and withdrew from membership of the Commune. He only waited till the spring, and then started with his family for the new settlement.

IV

As soon as Pahóm and his family arrived at their new abode, he applied for admission into the Commune of a large village. He stood treat to the Elders, and obtained the necessary documents. Five shares of Communal land were given him for his own and his sons' use: that is to say – 125 acres (not all together, but in different fields) besides the use of the Communal pasture. Pahóm put up the buildings he needed, and

---

1 Three rubles per *desyatina*.

bought cattle. Of the Communal land alone he had three times as much as at his former home, and the land was good corn-land. He was ten times better off than he had been. He had plenty of arable land and pasturage, and could keep as many head of cattle as he liked.

At first, in the bustle of building and settling down, Pahóm was pleased with it all, but when he got used to it he began to think that even here he had not enough land. The first year, he sowed wheat on his share of the Communal land, and had a good crop. He wanted to go on sowing wheat, but had not enough Communal land for the purpose, and what he had already used was not available; for in those parts wheat is only sown on virgin soil or on fallow land. It is sown for one or two years, and then the land lies fallow till it is again overgrown with prairie grass. There were many who wanted such land, and there was not enough for all; so that people quarrelled about it. Those who were better off, wanted it for growing wheat, and those who were poor, wanted it to let to dealers, so that they might raise money to pay their taxes. Pahóm wanted to sow more wheat; so he rented land from a dealer for a year. He sowed much wheat and had a fine crop, but the land was too far from the village – the wheat had to be carted more than ten miles. After a time Pahóm noticed that some peasant-dealers were living on separate farms, and were growing wealthy; and he thought:

'If I were to buy some freehold land, and have a homestead on it, it would be a different thing altogether. Then it would all be nice and compact.'

The question of buying freehold land recurred to him again and again.

He went on in the same way for three years: renting land and sowing wheat. The seasons turned out well and the crops were good, so that he began to lay money by. He might have gone on living contentedly, but he grew tired of having to rent other people's land every year, and having to scramble for it. Wherever there was good land to be had, the peasants would rush for it and it was taken up at once, so that unless you were sharp about it you got none. It happened in the third year that he and a dealer together rented a piece of pasture land from some peasants; and they had already ploughed it up, when there was some dispute, and the peasants went to law about it, and things fell out so that the labour was all lost.

'If it were my own land,' thought Pahóm, 'I should be independent, and there would not be all this unpleasantness.'

So Pahóm began looking out for land which he could buy; and he came across a peasant who had bought thirteen hundred acres, but having got into difficulties was willing to sell again cheap. Pahóm bargained and haggled with him, and at last they settled the price at 1,500 rubles, part in cash and part to be paid later. They had all but clinched the matter, when a passing dealer happened to stop at Pahóm's one day to get a feed for his horses. He drank tea with Pahóm, and they had a talk. The dealer said that he was just returning from the land of the Bashkírs, far away, where he had bought thirteen thousand acres of land, all for 1,000 rubles. Pahóm questioned him further, and the tradesman said:

'All one need do is to make friends with the chiefs. I gave away about one hundred rubles' worth of dressing-gowns and carpets, besides a case of tea, and I gave wine to those who would drink it; and I got the land for less than twopence an acre.[1] And he showed Pahóm the title-deeds, saying:

'The land lies near a river, and the whole prairie is virgin soil.'

Pahóm plied him with questions, and the tradesman said:

'There is more land there than you could cover if you walked a year, and it all belongs to the Bashkírs. They are as simple as sheep, and land can be got almost for nothing.'

'There now,' thought Pahóm, 'with my one thousand rubles, why should I get only thirteen hundred acres, and saddle myself with a debt besides. If I take it out there, I can get more than ten times as much for the money.'

V

PAHÓM inquired how to get to the place, and as soon as the tradesman had left him, he prepared to go there himself. He

[1] Five kopeks for a *desyatina*.

left his wife to look after the homestead, and started on his journey taking his man with him. They stopped at a town on their way, and bought a case of tea, some wine, and other presents, as the tradesman had advised. On and on they went until they had gone more than three hundred miles, and on the seventh day they came to a place where the Bashkírs had pitched their tents. It was all just as the tradesman had said. The people lived on the steppes, by a river, in felt-covered tents.[1] They neither tilled the ground, nor ate bread. Their cattle and horses grazed in herds on the steppe. The colts were tethered behind the tents, and the mares were driven to them twice a day. The mares were milked, and from the milk kumiss was made. It was the women who prepared kumiss, and they also made cheese. As far as the men were concerned, drinking kumiss and tea, eating mutton, and playing on their pipes, was all they cared about. They were all stout and merry, and all the summer long they never thought of doing any work. They were quite ignorant, and knew no Russian, but were good-natured enough.

As soon as they saw Pahóm, they came out of their tents and gathered round their visitor. An interpreter was found, and Pahóm told them he had come about some land. The Bashkírs seemed very glad; they took Pahóm and led him into one of the best tents, where they made him sit on some down cushions placed on a carpet, while they sat round him. They gave him tea and kumiss, and had a sheep killed, and gave him mutton to eat. Pahóm took presents out of his cart and distributed them among the Bashkírs, and divided amongst them the tea. The Bashkírs were delighted. They talked a great deal among themselves, and then told the interpreter to translate.

'They wish to tell you,' said the interpreter, 'that they like you, and that it is our custom to do all we can to please a guest and to repay him for his gifts. You have given us presents, now tell us which of the things we possess please you best, that we may present them to you.'

---

1 *Kibítkas*, as described in footnote on p. 105.

'What pleases me best here,' answered Pahóm, 'is your land. Our land is crowded, and the soil is exhausted; but you have plenty of land and it is good land. I never saw the like of it.'

The interpreter translated. The Bashkírs talked among themselves for a while. Pahóm could not understand what they were saying, but saw that they were much amused, and that they shouted and laughed. Then they were silent and looked at Pahóm while the interpreter said:

'They wish me to tell you that in return for your presents they will gladly give you as much land as you want. You have only to point it out with your hand and it is yours.'

The Bashkírs talked again for a while and began to dispute. Pahóm asked what they were disputing about, and the interpreter told him that some of them thought they ought to ask their Chief about the land and not act in his absence, while others thought there was no need to wait for his return.

VI

WHILE the Bashkírs were disputing, a man in a large fox-fur cap appeared on the scene. They all became silent and rose to their feet. The interpreter said, 'This is our Chief himself.'

Pahóm immediately fetched the best dressing-gown and five pounds of tea, and offered these to the Chief. The Chief accepted them, and seated himself in the place of honour. The Bashkírs at once began telling him something. The Chief listened for a while, then made a sign with his head for them to be silent, and addressing himself to Pahóm, said in Russian:

'Well, let it be so. Choose whatever piece of land you like; we have plenty of it.'

'How can I take as much as I like?' thought Pahóm. 'I must get a deed to make it secure, or else they may say, "It is yours," and afterwards may take it away again.'

'Thank you for your kind words,' he said aloud. 'You have much land, and I only want a little. But I should like to be sure which bit is mine. Could it not be measured and made over to me? Life and death are in God's hands. You good people give it to me, but your children might wish to take it away again.'

'You are quite right,' said the Chief. 'We will make it over to you.'

'I heard that a dealer had been here,' continued Pahóm, 'and that you gave him a little land, too, and signed title-deeds to that effect. I should like to have it done in the same way.'

The Chief understood.

'Yes,' replied he, 'that can be done quite easily. We have a scribe, and we will go to town with you and have the deed properly sealed.'

'And what will be the price?' asked Pahóm.

'Our price is always the same: one thousand rubles a day.'

Pahóm did not understand.

'A day? What measure is that? How many acres would that be?'

'We do not know how to reckon it out,' said the Chief. 'We sell it by the day. As much as you can go round on your feet in a day is yours, and the price is one thousand rubles a day.'

Pahóm was surprised.

'But in a day you can get round a large tract of land,' he said.

The Chief laughed.

'It will all be yours!' said he. 'But there is one condition: If you don't return on the same day to the spot whence you started, your money is lost.'

'But how am I to mark the way that I have gone?'

'Why, we shall go to any spot you like, and stay there. You must start from that spot and make your round, taking a spade with you. Wherever you think necessary, make a mark. At every turning, dig a hole and pile up the turf; then afterwards we will go round with a plough from hole to hole. You may make as large a circuit as you please, but before the sun sets you must return to the place you started from. All the land you cover will be yours.'

Pahóm was delighted. It was decided to start early next morning. They talked a while, and after drinking some more kumiss and eating some more mutton, they had tea again, and then the night came on. They gave Pahóm a feather-bed to sleep on, and the Bashkírs dispersed for the night, promising to assemble the next morning at daybreak and ride out before sunrise to the appointed spot.

VII

PAHÓM lay on the feather-bed, but could not sleep. He kept thinking about the land.

'What a large tract I will mark off!' thought he. 'I can easily do thirty-five miles in a day. The days are long now, and within a circuit of thirty-five miles what a lot of land there will be! I will sell the poorer land, or let it to peasants, but I'll pick out the best and farm it. I will buy two ox-teams, and hire two more labourers. About a hundred and fifty acres shall be plough-land, and I will pasture cattle on the rest.'

Pahóm lay awake all night, and dozed off only just before dawn. Hardly were his eyes closed when he had a dream. He thought he was lying in that same tent, and heard somebody chuckling outside. He wondered who it could be, and rose and went out, and he saw the Bashkír Chief sitting in front of the tent holding his sides and rolling about with laughter. Going nearer to the Chief, Pahóm asked: 'What are you laughing at?' But he saw that it was no longer the Chief, but the dealer who had recently stopped at his house and had told him about the land. Just as Pahóm was going to ask, 'Have you been here long?' he saw that it was not the dealer, but the peasant who had come up from the Volga, long ago, to Pahóm's old home. Then he saw that it was not the peasant either, but the Devil himself with hoofs and horns, sitting there and chuckling, and before him lay a man barefoot, prostrate on the ground, with only trousers and a shirt on. And Pahóm dreamt that he looked more attentively to see what sort of a man it was that was lying there, and he saw that the man was dead, and that it was himself! He awoke horror-struck.

'What things one does dream,' thought he.

Looking round he saw through the open door that the dawn was breaking.

'It's time to wake them up,' thought he. 'We ought to be starting.'

He got up, roused his man (who was sleeping in his cart), bade him harness; and went to call the Bashkírs.

'It's time to go to the steppe to measure the land,' he said.

The Bashkírs rose and assembled, and the Chief came too. Then they began drinking kumiss again, and offered Pahóm some tea, but he would not wait.

'If we are to go, let us go. It is high time,' said he.

VIII

THE Bashkírs got ready and they all started: some mounted on horses, and some in carts. Pahóm drove in his own small cart with his servant, and took a spade with him. When they reached the steppe, the morning red was beginning to kindle. They ascended a hillock (called by the Bashkírs a *shikhan*) and dismounting from their carts and their horses, gathered in one spot. The Chief came up to Pahóm and stretching out his arm towards the plain:

'See,' said he, 'all this, as far as your eye can reach, is ours. You may have any part of it you like.'

Pahóm's eyes glistened: it was all virgin soil, as flat as the palm of your hand, as black as the seed of a poppy, and in the hollows different kinds of grasses grew breast high.

The Chief took off his fox-fur cap, placed it on the ground and said:

'This will be the mark. Start from here, and return here again. All the land you go round shall be yours.'

Pahóm took out his money and put it on the cap. Then he took off his outer coat, remaining in his sleeveless under-coat. He unfastened his girdle and tied it tight below his stomach, put a little bag of bread into the breast of his coat, and tying a flask of water to his girdle, he drew up the tops of his boots, took the spade from his man, and stood ready to start. He considered for some moments which way he had better go – it was tempting everywhere.

'No matter,' he concluded, 'I will go towards the rising sun.'

He turned his face to the east, stretched himself, and waited for the sun to appear above the rim.

'I must lose no time,' he thought, 'and it is easier walking while it is still cool.'

The sun's rays had hardly flashed above the horizon, before Pahóm, carrying the spade over his shoulder, went down into the steppe.

Pahóm started walking neither slowly nor quickly. After having gone a thousand yards he stopped, dug a hole, and placed pieces of turf one on another to make it more visible. Then he went on; and now that he had walked off his stiffness he quickened his pace. After a while he dug another hole.

Pahóm looked back. The hillock could be distinctly seen in the sunlight, with the people on it, and the glittering tyres of the cart-wheels. At a rough guess Pahóm concluded that he had walked three miles. It was growing warmer; he took off his under-coat, flung it across his shoulder, and went on again. It had grown quite warm now; he looked at the sun, it was time to think of breakfast.

'The first shift is done, but there are four in a day, and it is too soon yet to turn. But I will just take off my boots,' said he to himself.

He sat down, took off his boots, stuck them into his girdle, and went on. It was easy walking now.

'I will go on for another three miles,' thought he, 'and then turn to the left. This spot is so fine, that it would be a pity to lose it. The further one goes, the better the land seems.'

He went straight on for a while, and when he looked round, the hillock was scarcely visible and the people on it looked like black ants, and he could just see something glistening there in the sun.

'Ah,' thought Pahóm, 'I have gone far enough in this direction, it is time to turn. Besides I am in a regular sweat, and very thirsty.'

He stopped, dug a large hole, and heaped up pieces of turf. Next he untied his flask, had a drink, and then turned sharply to the left. He went on and on; the grass was high, and it was very hot.

Pahóm began to grow tired: he looked at the sun and saw that it was noon.

'Well,' he thought, 'I must have a rest.'

He sat down, and ate some bread and drank some water; but he did not lie down, thinking that if he did he might fall asleep. After sitting a little while, he went on again. At first he walked easily: the food had strengthened him; but it had become terribly hot, and he felt sleepy; still he went on, thinking: 'An hour to suffer, a life-time to live.'

He went a long way in this direction also, and was about to turn to the left again, when he perceived a damp hollow: 'It would be a pity to leave that out,' he thought. 'Flax would do well there.' So he went on past the hollow, and dug a hole on the other side of it before he turned the corner. Pahóm looked towards the hillock. The heat made the air hazy: it seemed to be quivering, and through the haze the people on the hillock could scarcely be seen.

'Ah!' thought Pahóm, 'I have made the sides too long; I must make this one shorter.' And he went along the third side, stepping faster. He looked at the sun: it was nearly half-way to the horizon, and he had not yet done two miles of the third side of the square. He was still ten miles from the goal.

'No,' he thought, 'though it will make my land lop-sided, I must hurry back in a straight line now. I might go too far, and as it is I have a great deal of land.'

So Pahóm hurriedly dug a hole, and turned straight towards the hillock.

IX

PAHÓM went straight towards the hillock, but he now walked with difficulty. He was done up with the heat, his bare feet were cut and bruised, and his legs began to fail. He longed to rest, but it was impossible if he meant to get back before sunset. The sun waits for no man, and it was sinking lower and lower.

'Oh dear,' he thought, 'if only I have not blundered trying for too much! What if I am too late?'

He looked towards the hillock and at the sun. He was still far from his goal, and the sun was already near the rim.

Pahóm walked on and on; it was very hard walking, but he went quicker and quicker. He pressed on, but was still far from the place. He began running, threw away his coat, his boots, his flask, and his cap, and kept only the spade which he used as a support.

'What shall I do,' he thought again, 'I have grasped too much, and ruined the whole affair. I can't get there before the sun sets.'

And this fear made him still more breathless. Pahóm went on running, his soaking shirt and trousers stuck to him, and his mouth was parched. His breast was working like a blacksmith's bellows, his heart was beating like a hammer, and his legs were giving way as if they did not belong to him. Pahóm was seized with terror lest he should die of the strain.

Though afraid of death, he could not stop. 'After having run all that way they will call me a fool if I stop now,' thought he. And he ran on and on, and drew near and heard the Bashkírs yelling and shouting to him, and their cries inflamed his heart still more. He gathered his last strength and ran on.

The sun was close to the rim, and cloaked in mist looked large, and red as blood. Now, yes now, it was about to set! The sun was quite low, but he was also quite near his aim. Pahóm could already see the people on the hillock waving their arms to hurry him up. He could see the fox-fur cap on the ground, and the money on it, and the Chief sitting on the ground holding his sides. And Pahóm remembered his dream.

'There is plenty of land,' thought he, 'but will God let me live on it? I have lost my life, I have lost my life! I shall never reach that spot!'

Pahóm looked at the sun, which had reached the earth: one side of it had already disappeared. With all his remaining strength he rushed on, bending his body forward so that his legs could hardly follow fast enough to keep him from falling. Just as he reached the hillock it suddenly grew dark. He looked up – the sun had already set! He gave a cry: 'All my labour has been in vain,' thought he, and was about to stop, but he heard the Bashkírs still shouting, and remembered that though to him, from below, the sun seemed to have set, they on the hillock could still see it. He took a long breath and ran up the hillock. It was still light there. He reached the top and saw the cap. Before it sat the Chief laughing and holding his sides. Again Pahóm remembered his dream, and he uttered a cry: his legs gave way beneath him, he fell forward and reached the cap with his hands.

'Ah, that's a fine fellow!' exclaimed the Chief. 'He has gained much land!'

Pahóm's servant came running up and tried to raise him, but he saw that blood was flowing from his mouth. Pahóm was dead!

The Bashkírs clicked their tongues to show their pity.

His servant picked up the spade and dug a grave long enough for Pahóm to lie in, and buried him in it. Six feet from his head to his heels was all he needed.

A GRAIN AS BIG AS A
HEN'S EGG

ONE day some children found, in a ravine, a thing shaped like a grain of corn, with a groove down the middle, but as large as a hen's egg. A traveller passing by saw the thing, bought it from the children for a penny, and taking it to town sold it to the King as a curiosity.

The King called together his wise men, and told them to find out what the thing was. The wise men pondered and pondered and could not make head or tail of it, till one day, when the thing was lying on a window-sill, a hen flew in and pecked at it till she made a hole in it, and then everyone saw that it was a grain of corn. The wise men went to the King, and said:

'It is a grain of corn.'

At this the King was much surprised; and he ordered the learned men to find out when and where such corn had grown. The learned men pondered again, and searched in their books, but could find nothing about it. So they returned to the King and said:

'We can give you no answer. There is nothing about it in our books. You will have to ask the peasants; perhaps some of them may have heard from their fathers when and where grain grew to such a size.'

So the King gave orders that some very old peasant should be brought before him; and his servants found such a man and brought him to the King. Old and bent, ashy pale and toothless, he just managed with the help of two crutches to totter into the King's presence.

The King showed him the grain, but the old man could hardly see it; he took it, however, and felt it with his hands. The King questioned him, saying:

'Can you tell us, old man, where such grain as this grew? Have you ever bought such corn, or sown such in your fields?'

The old man was so deaf that he could hardly hear what the King said, and only understood with great difficulty.

'No!' he answered at last, 'I never sowed nor reaped any like it in my fields, nor did I ever buy any such. When we bought corn, the grains were always as small as they are now. But you might ask my father. He may have heard where such grain grew.'

So the King sent for the old man's father, and he was found and brought before the King. He came walking with one crutch. The King showed him the grain, and the old peasant, who was still able to see, took a good look at it. And the King asked him:

'Can you not tell us, old man, where corn like this used to grow? Have you ever bought any like it, or sown any in your fields?'

Though the old man was rather hard of hearing, he still heard better than his son had done.

'No,' he said, 'I never sowed nor reaped any grain like this in my field. As to buying, I never bought any, for in my time money was not yet in use. Everyone grew his own corn, and when there was any need we shared with one another. I do not know where corn like this grew. Ours was larger and yielded more flour than present-day grain, but I never saw any like this. I have, however, heard my father say that in his time the grain grew larger and yielded more flour than ours. You had better ask him.'

So the King sent for this old man's father, and they found him too, and brought him before the King. He entered walking easily and without crutches: his eye was clear, his hearing good, and he spoke distinctly. The King showed him the grain, and the old grandfather looked at it, and turned it about in his hand.

'It is long since I saw such a fine grain,' said he, and he bit a piece off and tasted it.

'It's the very same kind,' he added.

'Tell me, grandfather,' said the King, 'when and where was such corn grown? Have you ever bought any like it, or sown any in your fields?'

And the old man replied:

'Corn like this used to grow everywhere in my time. I lived on corn like this in my young days, and fed others on it. It was grain like this that we used to sow and reap and thresh.'

And the King asked:

'Tell me, grandfather, did you buy it anywhere, or did you grow it all yourself?'

The old man smiled.

'In my time,' he answered, 'no one ever thought of such a sin as buying or selling bread; and we knew nothing of money. Each man had corn enough of his own.'

'Then tell me, grandfather,' asked the King, 'where was your field, where did you grow corn like this?'

And the grandfather answered:

'My field was God's earth. Wherever I ploughed, there was my field. Land was free. It was a thing no man called his own. Labour was the only thing men called their own.'

'Answer me two more questions,' said the King. 'The first is, Why did the earth bear such grain then, and has ceased to do so now? And the second is, Why your grandson walks with two crutches, your son with one, and you yourself with none? Your eyes are bright, your teeth sound, and your speech clear and pleasant to the ear. How have these things come about?'

And the old man answered:

'These things are so, because men have ceased to live by their own labour, and have taken to depending on the labour of others. In the old time, men lived according to God's law. They had what was their own, and coveted not what others had produced.'

THE GODSON

'Ye have heard that it was said, An eye for an eye, and a tooth for a tooth, but I say unto you, Resist not him that is evil.' – *Matt*. v. 38, 39.

'Vengeance is mine; I will repay.' – *Rom*. xii. 19.

I

A son was born to a poor peasant. He was glad, and went to his neighbour to ask him to stand godfather to the boy. The neighbour refused – he did not like standing godfather to a poor man's child. The peasant asked another neighbour, but he too refused, and after that the poor father went to every house in the village, but found no one willing to be godfather to his son. So he set off to another village, and on the way he met a man who stopped and said:

'Good-day, my good man; where are you off to?'

'God has given me a child,' said the peasant, 'to rejoice my eyes in youth, to comfort my old age, and to pray for my soul after death. But I am poor, and no one in our village will stand godfather to him, so I am now on my way to seek a godfather for him elsewhere.'

'Let me be godfather,' said the stranger.

The peasant was glad, and thanked him, but added:

'And whom shall I ask to be godmother?'

'Go to the town,' replied the stranger, 'and, in the square, you will see a stone house with shop-windows in the front. At the entrance you will find the tradesman to whom it belongs. Ask him to let his daughter stand godmother to your child.'

The peasant hesitated.

'How can I ask a rich tradesman?' said he. 'He will despise me, and will not let his daughter come.'

'Don't trouble about that. Go and ask. Get everything ready by to-morrow morning, and I will come to the christening.'

The poor peasant returned home, and then drove to the town to find the tradesman. He had hardly taken his horse into the yard, when the tradesman himself came out.

217

'What do you want?' said he.

'Why, sir,' said the peasant, 'you see God has given me a son to rejoice my eyes in youth, to comfort my old age, and to pray for my soul after death. Be so kind as to let your daughter stand godmother to him.'

'And when is the christening?' said the tradesman.

'To-morrow morning.'

'Very well. Go in peace. She shall be with you at Mass to-morrow morning.'

The next day the godmother came, and the godfather also, and the infant was baptized. Immediately after the christening the godfather went away. They did not know who he was, and never saw him again.

II

THE child grew up to be a joy to his parents. He was strong, willing to work, clever and obedient. When he was ten years old his parents sent him to school to learn to read and write. What others learnt in five years, he learnt in one, and soon there was nothing more they could teach him.

Easter came round, and the boy went to see his godmother, to give her his Easter greeting.

'Father and mother,' said he when he got home again, 'where does my godfather live? I should like to give him my Easter greeting, too.'

And his father answered:

'We know nothing about your godfather, dear son. We often regret it ourselves. Since the day you were christened we have never seen him, nor had any news of him. We do not know where he lives, or even whether he is still alive.'

The son bowed to his parents.

'Father and mother,' said he, 'let me go and look for my godfather. I must find him and give him my Easter greeting.'

So his father and mother let him go; and the boy set off to find his godfather.

III

THE boy left the house and set out along the road. He had been walking for several hours when he met a stranger who stopped him and said:

'Good-day to you, my boy. Where are you going?'

And the boy answered:

'I went to see my godmother and to give her my Easter greeting, and when I got home I asked my parents where my godfather lives, that I might go and greet him also. They told me they did not know. They said he went away as soon as I was christened, and they know nothing about him, not even if he be still alive. But I wished to see my godfather, and so I have set out to look for him.'

Then the stranger said: 'I am your godfather.'

The boy was glad to hear this. After kissing his godfather three times for an Easter greeting, he asked him:

'Which way are you going now, godfather? If you are coming our way, please come to our house; but if you are going home, I will go with you.'

'I have no time now,' replied his godfather, 'to come to your house. I have business in several villages; but I shall return home again to-morrow. Come and see me then.'

'But how shall I find you, godfather?'

'When you leave home, go straight towards the rising sun, and you will come to a forest; going through the forest you will come to a glade. When you reach this glade sit down and rest awhile, and look around you and see what happens. On the further side of the forest you will find a garden, and in it a house with a golden roof. That is my home. Go up to the gate, and I will myself be there to meet you.'

And having said this the godfather disappeared from his godson's sight.

IV

THE boy did as his godfather had told him. He walked eastward until he reached a forest, and there he came to a glade, and in the midst of the glade he saw a pine tree to a branch of which was tied a rope supporting a heavy log of oak. Close under this log stood a wooden trough filled with honey. Hardly had the boy had time to wonder why the honey was placed there, and why the log hung above it, when he heard a crackling in the wood, and saw some bears approaching: a she-bear, followed by a yearling and three tiny cubs. The she-bear, sniffing the air, went straight to the trough, the cubs following her. She thrust her muzzle into the honey, and called the cubs to do the same. They scampered up and began to eat. As they did so, the log, which the she-bear had moved aside with her head, swung away a little and, returning, gave the cubs a push. Seeing this the she-bear shoved the log away with her paw. It swung further out and returned more forcibly, striking one cub on the back and another on the head. The cubs ran away howling with pain, and the mother, with a growl, caught the log in her fore paws and, raising it above her head, flung it away. The log flew high in the air, and the yearling, rushing to the trough, pushed his muzzle into the honey and began to suck noisily. The others also drew near, but they had not reached the trough when the log, flying back, struck the yearling on the head and killed him. The mother growled louder than before and, seizing the log, flung it from her with all her might. It flew higher than the branch it was tied to; so high that the rope slackened; and the she-bear returned to the trough, and the little cubs after her. The log flew higher and higher, then stopped, and began to fall. The nearer it came the faster it swung, and at last, at full speed, it crashed down on her head. The she-bear rolled over, her legs jerked, and she died! The cubs ran away into the forest.

V

THE boy watched all this in surprise, and then continued his way. Leaving the forest, he came upon a large garden in the midst of which stood a lofty palace with a golden roof. At the gate stood his godfather, smiling. He welcomed his godson, and led him through the gateway into the garden. The boy had never dreamed of such beauty and delight as surrounded him in that place.

Then his godfather led him into the palace, which was even more beautiful inside than outside. The godfather showed the boy through all the rooms: each brighter and finer than the other, but at last they came to one door that was sealed up.

'You see this door,' said he. 'It is not locked, but only sealed. It can be opened, but I forbid you to open it. You may live here, and go where you please, and enjoy all the delights of the place. My only command is – do not open that door! But should you ever do so, remember what you saw in the forest.'

Having said this the godfather went away. The godson remained in the palace, and life there was so bright and joyful that he thought he had only been there three hours, when he had really lived there thirty years. When thirty years had gone by, the godson happened to be passing the sealed door one day, and he wondered why his godfather had forbidden him to enter that room.

'I'll just look in and see what is there,' thought he, and he gave the door a push. The seals gave way, the door opened, and the godson entering saw a hall more lofty and beautiful than all the others, and in the midst of it a throne. He wandered about the hall for a while, and then mounted the steps and seated himself upon the throne. As he sat there he noticed a sceptre leaning against the throne, and took it in his hand. Hardly had he done so when the four walls of the hall suddenly disappeared. The godson looked around, and saw the whole world, and all that men were doing in it. He looked in front, and saw the sea with ships sailing on it. He looked to the right, and saw where strange heathen people lived. He looked to the left, and saw where men who were Christians, but not Russians, lived. He looked round, and on the fourth side, he saw Russian people, like himself.

'I will look,' said he, 'and see what is happening at home, and whether the harvest is good.'

He looked towards his father's fields and saw the sheaves standing in stooks. He began counting them to see whether there was much corn, when he noticed a peasant driving in a cart. It was night, and the godson thought it was his father coming to cart the corn by night. But as he looked he recognized Vasíly Koudryashóf, the thief, driving into the field and beginning to load the sheaves on to his cart. This made the godson angry, and he called out:

'Father, the sheaves are being stolen from our field!'

His father, who was out with the horses in the night-pasture, woke up.

'I dreamt the sheaves were being stolen,' said he. 'I will just ride down and see.'

So he got on a horse and rode out to the field. Finding Vasíly there, he called together other peasants to help him, and Vasíly was beaten, bound, and taken to prison.

Then the godson looked at the town, where his godmother lived. He saw that she was now married to a tradesman. She lay asleep, and her husband rose and went to his mistress. The godson shouted to her:

'Get up, get up, your husband has taken to evil ways.'

The godmother jumped up and dressed, and finding out where her husband was, she shamed and beat his mistress, and drove him away.

Then the godson looked for his mother, and saw her lying asleep in her cottage. And a thief crept into the cottage and began to break open the chest in which she kept her things. The mother awoke and screamed, and the robber seizing an axe, swung it over his head to kill her.

The godson could not refrain from hurling the sceptre at the robber. It struck him upon the temple, and killed him on the spot.

VI

As soon as the godson had killed the robber, the walls closed and the hall became just as it had been before.

Then the door opened and the godfather entered, and coming up to his godson he took him by the hand and led him down from the throne.

'You have not obeyed my command,' said he. 'You did one wrong thing, when you opened the forbidden door; another, when you mounted the throne and took my sceptre into your hands; and you have now done a third wrong, which has much increased the evil in the world. Had you sat here an hour longer, you would have ruined half mankind.'

Then the godfather led his godson back to the throne, and took the sceptre in his hand; and again the walls fell asunder and all things became visible. And the godfather said:

'See what you have done to your father. Vasíly has now been a year in prison, and has come out having learnt every kind of wickedness, and has become quite incorrigible. See, he has stolen two of your father's horses, and he is now setting fire to his barn. All this you have brought upon your father.'

The godson saw his father's barn breaking into flames, but his godfather shut off the sight from him, and told him to look another way.

'Here is your godmother's husband,' he said. 'It is a year since he left his wife, and now he goes after other women. His former mistress has sunk to still lower depths. Sorrow has driven his wife to drink. That's what you have done to your godmother.'

The godfather shut off this also, and showed the godson his father's house. There he saw his mother weeping for her sins, repenting, and saying:

'It would have been better had the robber killed me that night. I should not have sinned so heavily.'

'That', said the godfather, 'is what you have done to your mother.'

He shut this off also, and pointed downwards; and the godson saw two warders holding the robber in front of a prison-house.

And the godfather said:

'This man had murdered ten men. He should have expiated his sins himself, but by killing him you have taken his sins on yourself. Now you must answer for all his sins. That is what you have done to yourself. The she-bear pushed the log aside once, and disturbed her cubs; she pushed it again, and killed her yearling; she pushed it a third time, and was killed herself. You have done the same. Now I give you thirty years to go into the world and atone for the robber's sins. If you do not atone for them, you will have to take his place.'

'How am I to atone for his sins?' asked the godson.

And the godfather answered:

'When you have rid the world of as much evil as you have brought into it, you will have atoned both for your own sins and for those of the robber.'

'How can I destroy evil in the world?' the godson asked.

'Go out,' replied the godfather, 'and walk straight towards the rising sun. After a time you will come to a field with some men in it. Notice what they are doing, and teach them what you know. Then go on and note what you see. On the fourth day you will come to a forest. In the midst of the forest is a cell, and in the cell lives a hermit. Tell him all that has happened. He will teach you what to do. When you have done all he tells you, you will have atoned for your own and the robber's sins.'

And, having said this, the godfather led his godson out of the gate.

VII

THE godson went his way, and as he went he thought:

'How am I to destroy evil in the world? Evil is destroyed by banishing evil men, keeping them in prison, or putting them to death. How then am I to destroy evil without taking the sins of others upon myself?'

The godson pondered over it for a long time, but could come to no conclusion. He went on until he came to a field where corn was growing thick and good and ready for the reapers. The godson saw that a little calf had got in among the corn. Some men who were at hand saw it, and mounting their horses they chased it backwards and forwards through the corn. Each time the calf was about to come out of the corn, someone rode up and the calf got frightened and turned back again, and they all galloped after it, trampling down the corn. On the road stood a woman crying.

'They will chase my calf to death,' she said.

And the godson said to the peasants:

'What are you doing? Come out of the cornfield, all of you, and let the woman call her calf.'

The men did so; and the woman came to the edge of the cornfield and called to the calf. 'Come along, browney, come along,' said she. The calf pricked up its ears, listened a while, and then ran towards the woman of its own accord, and hid its head in her skirts, almost knocking her over. The men were glad, the woman was glad, and so was the little calf.

The godson went on, and he thought:

'Now I see that evil spreads evil. The more people try to drive away evil, the more the evil grows. Evil, it seems, cannot be destroyed by evil; but in what way it can be destroyed, I do not know. The calf obeyed its mistress and so all went well; but if it had not obeyed her, how could we have got it out of the field?'

The godson pondered again, but came to no conclusion, and continued his way.

VIII

HE went on until he came to a village. At the furthest end he stopped and asked leave to stay the night. The woman of the house was there alone, house-cleaning, and she let him in. The godson entered, and taking his seat upon the brick oven he watched what the woman was doing. He saw her finish scrubbing the room and begin scrubbing the table. Having done this, she began wiping the table with a dirty cloth. She wiped it from side to side – but it did not come clean. The soiled cloth left streaks of dirt. Then she wiped it the other way. The first streaks disappeared, but others came in their place. Then she wiped it from one end to the other, but again the same thing happened. The soiled cloth messed the table; when one streak was wiped off another was left on. The godson watched for awhile in silence, and then said:

'What are you doing, mistress?'

'Don't you see I'm cleaning up for the holiday? Only I can't manage this table, it won't come clean. I'm quite tired out.'

'You should rinse your cloth,' said the godson, 'before you wipe the table with it.'

The woman did so, and soon had the table clean.

'Thank you for telling me,' said she.

In the morning he took leave of the woman and went on his way. After walking a good while, he came to the edge of a forest. There he saw some peasants who were making wheel-rims of bent wood. Coming nearer, the godson saw that the men were going round and round, but could not bend the wood.

He stood and looked on, and noticed that the block, to which the piece of wood was fastened, was not fixed, but as the men moved round it went round too. Then the godson said:

'What are you doing, friends?'

'Why, don't you see, we are making wheel-rims. We have twice steamed the wood, and are quite tired out, but the wood will not bend.'

'You should fix the block, friends,' said the godson, 'or else it goes round when you do.'

The peasants took his advice and fixed the block, and then the work went on merrily.

The godson spent the night with them, and then went on. He walked all day and all night, and just before dawn he came upon some drovers encamped for the night, and lay down beside them. He saw that they had got all their cattle settled, and were trying to light a fire. They had taken dry twigs and lighted them, but before the twigs had time to burn up, they smothered them with damp brushwood. The brushwood hissed, and the fire smouldered and went out. Then the drovers brought more dry wood, lit it, and again put on the brushwood – and again the fire went out. They struggled with it for a long time, but could not get the fire to burn. Then the godson said:

'Do not be in such a hurry to put on the brushwood. Let the dry wood burn up properly before you put any on. When the fire is well alight you can put on as much as you please.'

The drovers followed his advice. They let the fire burn up fiercely before adding the brushwood, which then flared up so that they soon had a roaring fire.

The godson remained with them for a while, and then continued his way. He went on, wondering what the three things he had seen might mean; but he could not fathom them.

IX

THE godson walked the whole of that day, and in the evening came to another forest. There he found a hermit's cell, at which he knocked.

'Who is there?' asked a voice from within.

'A great sinner,' replied the godson. 'I must atone for another's sins as well as for my own.'

The hermit hearing this came out.

'What sins are those that you have to bear for another?'

The godson told him everything: about his godfather; about the she-bear with the cubs; about the throne in the sealed room; about the commands his godfather had given him, as well as about the peasants he had seen trampling down the corn, and the calf that ran out when its mistress called it.

'I have seen that one cannot destroy evil by evil,' said he, 'but I cannot understand how it is to be destroyed. Teach me how it can be done.'

'Tell me', replied the hermit, 'what else you have seen on your way.'

The godson told him about the woman washing the table, and the men making cart-wheels, and the drovers lighting their fire.

The hermit listened to it all, and then went back to his cell and brought out an old jagged axe.

'Come with me,' said he.

When they had gone some way, the hermit pointed to a tree.

'Cut it down,' he said.

The godson felled the tree.

'Now chop it into three,' said the hermit.

The godson chopped the tree into three pieces. Then the hermit went back to his cell, and brought out some blazing sticks.

'Burn those three logs,' said he.

So the godson made a fire, and burnt the three logs till only three charred stumps remained.

'Now plant them half in the ground, like this.'

The godson did so.

'You see that river at the foot of the hill. Bring water from there in your mouth, and water these stumps. Water this stump, as you taught the woman: this one, as you taught the wheelwrights: and this one, as you taught the drovers. When all three have taken root and from these charred stumps apple-trees have sprung, you will know how to destroy evil in men, and will have atoned for all your sins.'

Having said this, the hermit returned to his cell. The godson pondered for a long time, but could not understand what the hermit meant. Nevertheless he set to work to do as he had been told.

X

THE godson went down to the river, filled his mouth with water, and returning, emptied it on to one of the charred stumps. This he did again and again, and watered all three stumps. When he was hungry and quite tired out, he went to the cell to ask the old hermit for some food. He opened the door, and there upon a bench he saw the old man lying dead. The godson looked round for food, and he found some dried bread, and ate a little of it. Then he took a spade and set to work to dig the hermit's grave. During the night he carried water and watered the stumps, and in the day he dug the grave. He had hardly finished the grave, and was about to bury the corpse, when some people from the village came, bringing food for the old man.

The people heard that the old hermit was dead, and that he had given the godson his blessing, and left him in his place. So they buried the old man, gave the bread they had brought to the godson, and promising to bring him some more, they went away.

The godson remained in the old man's place. There he lived, eating the food people brought him, and doing as he had been told: carrying water from the river in his mouth and watering the charred stumps.

He lived thus for a year, and many people visited him. His fame spread abroad, as a holy man who lived in the forest and brought water from the bottom of a hill in his mouth to water charred stumps for the salvation of his soul. People flocked to see him. Rich merchants drove up bringing him presents, but he kept only the barest necessaries for himself, and gave the rest away to the poor.

And so the godson lived: carrying water in his mouth and watering the stumps half the day, and resting and receiving people the other half. And he began to think that this was the way he had been told to live, in order to destroy evil and atone for his sins.

He spent two years in this manner, not omitting for a single day to water the stumps. But still not one of them sprouted.

One day, as he sat in his cell, he heard a man ride past, singing as he went. The godson came out to see what sort of a man it was. He saw a strong young fellow, well dressed, and mounted on a handsome, well-saddled horse.

The godson stopped him, and asked him who he was, and where he was going.

'I am a robber,' the man answered, drawing rein. 'I ride about the highways killing people; and the more I kill, the merrier are the songs I sing.'

The godson was horror-struck, and thought:

'How can the evil be destroyed in such a man as this? It is easy to speak to those who come to me of their own accord and confess their sins. But this one boasts of the evil he does.'

So he said nothing, and turned away, thinking: 'What am I to do now? This robber may take to riding about here, and he will frighten away the people. They will leave off coming to me. It will be a loss to them, and I shall not know how to live.'

So the godson turned back, and said to the robber:

'People come to me here, not to boast of their sins, but to repent, and to pray for forgiveness. Repent of your sins, if you fear God; but if there is no repentance in your heart, then go away and never come here again. Do not trouble me, and do not frighten people away from me. If you do not hearken, God will punish you.'

The robber laughed:

'I am not afraid of God, and I will not listen to you. You are not my master,' said he. 'You live by your piety, and I by my robbery. We all must live. You may teach the old women who come to you, but you have nothing to teach me. And because you have reminded me of God, I will kill two more men to-morrow. I would kill you, but I do not want to soil my hands just now. See that in future you keep out of my way!'

Having uttered this threat, the robber rode away. He did not come again, and the godson lived in peace, as before, for eight more years.

XI

ONE night the godson watered his stumps, and, after returning to his cell, he sat down to rest, and watched the footpath, wondering if someone would soon come. But no one came at all that day. He sat alone till evening, feeling lonely and dull, and he thought about his past life. He remembered how the robber had reproached him for living by his piety; and he reflected on his way of life. 'I am not living as the hermit commanded me to,' thought he. 'The hermit laid a penance upon me, and I have made both a living and fame out of it; and have been so tempted by it, that now I feel dull when people do not come to me; and when they do come, I only rejoice because they praise my holiness. That is not how one should live. I have been led astray by love of praise. I have not atoned for my past sins, but have added fresh ones. I will go to another part of the forest where people will not find me; and I will live so as to atone for my old sins and commit no fresh ones.'

Having come to this conclusion the godson filled a bag with dried bread and, taking a spade, left the cell and started for a ravine he knew of in a lonely spot, where he could dig himself a cave and hide from the people.

As he was going along with his bag and his spade he saw the robber riding towards him. The godson was frightened, and started to run away, but the robber overtook him.

'Where are you going?' asked the robber.

The godson told him he wished to get away from the people and live somewhere where no one would come to him. This surprised the robber.

'What will you live on, if people do not come to see you?' asked he.

The godson had not even thought of this, but the robber's question reminded him that food would be necessary.

'On what God pleases to give me,' he replied.

The robber said nothing, and rode away.

'Why did I not say anything to him about his way of life?' thought the godson. 'He might repent now. To-day he seems in a gentler mood, and has not threatened to kill me.' And he shouted to the robber:

'You have still to repent of your sins. You cannot escape from God.'

The robber turned his horse, and drawing a knife from his girdle threatened the hermit with it. The latter was alarmed, and ran away further into the forest.

The robber did not follow him, but only shouted:

'Twice I have let you off, old man, but next time you come in my way I will kill you!'

Having said this, he rode away. In the evening when the godson went to water his stumps – one of them was sprouting! A little apple-tree was growing out of it.

XII

AFTER hiding himself from everybody, the godson lived all alone. When his supply of bread was exhausted, he thought: 'Now I must go and look for some roots to eat.' He had not gone far, however, before he saw a bag of dried bread hanging on a branch. He took it down, and as long as it lasted he lived upon that.

When he had eaten it all, he found another bagful on the same branch. So he lived on, his only trouble being his fear of the robber. Whenever he heard the robber passing, he hid, thinking:

'He may kill me before I have had time to atone for my sins.'

In this way he lived for ten more years. The one apple-tree continued to grow, but the other two stumps remained exactly as they were.

One morning the godson rose early and went to his work. By the time he had thoroughly moistened the ground round the stumps, he was tired out and sat down to rest. As he sat there he thought to himself:

'I have sinned, and have become afraid of death. It may be God's will that I should redeem my sins by death.'

Hardly had this thought crossed his mind when he heard the robber riding up, swearing at something. When the godson heard this, he thought:

'No evil and no good can befall me from anyone but from God.'

And he went to meet the robber. He saw the robber was not alone, but behind him on the saddle sat another man, gagged, and bound hand and foot. The man was doing nothing, but the robber was abusing him violently. The godson went up and stood in front of the horse.

'Where are you taking this man?' he asked.

'Into the forest,' replied the robber. 'He is a merchant's son, and will not tell me where his father's money is hidden. I am going to flog him till he tells me.'

And the robber spurred on his horse, but the godson caught hold of his bridle, and would not let him pass.

'Let this man go!' he said.

The robber grew angry, and raised his arm to strike.

'Would you like a taste of what I am going to give this man? Have I not promised to kill you? Let go!'

The godson was not afraid.

'You shall not go,' said he. 'I do not fear you. I fear no one but God, and He wills that I should not let you pass. Set this man free!'

The robber frowned, and snatching out his knife, cut the ropes with which the merchant's son was bound, and set him free.

'Get away both of you,' he said, 'and beware how you cross my path again.'

The merchant's son jumped down and ran away. The robber was about to ride on, but the godson stopped him again, and again spoke to him about giving up his evil life. The robber heard him to the end in silence, and then rode away without a word.

The next morning the godson went to water his stumps and lo! the second stump was sprouting. A second young apple-tree had begun to grow.

XIII

ANOTHER ten years had gone by. The godson was sitting quietly one day, desiring nothing, fearing nothing, and with a heart full of joy.

'What blessings God showers on men!' thought he. 'Yet how needlessly they torment themselves. What prevents them from living happily?'

And remembering all the evil in men, and the troubles they bring upon themselves, his heart filled with pity.

'It is wrong of me to live as I do,' he said to himself. 'I must go and teach others what I have myself learnt.'

Hardly had he thought this, when he heard the robber approaching. He let him pass, thinking:

'It is no good talking to him, he will not understand.'

That was his first thought, but he changed his mind and went out into the road. He saw that the robber was gloomy, and was riding with downcast eyes. The godson looked at him, pitied him, and running up to him laid his hand upon his knee.

'Brother, dear,' said he, 'have some pity on your own soul! In you lives the spirit of God. You suffer, and torment others, and lay up more and more suffering for the future. Yet God loves you, and has prepared such blessings for you. Do not ruin yourself utterly. Change your life!'

The robber frowned and turned away.

'Leave me alone!' said he.

But the godson held the robber still faster, and began to weep.

Then the robber lifted his eyes and looked at the godson. He looked at him for a long time, and alighting from his horse, fell on his knees at the godson's feet.

'You have overcome me, old man,' said he. 'For twenty years I have resisted you, but now you have conquered me. Do what you will with me, for I have no more power over myself. When you first tried to persuade me, it only angered me more. Only when you hid yourself from men did I begin to consider your words: for I saw then that you asked nothing of them for yourself. Since that day I have brought food for you, hanging it upon the tree.'

Then the godson remembered that the woman got her table clean only after she had rinsed her cloth. In the same way, it was only when he ceased caring about himself, and cleansed his own heart, that he was able to cleanse the hearts of others.

The robber went on.

'When I saw that you did not fear death, my heart turned.'

Then the godson remembered that the wheelwrights could not bend the rims until they had fixed their block. So, not till he had cast away the fear of death, and made his life fast in God, could he subdue this man's unruly heart.

'But my heart did not quite melt,' continued the robber, 'until you pitied me and wept for me.'

The godson, full of joy, led the robber to the place where the stumps were. And when they got there, they saw that from the third stump an apple-tree had begun to sprout. And the godson remembered that the drovers had not been able to light the damp wood until the fire had burnt up well. So it was only when his own heart burnt warmly, that another's heart had been kindled by it.

And the godson was full of joy that he had at last atoned for his sins.

He told all this to the robber, and died. The robber buried him, and lived as the godson had commanded him, teaching to others what the godson had taught him.

THE REPENTANT
SINNER

'And he said unto Jesus, Lord, remember me when thou comest into thy Kingdom. And Jesus said unto him, Verily I say unto thee, Today shalt thou be with me in paradise.' – *Luke* xxiii. 42, 43.

THERE was once a man who lived for seventy years in the world, and lived in sin all that time. He fell ill, but even then did not repent. Only at the last moment, as he was dying, he wept and said:

'Lord! forgive me, as Thou forgavest the thief upon the cross.'

And as he said these words, his soul left his body. And the soul of the sinner, feeling love towards God and faith in His mercy, went to the gates of heaven, and knocked, praying to be let into the heavenly kingdom.

Then a voice spoke from within the gate:

'What man is it that knocks at the gates of Paradise, and what deeds did he do during his life?'

And the voice of the Accuser replied, recounting all the man's evil deeds, and not a single good one.

And the voice from within the gates answered:

'Sinners cannot enter into the kingdom of heaven. Go hence!'

Then the man said:

'Lord, I hear thy voice, but cannot see thy face, nor do I know thy name.'

The voice answered:

'I am Peter, the Apostle.'

And the sinner replied.

'Have pity on me, Apostle Peter! Remember man's weakness, and God's mercy. Wert not thou a disciple of Christ? Didst not thou hear his teaching from his own lips, and hadst thou not his example before thee? Remember then how, when he sorrowed and was grieved in spirit, and three times asked thee to keep awake and pray, thou didst sleep, because thine eyes were heavy, and three times he found thee sleeping. So it was with me. Remember, also, how thou didst promise to be faithful unto death, and yet didst thrice deny him, when he was taken before Caiaphas. So it was with me. And remember, too, how when the cock crowed thou didst go out and didst weep bitterly. So it is with me. Thou canst not refuse to let me in.'

And the voice behind the gates was silent.

Then the sinner stood a little while, and again began to knock, and to ask to be let into the kingdom of heaven.

And he heard another voice behind the gates, which said:

'Who is this man, and how did he live on earth?'

And the voice of the Accuser again repeated all the sinner's evil deeds, and not a single good one.

And the voice from behind the gates replied:

'Go hence! Such sinners cannot live with us in Paradise.'

Then the sinner said:

'Lord, I hear thy voice, but I see thee not, nor do I know thy name.'

And the voice answered:

'I am David; king and prophet.'

The sinner did not despair, nor did he leave the gates of Paradise, but said:

'Have pity on me, King David! Remember man's weakness, and God's mercy. God loved thee and exalted thee among men. Thou hadst all: a kingdom, and honour, and riches, and wives, and children; but thou sawest from thy house-top the wife of a poor man, and sin entered into thee, and thou tookest the wife of Uriah, and didst slay him with the sword of the Ammonites. Thou, a rich man, didst take from the poor man his one ewe lamb, and didst kill him. I have done likewise. Remember, then, how thou didst repent, and how thou saidst, "I acknowledge my transgressions: my sin is ever before me?" I have done the same. Thou canst not refuse to let me in.'

And the voice from within the gates was silent.

The sinner having stood a little while, began knocking again, and asking to be let into the kingdom of heaven. And a third voice was heard within the gates, saying:

'Who is this man, and how has he spent his life on earth?'

And the voice of the Accuser replied for the third time, recounting the sinner's evil deeds, and not mentioning one good deed.

And the voice within the gates said:

'Depart hence! Sinners cannot enter into the kingdom of heaven.'

And the sinner said:

'Thy voice I hear, but thy face I see not, neither do I know thy name.'

Then the voice replied:

'I am John the Divine, the beloved disciple of Christ.'

And the sinner rejoiced and said:

'Now surely I shall be allowed to enter. Peter and David must let me in, because they know man's weakness and God's mercy; and thou wilt let me in, because thou lovest much. Was it not thou, John the Divine, who wrote that God is Love, and that he who loves not, knows not God? And in thine old age didst thou not say unto men: "Brethren, love one another." How, then, canst thou look on me with hatred, and drive me away? Either thou must renounce what thou hast said, or loving me, must let me enter the kingdom of heaven.'

And the gates of Paradise opened, and John embraced the repentant sinner and took him into the kingdom of heaven.

THE KREUTZER SONATA

But I say unto you, that every one that looketh on a woman to lust after her hath committed adultery with her already in his heart. *Matt.* v. 28.

The disciples say unto him, If the case of the man is so with his wife, it is not expedient to marry. But he said unto them, All men cannot receive this saying, but they to whom it is given. *Ibid.* xix. 10, 11.

The figures in text refer to the Appendix of readings contained in the lithographed version circulated subterraneously in Russia (see pp. 325–340) during the time that the book was banned by the censor.

I

It was early spring, and the second day of our journey.
Passengers going short distances entered and left our carriage,
but three others, like myself, had come all the way with the
train. One was a lady, plain and no longer young, who
smoked, had a harassed look, and wore a mannish coat and
cap; another was an acquaintance of hers, a talkative man of
about forty, whose things looked neat and new; the third was a
rather short man[1] who kept himself apart. He was not old, but
his curly hair had gone prematurely grey. His movements were
abrupt and his unusually glittering eyes moved rapidly from
one object to another. He wore an old overcoat, evidently
from a first-rate tailor, with an astrakhan collar, and a tall
astrakhan cap. When he unbuttoned his overcoat a sleeveless
Russian coat and embroidered shirt showed beneath it.
A peculiarity of this man was a strange sound he emitted,
something like a clearing of his throat, or a laugh begun and
sharply broken off.

All the way this man had carefully avoided making acquaintance or having any intercourse with his fellow passengers.
When spoken to by those near him he gave short and abrupt
answers, and at other times read, looked out of the window,
smoked, or drank tea and ate something he took out of an
old bag.

It seemed to me that his loneliness depressed him, and I made
several attempts to converse with him, but whenever our eyes
met, which happened often as he sat nearly opposite me, he
turned away and took up his book or looked out of the window.

Towards the second evening, when our train stopped at a
large station, this nervous man fetched himself some boiling

243

water and made tea. The man with the neat new things – a lawyer as I found out later – and his neighbour, the smoking lady with the mannish coat, went to the refreshment-room to drink tea.

During their absence several new passengers entered the carriage, among them a tall, shaven, wrinkled old man, evidently a tradesman, in a coat lined with skunk fur, and a cloth cap with an enormous peak. The tradesman sat down opposite the seats of the lady and the lawyer, and immediately started a conversation with a young man who had also entered at that station and, judging by his appearance, was a tradesman's clerk.[2]

I was sitting the other side of the gangway and as the train was standing still I could hear snatches of their conversation when nobody was passing between us. The tradesman began by saying that he was going to his estate which was only one station farther on; then as usual the conversation turned to prices and trade, and they spoke of the state of business in Moscow and then of the Nízhni-Nóvgorod Fair. The clerk began to relate how a wealthy merchant, known to both of them, had gone on the spree at the fair, but the old man interrupted him by telling of the orgies he had been at in former times at Kunávin Fair. He evidently prided himself on the part he had played in them, and[3] recounted with pleasure how he and some acquaintances, together with the merchant they had been speaking of, had once got drunk at Kunávin and played such a trick that he had to tell of it in a whisper. The clerk's roar of laughter filled the whole carriage; the old man laughed also, exposing two yellow teeth.

Not expecting to hear anything interesting, I got up to stroll about the platform till the train should start. At the carriage door I met the lawyer and the lady who were talking with animation as they approached.

'You won't have time,' said the sociable lawyer, 'the second bell will ring in a moment.'*

---

* It was customary in Russia for a first, second and third bell to ring before a train left a station.

And the bell did ring before I had gone the length of the train. When I returned, the animated conversation between the lady and the lawyer was proceeding. The old tradesman sat silent opposite to them, looking sternly before him, and occasionally mumbled disapprovingly as if chewing something.

'Then she plainly informed her husband,' the lawyer was smilingly saying as I passed him, 'that she was not able, and did not wish, to live with him since...'

He went on to say something I could not hear. Several other passengers came in after me. The guard passed, a porter hurried in, and for some time the noise made their voices inaudible. When all was quiet again the conversation had evidently turned from the particular case to general considerations.

The lawyer was saying that public opinion in Europe was occupied with the question of divorce, and that cases of 'that kind' were occurring more and more often in Russia. Noticing that his was the only voice audible, he stopped his discourse and turned to the old man.[4]

'Those things did not happen in the old days, did they?' he said, smiling pleasantly.

The old man was about to reply, but the train moved and he took off his cap, crossed himself, and whispered a prayer. The lawyer turned away his eyes and waited politely. Having finished his prayer and crossed himself three times the old man set his cap straight, pulled it well down over his forehead, changed his position, and began to speak.

'They used to happen even then, sir, but less often,' he said. 'As times are now they can't help happening. People have got too educated.'

The train moved faster and faster and jolted over the joints of the rails, making it difficult to hear, but being interested I moved nearer. The nervous man with the glittering eyes opposite me, evidently also interested, listened without changing his place.

'What is wrong with education?' said the lady, with a scarcely perceptible smile. 'Surely it can't be better to marry as they used to in the old days when the bride and bridegroom did not even see one another before the wedding,' she continued, answering not what her interlocutor had said but what she thought he would say, in the way many ladies have. 'Without knowing whether they loved, or whether they could love, they married just anybody, and were wretched all their lives. And you think that was better?' she said, evidently addressing me and the lawyer chiefly and least of all the old man with whom she was talking.

'They've got so very educated,' the tradesman reiterated, looking contemptuously at the lady and leaving her question unanswered.

'It would be interesting to know how you explain the connexion between education and matrimonial discord,' said the lawyer, with a scarcely perceptible smile.

The tradesman was about to speak, but the lady interrupted him.

'No,' she said, 'those times have passed.' But the lawyer stopped her.

'Yes, but allow the gentleman to express his views.'

'Foolishness comes from education,' the old man said categorically.

'They make people who don't love one another marry, and then wonder that they live in discord,' the lady hastened to say, turning to look at the lawyer, at me, and even at the clerk, who had got up and, leaning on the back of the seat, was smilingly listening to the conversation. 'It's only animals, you know, that can be paired off as their master likes; but human beings have their own inclinations and attachments,' said the lady, with an evident desire to annoy the tradesman.

'You should not talk like that, madam,' said the old man, 'animals are cattle, but human beings have a law given them.'

'Yes, but how is one to live with a man when there is no love?' the lady again hastened to express her argument, which probably seemed very new to her.[5]

'They used not to go into that,' said the old man in an impressive tone, 'it is only now that all this has sprung up. The least thing makes them say: "I will leave you!" The fashion has spread even to the peasants. "Here you are!" she says, "Here, take your shirts and trousers and I will go with Vánka; his head is curlier than yours." What can you say? The first thing that should be required of a woman is fear!'

The clerk glanced at the lawyer, at the lady, and at me, apparently suppressing a smile and prepared to ridicule or to approve of the tradesman's words according to the reception they met with.

'Fear of what?' asked the lady.

'Why this: Let her fear her husband! That fear!'

'Oh, the time for that, sir, has passed,' said the lady with a certain viciousness.

'No, madam, that time cannot pass. As she, Eve, was made from the rib of a man, so it will remain to the end of time,' said the old man, jerking his head with such sternness and such a victorious look that the clerk at once concluded that victory was on his side, and laughed loudly.

'Ah yes, that's the way you men argue,' said the lady unyieldingly, and turned to us. 'You have given yourselves freedom but want to shut women up in a tower.* You no doubt permit yourselves everything.'

'⁶No one is permitting anything, but a man does not bring offspring into the home; while a woman – a wife – is a leaky vessel,' the tradesman continued insistently. His tone was so impressive that it evidently vanquished his hearers, and even the lady felt crushed but still did not give in.

'Yes, but I think you will agree that a woman is a human being and has feelings as a man has. What is she to do then, if she does not love her husband?'

'Does not love!' said the tradesman severely, moving his brows and lips. 'She'll love, no fear!' This unexpected argument particularly pleased the clerk, and he emitted a sound of approval.

* Literally 'in the *terem*', the *terem* being the woman's quarter where in older times the women of a Russian family used to be secluded in oriental fashion.

'Oh, no, she won't!' the lady began, 'and when there is no love you can't enforce it.'

'Well, and supposing the wife is unfaithful, what then?' asked the lawyer.

'That is not admissible,' said the old man. 'One has to see to that.'

'But if it happens, what then? You know it does occur.'

'It happens among some, but not among us,' said the old man.[7]

All were silent. The clerk moved, came still nearer, and, evidently unwilling to be behindhand, began with a smile.

'Yes, a young fellow of ours had a scandal. It was a difficult case to deal with. It too was a case of a woman who was a bad lot. She began to play the devil, and the young fellow is respectable and cultured. At first it was with one of the office-clerks. The husband tried to persuade her with kindness. She would not stop, but played all sorts of dirty tricks. Then she began to steal his money. He beat her, but she only grew worse. Carried on intrigues, if I may mention it, with an unchristened Jew. What was he to do? He turned her out altogether and lives as a bachelor, while she gads about.'

'Because he is a fool,' said the old man. 'If he'd pulled her up properly from the first and not let her have her way, she'd be living with him, no fear! It's giving way at first that counts. Don't trust your horse in the field, or your wife in the house.'

At that moment the guard entered to collect the tickets for the next station. The old man gave up his.

'Yes, the female sex must be curbed in time or else all is lost!'

'Yes, but you yourself just now were speaking about the way married men amuse themselves at the Kunávin Fair,' I could not help saying.[8]

'That's a different matter,' said the old man and relapsed into silence.

When the whistle sounded the tradesman rose, got out his bag from under the seat, buttoned up his coat, and slightly lifting his cap went out of the carriage.

II

As soon as the old man had gone several voices were raised.

'A daddy of the old style!' remarked the clerk.

'A living Domostróy!'* said the lady. 'What barbarous views of women and marriage!'

'Yes, we are far from the European understanding of marriage,' said the lawyer.†

'The chief thing such people do not understand,' continued the lady, 'is that marriage without love is not marriage; that love alone sanctifies marriage, and that real marriage is only such as is sanctified by love.'

The clerk listened smilingly, trying to store up for future use all he could of the clever conversation.

In the midst of the lady's remarks we heard, behind me, a sound like that of a broken laugh or sob; and on turning round we saw my neighbour, the lonely grey-haired man with the glittering eyes, who had approached unnoticed during our conversation, which evidently interested him. He stood with his arms on the back of the seat, evidently much excited; his face was red[9] and a muscle twitched in his cheek.

'What kind of love . . . love . . . is it that sanctifies marriage?' he asked hesitatingly.[10]

Noticing the speaker's agitation, the lady tried to answer him as gently and fully as possible.

'True love . . . When such love exists between a man and a woman, then marriage is possible,' she said.

'Yes, but how is one to understand what is meant by "true love"?' said the gentleman with the glittering eyes timidly and with an awkward smile.

'Everybody knows what love is,' replied the lady, evidently wishing to break off her conversation with him.

'But I don't,' said the man. 'You must define what you understand . . . '

* *The Housebuilder,* a sixteenth-century manual, by the monk Silvester, on religion and household management.
† One Russian edition adds: 'First women's rights, the civil marriage, and then divorce, come as unsettled questions.'

'Why? It's very simple,' she said, but stopped to consider. 'Love? Love is an exclusive preference for one above everybody else,' said the lady.

'Preference for how long? A month, two days, or half an hour?' said the grey-haired man and began to laugh.

'Excuse me, we are evidently not speaking of the same thing.'

'Oh, yes! Exactly the same.'

'She means,' interposed the lawyer, pointing to the lady, 'that in the first place marriage must be the outcome of attachment – or love, if you please – and only where that exists is marriage sacred, so to speak. Secondly, that marriage when not based on natural attachment – love, if you prefer the word – lacks the element that makes it morally binding. Do I understand you rightly?' he added, addressing the lady.

The lady indicated her approval of his explanation by a nod of her head.

'It follows . . .' the lawyer continued – but the nervous man whose eyes now glowed as if aflame and who had evidently restrained himself with difficulty, began without letting the lawyer finish:

'Yes, I mean exactly the same thing, a preference for one person over everybody else, and I am only asking: a preference for how long?'

'For how long? For a long time; for life sometimes,' replied the lady, shrugging her shoulders.

'Oh, but that happens only in novels and never in real life. In real life this preference for one may last for years (that happens very rarely), more often for months, or perhaps for weeks, days, or hours,' he said, evidently aware that he was astonishing everybody by his views and pleased that it was so.

'Oh, what are you saying?' 'But no . . .' 'No, allow me . . .' we all three began at once. Even the clerk uttered an indefinite sound of disapproval.

'Yes, I know,' the grey-haired man shouted above our voices, 'you are talking about what is supposed to be, but I am speaking of what is. Every man experiences what you call love for every pretty woman[11].'

'Oh, what you say is awful! But the feeling that is called love does exist among people, and is given not for months or years, but for a lifetime!'

'No, it does not! Even if we should grant that a man might prefer a certain woman all his life, the woman in all probability would prefer someone else;[12] and so it always has been and still is in the world,' he said, and taking out his cigarette-case he began to smoke.

'But the feeling may be reciprocal,' said the lawyer.

'No, sir, it can't!' rejoined the other. 'Just as it cannot be that in a cartload of peas, two marked peas will lie side by side. Besides, it is not merely this impossibility, but the inevitable satiety.[13] To love one person for a whole lifetime is like saying that one candle will burn a whole life,' he said, greedily inhaling the smoke.

'But you are talking all the time about physical love. Don't you acknowledge love based on identity of ideals, on spiritual affinity?' asked the lady.

'Spiritual affinity! Identity of ideals!' he repeated, emitting his peculiar sound. 'But in that case why go to bed together? (Excuse my coarseness!) Or do people go to bed together because of the identity of their ideals?' he said, bursting into a nervous laugh.[14]

'But permit me,' said the lawyer. 'Facts contradict you. We do see that matrimony exists, that all mankind, or the greater part of it, lives in wedlock, and many people honourably live long married lives.'

The grey-haired man again laughed.

'First you say that marriage is based on love, and when I express a doubt as to the existence of a love other than sensual, you prove the existence of love by the fact that marriages exist. But marriages in our days are mere deception!'

'No, allow me!' said the lawyer. 'I only say that marriages have existed and do exist.'

'They do! But why? They have existed and do exist among people who see in marriage something sacramental, a mystery binding them in the sight of God. Among them marriages do exist. Among us, people marry regarding marriage as nothing but copulation, and the result is either deception or coercion.[15] When it is deception it is easier to bear. The husband and wife merely deceive people by pretending to be monogamists, while living polygamously. That is bad, but still bearable. But when, as most frequently happens, the husband and wife have undertaken the external duty of living together all their lives,[16] and begin to hate each other after a month, and wish to part but still continue to live together, it leads to that terrible hell which makes people take to drink, shoot themselves, and kill or poison themselves or one another,' he went on, speaking more and more rapidly, not allowing anyone to put in a word and becoming more and more excited. We all felt embarrassed.

'Yes, undoubtedly there are critical episodes in married life,' said the lawyer, wishing to end this disturbingly heated conversation.

'I see you have found out who I am!' said the grey-haired man softly, and with apparent calm.

'No, I have not that pleasure.'

'It is no great pleasure. I am that Pózdnyshev in whose life that critical episode occurred to which you alluded; the episode when he killed his wife,' he said, rapidly glancing at each of us.

No one knew what to say and all remained silent.

'Well, never mind,' he said with that peculiar sound of his. 'However, pardon me. Ah! ... I won't intrude on you.'

'Oh, no, if you please ... ' said the lawyer, himself not knowing 'if you please' what.

But Pózdnyshev, without listening to him, rapidly turned away and went back to his seat. The lawyer and the lady whispered together. I sat down beside Pózdnyshev in silence, unable to think of anything to say. It was too dark to read, so I shut my eyes pretending that I wished to go to sleep. So we travelled in silence to the next station.

At that station the lawyer and the lady moved into another car, having some time previously consulted the guard about it. The clerk lay down on the seat and fell asleep. Pózdnyshev kept smoking and drinking tea which he had made at the last station.

When I opened my eyes and looked at him he suddenly addressed me resolutely and irritably:

'Perhaps it is unpleasant for you to sit with me, knowing who I am? In that case I will go away.'

'Oh no, not at all.'

'Well then, won't you have some? Only it's very strong.'

He poured out some tea for me.

'They talk . . . and they always lie . . . ' he remarked.

'What are you speaking about?' I asked.

'Always about the same thing. About that love of theirs and what it is! Don't you want to sleep?'

'Not at all.'

'Then would you like me to tell you how that love led to what happened to me?'

'Yes, if it will not be painful for you.'

'No, it is painful for me to be silent. Drink the tea . . . or is it too strong?'

The tea was really like beer, but I drank a glass of it.*Just then the guard entered. Pózdnyshev followed him with angry eyes, and only began to speak after he had left.[17]

III

'WELL then, I'll tell you.[18] But do you really want to hear it?'

I repeated that I wished it very much. He paused, rubbed his face with his hands, and began:

'If I am to tell it, I must tell everything from the beginning: I must tell how and why I married, and the kind of man I was before my marriage.[19]

'Till my marriage I lived as everybody does, that is, everybody in our class. I am a landowner and a graduate of the university, and was a marshal of the gentry. Before my marriage I lived as everyone does, that is, dissolutely; and while living dissolutely I was convinced, like everybody in our class, that I was living as one has to. I thought I was a charming fellow and quite a moral man.[20] I was not a

---

* Tea in Russia is usually drunk out of tumblers.

seducer, had no unnatural tastes, did not make that the
chief purpose of my life as many of my associates did, but I
practised debauchery in a steady, decent way for health's
sake.[21] I avoided women who might tie my hands by having
a child or by attachment for me. However, there may have
been children and attachments, but I acted as if there were
not. And this I not only considered moral, but I was even
proud of it.'

He paused and gave vent to his peculiar sound, as he
evidently did whenever a new idea occurred to him.

'And you know, that is the chief abomination!'
he exclaimed. 'Dissoluteness does not lie in anything physical
– no kind of physical misconduct is debauchery; real
debauchery lies precisely in freeing oneself from moral
relations with a woman with whom you have physical
intimacy. And such emancipation I regarded as a merit.
I remember how I once worried because I had not had
an opportunity to pay a woman who gave herself to
me (having probably taken a fancy to me) and how I
only became tranquil after having sent her some money –
thereby intimating that I did not consider myself in any
way morally bound to her...Don't nod as if you agreed
with me,' he suddenly shouted at me. 'Don't I know
these things? We all, and you too unless you are a rare
exception, hold those same views, just as I used to. Never
mind, I beg your pardon, but the fact is that it's terrible,
terrible, terrible!'

'What is terrible?' I asked.

'That abyss of error in which we live[22] regarding women
and our relations with them. No, I can't speak calmly about it,
not because of that "episode", as he called it, in my life, but
because since that "episode" occurred my eyes have been
opened and I have seen everything in quite a different light.
Everything reversed, everything reversed!'

He lit a cigarette and began to speak, leaning his elbows on
his knees.

It was too dark to see his face, but, above the jolting of the
train, I could hear his impressive and pleasant voice.

IV

'Yes, only after such torments as I have endured, only by their means, have I understood where the root of the matter lies – understood what ought to be, and therefore seen all the horror of what is.[23]

'So you will see how and when that which led up to my "episode" began. It began when I was not quite sixteen. It happened when I still went to the grammar school and my elder brother was a first-year student at the university. I had not yet known any woman, but, like all the unfortunate children of our class, I was no longer an innocent boy. I had been depraved two years before that by other boys. Already woman, not some particular woman but woman as something to be desired, woman, every woman, woman's nudity, tormented me. My solitude was not pure. I was tormented, as ninety-nine per cent. of our boys are. I was horrified, I suffered, I prayed, and I fell. I was already depraved in imagination and in fact, but I had not yet taken the last step. I was perishing, but I had not yet laid hands on another human being. But one day a comrade of my brother's, a jolly student, a so-called good fellow, that is, the worst kind of good-for-nothing, who had taught us to drink and to play cards, persuaded us after a carousal to go *there*. We went. My brother was also still innocent, and he fell that same night. And I, a fifteen-year-old boy, defiled myself and took part in defiling a woman, without at all understanding what I was doing. I had never heard from any of my elders that what I was doing was wrong, you know. And indeed no one hears it now. It is true it is in the Commandments, but then the Commandments are only needed to answer the priest at Scripture examination, and even then they are not very necessary, not nearly as necessary as the commandment about the use of *ut* in conditional sentences in Latin.

'And so I never heard those older persons whose opinions I respected say that it was an evil. On the contrary, I heard people I respected say it was good. I had heard that my struggles and sufferings would be eased after that. I heard this and read it, and heard my elders say it would be good for my health, while from my comrades I heard that it was rather a fine, spirited thing to do. So in general I expected nothing but good from it. The risk of disease? But that too had been foreseen. A paternal government saw to that. It sees to the correct working of the brothels,* and makes profligacy safe for schoolboys. Doctors too deal with it for a consideration. That is proper. They assert that debauchery is good for the health, and they organize proper well-regulated debauchery. I know some mothers who attend to their sons' health in that sense. And science sends them to the brothels.'

'Why do you say "science"?' I asked.

'Why, who are the doctors? The priests of science. Who deprave youths[24] by maintaining that this is necessary for their health? They do.

'Yet if a one-hundredth part of the efforts devoted to the cure of syphilis were devoted to the eradication of debauchery, there would long ago not have been a trace of syphilis left. But as it is, efforts are made not to eradicate debauchery but to encourage it and to make debauchery safe. That is not the point however. The point is that with me – and with nine-tenths, if not more, not of our class only but of all classes, even the peasants – this terrible thing happens that happened to me; I fell not because I succumbed to the natural temptation of a particular woman's charm – no, I was not seduced by a woman – but I fell because, in the set around me, what was really a fall was regarded by some as a most legitimate function good for one's health, and by others as a very natural and not only excusable but even innocent amusement for a young man. I did not understand that it was a fall, but simply indulged in that half-pleasure, half-need, which, as was suggested to me, was natural at a certain age. I began to indulge in debauchery as I began to drink and to smoke. Yet in that first fall there was something special and pathetic. I remember that at once, on the

---

* In Russia, as in other continental countries and formerly in England, the *maisons de tolérance* were under the supervision of the government; doctors were employed to examine the women, and, as far as possible, see that they did not continue their trade when diseased.

spot before I left the room, I felt sad, so sad that I wanted to cry – to cry for the loss of my innocence and for my relationship with women, now sullied for ever. Yes, my natural, simple relationship with women was spoilt for ever. From that time I have not had, and could not have, pure relations with women. I had become what is called a libertine. To be a libertine is a physical condition like that of a morphinist, a drunkard, or a smoker. As a morphinist, a drunkard, or a smoker is no longer normal, so too a man who has known several women for his pleasure is not normal but is a man perverted for ever, a libertine. As a drunkard or a morphinist can be recognized at once by his face and manner, so it is with a libertine. A libertine may restrain himself, may struggle, but he will never have those pure, simple, clear, brotherly relations with a woman. By the way he looks at a young woman and examines her, a libertine can always be recognized. And I had become and I remained a libertine, and it was this that brought me to ruin.

V

'Ah, yes! After that things went from bad to worse, and there were all sorts of deviations. Oh, God! When I recall the abominations I committed in this respect I am seized with horror! And that is true of me, whom my companions, I remember, ridiculed for my so-called innocence. And when one hears of the "gilded youths", of officers, of the Parisians . . . ! And when all these gentlemen, and I – who have on our souls hundreds of the most varied and horrible crimes against women – when we thirty-year-old profligates, very carefully washed, shaved, perfumed, in clean linen and in evening dress or uniform, enter a drawing-room or ball-room, we are emblems of purity, charming!

'Only think of what ought to be, and of what is! When in society such a gentleman comes up to my sister or daughter, I, knowing his life, ought to go up to him, take him aside, and say quietly, "My dear fellow, I know the life you lead, and how and with whom you pass your nights. This is no place for you.

There are pure, innocent girls here. Be off!" That is what ought to be; but what happens is that when such a gentleman comes and dances, embracing our sister or daughter, we are jubilant, if he is rich and well-connected. Maybe after Rigulboche* he will honour my daughter! Even if traces of disease remain, no matter! They are clever at curing that nowadays. Oh, yes, I know several girls in the best society whom their parents enthusiastically gave in marriage to men suffering from a certain disease. Oh, oh . . . the abomination of it! But a time will come when this abomination and falsehood will be exposed!'

He made his strange noise several times and again drank tea. It was fearfully strong and there was no water with which to dilute it. I felt that I was much excited by the two glasses I had drunk. Probably the tea affected him too, for he became more and more excited. His voice grew increasingly mellow and expressive. He continually changed his position, now taking off his cap and now putting it on again, and his face changed strangely in the semi-darkness in which we were sitting.

'Well, so I lived till I was thirty, not abandoning for a moment the intention of marrying and arranging for myself a most elevated and pure family life. With that purpose I observed the girls suitable for that end,' he continued. 'I weltered in a mire of debauchery and at the same time was on the look-out for a girl pure enough to be worthy of me.

'I rejected many just because they were not pure enough to suit me, but at last I found one whom I considered worthy. She was one of two daughters of a once-wealthy Pénza landowner who had been ruined.

'25One evening after we had been out in a boat and had returned by moonlight, and I was sitting beside her admiring her curls and her shapely figure in a tight-fitting jersey, I suddenly decided that it was she! It seemed to me that evening that she understood all that I felt and thought, and that what I felt and thought was very lofty. In reality it was

* A notorious Parisian *cancanière*.

only that the jersey and the curls were particularly becoming to her and that after a day spent near her I wanted to be still closer.

'It is amazing how complete is the delusion that beauty is goodness. A handsome woman talks nonsense, you listen and hear not nonsense but cleverness. She says and does horrid things, and you see only charm. And if a handsome woman does not say stupid or horrid things, you at once persuade yourself that she is wonderfully clever and moral.

'I returned home in rapture, decided that she was the acme of moral perfection, and that therefore she was worthy to be my wife, and I proposed to her next day.

'[26]What a muddle it is! Out of a thousand men who marry (not only among us but unfortunately also among the masses) there is hardly one who has not already been married ten, a hundred, or even, like Don Juan, a thousand times, before his wedding.

'It is true as I have heard and have myself observed that there are nowadays some chaste young men who feel and know that this thing is not a joke but an important matter.

'God help them! But in my time there was not one such in ten thousand. And everybody knows this and pretends not to know it. In all the novels they describe in detail the heroes' feelings and the ponds and bushes beside which they walk, but when their great love for some maiden is described, nothing is said about what has happened to these interesting heroes before: not a word about their frequenting certain houses, or about the servant-girls, cooks, and other people's wives! If there are such improper novels they are not put into the hands of those who most need this information – the unmarried girls.

'We first pretend to these girls that the profligacy which fills half the life of our towns, and even of the villages, does not exist at all.

'Then we get so accustomed to this pretence that at last, like the English, we ourselves really begin to believe that we are all moral people and live in a moral world. The girls, poor things, believe this quite seriously. So too did my unfortunate wife. I remember how, when we were engaged,

I showed her my diary, from which she could learn something, if but a little, of my past, especially about my last *liaison*, of which she might hear from others, and about which I therefore felt it necessary to inform her. I remember her horror, despair, and confusion, when she learnt of it and understood it. I saw that she then wanted to give me up. And why did she not do so? . . . [27]'

He again made that sound, swallowed another mouthful of tea, and remained silent for a while.

VI

'No, after all, it is better, better so!' he exclaimed. 'It serves me right! But that's not to the point – I meant to say that it is only the unfortunate girls who are deceived.

'The mothers know it, especially mothers educated by their own husbands – they know it very well. While pretending to believe in the purity of men, they act quite differently. They know with what sort of bait to catch men for themselves and for their daughters.

'You see it is only we men who don't know (because we don't wish to know) what women know very well, that the most exalted poetic love, as we call it, depends not on moral qualities but on physical nearness and on the *coiffure*, and the colour and cut of the dress. Ask an expert coquette who has set herself the task of captivating a man, which she would prefer to risk: to be convicted in his presence of lying, of cruelty, or even of dissoluteness, or to appear before him in an ugly and badly made dress – she will always prefer the first. She knows that we are continually lying about high sentiments, but really only want her body and will therefore forgive any abomination except an ugly tasteless costume that is in bad style.

'A coquette knows that consciously, and every innocent girl knows it unconsciously just as animals do.

'That is why there are those detestable jerseys, bustles, and naked shoulders, arms, almost breasts. A woman, especially if she has passed the male school, knows very well that all the talk about elevated subjects is just talk, but that what a man wants is her body and all that presents it in the most deceptive but alluring light; and she acts accordingly.[28] If we only throw aside our familiarity with this indecency, which has become a second nature to us, and look at the life of our upper classes as it is, in all its shamelessness – why, it is simply a brothel ... You don't agree? Allow me, I'll prove it,' he said, interrupting me. 'You say that the women of our society have other interests in life than prostitutes have, but I say no, and will prove it. If people differ in the aims of their lives, by the inner content of their lives, this difference will necessarily be reflected in externals and their externals will be different. But look at those unfortunate despised women and at the highest society ladies: the same costumes, the same fashions, the same perfumes, the same exposure of arms, shoulders, and breasts, the same tight skirts over prominent bustles, the same passion for little stones, for costly, glittering objects, the same amusements, dances, music, and singing. As the former employ all means to allure, so do these others.[29]

VII

'Well, so these jerseys and curls and bustles caught me!

'It was very easy to catch me for I was brought up in the conditions in which amorous young people are forced like cucumbers in a hot-bed. You see our stimulating super-abundance of food, together with complete physical idleness, is nothing but a systematic excitement of desire.[30] Whether this astonishes you or not, it is so. Why, till quite recently I did not see anything of this myself, but now I have seen it. That is why it torments me that nobody knows this, and people talk such nonsense as that lady did.

'Yes, last spring some peasants were working in our neighbourhood on a railway embankment. The usual food of a young peasant is rye-bread, kvas, and onions; he keeps alive and is vigorous and healthy; his work is light agricultural work. When he goes to railway-work his rations are buckwheat porridge and a pound of meat a day. But he works off that pound of meat during his sixteen hours' work wheeling barrow-loads of half-a-ton weight, so it is just enough for him. But we who every day consume two pounds of meat, and game, and fish and all sorts of heating foods and drinks – where does that go to? Into excesses of sensuality. And if it goes there and the safety-valve is open, all is well; but try and close the safety-valve, as I closed it temporarily, and at once a stimulus arises which, passing[31] through the prism of our artificial life, expresses itself in utter infatuation, sometimes even platonic. And I fell in love as they all do.

'Everything was there to hand: raptures, tenderness, and poetry. In reality that love of mine was the result, on the one hand of her mamma's and the dressmakers' activity, and on the other of the super-abundance of food consumed by me while living an idle life. If on the one hand there had been no boating, no dressmaker with her waists and so forth, and had my wife been sitting at home in a shapeless dressing-gown, and had I on the other hand been in circumstances normal to man – consuming just enough food to suffice for the work I did, and had the safety-valve been open – it happened to be closed at the time – I should not have fallen in love and nothing of all this would have happened.

VIII

'WELL, and now it so chanced that everything combined – my condition, her becoming dress, and the satisfactory boating. It had failed twenty times but now it succeeded. Just like a trap! I am not joking. You see nowadays marriages are arranged that way – like traps. What is the natural way? The lass is ripe, she must be given in marriage. It seems very simple if the girl is not a fright and there are men wanting to marry. That is how it was done in olden times. The lass was grown up and her parents arranged the marriage.[32] So it was done, and is done, among all mankind – Chinese, Hindus, Mohammedans, and among our own working classes; so it is done among at least ninety-nine per cent. of the human race. Only among one per cent. or less, among us libertines, has it been discovered that that is not right, and something new has been invented. And what is this novelty? It is that the maidens sit round and the men walk about, as at a bazaar, choosing. And the maidens wait and think, but dare not say: "Me, please!" "No, me!" "Not her, but me!" "Look what shoulders and other things I have!" And we men stroll around and look,[33] and are very pleased. "Yes, I know! I won't be caught!" They stroll about and look, and are very pleased that everything is arranged like that for them. And then in an unguarded moment – snap! He is caught!'

'Then how ought it to be done?' I asked. 'Should the woman propose?'

'Oh, I don't know how; only if there's to be equality, let it be equality. If they have discovered that pre-arranged matches are degrading, why this is a thousand times worse! Then the rights and chances were equal, but here the woman is a slave in a bazaar[34] or the bait in a trap. Tell any mother, or the girl herself, the truth, that she is only occupied in catching a husband . . . oh dear! what an insult! Yet they all do it and have nothing else to do. What is so terrible is to see sometimes quite innocent poor young girls engaged on it. And again, if it were but done openly – but it is always done deceitfully. "Ah, the origin of species, how interesting!" "Oh, Lily takes such an interest in painting! And will you be going to the exhibition? How instructive!" And the troyka-drives, and shows, and symphonies! "Oh! how remarkable! My Lily is mad on music." "And why don't you share these convictions?" And boating . . . But their one thought is: "Take me, take me!" "Take my Lily!" "Or try – at least!" Oh, what an abomination! What falsehood!' he concluded, finishing his tea and beginning to put away the tea-things.

IX

'Y o u know,' he began while packing the tea and sugar into his bag. 'The domination of women from which the world suffers all arises from this.'

'What "domination of women"?' I asked. '[35]The rights, the legal privileges, are on the man's side.'

'Yes, yes! That's just it,' he interrupted me. 'That's just what I want to say. It explains the extraordinary phenomenon that on the one hand woman is reduced to the lowest stage of humiliation, while on the other she dominates. Just like the Jews: as they pay us back for their oppression by a financial domination, so it is with women. "Ah, you want us to be traders only, – all right, as traders we will dominate you!" say the Jews. "Ah, you want us to be merely objects of sensuality – all right, as objects of sensuality we will enslave you," say the women. Woman's lack of rights arises not from the fact that she must not vote or be a judge – to be occupied with such affairs is no privilege – but from the fact that she is not man's equal in sexual intercourse and has not the right to use a man or abstain from him as she likes – is not allowed to choose a man at her pleasure instead of being chosen by him. You say that is monstrous. Very well! Then a man must not have those rights either. As it is at present, a woman is deprived of that right while a man has it. And to make up for that right she acts on man's sensuality, and through his sensuality subdues him so that he only chooses formally, while in reality it is she who chooses. And once she has obtained these means she abuses them and acquires a terrible power over people.'

'But where is this special power?' I inquired.

'Where is it? Why everywhere, in everything! Go round the shops in any big town. There are goods worth millions and you cannot estimate the human labour expended on them, and look whether in nine-tenths of these shops there is anything for the use of men. All the luxuries of life are demanded and maintained by women.

'Count all the factories. An enormous proportion of them produce useless ornaments, carriages, furniture, and trinkets, for women. Millions of people, generations of slaves, perish at hard labour in factories merely to satisfy woman's caprice. Women, like queens, keep nine-tenths of mankind in bondage to heavy labour. And all because they have been abased and deprived of equal rights with men. And they revenge themselves by acting on our sensuality and catch us in their nets. Yes, it all comes of that.

'Women have made of themselves such an instrument for acting upon our sensuality that a man cannot quietly consort with a woman.[36] As soon as a man approaches a woman he succumbs to her stupefying influence and becomes intoxicated and crazy. I used formerly to feel uncomfortable and uneasy when I saw a lady dressed up for a ball, but now I am simply frightened and plainly see her as something dangerous and illicit. I want to call a policeman and ask for protection from the peril, and demand that the dangerous object be removed and put away.

'Ah, you are laughing!' he shouted at me, 'but it is not at all a joke. I am sure a time will come, and perhaps very soon, when people will understand this and will wonder how a society could exist in which actions were permitted which so disturb social tranquillity as those adornments of the body directly evoking sensuality, which we tolerate for women in our society. Why, it's like setting all sorts of traps along the paths and promenades – it is even worse! Why is gambling forbidden while women in costumes which evoke sensuality are not forbidden? They are a thousand times more dangerous!

X

'WELL, you see, I was caught that way. I was what is called in love. I not only imagined her to be the height of perfection, but during the time of our engagement I regarded myself also as the height of perfection. You know there is no rascal who cannot, if he tries, find rascals in some respects worse than himself, and who consequently cannot find reasons for pride and self-satisfaction. So it was with me: I was not marrying for money – covetousness had nothing to do with it – unlike the majority of my acquaintances who married for money or connexions – I was rich, she was poor. That was one thing. Another thing I prided myself on was that while others married intending to continue in future the same polygamous life they had lived before marriage, I was firmly resolved to be monogamous after marriage, and there was no limit to my pride on that score. Yes, I was a dreadful pig and imagined myself to be an angel.

'Our engagement did not last long. I cannot now think of that time without shame! What nastiness! Love is supposed to be spiritual and not sensual. Well, if the love is spiritual, a spiritual communion, then that spiritual communion should find expression in words, in conversations, in discourse. There was nothing of the kind. It used to be dreadfully difficult to talk when we were left alone. It was the labour of Sisyphus. As soon as we thought of something to say and said it, we had again to be silent, devising something else. There was nothing to talk about. All that could be said about the life that awaited us, our arrangements and plans, had been said, and what was there more? Now if we had been animals we should have known that speech was unnecessary; but here on the contrary it was necessary to speak, and there was nothing to say, because we were not occupied with what finds vent in speech. And moreover there was that ridiculous custom of giving sweets, of coarse gormandizing on sweets, and all those abominable preparations for the wedding: remarks about the house, the bedroom, beds, wraps, dressing-gowns, underclothing, costumes. You must remember that if one married according to the injunctions of Domostróy, as that old fellow was saying, then the feather-beds, the trousseau, and the bedstead – are all but details appropriate to the sacrament. But among us, when of ten who marry there are certainly nine who not only do not believe in the sacrament,[37] but do not even believe that what they are doing entails certain obligations – where scarcely one man out of a hundred has not been married before, and of fifty scarcely one is not preparing in advance to be unfaithful to his wife at every convenient opportunity – when the majority regard the going to church as only a special condition for obtaining possession of a certain woman – think what a dreadful significance all these details acquire. They show that the whole business is only that; they show that it is a kind of sale. An innocent girl is sold to a profligate, and the sale is accompanied by certain formalities.

XI

'THAT is how everybody marries and that is how I married, and the much vaunted honeymoon began. Why, its very name is vile!' he hissed viciously. 'In Paris I once went to see the sights, and noticing a bearded woman and a water-dog on a sign-board, I entered the show. It turned out to be nothing but a man in a woman's low-necked dress, and a dog done up in walrus skin and swimming in a bath. It was very far from being interesting; but as I was leaving, the showman politely saw me out and, addressing the public at the entrance, pointed to me and said, "Ask the gentleman whether it is not worth seeing! Come in, come in, one franc apiece!" I felt ashamed to say it was not worth seeing, and the showman had probably counted on that. It must be the same with those who have experienced the abomination of a honeymoon and who do not disillusion others. Neither did I disillusion anyone, but I do not now see why I should not tell the truth. Indeed, I think it needful to tell the truth about it. One felt awkward, ashamed, repelled, sorry, and above all dull, intolerably dull! It was something like what I felt when I learnt to smoke – when I felt sick and the saliva gathered in my mouth and I swallowed it and pretended that it was very pleasant. Pleasure from smoking, just as from that, if it comes at all, comes later. The husband must cultivate that vice in his wife in order to derive pleasure from it.'

'Why vice?' I said. 'You are speaking of the most natural human functions.'

'Natural?' he said. 'Natural? No, I may tell you that I have come to the conclusion that it is, on the contrary, *un*natural. Yes, quite *un*natural. Ask a child, ask an unperverted girl.[38]

'Natural, you say!

'It is natural to eat. And to eat is, from the very beginning, enjoyable, easy, pleasant, and not shameful; but this is horrid, shameful, and painful. No, it is unnatural! And an unspoilt girl, as I have convinced myself, always hates it.'[39]

'But how,' I asked, 'would the human race continue?'

'Yes, would not the human race perish?' he said irritably and ironically, as if he had expected this familiar and insincere objection. 'Teach abstention from child-bearing so that English lords may always gorge themselves – that is all right. Preach it for the sake of greater pleasure – that is all right; but just hint at abstention from child-bearing in the name of morality – and, my goodness, what a rumpus . . . ! Isn't there a danger that the human race may die out because they want to cease to be swine? But forgive me! This light is unpleasant, may I shade it?' he said, pointing to the lamp. I said I did not mind; and with the haste with which he did everything, he got up on the seat and drew the woollen shade over the lamp.

'All the same,' I said, 'if everyone thought this the right thing to do, the human race would cease to exist.'

He did not reply at once.

'You ask how the human race will continue to exist,' he said, having again sat down in front of me, and spreading his legs far apart he leant his elbows on his knees. 'Why should it continue?'

'Why? If not, we should not exist.'

'And why should we exist?'

'Why? In order to live, of course.'

'But why live?[40] If life has no aim, if life is given us for life's sake, there is no reason for living. And if it is so, then the Schopenhauers, the Hartmanns, and all the Buddhists as well, are quite right. But if life has an aim, it is clear that it ought to come to an end when that aim is reached. And so it turns out,' he said with noticeable agitation, evidently prizing his thought very highly. 'So it turns out. Just think: if the aim of humanity is goodness, righteousness, love – call it what you will – if it is what the prophets have said, that all mankind should be united together in love, that the spears should be beaten into pruning-hooks and so forth, what is it that hinders the attainment of this aim? The passions hinder it. Of all the passions the strongest, cruellest, and most stubborn is the sex-passion, physical love; and therefore if the passions are destroyed, including the strongest of them – physical love – the prophecies will be fulfilled, mankind will be brought into a unity, the aim of human existence will be attained, and there will be nothing further to live for. As long as mankind exists the ideal is before it, and of course not the rabbits' and pigs' ideal of breeding as fast as possible, nor that of monkeys or Parisians – to enjoy sex-passion in the most refined manner, but the ideal of goodness attained by continence and purity. Towards that people have always striven and still strive. You see what follows.

'It follows that physical love is a safety-valve. If the present generation has not attained its aim, it has not done so because of its passions, of which the sex-passion is the strongest. And if the sex-passion endures there will be a new generation and consequently the possibility of attaining the aim in the next generation. If the next one does not attain it, then the next after that may, and so on, till the aim is attained, the prophecies fulfilled, and mankind attains unity. If not, what would result? If one admits that God created men for the attainment of a certain aim, and created them mortal but sexless, or created them immortal, what would be the result? Why, if they were mortal but without the sex-passion, and died without attaining the aim, God would have had to create new people to attain his aim. If they were immortal, let us grant that (though it would be more difficult for the same people to correct their mistakes and approach perfection than for those of another generation) they might attain that aim after many thousands of years, but then what use would they be afterwards? What could be done with them? It is best as it is.... But perhaps you don't like that way of putting it? Perhaps you are an evolutionist? It comes to the same thing. The highest race of animals, the human race, in order to maintain itself in the struggle with other animals ought to unite into one whole like a swarm of bees, and not breed continually; it should bring up sexless members as the bees do; that is, again, it should strive towards continence and not towards inflaming desire – to which the whole system of our life is now directed.' He paused. 'The human race will cease? But can anyone doubt it, whatever his outlook on life may be? Why, it is as certain as death. According to all the teaching of the Church the end of the world will come, and according to all the teaching of science the same result is inevitable.

XII[41]

'IN our world it is just the reverse: even if a man does think of continence while he is a bachelor, once married he is sure to think continence no longer necessary. You know those wedding tours – the seclusion into which, with their parents' consent, the young couple go – are nothing but licensed debauchery. But a moral law avenges itself when it is violated. Hard as I tried to make a success of my honeymoon, nothing came of it. It was horrid, shameful, and dull, the whole time. And very soon I began also to experience a painful, oppressive feeling. That began very quickly. I think it was on the third or fourth day that I found my wife depressed. I began asking her the reason and embracing her, which in my view was all she could want, but she removed my arm and began to cry. What about? She could not say. But she felt sad and distressed. Probably her exhausted nerves suggested to her the truth as to the vileness of our relation but she did not know how to express it. I began to question her, and she said something about feeling sad without her mother. It seemed to me that this was untrue, and I began comforting her without alluding to her mother. I did not understand that she was simply depressed and her mother was merely an excuse. But she immediately took offence because I had not mentioned her mother, as though I did not believe her. She told me she saw that I did not love her. I reproached her with being capricious, and suddenly her face changed entirely and instead of sadness it expressed irritation, and with the most venomous words she began accusing me of selfishness and cruelty. I gazed at her. Her whole face showed complete coldness and hostility, almost hatred. I remember how horror-struck I was when I saw this. "How? What?" I thought. "Love is a union of souls – and instead of that there is this! Impossible, this is not she!" I tried to soften her, but encountered such an insuperable wall of cold virulent hostility that before I had time to turn round I too was seized with irritation and we said a great many unpleasant things to one another. The impression of that first quarrel was dreadful. I call it a quarrel, but it was not a quarrel but only the disclosure of the abyss that really existed between us. Amorousness was exhausted by the satisfaction of sensuality and we were left confronting one another in our true relation: that is, as two egotists quite alien to each other who wished to get as much pleasure as possible each from the other. I call what took place between us a quarrel, but it was not a quarrel, only the consequence of the cessation of sensuality – revealing our real relations to one another. I did not understand that this cold and hostile relation was our normal state, I did not understand it because at first this hostile attitude was very soon concealed from us by a renewal of redistilled sensuality, that is by love-making.

'I thought we had quarrelled and made it up again, and that it would not recur. But during that same first month of honeymoon a period of satiety soon returned, we again ceased to need one another, and another quarrel supervened. This second quarrel struck me even more painfully than the first. "So the first one was not an accident but was bound to happen and will happen again," I thought. I was all the more staggered by that second quarrel because it arose from such an impossible pretext. It had something to do with money, which I never grudged and could certainly not have grudged to my wife. I only remember that she gave the matter such a twist that some remark of mine appeared to be an expression of a desire on my part to dominate over her by means of money, to which I was supposed to assert an exclusive right – it was something impossibly stupid, mean, and not natural either to me or to her. I became exasperated, and upbraided her with lack of consideration for me. She accused me of the same thing, and it all began again. In her words and in the expression of her face and eyes I again noticed the cruel cold hostility that had so staggered me before. I had formerly quarrelled with my brother, my friends, and my father, but there had never,

I remember, been the special venomous malice which there was here. But after a while this mutual hatred was screened by amorousness, that is sensuality, and I still consoled myself with the thought that these two quarrels had been mistakes and could be remedied. But then a third and a fourth quarrel followed and I realized that it was not accidental, but that it was bound to happen and would happen so, and I was horrified at the prospect before me. At the same time I was tormented by the terrible thought that I alone lived on such bad terms with my wife, so unlike what I had expected, whereas this did not happen between other married couples. I did not know then that it is our common fate, but that everybody imagines, just as I did, that it is their peculiar misfortune, and everyone conceals this exceptional and shameful misfortune not only from others but even from himself and does not acknowledge it to himself.

'It began during the first days and continued all the time, ever increasing and growing more obdurate. In the depths of my soul I felt from the first weeks that I was lost, that things had not turned out as I expected, that marriage was not only no happiness but a very heavy burden; but like everybody else I did not wish to acknowledge this to myself (I should not have acknowledged it even now but for the end that followed) and I concealed it not only from others but from myself too. Now I am astonished that I failed to see my real position. It might have been seen from the fact that the quarrels began on pretexts it was impossible to remember when they were over. Our reason was not quick enough to *devise* sufficient excuses for the animosity that always existed between us.[42] But more striking still was the insufficiency of the excuses for our reconciliations. Sometimes there were words, explanations, even tears, but sometimes . . . oh! it is disgusting even now to think of it – after the most cruel words to one another, came sudden silent glances, smiles, kisses, embraces. . . . Faugh, how horrid! How is it I did not then see all the vileness of it?'

XIII

T w o fresh passengers entered and settled down on the farthest seats. He was silent while they were seating themselves but as soon as they had settled down continued, evidently not for a moment losing the thread of his idea.

[43]'You know, what is vilest about it,' he began, 'is that in theory love is something ideal and exalted, but in practice it is something abominable, swinish, which it is horrid and shameful to mention or remember. It is not for nothing that nature has made it disgusting and shameful. And if it is disgusting and shameful one must understand that it is so. But here, on the contrary, people pretend that what is disgusting and shameful is beautiful and lofty. What were the first symptoms of my love? Why that I gave way to animal excesses, not only without shame but being somehow even proud of the possibility of these physical excesses, and without in the least considering either her spiritual or even her physical life. I wondered what embittered us against one another, yet it was perfectly simple: that animosity was nothing but the protest of our human nature against the animal nature that overpowered it.

'I was surprised at our enmity to one another; yet it could not have been otherwise. That hatred was nothing but the mutual hatred of accomplices in a crime – both for the incitement to the crime and for the part taken in it. What was it but a crime when she, poor thing, became pregnant in the first month and our *swinish* connexion continued? You think I am straying from my subject? Not at all! I am telling you *how* I killed my wife. They asked me at the trial with what and how I killed her. Fools! They thought I killed her with a knife, on the 5th of October. It was not then I killed her, but much earlier. Just as they are all now killing, all, all. . . .'

'But with what?' I asked.

'That is just what is so surprising, that nobody wants to see what is so clear and evident, what doctors ought to know and preach, but are silent about. Yet the matter is very simple. Men and women are created like the animals so that physical love is followed by pregnancy and then by suckling – conditions under which physical love is bad for the woman and for her child. There are an equal number of men and women. What follows from this? It seems clear, and no great wisdom is needed to draw the conclusion that animals do, namely, the need of continence. But no. Science has been able to discover some kind of leucocytes that run about in the blood, and all sorts of useless nonsense, but cannot understand that. At least one does not hear of science teaching it!

'And so a woman has only two ways out: one is to make a monster of herself, to destroy and go on destroying within herself to such degree as may be necessary the capacity of being a woman, that is, a mother, in order that a man may quietly and continuously get his enjoyment; the other way out – and it is not even a way out but a simple, coarse, and direct violation of the laws of nature – practised in all so-called decent families – is that, contrary to her nature, the woman must be her husband's mistress even while she is pregnant or nursing – must be what not even an animal descends to, and for which her strength is insufficient. That is what causes nerve troubles and hysteria in our class, and among the peasants causes what they call being "possessed by the devil" – epilepsy. You will notice that no pure maidens are ever "possessed", but only married women living with their husbands. That is so here, and it is just the same in Europe. All the hospitals for hysterical women are full of those who have violated nature's law. The epileptics and Charcot's patients are complete wrecks you know, but the world is full of half-crippled women. Just think of it, what a great work goes on within a woman when she conceives or when she is nursing an infant. That is growing which will continue us and replace us. And this sacred work is violated – by what? It is terrible to think of it! And they prate about the freedom and the rights of women! It is as if cannibals fattened their captives to be eaten, and at the same time declared that they were concerned about their prisoners' rights and freedom.'

All this was new to me and startled me.

'What is one to do? If that is so,' I said, 'it means that one may love one's wife once in two years, yet men . . .'

'Men must!' he interrupted me. 'It is again those precious priests of science who have persuaded everybody of that.[44] Imbue a man with the idea that he requires vodka, tobacco, or opium, and all these things will be indispensable to him. It seems that God did not understand what was necessary and therefore, omitting to consult those wizards, arranged things badly. You see matters do not tally. They have decided that it is essential for a man to satisfy his desires, and the bearing and nursing of children comes and interferes with it and hinders the satisfaction of that need. What is one to do then? Consult the wizards! They will arrange it. And they have devised something. Oh! when will those wizards with their deceptions be dethroned? It is high time! It has come to such a point that people go mad and shoot themselves and all because of this. How could it be otherwise? The animals seem to know that their progeny continue their race, and they keep to a certain law in this matter. Man alone neither knows it nor wishes to know, but is concerned only to get all the pleasure he can. And who is doing that? The lord of nature – man! Animals, you see, only come together at times when they are capable of producing progeny, but the filthy lord of nature is at it any time if only it pleases him! And as if that were not sufficient, he exalts this apish occupation into the most precious pearl of creation, into love. In the name of this love, that is, this filth, he destroys – what? Why, half the human race! All the women who might help the progress of mankind towards truth and goodness he converts, for the sake of his pleasure, into enemies instead of helpmates. See what it is that everywhere impedes the forward movement of mankind. Women! And why are they what they are? Only because of that. Yes, yes . . . ' he repeated several times, and began to move about, and to get out his cigarettes and to smoke, evidently trying to calm himself.

XIV

'I TOO lived like a pig of that sort,' he continued in his former tone. 'The worst thing about it was that while living that horrid life I imagined that, because I did not go after other women, I was living an honest family life, that I was a moral man and in no way blameworthy, and if quarrels occurred it was her fault and resulted from her character.

'Of course the fault was not hers. She was like everybody else – like the majority of women. She had been brought up as the position of women in our society requires, and as therefore all women of the leisured classes without exception are brought up and cannot help being brought up. People talk about some new kind of education for women. It is all empty words: their education is exactly what it has to be in view of our unfeigned, real, general opinion about women.[45]

'The education of women will always correspond to men's opinion about them. Don't we know how men regard women:[46] *Wein, Weib, und Gesang*, and what the poets say in their verses? Take all poetry, all pictures and sculpture, beginning with love poems[47] and the nude Venuses and Phrynes, and you will see that woman is an instrument of enjoyment; she is so on the Trubá and the Grachévka,* and also at the Court balls.† And note the devil's cunning: if they are here for enjoyment and pleasure, let it be known that it is pleasure and that woman is a sweet morsel. But no, first the knights-errant declare that they worship women (worship her, and yet regard her as an instrument of enjoyment), and now people assure us that they respect women. Some give up their places to her, pick up her handkerchief; others acknowledge her right to occupy all positions and to take part in the government, and so on. They do all that, but their outlook on her remains the same. She is a means of enjoyment. Her body is a means of enjoyment. And she knows this. It is just as it is with slavery. Slavery, you know, is nothing else than the exploitation by some of the unwilling labour of many. Therefore to get rid of slavery it is necessary that people should not wish to profit by the forced labour of others and should consider it a sin and a shame. But they go and abolish the external form of slavery and arrange so that one can no longer buy and sell slaves, and they imagine and assure

* Streets in Moscow in which brothels were numerous.
† In the printed and censored Russian edition the word 'Court' was changed to 'most refined'.

themselves that slavery no longer exists, and do not see or wish to see that it does, because people still want and consider it good and right to exploit the labour of others. And as long as they consider that good, there will always be people stronger or more cunning than others who will succeed in doing it. So it is with the emancipation of woman: the enslavement of woman lies simply in the fact that people desire, and think it good, to avail themselves of her as a tool of enjoyment. Well, and they liberate woman, give her all sorts of rights equal to man, but continue to regard her as an instrument of enjoyment, and so educate her in childhood and afterwards by public opinion. And there she is, still the same humiliated and depraved slave, and the man still a depraved slave-owner.

[48]'They emancipate women in universities and in law courts, but continue to regard her as an object of enjoyment. Teach her, as she is taught among us, to regard herself as such, and she will always remain an inferior being. Either with the help of those scoundrels the doctors she will prevent the conception of offspring – that is, will be a complete prostitute, lowering herself not to the level of an animal but to the level of a thing – or she will be what the majority of women are, mentally diseased, hysterical, unhappy, and lacking capacity for spiritual development. High schools and universities cannot alter that. It can only be changed by a change in men's outlook on women and women's way of regarding themselves. It will change only when woman regards virginity as the highest state, and does not, as at present, consider the highest state of a human being a shame and a disgrace. While that is not so, the ideal of every girl, whatever her education may be, will continue to be to attract as many men as possible, as many males as possible, so as to have the possibility of choosing.

'But the fact that one of them knows more mathematics, and another can play the harp, makes no difference. A woman is happy and attains all she can desire when she has bewitched man. Therefore the chief aim of a woman is to be able to bewitch him. So it has been and will be. So it is in her maiden life in our society, and so it continues to be in her married life. For a maiden this is necessary in order to have a choice, for the married woman in order to have power over her husband.

'The one thing that stops this or at any rate suppresses it for a time, is children, and then only if the mother is not a monster, that is, if she nurses them herself. But here the doctors again come in.

'My wife, who wanted to nurse, and did nurse the four later children herself, happened to be unwell after the birth of her first child. And those doctors, who cynically undressed her and felt her all over – for which I had to thank them and pay them money – those dear doctors considered that she must not nurse the child; and that first time she was deprived of the only means which might have kept her from coquetry. We engaged a wet-nurse, that is, we took advantage of the poverty, the need, and the ignorance of a woman, tempted her away from her own baby to ours, and in return gave her a fine head-dress with gold lace.* But that is not the point. The point is that during that time when my wife was free from pregnancy and from suckling, the feminine coquetry which had lain dormant within her manifested itself with particular force. And coinciding with this the torments of jealousy rose up in me with special force. They tortured me all my married life, as they cannot but torture all husbands who live with their wives as I did with mine, that is, immorally.

XV[49]

'DURING the whole of my married life I never ceased to be tormented by jealousy, but there were periods when I specially suffered from it. One of these periods was when, after the birth of our first child, the doctors forbade my wife to nurse it. I was particularly jealous at that time, in the first place because my wife was experiencing that unrest natural to a mother which is sure to be aroused when the natural course of life is needlessly violated; and secondly, because seeing how easily she abandoned her moral obligations as a mother, I rightly though unconsciously concluded that it would be equally easy for

* In Russia wet-nurses were usually provided with an elaborate national costume by their employers.

her to disregard her duty as a wife, especially as she was quite well and in spite of the precious doctors' prohibition was able to nurse her later children admirably.'

'I see you don't like doctors,' I said, noticing a peculiarly malevolent tone in his voice whenever he alluded to them.

'It is not a case of liking or disliking. They have ruined my life as they have ruined and are ruining the lives of thousands and hundreds of thousands of human beings, and I cannot help connecting the effect with the cause. I understand that they want to earn money like lawyers and others, and I would willingly give them half my income, and all who realize what they are doing would willingly give them half of their possessions, if only they would not interfere with our family life and would never come near us. I have not collected evidence, but I know dozens of cases (there are any number of them!) where they have killed a child in its mother's womb asserting that she could not give it birth, though she has had children quite safely later on; or they have killed the mother on the pretext of performing some operation. No one reckons these murders any more than they reckoned the murders of the Inquisition, because it is supposed that it is done for the good of mankind. It is impossible to number all the crimes they commit. But all those crimes are as nothing compared to the moral corruption of materialism they introduce into the world, especially through women.

'I don't lay stress on the fact that if one is to follow their instructions, then on account of the infection which exists everywhere and in everything, people would not progress towards greater unity but towards separation; for according to their teaching we ought all to sit apart and not remove the carbolic atomizer from our mouths (though now they have discovered that even that is of no avail). But that does not matter either. The principal poison lies in the demoralization of the world, especially of women.

'To-day one can no longer say: "You are not living rightly, live better." One can't say that, either to oneself or to anyone else. If you live a bad life it is caused by the abnormal function-ing of your nerves, &c. So you must go to them, and they will prescribe eight penn'orth of medicine from a chemist, which you must take!

'You get still worse: then more medicine and the doctor again. An excellent trick!

'That however is not the point. All I wish to say is that she nursed her babies perfectly well and that only her pregnancy and the nursing of her babies saved me from the torments of jealousy. Had it not been for that it would all have happened sooner. The children saved me and her. In eight years she had five children and nursed all except the first herself.'

'And where are your children now?' I asked.

'The children?' he repeated in a frightened voice.

'Forgive me, perhaps it is painful for you to be reminded of them.'

'No, it does not matter. My wife's sister and brother have taken them. They would not let me have them. I gave them my estate, but they did not give them up to me. You know I am a sort of lunatic. I have left them now and am going away. I have seen them, but they won't let me have them because I might bring them up so that they would not be like their parents, and they have to be just like them. Oh well, what is to be done? Of course they won't let me have them and won't trust me. Besides, I do not know whether I should be able to bring them up. I think not. I am a ruin, a cripple. Still I have one thing in me. I know! Yes, that is true, I know what others are far from knowing.

'Yes, my children are living and growing up just such savages as everybody around them. I saw them, saw them three times. I can do nothing for them, nothing. I am now going to my place in the south. I have a little house and a small garden there.

'Yes, it will be a long time before people learn what I know. How much of iron and other metal there is in the sun and the stars is easy to find out, but anything that exposes our swinishness is difficult, terribly difficult!

'You at least listen to me, and I am grateful for that.

XVI

'YOU mentioned my children. There again, what terrible lies are told about children! Children a blessing from God, a joy! That is all a lie. It was so once upon a time, but now it is not so at all. Children are a torment and nothing else. Most mothers feel this quite plainly, and sometimes inadvertently say so. Ask most mothers of our propertied classes and they will tell you that they do not want to have children for fear of their falling ill and dying.[50] They don't want to nurse* them if they do have them, for fear of becoming too much attached to them and having to suffer. The pleasure a baby gives them by its loveliness, its little hands and feet, and its whole body, is not as great as the suffering caused by the very fear of its possibly falling ill and dying, not to speak of its actual illness or death. After weighing the advantages and disadvantages it seems disadvantageous, and therefore undesirable, to have children. They say this quite frankly and boldly, imagining that these feelings of theirs arise from their love of children, a good and laudable feeling of which they are proud. They do not notice that by this reflection they plainly repudiate love, and only affirm their own selfishness. They get less pleasure from a baby's loveliness than suffering from fear on its account, and therefore the baby they would love is not wanted. They do not sacrifice themselves for a beloved being, but sacrifice a being whom they might love, for their own sakes.

'It is clear that this is not love but selfishness. But one has not the heart to blame them – the mothers in well-to-do families – for that selfishness, when one remembers how dreadfully they suffer on account of their children's health, again thanks to the influence of those same doctors among our well-to-do classes. Even now, when I do but remember my wife's life and the condition she was in during the first years when we had three or four children and she was absorbed in them, I am seized

---

* The practice of employing wet-nurses was very much more general in Russia than in the English-speaking countries.

with horror! We led no life at all, but were in a state of constant
danger, of escape from it, recurring danger, again followed by
a desperate struggle and another escape – always as if we were
on a sinking ship. Sometimes it seemed to me that this was
done on purpose and that she pretended to be anxious about
the children in order to subdue me. It solved all questions in
her favour with such tempting simplicity. It sometimes seemed
as if all she did and said on these occasions was pretence. But
no! She herself suffered terribly, and continually tormented
herself about the children and their health and illnesses. It was
torture for her and for me too;[51] and it was impossible for her
not to suffer. After all, the attachment to her children, the
animal need of feeding, caressing, and protecting them, was
there as with most women, but there was not the lack of
imagination and reason that there is in animals. A hen is not
afraid of what may happen to her chick, does not know all the
diseases that may befall it, and does not know all those rem-
edies with which people imagine that they can save from
illness and death. And for a hen her young are not a source
of torment. She does for them what it is natural and pleasurable
for her to do; her young ones are a pleasure to her. When a
chick falls ill her duties are quite definite: she warms and feeds
it. And doing this she knows that she is doing all that is
necessary. If her chick dies she does not ask herself why it
died, or where it has gone to; she cackles for a while, and then
leaves off and goes on living as before. But for our unfortunate
women, my wife among them, it was not so. Not to mention
illnesses and how to cure them, she was always hearing and
reading from all sides endless rules for the rearing and educat-
ing of children, which were continually being superseded by
others. This is the way to feed a child: feed it in this way, on
such a thing; no, not on such a thing, but in this way; clothes,
drinks, baths, putting to bed, walking, fresh air, – for all these
things we, especially she, heard of new rules every week, just as
if children had only begun to be born into the world since
yesterday. And if a child that had not been fed or bathed in the
right way or at the right time fell ill, it appeared that we were
to blame for not having done what we ought.

'That was so while they were well. It was a torment even then. But if one of them happened to fall ill, it was all up: a regular hell! It is supposed that illness can be cured and that there is a science about it, and people – doctors – who know about it. Ah, but not all of them know – only the very best. When a child is ill one must get hold of the very best one, the one who saves, and then the child is saved; but if you don't get that doctor, or if you don't live in the place where that doctor lives, the child is lost. This was not a creed peculiar to her, it is the creed of all the women of our class, and she heard nothing else from all sides. Catherine Semënovna lost two children because Iván Zakhárych was not called in in time, but Iván Zakhárych saved Mary Ivánovna's eldest girl, and the Petróvs moved in time to various hotels by the doctor's advice, and the children remained alive; but if they had not been segregated the children would have died.[52] Another who had a delicate child moved south by the doctor's advice and saved the child. How can she help being tortured and agitated all the time, when the lives of the children for whom she has an animal attachment depend on her finding out in time what Iván Zakhárych will say! But what Iván Zakhárych will say nobody knows, and he himself least of all, for he is well aware that he knows nothing and therefore cannot be of any use, but just shuffles about at random so that people should not cease to believe that he knows something or other. You see, had she been wholly an animal she would not have suffered so, and if she had been quite a human being she would have had faith in God and would have said and thought, as a believer does: "The Lord gave and the Lord hath taken away. One can't escape from God."

'Our whole life with the children, for my wife and con-sequently for me, was not a joy but a torment. How could she help torturing herself? She tortured herself incessantly. Some-times when we had just made peace after some scene of jealousy, or simply after a quarrel, and thought we should be able to live, to read, and to think a little, we had no sooner settled down to some occupation than the news came that Vásya was being sick, or Másha showed symptoms of dysentery, or Andrúsha had a rash, and there was an end to peace, it was not life any more. Where was one to drive to? For what doctor? How isolate the child? And then it's a case of enemas, temperatures, medicines, and doctors. Hardly is that over before something else begins. We had no regular settled family life but only, as I have already said, continual escapes from imaginary and real dangers. It is like that in most families nowadays you know, but in my family it was especially acute. My wife was a child-loving and a credulous woman.

'So the presence of children not only failed to improve our life but poisoned it. Besides, the children were a new cause of dissension. As soon as we had children they became the means and the object of our discord, and more often the older they grew. They were not only the object of discord but the weapons of our strife. We used our children, as it were, to fight one another with. Each of us had a favourite weapon among them for our strife. I used to fight her chiefly through Vásya, the eldest boy, and she me through Lisa. Besides that, as they grew older and their characters became defined, it came about that they grew into allies whom each of us tried to draw to his or her side. They, poor things, suffered terribly from this, but we, with our incessant warfare, had no time to think of that. The girl was my ally, and the eldest boy, who resembled his mother and was her favourite, was often hateful to me.

XVII

'WELL, and so we lived.[53] Our relations to one another grew more and more hostile and at last reached a stage where it was not disagreement that caused hostility but hostility that caused disagreement. Whatever she might say I disagreed with beforehand, and it was just the same with her.

'In the fourth year we both, it seemed, came to the conclusion that we could not understand one another or agree with one another. We no longer tried to bring any dispute to a conclusion. We invariably kept to our own opinions even about the most trivial questions,[54] but especially about the children. As I now recall them the views I maintained were not at all so dear to me that I could not have given them up; but she was of the opposite opinion and to yield meant yielding to her, and that I could not do. It was the same with her. She probably considered herself quite in the right towards me, and as for me I always thought myself a saint towards her. When we were alone together we were doomed almost to silence, or to conversations such as I am convinced animals can carry on with one another: "What is the time? Time to go to bed. What is to-day's dinner? Where shall we go? What is there in the papers? Send for the doctor; Másha has a sore throat." We only needed to go a hairbreadth beyond this impossibly limited circle of conversation for irritation to flare up.[55] We had collisions and acrimonious words about the coffee, a table-cloth, a trap, a lead at bridge,* all of them things that could not be of any importance to either of us. In me at any rate there often raged a terrible hatred of her. Sometimes I watched her pouring out tea, swinging her leg, lifting a spoon to her mouth, smacking her lips and drawing in some liquid, and I hated her for these things as though they were the worst possible actions. I did not then notice that the periods of anger corresponded quite regularly and exactly to the periods of what we called love. A period of love – then a period of animosity; an energetic period of love, then a long period of animosity; a weaker manifestation of love, and a shorter period of animosity. We did not then understand that this love and animosity were one and the same animal feeling only at opposite poles. To live like that would have been awful had we understood our position; but we neither understood nor saw it. Both salvation and punishment for man lie in the fact that if he lives wrongly he can befog himself so as not to see the misery of his position. And this we did. She tried to forget herself in intense and always hurried occupation with household affairs, busying herself with the arrangements of the

* The card-game named in the original, and then much played in Russia, was *vint*, which resembles bridge.

house, her own and the children's clothes, their lessons, and
their health;[56] while I had my own occupations: wine, my
office duties, shooting, and cards. We were both continually
occupied, and we both felt that the busier we were the nastier
we might be to each other. "It's all very well for you to
grimace," I thought, "but you have harassed me all night
with your scenes, and I have a meeting on." "It's all very
well for you," she not only thought but said, "but I have
been awake all night with the baby." Those new theories of
hypnotism, psychic diseases, and hysterics are not a simple
folly, but a dangerous and repulsive one. Charcot would
certainly have said that my wife was hysterical, and that I was
abnormal, and he would no doubt have tried to cure me. But
there was nothing to cure.[57]

'Thus we lived in a perpetual fog, not seeing the condition
we were in. And if what did happen had not happened,
I should have gone on living so to old age and should have
thought, when dying, that I had led a good life. I should not
have realized the abyss of misery and the horrible falsehood in
which I wallowed.

'We were like two convicts hating each other and
chained together, poisoning one another's lives and trying
not to see it. I did not then know that ninety-nine per
cent. of married people live in a similar hell to the one I
was in and that it cannot be otherwise. I did not then
know this either about others or about myself.

'It is strange what coincidences there are in regular, or even in
irregular, lives! Just when the parents find life together unendurable, it becomes necessary to move to town for the children's education.'

He stopped, and once or twice gave vent to his strange
sounds, which were now quite like suppressed sobs. We were
approaching a station.

'What is the time?' he asked.

I looked at my watch. It was two o'clock.

'You are not tired?' he asked.

'No, but you are?'

'I am suffocating. Excuse me, I will walk up and down and drink some water.'

He went unsteadily through the carriage. I remained alone thinking over what he had said, and I was so engrossed in thought that I did not notice when he re-entered by the door at the other end of the carriage.

XVIII

'Yes, I keep diverging,' he began. 'I have thought much over it. I now see many things differently and I want to express it.

'Well, so we lived in town.[58] In town a man can live for a hundred years without noticing that he has long been dead and has rotted away. He has no time to take account of himself, he is always occupied. Business affairs, social intercourse, health, art, the children's health and their education. Now one has to receive so-and-so and so-and-so, go to see so-and-so and so-and-so; now one has to go and look at this, and hear this man or that woman. In town, you know, there are at any given moment one or two, or even three, celebrities whom one must on no account miss seeing. Then one has to undergo a treatment oneself or get someone else attended to, then there are teachers, tutors, and governesses, but one's own life is quite empty. Well, so we lived and felt less the painfulness of living together. Besides at first we had splendid occupations, arranging things in a new place, in new quarters; and we were also occupied in going from the town to the country and back to town again.

'We lived so through one winter, and the next there occurred, unnoticed by anyone, an apparently unimportant thing, but the cause of all that happened later.

'She was not well and the doctors told her not to have children, and taught her how to avoid it. To me it was disgusting. I struggled against it, but she with frivolous obstinacy insisted on having her own way and I submitted. The last excuse for our swinish life – children – was then taken away, and life became viler than ever.

'To a peasant, a labouring man, children are necessary; though it is hard for him to feed them, still he needs them, and therefore his marital relations have a justification. But to us who have children, more children are unnecessary; they are an additional care and expense, a further division of property, and a burden. So our swinish life has no justification. We either artificially deprive ourselves of children or regard them as a misfortune, the consequences of carelessness, and that is still worse.

'We have no justification. But we have fallen morally so low that we do not even feel the need of any justification.

'The majority of the present educated world devote themselves to this kind of debauchery without the least qualm of conscience.

'There is indeed nothing that can feel qualms, for conscience in our society is non-existent, unless one can call public opinion and the criminal law a "conscience". In this case neither the one nor the other is infringed: there is no reason to be ashamed of public opinion for everybody acts in the same way – Mary Pávlovna, Iván Zakhárych, and the rest. Why breed paupers or deprive oneself of the possibility of social life? There is no need to fear or be ashamed in face of the criminal law either. Those shameless hussies, or soldiers' wives, throw their babies into ponds or wells, and they of course must be put in prison, but we do it all at the proper time and in a clean way.

'We lived like that for another two years. The means employed by those scoundrel-doctors evidently began to bear fruit; she became physically stouter and handsomer, like the late beauty of summer's end. She felt this and paid attention to her appearance. She developed a provocative kind of beauty which made people restless. She was in the full vigour of a well-fed and excited woman of thirty who is not bearing children. Her appearance disturbed people. When she passed men she attracted their notice. She was like a fresh, well-fed, harnessed horse, whose bridle has been removed. There was no bridle, as is the case with ninety-nine hundredths of our women. And I felt this – and was frightened.'

XIX

He suddenly rose and sat down close to the window.

'Pardon me,' he muttered and, with his eyes fixed on the window, he remained silent for about three minutes. Then he sighed deeply and moved back to the seat opposite mine. His face was quite changed, his eyes looked pathetic, and his lips puckered strangely, almost as if he were smiling. 'I am rather tired but I will go on with it. We have still plenty of time, it is not dawn yet. Ah, yes,' he began after lighting a cigarette, 'she grew plumper after she stopped having babies, and her malady – that everlasting worry about the children – began to pass . . . at least not actually to pass, but she as it were woke up from an intoxication, came to herself, and saw that there was a whole divine world with its joys which she had forgotten, but a divine world she did not know how to live in and did not at all understand. "I must not miss it! Time is passing and won't come back!" So, I imagine, she thought, or rather felt, nor could she have thought or felt differently: she had been brought up in the belief that there was only one thing in the world worthy of attention – love. She had married and received something of that love, but not nearly what had been promised and was expected. Even that had been accompanied by many disappointments and sufferings, and then this unexpected torment: so many children! The torments exhausted her. And then, thanks to the obliging doctors, she learnt that it is possible to avoid having children. She was very glad, tried it, and became alive again for the one thing she knew – for love. But love with a husband, befouled by jealousy and all kinds of anger, was no longer the thing she wanted. She had visions of some other, clean, new love; at least I thought she had. And she began to look about her as if expecting something. I saw this and could not help feeling anxious. It happened again and again that while talking to me, as usual through other people – that is, telling a third person what she meant for me – she boldly, without remembering that she had expressed the opposite opinion an hour before, declared, though half-jokingly, that a mother's cares are a fraud, and that it is not worth while to devote one's life to children when one is young and can enjoy life. She gave less attention to the children, and less frenziedly than before, but gave more and more attention to herself, to her appearance (though she tried to conceal this), and to her pleasures, even to her accomplishments. She again enthusiastically took to the piano which she had quite abandoned, and it all began from that.'

He turned his weary eyes to the window again but, evidently making an effort, immediately continued once more.

'Yes, that man made his appearance . . .' he became confused and once or twice made that peculiar sound with his nose.

I could see that it was painful for him to name that man, to recall him, or speak about him. But he made an effort and, as if he had broken the obstacle that hindered him, continued resolutely.

'He was a worthless man in my opinion and according to my estimate. And not because of the significance he acquired in my life but because he really was so. However, the fact that he was a poor sort of fellow only served to show how irresponsible she was. If it had not been he then it would have been another. It had to be!'

Again he paused. 'Yes, he was a musician, a violinist; not a professional, but a semi-professional semi-society man.

'His father, a landowner, was a neighbour of my father's. He had been ruined, and his children – there were three boys – had obtained settled positions; only this one, the youngest, had been handed over to his godmother in Paris. There he was sent to the *Conservatoire* because he had a talent for music, and he came out as a violinist and played at concerts. He was a man . . .' Having evidently intended to say something bad about him, Pózdnyshev restrained himself and rapidly said: 'Well, I don't really know how he lived, I only know that he returned to Russia that year and appeared in my house.

'With moist almond-shaped eyes, red smiling lips, a small waxed moustache, hair done in the latest fashion, and an insipidly pretty face, he was what women call "not bad looking". His figure was weak though not misshapen, and he had a specially developed posterior, like a woman's, or such as Hottentots are said to have. They too are reported to be musical. Pushing himself as far as possible into familiarity, but sensitive and always ready to yield at the slightest resistance, he maintained his dignity in externals, wore buttoned boots of a special Parisian fashion, bright-coloured ties, and other things foreigners acquire in Paris, which by their noticeable novelty always attract women. There was an affected external gaiety in his manner. That manner, you know, of speaking about everything in allusions and unfinished sentences, as if you knew it all, remembered it, and could complete it yourself.

'It was he with his music who was the cause of it all. You know at the trial the case was put as if it was all caused by jealousy. No such thing, that is, I don't mean "no such thing", it was and yet it was not. At the trial it was decided that I was a wronged husband and that I had killed her while defending my outraged honour (that is the phrase they employ, you know). That is why I was acquitted. I tried to explain matters at the trial but they took it that I was trying to rehabilitate my wife's honour.

'What my wife's relations with that musician may have been has no meaning for me, or for her either. What has a meaning is what I have told you about – my swinishness. The whole thing was an outcome of the terrible abyss between us of which I have told you – that dreadful tension of mutual hatred which made the first excuse sufficient to produce a crisis. The quarrels between us had for some time past become frightful, and were all the more startling because they alternated with similarly intense animal passion.

'If he had not appeared there would have been someone else. If the occasion had not been jealousy it would have been something else. I maintain that all husbands who live as I did, must either live dissolutely, separate, or kill themselves or their wives as I have done. If there is anybody who has not done so, he is a rare exception. Before I ended as I did, I had several times been on the verge of suicide, and she too had repeatedly tried to poison herself.

XX

'Well, that is how things were going not long before it happened. We seemed to be living in a state of truce and had no reason to infringe it. Then we chanced to speak about a dog which I said had been awarded a medal at an exhibition. She remarked "Not a medal, but an honourable mention." A dispute ensues. We jump from one subject to another, reproach one another, "Oh, that's nothing new, it's always been like that." "You said . . ." "No, I didn't say so." "Then I am telling lies! . . ." You feel that at any moment that dreadful quarrelling which makes you wish to kill yourself or her will begin. You know it will begin immediately, and fear it like fire and therefore wish to restrain yourself, but your whole being is seized with fury. She being in the same or even a worse condition purposely misinterprets every word you say, giving it a wrong meaning. Her every word is venomous; where she alone knows that I am most sensitive, she stabs. It gets worse and worse. I shout: "Be quiet!" or something of that kind.

'She rushes out of the room and into the nursery. I try to hold her back in order to finish what I was saying, to prove my point, and I seize her by the arm. She pretends that I have hurt her and screams: "Children, your father is striking me!" I shout: "Don't lie!" "But it's not the first time!" she screams, or something like that. The children rush to her. She calms them down. I say, "Don't sham!" She says, "Everything is sham in your eyes, you would kill anyone and say they were shamming. Now I have understood you. That's just what you want!" "Oh, I wish you were dead as a dog!" I shout. I remember how those dreadful words horrified me. I never thought I could utter such dreadful, coarse words, and am surprised that they escaped me. I shout them and rush away into my study and sit down and smoke. I hear her go out into the hall preparing to go away. I ask, "Where are you going to?" She does not reply. "Well, devil take her," I say to myself, and go back to my study and lie down and smoke. A thousand different plans of how to revenge myself on her and get rid of her, and how to improve matters and go on as if nothing had happened, come into my head. I think all that and go on smoking and smoking. I think of running away from her, hiding myself, going to America. I get as far as dreaming of how I shall get rid of her, how splendid that will be, and how I shall unite with another, an admirable woman – quite different. I shall get rid of her either by her dying or by a divorce, and I plan how it is to be done. I notice that I am getting confused and not thinking of what is necessary, and to prevent myself from perceiving that my thoughts are not to the point I go on smoking.

'Life in the house goes on. The governess comes in and asks: "Where is madame? When will she be back?" The footman asks whether he is to serve tea. I go to the dining-room. The children, especially Lisa who already understands, gaze inquiringly and disapprovingly at me. We drink tea in silence. She has still not come back. The evening passes, she has not returned, and two different feelings alternate within me. Anger because she torments me and all the children by her absence which will end by her returning; and fear that she will not return but will do something to herself. I would go to fetch her, but where am I to look for her? At her sister's? But it would be so stupid to go and ask. And it's all the better: if she is bent on tormenting someone, let her torment herself. Besides that is what she is waiting for; and next time it would be worse still. But suppose she is not with her sister but is doing something to herself, or has already done it! It's past ten, past eleven! I don't go to the bedroom – it would be stupid to lie there alone waiting – but I'll not lie down here either. I wish to occupy my mind, to write a letter or to read, but I can't do anything. I sit alone in my study, tortured, angry, and listening. It's three o'clock, four o'clock, and she is not back. Towards morning I fall asleep. I wake up, she has still not come!

'Everything in the house goes on in the usual way, but all are perplexed and look at me inquiringly and reproachfully, considering me to be the cause of it all. And in me the same struggle still continues: anger that she is torturing me, and anxiety for her.

'At about eleven in the morning her sister arrives as her envoy. And the usual talk begins. "She is in a terrible state. What does it all mean?" "After all, nothing has happened." I speak of her impossible character and say that I have not done anything.

'"But, you know, it can't go on like this," says her sister.

'"It's all her doing and not mine," I say. "I won't take the first step.[59] If it means separation, let it be separation."

'My sister-in-law goes away having achieved nothing. I had boldly said that I would not take the first step; but after her departure, when I came out of my study and saw the children piteous and frightened, I was prepared to take the first step. I should be glad to do it, but[60] I don't know how. Again I pace up and down and smoke; at lunch I drink vodka and wine and attain what I unconsciously desire – I no longer see the stupidity and humiliation of my position.

'At about three she comes. When she meets me she does not speak. I imagine that she has submitted, and begin to say that I had been provoked by her reproaches. She, with the same stern expression on her terribly harassed face, says that she has not come for explanations but to fetch the children, because we cannot live together. I begin telling her that the fault is not mine and that she provoked me beyond endurance. She looks severely and solemnly at me and says: "Do not say any more, you will repent it." I tell her that I cannot stand comedies. Then she cries out something I don't catch, and rushes into her room. The key clicks behind her, – she has locked herself in. I try the door, but getting no answer, go away angrily. Half an hour later Lisa runs in crying. "What is it? Has anything happened?" "We can't hear mamma." We go. I pull at the double doors with all my might. The bolt had not been firmly secured, and the two halves both open. I approach the bed, on which she is lying awkwardly in her petticoats and with a pair of high boots on. An empty opium bottle is on the table. She is brought to herself. Tears follow, and a reconciliation. No, not a reconciliation: in the heart of each there is still the old animosity, with the additional irritation produced by the pain of this quarrel which each attributes to the other. But one must of course finish it all somehow, and life goes on in the old way. And so the same kind of quarrel, and even worse ones, occurred continually: once a week, once a month, or at times every day. It was always the same. Once I had already procured a passport to go abroad – the quarrel had continued for two days. But there was again a partial explanation, a partial reconciliation, and I did not go.

XXI

'So those were our relations when that man appeared. He arrived in Moscow – his name is Trukhachévski – and came to my house. It was in the morning. I received him. We had once been on familiar terms and he tried to maintain a familiar tone by using non-committal expressions, but I definitely adopted a conventional tone and he at once submitted to it. I disliked him from the first glance.[61] But curiously enough a strange and fatal force led me not to repulse him, not to keep him away, but on the contrary to invite him to the house. After all, what could have been simpler than to converse with him coldly, and say good-bye without introducing him to my wife? But no, as if purposely, I began talking about his playing, and said I had been told he had given up the violin. He replied that, on the contrary, he now played more than ever. He referred to the fact that there had been a time when I myself played. I said I had given it up but that my wife played well. It is an astonishing thing[62] that from the first day, from the first hour of my meeting him, my relations with him were such as they might have been only after all that subsequently happened.[63] There was something strained in them: I noticed every word, every expression he or I used, and attributed importance to them.

'I introduced him to my wife. The conversation immediately turned to music, and he offered to be of use to her by playing with her. My wife was, as usual of late, very elegant, attractive, and disquietingly beautiful. He evidently pleased her at first sight. Besides she was glad that she would have someone to accompany her on a violin, which she was so fond of that she used to engage a violinist from the theatre for the purpose; and her face reflected her pleasure. But catching sight of me she at once understood my feeling and changed her expression, and a game of mutual deception began. I smiled pleasantly to appear as if I liked it. He, looking at my wife as all immoral men look at pretty women, pretended that he was only interested in the subject of the conversation – which no longer interested him at all; while she tried to seem indifferent, though my false smile of jealousy with which she was familiar, and his lustful gaze, evidently excited her. I saw that from their first encounter her eyes were particularly bright and, probably as a result of my jealousy, it seemed as if an electric current had been established between them, evoking as it were an identity of expressions, looks, and smiles. She blushed and he blushed. She smiled and he smiled. We spoke about music, Paris, and all sorts of trifles. Then he rose to go, and stood smilingly, holding his hat against his twitching thigh and looking now at her and now at me, as if in expectation of what we would do. I remember that instant just because at that moment I might not have invited him, and then nothing would have happened. But I glanced at him and at her and said silently to myself, "Don't suppose that I am jealous," "or that I am afraid of you," I added mentally addressing him, and I invited him to come some evening and bring his violin to play with my wife. She glanced at me with surprise, flushed, and as if frightened began to decline, saying that she did not play well enough. This refusal irritated me still more, and I insisted the more on his coming. I remember the curious feeling with which I looked at the back of his head, with the black hair parted in the middle contrasting with the white nape of his neck, as he went out with his peculiar springing gait suggestive of some kind of a bird. I could not conceal from myself that that man's presence tormented me. "It depends on me," I reflected, "to act so as to see nothing more of him. But that would be to admit that I am afraid of him. No, I am not afraid of him; it would be too humiliating," I said to myself. And there in the ante-room, knowing that my wife heard me, I insisted that he should come that evening with his violin. He promised to do so, and left.

'In the evening he brought his violin and they played. But it took a long time to arrange matters – they had not the music they wanted, and my wife could not without preparation play what they had. I was very fond of music and sympathized with their playing, arranging a music-stand for him and turning over the pages. They played a few things, some songs without words, and a little sonata by Mozart. They played splendidly,[64] and he had an exceptionally fine tone. Besides that, he had a refined and elevated taste not at all in correspondence with his character.

'He was of course a much better player than my wife, and he helped her, while at the same time politely praising her playing. He behaved himself very well. My wife seemed interested only in music and was very simple and natural.[65] But though I pretended to be interested in the music I was tormented by jealousy all the evening.

'From the first moment his eyes met my wife's I saw that the animal in each of them, regardless of all conditions of their position and of society, asked, "May I?" and answered, "Oh, yes, certainly." I saw that he had not at all expected to find my wife, a Moscow lady, so attractive, and that he was very pleased. For he had no doubt whatever that she was *willing*. The only crux was whether that unendurable husband could hinder them. Had I been pure I should not have understood this, but, like the majority of men, I had myself regarded women in that way before I married and therefore could read his mind like a manuscript. I was particularly tormented because I saw without doubt that she had no other feeling towards me than a continual irritation only occasionally interrupted by the habitual sensuality; but that this man – by his external refinement and novelty and still more by his undoubtedly great talent for music, by the nearness that comes of playing together, and by the influence music, especially the violin, exercises on impressionable natures – was sure not only to please but certainly and without the least hesitation to conquer, crush, bind her, twist her round his little finger and do whatever he liked with her. I could not help seeing this and I suffered terribly. But for all that, or perhaps on account of it, some force obliged me against my will to be not merely polite but amiable to him. Whether I did it for my wife or for him, to show that I was not afraid of him, or whether I did it to deceive myself – I don't know, but I know that from the first I could not behave naturally with him. In order not to yield to my wish to kill him there and then, I had to make much of him. I gave him expensive wines at supper, went into raptures over his playing, spoke to him with a particularly amiable smile, and invited him to dine and play with my wife again the next Sunday. I told him I would ask a few friends who were fond of music to hear him. And so it ended.'

Greatly agitated, Pózdnyshev changed his position and emitted his peculiar sound.

'It is strange how the presence of that man acted on me,' he began again, with an evident effort to keep calm. 'I come home from the Exhibition a day or two later, enter the ante-room, and suddenly feel something heavy, as if a stone had fallen on my heart, and I cannot understand what it is. It was that passing through the ante-room I noticed something which reminded me of him. I realized what it was only in my study, and went back to the ante-room to make sure. Yes, I was not mistaken, there was his overcoat. A fashionable coat, you know. (Though I did not realize it, I observed everything connected with him with extraordinary attention.) I inquire: sure enough he is there. I pass on to the dancing-room, not through the drawing-room but through the schoolroom. My daughter, Lisa, sits reading a book and the nurse sits with the youngest boy at the table, making a lid of some kind spin round. The door to the dancing-room is shut but I hear the sound of a rhythmic arpeggio and his[66] and her voices. I listen, but cannot make out anything.

'Evidently the sound of the piano is purposely made to drown the sound of their voices, their kisses... perhaps. My God! What was aroused in me! Even to think of the beast that then lived in me fills me with horror! My heart suddenly contracted, stopped, and then began to beat like a hammer. My chief feeling, as usual whenever I was enraged, was one of self-pity. "In the presence of the children! of their nurse!"[67]

thought I. Probably I looked awful, for Lisa gazed at me with strange eyes. "What am I to do?" I asked myself. "Go in? I can't: heaven only knows what I should do. But neither can I go away." The nurse looked at me as if she understood my position.[68] "But it is impossible not to go in," I said to myself, and I quickly opened the door. He was sitting at the piano playing those arpeggios with his large white upturned fingers. She was standing in the curve of the piano, bending over some open music. She was the first to see or hear, and glanced at me. Whether she was frightened and pretended not to be, or whether she was really not frightened, anyway she did not start or move but only blushed, and that not at once.

' "How glad I am that you have come: we have not decided what to play on Sunday," she said in a tone she would not have used to me had we been alone. This and her using the word "we" of herself and him, filled me with indignation. I greeted him silently.

'He pressed my hand, and at once, with a smile which I thought distinctly ironic, began to explain that he had brought some music to practise for Sunday, but that they disagreed about what to play: a classical but more difficult piece, namely Beethoven's sonata for the violin, or a few little pieces. It was all so simple and natural that there was nothing one could cavil at, yet I felt certain that it was all untrue and that they had agreed how to deceive me.

'Among the most distressing conditions of life for a jealous man (and everyone is jealous in our world) are certain society conventions which allow a man and woman the greatest and most dangerous proximity. You would become a laughing-stock to others if you tried to prevent such nearness at balls, or the nearness of doctors to their women–patients, or of people occupied with art, sculpture, and especially music. A couple are occupied with the noblest of arts, music; this demands a certain nearness, and there is nothing reprehensible in that and only a stupid jealous husband can see anything undesirable in it.[69] Yet everybody knows that it is by means of those very pursuits, especially of music, that the greater part of the adulteries in our society occur. I evidently confused them by the confusion I betrayed: for a long time I could not speak. I was like a bottle held upside down from which the water does not flow because it is too full. I wanted to abuse him and to turn him out, but again felt that I must treat him courteously and amiably. And I did so. I acted as though I approved of it all, and again because of the strange feeling which made me behave to him the more amiably the more his presence distressed me. I told him that I trusted his taste and advised her to do the same. He stayed as long as was necessary to efface the unpleasant impression caused by my sudden entrance – looking frightened and remaining silent – and then left, pretending that it was now decided what to play next day. I was however fully convinced that compared to what interested them the question of what to play was quite indifferent.

'I saw him out to the ante-room with special politeness. (How could one do less than accompany a man who had come to disturb the peace and destroy the happiness of a whole family?) And I pressed his soft white hand with particular warmth.

XXII

'I DID not speak to her all that day – I could not. Nearness to her aroused in me such hatred of her that I was afraid of myself. At dinner in the presence of the children she asked me when I was going away. I had to go next week to the District Meetings of the Zémstvo. I told her the date. She asked whether I did not want anything for the journey. I did not answer but sat silent at table and then went in silence to my study. Latterly she used never to come to my room, especially not at that time of day. I lay in my study filled with anger. Suddenly I heard her familiar step, and the terrible, monstrous idea entered my head that she, like Uriah's wife, wished to conceal the sin she had already committed and that that was why she was coming to me at such an unusual time. "Can she be coming to me?" thought I, listening to her approaching footsteps. "If she is coming here, then I am right," and an inexpressible hatred of her took possession of me. Nearer and nearer came the steps. Is it possible that she won't pass on to the dancing-room? No, the door creaks and in the doorway appears her tall[70] handsome figure, on her face and in her eyes a timid ingratiating look which she tries to hide, but which I see and the meaning of which I know. I almost choked, so long did I hold my breath, and still looking at her I grasped my cigarette-case and began to smoke.

' "Now how can you? One comes to sit with you for a bit, and you begin smoking" – and she sat down close to me on the sofa, leaning against me. I moved away so as not to touch her.

' "I see you are dissatisfied at my wanting to play on Sunday," she said.

' "I am not at all dissatisfied," I said.

' "As if I don't see!"

' "Well, I congratulate you on seeing. But I only see that you behave like a coquette. . . . You always find pleasure in all kinds of vileness, but to me it is terrible!"

' "Oh, well, if you are going to scold like a cabman I'll go away."

' "Do, but remember that if you don't value the family honour, I value not you (devil take you) but the honour of the family!"

' "But what is the matter? What?"

' "Go away, for God's sake be off!"

'Whether she pretended not to understand what it was about or really did not understand, at any rate she took offence, grew angry, and did not go away but stood in the middle of the room.

' "You have really become impossible," she began.[71] "You have a character that even an angel could not put up with." And as usual trying to sting me as painfully as possible, she reminded me of my conduct to my sister (an incident when, being exasperated, I said rude things to my sister); she knew I was distressed about it and she stung me just on that spot. "After that, nothing from you will surprise me," she said.

' "Yes! Insult me, humiliate me, disgrace me, and then put the blame on me," I said to myself, and suddenly I was seized by such terrible rage as I had never before experienced.

'For the first time I wished to give physical expression to that rage. I jumped up and went towards her; but just as I jumped up I remember becoming conscious of my rage and asking myself: "Is it right to give way to this feeling?" and at once I answered that it was right, that it would frighten her, and instead of restraining my fury I immediately began inflaming it still further, and was glad it burnt yet more fiercely within me.

' "Be off, or I'll kill you!" I shouted,[72] going up to her and seizing her by the arm. I consciously intensified the anger in my voice as I said this. And I suppose I was terrible, for she was so frightened that she had not even the strength to go away, but only said: "Vásya, what is it? What is the matter with you?"

' "Go!" I roared louder still.[73] "No one but you can drive me to fury. I do not answer for myself!"

'Having given reins to my rage, I revelled in it and wished to do something still more unusual to show the extreme degree of my anger. I felt a terrible desire to beat her, to kill her, but knew that this would not do, and so[74] to give vent to my fury I seized a paper-weight from my table, again shouting "Go!" and hurled it to the floor near her. I aimed it very exactly past her. Then she left the room, but stopped at the doorway, and immediately, while she still saw it (I did it so that she might see), I began snatching things from the table – candlesticks and ink-stand – and hurling them on the floor still shouting "Go! Get out! I don't answer for myself!" She went away – and I immediately stopped.

'An hour later the nurse came to tell me that my wife was in hysterics. I went to her; she sobbed, laughed, could not speak, and her whole body was convulsed. She was not pretending, but was really ill.[75]

'Towards morning she grew quiet, and we made peace under the influence of the feeling we called love.

'In the morning when, after our reconciliation, I confessed to her that I was jealous of Trukhachévski, she was not at all confused, but laughed most naturally; so strange did the very possibility of an infatuation for such a man seem to her, she said.

' "Could a decent woman have any other feeling for such a man than the pleasure of his music? Why, if you like I am ready never to see him again...not even on Sunday, though every-body has been invited. Write and tell him that I am ill, and there's an end of it! Only it is unpleasant that anyone, espe-cially he himself, should imagine that he is dangerous. I am too proud to allow anyone to think that of me!"

'And you know, she was not lying, she believed what she was saying; she hoped by those words to evoke in herself contempt for him and so to defend herself from him, but she did not succeed in doing so. Everything was against her, especially that accursed music. So it all ended, and on the Sunday the guests assembled and they again played together.

XXIII

'I suppose it is hardly necessary to say that I was very vain: if one is not vain there is nothing to live for in our usual way of life. So on that Sunday I arranged the dinner and the musical evening with much care. I bought the provisions myself and invited the guests.

'Towards six the visitors assembled. He came in evening dress with diamond studs that showed bad taste. He behaved in a free and easy manner, answered everything hurriedly with a smile of agreement and understanding, you know, with that peculiar expression which seems to say that all you may do or say is just what he expected. Everything that was not in good taste about him I noticed with particular pleasure, because it ought all to have had the effect of tranquillizing me and showing that he was so far beneath my wife that, as she had said, she could not lower herself to his level. I did not now allow myself to be jealous.[76] In the first place I had worried through that torment and needed rest, and secondly I wanted to believe my wife's assurances and did believe them. But though I was not jealous I was nevertheless not natural with either of them, and at dinner and during the first half of the evening before the music began I still followed their move-ments and looks.

'The dinner was, as dinners are, dull and pretentious. The music began pretty early.[77] Oh, how I remember every detail of that evening! I remember how he brought in his violin, unlocked the case, took off the cover a lady had embroidered for him, drew out the violin, and began tuning it. I remember how my wife sat down at the piano with pretended unconcern, under which I saw that she was trying to conceal great timidity – chiefly as to her own ability – and then the usual A on the piano began, the pizzicato of the violin, and the arrangement of the music. Then I remember how they glanced at one another, turned to look at the audience who were seating themselves, said something to one another, and began. He took the first chords. His face grew serious, stern, and sympathetic, and listening to the sounds he produced, he touched the strings with careful fingers. The piano answered him. The music began. . . .'

Pózdnyshev paused and produced his strange sound several times in succession. He tried to speak, but sniffed, and stopped.

'They played Beethoven's Kreutzer Sonata,' he continued. 'Do you know the first presto? You do?' he cried.[78] 'Ugh! Ugh! It is a terrible thing, that sonata. And especially that part. And in general music is a dreadful thing! What is it? I don't understand it. What is music? What does it do? And why does it do what it does? They say music exalts the soul. Nonsense, it is not true! It has an effect, an awful effect – I am speaking of myself – but not of an exalting kind. It has neither an exalting nor a debasing effect but it produces agitation. How can I put it? Music makes me forget myself, my real position; it transports me to some other position not my own. Under the influence of music it seems to me that I feel what I do not really feel, that I understand what I do not understand, that I can do what I cannot do. I explain it by the fact that music acts like yawning, like laughter: I am not sleepy, but I yawn when I see someone yawning; there is nothing for me to laugh at, but I laugh when I hear people laughing.

'Music carries me immediately and directly into the mental condition in which the man was who composed it. My soul merges with his and together with him I pass from one condition into another, but why this happens I don't know. You see, he who wrote, let us say, the Kreutzer Sonata – Beethoven – knew of course why he was in that condition; that condition caused him to do certain actions and therefore that condition had a meaning for him, but for me – none at all. That is why music only agitates and doesn't lead to a conclusion. Well, when a military march is played the soldiers march to the music and the music has achieved its object. A dance is played, I dance and the music has achieved its object. Mass has been sung, I receive Communion, and that music too has reached a conclusion. Otherwise it is only agitating, and what ought to be done in that agitation is lacking. That is why music sometimes acts so dreadfully, so terribly. In China, music is a State affair. And that is as it should be. How can one allow anyone who pleases to hypnotize another, or many others, and do what he likes with them? And especially that this hypnotist should be the first immoral man who turns up?

'It is a terrible instrument in the hands of any chance user! Take that Kreutzer Sonata for instance, how can that first presto be played in a drawing-room among ladies in low-necked dresses? To hear that played, to clap a little, and then to eat ices and talk of the latest scandal? Such things should only be played on certain important significant occasions, and then only when certain actions answering to such music are wanted; play it then and do what the music has moved you to. Otherwise an awakening of energy and feeling unsuited both to the time and the place, to which no outlet is given, cannot but act harmfully. At any rate that piece had a terrible effect on me; it was as if quite new feelings, new possibilities, of which I had till then been unaware, had been revealed to me. "That's how it is: not at all as I used to think and live, but that way," something seemed to say within me. What this new thing was that had been revealed to me I could not explain to myself, but the consciousness of this new condition was very joyous.[79] All those same people, including my wife and him, appeared in a new light.[80]

'After that allegro they played the beautiful, but common and unoriginal, andante with trite variations, and the very weak finale. Then, at the request of the visitors, they played Ernst's Elegy and a few small pieces. They were all good, but they did not produce on me a one-hundredth part of the impression the first piece had. The effect of the first piece formed the background for them all.

'I felt light-hearted and cheerful the whole evening. I had never seen my wife as she was that evening. Those shining eyes, that severe, significant expression while she played, and her melting languor and feeble, pathetic, and blissful smile after they had finished. I saw all that but did not attribute any meaning to it except that she was feeling what I felt, and that to her as to me new feelings, never before experienced, were revealed or, as it were, recalled.[81] The evening ended satisfactorily and the visitors departed.

'Knowing that I had to go away to attend the Zémstvo Meetings two days later, Trukhachévski on leaving said he hoped to repeat the pleasure of that evening when he next came to Moscow. From this I concluded that he did not consider it possible to come to my house during my absence, and this pleased me.

'It turned out that as I should not be back before he left town, we should not see one another again.

'For the first time I pressed his hand with real pleasure, and thanked him for the enjoyment he had given us. In the same way he bade a final farewell to my wife. Their leave-taking seemed to be most natural and proper. Everything was splendid. My wife and I were both very well satisfied with our evening party.[82]

XXIV

'Two days later I left for the Meetings, parting from my wife in the best and most tranquil of moods.

'In the district there was always an enormous amount to do and a quite special life, a special little world of its own. I spent two ten-hour days at the Council. A letter from my wife was brought me on the second day and I read it there and then.

'She wrote about the children, about uncle, about the nurse, about shopping, and among other things she mentioned, as a most natural occurrence, that Trukhachévski had called, brought some music he had promised, and had offered to play again, but that she had refused.

'I did not remember his having promised any music, but thought he had taken leave for good, and I was therefore unpleasantly struck by this. I was however so busy that I had no time to think of it, and it was only in the evening when I had returned to my lodgings that I re-read her letter.

'Besides the fact that Trukhachévski had called at my house during my absence, the whole tone of the letter seemed to me unnatural. The mad beast of jealousy began to growl in its kennel and wanted to leap out, but I was afraid of that beast and quickly fastened him in. "What an abominable feeling this jealousy is!" I said to myself. "What could be more natural than what she writes?"

'I went to bed and began thinking about the affairs awaiting me next day. During those Meetings, sleeping in a new place, I usually slept badly, but now I fell asleep very quickly. And as sometimes happens, you know, you feel a kind of electric shock and wake up. So I awoke thinking of her, of my physical love for her, and of Trukhachévski, and of everything being accomplished between them. Horror and rage compressed my heart. But I began to reason with myself. "What nonsense!" said I to myself. "There are no grounds to go on, there is nothing and there has been nothing. How can I so degrade her and myself as to imagine such horrors? He is a sort of hired violinist, known as a worthless fellow, and suddenly an honourable woman, the respected mother of a family, *my* wife.... What absurdity!" So it seemed to me on the one hand. "How could it help being so?" it seemed on the other. "How could that simplest and most intelligible thing help happening – that for the sake of which I married her, for the sake of which I have been living with her, what alone I wanted of her, and which others including this musician must therefore also want? He is an unmarried man, healthy (I remember how he crunched the gristle of a cutlet and how greedily his red lips clung to the glass of wine), well-fed, plump, and not merely unprincipled but evidently making it a principle to accept the pleasures that present themselves. And they have music, that most exquisite voluptuousness of the senses, as a link between them. What then could make him refrain? She? But who is she? She was, and still is, a mystery. I don't know her. I only know her as an animal. And nothing can or should restrain an animal."

'Only then did I remember their faces that evening when, after the Kreutzer Sonata, they played some impassioned little piece, I don't remember by whom, impassioned to the point of obscenity. "How dared I go away?" I asked myself, remembering their faces. Was it not clear that everything had happened between them that evening? Was it not evident already then that there was not only no barrier between them, but that they both, and she chiefly, felt a certain measure of shame after what had happened? I remember her weak, piteous, and beatific smile as she wiped the perspiration from her flushed face when I came up to the piano. Already then they avoided looking at one another, and only at supper when he was pouring out some water for her, they glanced at each other with the vestige of a smile. I now recalled with horror the glance and scarcely perceptible smile I had then caught. "Yes, it is all over," said one voice, and immediately the other voice said something entirely different. "Something has come over you, it can't be that it is so," said that other voice. It felt uncanny lying in the dark and I struck a light, and felt a kind of terror in that little room with its yellow wall-paper. I lit a cigarette and, as always happens when one's thoughts go round and round in a circle of insoluble contradictions, I smoked, taking one cigarette after another in order to befog myself so as not to see those contradictions.

'I did not sleep all night, and at five in the morning,[83] having decided that I could not continue in such a state of tension, I rose, woke the caretaker who attended me and sent him to get horses. I sent a note to the Council saying that I had been recalled to Moscow on urgent business and asking that one of the members should take my place. At eight o'clock I got into my trap and started.'

XXV

THE conductor entered and seeing that our candle had burnt down put it out, without supplying a fresh one. The day was dawning. Pózdnyshev was silent, but sighed deeply all the time the conductor was in the carriage. He continued his story only after the conductor had gone out, and in the semi-darkness of the carriage only the rattle of the windows of the moving carriage and the rhythmic snoring of the clerk could be heard. In the half-light of dawn I could not see Pózdnyshev's face at all, but only heard his voice becoming ever more and more excited and full of suffering.

'I had to travel twenty-four miles by road and eight hours by rail. It was splendid driving. It was frosty autumn weather, bright and sunny. The roads were in that condition when the tyres leave their dark imprint on them, you know. They were smooth, the light brilliant, and the air invigorating. It was pleasant driving in the tarantas. When it grew lighter and I had started I felt easier. Looking at the houses, the fields, and the passers-by, I forgot where I was going. Sometimes I felt that I was simply taking a drive,[84] and that nothing of what was calling me back had taken place. This oblivion was peculiarly enjoyable. When I remembered where I was going to, I said to myself, "We shall see when the time comes; I must not think about it." When we were half-way an incident occurred which detained me and still further distracted my thoughts. The tarantas[85] broke down and had to be repaired. That break-down had a very important effect, for it caused me to arrive in Moscow at midnight, instead of at seven o'clock as I had expected, and to reach home between twelve and one, as I missed the express and had to travel by an ordinary train. Going to fetch a cart, having the tarantas mended, settling up, tea at the inn, a talk with the inn-keeper – all this still further diverted my attention. It was twilight before all was ready and I started again. By night it was even pleasanter driving than during the day. There was a new moon, a slight frost, still good roads, good horses, and a jolly driver, and as I went on I enjoyed it, hardly thinking at all of what lay before me; or perhaps I enjoyed it just because I knew what awaited me and was saying good-bye to the joys of life. But that tranquil mood, that ability to suppress my feelings, ended with my drive. As soon as I entered the train something entirely different began. That eight-hour journey in a railway carriage was something dreadful, which I shall never forget all my life. Whether it was that having taken my seat in the carriage I vividly imagined myself as having already arrived, or that railway travelling has such an exciting effect on people, at any rate from the moment I sat down in the train I could no longer control my imagination, and with extraordinary vividness which inflamed my jealousy it painted incessantly, one after another, pictures[86] of what had gone on in my absence, of how she had been false to me. I burnt with indignation, anger, and a peculiar feeling of intoxication with my own humiliation, as I gazed at those pictures, and I could not tear myself away from them; I could not help looking at them, could not efface them, and could not help evoking them.

'That was not all. The more I gazed at those imaginary pictures the stronger grew my belief in their reality.[87] The vividness with which they presented themselves to me seemed to serve as proof that what I imagined was real. It was as if some devil against my will invented and suggested to me the most terrible reflections. An old conversation I had had with Trukhachévski's brother came to my mind, and in a kind of ecstasy I rent my heart with that conversation, making it refer to Trukhachévski and my wife.

'That had occurred long before, but I recalled it. Trukhachévski's brother, I remember, in reply to a question whether he frequented houses of ill-fame, had said that a decent man would not go to places where there was danger of infection and it was dirty and nasty, since he could always find a decent woman. And now his brother had found my wife! "True, she is not in her first youth, has lost a side-tooth, and there is a slight puffiness about her; but it can't be helped, one has to take advantage of what one can get," I imagined him to be thinking. "Yes, it is condescending of him to take her for his mistress!" I said to myself. "And she is safe...." "No, it is impossible!" I thought horror-struck. "There is nothing of the kind, nothing! There are not even any grounds for suspecting such things. Didn't she tell me that the very thought that I could be jealous of him was degrading to her? Yes, but she is lying, she is always lying!"[88] I exclaimed, and everything began anew.... There were only two other people in the carriage; an old woman and her husband, both very taciturn, and even they got out at one of the stations and I was quite alone. I was like a caged animal: now I jumped up and went to the window, now I began to walk up and down trying to speed the carriage up; but the carriage with all its seats and windows went jolting on in the same way, just as ours does....'

Pózdnyshev jumped up, took a few steps, and sat down again.

'Oh, I am afraid, afraid of railway carriages, I am seized with horror. Yes, it is awful!' he continued. 'I said to myself, "I will think of something else. Suppose I think of the inn-keeper where I had tea," and there in my mind's eye appears the inn-keeper with his long beard and his grandson, a boy of the age of my Vásya. "My Vásya! He will see how the musician kisses his mother. What will happen in his poor soul? But what does she care? She loves"[89] ... and again the same thing rose up in me. "No, no ... I will think about the inspection of the District Hospital. Oh, yes, about the patient who complained of the doctor yesterday. The doctor has a moustache like Tru-khachévski's. And how impudent he is ... they both deceived me when he said he was leaving Moscow," and it began afresh. Everything I thought of had some connexion with them. I suffered dreadfully. The chief cause of the suffering was my ignorance, my doubt, and the contradictions within me: my not knowing whether I ought to love or hate her. My suffering was of a strange kind. I felt a hateful consciousness of my humiliation and of his victory, but a terrible hatred for her. "It will not do to put an end to myself and leave her; she must at least suffer to some extent, and at least understand that I have suffered," I said to myself. I got out at every station to divert my mind. At one station I saw some people drinking, and I immediately drank some vodka. Beside me stood a Jew who was also drinking. He began to talk, and to avoid being alone in my carriage I went with him into his dirty third-class carriage reeking with smoke and bespattered with shells of sunflower seeds. There I sat down beside him and he chattered a great deal and told anecdotes. I listened to him, but could not take in what he was saying because I continued to think about my own affairs. He noticed this and demanded my attention. Then I rose and went back to my carriage. "I must think it over," I said to myself. "Is what I suspect true, and is there any reason for me to suffer?" I sat down, wishing to think it over calmly, but immediately, instead of calm reflection, the same thing began again: instead of reflection, pictures and fancies. "How often I have suffered like this," I said to myself (recalling former similar attacks of jealousy), "and afterwards it all ended in nothing. So it will be now perhaps, yes certainly it will. I shall find her calmly asleep, she will wake up, be pleased to see me, and by her words and looks I shall know that there has been nothing and that this is all nonsense. Oh, how good that would be! But no, that has happened too often and won't happen again now," some voice seemed to say; and it began again. Yes, that was where the punishment lay! I wouldn't take a young man to a lock-hospital to knock the hankering after women out of him, but into my soul, to see the devils that were rending it! What was terrible, you know, was that I considered myself to have a complete right to her body as if it were my own, and yet at the same time I felt I could not control that body, that it was not mine and she could dispose of it as she pleased, and that she wanted to dispose of it not as I wished her to. And I could do nothing either to her or to him. He, like Vánka the Steward,* could sing a song before the gallows of how he kissed the sugared lips and so forth. And he would triumph. If she has not yet done it but wishes to – and I know that she does wish to – it is still worse; it would be

---

* *Vánka the Steward* is the subject and name of some old Russian poems. Vánka seduces his master's wife, boasts of having done so, and is hanged.

better if she had done it and I knew it, so that there would be an end to this uncertainty. I could not have said what it was I wanted. I wanted her not to desire that which she was bound to desire. It was utter insanity.

XXVI

'At the last station but one, when the conductor had been to collect the tickets, I gathered my things together and went out onto the brake-platform, and the consciousness that the crisis was at hand still further increased my agitation. I felt cold, and my jaw trembled so that my teeth chattered. I automatically left the terminus with the crowd, took a cab, got in, and drove off. I rode looking at the few passers-by, the night-watch-men,[90] and the shadows of my trap thrown by the street lamps, now in front and now behind me, and did not think of anything. When we had gone about half a mile my feet felt cold, and I remembered that I had taken off my woollen stockings in the train and put them in my satchel. "Where is the satchel? Is it here? Yes." And my wicker trunk? I remembered that I had entirely forgotten about my luggage, but finding that I had the luggage-ticket I decided that it was not worth while going back for it, and so continued my way.

[91]"Try now as I will, I cannot recall my state of mind at the time. What did I think? What did I want? I don't know at all. All I remember is a consciousness that something dreadful and very important in my life was imminent. Whether that import-ant event occurred because I thought it would, or whether I had a presentiment of what was to happen, I don't know. It may even be that after what has happened all the foregoing moments have acquired a certain gloom in my mind. I drove up to the front porch. It was past midnight. Some cabmen were waiting in front of the porch expecting, from the fact that there were lights in the windows, to get fares. (The lights were in our flat, in the dancing-room and drawing-room.) Without considering why it was still light in our windows so late, I went upstairs in the same state of expectation of something dreadful, and rang. Egór, a kind, willing, but very

stupid footman, opened the door. The first thing my eyes fell on in the hall was a man's cloak hanging on the stand with other outdoor coats. I ought to have been surprised but was not, for I had expected it. "That's it!" I said to myself. When I asked Egór who the visitor was and he named Trukha-chévski, I inquired whether there was anyone else. He replied, "Nobody, sir." I remember that he replied in a tone as if he wanted to cheer me and dissipate my doubts of there being anybody else there. "So it is, so it is," I seemed to be saying to myself. "And the children?" "All well, heaven be praised. In bed, long ago."

'I could not breathe, and could not check the trembling of my jaw. "Yes, so it is not as I thought: I used to expect a misfortune but things used to turn out all right and in the usual way. Now it is not as usual, but is all as I pictured to myself. I thought it was only fancy, but here it is, all real. Here it all is . . . !"

'I almost began to sob, but the devil immediately suggested to me: "Cry, be sentimental, and they will get away quietly. You will have no proof and will continue to suffer and doubt all your life." And my self-pity immediately vanished, and[92] a strange sense of joy arose in me, that my torture would now be over, that now I could punish her, could get rid of her, and could vent my anger. And I gave vent to it – I became a beast, a cruel and cunning beast.

'"Don't!" I said to Egór, who was about to go to the drawing-room. "Here is my luggage-ticket, take a cab as quick as you can and go and get my luggage. Go!" He went down the passage to fetch his overcoat. Afraid that he might alarm them, I went as far as his little room and waited while he put on his overcoat. From the drawing-room, beyond another room, one could hear voices and the clatter of knives and plates. They were eating and had not heard the bell. "If only they don't come out now," thought I. Egór put on his overcoat, which had an astrakhan collar, and went out. I locked the door after him and felt creepy when I knew I was alone and must act at once. How, I did not yet know. I only knew that all was now over, that there could be no doubt as to her guilt, and that I should punish her immediately and end my relations with her.

'Previously I had doubted and had thought: "Perhaps after all it's not true, perhaps I am mistaken." But now it was so no longer. It was all irrevocably decided. "Without my knowledge she is alone with him at night! That is a complete disregard of everything! Or worse still: it is intentional boldness and impudence in crime, that the boldness may serve as a sign of innocence. All is clear. There is no doubt." I only feared one thing – their parting hastily, inventing some fresh lie, and thus depriving me of clear evidence[93] and of the possibility of proving the fact. So as to catch them more quickly I went on tiptoe to the dancing-room where they were, not through the drawing-room but through the passage and nurseries.

'In the first nursery slept the boys. In the second nursery the nurse moved and was about to wake, and I imagined to myself what she would think when she knew all; and such pity for myself seized me at that thought that I could not restrain my tears, and not to wake the children I ran on tiptoe into the passage and on into my study, where I fell sobbing on the sofa.

' "I, an honest man, I, the son of my parents, I, who have all my life dreamt of the happiness of married life; I, a man who was never unfaithful to her.... And now! Five children, and she is embracing a musician because he has red lips!

' "No, she is not a human being. She is a bitch, an abominable bitch! In the next room to her children whom she has all her life pretended to love. And writing to me as she did! Throwing herself so barefacedly on his neck! But what do I know? Perhaps she long ago carried on with the footmen, and so got the children who are considered mine!

' "To-morrow I should have come back and she would have met me with her fine coiffure, with her elegant waist and her indolent, graceful movements" (I saw all her attractive, hateful face), "and that beast of jealousy would for ever have sat in my heart lacerating it. What will the nurse think? ... And Egór? And poor little Lisa! She already understands something. Ah, that impudence, those lies! And that animal sensuality which I know so well," I said to myself.

'I tried to get up but could not. My heart was beating so that I could not stand on my feet. "Yes, I shall die of a stroke. She will kill me. That is just what she wants. What is killing to her? But no, that would be too advantageous for her and I will not give her that pleasure. Yes, here I sit while they eat and laugh and . . . Yes, though she was no longer in her first freshness he did not disdain her. For in spite of that she is not bad looking, and above all she is at any rate not dangerous to his precious health. And why did I not throttle her then?" I said to myself, recalling the moment when, the week before, I drove her out of my study and hurled things about. I vividly recalled the state I had then been in; I not only recalled it, but again felt the need to strike and destroy that I had felt then. I remember how I wished to act, and how all considerations except those necessary for action went out of my head. I entered into that condition when an animal or a man, under the influence of physical excitement at a time of danger, acts with precision and deliberation but without losing a moment and always with a single definite aim in view.

'The first thing I did was to take off my boots and, in my socks, approach the sofa, on the wall above which guns and daggers were hung. I took down a curved Damascus dagger that had never been used and was very sharp. I drew it out of its scabbard. I remember the scabbard fell behind the sofa, and I remember thinking "I must find it afterwards or it will get lost". Then I took off my overcoat which I was still wearing, and stepping softly in my socks I went there.[94]

XXVII

'HAVING crept up stealthily to the door, I suddenly opened it.[95] I remember the expression of their faces. I remember that expression because it gave me a painful pleasure – it was an expression of terror. That was just what I wanted. I shall never forget the look of desperate terror that appeared on both their faces the first instant they saw me. He I think was sitting at the table, but on seeing or hearing me he jumped to his feet and stood with his back to the cupboard. His face expressed nothing but quite unmistakable terror. Her face too expressed terror but there was something else besides. If it had expressed only terror, perhaps what happened might not have happened; but on her face there was, or at any rate so it seemed to me at the first moment, also an expression of regret and annoyance that love's raptures and her happiness with him had been disturbed. It was as if she wanted nothing but that her present happiness should not be interfered with. These expressions remained on their faces but an instant. The look of terror on his changed immediately to one of inquiry: might he, or might he not, begin lying? If he might, he must begin at once; if not, something else would happen. But what? . . . He looked inquiringly at her face. On her face the look of vexation and regret changed as she looked at him (so it seemed to me) to one of solicitude for him.

'For an instant I stood in the doorway holding the dagger behind my back.

'At that moment he smiled, and in a ridiculously indifferent tone remarked: "And we have been having some music."

'"What a surprise!" she began, falling into his tone. But neither of them finished; the same fury I had experienced the week before overcame me. Again I felt that need of destruction, violence, and a transport of rage, and yielded to it. Neither finished what they were saying. That something else began which he had feared and which immediately destroyed all they were saying. I rushed towards her, still hiding the dagger that he might not prevent my striking her in the side under her breast. I selected that spot from the first. Just as I rushed at her he saw it, and – a thing I never expected of him – seized me by the arm and shouted: "Think what you are doing! . . . Help, someone! . . ."

'I snatched my arm away and rushed at him in silence. His eyes met mine and he suddenly grew as pale as a sheet to his very lips. His eyes flashed in a peculiar way, and – what again I had not expected – he darted under the piano and out at the door. I was going to rush after him, but a weight hung on my left arm. It was she. I tried to free myself, but she hung on yet more heavily and would not let me go. This unexpected hindrance, the weight, and her touch which was loathsome to me, inflamed me still more. I felt that I was quite mad and that I must look frightful, and this delighted me. I swung my left arm with all my might, and my elbow hit her straight in the face. She cried out and let go my arm. I wanted to run after him, but remembered that it is ridiculous to run after one's wife's lover in one's socks; and I did not wish to be ridiculous but terrible. In spite of the fearful frenzy I was in, I was all the time aware of the impression I might produce on others, and was even partly guided by that impression. I turned towards her. She fell on the couch, and holding her hand to her bruised eyes, looked at me. Her face showed fear and hatred of me, the enemy, as a rat's does when one lifts the trap in which it has been caught. At any rate I saw nothing in her expression but this fear and hatred of me. It was just the fear and hatred of me which would be evoked by love for another. But still I might perhaps have restrained myself and not done what I did had she remained silent. But she suddenly began to speak and to catch hold of the hand in which I held the dagger.

'"Come to yourself! What are you doing? What is the matter? There has been nothing, nothing, nothing.... I swear it!"

'I might still have hesitated, but those last words of hers, from which I concluded just the opposite – that everything had happened – called forth a reply. And the reply had to correspond to the temper to which I had brought myself, which continued to increase and had to go on increasing. Fury, too, has its laws.

'"Don't lie, you wretch!" I howled, and seized her arm with my left hand, but she wrenched herself away. Then, still without letting go of the dagger, I seized her by the throat with my left hand, threw her backwards, and began throttling her. What a firm neck it was ...! She seized my hand with both hers trying to pull it away from her throat, and as if I had only waited for that, I struck her with all my might with the dagger in the side below the ribs.

'When people say they don't remember what they do in a fit of fury, it is rubbish, falsehood. I remembered everything and did not for a moment lose consciousness of what I was doing. The more frenzied I became the more brightly the light of consciousness burnt in me, so that I could not help knowing everything I did. I knew what I was doing every second. I cannot say that I knew beforehand what I was going to do; but I knew what I was doing when I did it, and even I think a little before, as if to make repentance possible and to be able to tell myself that I could stop. I knew I was hitting below the ribs and that the dagger would enter. At the moment I did it I knew I was doing an awful thing such as I had never done before, which would have terrible consequences. But that consciousness passed like a flash of lightning and the deed immediately followed the consciousness. I realized the action with extraordinary clearness. I felt, and remember, the momentary resistance of her corset and of something else, and then the plunging of the dagger into something soft. She seized the dagger with her hands, and cut them, but could not hold it back.

'For a long time afterwards, in prison when the moral change had taken place in me, I thought of that moment, recalled what I could of it, and considered it. I remembered that for an instant, only an instant, before the action I had a terrible consciousness that I was killing, had killed, a defenceless woman, my wife! I remember the horror of that consciousness and conclude from that, and even dimly remember, that having plunged the dagger in I pulled it out immediately, trying to remedy what had been done and to stop it. I stood for a second motionless waiting to see what would happen, and whether it could be remedied.

'She jumped to her feet and screamed: "Nurse! He has killed me."

'Having heard the noise the nurse was standing by the door. I continued to stand waiting, and not believing the truth. But the blood rushed from under her corset.[96] Only then did I understand that it could not be remedied, and I immediately decided that it was not necessary it should be, that I had done what I wanted and had to do. I waited till she fell down, and the nurse, crying "Good God!" ran to her, and only then did I throw away the dagger and leave the room.

' "I must not be excited; I must know what I am doing," I said to myself without looking at her and at the nurse. The nurse was screaming – calling for the maid. I went down the passage, sent the maid, and went into my study. "What am I to do now?" I asked myself, and immediately realized what it must be. On entering the study I went straight to the wall, took down a revolver and examined it – it was loaded – I put it on the table. Then I picked up the scabbard from behind the sofa and sat down there.

'I sat thus for a long time. I did not think of anything or call anything to mind. I heard the sounds of bustling outside. I heard someone drive up, then someone else. Then I heard and saw Egór bring into the room my wicker trunk he had fetched. As if anyone wanted that!

' "Have you heard what has happened?" I asked. "Tell the yard-porter to inform the police." He did not reply, and went away. I rose, locked the door, got out my cigarettes and matches and began to smoke. I had not finished the cigarette before sleep overpowered me. I must have slept for a couple of hours. I remember dreaming that she and I were friendly together, that we had quarrelled but were making it up, there was something rather in the way, but we were friends. I was awakened by someone knocking at the door. "That is the police!" I thought, waking up. "I have committed murder, I think. But perhaps it is *she*, and nothing has happened." There was again a knock at the door. I did not answer, but was trying to solve the question whether it had happened or not. Yes, it had! I remembered the resistance of the corset and the plunging in of the dagger, and a cold shiver ran down my back. "Yes, it has. Yes, and now I must do away with myself too," I thought. But I thought this knowing that I should *not* kill myself. Still I got up and took the revolver in my hand. But it is strange: I remember how I had many times been near suicide, how even that day on the railway it had seemed easy, easy just because I thought how it would stagger her – now I was not only unable to kill myself but even to think of it. "Why should

I do it?" I asked myself, and there was no reply. There was more knocking at the door. "First I must find out who is knocking. There will still be time for this." I put down the revolver and covered it with a newspaper. I went to the door and unlatched it. It was my wife's sister, a kindly, stupid widow. "Vásya, what is this?" and her ever ready tears began to flow.

' "What do you want?" I asked rudely. I knew I ought not to be rude to her and had no reason to be, but I could think of no other tone to adopt.

' "Vásya, she is dying! Iván Zakhárych says so." Iván Zakhárych was her doctor and adviser.

' "Is he here?" I asked, and all my animosity against her surged up again. "Well, what of it?"

' "Vásya, go to her. Oh, how terrible it is!" said she.

' "Shall I go to her?" I asked myself, and immediately decided that I must go to her. Probably it is always done, when a husband has killed his wife, as I had – he must certainly go to her. "If that is what is done, then I must go," I said to myself. "If necessary I shall always have time," I reflected, referring to the shooting of myself, and I went to her. "Now we shall have phrases, grimaces, but I will not yield to them," I thought. "Wait," I said to her sister, "it is silly without boots, let me at least put on slippers."

XXVIII

'WONDERFUL to say, when I left my study and went through the familiar rooms, the hope that nothing had happened again awoke in me; but the smell of that doctor's nastiness – iodoform and carbolic – took me aback. "No, it had happened." Going down the passage past the nursery I saw little Lisa. She looked at me with frightened eyes. It even seemed to me that all the five children were there and all looked at me. I approached the door, and the maid opened it from inside for me and passed out. The first thing that caught my eye was her light-grey dress thrown on a chair and all stained black with blood. She was lying on one of the twin beds (on mine because it was easier to get at), with her knees raised. She lay in a very sloping position supported by pillows, with her dressing jacket unfastened. Something had been put on the wound. There was a heavy smell of iodoform in the room. What struck me first and most of all was her swollen and bruised face, blue on part of the nose and under the eyes. This was the result of the blow with my elbow when she had tried to hold me back. There was nothing beautiful about her, but something repulsive as it seemed to me. I stopped on the threshold. "Go up to her, do," said her sister. "Yes, no doubt she wants to confess," I thought. "Shall I forgive her? Yes, she is dying and may be forgiven," I thought, trying to be magnanimous. I went up close to her. She raised her eyes to me with difficulty, one of them was black, and with an effort said falteringly:

'"You've got your way, killed..." and through the look of suffering and even the nearness of death her face had the old expression of cold animal hatred that I knew so well. "I shan't... let you have... the children, all the same.... She (her sister) will take..."

'Of what to me was the most important matter, her guilt, her faithlessness, she seemed to consider it beneath her to speak.

'"Yes, look and admire what you have done," she said looking towards the door, and she sobbed. In the doorway stood her sister with the children. "Yes, see what you have done."

'I looked at the children and at her bruised disfigured face, and for the first time I forgot myself, my rights, my pride, and for the first time saw a human being in her.[97] And so insignificant did all that had offended me, all my jealousy, appear, and so important what I had done, that I wished to fall with my face to her hand, and say: "Forgive me," but dared not do so.

'She lay silent with her eyes closed, evidently too weak to say more. Then her disfigured face trembled and puckered. She pushed me feebly away.

'"Why did it all happen? Why?"

'"Forgive me," I said.

[98]'"Forgive! That's all rubbish!... Only not to die!..." she cried, raising herself, and her glittering eyes were bent on me. "Yes, you have had your way!...I hate you! Ah! Ah!" she cried, evidently already in delirium and frightened at something. "Shoot! I'm not afraid!... Only kill everyone...! He has gone...! Gone...!"

'After that the delirium continued all the time. She did not recognize[99] anyone. She died towards noon that same day. Before that they had taken me to the police-station and from there to prison. There, during the eleven months I remained awaiting trial, I examined myself and my past, and understood it. I began to understand it on the third day: on the third day they took me *there...*'

He was going on but, unable to repress his sobs, he stopped. When he recovered himself he continued:

'I only began to understand when I saw her in her coffin...'

He gave a sob, but immediately continued hurriedly:

'Only when I saw her dead face did I understand all that I had done. I realized that I, I, had killed her; that it was my doing that she, living, moving, warm, had now become motionless, waxen, and cold, and that this could never, anywhere, or by any means, be remedied. He who has not lived through it cannot understand.... Ugh! Ugh! Ugh!...' he cried several times and then was silent.

We sat in silence a long while. He kept sobbing and trembling as he sat opposite me without speaking. His face had grown narrow and elongated and his mouth seemed to stretch right across it.

'Yes,' he suddenly said. 'Had I then known what I know now, everything would have been different. Nothing would have induced me to marry her.... I should not have married at all.'

Again we remained silent for a long time.

[100]'Well, forgive me....'* He turned away from me and lay down on the seat, covering himself up with his plaid. At

---

* In Russian the word for 'forgive me' is very similar to that for 'good-bye', and is sometimes used in place of the latter.

the station where I had to get out (it was at eight o'clock in the morning) I went up to him to say good-bye. Whether he was asleep or only pretended to be, at any rate he did not move. I touched him with my hand. He uncovered his face, and I could see he had not been asleep.

'Good-bye,' I said, holding out my hand. He gave me his and smiled slightly, but so piteously that I felt ready to weep.

'Yes, forgive me . . .' he said, repeating the same words with which he had concluded his story.

APPENDIX

The following are the readings of the lithograph:

1 *Add*: with remarkable glittering eyes of an indefinite colour, which attracted attention. *Some of the description that follows is omitted.*

2 *Read*: At first the clerk said that the place opposite was engaged; to which the old man replied that he was only going as far as the next station.

3 *Read*: considering probably that this did not at all infringe the dignity his figure and manner denoted, . . .

4 *For the above paragraph read*: 'And then come discord, financial troubles, mutual recrimination, and the married couple separate,' said the lawyer.

5 *In place of the two preceding lines, read*: said the lady, evidently encouraged by the general attention and approval.

6 *The old man here replies*: 'Men are a different matter.' *And the lady says*: 'Then to a man, in your opinion, everything is permitted.'

7 *Add*: 'Or if some stupid man cannot control his wife – it serves him right. But all the same one must not create a scandal about it. Love or don't love, but don't break up the home. Every husband can keep his wife in order, he has the right to do it. Only a fool can't manage it.'

8 *In place of this paragraph read*: 'But you yourself may go on the spree with the girls at Kunávin,' said the lawyer with a smile.

9 *Add*: a vein on his forehead stood out,

10 *The lithograph here reads differently, and the words that follow are*: 'How do you mean "what kind of love"?' said the lady. 'The ordinary love of married couples.'

'But how can ordinary love sanctify marriage?' continued the nervous gentleman. He was as agitated as though he were angry and wished to speak unpleasantly to the lady. She felt this and was also agitated.

'How? Very simply,' said she. The nervous gentleman at once seized on the word.

'No, not simply!'

11 *Add*: and least of all for his wife. That is what the proverb says, and it is a true one. "Another's wife is a swan, but one's own is bitter wormwood."

325

12 *Read*: Even if one admits that Menelaus might prefer Helen for his whole lifetime, Helen would prefer Paris.

13 *Add*: ... of Helen with Menelaus or vice versa. The only difference is that with one it comes sooner and with another later. It is only written in stupid novels that they loved one another all their lives, and only children can believe that.

14 *Add*: 'This identity of ideals does not occur among old people, but always between handsome and young ones. And I assert that love, real love, does not sanctify marriage as we are accustomed to suppose for one's whole life, but on the contrary destroys it.'

15 *Add*: And we feel this, and to avoid it we preach "love". In reality the preaching of free love is only a call to return to the mingling of the sexes – excuse me,' said he, turning to the lady, 'to fornication. The old basis has worn out, and we must find a new one, but not preach depravity!' He had become so excited that we all remained silent and looked at him.

'And at present the transition stage is terrible. People feel that it will not do to allow adultery, and that sexual relations must in some way be defined; but bases for this are lacking, except the old ones in which no one any longer believes. And people go on getting married in the old way without believing in what they are doing, and the result is either deception or coercion.

16 *Add*: and do not themselves know why or what for,

17 *Add*: In the course of his story he did not once stop after that, and not even the entry of fresh passengers interrupted him. During his narration his face completely changed several times so that nothing resembling the former face remained: his eyes, his mouth, his moustache and even his beard were all different – it was a beautiful, touching, new face. These changes occurred suddenly in the dim light, and for some five minutes there was one face and it was impossible to see the former face, and then, one did not know how, another face appeared and again it was impossible to see it otherwise.

18 *Add*: ... my life and all my terrible story. Terrible, really terrible. The whole story is more terrible than the end.

19 *Add*: In the first place let me tell you who I am. I am the son of a rich landowner in the steppes, and I took a degree in law at the university. I married when I was rather over thirty, but before telling of my marriage I must say how I lived previously and how I regarded family life.

20 *Add*: This – the fact that I considered myself moral – came about because in our family there was not any of that particular specialized vice which was so common in our landowning class, and therefore, being brought up in a family where neither my father nor my mother was unfaithful, I nursed the dream of a most elevated and poetic family life from my early years. My wife had to be the height of perfection. Our mutual love had to be most elevated. The purity of our family life was to be dove-like. So I thought, and I praised myself all the time for having such elevated

thoughts. And at the same time, for ten years, I lived as an adult, in no haste to get married, and led what I called a respectable, reasonable, bachelor life.

21 *Add*: and I was naïvely confident that I was quite a moral man. The women I was intimate with were not mine, and I had nothing to do with them except for the pleasure they afforded me. And I saw nothing disgraceful in this.

22 *Add*: ... in regard to the real woman-question...'

'That is to say... what do you understand to be the real woman-question?'

'The question of what this organic creature that is distinct from man is, and how she herself and men also should regard her.

23 *For this paragraph read*: 'Yes, for ten years I lived in most disgraceful debauchery, dreaming of a pure, elevated love—and even in the name of that love. Yes, I want to tell of how I killed my wife, and to tell that I must tell how I became depraved.

'I killed her before I met her; I killed a woman the first time I knew one without loving her, and it was already then that I killed my wife.

24 *Read*: Who deprave youths? They do! Who deprave women by devising means for them and teaching them not to bear children? Who treat syphilis with enthusiasm? They.'

'But why not treat syphilis?'

'Because to cure syphilis is the same as to safeguard vice; it is the same as the Foundlings Hospital for discarded babies.'

'No, not the same... *Then omit to end of paragraph*.

25 *Insert here*: To tell the truth without false shame, I was trapped and caught. Her mamma – her papa was dead – arranged all sorts of traps and one of them – namely boating – succeeded.

26 *Insert*: No, say what you will, we live up to our ears in such a swamp of lies that unless we have our heads bumped, as I did, we cannot come to our senses.

27 *Add*: How fortunate that would have been for us!

28 *Add*: If we only reject the conventional explanations of why and for what reason these things are done, if we ...

29 *Add*: There is no difference. Strictly defining the matter, one must say that prostitutes for short terms are usually despised, while prostitutes for long terms are respected.

30 *Add*: The men of our circle are kept and fed like breeding stallions. It is only necessary, you know, to close the safety-valve – that is, for a vicious young man to live a continent life for a little while – and immediately a terrible restlessness and excitement is caused, which passing through the prism of the artificial conditions of our social life shows itself in the guise of falling in love. Our love affairs and marriages, for the most part, are conditioned by our food. You are surprised: one ought to be surprised that we have not noticed it sooner.

31 *Read*: through the prism of novels, stories, verses, music – through the idle, luxurious setting of our life – and there will be amorousness of the purest water.

32 *Read*: ...her parents, knowing more of life and not distracted by a momentary infatuation, but yet loving her not less than they loved themselves – arranged the marriage.

33 *Instead of the following lines, read*: and we talk of woman's rights, of "freedom" which is somehow obtainable at university lectures.'

34 *Add*: and as she cannot consent to be a slave and cannot herself propose, there begins that other abominable lie which is sometimes called "coming out into society", and sometimes "amusing themselves", and which is nothing but husband-hunting.

35 *Add*: 'They all complain that they are deprived of rights and are oppressed.

36 *Add*: Look at the people's fêtes, and at our balls and parties. Woman knows how she acts, you can see that by her triumphant smile.

37 *Add*: whether they believe in that or not – is unimportant.

38 *Add*: My sister, when very young, married a man twice her age and a debauchee. I remember how astonished we were the night of the wedding, when she ran out of her bedroom in tears and, shaking all over, said that she could on no account, on no account, even tell us what he had wanted to do to her.

39 *Add*: A pure girl only wants children. Children, – yes, but not a husband.'

'How then,' I said with astonishment, 'how is the human race to be continued?'

'And why should it be continued?' was his unexpected rejoinder.

40 *Add*: You know that Schopenhauer, Hartmann, and all the Buddhists too, declare that it is a blessing not to live. And they are so far right that welfare for humanity coincides with self-annihilation, only they have not expressed themselves rightly: they say that the human race should destroy itself to escape from suffering – that its aim should be self-destruction. That is wrong. The aim of humanity cannot be to escape from suffering by self-destruction, because sufferings are the result of activity, and the aim of an activity cannot be to destroy its consequences. The aim both of men and of humanity is blessedness. For the attainment of blessedness a law has been given to humanity which it should fulfil. The law is that of the union of mankind.

41 *In the lithographed version there are a number of small differences in the last paragraphs of Chapter XI, and Chapter XII commences with the words*: 'It is a strange story,' said I.

'What is there strange about it? According to all Church teaching the end of the world is coming, and according to all that science teaches the same thing is inevitable. So what is there strange in the fact that moral teaching reaches the same result? "He that is able to receive it, let him receive it," said

Christ. And I understand that just as he said it. For morality to exist between people in sexual relations it is necessary that the aim they set themselves should be complete chastity. In striving towards chastity, man falls; he falls, and the result is a moral marriage; but if, as in our society, man aims directly at physical love, then though it may clothe itself in the pseudo-moral form of marriage, that will merely be permitted debauchery with one woman – and will none the less be an immoral life, such as that in which I perished and destroyed her, and such as among us is called moral family life. Note what a perverse conception exists among us, when the happiest position for a man – that of freedom, celibacy – is considered pitiable and ridiculous. And the highest ideal, the best position, for a woman – that of being pure, a vestal, a virgin – is a thing to be afraid of and a subject for ridicule in our society. How many and many young girls have offered up their purity to that Moloch of opinion by marrying good-for-nothing fellows, merely to avoid remaining virgin, which is the highest state. For fear that she may remain in that highest state she ruins herself! But I did not then understand that the words in the Gospel – that he who looks upon a woman with desire has already committed adultery with her in his heart – refer not to other wives only, but specially and chiefly to one's own. I did not understand that, and thought that this honeymoon and my behaviour on this honeymoon were most excellent, and that to satisfy desire with my own wife was a perfectly right thing. *Then follow in the lithographed version the words*: You know those wedding tours, &c.

42 *Read*: As happens with mirthful young people who, unable to devise funny things to laugh at quickly enough, laugh at their own laughter, so we had not time to devise excuses for our hatred.

43 *Read*: 'We all – men and women – are brought up to a kind of veneration for that feeling which we are accustomed to call love. From childhood I prepared to fall in love, and I fell in love; all my youth I was in love and was glad to be so. It was instilled into me that there was no nobler and more exalted business in the world than to be in love. Well at last the expected feeling comes, and a man devotes himself to it. But that is where the deception appears. In theory love is something ideal . . .

44 *Add*: I would order them – those wizards – to perform the office of those women who, in their opinion, are necessary to men – and then let them talk!

45 *Add*: According to the view existing in our society a woman's vocation is to afford pleasure to man, and the education given her corresponds with this view. From childhood she learns only how to be more attractive. Girls are all taught to think entirely of that. As serfs were brought up to satisfy their masters and it could not be otherwise, so also all our women are educated to attract men and this too cannot be otherwise. But you will perhaps say that this is true only of badly brought-up girls – those who among us are contemptuously called "young ladies" – you will say there is another, a serious education, supplied in high-schools – even classical ones

LEO TOLSTOY

– in midwifery, and in medical and university courses. That is not true. All female education of whatever kind has in view only the capture of men. Some girls captivate men by music and curls; others by learning and by political services. But the aim is always the same and cannot be other, because there is no other than that of charming a man so as to capture him. Can you imagine courses for women, and scholarship for women, without men: that is to say, that they should be educated but that men should not know about it? I cannot! No bringing up, no education, can alter this as long as woman's highest ideal remains marriage, and not virginity and freedom from sensuality. Till then she will be a slave. You know one need only think – forgetting how customary they are – of the conditions in which our young ladies are brought up, and we shall be surprised not at the vice which rules among the women of our propertied classes, but on the contrary that there is so little vice. Only think of the finery from early childhood, the adorning of herself, the cleanliness, the grace, the music, the reading of verses and novels, the songs and theatres and concerts for external and internal application, that is those they hear and those in which they perform. And with it all their complete physical idleness and the food they eat, with so much sweetness and so much fat in it. You see, it is only because it is all wrapped up and concealed that we do not know what those unfortunate girls suffer from the excitation of their sensuality: nine out of ten suffer and are unendurably tormented at the period of adolescence and later, if they do not get married by twenty. You know it is only that we do not want to see it, but anyone who has eyes sees that the majority of these unfortunates are so excited by this concealed sensuality (it is well if it is concealed) that they can do nothing, they only begin to live in the presence of a man. Their whole life is passed in preparations for coquetry and in coquetting. In the presence of men they overflow with life and become animated with sensual energy, but as soon as the man goes away their energy all droops and they cease to live. And this is not with some particular man but with any man, if only he is not quite repulsive. You will say, that is exceptional. No, this is the rule. Only it shows itself more strongly in some girls and less in others; none of them however lives a full life of her own, but only in dependence on man. When he is absent they are all alike and cannot help being alike, because for them all to attract to themselves as many men as possible is the highest ideal both of their girlhood and of their married life. And from this arises a feeling stronger than that one which I will not call their feminine vanity – the animal need of every female animal to attract to herself as many males as possible in order to have a chance of choosing. So it is in their girlhood and so it continues to be after marriage.

46 *Insert*: You must understand that in our world an opinion exists, shared by everyone, that woman is there to afford man enjoyment (and vice versa probably, but I don't know about that, I know my own part).

47 *Add*: from Pushkin's lines about "little feet".

48 *Read*: 'The emancipation of woman lies not in universities and law-courts but in the bedroom. Yes, and the struggle against prostitution lies not in the brothels but in the families.'

The arrangement of this chapter differs in the two versions, and the following passage occurs in the lithographed but is omitted in the printed version:

'But why so?' I asked.

'That is what is surprising – that no one wishes to know what is so clear and evident, and what the doctors ought to know and to preach, but about which they are silent. Man desires the law of nature – children; but the coming of children presents an obstacle to continuous enjoyment, and people who only desire continuous enjoyment have to devise means to evade that obstacle. And they have devised three such means. One is, by the receipt the rascals give, to cripple the woman by making her barren – which has always been, and must be, a misfortune for a woman – then man can quietly and constantly enjoy himself; the second way is polygamy, not honourable polygamy as among the Mohammedans but our base European polygamy, replete with falsehood and hypocrisy; and there is the third evasion – which is not even an evasion, but a simple, coarse, direct infringement of the laws of nature, and which is committed by all the husbands among the peasants and by most husbands in our so-called honourable families. I too lived in that way. We have not even reached the level of Europe, of Paris, of the *Zwei Kinder System*, or of the Mohammedans, and we have devised nothing of our own because we have not thought at all about the matter. We feel that there is something nasty in the one plan and in the other, and we wish to have families, but our barbarous view of woman remains the same and the result is yet worse. A woman with us must at one and the same time be pregnant and be her husband's mistress – must be a nursing mother and his mistress. But her strength cannot stand it.'

49 *The lithographed version of Chapter XV begins with a long section on jealousy, omitted in the printed version*:

'Yes, jealousy is one of the secrets of marriage that are known to all and hidden from everybody. Besides the general reason for married couples' hatred of one another – which is their co-operation in defiling a human being – mutual jealousy is continually gnawing at them. But by mutual agreement it is generally decided to conceal this from everyone, and it is so concealed. Knowing that this is so, each assumes that it is an unhappy peculiarity of his own and not the common lot. So it was with me. So it must be. Jealousy must exist between married couples who live immorally with one another. If they are both unable to sacrifice their own pleasure for the welfare of their child, each rightly concludes that the other will certainly not sacrifice pleasure – I will not say for welfare or tranquillity (for one may sin so as not to be found out), but – merely for conscience's sake. Each knows that no strong moral obstacle to unfaithfulness exists in the other. They know this because they infringe the demands of morality with one another, and therefore they distrust and watch each other. Oh, what an awful feeling jealousy is! I am not speaking of that real jealousy which at any rate has some basis. That real jealousy is tormenting but it has, and promises, a result; but I am speaking of the unconscious jealousy which inevitably accompanies every immoral marriage, and which, having no definite cause, has also no end. The other is an abscess on a tooth, but this is a tooth aching with its bone – unchanging pain day and night, and again day and night, and unendingly. This jealousy is dreadful, really dreadful! It is like this: a young man is pleasantly talking to my wife and looking at her, as it seems to me, examining her body. How dare he think about her, or dream of a romance with her! But she not merely tolerates it, she is apparently quite pleased. I even see that she is behaving in the same way to him as he is doing to her. And in my soul there arises such a hatred of her that every word of hers and every gesture becomes repulsive. She notices this, and does not know what she is to do, and she puts on an air of animated indifference. "Ah! I suffer and she finds it amusing, she is well satisfied!" And the hatred increases tenfold but I dare not give it vent, for in the depth of my soul I know that there is no real ground for it. And I sit, pretending to be indifferent, and put on an air of special regard and politeness towards him. Then I become angry with myself and wish to get out of the room and leave them alone, and I really go out. But as soon as I am out I am seized with horror at what is going on in my absence. I go back – inventing some excuse for doing so; or sometimes I do not re-enter the room but stop at the door and listen. How can she humiliate herself and me, putting me – me – in such a mean position of suspicion and eaves-dropping! What meanness! Oh, the nasty beast! And he, he! What about him? He is what all men are, what I was when a bachelor. For him it is a pleasure. He even smiles when he looks at me as though saying: "What can you say about it? It is my turn now!" Oh, that feeling is terrible! The sting of that feeling is terrible: I had only to let loose that feeling on anyone if but once – it was enough if once I suspected a man of having designs on my wife – and that man was for ever spoilt for me, as if vitriol had been poured over him. It was enough for me to be jealous of a man once and I could never afterwards renew simple human relations with him. For ever after that, our eyes flashed when we looked at one another. As for my wife, whom I deluged with quantities of this vitriol of jealous hatred, I entirely disfigured her. During this period of unfounded hatred, I quite dethroned and shamed her in my imagination. I imagined the most impossible tricks on her part. I suspected her, I am ashamed to say, of behaving like the queen in the *Arabian Nights*: being unfaithful to me with a slave almost before my very eyes, and then laughing at me. So that with each fresh access of jealousy (I am still speaking of groundless jealousy) I fell into an already prepared rut of filthy suspicions about her and I made the rut deeper and deeper. She did the same. If I had reasons for jealousy, she, knowing my past, had a thousand times more. And she was even more jealous of me. And the sufferings I experienced from her jealousy were quite different and were also very severe. They occurred like this: we are living more or less quietly; I am even merry and tranquil, when we happen to begin a most ordinary conversation and all at once she does not agree with things she had always agreed with. More than that, I notice that she is becoming irritable without a cause. I think she is upset or that what we are saying is really unpleasant to her. But we turn to something else and the same thing happens, she again attacks me and is again irritable. I am astonished and seek the cause of this. What is it all about? She becomes silent, replies in monosyllables, or when she speaks is evidently hinting at something. I begin to guess that the reason of it is that I have taken a walk in the garden with her cousin, with whom I never even thought of anything wrong, or there is some cause of that kind. I begin to guess at it but cannot mention it. Were I to do so I should confirm her suspicions. I begin to investigate and to interrogate her. She does not reply but guesses that I have understood what it is, and she feels still more strongly confirmed in her suspicions. "What is the matter with you?" I ask. "Nothing, I am the same as usual," she says; but like a lunatic she utters meaningless, inexplicable, and bitter words. Sometimes I endure it, but sometimes I burst out and become irritable myself, and then a flood of abuse pours forth and I am convicted of some imaginary offence. And all this is carried to an extreme with sobs and tears, and she rushes out of the house to most unusual places. I begin to search for her. I am uneasy as to what the servants and children will think but there is nothing for it. She is in such a state that I feel she may do anything. I run after her and look for her. I spend tormenting nights. And finally, with exhausted nerves, after most cruel words and accusations, we both become tranquillized again.

50 *The lithographed version varies here considerably from the printed version, though in some passages the one repeats the other. The lithograph runs as follows*:

That is why they do not wish to suckle them: "If I suckle him," they say, "I shall love him too much – and what shall I do then if he dies?" It seems that they would prefer it if their children were gutta-percha, so that they could not be ill or die but could always be mended. Think what a muddle goes on in the heads and hearts of these unfortunate women. That is why they do nasty things to prevent births: so as not to love! Love – the most joyful condition of the soul – seems to them a danger. And why is this so? Because when a man or woman does not live as a human being should, he or she is much worse than a beast. You see, our women are unable to regard a child otherwise than as a pleasure. It is true that the birth is painful, but its little hands. . . . Ah, its little feet! Ah, it smiles! Ah, what a darling little body it has! Ah, and it smacks its lips and hiccups! In a word, the animal maternal instinct is sensual. There is in it no thought at all of the mysterious meaning of the arrival of a new human being who will replace us. There is nothing of what is said and done in baptism. You know, nobody believes in baptism, and yet that was really a reminder of the human importance of the baby. People have given that up, they do not believe in it, but they have not replaced it in any way, and only the ribbons and lace and little hands and feet have remained. The animal part has remained. But the thing is that an animal does not possess imagination or foresight or reflections or doctors – yes – again those doctors! Take a hen or a cow: when a chicken gets the pip or a calf dies she cackles a bit or lows a little, and goes on living as before. When among us a child falls ill – what happens? How is it to be treated? Where is it to be nursed? What doctor must we call in? Where is one to drive to? And if it should die – where will the little hands and little feet be then? Why has it all happened so? Why do we have this suffering? A cow does not ask this, and this is why our children are a torment. A cow has no imagination, and therefore cannot think of how she might have saved her offspring by doing so-and-so and so-and-so; and therefore her grief, mingling with her physical condition and continuing for a certain limited time, is not a condition of grief which is augmented by physical idleness and satiation till it becomes despair. She has not a reason which asks, "Why has this happened? Why were all these sufferings endured, why did I love the babies – if they had to die?" The cow has no reason which could say that in future it will be better not to bear offspring or if that happens accidentally then not to suckle it and in general not to love it, or things will be worse for her. But that is how our women reason. And it shows that when a human being does not live humanly, it is worse for him or her than for a beast.'

'Then what, in your opinion, is the human way in which one should treat children?' I asked.

'How? Love them humanly.'

'Well, don't mothers love their children?'

'Not like human beings, they hardly ever do that, and therefore they do not even love them in dog-fashion. Just notice: a hen, a goose, a she-wolf, are always unattainable models of animal love for our women. Few women would at the risk of their lives rush at an elephant to take their baby from him, but no hen, and no she-crow even, would fail to fly at a dog; and each of them would sacrifice itself for its children, while few women would do so. Notice that a human mother can refrain from physical love of her children while an animal cannot do so. Well, is that because a woman is inferior to an animal? No, but because she is superior (though "superior" is incorrect; she is not "superior", but is a different creature). She has other obligations – human ones; she can refrain from animal love and can transfer her love to the child's soul. That is becoming to a human mother, and that is what never is done in our society. We read of the heroism of mothers who sacrifice their children for the sake of something higher, and it seems to us that these cases are merely stories of ancient times, which have no relation to us. But yet I think that if a mother has nothing for the sake of which she can sacrifice her animal feelings for her child, and if she transfers the spiritual force, which has been left unapplied, to attempting the impossible – the physical preservation of her child – in which attempt the doctors will assist her, it will be much worse for her, and she will suffer, as she actually does suffer! So it was with my wife. Whether there was one child or five – it was always the same. It was even a little better when we had five of them. Our whole life was continually poisoned by fear on the children's account – fear of their real or imaginary illnesses – and even by their very presence. I at any rate, during my whole married life, always felt that my life and all my interests continually hung by a hair, and depended on the children's health and condition and lessons. Children are of course an important matter, but then we all have to live! In our times the grown-ups are not allowed to live. They have no proper life: the life of the whole family hangs every second by a hair; and family life, life for the married couple, is lacking. No matter what important affair you may have, if you suddenly hear that Vásya has vomited, or Lisa's motion shows signs of blood, everything has instantly to be left, forgotten, thrown away. Everything else is insignificant.... The only important things are the doctors, the enemas, the temperatures: not to mention the fact that you can never begin a conversation without it happening at the most interesting part that Pétya runs in with a troubled face to ask whether he is to eat an apple or which jacket he is to put on, or without the nurse bringing in a shrieking baby. There is no regular firm family life. How you are to live, where to live, and therefore what your occupation is to be, all depends on the children's health; while their health does not depend on anyone, but, thanks to the doctors who say that they can preserve their health, your whole life may be disturbed at any moment. There is no life; it is a constant peril.'

51 *Add*: But besides this, the children were for her also a means of forgetting herself – an intoxication. I often noticed that when she was upset about anything she felt better if one of the children fell ill and she could revert to that state of intoxication. But it was an involuntary intoxication; there was nothing evil about it.

52 *Add*: Of course the doctors confirmed all this with an air of importance and encouraged her in the belief. She would have been glad not to be afraid, but the doctor dropped a word or two about "blood-poisoning", "scarlatina", or (God forbid) "dysentery" – and it was all up! Nor could it be otherwise. You see, if among us women had, as in olden times, a belief that "The Lord gave, and the Lord hath taken away", that a young child's angel-soul goes to God and it is better for him – the dead child – to die in innocence than to die later on in sin, and so forth, which is what people did believe, you know – if they had any faith of that sort, they could bear the children's illnesses more quietly; but now there is nothing of that sort left – not a trace of it. There is no belief of that kind. But one must have faith in something, and they have faith – a senseless faith – in medicine – and not even in medicine but in doctors. One woman in I. I., and another in P. P.; and like religious believers they do not see the absurdity of their faith but believe *quia absurdum*. You know, if they did not believe irrationally, they would see the absurdity of what those brigands prescribe – the whole of it. Scarlatina is an infectious disease; on account of it, in a large town, half the family has to move into an hotel (they twice made us move in that way). But, you see, everyone in a town is a centre of innumerable diameters which carry the threads of all kinds of infection, and there is no possibility of

avoiding them: the baker, the tailor, the laundress, and the cabman. So that for everyone who moves out of his own house to another place to escape an infection he knows of, I will undertake to find, in that other place, another infection – if not the very same infection – as near at hand. But that is not enough. We all know of rich people who after diphtheria have had every-thing in their house destroyed, and in that house when freshly done up, have themselves fallen ill; and we all know of dozens of people who have remained with the sick ones and have not been infected. And so it is with everything; one only need keep one's ears open. One woman tells another that her doctor is a good one. The other replies: "What are you saying? Why, he killed so-and-so." And vice versa. Well, bring a country doctor to a lady and she won't trust him; but bring another doctor in a carriage, who knows precisely as much and who treats his patients on the basis of the same books and the same experiments, and tell her that he must be paid £10 for each visit, and she will believe in him. The root of the matter is that our women are savages. They have no faith in God, and so some of them believe in an evil eye cast by wicked people and others in Doctor I. P. because he charges high fees. If they had faith they would know that scarlatina and so forth is not at all so terrible, for it cannot injure what one can and should love – namely, the soul, and that sickness and death which none of us can avoid may occur. But as there is no faith in God they only love physically and all their energy is directed towards preserving life, which cannot be done, and which only the doctors assure fools, and especially she-fools, that they can save. And so they have to be called in. Therefore having children, far from improving our relations to one another, did not unite us but on the contrary divided us.

53 *In the lithographed version the chapter continues*: At first we lived in the country, and later on in town. What I chiefly felt was that I was a man, and that a man, as I understood it, ought to be master, but that I had fallen under my wife's slipper, as the saying is, and could not manage to escape from under it. What chiefly kept me under her slipper was the children. I wished to get up and assert my authority, but it never came off. She had the children and, supporting herself on them, she ruled. I did not then understand that she was sure to rule, chiefly because when she married she was morally immea-surably superior to me as all maidens always are to man, because they are immeasurably purer than he. Notice this surprising fact, that a woman, an average woman of our circle, is usually a very poor creature, lacking moral bases, an egotist, a chatterbox, and wrong-headed, but a maiden, an ordinary maiden, a girl up to twenty years of age, is for the most part a charming creature ready for everything noble and good. Why is that so? Clearly it is because the husbands pervert their wives and bring them morally down to their own lower level. In fact if boys and girls are born equal the advantage on the girls' side is still enormous. In the first place a girl is not exposed to those vicious conditions to which we are exposed; she has not the smoking, the wine, the cards, the schools, the comrades, or the state-service we have,

and secondly and chiefly she is physically virgin. And so a maiden when she marries is always superior to her husband. She is superior to him while she is a maiden, and when she becomes a married woman, in our circle where the men are under no direct compulsion to earn their own maintenance, she usually becomes superior to him also by the greater importance of her occupation when she begins to bear children and to feed them. A woman when bearing and nursing, clearly sees that her occupation is more important than the man's – who sits on the County Council,* in Courts of Justice, or in the Senate. She knows that in all such affairs the one important thing is to get money. But money can be got in various other ways, and therefore the getting of it is not so indubitably necessary as the feeding of a child. So that the woman is certainly superior to the man and ought to rule him. But a man of our circle not only does not acknowledge this, but on the contrary always looks down on woman from the height of his grandeur, and despises her activity. So my wife despised me and my County activities, on the ground that she bore and nursed children. While I, supported by the established masculine view, considered that a woman's fussing: "swaddlings, teats, and teething," as I jokingly called it, is a most contemptible activity which one may and should jest about. "The women know how to attend to that." So besides all other causes we were also separated by mutual contempt.

54 *Instead of the next nine lines, read*: To people who were quite strangers to us she and I spoke of various subjects, but not with one another. Sometimes hearing how she spoke to other people in my presence, I said to myself: "What lies she is telling!" And I was surprised that the person she was speaking to did not see that she was pretending.

55 *Add*: The periods of what we called love occurred as often as before, but were barer, coarser, and lacked any cover. But they did not last long and were immediately followed by periods of quite causeless anger springing up on most unintelligible grounds.

56 *Add*: All these were occupations that were not directly necessary, but she always behaved as if her life and that of the children depended on the pies with the soup not being burnt, on the curtain being hung up, the dress finished, the lesson learnt, and some medicine or other taken. It was clear to me that all this was for her mainly a means of forgetting herself, an intoxication, such as was for me the intoxication of my service, shooting, or cards. It is true that besides these I also had intoxication in its direct meaning – drunkenness: with tobacco, of which I smoked an enormous quantity, and alcohol with which I did not actually get drunk, but of which I took some vodka before meals and a couple of tumblers of wine during meals, so that a continual fog screened from us the discord of our life.

57 *Add*: All this mental illness of ours occurred simply because we lived immorally. We suffered from our immoral life, and to smother our suffering

* The *Zémskoe Sobránie*, work in the administration of which was paid for.

we committed various abnormal acts – just what those doctors call "indications of mental disease" – hysterics. The cure for these illnesses does not lie with Charcot, nor with them. It cannot be cured by any suggestions or bromides, but it is necessary to recognize what the pain comes from. It is like sitting down on a nail: if you notice the nail, or see what is wrong in your life and cease to do it, the pain will cease and there will be nothing to smother. The wrongness of our life caused the pain, caused my torments of jealousy and my need of going out shooting, of cards, and above all of wine and tobacco to keep myself in a constant state of intoxication. From that wrongness of life arose also her passionate relation to all her occupations, her instability of mood – now gloomy, now terribly gay, – and her volubility – it all came from the constant need of diverting her attention from herself and her life. It was a constant intoxication with this or that work, which always had to be done in a hurry.

58 *Add*: Unhappy people can get on better in town.

59 *Instead of the following line, read*: Divorce, well then divorce!" My sister-in-law would not admit that idea.

60 *Read*: but I have bound myself by my own words.

61 *Read*: disliked him and understood that he was a dirty adulterer, and I began to be jealous of him even before he saw my wife.

62 *Read*: why, in the important events of our life, in those which decide a man's fate – as mine was decided then – why, there is no distinction between past and future.

63 *Instead of the following three lines, read*: I had a consciousness of some terrible calamity connected with that man. But for all that I could not help being affable with him.

64 *Read*: He played excellently, with a strong and tender tone; difficulties did not exist for him. As soon as he began to play his face altered, became serious and far more sympathetic; he was of course a much better player than my wife and helped her simply and naturally.

65 *Read*: . . . simple and pleasant. During the whole evening I seemed not only to the others, but to myself, to be solely interested in the music, while in reality I was unceasingly tormented by jealousy. From the first moment that his eyes met my wife's I saw that he looked at her as at a woman who was not unpleasant and with whom on occasion it would not be unpleasant to have a liaison. Had I been pure I should not have thought about what he might think of her, but like most men I also thought about women, and therefore understood him and was tormented by it.

66 *Read*: his restrained voice and her refusal. She seemed to say "but no", and something more. It was as if someone was intentionally smothering the words. My God, what then arose in me! What I imagined!

67 *Add*: She will disgrace me! I will go away – but I can't.

68 *Add*: and advised me to see it out.

69 *Add*: A husband ought not to think so, and still less should he shove his nose in and hinder things.

70 *Read*: graceful, indolent, subtle figure,

71 *Add*: or something of that kind about my character.

72 *Instead of the next six lines, read*: and I turned her round and gave her a violent push. "What is the matter with you? Recollect yourself!" said she.

73 *Add*: rolling my eyes.

74 *Read*: I restrained myself and

75 *Add*: We sent for the doctor, and I attended her all night.

76 *Add*: . . . not so much on account of my wife's assurances, as on account of the tormenting suffering I had experienced from my jealousy.

77 *Add*: He went to fetch his violin. My wife went to the piano and began selecting the music.

78 *Add*: and long remained silent.

79 *Add*: In this new condition jealousy had no place.

80 *Add*: That music drew me into some world in which jealousy no longer had place. Jealousy and the feeling that evoked it seemed trifles not worth considering.

81 *Instead of the next eleven lines, read*: I hardly felt jealous all the evening. I had to go to the Meetings in two days' time, and he, when leaving, collected all his music and inquired when I should be back, as he wished to say good-bye before his own departure. . . . It appeared that I should hardly be back before he left Moscow, so we bade one another a definite good-bye.

82 *Add*: We spoke in very general terms of the impressions produced by the music, but we were nearer and more friendly to one another that evening, in a way we had seldom been of late.

83 *Read*: while it was still dark,

84 *Add*: and as if I should drive on like that to the end of my life and of the world,

85 *Add*: which was quite a new one,

86 *Add*: one more cynical than another,

87 *Add*: forgetting that there was no ground for this.

88 *Instead of the next line, read*: I cried out, and began to groan.

89 *Add*: And the same thing began again within me. I suffered as I never had suffered before. I did not know what to do with myself, and the thought occurred to me – and it pleased me very much – of getting out onto the line, lying down under the train, and finishing everything. The one thing that hindered my doing this was my self-pity, which immediately evoked hatred of her and of him. Of him not so much. Regarding him I had a strange feeling of my own humiliation and of his victory, but of her I felt terrible hatred. It will not do to finish myself off and to leave her, it is necessary that she should suffer.

90 *Instead of the following words, read*: and read the shop sign-boards,

91 *Instead of the next sentence, read*: I cannot at all explain to myself now why I was in such a hurry.

92 *Read*: there arose in me an animal craving for physical, agile, cunning, and decisive action.

93 *Read*: and of the tormenting pleasure of punishing, and executing.

94 *In the lithograph the chapter ends with the words*: I do not know how I went, with what steps, whether I ran or only walked, through which rooms I went on my way to the drawing-room, how I opened the door or how I entered the room – I remember nothing of all that.

95 *In the lithograph this first sentence is omitted.*

96 *Add*: as from a spring.

97 *Add*: – a sister.

98 *Read*: ' "Yes, if you had not killed me!" she suddenly exclaimed, and her eyes glittered feverishly.

99 *The sentence ends*: the children, not even Lisa who rushed up to her.

100 *In the lithograph the conclusion is different, the last paragraph being as follows*: Yes, that is what I have done, and what I have gone through. Yes, a man should understand that the real meaning of the words in the Gospel – Matthew v. 28 – where it says that everyone that looketh on a woman to lust after her commits adultery, relates to woman, his fellow human being – not merely to casual women or strangers, but above all to his own wife.

THE DEVIL

But I say unto you, that every one that looketh on a woman to lust after her hath committed adultery with her already in his heart.

And if thy right eye causeth thee to stumble, pluck it out, and cast it from thee: for it is profitable for thee that one of thy members should perish, and not thy whole body be cast into hell.

And if thy right hand causeth thee to stumble, cut it off, and cast it from thee: for it is profitable for thee that one of thy members should perish, and not thy whole body go into hell. *Matthew* v. 28, 29, 30.

I

A BRILLIANT career lay before Eugène Irténev. He had everything necessary to attain it: an admirable education at home, high honours when he graduated in law at Petersburg University, and connexions in the highest society through his recently deceased father; he had also already begun service in one of the Ministries under the protection of the Minister. Moreover he had a fortune; even a large one, though insecure. His father had lived abroad and in Petersburg, allowing his sons, Eugène and Andrew (who was older than Eugène and in the Horse Guards), six thousand rubles a year each, while he himself and his wife spent a great deal. He only used to visit his estate for a couple of months in summer and did not concern himself with its direction, entrusting it all to an unscrupulous manager who also failed to attend to it, but in whom he had complete confidence.

After the father's death, when the brothers began to divide the property, so many debts were discovered that their lawyer even advised them to refuse the inheritance and retain only an estate left them by their grandmother, which was valued at a hundred thousand rubles. But a neighbouring landed proprietor who had done business with old Irténev, that is to say, who had promissory notes from him and had come to Petersburg on that account, said that in spite of the debts they could straighten out affairs so as to retain a large fortune (it would only be necessary to sell the forest and some outlying land, retaining the rich Semënov estate with four thousand desyatins of black earth, the sugar factory, and two hundred desyatins of water-meadows) if one devoted oneself to the management of the estate, settled there, and farmed it wisely and economically.

And so, having visited the estate in spring (his father had died in Lent), Eugène looked into everything, resolved to retire from the Civil Service, settle in the country with his mother, and undertake the management with the object of preserving the main estate. He arranged with his brother, with whom he was very friendly, that he would pay him either four thousand rubles a year, or a lump sum of eighty thousand, for which Andrew would hand over to him his share of the inheritance.

So he arranged matters and, having settled down with his mother in the big house, began managing the estate eagerly, yet cautiously.

It is generally supposed that conservatives are usually old people, and that those in favour of change are the young. That is not quite correct. Usually conservatives are young people: those who want to live but who do not think about how to live, and have not time to think, and therefore take as a model for themselves a way of life that they have seen.

Thus it was with Eugène. Having settled in the village, his aim and ideal was to restore the form of life that had existed, not in his father's time – his father had been a bad manager – but in his grandfather's. And now he tried to resurrect the general spirit of his grandfather's life – in the house, the garden, and in the estate management – of course with changes suited to the times – everything on a large scale – good order, method, and everybody satisfied. But to do this entailed much work. It was necessary to meet the demands of the creditors and the banks, and for that purpose to sell some land and arrange renewals of credit. It was also necessary to get money to carry on (partly by farming out land, and partly by hiring labour) the immense operations on the Semënov estate, with its four hundred desyatins of ploughland and its sugar factory, and to deal with the garden so that it should not seem to be neglected or in decay.

There was much work to do, but Eugène had plenty of strength – physical and mental. He was twenty-six, of medium height, strongly built, with muscles developed by gymnastics. He was full-blooded and his whole neck was very red, his teeth and lips were bright, and his hair soft and curly though not thick. His only physical defect was short-sightedness, which he had himself developed by using spectacles, so that he could not now do without a pince-nez, which had already formed a line on the bridge of his nose.

Such he was physically. For his spiritual portrait it might be said that the better people knew him the better they liked him. His mother had always loved him more than anyone else, and now after her husband's death she concentrated on him not only her whole affection but her whole life. Nor was it only his mother who so loved him. All his comrades at the high school and the university not merely liked him very much, but respected him. He had this effect on all who met him. It was impossible not to believe what he said, impossible to suspect any deception or falseness in one who had such an open, honest face and in particular such eyes.

In general his personality helped him much in his affairs. A creditor who would have refused another trusted him. The clerk, the village Elder, or a peasant, who would have played a dirty trick and cheated someone else, forgot to deceive under the pleasant impression of intercourse with this kindly, agreeable, and above all candid man.

It was the end of May. Eugène had somehow managed in town to get the vacant land freed from the mortgage, so as to sell it to a merchant, and had borrowed money from that same merchant to replenish his stock, that is to say, to procure horses, bulls, and carts, and in particular to begin to build a necessary farm-house. The matter had been arranged. The timber was being carted, the carpenters were already at work, and manure for the estate was being brought on eighty carts, but everything still hung by a thread.

II

AMID these cares something came about which though unimportant tormented Eugène at the time. As a young man he had lived as all healthy young men live, that is, he had had relations with women of various kinds. He was not a libertine but neither, as he himself said, was he a monk. He only turned to this, however, in so far as was necessary for physical health and to have his mind free, as he used to say. This had begun when he was sixteen and had gone on satisfactorily – in the sense that he had never given himself up to debauchery, never once been infatuated, and had never contracted a disease. At first he had had a seamstress in Petersburg, then she got spoilt and he made other arrangements, and that side of his affairs was so well secured that it did not trouble him.

But now he was living in the country for the second month and did not at all know what he was to do. Compulsory self-restraint was beginning to have a bad effect on him.

Must he really go to town for that purpose? And where to? How? That was the only thing that disturbed him; but as he was convinced that the thing was necessary and that he needed it, it really became a necessity, and he felt that he was not free and that his eyes involuntarily followed every young woman.

He did not approve of having relations with a married woman or a maid in his own village. He knew by report that both his father and grandfather had been quite different in this matter from other landowners of that time. At home they had never had any entanglements with peasant-women, and he had decided that he would not do so either; but afterwards, feeling himself ever more and more under compulsion and imagining with horror what might happen to him in the neighbouring country town, and reflecting on the fact that the days of serfdom were now over, he decided that it might be done on the spot. Only it must be done so that no one should know of it, and not for the sake of debauchery but merely for health's sake – as he said to himself. And when he had decided this he became still more restless. When talking to the village Elder, the peasants, or the carpenters, he involuntarily brought the conversation round to women, and when it turned to women he kept it on that theme. He noticed the women more and more.

III

To settle the matter in his own mind was one thing but to carry it out was another. To approach a woman himself was impossible. Which one? Where? It must be done through someone else, but to whom should he speak about it?

He happened to go into a watchman's hut in the forest to get a drink of water. The watchman had been his father's huntsman, and Eugène Ivánich chatted with him, and the man began telling some strange tales of hunting sprees. It occurred to Eugène Ivánich that it would be convenient to arrange matters in this hut, or in the wood, only he did not know how to manage it and whether old Daniel would undertake the arrangement. 'Perhaps he will be horrified at such a proposal and I shall have disgraced myself, but perhaps he will agree to it quite simply.' So he thought while listening to Daniel's stories. Daniel was telling how once when they had been stopping at the hut of the sexton's wife in an outlying field, he had brought a woman for Fëdor Zakhárich Pryánishnikov.

'It will be all right,' thought Eugène.

'Your father, may the kingdom of heaven be his, did not go in for nonsense of that kind.'

'It won't do,' thought Eugène. But to test the matter he said: 'How was it you engaged in such bad things?'

'But what was there bad in it? She was glad, and Fëdor Zakhárich was satisfied, very satisfied. I got a ruble. Why, what was he to do? He too is a lively limb apparently, and drinks wine.'

'Yes, I may speak,' thought Eugène, and at once proceeded to do so.

'And do you know, Daniel, I don't know how to endure it,' – he felt himself going scarlet.

Daniel smiled.

'I am not a monk – I have been accustomed to it.'

He felt that what he was saying was stupid, but was glad to see that Daniel approved.

'Why of course, you should have told me long ago. It can all be arranged,' said he: 'only tell me which one you want.'

'Oh, it is really all the same to me. Of course not an ugly one, and she must be healthy.'

'I understand!' said Daniel briefly. He reflected.

'Ah! There is a tasty morsel,' he began. Again Eugène went red. 'A tasty morsel. See here, she was married last autumn.' Daniel whispered, – 'and he hasn't been able to do anything. Think what that is worth to one who wants it!'

Eugène even frowned with shame.

'No, no,' he said. 'I don't want that at all. I want, on the contrary' (what could the contrary be?), 'on the contrary I only want that she should be healthy and that there should be as little fuss as possible – a woman whose husband is away in the army or something of that kind.'

'I know. It's Stepanída I must bring you. Her husband is away in town, just the same as a soldier. And she is a fine woman, and clean. You will be satisfied. As it is I was saying to her the other day – you should go, but she . . . '

'Well then, when is it to be?'

'To-morrow if you like. I shall be going to get some tobacco and I will call in, and at the dinner-hour come here, or to the bath-house behind the kitchen garden. There will be nobody about. Besides after dinner everybody takes a nap.'

'All right then.'

A terrible excitement seized Eugène as he rode home. 'What will happen? What is a peasant woman like? Suppose it turns out that she is hideous, horrible? No, she is handsome,' he told himself, remembering some he had been noticing. 'But what shall I say? What shall I do?'

He was not himself all that day. Next day at noon he went to the forester's hut. Daniel stood at the door and silently and significantly nodded towards the wood. The blood rushed to Eugène's heart, he was conscious of it and went to the kitchen-garden. No one was there. He went to the bath-house – there was no one about, he looked in, came out, and suddenly heard the crackling of a breaking twig. He looked round – and she was standing in the thicket beyond the little ravine. He rushed there across the ravine. There were nettles in it which he had not noticed. They stung him and, losing the pince-nez from his nose, he ran up the slope on the farther side. She stood there, in a white embroidered apron, a red-brown skirt, and a bright red kerchief, barefoot, fresh, firm, and handsome, and smiling shyly.

'There is a path leading round – you should have gone round,' she said. 'I came long ago, ever so long.'

He went up to her and, looking her over, touched her.

A quarter of an hour later they separated; he found his pince-nez, called in to see Daniel, and in reply to his question: 'Are you satisfied, master?' gave him a ruble and went home.

He was satisfied. Only at first had he felt ashamed, then it had passed off. And everything had gone well. The best thing was that he now felt at ease, tranquil and vigorous. As for her, he had not even seen her thoroughly. He remembered that she was clean, fresh, not bad-looking, and simple, without any pretence. 'Whose wife is she?' said he to himself. 'Péchnikov's,' Daniel said. What Péchnikov is that? There are two households of that name. Probably she is old Michael's daughter-in-law. Yes, that must be it. His son does live in Moscow. I'll ask Daniel about it some time.'

From then onward that previously important drawback to country life – enforced self-restraint – was eliminated. Eugène's freedom of mind was no longer disturbed and he was able to attend freely to his affairs.

And the matter Eugène had undertaken was far from easy: before he had time to stop up one hole a new one would unexpectedly show itself, and it sometimes seemed to him that he would not be able to go through with it and that it would end in his having to sell the estate after all, which would mean that all his efforts would be wasted and that he had failed to accomplish what he had undertaken. That prospect disturbed him most of all.

All this time more and more debts of his father's unexpectedly came to light. It was evident that towards the end of his life he had borrowed right and left. At the time of the settlement in May, Eugène had thought he at last knew everything, but in the middle of the summer he suddenly received a letter from which it appeared that there was still a debt of twelve thousand rubles to the widow Esípova. There was no promissory note, but only an ordinary receipt which his lawyer told him could be disputed. But it did not enter Eugène's head to refuse to pay a debt of his father's merely because the document could be challenged. He only wanted to know for certain whether there had been such a debt.

'Mamma! Who is Kalériya Vladímirovna Esípova?' he asked his mother when they met as usual for dinner.

'Esípova? She was brought up by your grandfather. Why?' Eugène told his mother about the letter.

'I wonder she is not ashamed to ask for it. Your father gave her so much!'

'But do we owe her this?'

'Well now, how shall I put it? It is not a debt. Papa, out of his unbounded kindness . . .'

'Yes, but did Papa consider it a debt?'

'I cannot say. I don't know. I only know it is hard enough for you without that.'

Eugène saw that Mary Pávlovna did not know what to say, and was as it were sounding him.

'I see from what you say that it must be paid,' said he. 'I will go to see her to-morrow and have a chat, and see if it cannot be deferred.'

'Ah, how sorry I am for you, but you know that will be best. Tell her she must wait,' said Mary Pávlovna, evidently tranquillized and proud of her son's decision.

Eugène's position was particularly hard because his mother, who was living with him, did not at all realize his position. She had been so accustomed all her life long to live extravagantly that she could not even imagine to herself the position her son was in, that is to say, that to-day or to-morrow matters might shape themselves so that they would have nothing left and he would have to sell everything and live and support his mother on what salary he could earn, which at the very most would be two thousand rubles. She did not understand that they could only save themselves from that position by cutting down expense in everything, and so she could not understand why Eugène was so careful about trifles, in expenditure on gardeners, coachmen, servants – even on food. Also, like most widows, she nourished feelings of devotion to the memory of her departed spouse quite different from those she had felt for him while he lived, and she did not admit the thought that anything the departed had done or arranged could be wrong or could be altered.

Eugène by great efforts managed to keep up the garden and the conservatory with two gardeners, and the stables with two coachmen. And Mary Pávlovna naïvely thought that she was sacrificing herself for her son and doing all a mother could do, by not complaining of the food which the old man-cook prepared, of the fact that the paths in the park were not all swept clean, and that instead of footmen they had only a boy.

So, too, concerning this new debt, in which Eugène saw an almost crushing blow to all his undertakings, Mary Pávlovna only saw an incident displaying Eugène's noble nature. Moreover she did not feel much anxiety about Eugène's position, because she was confident that he would make a brilliant marriage which would put everything right. And he could make a very brilliant marriage: she knew a dozen families who would be glad to give their daughters to him. And she wished to arrange the matter as soon as possible.

IV

EUGÈNE himself dreamt of marriage, but not in the same way as his mother. The idea of using marriage as a means of putting his affairs in order was repulsive to him. He wished to marry honourably, for love. He observed the girls whom he met and those he knew, and compared himself with them, but no decision had yet been taken. Meanwhile, contrary to his expectations, his relations with Stepanída continued, and even acquired the character of a settled affair. Eugène was so far from debauchery, it was so hard for him secretly to do this thing which he felt to be bad, that he could not arrange these meetings himself and even after the first one hoped not to see Stepanída again; but it turned out that after some time the same restlessness (due he believed to that cause) again overcame him. And his restlessness this time was no longer impersonal, but suggested just those same bright, black eyes, and that deep voice, saying, 'ever so long', that same scent of something fresh and strong, and that same full breast lifting the bib of her apron, and all this in that hazel and maple thicket, bathed in bright sunlight.

Though he felt ashamed he again approached Daniel. And again a rendezvous was fixed for midday in the wood. This time Eugène looked her over more carefully and everything about her seemed attractive. He tried talking to her and asked about her husband. He really was Michael's son and lived as a coachman in Moscow.

'Well, then, how is it you . . .' Eugène wanted to ask how it was she was untrue to him.

'What about "how is it"?' asked she. Evidently she was clever and quick-witted.

'Well, how is it you come to me?'

'There now,' said she merrily. 'I bet he goes on the spree there. Why shouldn't I?'

Evidently she was putting on an air of sauciness and assurance, and this seemed charming to Eugène. But all the same he did not himself fix a rendezvous with her. Even when she proposed that they should meet without the aid of Daniel, to whom she seemed not very well disposed, he did not consent. He hoped that this meeting would be the last. He liked her. He thought such intercourse was necessary for him and that there was nothing bad about it, but in the depth of his soul there was a stricter judge who did not approve of it and hoped that this would be the last time, or if he did not hope that, at any rate did not wish to participate in arrangements to repeat it another time.

So the whole summer passed, during which they met a dozen times and always by Daniel's help. It happened once that she could not be there because her husband had come home, and Daniel proposed another woman, but Eugène refused with disgust. Then the husband went away and the meetings continued as before, at first through Daniel, but afterwards he simply fixed the time and she came with another woman, Prókhorova – as it would not do for a peasant-woman to go about alone.

Once at the very time fixed for the rendezvous a family came to call on Mary Pávlovna, with the very girl she wished

Eugène to marry, and it was impossible for Eugène to get away. As soon as he could do so, he went out as though to the threshing-floor, and round by the path to their meeting-place in the wood. She was not there, but at the accustomed spot everything within reach had been broken – the black alder, the hazel-twigs, and even a young maple the thickness of a stake. She had waited, had become excited and angry, and had skittishly left him a remembrance. He waited and waited, and then went to Daniel to ask him to call her for to-morrow. She came and was just as usual.

So the summer passed. The meetings were always arranged in the wood, and only once, when it grew towards autumn, in the shed that stood in her backyard.

It did not enter Eugène's head that these relations of his had any importance for him. About her he did not even think. He gave her money and nothing more. At first he did not know and did not think that the affair was known and that she was envied throughout the village, or that her relations took money from her and encouraged her, and that her conception of any sin in the matter had been quite obliterated by the influence of the money and her family's approval. It seemed to her that if people envied her, then what she was doing was good.

'It is simply necessary for my health,' thought Eugène. 'I grant it is not right, and though no one says anything, everybody, or many people, know of it. The woman who comes with her knows. And once she knows she is sure to have told others. But what's to be done? I am acting badly,' thought Eugène, 'but what's one to do? Anyhow it is not for long.'

What chiefly disturbed Eugène was the thought of the husband. At first for some reason it seemed to him that the husband must be a poor sort, and this as it were partly justified his conduct. But he saw the husband and was struck by his appearance: he was a fine fellow and smartly dressed, in no way a worse man than himself, but surely better. At their next meeting he told her he had seen her husband and had been surprised to see that he was such a fine fellow.

'There's not another man like him in the village,' said she proudly.

This surprised Eugène, and the thought of the husband tormented him still more after that. He happened to be at Daniel's one day and Daniel, having begun chatting, said to him quite openly:

'And Michael asked me the other day: "Is it true that the master is living with my wife?" I said I did not know. Anyway, I said, better with the master than with a peasant.'

'Well, and what did he say?'

'He said: "Wait a bit. I'll get to know and I'll give it her all the same." '

'Yes, if the husband returned to live here I would give her up,' thought Eugène.

But the husband lived in town and for the present their intercourse continued.

'When necessary I will break it off, and there will be nothing left of it,' thought he.

And this seemed to him certain, especially as during the whole summer many different things occupied him very fully: the erection of the new farm-house, and the harvest, and building, and above all meeting the debts and selling the waste land. All these were affairs that completely absorbed him and on which he spent his thoughts when he lay down and when he got up. All that was real life. His intercourse – he did not even call it connexion – with Stepanída he paid no attention to. It is true that when the wish to see her arose it came with such strength that he could think of nothing else. But this did not last long. A meeting was arranged, and he again forgot her for a week or even for a month.

In autumn Eugène often rode to town, and there became friendly with the Ánnenskis. They had a daughter who had just finished the Institute.[1] And then, to Mary Pávlovna's great grief, it happened that Eugène 'cheapened himself', as she

---

1 The Institute was a boarding-school for the daughters of the nobility and gentry, in which great attention was paid to the manners and accomplishments of the pupils.

expressed it, by falling in love with Liza Ánnenskaya and proposing to her.

From that time his relations with Stepanída ceased.

V

I T is impossible to explain why Eugène chose Liza Ánnens-kaya, as it is always impossible to explain why a man chooses this and not that woman. There were many reasons – positive and negative. One reason was that she was not a very rich heiress such as his mother sought for him, another that she was naïve and to be pitied in her relations with her mother, another that she was not a beauty who attracted general attention to herself, and yet she was not bad-looking. But the chief reason was that his acquaintance with her began at the time when he was ripe for marriage. He fell in love because he knew that he would marry.

Liza Ánnenskaya was at first merely pleasing to Eugène, but when he decided to make her his wife his feelings for her became much stronger. He felt that he was in love.

Liza was tall, slender, and long. Everything about her was long; her face, and her nose (not prominently but downwards), and her fingers, and her feet. The colour of her face was very delicate, creamy white and delicately pink; she had long, soft, and curly, light-brown hair, and beautiful eyes, clear, mild, and confiding. Those eyes especially struck Eugène, and when he thought of Liza he always saw those clear, mild, confiding eyes.

Such was she physically; he knew nothing of her spiritually, but only saw those eyes. And those eyes seemed to tell him all he needed to know. The meaning of their expression was this:

While still in the Institute, when she was fifteen, Liza used continually to fall in love with all the attractive men she met and was animated and happy only when she was in love. After leaving the Institute she continued to fall in love in just the same way with all the young men she met, and of course fell in love with Eugène as soon as she made his acquaintance. It was this being in love which gave her eyes that particular

expression which so captivated Eugène. Already that winter
she had been in love with two young men at one and the same
time, and blushed and became excited not only when they
entered the room but whenever their names were mentioned.
But afterwards, when her mother hinted to her that Irténev
seemed to have serious intentions, her love for him increased
so that she became almost indifferent to the two previous
attractions, and when Irténev began to come to their balls
and parties and danced with her more than with others and
evidently only wished to know whether she loved him, her
love for him became painful. She dreamed of him in her sleep
and seemed to see him when she was awake in a dark room,
and everyone else vanished from her mind. But when he
proposed and they were formally engaged, and when they
had kissed one another and were a betrothed couple, then
she had no thoughts but of him, no desire but to be with him,
to love him, and to be loved by him. She was also proud of
him and felt emotional about him and herself and her love, and
quite melted and felt faint from love of him.

The more he got to know her the more he loved her. He
had not at all expected to find such love, and it strengthened
his own feeling still more.

VI

TOWARDS spring he went to his estate at Semënovskoe to
have a look at it and to give directions about the management,
and especially about the house which was being done up for
his wedding.

Mary Pávlovna was dissatisfied with her son's choice, not
only because the match was not as brilliant as it might have
been, but also because she did not like Varvára Alexéevna, his
future mother-in-law. Whether she was good-natured or not
she did not know and could not decide, but that she was not
well-bred, not *comme il faut* – 'not a lady' as Mary Pávlovna said
to herself – she saw from their first acquaintance, and this
distressed her; distressed her because she was accustomed to
value breeding and knew that Eugène was sensitive to it, and

she foresaw that he would suffer much annoyance on this account. But she liked the girl. Liked her chiefly because Eugène did. One could not help loving her, and Mary Pávlovna was quite sincerely ready to do so.

Eugène found his mother contented and in good spirits. She was getting everything straight in the house and preparing to go away herself as soon as he brought his young wife. Eugène persuaded her to stay for the time being, and the future remained undecided.

In the evening after tea Mary Pávlovna played patience as usual. Eugène sat by, helping her. This was the hour of their most intimate talks. Having finished one game and while preparing to begin another, she looked up at him and, with a little hesitation, began thus:

'I wanted to tell you, Jénya – of course I do not know, but in general I wanted to suggest to you – that before your wedding it is absolutely necessary to have finished with all your bachelor affairs so that nothing may disturb either you or your wife. God forbid that it should. You understand me?'

And indeed Eugène at once understood that Mary Pávlovna was hinting at his relations with Stepanída which had ended in the previous autumn, and that she attributed much more importance to those relations than they deserved, as solitary women always do. Eugène blushed, not from shame so much as from vexation that good-natured Mary Pávlovna was bothering – out of affection no doubt, but still was bothering – about matters that were not her business and that she did not and could not understand. He answered that there was nothing that needed concealment, and that he had always conducted himself so that there should be nothing to hinder his marrying.

'Well, dear, that is excellent. Only, Jénya . . . don't be vexed with me,' said Mary Pávlovna, and broke off in confusion.

Eugène saw that she had not finished and had not said what she wanted to. And this was confirmed when a little later she began to tell him how, in his absence, she had been asked to stand godmother at . . . the Péchnikovs.

Eugène flushed again, not with vexation or shame this time, but with some strange consciousness of the importance of what was about to be told him – an involuntary consciousness quite at variance with his conclusions. And what he expected happened. Mary Pávlovna, as if merely by way of conversation, mentioned that this year only boys were being born – evidently a sign of a coming war. Both at the Vásins and the Péchnikovs the young wife had a first child – at each house a boy. Mary Pávlovna wanted to say this casually, but she herself felt ashamed when she saw the colour mount to her son's face and saw him nervously removing, tapping, and replacing his pince-nez and hurriedly lighting a cigarette. She became silent. He too was silent and could not think how to break that silence. So they both understood that they had understood one another.

'Yes, the chief thing is that there should be justice and no favouritism in the village – as under your grandfather.'

'Mamma,' said Eugène suddenly, 'I know why you are saying this. You have no need to be disturbed. My future family-life is so sacred to me that I should not infringe it in any case. And as to what occurred in my bachelor days, that is quite ended. I never formed any union and no one has any claims on me.'

'Well, I am glad,' said his mother. 'I know how noble your feelings are.'

Eugène accepted his mother's words as a tribute due to him, and did not reply.

Next day he drove to town thinking of his fiancée and of anything in the world except of Stepanída. But, as if purposely to remind him, on approaching the church he met people walking and driving back from it. He met old Matvéy with Simon, some lads and girls, and then two women, one elderly, the other, who seemed familiar, smartly dressed and wearing a bright-red kerchief. This woman was walking lightly and boldly, carrying a child in her arms. He came up to them, and the elder woman bowed, stopping in the old-fashioned way, but the young woman with the child only bent her head, and from under the kerchief gleamed familiar, merry, smiling eyes.

Yes, this was she, but all that was over and it was no use looking at her: 'and the child may be mine', flashed through his mind. No, what nonsense! There was her husband, she used to see him. He did not even consider the matter further, so settled in his mind was it that it had been necessary for his health – he had paid her money and there was no more to be said; there was, there had been, and there could be, no question of any union between them. It was not that he stifled the voice of conscience, no – his conscience simply said nothing to him. And he thought no more about her after the conversation with his mother and this meeting. Nor did he meet her again.

Eugène was married in town the week after Easter, and left at once with his young wife for his country estate. The house had been arranged as usual for a young couple. Mary Pávlovna wished to leave, but Eugène begged her to remain, and Liza still more strongly, and she only moved into a detached wing of the house.

And so a new life began for Eugène.

VII

THE first year of his marriage was a hard one for Eugène. It was hard because affairs he had managed to put off during the time of his courtship now, after his marriage, all came upon him at once.

To escape from debts was impossible. An outlying part of the estate was sold and the most pressing obligations met, but others remained, and he had no money. The estate yielded a good revenue, but he had had to send payments to his brother and to spend on his own marriage, so that there was no ready money and the factory could not carry on and would have to be closed down. The only way of escape was to use his wife's money; and Liza, having realized her husband's position, insisted on this herself. Eugène agreed, but only on condition that he should give her a mortgage on half his estate, which he did. Of course this was done not for his wife's sake, who felt offended at it, but to appease his mother-in-law.

These affairs with various fluctuations of success and failure helped to poison Eugène's life that first year. Another thing was his wife's ill-health. That same first year in autumn, seven months after their marriage, a misfortune befell Liza. She was driving out to meet her husband on his return from town, and the quiet horse became rather playful and she was frightened and jumped out. Her jump was comparatively fortunate – she might have been caught by the wheel – but she was pregnant, and that same night the pains began and she had a miscarriage from which she was long in recovering. The loss of the expected child and his wife's illness, together with the disorder in his affairs, and above all the presence of his mother-in-law, who arrived as soon as Liza fell ill – all this together made the year still harder for Eugène.

But notwithstanding these difficult circumstances, towards the end of the first year Eugène felt very well. First of all his cherished hope of restoring his fallen fortune and renewing his grandfather's way of life in a new form, was approaching accomplishment, though slowly and with difficulty. There was no longer any question of having to sell the whole estate to meet the debts. The chief estate, though transferred to his wife's name, was saved, and if only the beet crop succeeded and the price kept up, by next year his position of want and stress might be replaced by one of complete prosperity. That was one thing.

Another was that however much he had expected from his wife, he had never expected to find in her what he actually found. He found not what he had expected, but something much better. Raptures of love – though he tried to produce them – did not take place or were very slight, but he discovered something quite different, namely, that he was not merely more cheerful and happier but that it had become easier to live. He did not know why this should be so, but it was.

And it was so because immediately after marriage his wife decided that Eugène Irténev was superior to anyone else in the world: wiser, purer, and nobler than they, and that therefore it was right for everyone to serve him and please him; but that as it was impossible to make everyone do this, she must do it herself to the limit of her strength. And she did; directing all her strength of mind towards learning and guessing what he liked, and then doing just that thing, whatever it was and however difficult it might be.

She had the gift which furnishes the chief delight of intercourse with a loving woman: thanks to her love of her husband she penetrated into his soul. She knew his every state and his every shade of feeling – better it seemed to him than he himself – and she behaved correspondingly and therefore never hurt his feelings, but always lessened his distresses and strengthened his joys. And she understood not only his feelings but also his joys. Things quite foreign to her – concerning the farming, the factory, or the appraisement of others – she immediately understood so that she could not merely converse with him, but could often, as he himself said, be a useful and irreplaceable counsellor. She regarded affairs and people and everything in the world only through his eyes. She loved her mother, but having seen that Eugène disliked his mother-in-law's interference in their life she immediately took her husband's side, and did so with such decision that he had to restrain her.

Besides all this she had very good taste, much tact, and above all she had repose. All that she did, she did unnoticed; only the results of what she did were observable, namely, that always and in everything there was cleanliness, order, and elegance. Liza had at once understood in what her husband's ideal of life consisted, and she tried to attain, and in the arrangement and order of the house did attain, what he wanted. Children it is true were lacking, but there was hope of that also. In winter she went to Petersburg to see a specialist and he assured them that she was quite well and could have children.

And this desire was accomplished. By the end of the year she was again pregnant.

The one thing that threatened, not to say poisoned, their happiness was her jealousy – a jealousy she restrained and did not exhibit, but from which she often suffered. Not only might Eugène not love any other woman – because there was not a woman on earth worthy of him (as to whether she herself was worthy or not she never asked herself), – but not a single woman might therefore dare to love him.

VIII

THIS was how they lived: he rose early, as he always had done, and went to see to the farm or the factory where work was going on, or sometimes to the fields. Towards ten o'clock he would come back for his coffee, which they had on the veranda: Mary Pávlovna, an uncle who lived with them, and Liza. After a conversation which was often very animated while they drank their coffee, they dispersed till dinner-time. At two o'clock they dined and then went for a walk or a drive. In the evening when he returned from his office they drank their evening tea and sometimes he read aloud while she worked, or when there were guests they had music or conversation. When he went away on business he wrote to his wife and received letters from her every day. Sometimes she accompanied him, and then they were particularly merry. On his name-day and on hers guests assembled, and it pleased him to see how well she managed to arrange things so that everybody enjoyed coming. He saw and heard that they all admired her – the young, agreeable hostess – and he loved her still more for this.

All went excellently. She bore her pregnancy easily and, though they were afraid, they both began making plans as to how they would bring the child up. The system of education and the arrangements were all decided by Eugène, and her only wish was to carry out his desires obediently. Eugène on his part read up medical works and intended to bring the child up according to all the precepts of science. She of course agreed to everything and made preparations, making warm and also cool 'envelopes',[1] and preparing a cradle. Thus the second year of their marriage arrived and the second spring.

IX

IT was just before Trinity Sunday. Liza was in her fifth month, and though careful she was still brisk and active. Both his

---

1 An 'envelope' was a small mattress with a coverlet attached, on which babies were carried about.

mother and hers were living in the house, but under pretext of watching and safeguarding her only upset her by their tiffs. Eugène was specially engrossed with a new experiment for the cultivation of sugar-beet on a large scale.

Just before Trinity Liza decided that it was necessary to have a thorough house-cleaning as it had not been done since Easter, and she hired two women by the day to help the servants wash the floors and windows, beat the furniture and the carpets, and put covers on them. These women came early in the morning, heated the coppers, and set to work. One of the two was Stepanída, who had just weaned her baby boy and had begged for the job of washing the floors through the office-clerk – whom she now carried on with. She wanted to have a good look at the new mistress. Stepanída was living by herself as formerly, her husband being away, and she was up to tricks as she had formerly been first with old Daniel (who had once caught her taking some logs of firewood), afterwards with the master, and now with the young clerk. She was not concerning herself any longer about her master. 'He has a wife now,' she thought. But it would be good to have a look at the lady and at her establishment: folk said it was well arranged.

Eugène had not seen her since he had met her with the child. Having a baby to attend to she had not been going out to work, and he seldom walked through the village. That morning, on the eve of Trinity Sunday, he got up at five o'clock and rode to the fallow land which was to be sprinkled with phosphates, and had left the house before the women were about, and while they were still engaged lighting the copper fires.

He returned to breakfast merry, contented, and hungry; dismounting from his mare at the gate and handing her over to the gardener. Flicking the high grass with his whip and repeating a phrase he had just uttered, as one often does, he walked towards the house. The phrase was: 'phosphates justify' – what or to whom, he neither knew nor reflected.

They were beating a carpet on the grass. The furniture had been brought out.

'There now! What a house-cleaning Liza has undertaken!... Phosphates justify.... What a manageress she is!

A manageress! Yes, a manageress,' said he to himself, vividly imagining her in her white wrapper and with her smiling joyful face, as it nearly always was when he looked at her. 'Yes, I must change my boots, or else "phosphates justify", that is, smell of manure, and the manageress is in such a condition. Why "in such a condition"? Because a new little Irténev is growing there inside her,' he thought. 'Yes, phosphates justify,' and smiling at his thoughts he put his hand to the door of his room.

But he had not time to push the door before it opened of itself and he came face to face with a woman coming towards him carrying a pail, barefoot and with sleeves turned up high. He stepped aside to let her pass and she too stepped aside, adjusting her kerchief with a wet hand.

'Go on, go on, I won't go in, if you . . . ' began Eugène and suddenly stopped, recognizing her.

She glanced merrily at him with smiling eyes, and pulling down her skirt went out at the door.

'What nonsense! . . . It is impossible,' said Eugène to himself, frowning and waving his hand as though to get rid of a fly, displeased at having noticed her. He was vexed that he had noticed her and yet he could not take his eyes from her strong body, swayed by her agile strides, from her bare feet, or from her arms and shoulders, and the pleasing folds of her shirt and the handsome skirt tucked up high above her white calves.

'But why am I looking?' said he to himself, lowering his eyes so as not to see her. 'And anyhow I must go in to get some other boots.' And he turned back to go into his own room, but had not gone five steps before he again glanced round to have another look at her without knowing why or wherefore. She was just going round the corner and also glanced at him.

'Ah, what am I doing!' said he to himself. 'She may think . . . It is even certain that she already does think . . . '

He entered his damp room. Another woman, an old and skinny one, was there, and was still washing it. Eugène passed on tiptoe across the floor, wet with dirty water, to the wall where his boots stood, and he was about to leave the room when the woman herself went out.

'This one has gone and the other, Stepanída, will come here alone,' someone within him began to reflect.

'My God, what am I thinking of and what am I doing!' He seized his boots and ran out with them into the hall, put them on there, brushed himself, and went out onto the veranda where both the mammas were already drinking coffee. Liza had evidently been expecting him and came onto the veranda through another door at the same time.

'My God! If she, who considers me so honourable, pure, and innocent – if she only knew!' – thought he.

Liza as usual met him with shining face. But to-day some-how she seemed to him particularly pale, yellow, long, and weak.

X

DURING coffee, as often happened, a peculiarly feminine kind of conversation went on which had no logical sequence but which evidently was connected in some way for it went on uninterruptedly.

The two old ladies were pin-pricking one another, and Liza was skilfully manœuvring between them.

'I am so vexed that we had not finished washing your room before you got back,' she said to her husband. 'But I do so want to get everything arranged.'

'Well, did you sleep well after I got up?'

'Yes, I slept well and I feel well.'

'How can a woman be well in her condition during this intolerable heat, when her windows face the sun,' said Varvára Alexéevna, her mother. 'And they have no venetian-blinds or awnings. I always had awnings.'

'But you know we are in the shade after ten o'clock,' said Mary Pávlovna.

'That's what causes fever; it comes of dampness,' said Var-vára Alexéevna, not noticing that what she was saying did not agree with what she had just said. 'My doctor always says that it is impossible to diagnose an illness unless one knows the patient. And he certainly knows, for he is the leading physician and we pay him a hundred rubles a visit. My late husband did not believe in doctors, but he did not grudge me anything.'

'How can a man grudge anything to a woman when perhaps her life and the child's depend . . .'

'Yes, when she has means a wife need not depend on her husband. A good wife submits to her husband,' said Varvára Alexéevna – 'only Liza is too weak after her illness.'

'Oh no, mamma, I feel quite well. But why have they not brought you any boiled cream?'

'I don't want any. I can do with raw cream.'

'I offered some to Varvára Alexéevna, but she declined,' said Mary Pávlovna, as if justifying herself.

'No, I don't want any to-day.' And as if to terminate an unpleasant conversation and yield magnanimously, Varvára Alexéevna turned to Eugène and said: 'Well, and have you sprinkled the phosphates?'

Liza ran to fetch the cream.

'But I don't want it. I don't want it.'

'Liza, Liza, go gently,' said Mary Pávlovna. 'Such rapid movements do her harm.'

'Nothing does harm if one's mind is at peace,' said Varvára Alexéevna as if referring to something, though she knew that there was nothing her words could refer to.

Liza returned with the cream and Eugène drank his coffee and listened morosely. He was accustomed to these conversations, but to-day he was particularly annoyed by its lack of sense. He wanted to think over what had happened to him but this chatter disturbed him. Having finished her coffee Varvára Alexéevna went away in a bad humour. Liza, Eugène, and Mary Pávlovna stayed behind, and their conversation was simple and pleasant. But Liza, being sensitive, at once noticed that something was tormenting Eugène, and she asked him whether anything unpleasant had happened. He was not prepared for this question and hesitated a little before replying that there had been nothing. This reply made Liza think all the more. That something was tormenting him, and greatly tormenting, was as evident to her as that a fly had fallen into the milk, yet he would not speak of it. What could it be?

XI

AFTER breakfast they all dispersed. Eugène as usual went to his study, but instead of beginning to read or write his letters, he sat smoking one cigarette after another and thinking. He was terribly surprised and disturbed by the unexpected recrudescence within him of the bad feeling from which he had thought himself free since his marriage. Since then he had not once experienced that feeling, either for her – the woman he had known – or for any other woman except his wife. He had often felt glad of this emancipation, and now suddenly a chance meeting, seemingly so unimportant, revealed to him the fact that he was not free. What now tormented him was not that he was yielding to that feeling and desired her – he did not dream of so doing – but that the feeling was awake within him and he had to be on his guard against it. He had no doubt but that he would suppress it.

He had a letter to answer and a paper to write, and sat down at his writing-table and began to work. Having finished it and quite forgotten what had disturbed him, he went out to go to the stables. And again as ill-luck would have it, either by unfortunate chance or intentionally, as soon as he stepped from the porch a red skirt and red kerchief appeared from round the corner, and she went past him swinging her arms and swaying her body. She not only went past him, but on passing him ran, as if playfully, to overtake her fellow-servant.

Again the bright midday, the nettles, the back of Daniel's hut, and in the shade of the plane-trees her smiling face biting some leaves, rose in his imagination.

'No, it is impossible to let matters continue so,' he said to himself, and waiting till the women had passed out of sight he went to the office.

It was just the dinner-hour and he hoped to find the steward still there, and so it happened. The steward was just waking up from his after-dinner nap, and stretching himself and yawning was standing in the office, looking at the herdsman who was telling him something.

'Vasíli Nikoláich!' said Eugène to the steward.

'What is your pleasure?'

'I want to speak to you.'

'What is your pleasure?'

'Just finish what you are saying.'

'Aren't you going to bring it in?' said Vasíli Nikoláich to the herdsman.

'It's heavy, Vasíli Nikoláich.'

'What is it?' asked Eugène.

'Why, a cow has calved in the meadow. Well, all right, I'll order them to harness a horse at once. Tell Nicholas Lysúkh to get out the dray cart.'

The herdsman went out.

'Do you know,' began Eugène, flushing and conscious that he was doing so, 'do you know, Vasíli Nikoláich, while I was a bachelor I went off the track a bit. . . . You may have heard . . . '

Vasíli Nikoláich, evidently sorry for his master, said with smiling eyes: 'Is it about Stepanída?'

'Why, yes. Look here. Please, please do not engage her to help in the house. You understand, it is very awkward for me . . . '

'Yes, it must have been Ványa the clerk who arranged it.'

'Yes, please . . . and hadn't the rest of the phosphates better be strewn?' said Eugène, to hide his confusion.

'Yes, I am just going to see to it.'

So the matter ended, and Eugène calmed down, hoping that as he had lived for a year without seeing her, so things would go on now. 'Besides, Vasíli Nikoláich will speak to Iván the clerk; Iván will speak to her, and she will understand that I don't want it,' said Eugène to himself, and he was glad that he had forced himself to speak to Vasíli Nikoláich, hard as it had been to do so.

'Yes, it is better, much better, than that feeling of doubt, that feeling of shame.' He shuddered at the mere remembrance of his sin in thought.

XII

THE moral effort he had made to overcome his shame and speak to Vasíli Nikoláich tranquillized Eugène. It seemed to him that the matter was all over now. Liza at once noticed that he was quite calm, and even happier than usual. 'No doubt he was upset by our mothers pin-pricking one another. It really is disagreeable, especially for him who is so sensitive and noble, always to hear such unfriendly and ill-mannered insinuations,' thought she.

The next day was Trinity Sunday. It was a beautiful day, and the peasant-women, on their way into the woods to plait wreaths, came, according to custom, to the landowner's home and began to sing and dance. Mary Pávlovna and Varvára Alexéevna came out onto the porch in smart clothes, carrying sunshades, and went up to the ring of singers. With them, in a jacket of Chinese silk, came out the uncle, a flabby libertine and drunkard, who was living that summer with Eugène.

As usual there was a bright, many-coloured ring of young women and girls, the centre of everything, and around these from different sides like attendant planets that had detached themselves and were circling round, went girls hand in hand, rustling in their new print gowns; young lads giggling and running backwards and forwards after one another; full-grown lads in dark blue or black coats and caps and with red shirts, who unceasingly spat out sunflower-seed shells; and the domestic servants or other outsiders watching the dance-circle from aside. Both the old ladies went close up to the ring, and Liza accompanied them in a light blue dress, with light blue ribbons on her head, and with wide sleeves under which her long white arms and angular elbows were visible.

Eugène did not wish to come out, but it was ridiculous to hide, and he too came out onto the porch smoking a cigarette, bowed to the men and lads, and talked with one of them. The women meanwhile shouted a dance-song with all their might, snapping their fingers, clapping their hands, and dancing.

'They are calling for the master,' said a youngster coming up to Eugène's wife, who had not noticed the call. Liza called Eugène to look at the dance and at one of the women dancers who particularly pleased her. This was Stepanída. She wore a yellow skirt, a velveteen sleeveless jacket and a silk kerchief, and was broad, energetic, ruddy, and merry. No doubt she danced well. He saw nothing.

'Yes, yes,' he said, removing and replacing his pince-nez. 'Yes, yes,' he repeated. 'So it seems I cannot be rid of her,' he thought.

He did not look at her, fearing her attraction, and just on that account what his passing glance caught of her seemed to him especially attractive. Besides this he saw by her sparkling look that she saw him and saw that he admired her. He stood there as long as propriety demanded, and seeing that Varvára Alexéevna had called her 'my dear' senselessly and insincerely and was talking to her, he turned aside and went away.

He went into the house in order not to see her, but on reaching the upper storey he approached the window, without knowing how or why, and as long as the women remained at the porch he stood there and looked and looked at her, feasting his eyes on her.

He ran, while there was no one to see him, and then went with quiet steps onto the veranda, and from there, smoking a cigarette, he passed through the garden as if going for a stroll, and followed the direction she had taken. He had not gone two steps along the alley before he noticed behind the trees a velveteen sleeveless jacket, with a pink and yellow skirt and a red kerchief. She was going somewhere with another woman. 'Where are they going?'

And suddenly a terrible desire scorched him as though a hand were seizing his heart. As if by someone else's wish he looked round and went towards her.

'Eugène Ivánich, Eugène Ivánich! I have come to see your honour,' said a voice behind him, and Eugène, seeing old Samókhin who was digging a well for him, roused himself and turning quickly round went to meet Samókhin. While speaking with him he turned sideways and saw that she and the woman who was with her went down the slope, evidently to the well or making an excuse of the well, and having stopped there a little while ran back to the dance-circle.

XIII

AFTER talking to Samókhin, Eugène returned to the house as depressed as if he had committed a crime. In the first place she had understood him, believed that he wanted to see her, and desired it herself. Secondly that other woman, Anna Prókhorova, evidently knew of it.

Above all he felt that he was conquered, that he was not master of his own will but that there was another power moving him, that he had been saved only by good fortune, and that if not to-day then to-morrow or a day later, he would perish all the same.

'Yes, perish,' he did not understand it otherwise: to be unfaithful to his young and loving wife with a peasant-woman in the village, in the sight of everyone – what was it but to perish, perish utterly, so that it would be impossible to live? No, something must be done.

'My God, my God! What am I to do? Can it be that I shall perish like this?' said he to himself. 'Is it not possible to do anything? Yet something must be done. Do not think about her' – he ordered himself. 'Do not think!' and immediately he began thinking and seeing her before him, and seeing also the shade of the plane-tree.

He remembered having read of a hermit who, to avoid the temptation he felt for a woman on whom he had to lay his hand to heal her, thrust his other hand into a brazier and burnt his fingers. He called that to mind. 'Yes, I am ready to burn my fingers rather than to perish.' He looked round to make sure that there was no one in the room, lit a candle, and put a finger into the flame. 'There, now think about her,' he said to himself ironically. It hurt him and he withdrew his smoke-stained finger, threw away the match, and laughed at himself. What nonsense! That was not what had to be done. But it was necessary to do something, to avoid seeing her – either to go away himself or to send her away. Yes – send her away. Offer her husband money to remove to town or to another village. People would hear of it and would talk about it. Well, what of that? At any rate it was better than this danger. 'Yes, that must be done,' he said to himself, and at that very moment he was looking at her without moving his eyes. 'Where is she going?' he suddenly asked himself. She, it seemed to him, had seen him at the window and now, having glanced at him and taken another woman by the hand, was going towards the garden swinging her arm briskly. Without knowing why or wherefore, merely in accord with what he had been thinking, he went to the office.

Vasíli Nikoláich in holiday costume and with oiled hair was sitting at tea with his wife and a guest who was wearing an oriental kerchief.

'I want a word with you, Vasíli Nikoláich!'

'Please say what you want to. We have finished tea.'

'No. I'd rather you came out with me.'

'Directly; only let me get my cap. Tánya, put out the samovar,' said Vasíli Nikoláich, stepping outside cheerfully.

It seemed to Eugène that Vasíli had been drinking, but what was to be done? It might be all the better – he would sympathize with him in his difficulties the more readily.

'I have come again to speak about that same matter, Vasíli Nikoláich,' said Eugène – 'about that woman.'

'Well, what of her? I told them not to take her again on any account.'

'No, I have been thinking in general, and this is what I wanted to take your advice about. Isn't it possible to get them away, to send the whole family away?'

'Where can they be sent?' said Vasíli, disapprovingly and ironically as it seemed to Eugène.

'Well, I thought of giving them money, or even some land in Koltóvski, – so that she should not be here.'

'But how can they be sent away? Where is he to go – torn up from his roots? And why should you do it? What harm can she do you?'

'Ah, Vasíli Nikoláich, you must understand that it would be dreadful for my wife to hear of it.'

'But who will tell her?'

'How can I live with this dread? The whole thing is very painful for me.'

'But really, why should you distress yourself? Whoever stirs up the past – out with his eye! Who is not a sinner before God and to blame before the Tsar, as the saying is?'

'All the same it would be better to get rid of them. Can't you speak to the husband?'

'But it is no use speaking! Eh, Eugène Ivánich, what is the matter with you? It is all past and forgotten. All sorts of things happen. Who is there that would now say anything bad of you? Everybody sees you.'

'But all the same go and have a talk with him.'

'All right, I will speak to him.'

Though he knew that nothing would come of it, this talk somewhat calmed Eugène. Above all, it made him feel that through excitement he had been exaggerating the danger.

Had he gone to meet her by appointment? It was impossible. He had simply gone to stroll in the garden and she had happened to run out at the same time.

XIV

AFTER dinner that very Trinity Sunday Liza while walking from the garden to the meadow, where her husband wanted to show her the clover, took a false step and fell when crossing a little ditch. She fell gently, on her side; but she gave an exclamation, and her husband saw an expression in her face not only of fear but of pain. He was about to help her up, but she motioned him away with her hand.

'No, wait a bit, Eugène,' she said, with a weak smile, and looked up guiltily as it seemed to him. 'My foot only gave way under me.'

'There, I always say,' remarked Varvára Alexéevna, 'can anyone in her condition possibly jump over ditches?'

'But it is all right, mamma. I shall get up directly.' With her husband's help she did get up, but she immediately turned pale, and looked frightened.

'Yes, I am not well!' and she whispered something to her mother.

'Oh, my God, what have you done! I said you ought not to go there,' cried Varvára Alexéevna. 'Wait – I will call the servants. She must not walk. She must be carried!'

'Don't be afraid, Liza, I will carry you,' said Eugène, putting his left arm round her. 'Hold me by the neck. Like that.' And stooping down he put his right arm under her knees and lifted her. He could never afterwards forget the suffering and yet beatific expression of her face.

'I am too heavy for you, dear,' she said with a smile. 'Mamma is running, tell her!' And she bent towards him and kissed him. She evidently wanted her mother to see how he was carrying her.

Eugène shouted to Varvára Alexéevna not to hurry, and that he would carry Liza home. Varvára Alexéevna stopped and began to shout still louder.

'You will drop her, you'll be sure to drop her. You want to destroy her. You have no conscience!'

'But I am carrying her excellently.'

'I do not want to watch you killing my daughter, and I can't.' And she ran round the bend in the alley.

'Never mind, it will pass,' said Liza, smiling.

'Yes. If only it does not have consequences like last time.'

'No. I am not speaking of that. That is all right. I mean mamma. You are tired. Rest a bit.'

But though he found it heavy, Eugène carried his burden proudly and gladly to the house and did not hand her over to the housemaid and the man-cook whom Varvára Alexéevna had found and sent to meet them. He carried her to the bedroom and put her on the bed.

'Now go away,' she said, and drawing his hand to her she kissed it. 'Ánnushka and I will manage all right.'

Mary Pávlovna also ran in from her rooms in the wing. They undressed Liza and laid her on the bed. Eugène sat in the drawing-room with a book in his hand, waiting. Varvára Alexéevna went past him with such a reproachfully gloomy air that he felt alarmed.

'Well, how is it?' he asked.

'How is it? What's the good of asking? It is probably what you wanted when you made your wife jump over the ditch.'

'Varvára Alexéevna!' he cried. 'This is impossible. If you want to torment people and to poison their life' (he wanted to say, 'then go elsewhere to do it,' but restrained himself). 'How is it that it does not hurt you?'

'It is too late now.' And shaking her cap in a triumphant manner she passed out by the door.

The fall had really been a bad one; Liza's foot had twisted awkwardly and there was danger of her having another miscarriage. Everyone knew that there was nothing to be done but that she must just lie quietly, yet all the same they decided to send for a doctor.

'Dear Nikoláy Semënich,' wrote Eugène to the doctor, 'you have always been so kind to us that I hope you will not refuse to come to my wife's assistance. She ...' and so on. Having written the letter he went to the stables to arrange about the horses and the carriage. Horses had to be got ready to bring the doctor and others to take him back. When an estate is not run on a large scale, such things cannot be quickly decided but have to be considered. Having arranged it all and dispatched the coachman, it was past nine before he got back to the house. His wife was lying down, and said that she felt perfectly well and had no pain. But Varvára Alexéevna was sitting with a lamp screened from Liza by some sheets of music and knitting a large red coverlet, with a mien that said that after what had happened peace was impossible, but that she at any rate would do her duty no matter what anyone else did.

Eugène noticed this, but, to appear as if he had not done so, tried to assume a cheerful and tranquil air and told how he had chosen the horses and how capitally the mare, Kabúshka, had galloped as left trace-horse in the troyka.

'Yes, of course, it is just the time to exercise the horses when help is needed. Probably the doctor will also be thrown into the ditch,' remarked Varvára Alexéevna, examining her knitting from under her pince-nez and moving it close up to the lamp.

'But you know we had to send one way or other, and I made the best arrangement I could.'

'Yes, I remember very well how your horses galloped with me under the arch of the gateway.' This was a long-standing fancy of hers, and Eugène now was injudicious enough to remark that that was not quite what had happened.

'It is not for nothing that I have always said, and have often remarked to the prince, that it is hardest of all to live with people who are untruthful and insincere. I can endure anything except that.'

'Well, if anyone has to suffer more than another, it is certainly I,' said Eugène. 'But you . . .'

'Yes, it is evident.'

'What?'

'Nothing, I am only counting my stitches.'

Eugène was standing at the time by the bed and Liza was looking at him, and one of her moist hands outside the coverlet caught his hand and pressed it. 'Bear with her for my sake. You know she cannot prevent our loving one another,' was what her look said.

'I won't do so again. It's nothing,' he whispered, and he kissed her damp, long hand and then her affectionate eyes, which closed while he kissed them.

'Can it be the same thing over again?' he asked. 'How are you feeling?'

'I am afraid to say for fear of being mistaken, but I feel that he is alive and will live,' said she, glancing at her stomach.

'Ah, it is dreadful, dreadful to think of.'

Notwithstanding Liza's insistence that he should go away, Eugène spent the night with her, hardly closing an eye and ready to attend on her.

But she passed the night well, and had they not sent for the doctor she would perhaps have got up.

By dinner-time the doctor arrived and of course said that though if the symptoms recurred there might be cause for apprehension, yet actually there were no positive symptoms, but as there were also no contrary indications one might suppose on the one hand that – and on the other hand that . . . And therefore she must lie still, and that 'though I do not like prescribing, yet all the same she should take this

mixture and should lie quiet'. Besides this, the doctor gave
Varvára Alexéevna a lecture on woman's anatomy, during
which Varvára Alexéevna nodded her head significantly. Having received his fee, as usual into the backmost part of his palm,
the doctor drove away and the patient was left to lie in bed for
a week.

XV

EUGÈNE spent most of his time by his wife's bedside, talking
to her, reading to her, and what was hardest of all, enduring
without murmur Varvára Alexéevna's attacks, and even con-
triving to turn these into jokes.

But he could not stay at home all the time. In the first place
his wife sent him away, saying that he would fall ill if he always
remained with her; and secondly the farming was progressing
in a way that demanded his presence at every step. He could
not stay at home, but had to be in the fields, in the wood, in
the garden, at the threshing-floor; and everywhere he was
pursued not merely by the thought but by the vivid image of
Stepanída, and he only occasionally forgot her. But that would
not have mattered, he could perhaps have mastered his feeling;
what was worst of all was that, whereas he had previously lived
for months without seeing her, he now continually came
across her. She evidently understood that he wished to
renew relations with her and tried to come in his way.
Nothing was said either by him or by her, and therefore
neither he nor she went directly to a rendezvous, but only
sought opportunities of meeting.

The most possible place for them to meet was in the forest,
where peasant-women went with sacks to collect grass for
their cows. Eugène knew this and therefore went there
every day. Every day he told himself that he would not
go, and every day it ended by his making his way to the forest
and, on hearing the sound of voices, standing behind the
bushes with sinking heart looking to see if she was there.

Why he wanted to know whether it was she who was there,
he did not know. If it had been she and she had been alone, he

would not have gone to her – so he believed – he would have run away; but he wanted to see her.

Once he met her. As he was entering the forest she came out of it with two other women, carrying a heavy sack full of grass on her back. A little earlier he would perhaps have met her in the forest. Now, with the other women there, she could not go back to him. But though he realized this impossibility, he stood for a long time behind a hazel-bush, at the risk of attracting the other women's attention. Of course she did not return, but he stayed there a long time. And, great heavens, how delightful his imagination made her appear to him! And this not only once, but five or six times, and each time more intensely. Never had she seemed so attractive, and never had he been so completely in her power.

He felt that he had lost control of himself and had become almost insane. His strictness with himself had not weakened a jot; on the contrary he saw all the abomination of his desire and even of his action, for his going to the wood was an action. He knew that he only need come near her anywhere in the dark, and if possible touch her, and he would yield to his feelings. He knew that it was only shame before people, before her, and no doubt before himself also, that restrained him. And he knew too that he had sought conditions in which that shame would not be apparent – darkness or proximity – in which it would be stifled by animal passion. And therefore he knew that he was a wretched criminal, and despised and hated himself with all his soul. He hated himself because he still had not surrendered: every day he prayed God to strengthen him, to save him from perishing; every day he determined that from to-day onward he would not take a step to see her, and would forget her. Every day he devised means of delivering himself from this enticement, and he made use of those means.

But it was all in vain.

One of the means was continual occupation; another was intense physical work and fasting; a third was imagining clearly to himself the shame that would fall upon him when every-body knew of it – his wife, his mother-in-law, and the folk around. He did all this and it seemed to him that he was conquering, but midday came — the hour of their former meetings and the hour when he had met her carrying the grass — and he went to the forest. Thus five days of torment passed. He only saw her from a distance, and did not once encounter her.

XVI

LIZA was gradually recovering, she could move about and was only uneasy at the change that had taken place in her husband, which she did not understand.

Varvára Alexéevna had gone away for a while, and the only visitor was Eugène's uncle. Mary Pávlovna was as usual at home.

Eugène was in his semi-insane condition when there came two days of pouring rain, as often happens after thunder in June. The rain stopped all work. They even ceased carting manure on account of the dampness and dirt. The peasants remained at home. The herdsmen wore themselves out with the cattle, and eventually drove them home. The cows and sheep wandered about in the pasture-land and ran loose in the grounds. The peasant-women, barefoot and wrapped in shawls, splashing through the mud, rushed about to seek the runaway cows. Streams flowed everywhere along the paths, all the leaves and all the grass were saturated with water, and streams flowed unceasingly from the spouts into the bubbling puddles.

Eugène sat at home with his wife, who was particularly wearisome that day. She questioned Eugène several times as to the cause of his discontent, and he replied with vexation that nothing was the matter. She ceased questioning him but was still distressed.

They were sitting after breakfast in the drawing-room. His uncle for the hundredth time was recounting fabrications about his society acquaintances. Liza was knitting a jacket and sighed, complaining of the weather and of a pain in the small of her back. The uncle advised her to lie down, and asked for vodka for himself. It was terribly dull for Eugène in the house. Everything was weak and dull. He read a book and a magazine, but understood nothing of them.

'I must go out and look at the rasping-machine they brought yesterday,' said he, and got up and went out.

'Take an umbrella with you.'

'Oh, no, I have a leather coat. And I am only going as far as the boiling-room.'

He put on his boots and his leather coat and went to the factory; and he had not gone twenty steps before he met her coming towards him, with her skirts tucked up high above her white calves. She was walking, holding down the shawl in which her head and shoulders were wrapped.

'Where are you going?' said he, not recognizing her the first instant. When he recognized her it was already too late. She stopped, smiling, and looked long at him.

'I am looking for a calf. Where are you off to in such weather?' said she, as if she were seeing him every day.

'Come to the shed,' said he suddenly, without knowing how he said it. It was as if someone else had uttered the words.

She bit her shawl, winked, and ran in the direction which led from the garden to the shed, and he continued his path, intending to turn off beyond the lilac-bush and go there too.

'Master,' he heard a voice behind him. 'The mistress is calling you, and wants you to come back for a minute.'

This was Mísha, his man-servant.

'My God! This is the second time you have saved me,' thought Eugène, and immediately turned back. His wife reminded him that he had promised to take some medicine at the dinner-hour to a sick woman, and he had better take it with him.

While they were getting the medicine some five minutes elapsed, and then, going away with the medicine, he hesitated to go direct to the shed lest he should be seen from the house, but as soon as he was out of sight he promptly turned and made his way to it. He already saw her in imagination inside the shed smiling gaily. But she was not there, and there was nothing in the shed to show that she had been there.

He was already thinking that she had not come, had not heard or understood his words – he had muttered them through his nose as if afraid of her hearing them – or perhaps she had not wanted to come. 'And why did I imagine that she would rush to me? She has her own husband; it is only I who am such a wretch as to have a wife, and a good one, and to run after another.' Thus he thought sitting in the shed, the thatch of which had a leak and dripped from its straw. 'But how delightful it would be if she did come – alone here in this rain. If only I could embrace her once again, then let happen what may. But I could tell if she has been here by her footprints,' he reflected. He looked at the trodden ground near the shed and at the path overgrown by grass, and the fresh print of bare feet, and even of one that had slipped, was visible. 'Yes, she has been here. Well, now it is settled. Wherever I may see her I shall go straight to her. I will go to her at night.' He sat for a long time in the shed and left it exhausted and crushed. He delivered the medicine, returned home, and lay down in his room to wait for dinner.

XVII

BEFORE dinner Liza came to him and, still wondering what could be the cause of his discontent, began to say that she was afraid he did not like the idea of her going to Moscow for her confinement, and that she had decided that she would remain at home and on no account go to Moscow. He knew how she feared both her confinement itself and the risk of not having a healthy child, and therefore he could not help being touched at seeing how ready she was to sacrifice everything for his sake. All was so nice, so pleasant, so clean, in the house; and in his soul it was so dirty, despicable, and foul. The whole evening Eugène was tormented by knowing that notwithstanding his sincere repulsion at his own weakness, notwithstanding his firm intention to break off, – the same thing would happen again to-morrow.

'No, this is impossible,' he said to himself, walking up and down in his room. 'There must be some remedy for it. My God! What am I to do?'

Someone knocked at the door as foreigners do. He knew this must be his uncle. 'Come in,' he said.

The uncle had come as a self-appointed ambassador from Liza.

'Do you know, I really do notice that there is a change in you,' he said, – 'and Liza – I understand how it troubles her. I understand that it must be hard for you to leave all the business you have so excellently started, but *que veux-tu?*[1] I should advise you to go away. It will be more satisfactory both for you and for her. And do you know, I should advise you to go to the Crimea. The climate is beautiful and there is an excellent *accoucheur* there, and you would be just in time for the best of the grape season.'

'Uncle,' Eugène suddenly exclaimed. 'Can you keep a secret? A secret that is terrible to me, a shameful secret.'

'Oh, come – do you really feel any doubt of me?'

'Uncle, you can help me. Not only help, but save me!' said Eugène. And the thought of disclosing his secret to his uncle whom he did not respect, the thought that he would show himself in the worst light and humiliate himself before him, was pleasant. He felt himself to be despicable and guilty, and wished to punish himself.

'Speak, my dear fellow, you know how fond I am of you,' said the uncle, evidently well content that there was a secret and that it was a shameful one, and that it would be communicated to him, and that he could be of use.

'First of all I must tell you that I am a wretch, a good-for-nothing, a scoundrel – a real scoundrel.'

'Now what are you saying . . .' began his uncle, as if he were offended.

'What! Not a wretch when I – Liza's husband, Liza's! One has only to know her purity, her love – and that I, her husband, want to be untrue to her with a peasant-woman!'

'What is this? Why do you want to – you have not been unfaithful to her?'

---

1 What would you have?

'Yes, at least just the same as being untrue, for it did not depend on me. I was ready to do so. I was hindered, or else I should . . . now. I do not know what I should have done . . .'

'But please, explain to me . . .'

'Well, it is like this. When I was a bachelor I was stupid enough to have relations with a woman here in our village. That is to say, I used to have meetings with her in the forest, in the field . . .'

'Was she pretty?' asked his uncle.

Eugène frowned at this question, but he was in such need of external help that he made as if he did not hear it, and continued:

'Well, I thought this was just casual and that I should break it off and have done with it. And I did break it off before my marriage. For nearly a year I did not see her or think about her.' It seemed strange to Eugène himself to hear the description of his own condition. 'Then suddenly, I don't myself know why – really one sometimes believes in witchcraft – I saw her, and a worm crept into my heart; and it gnaws. I reproach myself, I understand the full horror of my action, that is to say, of the act I may commit any moment, and yet I myself turn to it, and if I have not committed it, it is only because God preserved me. Yesterday I was on my way to see her when Liza sent for me.'

'What, in the rain?'

'Yes. I am worn out, Uncle, and have decided to confess to you and to ask your help.'

'Yes, of course, it's a bad thing on your own estate. People will get to know. I understand that Liza is weak and that it is necessary to spare her, but why on your own estate?'

Again Eugène tried not to hear what his uncle was saying, and hurried on to the core of the matter.

'Yes, save me from myself. That is what I ask of you. To-day I was hindered by chance. But to-morrow or next time no one will hinder me. And she knows now. Don't leave me alone.'

'Yes, all right,' said his uncle, – 'but are you really so much in love?'

'Oh, it is not that at all. It is not that, it is some kind of power that has seized me and holds me. I do not know what to do. Perhaps I shall gain strength, and then . . .'

'Well, it turns out as I suggested,' said his uncle. 'Let us be off to the Crimea.'

'Yes, yes, let us go, and meanwhile you will be with me and will talk to me.'

XVIII

THE fact that Eugène had confided his secret to his uncle, and still more the sufferings of his conscience and the feeling of shame he experienced after that rainy day, sobered him. It was settled that they would start for Yálta in a week's time. During that week Eugène drove to town to get money for the journey, gave instructions from the house and from the office concerning the management of the estate, again became gay and friendly with his wife, and began to awaken morally.

So without having once seen Stepanída after that rainy day he left with his wife for the Crimea. There he spent an excellent two months. He received so many new impressions that it seemed to him that the past was obliterated from his memory. In the Crimea they met former acquaintances and became particularly friendly with them, and they also made new acquaintances. Life in the Crimea was a continual holiday for Eugène, besides being instructive and beneficial. They became friendly there with the former Marshal of the Nobility of their province, a clever and liberal-minded man who became fond of Eugène and coached him, and attracted him to his Party.

At the end of August Liza gave birth to a beautiful, healthy daughter, and her confinement was unexpectedly easy.

In September they returned home, the four of them, including the baby and its wet-nurse, as Liza was unable to nurse it herself. Eugène returned home entirely free from the former horrors and quite a new and happy man. Having gone through all that a husband goes through when his wife bears a child, he loved her more than ever. His feeling for the child when he took it in his arms was a funny, new, very pleasant and, as it were, a tickling feeling. Another new thing in his life now was that, besides his occupation with the estate, thanks to his acquaintance with Dúmchin (the ex-Marshal) a new interest occupied his mind, that of the Zémstvo – partly an ambitious interest, partly a feeling of duty. In October there was to be a special Assembly, at which he was to be elected. After arriving home he drove once to town and another time to Dúmchin.

Of the torments of his temptation and struggle he had forgotten even to think, and could with difficulty recall them to mind. It seemed to him something like an attack of insanity he had undergone.

To such an extent did he now feel free from it that he was not even afraid to make inquiries on the first occasion when he remained alone with the steward. As he had previously spoken to him about the matter he was not ashamed to ask.

'Well, and is Sídor Péchnikov still away from home?' he inquired.

'Yes, he is still in town.'

'And his wife?'

'Oh, she is a worthless woman. She is now carrying on with Zenóvi. She has gone quite on the loose.'

'Well, that is all right,' thought Eugène. 'How wonderfully indifferent to it I am! How I have changed.'

XIX

ALL that Eugène had wished had been realized. He had obtained the property, the factory was working successfully, the beet-crops were excellent, and he expected a large income; his wife had borne a child satisfactorily, his mother-in-law had left, and he had been unanimously elected to the Zémstvo.

He was returning home from town after the election. He had been congratulated and had had to return thanks. He had had dinner and had drunk some five glasses of champagne. Quite new plans of life now presented themselves to him, and he was thinking about these as he drove home. It was the

Indian summer: an excellent road and a hot sun. As he approached his home Eugène was thinking of how, as a result of this election, he would occupy among the people the position he had always dreamed of; that is to say, one in which he would be able to serve them not only by production, which gave employment, but also by direct influence. He imagined what his own and the other peasants would think of him in three years' time. 'For instance this one,' he thought, driving just then through the village and glancing at a peasant who with a peasant-woman was crossing the street in front of him carrying a full water-tub. They stopped to let his carriage pass. The peasant was old Péchnikov, and the woman was Stepanída. Eugène looked at her, recognized her, and was glad to feel that he remained quite tranquil. She was still as good-looking as ever, but this did not touch him at all. He drove home.

'Well, may we congratulate you?' said his uncle.

'Yes, I was elected.'

'Capital! We must drink to it!'

Next day Eugène drove about to see to the farming which he had been neglecting. At the outlying farmstead a new threshing machine was at work. While watching it Eugène stepped among the women, trying not to take notice of them; but try as he would he once or twice noticed the black eyes and red kerchief of Stepanída, who was carrying away the straw. Once or twice he glanced sideways at her and felt that something was happening, but could not account for it to himself. Only next day, when he again drove to the threshing-floor and spent two hours there quite unnecessarily, without ceasing to caress with his eyes the familiar, handsome figure of the young woman, did he feel that he was lost, irremediably lost. Again those torments! Again all that horror and fear, and there was no saving himself.

What he expected happened to him. The evening of the next day, without knowing how, he found himself at her backyard, by her hay-shed, where in autumn they had once had a meeting. As though having a stroll, he stopped there lighting a cigarette. A neighbouring peasant-woman saw him, and as he turned back he heard her say to someone: 'Go, he is waiting for you – on my dying word he is standing there. Go, you fool!'

He saw how a woman – she – ran to the hay-shed; but as a peasant had met him it was no longer possible for him to turn back, and so he went home.

XX

WHEN he entered the drawing-room everything seemed strange and unnatural to him. He had risen that morning vigorous, determined to fling it all aside, to forget it and not allow himself to think about it. But without noticing how it occurred he had all the morning not merely not interested himself in the work, but tried to avoid it. What had formerly cheered him and been important was now insignificant. Unconsciously he tried to free himself from business. It seemed to him that he had to do so in order to think and to plan. And he freed himself and remained alone. But as soon as he was alone he began to wander about in the garden and the forest. And all those spots were besmirched in his recollection by memories that gripped him. He felt that he was walking in the garden and pretending to himself that he was thinking out something, but that really he was not thinking out anything, but insanely and unreasonably expecting her; expecting that by some miracle she would be aware that he was expecting her, and would come here at once and go somewhere where no one would see them, or would come at night when there would be no moon, and no one, not even she herself, would see – on such a night she would come and he would touch her body. . . .

'There now, talking of breaking off when I wish to,' said he to himself. 'Yes, and that is having a clean healthy woman for one's health's sake! No, it seems one can't play with her like that. I thought I had taken her, but it was she who took me; took me and does not let me go. Why, I thought I was free, but I was not free and was deceiving myself when I married. It was all nonsense – fraud. From the time I had her I experienced a new feeling, the real feeling of a husband. Yes, I ought to have lived with her.

'One of two lives is possible for me: that which I began with Liza: service, estate management, the child, and people's respect. If that is life, it is necessary that she, Stepanída, should not be there. She must be sent away, as I said, or destroyed so that she shall not exist. And the other life – is this: For me to take her away from her husband, pay him money, disregard the shame and disgrace, and live with her. But in that case it is necessary that Liza should not exist, nor Mimi (the baby). No, that is not so, the baby does not matter, but it is necessary that there should be no Liza – that she should go away – that she should know, curse me, and go away. That she should know that I have exchanged her for a peasant-woman, that I am a deceiver and a scoundrel! – No, that is too terrible! It is impossible. But it might happen,' he went on thinking, – 'it might happen that Liza might fall ill and die. Die, and then everything would be capital.

'Capital! Oh, scoundrel! No, if someone must die it should be Stepanída. If she were to die, how good it would be.

'Yes, that is how men come to poison or kill their wives or lovers. Take a revolver and go and call her, and instead of embracing her, shoot her in the breast and have done with it.

'Really she is – a devil. Simply a devil. She has possessed herself of me against my own will.

'Kill? Yes. There are only two ways out: to kill my wife or her. For it is impossible to live like this.[1] It is impossible! I must consider the matter and look ahead. If things remain as they are what will happen? I shall again be saying to myself that I do not wish it and that I will throw her off, but it will be merely words; in the evening I shall be at her backyard, and she will know it and will come out. And if people know of it and tell my wife, or if I tell her myself – for I can't lie – I shall not be able to live so. I cannot! People will know. They will all know – Parásha and the blacksmith. Well, is it possible to live so?

[1] At this place the alternative ending, printed at the end of the story, begins.

'Impossible! There are only two ways out: to kill my wife, or to kill her. Yes, or else . . . Ah, yes, there is a third way: to kill myself,' said he softly, and suddenly a shudder ran over his skin. 'Yes, kill myself, then I shall not need to kill them.' He became frightened, for he felt that only that way was possible. He had a revolver. 'Shall I really kill myself? It is something I never thought of – how strange it will be . . . '

He returned to his study and at once opened the cupboard where the revolver lay, but before he had taken it out of its case his wife entered the room.

XXI

HE threw a newspaper over the revolver.

'Again the same!' said she aghast when she had looked at him.

'What is the same?'

'The same terrible expression that you had before and would not explain to me. Jénya, dear one, tell me about it. I see that you are suffering. Tell me and you will feel easier. Whatever it may be, it will be better than for you to suffer so. Don't I know that it is nothing bad?'

'You know? While . . . '

'Tell me, tell me, tell me. I won't let you go.'

He smiled a piteous smile.

'Shall I? – No, it is impossible. And there is nothing to tell.'

Perhaps he might have told her, but at that moment the wet-nurse entered to ask if she should go for a walk. Liza went out to dress the baby.

'Then you will tell me? I will be back directly.'

'Yes, perhaps . . . '

She never could forget the piteous smile with which he said this. She went out.

Hurriedly, stealthily like a robber, he seized the revolver and took it out of its case. It was loaded, yes, but long ago, and one cartridge was missing.

'Well, how will it be?' He put it to his temple and hesitated a little, but as soon as he remembered Stepanída – his decision not to see her, his struggle, temptation, fall, and renewed struggle – he shuddered with horror. 'No, this is better,' and he pulled the trigger...

When Liza ran into the room – she had only had time to step down from the balcony – he was lying face downwards on the floor: black, warm blood was gushing from the wound, and his corpse was twitching.

There was an inquest. No one could understand or explain the suicide. It never even entered his uncle's head that its cause could be anything in common with the confession Eugène had made to him two months previously.

Varvára Alexéevna assured them that she had always foreseen it. It had been evident from his way of disputing. Neither Liza nor Mary Pávlovna could at all understand why it had happened, but still they did not believe what the doctors said, namely, that he was mentally deranged – a psychopath. They were quite unable to accept this, for they knew he was saner than hundreds of their acquaintances.

And indeed if Eugène Irténev was mentally deranged everyone is in the same case; the most mentally deranged people are certainly those who see in others indications of insanity they do not notice in themselves.

VARIATION OF THE CONCLUSION OF 'THE DEVIL'

'To kill, yes. There are only two ways out: to kill my wife, or to kill her. For it is impossible to live like this,' said he to himself, and going up to the table he took from it a revolver and, having examined it – one cartridge was wanting – he put it in his trouser pocket.

'My God! What am I doing?' he suddenly exclaimed, and folding his hands he began to pray.

'O God, help me and deliver me! Thou knowest that I do not desire evil, but by myself am powerless. Help me,' said he, making the sign of the cross on his breast before the icon.

'Yes, I can control myself. I will go out, walk about and think things over.'

He went to the entrance-hall, put on his overcoat and went out onto the porch. Unconsciously his steps took him past the garden along the field path to the outlying farmstead. There the threshing machine was still droning and the cries of the driver-lads were heard. He entered the barn. She was there. He saw her at once. She was raking up the corn, and on seeing him she ran briskly and merrily about, with laughing eyes, raking up the scattered corn with agility. Eugène could not help watching her though he did not wish to do so. He only recollected himself when she was no longer in sight. The clerk informed him that they were now finishing threshing the corn that had been beaten down – that was why it was going slower and the output was less. Eugène went up to the drum, which occasionally gave a knock as sheaves not evenly fed in passed under it, and he asked the clerk if there were many such sheaves of beaten-down corn.

'There will be five cartloads of it.'

'Then look here . . . ' began Eugène, but he did not finish the sentence. She had gone close up to the drum and was raking the corn from under it, and she scorched him with her laughing eyes. That look spoke of a merry, careless love between them, of the fact that she knew he wanted her and had come to her shed, and that she as always was ready to live and be merry with him regardless of all conditions or consequences. Eugène felt himself to be in her power but did not wish to yield.

He remembered his prayer and tried to repeat it. He began saying it to himself, but at once felt that it was useless. A single thought now engrossed him entirely: how to arrange a meeting with her so that the others should not notice it.

'If we finish this lot to-day, are we to start on a fresh stack or leave it till to-morrow?' asked the clerk.

'Yes, yes,' replied Eugène, involuntarily following her to the heap to which with the other women she was raking the corn.

'But can I really not master myself?' said he to himself. 'Have I really perished? O God! But there is no God. There is only a devil. And it is she. She has possessed me. But I won't, I won't! A devil, yes, a devil.'

Again he went up to her, drew the revolver from his pocket and shot her, once, twice, thrice, in the back. She ran a few steps and fell on the heap of corn.

'My God, my God! What is that?' cried the women.

'No, it was not an accident. I killed her on purpose,' cried Eugène. 'Send for the police-officer.'

He went home and went to his study and locked himself in, without speaking to his wife.

'Do not come to me,' he cried to her through the door. 'You will know all about it.'

An hour later he rang, and bade the man-servant who answered the bell: 'Go and find out whether Stepanída is alive.'

The servant already knew all about it, and told him she had died an hour ago.

'Well, all right. Now leave me alone. When the police-officer or the magistrate comes, let me know.'

The police-officer and magistrate arrived next morning, and Eugène, having bidden his wife and baby farewell, was taken to prison.

He was tried. It was during the early days of trial by jury,[1] and the verdict was one of temporary insanity, and he was sentenced only to perform church penance.

He had been kept in prison for nine months and was then confined in a monastery for one month.

He had begun to drink while still in prison, continued to do so in the monastery, and returned home an enfeebled, irresponsible drunkard.

Varvára Alexéevna assured them that she had always predicted this. It was, she said, evident from the way he disputed. Neither Liza nor Mary Pávlovna could understand how the affair had happened, but for all that, they did not believe what the doctors said, namely, that he was mentally deranged – a psychopath. They could not accept that, for they knew that he was saner than hundreds of their acquaintances.

---

1 Trial by jury was introduced in 1864, and at first the juries were inclined to be extremely lenient to the prisoners.

And indeed, if Eugène Irténev was mentally deranged when he committed this crime, then everyone is similarly insane. The most mentally deranged people are certainly those who see in others indications of insanity they do not notice in themselves.

FATHER SERGIUS

I

In Petersburg in the eighteen-forties a surprising event occurred. An officer of the Cuirassier Life Guards, a handsome prince who everyone predicted would become aide-de-camp to the Emperor Nicholas I and have a brilliant career, left the service, broke off his engagement to a beautiful maid of honour, a favourite of the Empress's, gave his small estate to his sister, and retired to a monastery to become a monk.

This event appeared extraordinary and inexplicable to those who did not know his inner motives, but for Prince Stepán Kasátsky himself it all occurred so naturally that he could not imagine how he could have acted otherwise.

His father, a retired colonel of the Guards, had died when Stepán was twelve, and sorry as his mother was to part from her son, she entered him at the Military College as her deceased husband had intended.

The widow herself, with her daughter Varvára, moved to Petersburg to be near her son and have him with her for the holidays.

The boy was distinguished both by his brilliant ability and by his immense self-esteem. He was first both in his studies – especially in mathematics, of which he was particularly fond – and also in drill and in riding. Though of more than average height, he was handsome and agile, and he would have been an altogether exemplary cadet had it not been for his quick temper. He was remarkably truthful, and was neither dissipated nor addicted to drink. The only faults that marred his conduct were fits of fury to which he was subject and during which he lost control of himself and became like a wild animal. He once nearly threw out of the window another cadet who

397

had begun to tease him about his collection of minerals. On another occasion he came almost completely to grief by flinging a whole dish of cutlets at an officer who was acting as steward, attacking him and, it was said, striking him for having broken his word and told a barefaced lie. He would certainly have been reduced to the ranks had not the Director of the College hushed up the whole matter and dismissed the steward.

By the time he was eighteen he had finished his College course and received a commission as lieutenant in an aristocratic regiment of the Guards.

The Emperor Nicholas Pávlovich (Nicholas I) had noticed him while he was still at the College, and continued to take notice of him in the regiment, and it was on this account that people predicted for him an appointment as aide-de-camp to the Emperor. Kasátsky himself strongly desired it, not from ambition only but chiefly because since his cadet days he had been passionately devoted to Nicholas Pávlovich. The Emperor had often visited the Military College and every time Kasátsky saw that tall erect figure, with breast expanded in its military overcoat, entering with brisk step, saw the cropped side-whiskers, the moustache, the aquiline nose, and heard the sonorous voice exchanging greetings with the cadets, he was seized by the same rapture that he experienced later on when he met the woman he loved. Indeed, his passionate adoration of the Emperor was even stronger: he wished to sacrifice something – everything, even himself – to prove his complete devotion. And the Emperor Nicholas was conscious of evoking this rapture and deliberately aroused it. He played with the cadets, surrounded himself with them, treating them sometimes with childish simplicity, sometimes as a friend, and then again with majestic solemnity. After that affair with the officer, Nicholas Pávlovich said nothing to Kasátsky, but when the latter approached he waved him away theatrically, frowned, shook his finger at him, and afterwards when leaving, said: 'Remember that I know everything. There are some things I would rather not know, but they remain here,' and he pointed to his heart.

When on leaving College the cadets were received by the Emperor, he did not again refer to Kasátsky's offence, but told them all, as was his custom, that they should serve him and the fatherland loyally, that he would always be their best friend, and that when necessary they might approach him direct. All the cadets were as usual greatly moved, and Kasátsky even shed tears, remembering the past, and vowed that he would serve his beloved Tsar with all his soul.

When Kasátsky took up his commission his mother moved with her daughter first to Moscow and then to their country estate. Kasátsky gave half his property to his sister and kept only enough to maintain himself in the expensive regiment he had joined.

To all appearance he was just an ordinary, brilliant young officer of the Guards making a career for himself; but intense and complex strivings went on within him. From early childhood his efforts had seemed to be very varied, but essentially they were all one and the same. He tried in everything he took up to attain such success and perfection as would evoke praise and surprise. Whether it was his studies or his military exercises, he took them up and worked at them till he was praised and held up as an example to others. Mastering one subject he took up another, and obtained first place in his studies. For example, while still at College he noticed in himself an awkwardness in French conversation, and contrived to master French till he spoke it as well as Russian, and then he took up chess and became an excellent player.

Apart from his main vocation, which was the service of his Tsar and the fatherland, he always set himself some particular aim, and however unimportant it was, devoted himself completely to it and lived for it until it was accomplished. And as soon as it was attained another aim would immediately present itself, replacing its predecessor. This passion for distinguishing himself, or for accomplishing something in order to distinguish himself, filled his life. On taking up his commission he set himself to acquire the utmost perfection in knowledge of the service, and very soon became a model officer, though still with the same fault of ungovernable irascibility, which here in the service again led him to commit actions inimical to his success. Then he took to reading, having once in conversation in society felt himself deficient in general education – and again achieved his purpose. Then, wishing to secure a brilliant position in high society, he learnt to dance excellently and very soon was invited to all the balls in the best circles, and to some of their evening gatherings. But this did not satisfy him: he was accustomed to being first, and in this society was far from being so.

The highest society then consisted, and I think always and everywhere does consist, of four sorts of people: rich people who are received at Court, people not wealthy but born and brought up in Court circles, rich people who ingratiate themselves into the Court set, and people neither rich nor belonging to the Court but who ingratiate themselves into the first and second sets.

Kasátsky did not belong to the first two sets, but was readily welcomed in the others. On entering society he determined to have relations with some society lady, and to his own surprise quickly accomplished this purpose. He soon realized, however, that the circles in which he moved were not the highest, and that though he was received in the highest spheres he did not belong to them. They were polite to him, but showed by their whole manner that they had their own set and that he was not of it. And Kasátsky wished to belong to that inner circle. To attain that end it would be necessary to be an aide-de-camp to the Emperor – which he expected to become – or to marry into that exclusive set, which he resolved to do. And his choice fell on a beauty belonging to the Court, who not merely belonged to the circle into which he wished to be accepted, but whose friendship was coveted by the very highest people and those most firmly established in that highest circle. This was Countess Korotkóva. Kasátsky began to pay court to her, and not merely for the sake of his career. She was extremely attractive and he soon fell in love with her. At first she was noticeably cool towards him, but then suddenly changed and became gracious, and her mother gave him pressing invitations to visit them. Kasátsky proposed and was accepted. He was surprised at the facility with which he attained such happiness. But though he noticed something strange and unusual in the behaviour towards him of both mother and daughter, he was blinded by being so deeply in love, and did not realize what almost the whole town knew – namely, that his fiancée had been the Emperor Nicholas's mistress the previous year.

Two weeks before the day arranged for the wedding, Kasátsky was at Tsárskoe Seló at his fiancée's country place. It was a hot day in May. He and his betrothed had walked about the garden and were sitting on a bench in a shady linden alley. Mary's white muslin dress suited her particularly well, and she seemed the personification of innocence and love as she sat, now bending her head, now gazing up at the very tall and handsome man who was speaking to her with particular tenderness and self-restraint, as if he feared by word or gesture to offend or sully her angelic purity.

Kasátsky belonged to those men of the eighteen-forties (they are now no longer to be found) who while deliberately and without any conscientious scruples condoning impurity in themselves, required ideal and angelic purity in their women, regarded all unmarried women of their circle as possessed of such purity, and treated them accordingly. There was much that was false and harmful in this outlook, as concerning the laxity the men permitted themselves, but in regard to the women that old-fashioned view (sharply differing from that held by young people to-day who see in every girl merely a female seeking a mate) was, I think, of value. The girls, perceiving such adoration, endeavoured with more or less success to be goddesses.

Such was the view Kasátsky held of women, and that was how he regarded his fiancée. He was particularly in love that day, but did not experience any sensual desire for her. On the contrary he regarded her with tender adoration as something unattainable.

He rose to his full height, standing before her with both hands on his sabre.

'I have only now realized what happiness a man can experience! And it is you, my darling, who have given me this happiness,' he said with a timid smile.

Endearments had not yet become usual between them, and feeling himself morally inferior he felt terrified at this stage to use them to such an angel.

'It is thanks to you that I have come to know myself. I have learnt that I am better than I thought.'

'I have known that for a long time. That was why I began to love you.'

Nightingales trilled near by and the fresh leafage rustled, moved by a passing breeze.

He took her hand and kissed it, and tears came into his eyes.

She understood that he was thanking her for having said she loved him. He silently took a few steps up and down, and then approached her again and sat down.

'You know . . . I have to tell you . . . I was not disinterested when I began to make love to you. I wanted to get into society; but later . . . how unimportant that became in comparison with you – when I got to know you. You are not angry with me for that?'

She did not reply but merely touched his hand. He understood that this meant: 'No, I am not angry.'

'You said . . .' He hesitated. It seemed too bold to say. 'You said that you began to love me. I believe it – but there is something that troubles you and checks your feeling. What is it?'

'Yes – now or never!' thought she. 'He is bound to know of it anyway. But now he will not forsake me. Ah, if he should, it would be terrible!' And she threw a loving glance at his tall, noble, powerful figure. She loved him now more than she had loved the Tsar, and apart from the Imperial dignity would not have preferred the Emperor to him.

'Listen! I cannot deceive you. I have to tell you. You ask what it is? It is that I have loved before.'

She again laid her hand on his with an imploring gesture. He was silent.

'You want to know who it was? It was – the Emperor.'

'We all love him. I can imagine you, a schoolgirl at the Institute . . .'

'No, it was later. I was infatuated, but it passed . . . I must tell you . . .'

'Well, what of it?'

'No, it was not simply —' She covered her face with her hands.

'What? You gave yourself to him?'

She was silent.

'His mistress?'

She did not answer.

He sprang up and stood before her with trembling jaws, pale as death. He now remembered how the Emperor, meeting him on the Névsky, had amiably congratulated him.

'O God, what have I done! Stíva!'

'Don't touch me! Don't touch me! Oh, how it pains!'

He turned away and went to the house. There he met her mother.

'What is the matter, Prince? I ...' She became silent on seeing his face. The blood had suddenly rushed to his head.

'You knew it, and used me to shield them! If you weren't a woman ...!' he cried, lifting his enormous fist, and turning aside he ran away.

Had his fiancée's lover been a private person he would have killed him, but it was his beloved Tsar.

Next day he applied both for furlough and his discharge, and professing to be ill, so as to see no one, he went away to the country.

He spent the summer at his village arranging his affairs. When summer was over he did not return to Petersburg, but entered a monastery and there became a monk.

His mother wrote to try to dissuade him from this decisive step, but he replied that he felt God's call which transcended all other considerations. Only his sister, who was as proud and ambitious as he, understood him.

She understood that he had become a monk in order to be above those who considered themselves his superiors. And she understood him correctly. By becoming a monk he showed contempt for all that seemed most important to others and had seemed so to him while he was in the service, and he now ascended a height from which he could look down on those he had formerly envied. ... But it was not this alone, as his sister

Varvára supposed, that influenced him. There was also in him something else — a sincere religious feeling which Varvára did not know, which intertwined itself with the feeling of pride and the desire for pre-eminence, and guided him. His disillusionment with Mary, whom he had thought of angelic purity, and his sense of injury, were so strong that they brought him to despair, and the despair led him — to what? To God, to his childhood's faith which had never been destroyed in him.

II

KASÁTSKY entered the monastery on the feast of the Intercession of the Blessed Virgin.[1] The Abbot of that monastery was a gentleman by birth, a learned writer and a *stárets*, that is, he belonged to that succession of monks originating in Walachia who each choose a director and teacher whom they implicitly obey. This Superior had been a disciple of the *stárets* Ambrose, who was a disciple of Makarius, who was a disciple of the *stárets* Leonid, who was a disciple of Païssy Velichkóvsky.

To this Abbot Kasátsky submitted himself as to his chosen director. Here in the monastery, besides the feeling of ascendency over others that such a life gave him, he felt much as he had done in the world: he found satisfaction in attaining the greatest possible perfection outwardly as well as inwardly. As in the regiment he had been not merely an irreproachable officer but had even exceeded his duties and widened the borders of perfection, so also as a monk he tried to be perfect, and was always industrious, abstemious, submissive, and meek, as well as pure both in deed and in thought, and obedient. This last quality in particular made life far easier for him. If many of the demands of life in the monastery, which was near the capital and much frequented, did not please him and were temptations to him, they were all nullified by obedience: 'It is not for me to reason; my business is to do the task set me, whether it be standing beside the relics, singing in the choir, or making up accounts in the monastery guest-house.' All possibility of

[1] 1st October o.s.

doubt about anything was silenced by obedience to the *stárets*. Had it not been for this, he would have been oppressed by the length and monotony of the church services, the bustle of the many visitors, and the bad qualities of the other monks. As it was, he not only bore it all joyfully but found in it solace and support. 'I don't know why it is necessary to hear the same prayers several times a day, but I know that it is necessary; and knowing this I find joy in them.' His director told him that as material food is necessary for the maintenance of the life of the body, so spiritual food – the church prayers – is necessary for the maintenance of the spiritual life. He believed this, and though the church services, for which he had to get up early in the morning, were a difficulty, they certainly calmed him and gave him joy. This was the result of his consciousness of humility, and the certainty that whatever he had to do, being fixed by the *stárets*, was right.

The interest of his life consisted not only in an ever greater and greater subjugation of his will, but in the attainment of all the Christian virtues, which at first seemed to him easily attainable. He had given his whole estate to his sister and did not regret it, he had no personal claims, humility towards his inferiors was not merely easy for him but afforded him pleasure. Even victory over the sins of the flesh, greed and lust, was easily attained. His director had specially warned him against the latter sin, but Kasátsky felt free from it and was glad.

One thing only tormented him – the remembrance of his fiancée; and not merely the remembrance but the vivid image of what might have been. Involuntarily he recalled a lady he knew who had been a favourite of the Emperor's, but had afterwards married and become an admirable wife and mother. The husband had a high position, influence and honour, and a good and penitent wife.

In his better hours Kasátsky was not disturbed by such thoughts, and when he recalled them at such times he was merely glad to feel that the temptation was past. But there were moments when all that made up his present life suddenly grew dim before him, moments when, if he did not cease to believe in the aims he had set himself, he ceased to see them and could evoke no confidence in them but was seized by a remembrance of, and – terrible to say – a regret for, the change of life he had made.

The only thing that saved him in that state of mind was obedience and work, and the fact that the whole day was occupied by prayer. He went through the usual forms of prayer, he bowed in prayer, he even prayed more than usual, but it was lip-service only and his soul was not in it. This condition would continue for a day, or sometimes for two days, and would then pass of itself. But those days were dreadful. Kasátsky felt that he was neither in his own hands nor in God's, but was subject to something else. All he could do then was to obey the *stárets*, to restrain himself, to undertake nothing, and simply to wait. In general all this time he lived not by his own will but by that of the *stárets*, and in this obedience he found a special tranquillity.

So he lived in his first monastery for seven years. At the end of the third year he received the tonsure and was ordained to the priesthood by the name of Sergius. The profession was an important event in his inner life. He had previously experienced a great consolation and spiritual exaltation when receiving communion, and now when he himself officiated, the performance of the preparation filled him with ecstatic and deep emotion. But subsequently that feeling became more and more deadened, and once when he was officiating in a depressed state of mind he felt that the influence produced on him by the service would not endure. And it did in fact weaken till only the habit remained.

In general in the seventh year of his life in the monastery Sergius grew weary. He had learnt all there was to learn and had attained all there was to attain, there was nothing more to do and his spiritual drowsiness increased. During this time he heard of his mother's death and his sister Varvára's marriage, but both events were matters of indifference to him. His whole attention and his whole interest were concentrated on his inner life.

In the fourth year of his priesthood, during which the Bishop had been particularly kind to him, the *stárets* told him that he ought not to decline it if he were offered an appointment to higher duties. Then monastic ambition, the very thing he had found so repulsive in other monks, arose within him. He was assigned to a monastery near the metropolis. He wished to refuse but the *stárets* ordered him to accept the appointment. He did so, and took leave of the *stárets* and moved to the other monastery.

The exchange into the metropolitan monastery was an important event in Sergius's life. There he encountered many temptations, and his whole will-power was concentrated on meeting them.

In the first monastery, women had not been a temptation to him, but here that temptation arose with terrible strength and even took definite shape. There was a lady known for her frivolous behaviour who began to seek his favour. She talked to him and asked him to visit her. Sergius sternly declined, but was horrified by the definiteness of his desire. He was so alarmed that he wrote about it to the *stárets*. And in addition, to keep himself in hand, he spoke to a young novice and, conquering his sense of shame, confessed his weakness to him, asking him to keep watch on him and not let him go anywhere except to service and to fulfil his duties.

Besides this a great pitfall for Sergius lay in the fact of his extreme antipathy to his new Abbot, a cunning worldly man who was making a career for himself in the Church. Struggle with himself as he might, he could not master that feeling. He was submissive to the Abbot, but in the depths of his soul he never ceased to condemn him. And in the second year of his residence at the new monastery that ill-feeling broke out.

The Vigil service was being performed in the large church on the eve of the feast of the Intercession of the Blessed Virgin, and there were many visitors. The Abbot himself was conducting the service. Father Sergius was standing in his usual place and praying: that is, he was in that condition of struggle which always occupied him during the service, especially in the large church when he was not himself conducting the

service. This conflict was occasioned by his irritation at the
presence of fine folk, especially ladies. He tried not to see them
or to notice all that went on: how a soldier conducted them,
pushing the common people aside, how the ladies pointed out
the monks to one another – especially himself and a monk
noted for his good looks. He tried as it were to keep his mind
in blinkers, to see nothing but the light of the candles on the
altar-screen, the icons, and those conducting the service. He
tried to hear nothing but the prayers that were being chanted
or read, to feel nothing but self-oblivion in consciousness of
the fulfilment of duty – a feeling he always experienced when
hearing or reciting in advance the prayers he had so often
heard.

So he stood, crossing and prostrating himself when necessary, and struggled with himself, now giving way to cold
condemnation and now to a consciously evoked obliteration
of thought and feeling. Then the sacristan, Father Nicodemus
– also a great stumbling-block to Sergius who involuntarily
reproached him for flattering and fawning on the Abbot –
approached him and, bowing low, requested his presence
behind the holy gates. Father Sergius straightened his mantle,
put on his biretta, and went circumspectly through the crowd.

'*Lise, regarde à droite, c'est lui!*'[1] he heard a woman's voice say.
'*Où, où? Il n'est pas tellement beau.*'[2]

He knew that they were speaking of him. He heard them
and, as always at moments of temptation, he repeated the
words, 'Lead us not into temptation', and bowing his head
and lowering his eyes went past the ambo and in by the north
door, avoiding the canons in their cassocks who were just then
passing the altar-screen. On entering the sanctuary he bowed,
crossing himself as usual and bending double before the icons.
Then, raising his head but without turning, he glanced out of
the corner of his eye at the Abbot, whom he saw standing
beside another glittering figure.

1 'Lise, look to the right. That is he.'
2 'Where? Where? He is not so very handsome.'

The Abbot was standing by the wall in his vestments. Having freed his short plump hands from beneath his chasuble he had folded them over his fat body and protruding stomach, and fingering the cords of his vestments was smilingly saying something to a military man in the uniform of a general of the Imperial suite, with its insignia and shoulder-knots which Father Sergius's experienced eye at once recognized. This general had been the commander of the regiment in which Sergius had served. He now evidently occupied an important position, and Father Sergius at once noticed that the Abbot was aware of this and that his red face and bald head beamed with satisfaction and pleasure. This vexed and disgusted Father Sergius, the more so when he heard that the Abbot had only sent for him to satisfy the general's curiosity to see a man who had formerly served with him, as he expressed it.

'Very pleased to see you in your angelic guise,' said the general, holding out his hand. 'I hope you have not forgotten an old comrade.'

The whole thing – the Abbot's red, smiling face amid its fringe of grey, the general's words, his well-cared-for face with its self-satisfied smile and the smell of wine from his breath and of cigars from his whiskers – revolted Father Sergius. He bowed again to the Abbot and said:

'Your reverence deigned to send for me?' – and stopped, the whole expression of his face and eyes asking why.

'Yes, to meet the general,' replied the Abbot.

'Your reverence, I left the world to save myself from temptation,' said Father Sergius, turning pale and with quivering lips. 'Why do you expose me to it during prayers and in God's house?'

'You may go! Go!' said the Abbot, flaring up and frowning.

Next day Father Sergius asked pardon of the Abbot and of the brethren for his pride, but at the same time, after a night spent in prayer, he decided that he must leave this monastery, and he wrote to the *stárets* begging permission to return to him. He wrote that he felt his weakness and incapacity to struggle against temptation without his help, and penitently confessed his sin of pride. By return of post came a letter from the *stárets*, who wrote that Sergius's pride was the cause of all that had happened. The old man pointed out that his fits of anger were due to the fact that in refusing all clerical honours he humiliated himself not for the sake of God but for the sake of his pride. 'There now, am I not a splendid man not to want anything?' That was why he could not tolerate the Abbot's action. 'I have renounced everything for the glory of God, and here I am exhibited like a wild beast!' 'Had you renounced vanity for God's sake you would have borne it. Worldly pride is not yet dead in you. I have thought about you, Sergius my son, and prayed also, and this is what God has suggested to me. At the Tambóv hermitage the anchorite Hilary, a man of saintly life, has died. He had lived there eighteen years. The Tambóv Abbot is asking whether there is not a brother who would take his place. And here comes your letter. Go to Father Païssy of the Tambóv Monastery. I will write to him about you, and you must ask for Hilary's cell. Not that you can replace Hilary, but you need solitude to quell your pride. May God bless you!'

Sergius obeyed the *stárets*, showed his letter to the Abbot, and having obtained his permission, gave up his cell, handed all his possessions over to the monastery, and set out for the Tambóv hermitage.

There the Abbot, an excellent manager of merchant origin, received Sergius simply and quietly and placed him in Hilary's cell, at first assigning to him a lay brother but afterwards leaving him alone, at Sergius's own request. The cell was a dual cave, dug into the hillside, and in it Hilary had been buried. In the back part was Hilary's grave, while in the front was a niche for sleeping, with a straw mattress, a small table, and a shelf with icons and books. Outside the outer door, which fastened with a hook, was another shelf on which, once a day, a monk placed food from the monastery.

And so Sergius became a hermit.

III

AT Carnival time, in the sixth year of Sergius's life at the hermitage, a merry company of rich people, men and women from a neighbouring town, made up a troyka-party, after a meal of carnival-pancakes and wine. The company consisted of two lawyers, a wealthy landowner, an officer, and four ladies. One lady was the officer's wife, another the wife of the landowner, the third his sister – a young girl – and the fourth a divorcée, beautiful, rich, and eccentric, who amazed and shocked the town by her escapades.

The weather was excellent and the snow-covered road smooth as a floor. They drove some seven miles out of town, and then stopped and consulted as to whether they should turn back or drive farther.

'But where does this road lead to?' asked Makóvkina, the beautiful divorcée.

'To Tambóv, eight miles from here,' replied one of the lawyers, who was having a flirtation with her.

'And then where?'

'Then on to L—, past the Monastery.'

'Where that Father Sergius lives?'

'Yes.'

'Kasátsky, the handsome hermit?'

'Yes.'

'*Mesdames and messieurs*, let us drive on and see Kasátsky! We can stop at Tambóv and have something to eat.'

'But we shouldn't get home to-night!'

'Never mind, we will stay at Kasátsky's.'

'Well, there is a very good hostelry at the Monastery. I stayed there when I was defending Mákhin.'

'No, I shall spend the night at Kasátsky's!'

'Impossible! Even your omnipotence could not accomplish that!'

'Impossible? Will you bet?'

'All right! If you spend the night with him, the stake shall be whatever you like.'

'*A discrétion!*'

'But on your side too!'

'Yes, of course. Let us drive on.'

Vodka was handed to the drivers, and the party got out a box of pies, wine, and sweets for themselves. The ladies wrapped up in their white dogskins. The drivers disputed as to whose troyka should go ahead, and the youngest, seating himself sideways with a dashing air, swung his long knout and shouted to the horses. The troyka-bells tinkled and the sledge-runners squeaked over the snow.

The sledges swayed hardly at all. The shaft-horse, with his tightly bound tail under his decorated breechband, galloped smoothly and briskly; the smooth road seemed to run rapidly backwards, while the driver dashingly shook the reins. One of the lawyers and the officer sitting opposite talked nonsense to Makóvkina's neighbour, but Makóvkina herself sat motionless and in thought, tightly wrapped in her fur. 'Always the same and always nasty! The same red shiny faces smelling of wine and cigars! The same talk, the same thoughts, and always about the same things! And they are all satisfied and confident that it should be so, and will go on living like that till they die. But I can't. It bores me. I want something that would upset it all and turn it upside down. Suppose it happened to us as to those people – at Sarátov was it? – who kept on driving and froze to death.... What would our people do? How would they behave? Basely, for certain. Each for himself. And I too should act badly. But I at any rate have beauty. They all know it. And how about that monk? Is it possible that he has become indifferent to it? No! That is the one thing they all care for – like that cadet last autumn. What a fool he was!'

'Iván Nikoláevich!' she said aloud.

'What are your commands?'

'How old is he?'

'Who?'

'Kasátsky.'

'Over forty, I should think.'

'And does he receive all visitors?'

'Yes, everybody, but not always.'

'Cover up my feet. Not like that – how clumsy you are! No! More, more – like that! But you need not squeeze them!'

So they came to the forest where the cell was.

Makóvkina got out of the sledge, and told them to drive on. They tried to dissuade her, but she grew irritable and ordered them to go on.

When the sledges had gone she went up the path in her white dogskin coat. The lawyer got out and stopped to watch her.

It was Father Sergius's sixth year as a recluse, and he was now forty-nine. His life in solitude was hard – not on account of the fasts and the prayers (they were no hardship to him) but on account of an inner conflict he had not at all anticipated. The sources of that conflict were two: doubts, and the lust of the flesh. And these two enemies always appeared together. It seemed to him that they were two foes, but in reality they were one and the same. As soon as doubt was gone so was the lustful desire. But thinking them to be two different fiends he fought them separately.

'O my God, my God!' thought he. 'Why dost thou not grant me faith? There is lust, of course: even the saints had to fight that – Saint Anthony and others. But they had faith, while I have moments, hours, and days, when it is absent. Why does the whole world, with all its delights, exist if it is sinful and must be renounced? Why hast Thou created this temptation? Temptation? Is it not rather a temptation that I wish to abandon all the joys of earth and prepare something for myself there where perhaps there is nothing?' And he became horrified and filled with disgust at himself. 'Vile creature! And it is you who wish to become a saint!' he upbraided himself, and he began to pray. But as soon as he started to pray he saw himself vividly as he had been at the Monastery, in a majestic post in biretta and mantle, and he shook his head. 'No, that is not right. It is deception. I may deceive others, but not myself or God. I am not a majestic man, but a pitiable and ridiculous one!' And he threw back the folds of his cassock and smiled as he looked at his thin legs in their underclothing.

Then he dropped the folds of the cassock again and began reading the prayers, making the sign of the cross and prostrating himself. 'Can it be that this couch will be my bier?' he read.

And it seemed as if a devil whispered to him: 'A solitary couch is itself a bier. Falsehood!' And in imagination he saw the shoulders of a widow with whom he had lived. He shook himself, and went on reading. Having read the precepts he took up the Gospels, opened the book, and happened on a passage he often repeated and knew by heart: 'Lord, I believe. Help thou my unbelief!' – and he put away all the doubts that had arisen. As one replaces an object of insecure equilibrium, so he carefully replaced his belief on its shaky pedestal and carefully stepped back from it so as not to shake or upset it. The blinkers were adjusted again and he felt tranquillized, and repeating his childhood's prayer: 'Lord, receive me, receive me!' he felt not merely at ease, but thrilled and joyful. He crossed himself and lay down on the bedding on his narrow bench, tucking his summer cassock under his head. He fell asleep at once, and in his light slumber he seemed to hear the tinkling of sledge-bells. He did not know whether he was dreaming or awake, but a knock at the door aroused him. He sat up, distrusting his senses, but the knock was repeated. Yes, it was a knock close at hand, at his door, and with it the sound of a woman's voice.

'My God! Can it be true, as I have read in the *Lives of the Saints*, that the devil takes on the form of a woman? Yes – it is a woman's voice. And a tender, timid, pleasant voice. Phui!' And he spat to exorcize the devil. 'No, it was only my imagination,' he assured himself, and he went to the corner where his lectern stood, falling on his knees in the regular and habitual manner which of itself gave him consolation and satisfaction. He sank down, his hair hanging over his face, and pressed his head, already going bald in front, to the cold damp strip of drugget on the draughty floor. He read the psalm old Father Pímon had told him warded off temptation. He easily raised his light and emaciated body on his strong sinewy legs and tried to continue saying his prayers, but instead of doing so he involuntarily strained his hearing. He wished to hear more. All was quiet. From the corner of the roof regular drops continued to fall into the tub below. Outside was a mist and fog eating into the snow that lay on the ground. It was still, very still. And suddenly there was a rustling at the window and a voice – that same tender, timid voice, which could only belong to an attractive woman – said:

'Let me in, for Christ's sake!'

It seemed as though his blood had all rushed to his heart and settled there. He could hardly breathe. 'Let God arise and let his enemies be scattered . . .'

'But I am not a devil!' It was obvious that the lips that uttered this were smiling. 'I am not a devil, but only a sinful woman who has lost her way, not figuratively but literally!' She laughed. 'I am frozen and beg for shelter.'

He pressed his face to the window, but the little icon-lamp was reflected by it and shone on the whole pane. He put his hands to both sides of his face and peered between them. Fog, mist, a tree, and – just opposite him – she herself. Yes, there, a few inches from him, was the sweet, kindly frightened face of a woman in a cap and a coat of long white fur, leaning towards him. Their eyes met with instant recognition: not that they had ever known one another, they had never met before, but by the look they exchanged they – and he particularly – felt that they knew and understood one another. After that glance to imagine her to be a devil and not a simple, kindly, sweet, timid woman, was impossible.

'Who are you? Why have you come?' he asked.

'Do please open the door!' she replied, with capricious authority. 'I am frozen. I tell you I have lost my way.'

'But I am a monk – a hermit.'

'Oh, do please open the door – or do you wish me to freeze under your window while you say your prayers?'

'But how have you . . .'

'I shan't eat you. For God's sake let me in! I am quite frozen.'

She really did feel afraid, and said this in an almost tearful voice.

He stepped back from the window and looked at an icon of the Saviour in His crown of thorns. 'Lord, help me! Lord, help me!' he exclaimed, crossing himself and bowing low. Then he went to the door, and opening it into the tiny porch, felt for the hook that fastened the outer door and began to lift it. He heard steps outside. She was coming from the window to the door. 'Ah!' she suddenly exclaimed, and he understood that she had stepped into the puddle that the dripping from the roof had formed at the threshold. His hands trembled, and he could not raise the hook of the tightly closed door.

'Oh, what are you doing? Let me in! I am all wet. I am frozen! You are thinking about saving your soul and are letting me freeze to death...'

He jerked the door towards him, raised the hook, and without considering what he was doing, pushed it open with such force that it struck her.

'Oh – *pardon!*' he suddenly exclaimed, reverting completely to his old manner with ladies.

She smiled on hearing that *pardon*. 'He is not quite so terrible, after all,' she thought. 'It's all right. It is you who must pardon me,' she said, stepping past him. 'I should never have ventured, but such an extraordinary circumstance...'

'If you please!' he uttered, and stood aside to let her pass him. A strong smell of fine scent, which he had long not encountered, struck him. She went through the little porch into the cell where he lived. He closed the outer door without fastening the hook, and stepped in after her.

'Lord Jesus Christ, Son of God, have mercy on me a sinner! Lord, have mercy on me a sinner!' he prayed unceasingly, not merely to himself but involuntarily moving his lips. 'If you please!' he said to her again. She stood in the middle of the room, moisture dripping from her to the floor as she looked him over. Her eyes were laughing.

'Forgive me for having disturbed your solitude. But you see what a position I am in. It all came about from our starting from town for a sledge-drive, and my making a bet that I would walk back by myself from the Vorobëvka to the town. But then I lost my way, and if I had not happened to come upon your cell...' She began lying, but his face confused her so that she could not continue, but became silent. She had not expected him to be at all such as he was. He was not as handsome as she had imagined, but was nevertheless beautiful in her eyes: his greyish hair and beard, slightly curling, his fine, regular nose, and his eyes like glowing coal when he looked at her, made a strong impression on her.

He saw that she was lying.

'Yes . . . so,' said he, looking at her and again lowering his eyes. 'I will go in there, and this place is at your disposal.'

And taking down the little lamp, he lit a candle, and bowing low to her went into the small cell beyond the partition, and she heard him begin to move something about there. 'Probably he is barricading himself in from me!' she thought with a smile, and throwing off her white dogskin cloak she tried to take off her cap, which had become entangled in her hair and in the woven kerchief she was wearing under it. She had not got at all wet when standing under the window, and had said so only as a pretext to get him to let her in. But she really had stepped into the puddle at the door, and her left foot was wet up to the ankle and her overshoe full of water. She sat down on his bed – a bench only covered by a bit of carpet – and began to take off her boots. The little cell seemed to her charming. The narrow little room, some seven feet by nine, was as clean as glass. There was nothing in it but the bench on which she was sitting, the book-shelf above it, and a lectern in the corner. A sheepskin coat and a cassock hung on nails by the door. Above the lectern was the little lamp and an icon of Christ in His crown of thorns. The room smelt strangely of perspiration and of earth. It all pleased her – even that smell. Her wet feet, especially one of them, were uncomfortable, and she quickly began to take off her boots and stockings without ceasing to smile, pleased not so much at having achieved her object as because she perceived that she had abashed that charming, strange, striking, and attractive man. 'He did not respond, but what of that?' she said to herself.

'Father Sergius! Father Sergius! Or how does one call you?'

'What do you want?' replied a quiet voice.

'Please forgive me for disturbing your solitude, but really I could not help it. I should simply have fallen ill. And I don't know that I shan't now. I am all wet and my feet are like ice.'

'Pardon me,' replied the quiet voice. 'I cannot be of any assistance to you.'

'I would not have disturbed you if I could have helped it. I am only here till daybreak.'

He did not reply and she heard him muttering something, probably his prayers.

'You will not be coming in here?' she asked, smiling. 'For I must undress to dry myself.'

He did not reply, but continued to read his prayers.

'Yes, that is a man!' thought she, getting her dripping boot off with difficulty. She tugged at it, but could not get it off. The absurdity of it struck her and she began to laugh almost inaudibly. But knowing that he would hear her laughter and would be moved by it just as she wished him to be, she laughed louder, and her laughter – gay, natural, and kindly – really acted on him just in the way she wished.

'Yes, I could love a man like that – such eyes and such a simple noble face, and passionate too despite all the prayers he mutters!' thought she. 'You can't deceive a woman in these things. As soon as he put his face to the window and saw me, he understood and knew. The glimmer of it was in his eyes and remained there. He began to love me and desired me. Yes – desired!' said she, getting her overshoe and her boot off at last and starting to take off her stockings. To remove those long stockings fastened with elastic it was necessary to raise her skirts. She felt embarrassed and said:

'Don't come in!'

But there was no reply from the other side of the wall. The steady muttering continued and also a sound of moving.

'He is prostrating himself to the ground, no doubt,' thought she. 'But he won't bow himself out of it. He is thinking of me just as I am thinking of him. He is thinking of these feet of mine with the same feeling that I have!' And she pulled off her wet stockings and put her feet up on the bench, pressing them under her. She sat a while like that with her arms round her knees and looking pensively before her. 'But it is a desert, here in this silence. No one would ever know....'

She rose, took her stockings over to the stove, and hung them on the damper. It was a queer damper, and she turned it about, and then, stepping lightly on her bare feet, returned to the bench and sat down there again with her feet up.

There was complete silence on the other side of the partition. She looked at the tiny watch that hung round her neck. It was two o'clock. 'Our party should return about three!' She had not more than an hour before her. 'Well, am I to sit like this all alone? What nonsense! I don't want to. I will call him at once.'

'Father Sergius, Father Sergius! Sergéy Dmítrich! Prince Kasátsky!'

Beyond the partition all was silent.

'Listen! This is cruel. I would not call you if it were not necessary. I am ill. I don't know what is the matter with me!' she exclaimed in a tone of suffering. 'Oh! Oh!' she groaned, falling back on the bench. And strange to say she really felt that her strength was failing, that she was becoming faint, that everything in her ached, and that she was shivering with fever.

'Listen! Help me! I don't know what is the matter with me. Oh! Oh!' She unfastened her dress, exposing her breast, and lifted her arms, bare to the elbow. 'Oh! Oh!'

All this time he stood on the other side of the partition and prayed. Having finished all the evening prayers, he now stood motionless, his eyes looking at the end of his nose, and mentally repeated with all his soul: 'Lord Jesus Christ, Son of God, have mercy upon me!'

But he had heard everything. He had heard how the silk rustled when she took off her dress, how she stepped with bare feet on the floor, and had heard how she rubbed her feet with her hand. He felt his own weakness, and that he might be lost at any moment. That was why he prayed unceasingly. He felt rather as the hero in the fairy-tale must have felt when he had to go on and on without looking round. So Sergius heard and felt that danger and destruction were there, hovering above and around him, and that he could only save himself by not looking in that direction for an instant. But suddenly the desire to look seized him. At the same instant she said:

'This is inhuman. I may die. . . .'

'Yes, I will go to her, but like the Saint who laid one hand on the adulteress and thrust his other into the brazier. But there is no brazier here.' He looked round. The lamp! He put his finger over the flame and frowned, preparing himself to suffer. And for a rather long time, as it seemed to him, there was no sensation, but suddenly – he had not yet decided whether it was painful enough – he writhed all over, jerked his hand away, and waved it in the air. 'No, I can't stand that!'

'For God's sake come to me! I am dying! Oh!'

'Well – shall I perish? No, not so!'

'I will come to you directly,' he said, and having opened his door, he went without looking at her through the cell into the porch where he used to chop wood. There he felt for the block and for an axe which leant against the wall.

'Immediately!' he said, and taking up the axe with his right hand he laid the forefinger of his left hand on the block, swung the axe, and struck with it below the second joint. The finger flew off more lightly than a stick of similar thickness, and bounding up, turned over on the edge of the block and then fell to the floor.

He heard it fall before he felt any pain, but before he had time to be surprised he felt a burning pain and the warmth of flowing blood. He hastily wrapped the stump in the skirt of his cassock, and pressing it to his hip went back into the room, and standing in front of the woman, lowered his eyes and asked in a low voice: 'What do you want?'

She looked at his pale face and his quivering left cheek, and suddenly felt ashamed. She jumped up, seized her fur cloak, and throwing it round her shoulders, wrapped herself up in it.

'I was in pain. . . . I have caught cold . . . I . . . Father Sergius . . . I . . .'

He let his eyes, shining with a quiet light of joy, rest upon her, and said:

'Dear sister, why did you wish to ruin your immortal soul? Temptations must come into the world, but woe to him by whom temptation comes. Pray that God may forgive us!'

She listened and looked at him. Suddenly she heard the sound of something dripping. She looked down and saw that blood was flowing from his hand and down his cassock.

'What have you done to your hand?' She remembered the sound she had heard, and seizing the little lamp ran out into the porch. There on the floor she saw the bloody finger. She returned with her face paler than his and was about to speak to him, but he silently passed into the back cell and fastened the door.

'Forgive me!' she said. 'How can I atone for my sin?'

'Go away.'

'Let me tie up your hand.'

'Go away from here.'

She dressed hurriedly and silently, and when ready sat waiting in her furs. The sledge-bells were heard outside.

'Father Sergius, forgive me!'

'Go away. God will forgive.'

'Father Sergius! I will change my life. Do not forsake me!'

'Go away.'

'Forgive me – and give me your blessing!'

'In the name of the Father and of the Son and of the Holy Ghost!' – she heard his voice from behind the partition. 'Go!'

She burst into sobs and left the cell. The lawyer came forward to meet her.

'Well, I see I have lost the bet. It can't be helped. Where will you sit?'

'It is all the same to me.'

She took a seat in the sledge, and did not utter a word all the way home.

A year later she entered a convent as a novice, and lived a strict life under the direction of the hermit Arsény, who wrote letters to her at long intervals.

IV

FATHER SERGIUS lived as a recluse for another seven years.

At first he accepted much of what people brought him – tea,

sugar, white bread, milk, clothing, and fire-wood. But as time went on he led a more and more austere life, refusing everything superfluous, and finally he accepted nothing but rye-bread once a week. Everything else that was brought him he gave to the poor who came to him. He spent his entire time in his cell, in prayer or in conversation with callers, who became more and more numerous as time went on. Only three times a year did he go out to church, and when necessary he went out to fetch water and wood.

The episode with Makóvkina had occurred after five years of his hermit life. That occurrence soon became generally known – her nocturnal visit, the change she underwent, and her entry into a convent. From that time Father Sergius's fame increased. More and more visitors came to see him, other monks settled down near his cell, and a church was erected there and also a hostelry. His fame, as usual exaggerating his feats, spread ever more and more widely. People began to come to him from a distance, and began bringing invalids to him whom they declared he cured.

His first cure occurred in the eighth year of his life as a hermit. It was the healing of a fourteen-year-old boy, whose mother brought him to Father Sergius insisting that he should lay his hand on the child's head. It had never occurred to Father Sergius that he could cure the sick. He would have regarded such a thought as a great sin of pride; but the mother who brought the boy implored him insistently, falling at his feet and saying: 'Why do you, who heal others, refuse to help my son?' She besought him in Christ's name. When Father Sergius assured her that only God could heal the sick, she replied that she only wanted him to lay his hands on the boy and pray for him. Father Sergius refused and returned to his cell. But next day (it was in autumn and the nights were already cold) on going out for water he saw the same mother with her son, a pale boy of fourteen, and was met by the same petition.

He remembered the parable of the unjust judge, and though he had previously felt sure that he ought to refuse, he now began to hesitate and, having hesitated, took to prayer and prayed until a decision formed itself in his soul. This decision was, that he ought to accede to the woman's request and that her faith might save her son. As for himself, he would in this case be but an insignificant instrument chosen by God.

And going out to the mother he did what she asked – laid his hand on the boy's head and prayed.

The mother left with her son, and a month later the boy recovered, and the fame of the holy healing power of the *stárets* Sergius (as they now called him) spread throughout the whole district. After that, not a week passed without sick people coming, riding or on foot, to Father Sergius; and having acceded to one petition he could not refuse others, and he laid his hands on many and prayed. Many recovered, and his fame spread more and more.

So seven years passed in the Monastery and thirteen in his hermit's cell. He now had the appearance of an old man: his beard was long and grey, but his hair, though thin, was still black and curly.

V

FOR some weeks Father Sergius had been living with one persistent thought: whether he was right in accepting the position in which he had not so much placed himself as been placed by the Archimandrite and the Abbot. That position had begun after the recovery of the fourteen-year-old boy. From that time, with each month, week, and day that passed, Sergius felt his own inner life wasting away and being replaced by external life. It was as if he had been turned inside out.

Sergius saw that he was a means of attracting visitors and contributions to the Monastery, and that therefore the author-ities arranged matters in such a way as to make as much use of him as possible. For instance, they rendered it impossible for him to do any manual work. He was supplied with everything he could want, and they only demanded of him that he should not refuse his blessing to those who came to seek it. For his convenience they appointed days when he would receive. They arranged a reception-room for men, and a place was railed in so that he should not be pushed over by the crowds of women visitors, and so that he could conveniently bless those who came.

They told him that people needed him, and that fulfilling Christ's law of love he could not refuse their demand to see him, and that to avoid them would be cruel. He could not but agree with this, but the more he gave himself up to such a life the more he felt that what was internal became external, and that the fount of living water within him dried up, and that what he did now was done more and more for men and less and less for God.

Whether he admonished people, or simply blessed them, or prayed for the sick, or advised people about their lives, or listened to expressions of gratitude from those he had helped by precepts, or alms, or healing (as they assured him) – he could not help being pleased at it, and could not be indifferent to the results of his activity and to the influence he exerted. He thought himself a shining light, and the more he felt this the more was he conscious of a weakening, a dying down of the divine light of truth that shone within him.

'In how far is what I do for God and in how far is it for men?' That was the question that insistently tormented him and to which he was not so much unable to give himself an answer as unable to face the answer.

In the depth of his soul he felt that the devil had substituted an activity for men in place of his former activity for God. He felt this because, just as it had formerly been hard for him to be torn from his solitude so now that solitude itself was hard for him. He was oppressed and wearied by visitors, but at the bottom of his heart he was glad of their presence and glad of the praise they heaped upon him.

There was a time when he decided to go away and hide. He even planned all that was necessary for that purpose. He prepared for himself a peasant's shirt, trousers, coat, and cap. He explained that he wanted these to give to those who asked. And he kept these clothes in his cell, planning how he would put them on, cut his hair short, and go away. First he would go some three hundred versts by train, then he would leave the train and walk from village to village. He asked an old man who had been a soldier how he tramped: what people gave him, and what shelter they allowed him. The soldier told him where people were most charitable, and where they would take a wanderer in for the night, and Father Sergius intended to avail himself of this information. He even put on those clothes one night in his desire to go, but he could not decide what was best – to remain or to escape. At first he was in doubt, but afterwards this indecision passed. He submitted to custom and yielded to the devil, and only the peasant garb reminded him of the thought and feeling he had had.

Every day more and more people flocked to him and less and less time was left him for prayer and for renewing his spiritual strength. Sometimes in lucid moments he thought he was like a place where there had once been a spring. 'There used to be a feeble spring of living water which flowed quietly from me and through me. That was true life, the time when she tempted me!' (He always thought with ecstasy of that night and of her who was now Mother Agnes.) She had tasted of that pure water, but since then there had not been time for it to collect before thirsty people came crowding in and pushing one another aside. And they had trampled everything down and nothing was left but mud.

So he thought in rare moments of lucidity, but his usual state of mind was one of weariness and a tender pity for himself because of that weariness.

It was in spring, on the eve of the mid-Pentecostal feast. Father Sergius was officiating at the Vigil Service in his hermitage church, where the congregation was as large as the little church could hold – about twenty people. They were all well-to-do proprietors or merchants. Father Sergius admitted anyone, but a selection was made by the monk in attendance and by an assistant who was sent to the hermitage every day from the Monastery. A crowd of some eighty people – pilgrims and peasants, and especially peasant-women – stood outside waiting for Father Sergius to come out and bless them. Meanwhile he conducted the service, but at the point at which he went out to the tomb of his predecessor, he staggered and would have fallen had he not been caught by a merchant standing behind him and by the monk acting as deacon.

'What is the matter, Father Sergius? Dear man! O Lord!' exclaimed the women. 'He is as white as a sheet!'

But Father Sergius recovered immediately, and though very pale, he waved the merchant and the deacon aside and continued to chant the service.

Father Seraphim, the deacon, the acolytes, and Sófya Iván-ovna, a lady who always lived near the hermitage and tended Father Sergius, begged him to bring the service to an end.

'No, there's nothing the matter,' said Father Sergius, slightly smiling from beneath his moustache and continuing the service. 'Yes, that is the way the Saints behaved!' thought he.

'A holy man – an angel of God!' he heard just then the voice of Sófya Ivánovna behind him, and also of the merchant who had supported him. He did not heed their entreaties, but went on with the service. Again crowding together they all made their way by the narrow passages back into the little church, and there, though abbreviating it slightly, Father Sergius completed vespers.

Immediately after the service Father Sergius, having pronounced the benediction on those present, went over to the bench under the elm tree at the entrance to the cave. He wished to rest and breathe the fresh air – he felt in need of it. But as soon as he left the church the crowd of people rushed to him soliciting his blessing, his advice, and his help. There were pilgrims who constantly tramped from one holy place to another and from one *stárets* to another, and were always entranced by every shrine and every *stárets*. Father Sergius knew this common, cold, conventional, and most irreligious type. There were pilgrims, for the most part discharged soldiers, unaccustomed to a settled life, poverty-stricken, and many of them drunken old men, who tramped from monastery to monastery merely to be fed. And there were rough peasants and peasant-women who had come with their selfish requirements, seeking cures or to have doubts about quite practical affairs solved for them: about marrying off a daughter, or hiring a shop, or buying a bit of land, or how to atone for having overlaid a child or having an illegitimate one.

All this was an old story and not in the least interesting to him. He knew he would hear nothing new from these folk, that they would arouse no religious emotion in him; but he liked to see the crowd to which his blessing and advice was necessary and precious, so while that crowd oppressed him it also pleased him. Father Seraphim began to drive them away, saying that Father Sergius was tired. But Father Sergius, remembering the words of the Gospel: 'Forbid them' (children) 'not to come unto me', and feeling tenderly towards himself at this recollection, said they should be allowed to approach.

He rose, went to the railing beyond which the crowd had gathered, and began blessing them and answering their questions, but in a voice so weak that he was touched with pity for himself. Yet despite his wish to receive them all he could not do it. Things again grew dark before his eyes, and he staggered and grasped the railings. He felt a rush of blood to his head and first went pale and then suddenly flushed.

'I must leave the rest till to-morrow. I cannot do more to-day,' and, pronouncing a general benediction, he returned to the bench. The merchant again supported him, and leading him by the arm helped him to be seated.

'Father!' came voices from the crowd. 'Dear Father! Do not forsake us. Without you we are lost!'

The merchant, having seated Father Sergius on the bench under the elm, took on himself police duties and drove the people off very resolutely. It is true that he spoke in a low voice so that Father Sergius might not hear him, but his words were incisive and angry.

'Be off, be off! He has blessed you, and what more do you want? Get along with you, or I'll wring your necks! Move on there! Get along, you old woman with your dirty leg-bands! Go, go! Where are you shoving to? You've been told that it is finished. To-morrow will be as God wills, but for to-day he has finished!'

'Father! Only let my eyes have a glimpse of his dear face!' said an old woman.

'I'll glimpse you! Where are you shoving to?'

Father Sergius noticed that the merchant seemed to be acting roughly, and in a feeble voice told the attendant that the people should not be driven away. He knew that they would be driven away all the same, and he much desired to be left alone and to rest, but he sent the attendant with that message to produce an impression.

'All right, all right! I am not driving them away. I am only remonstrating with them,' replied the merchant. 'You know they wouldn't hesitate to drive a man to death. They have no pity, they only consider themselves. . . . You've been told you cannot see him. Go away! To-morrow!' And he got rid of them all.

He took all these pains because he liked order and liked to domineer and drive the people away, but chiefly because he wanted to have Father Sergius to himself. He was a widower with an only daughter who was an invalid and unmarried, and whom he had brought fourteen hundred versts to Father Sergius to be healed. For two years past he had been taking her to different places to be cured: first to the university clinic in the chief town of the province, but that did no good; then to a peasant in the province of Samára, where she got a little better; then to a doctor in Moscow to whom he paid much money, but this did no good at all. Now he had been told that Father Sergius wrought cures, and had brought her to him. So when all the people had been driven away he approached Father Sergius, and suddenly falling on his knees loudly exclaimed:

'Holy Father! Bless my afflicted offspring that she may be healed of her malady. I venture to prostrate myself at your holy feet.'

And he placed one hand on the other, cup-wise. He said and did all this as if he were doing something clearly and firmly appointed by law and usage – as if one must and should ask for a daughter to be cured in just this way and no other. He did it with such conviction that it seemed even to Father Sergius that it should be said and done in just that way, but nevertheless he bade him rise and tell him what the trouble was. The merchant said that his daughter, a girl of twenty-two, had fallen ill two years ago, after her mother's sudden death. She had moaned (as he expressed it) and since then had not been herself. And now he had brought her fourteen hundred versts and she was waiting in the hostelry till Father Sergius should give orders to bring her. She did not go out during the day, being afraid of the light, and could only come after sunset.

'Is she very weak?' asked Father Sergius.

'No, she has no particular weakness. She is quite plump, and is only "nerastenic" the doctors say. If you will only let me bring her this evening, Father Sergius, I'll fly like a spirit to fetch her. Holy Father! Revive a parent's heart, restore his line, save his afflicted daughter by your prayers!' And the merchant again threw himself on his knees and bending sideways, with his head resting on his clenched fists, remained stock still. Father Sergius again told him to get up, and thinking how heavy his activities were and how he went through with them patiently notwithstanding, he sighed heavily and after a few seconds of silence, said:

'Well, bring her this evening. I will pray for her, but now I am tired...' and he closed his eyes. 'I will send for you.'

The merchant went away, stepping on tiptoe, which only made his boots creak the louder, and Father Sergius remained alone.

His whole life was filled by church services and by people who came to see him, but to-day had been a particularly difficult one. In the morning an important official had arrived and had had a long conversation with him; after that a lady had come with her son. This son was a sceptical young professor whom the mother, an ardent believer and devoted to Father Sergius, had brought that he might talk to him. The conversation had been very trying. The young man, evidently not wishing to have a controversy with a monk, had agreed with him in everything as with someone who was mentally inferior. Father Sergius saw that the young man did not believe but yet was satisfied, tranquil, and at ease, and the memory of that conversation now disquieted him.

'Have something to eat, Father,' said the attendant.

'All right, bring me something.'

The attendant went to a hut that had been arranged some ten paces from the cave, and Father Sergius remained alone.

The time was long past when he had lived alone doing everything for himself and eating only rye-bread, or rolls prepared for the church. He had been advised long since that he had no right to neglect his health, and he was given wholesome, though Lenten, food. He ate sparingly, though much more than he had done, and often he ate with much pleasure, and not as formerly with aversion and a sense of guilt. So it was now. He had some gruel, drank a cup of tea, and ate half a white roll.

The attendant went away, and Father Sergius remained alone under the elm tree.

It was a wonderful May evening, when the birches, aspens, elms, wild cherries, and oaks, had just burst into foliage.

The bush of wild cherries behind the elm tree was in full bloom and had not yet begun to shed its blossoms, and the nightingales – one quite near at hand and two or three others in the bushes down by the river – burst into full song after some preliminary twitters. From the river came the far-off songs of peasants returning, no doubt, from their work. The sun was setting behind the forest, its last rays glowing through the leaves. All that side was brilliant green, the other side with the elm tree was dark. The cockchafers flew clumsily about, falling to the ground when they collided with anything.

After supper Father Sergius began to repeat a silent prayer: 'O Lord Jesus Christ, Son of God, have mercy upon us!' and then he read a psalm, and suddenly in the middle of the psalm a sparrow flew out from the bush, alighted on the ground, and hopped towards him chirping as it came, but then it took fright at something and flew away. He said a prayer which referred to his abandonment of the world, and hastened to finish it in order to send for the merchant with the sick daughter. She interested him in that she presented a distraction, and because both she and her father considered him a saint whose prayers were efficacious. Outwardly he disavowed that idea, but in the depths of his soul he considered it to be true.

He was often amazed that this had happened, that he, Stepán Kasátsky, had come to be such an extraordinary saint and even a worker of miracles, but of the fact that he was such there could not be the least doubt. He could not fail to believe in the miracles he himself witnessed, beginning with the sick boy and ending with the old woman who had recovered her sight when he had prayed for her.

Strange as it might be, it was so. Accordingly the merchant's daughter interested him as a new individual who had faith in him, and also as a fresh opportunity to confirm his healing powers and enhance his fame. 'They bring people a thousand versts and write about it in the papers. The Emperor knows of it, and they know of it in Europe, in unbelieving Europe' – thought he. And suddenly he felt ashamed of his vanity and again began to pray. 'Lord, King of Heaven, Comforter, Soul of Truth! Come and enter into me and cleanse me from all sin and save and bless my soul. Cleanse me from the sin of worldly vanity that troubles me!' he repeated, and he remembered how often he had prayed about this and how vain till now his prayers had been in that respect. His prayers worked miracles for others, but in his own case God had not granted him liberation from this petty passion.

He remembered his prayers at the commencement of his life at the hermitage, when he prayed for purity, humility, and love, and how it seemed to him then that God heard his prayers. He had retained his purity and had chopped off his finger. And he lifted the shrivelled stump of that finger to his lips and kissed it. It seemed to him now that he had been humble then when he had always seemed loathsome to himself on account of his sinfulness; and when he remembered the tender feelings with which he had then met an old man who was bringing a drunken soldier to him to ask alms; and how he had received *her*, it seemed to him that he had then possessed love also. But now? And he asked himself whether he loved anyone, whether he loved Sófya Ivánovna, or Father Seraphim, whether he had any feeling of love for all who had come to him that day – for that learned young man with whom he had had that instructive discussion in which he was concerned

only to show off his own intelligence and that he had not
lagged behind the times in knowledge. He wanted and needed
their love, but felt none towards them. He now had neither
love nor humility nor purity.

He was pleased to know that the merchant's daughter
was twenty-two, and he wondered whether she was good-
looking. When he inquired whether she was weak, he really
wanted to know if she had feminine charm.

'Can I have fallen so low?' he thought. 'Lord, help me!
Restore me, my Lord and God!' And he clasped his hands and
began to pray.

The nightingales burst into song, a cockchafer knocked
against him and crept up the back of his neck. He brushed it
off. 'But does He exist? What if I am knocking at a door
fastened from outside? The bar is on the door for all to see.
Nature – the nightingales and the cockchafers – is that bar.
Perhaps the young man was right.' And he began to pray
aloud. He prayed for a long time till these thoughts vanished
and he again felt calm and confident. He rang the bell and told
the attendant to say that the merchant might bring his daughter
to him now.

The merchant came, leading his daughter by the arm. He
led her into the cell and immediately left her.

She was a very fair girl, plump and very short, with a pale,
frightened, childish face and a much developed feminine
figure. Father Sergius remained seated on the bench at the
entrance and when she was passing and stopped beside him for
his blessing he was aghast at himself for the way he looked at
her figure. As she passed by him he was acutely conscious of
her femininity, though he saw by her face that she was sensual
and feeble-minded. He rose and went into the cell. She was
sitting on a stool waiting for him, and when he entered she
rose.

'I want to go back to Papa,' she said.

'Don't be afraid,' he replied. 'What are you suffering from?'

'I am in pain all over,' she said, and suddenly her face lit up
with a smile.

'You will be well,' said he. 'Pray!'

'What is the use of praying? I have prayed and it does no good' – and she continued to smile. 'I want you to pray for me and lay your hands on me. I saw you in a dream.'

'How did you see me?'

'I saw you put your hands on my breast like that.' She took his hand and pressed it to her breast. 'Just here.'

He yielded his right hand to her.

'What is your name?' he asked, trembling all over and feeling that he was overcome and that his desire had already passed beyond control.

'Marie. Why?'

She took his hand and kissed it, and then put her arm round his waist and pressed him to herself.

'What are you doing?' he said. 'Marie, you are a devil!'

'Oh, perhaps. What does it matter?'

And embracing him she sat down with him on the bed.

At dawn he went out into the porch.

'Can this all have happened? Her father will come and she will tell him everything. She is a devil! What am I to do? Here is the axe with which I chopped off my finger.' He snatched up the axe and moved back towards the cell.

The attendant came up.

'Do you want some wood chopped? Let me have the axe.'

Sergius yielded up the axe and entered the cell. She was lying there asleep. He looked at her with horror, and passed on beyond the partition, where he took down the peasant clothes and put them on. Then he seized a pair of scissors, cut off his long hair, and went out along the path down the hill to the river, where he had not been for more than three years.

A road ran beside the river and he went along it and walked till noon. Then he went into a field of rye and lay down there. Towards evening he approached a village, but without entering it went towards the cliff that overhung the river. There he again lay down to rest.

It was early morning, half an hour before sunrise. All was damp and gloomy and a cold early wind was blowing from the west. 'Yes, I must end it all. There is no God. But how am I to end it? Throw myself into the river? I can swim and should not drown. Hang myself? Yes, just throw this sash over a branch.' This seemed so feasible and so easy that he felt horrified. As usual at moments of despair he felt the need of prayer. But there was no one to pray to. There was no God. He lay down resting on his arm, and suddenly such a longing for sleep overcame him that he could no longer support his head on his hand, but stretched out his arm, laid his head upon it, and fell asleep. But that sleep lasted only for a moment. He woke up immediately and began not to dream but to remember.

He saw himself as a child in his mother's home in the country. A carriage drives up, and out of it steps Uncle Nicholas Sergéevich, with his long, spade-shaped, black beard, and with him Páshenka, a thin little girl with large mild eyes and a timid pathetic face. And into their company of boys Páshenka is brought and they have to play with her, but it is dull. She is silly, and it ends by their making fun of her and forcing her to show how she can swim. She lies down on the floor and shows them, and they all laugh and make a fool of her. She sees this and blushes red in patches and becomes more pitiable than before, so pitiable that he feels ashamed and can never forget that crooked, kindly, submissive smile. And Sergius remembered having seen her since then. Long after, just before he became a monk, she had married a landowner who squandered all her fortune and was in the habit of beating her. She had had two children, a son and a daughter, but the son had died while still young. And Sergius remembered having seen her very wretched. Then again he had seen her in the Monastery when she was a widow. She had been still the same, not exactly stupid, but insipid, insignificant, and pitiable. She had come with her daughter and her daughter's fiancé. They were already poor at that time and later on he had heard that she was living in a small provincial town and was very poor.

'Why am I thinking about her?' he asked himself, but he could not cease doing so. 'Where is she? How is she getting on? Is she still as unhappy as she was then when she had to show us how to swim on the floor? But why should I think about her? What am I doing? I must put an end to myself.'

And again he felt afraid, and again, to escape from that thought, he went on thinking about Páshenka.

So he lay for a long time, thinking now of his unavoidable end and now of Páshenka. She presented herself to him as a means of salvation. At last he fell asleep, and in his sleep he saw an angel who came to him and said: 'Go to Páshenka and learn from her what you have to do, what your sin is, and wherein lies your salvation.'

He awoke, and having decided that this was a vision sent by God, he felt glad, and resolved to do what had been told him in the vision. He knew the town where she lived. It was some three hundred versts (two hundred miles) away, and he set out to walk there.

VI

PÁSHENKA had already long ceased to be Páshenka and had become old, withered, wrinkled Praskóvya Mikháylovna,[1] mother-in-law of that failure, the drunken official Mavríkyev. She was living in the country town where he had had his last appointment, and there she was supporting the family: her daughter, her ailing neurasthenic son-in-law, and her five grandchildren. She did this by giving music lessons to trades-men's daughters, giving four and sometimes five lessons a day of an hour each, and earning in this way some sixty rubles [£6] a month. So they lived for the present, in expectation of another appointment. She had sent letters to all her relations and acquaintances asking them to obtain a post for her son-in-law, and among the rest she had written to Sergius, but that letter had not reached him.

It was a Saturday, and Praskóvya Mikháylovna was herself mixing dough for currant bread such as the serf-cook on her father's estate used to make so well. She wished to give her grandchildren a treat on the Sunday.

1 Páshenka is a familiar pet name. Praskóvya Mikháylovna (Michael's daughter) is the full Christian name and patronymic proper when formally addressing an adult.

Másha, her daughter, was nursing her youngest child, the eldest boy and girl were at school, and her son-in-law was asleep, not having slept during the night. Praskóvya Mikháylovna had remained awake too for a great part of the night, trying to soften her daughter's anger against her husband.

She saw that it was impossible for her son-in-law, a weak creature, to be other than he was, and realized that his wife's reproaches could do no good – so she used all her efforts to soften those reproaches and to avoid recrimination and anger. Unkindly relations between people caused her actual physical suffering. It was so clear to her that bitter feelings do not make anything better, but only make everything worse. She did not in fact think about this: she simply suffered at the sight of anger as she would from a bad smell, a harsh noise, or from blows on her body.

She had – with a feeling of self-satisfaction – just taught Lukérya how to mix the dough, when her six-year-old grandson Mísha, wearing an apron and with darned stockings on his crooked little legs, ran into the kitchen with a frightened face.

'Grandma, a dreadful old man wants to see you.'

Lukérya looked out at the door.

'There is a pilgrim of some kind, a man . . . '

Praskóvya Mikháylovna rubbed her thin elbows against one another, wiped her hands on her apron and went upstairs to get a five-kopek piece [about a penny] out of her purse for him, but remembering that she had nothing less than a ten-kopek piece she decided to give him some bread instead. She returned to the cupboard, but suddenly blushed at the thought of having grudged the ten-kopek piece, and telling Lukérya to cut a slice of bread, went upstairs again to fetch it. 'It serves you right,' she said to herself. 'You must now give twice over.'

She gave both the bread and the money to the pilgrim, and when doing so – far from being proud of her generosity – she excused herself for giving so little. The man had such an imposing appearance.

Though he had tramped two hundred versts as a beggar, though he was tattered and had grown thin and weather-beaten, though he had cropped his long hair and was wearing a peasant's cap and boots, and though he bowed very humbly, Sergius still had the impressive appearance that made him so attractive. But Praskóvya Mikháylovna did not recognize him. She could hardly do so, not having seen him for almost twenty years.

'Don't think ill of me, Father. Perhaps you want something to eat?'

He took the bread and the money, and Praskóvya Mikháylovna was surprised that he did not go, but stood looking at her.

'Páshenka, I have come to you! Take me in . . .'

His beautiful black eyes, shining with the tears that started in them, were fixed on her with imploring insistence. And under his greyish moustache his lips quivered piteously.

Praskóvya Mikháylovna pressed her hands to her withered breast, opened her mouth, and stood petrified, staring at the pilgrim with dilated eyes.

'It can't be! Stěpa! Sergéy! Father Sergius!'

'Yes, it is I,' said Sergius in a low voice. 'Only not Sergius, or Father Sergius, but a great sinner, Stepán Kasátsky – a great and lost sinner. Take me in and help me!'

'It's impossible! How have you so humbled yourself? But come in.'

She reached out her hand, but he did not take it and only followed her in.

But where was she to take him? The lodging was a small one. Formerly she had had a tiny room, almost a closet, for herself, but later she had given it up to her daughter, and Másha was now sitting there rocking the baby.

'Sit here for the present,' she said to Sergius, pointing to a bench in the kitchen.

He sat down at once, and with an evidently accustomed movement slipped the straps of his wallet first off one shoulder and then off the other.

'My God, my God! How you have humbled yourself, Father! Such great fame, and now like this . . .'

Sergius did not reply, but only smiled meekly, placing his wallet under the bench on which he sat.

'Másha, do you know who this is?' – And in a whisper Praskóvya Mikháylovna told her daughter who he was, and together they then carried the bed and the cradle out of the tiny room and cleared it for Sergius.

Praskóvya Mikháylovna led him into it.

'Here you can rest. Don't take offence . . . but I must go out.'

'Where to?'

'I have to go to a lesson. I am ashamed to tell you, but I teach music!'

'Music? But that is good. Only just one thing, Praskóvya Mikháylovna, I have come to you with a definite object. When can I have a talk with you?'

'I shall be very glad. Will this evening do?'

'Yes. But one thing more. Don't speak about me, or say who I am. I have revealed myself only to you. No one knows where I have gone to. It must be so.'

'Oh, but I have told my daughter.'

'Well, ask her not to mention it.'

And Sergius took off his boots, lay down, and at once fell asleep after a sleepless night and a walk of nearly thirty miles.

When Praskóvya Mikháylovna returned, Sergius was sitting in the little room waiting for her. He did not come out for dinner, but had some soup and gruel which Lukérya brought him.

'How is it that you have come back earlier than you said?' asked Sergius. 'Can I speak to you now?'

'How is it that I have the happiness to receive such a guest? I have missed one of my lessons. That can wait . . . I had always been planning to go to see you. I wrote to you, and now this good fortune has come.'

'Páshenka, please listen to what I am going to tell you as to a confession made to God at my last hour. Páshenka, I am not a holy man, I am not even as good as a simple ordinary man, I am a loathsome, vile, and proud sinner who has gone astray, and who, if not worse than everyone else, is at least worse than most very bad people.'

Páshenka looked at him at first with staring eyes. But she

believed what he said, and when she had quite grasped it she touched his hand, smiled pityingly, and said:

'Perhaps you exaggerate, Stíva?'

'No, Páshenka. I am an adulterer, a murderer, a blasphemer, and a deceiver.'

'My God! How is that?' exclaimed Praskóvya Mikháylovna.

'But I must go on living. And I, who thought I knew everything, who taught others how to live – I know nothing and ask you to teach me.'

'What are you saying, Stíva? You are laughing at me. Why do you always make fun of me?'

'Well, if you think I am jesting you must have it as you please. But tell me all the same how you live, and how you have lived your life.'

'I? I have lived a very nasty, horrible life, and now God is punishing me as I deserve. I live so wretchedly, so wretchedly . . .'

'How was it with your marriage? How did you live with your husband?'

'It was all bad. I married because I fell in love in the nastiest way. Papa did not approve. But I would not listen to anything and just got married. Then instead of helping my husband I tormented him by my jealousy, which I could not restrain.'

'I heard that he drank . . .'

'Yes, but I did not give him any peace. I always reproached him, though you know it is a disease! He could not refrain from it. I now remember how I tried to prevent his having it, and the frightful scenes we had!'

And she looked at Kasátsky with beautiful eyes, suffering from the remembrance.

Kasátsky remembered how he had been told that Páshenka's husband used to beat her, and now, looking at her thin withered neck with prominent veins behind her ears, and her scanty coil of hair, half grey half auburn, he seemed to see just how it had occurred.

'Then I was left with two children and no means at all.'

'But you had an estate!'

'Oh, we sold that while Vásya was still alive, and the money was all spent. We had to live, and like all our young ladies I did not know how to earn anything. I was particularly useless and helpless. So we spent all we had. I taught the children and improved my own education a little. And then Mítya fell ill when he was already in the fourth form, and God took him. Másha fell in love with Ványa, my son-in-law. And – well, he is well-meaning but unfortunate. He is ill.'

'Mamma!' – her daughter's voice interrupted her – 'Take Mítya! I can't be in two places at once.'

Praskóvya Mikháylovna shuddered, but rose and went out of the room, stepping quickly in her patched shoes. She soon came back with a boy of two in her arms, who threw himself backwards and grabbed at her shawl with his little hands.

'Where was I? Oh yes, he had a good appointment here, and his chief was a kind man too. But Ványa could not go on, and had to give up his position.'

'What is the matter with him?'

'Neurasthenia – it is a dreadful complaint. We consulted a doctor, who told us he ought to go away, but we had no means. . . . I always hope it will pass of itself. He has no particular pain, but . . .'

'Lukérya!' cried an angry and feeble voice. 'She is always sent away when I want her. Mamma . . .'

'I'm coming!' Praskóvya Mikháylovna again interrupted herself. 'He has not had his dinner yet. He can't eat with us.'

She went out and arranged something, and came back wiping her thin dark hands.

'So that is how I live. I always complain and am always dissatisfied, but thank God the grandchildren are all nice and healthy, and we can still live. But why talk about me?'

'But what do you live on?'

'Well, I earn a little. How I used to dislike music, but how useful it is to me now!' Her small hand lay on the chest of drawers beside which she was sitting, and she drummed an exercise with her thin fingers.

'How much do you get for a lesson?'

'Sometimes a ruble, sometimes fifty kopeks, or sometimes thirty.[1] They are all so kind to me.'

1 'Sometimes two shillings, sometimes one, or sometimes sevenpence.'

'And do your pupils get on well?' asked Kasátsky with a slight smile.

Praskóvya Mikháylovna did not at first believe that he was asking seriously, and looked inquiringly into his eyes.

'Some of them do. One of them is a splendid girl – the butcher's daughter – such a good kind girl! If I were a clever woman I ought, of course, with the connexions Papa had, to be able to get an appointment for my son-in-law. But as it is I have not been able to do anything, and have brought them all to this – as you see.'

'Yes, yes,' said Kasátsky, lowering his head. 'And how is it, Páshenka – do you take part in church life?'

'Oh, don't speak of it. I am so bad that way, and have neglected it so! I keep the fasts with the children and sometimes go to church, and then again sometimes I don't go for months. I only send the children.'

'But why don't you go yourself?'

'To tell the truth' (she blushed) 'I am ashamed, for my daughter's sake and the children's, to go there in tattered clothes, and I haven't anything else. Besides, I am just lazy.'

'And do you pray at home?'

'I do. But what sort of prayer is it? Only mechanical. I know it should not be like that, but I lack real religious feeling. The only thing is that I know how bad I am...'

'Yes, yes, that's right!' said Kasátsky, as if approvingly.

'I'm coming! I'm coming!' she replied to a call from her son-in-law, and tidying her scanty plait she left the room.

But this time it was long before she returned. When she came back, Kasátsky was sitting in the same position, his elbows resting on his knees and his head bowed. But his wallet was strapped on his back.

When she came in, carrying a small tin lamp without a shade, he raised his fine weary eyes and sighed very deeply.

'I did not tell them who you are,' she began timidly. 'I only said that you are a pilgrim, a nobleman, and that I used to know you. Come into the dining-room for tea.'

'No...'

'Well then, I'll bring some to you here.'

'No, I don't want anything. God bless you, Páshenka! I am going now. If you pity me, don't tell anyone that you have seen me. For the love of God don't tell anyone. Thank you. I would bow to your feet but I know it would make you feel awkward. Thank you, and forgive me for Christ's sake!'

'Give me your blessing.'

'God bless you! Forgive me for Christ's sake!'

He rose, but she would not let him go until she had given him bread and butter and rusks. He took it all and went away.

It was dark, and before he had passed the second house he was lost to sight. She only knew he was there because the dog at the priest's house was barking.

'So that is what my dream meant! Páshenka is what I ought to have been but failed to be. I lived for men on the pretext of living for God; while she lives for God imagining that she lives for men. Yes, one good deed – a cup of water given without thought of reward – is worth more than any benefit I imagined I was bestowing on people. But after all was there not some share of sincere desire to serve God?' he asked himself, and the answer was: 'Yes, there was, but it was all soiled and overgrown by desire for human praise. Yes, there is no God for the man who lives, as I did, for human praise. I will now seek Him!'

And he walked from village to village as he had done on his way to Páshenka, meeting and parting from other pilgrims, men and women, and asking for bread and a night's rest in Christ's name. Occasionally some angry housewife scolded him, or a drunken peasant reviled him, but for the most part he was given food and drink and even something to take with him. His noble bearing disposed some people in his favour, while others on the contrary seemed pleased at the sight of a gentleman who had come to beggary.

But his gentleness prevailed with everyone.

Often, finding a copy of the Gospels in a hut he would read it aloud, and when they heard him the people were always touched and surprised, as at something new yet familiar.

When he succeeded in helping people, either by advice, or by his knowledge of reading and writing, or by settling some quarrel, he did not wait to see their gratitude but went away directly afterwards. And little by little God began to reveal Himself within him.

Once he was walking along with two old women and a soldier. They were stopped by a party consisting of a lady and gentleman in a gig and another lady and gentleman on horseback. The husband was on horseback with his daughter, while in the gig his wife was driving with a Frenchman, evidently a traveller.

The party stopped to let the Frenchman see the pilgrims who, in accord with a popular Russian superstition, tramped about from place to place instead of working.

They spoke French, thinking that the others would not understand them.

'*Demandez-leur,*' said the Frenchman, '*s'ils sont bien sûr de ce que leur pèlerinage est agréable à Dieu.*'[1]

The question was asked, and one old woman replied: 'As God takes it. Our feet have reached the holy places, but our hearts may not have done so.'

They asked the soldier. He said that he was alone in the world and had nowhere else to go.

They asked Kasátsky who he was.

'A servant of God.'

'*Qu'est-ce qu'il dit? Il ne répond pas.*'[2]

'*Il dit qu'il est un serviteur de Dieu. Cela doit être un fils de prêtre. Il a de la race. Avez-vous de la petite monnaie?*'[3]

The Frenchman found some small change and gave twenty kopeks to each of the pilgrims.

'*Mais dites-leur que ce n'est pas pour les cierges que je leur donne, mais pour qu'ils se régalent de thé. Chay, chay pour vous, mon vieux!*'[4] he said with a smile. And he patted Kasátsky on the shoulder with his gloved hand.

---

1 'Ask them whether they are quite sure that their pilgrimage pleases God.'
2 'What does he say? He does not answer.'
3 'He says that he is a servant of God. That one is probably a priest's son. He is not a common man. Have you any small change?'
4 'But tell them that I give it them not to spend on church candles, but that they should have some tea. Tea, tea for you, old fellow.'

'May Christ bless you,' replied Kasátsky without replacing his cap and bowing his bald head.

He rejoiced particularly at this meeting, because he had disregarded the opinion of men and had done the simplest, easiest thing – humbly accepted twenty kopeks and given them to his comrade, a blind beggar. The less importance he attached to the opinion of men the more did he feel the presence of God within him.

For eight months Kasátsky tramped on in this manner, and in the ninth month he was arrested for not having a passport. This happened at a night-refuge in a provincial town where he had passed the night with some pilgrims. He was taken to the police-station, and when asked who he was and where was his passport, he replied that he had no passport and that he was a servant of God. He was classed as a tramp, sentenced, and sent to live in Siberia.

In Siberia he has settled down as the hired man of a well-to-do peasant, in which capacity he works in the kitchen-garden, teaches children, and attends to the sick.

THE EMPTY DRUM

(A FOLK-TALE LONG CURRENT IN
THE REGION OF THE VOLGA)

EMELYÁN was a labourer and worked for a master. Crossing the meadows one day on his way to work, he nearly trod on a frog that jumped right in front of him, but he just managed to avoid it. Suddenly he heard someone calling to him from behind.

Emelyán looked round and saw a lovely lassie, who said to him: 'Why don't you get married, Emelyán?'

'How can I marry, my lass?' said he. 'I have but the clothes I stand up in, nothing more, and no one would have me for a husband.'

'Take me for a wife,' said she.

Emelyán liked the maid. 'I should be glad to,' said he, 'but where and how could we live?'

'Why trouble about that?' said the girl. 'One only has to work more and sleep less, and one can clothe and feed oneself anywhere.'

'Very well then, let us marry,' said Emelyán. 'Where shall we go to?'

'Let us go to town.'

So Emelyán and the lass went to town, and she took him to a small hut on the very edge of the town, and they married and began housekeeping.

One day the King, driving through the town, passed by Emelyán's hut. Emelyán's wife came out to see the King. The King noticed her and was quite surprised.

'Where did such a beauty come from?' said he; and stopping his carriage he called Emelyán's wife and asked her: 'Who are you?'

'The peasant Emelyán's wife,' said she.

447

'Why did you, who are such a beauty, marry a peasant?' said the King. 'You ought to be a queen!'

'Thank you for your kind words,' said she, 'but a peasant husband is good enough for me.'

The King talked to her awhile and then drove on. He returned to the palace, but could not get Emelyán's wife out of his head. All night he did not sleep, but kept thinking how to get her for himself. He could think of no way of doing it, so he called his servants and told them they must find a way.

The King's servants said: 'Command Emelyán to come to the palace to work, and we will work him so hard that he will die. His wife will be left a widow, and then you can take her for yourself.'

The messengers followed their advice. He sent an order that Emelyán should come to the palace as a workman, and that he should live at the palace, and his wife with him.

The messengers came to Emelyán and gave him the King's message. His wife said, 'Go, Emelyán; work all day, but come back home at night.'

So Emelyán went, and when he got to the palace the King's steward asked him, 'Why have you come alone, without your wife?'

'Why should I drag her about?' said Emelyán. 'She has a house to live in.'

At the King's palace they gave Emelyán work enough for two. He began the job not hoping to finish it; but when evening came, lo and behold! it was all done. The steward saw that it was finished, and set him four times as much for next day.

Emelyán went home. Everything there was swept and tidy; the oven was heated, his supper was cooked and ready, and his wife sat by the table sewing and waiting for his return. She greeted him, laid the table, gave him to eat and drink, and then began to ask him about his work.

'Ah!' said he, 'it's a bad business: they give me tasks beyond my strength, and want to kill me with work.'

'Don't fret about the work,' said she, 'don't look either before or behind to see how much you have done or how much there is left to do; only keep on working and all will be right.'

So Emelyán lay down and slept. Next morning he went to work again and worked without once looking round. And, lo and behold! by the evening it was all done, and before dark he came home for the night.

Again and again they increased Emelyán's work, but he always got through it in good time and went back to his hut to sleep. A week passed, and the King's servants saw they could not crush him with rough work, so they tried giving him work that required skill. But this, also, was of no avail. Carpentering, and masonry, and roofing, whatever they set him to do, Emelyán had it ready in time, and went home to his wife at night. So a second week passed.

Then the King called his servants and said: 'Am I to feed you for nothing? Two weeks have gone, and I don't see that you have done anything. You were going to tire Emelyán out with work, but I see from my windows how he goes home every evening – singing cheerfully! Do you mean to make a fool of me?'

The King's servants began to excuse themselves. 'We tried our best to wear him out with rough work,' they said, 'but nothing was too hard for him; he cleared it all off as though he had swept it away with a broom. There was no tiring him out. Then we set him to tasks needing skill, which we did not think he was clever enough to do, but he managed them all. No matter what one sets him, he does it all, no one knows how. Either he or his wife must know some spell that helps them. We ourselves are sick of him, and wish to find a task he cannot master. We have now thought of setting him to build a cathedral in a single day. Send for Emelyán, and order him to build a cathedral in front of the palace in a single day. Then, if he does not do it, let his head be cut off for disobedience.'

The King sent for Emelyán. 'Listen to my command,' said he: 'build me a new cathedral on the square in front of my palace, and have it ready by to-morrow evening. If you have it ready I will reward you, but if not I will have your head cut off.'

When Emelyán heard the King's command he turned away and went home. 'My end is near,' thought he. And coming to his wife, he said: 'Get ready, wife, we must fly from here, or I shall be lost by no fault of my own.'

'What has frightened you so?' said she, 'and why should we run away?'

'How can I help being frightened? The King has ordered me, to-morrow, in a single day, to build him a cathedral. If I fail he will cut my head off. There is only one thing to be done: we must fly while there is yet time.'

But his wife would not hear of it. 'The King has many soldiers,' said she. 'They would catch us anywhere. We cannot escape from him, but must obey him as long as strength holds out.'

'How can I obey him when the task is beyond my strength?'

'Eh, goodman, don't be downhearted. Eat your supper now, and go to sleep. Rise early in the morning and all will get done.'

So Emelyán lay down and slept. His wife roused him early next day. 'Go quickly,' said she, 'and finish the cathedral. Here are nails and a hammer; there is still enough work there for a day.'

Emelyán went into the town, reached the palace square, and there stood a large cathedral not quite finished. Emelyán set to work to do what was needed, and by the evening all was ready.

When the King awoke he looked out from his palace, and saw the cathedral, and Emelyán going about driving in nails here and there. And the King was not pleased to have the cathedral – he was annoyed at not being able to condemn Emelyán and take his wife. Again he called his servants. 'Emelyán has done this task also,' said the King, 'and there is no excuse for putting him to death. Even this work was not too hard for him. You must find a more cunning plan, or I will cut off your heads as well as his.'

So his servants planned that Emelyán should be ordered to make a river round the palace, with ships sailing on it. And the King sent for Emelyán and set him this new task.

'If', said he, 'you could build a cathedral in one night, you can also do this. To-morrow all must be ready. If not, I will have your head off.'

Emelyán was more downcast than before, and returned to his wife sad at heart.

'Why are you so sad?' said his wife. 'Has the King set you a fresh task?'

Emelyán told her about it. 'We must fly,' said he.

But his wife replied: 'There is no escaping the soldiers; they will catch us wherever we go. There is nothing for it but to obey.'

'How can I do it?' groaned Emelyán.

'Eh! eh! goodman,' said she, 'don't be downhearted. Eat your supper now, and go to sleep. Rise early, and all will get done in good time.'

So Emelyán lay down and slept. In the morning his wife woke him. 'Go', said she, 'to the palace – all is ready. Only, near the wharf in front of the palace, there is a mound left; take a spade and level it.'

When the King awoke he saw a river where there had not been one; ships were sailing up and down, and Emelyán was levelling a mound with a spade. The King wondered, but was pleased neither with the river nor with the ships, so vexed was he at not being able to condemn Emelyán. 'There is no task,' thought he, 'that he cannot manage. What is to be done?' And he called his servants and again asked their advice.

'Find some task,' said he, 'which Emelyán cannot compass. For whatever we plan he fulfils, and I cannot take his wife from him.'

The King's servants thought and thought, and at last devised a plan. They came to the King and said: 'Send for Emelyán and say to him: "Go to there, don't know where", and bring back "that, don't know what". Then he will not be able to escape you. No matter where he goes, you can say that he has not gone to the right place, and no matter what he brings, you can say it is not the right thing. Then you can have him beheaded and can take his wife.'

The King was pleased. 'That is well thought of,' said he. So the King sent for Emelyán and said to him: 'Go to "there, don't know where", and bring back "that, don't know what". If you fail to bring it, I will have you beheaded.'

Emelyán returned to his wife and told her what the King had said. His wife became thoughtful.

'Well,' said she, 'they have taught the King how to catch you. Now we must act warily.' So she sat and thought, and at last said to her husband: 'You must go far, to our Grandam – the old peasant woman, the mother of soldiers – and you must ask her aid. If she helps you to anything, go straight to the palace with it. I shall be there: I cannot escape them now. They will take me by force, but it will not be for long. If you do everything as Grandam directs, you will soon save me.'

So the wife got her husband ready for the journey. She gave him a wallet, and also a spindle. 'Give her this,' said she. 'By this token she will know that you are my husband.' And his wife showed him his road.

Emelyán set off. He left the town behind, and came to where some soldiers were being drilled. Emelyán stood and watched them. After drill the soldiers sat down to rest. Then Emelyán went up to them and asked: 'Do you know, brothers, the way to "there, don't know where"? and how I can get "that, don't know what"?'

The soldiers listened to him with surprise. 'Who sent you on this errand?' said they.

'The King,' said he.

'We ourselves,' said they, 'from the day we became soldiers, go we "don't know where", and never yet have we got there; and we seek we "don't know what", and cannot find it. We cannot help you.'

Emelyán sat a while with the soldiers and then went on again. He trudged many a mile, and at last came to a wood. In the wood was a hut, and in the hut sat an old, old woman, the mother of peasant soldiers, spinning flax and weeping. And as she spun she did not put her fingers to her mouth to wet them with spittle, but to her eyes to wet them with tears. When the old woman saw Emelyán she cried out at him: 'Why have you come here?' Then Emelyán gave her the spindle, and said his wife had sent it.

The old woman softened at once, and began to question him. And Emelyán told her his whole life: how he married the lass; how they went to live in the town; how he had worked, and what he had done at the palace; how he built the cathedral, and made a river with ships on it, and how the King had now told him to go to 'there, don't know where', and bring back 'that, don't know what'.

The Grandam listened to the end, and ceased weeping. She muttered to herself: 'The time has surely come,' and said to him: 'All right, my lad. Sit down now, and I will give you something to eat.'

Emelyán ate, and then the Grandam told him what to do. 'Here', said she, 'is a ball of thread; roll it before you, and follow where it goes. You must go far till you come right to the sea. When you get there, you will see a great city. Enter the city and ask for a night's lodging at the furthest house. There look out for what you are seeking.'

'How shall I know it when I see it, Granny?' said he.

'When you see something men obey more than father or mother, that is it. Seize that, and take it to the King. When you bring it to the King, he will say it is not right, and you must answer: "If it is not the right thing it must be smashed," and you must beat it, and carry it to the river, break it in pieces, and throw it into the water. Then you will get your wife back and my tears will be dried.'

Emelyán bade farewell to the Grandam and began rolling his ball before him. It rolled and rolled until at last it reached the sea. By the sea stood a great city, and at the further end of the city was a big house. There Emelyán begged for a night's lodging, and was granted it. He lay down to sleep, and in the morning awoke and heard a father rousing his son to go and cut wood for the fire. But the son did not obey. 'It is too early,' said he, 'there is time enough.' Then Emelyán heard the mother say, 'Go, my son, your father's bones ache; would you have him go himself? It is time to be up!'

But the son only murmured some words and fell asleep again. Hardly was he asleep when something thundered and rattled in the street. Up jumped the son and quickly putting on his clothes ran out into the street. Up jumped Emelyán, too, and ran after him to see what it was that a son obeys more than father or mother. What he saw was a man walking along the street carrying, tied to his stomach, a thing which he beat with sticks, and *that* it was that rattled and thundered so, and that the son had obeyed. Emelyán ran up and had a look at it. He saw it was round, like a small tub, with a skin stretched over both ends, and he asked what it was called.

He was told, 'A drum.'

'And is it empty?'

'Yes, it is empty.'

Emelyán was surprised. He asked them to give the thing to him, but they would not. So Emelyán left off asking, and followed the drummer. All day he followed, and when the drummer at last lay down to sleep, Emelyán snatched the drum from him and ran away with it.

He ran and ran, till at last he got back to his own town. He went to see his wife, but she was not at home. The day after he went away, the King had taken her. So Emelyán went to the palace, and sent in a message to the King: 'He has returned who went to "there, don't know where", and he has brought with him "that, don't know what".'

They told the King, and the King said he was to come again next day.

But Emelyán said, 'Tell the King I am here to-day, and have brought what the King wanted. Let him come out to me, or I will go in to him!'

The King came out. 'Where have you been?' said he.

Emelyán told him.

'That's not the right place,' said the King. 'What have you brought?'

Emelyán pointed to the drum, but the King did not look at it. 'That is not it.'

'If it is not the right thing,' said Emelyán, 'it must be smashed, and may the devil take it!'

And Emelyán left the palace, carrying the drum and beating it. And as he beat it all the King's army ran out to follow Emelyán, and they saluted him and waited his commands.

The King, from his window, began to shout at his army telling them not to follow Emelyán. They did not listen to what he said, but all followed Emelyán.

When the King saw that, he gave orders that Emelyán's wife should be taken back to him, and he sent to ask Emelyán to give him the drum.

'It can't be done,' said Emelyán. 'I was told to smash it and to throw the splinters into the river.'

So Emelyán went down to the river carrying the drum, and the soldiers followed him. When he reached the river bank Emelyán smashed the drum to splinters, and threw the splinters into the stream. And then all the soldiers ran away.

Emelyán took his wife and went home with her. And after that the King ceased to trouble him; and so they lived happily ever after.

FRANÇOISE

(TOLSTOY'S ADAPTATION OF A STORY BY GUY DE MAUPASSANT)

I

ON the 3rd of May 1882 a three-masted sailing vessel, *Notre-Dame-des-Vents*, left Havre for the China Seas. After discharging her cargo in China, she took on board a fresh freight for Buenos Aires, from whence she carried other goods to Brazil.

Apart from these long voyages, the vessel was so much delayed by damages, repairs, calms that continued for months, gales which drove her far out of her course, adventures at sea, and various accidents, that it was four years before she returned to France. At last however, on the 8th of May 1886, she reached Marseilles with a cargo of American tinned fruit.

When the ship left Havre she had on board a captain, a mate, and fourteen sailors. During the voyage one sailor died, four were lost in various adventures, and of those that had sailed from France only nine returned home. In place of these men struck off the list, two Americans had been engaged, besides one negro, and a Swede who had been picked up in a drink-shop at Singapore.

The sails were furled and all the rigging made taut. A tug took them in tow and, steaming noisily, drew the vessel to the line of ships moored at the quay. The sea was calm, only a slight swell plashed on the shore. The vessel took her place in the line of those ranged along the quay, where cheek by jowl stood ships large and small, of all sizes, shapes, and kinds, from every country in the world. *Notre-Dame-des-Vents* lay between an Italian brig and an English schooner, which had both crowded up to make room for their new companion.

As soon as the captain had got rid of the custom-house officers and port officials, he gave leave to the greater part of the crew to go ashore for the night.

459

It was a warm summer night. The streets of Marseilles were lighted up and were pervaded by the smell of food, the buzz of conversation, and the noise of traffic interspersed by sounds of gaiety.

The sailors from *Notre-Dame-des-Vents* had not been on shore for four months and now on landing went about timidly in pairs, like strangers unused to a town. They wandered about the streets nearest the quay, looking around them like dogs sniffing about in search of something. It was four months since they had seen a woman. In front walked Celestin Duclos, a strong and agile fellow who always took the lead when they went ashore. He knew how to find the right places and how to get out of a scrape when necessary. He avoided such broils as sailors frequently engage in when they go ashore, but he went the pace with his comrades and could stand up for himself.

For some time the sailors strolled about those streets which run down to the sea like sewers, filled with an oppressive smell rising from their damp cellars and musty attics. At last Celestin chose a narrow side-street where large, prominent lamps shone over the doors of the houses, and into this he turned. The others followed him, grinning and singing. Numbers were painted in huge figures on the coloured glass of these lamps. In the low doorways, on straw-plaited chairs, sat women in aprons. They rushed out at the sight of the sailors, and running into the street threw themselves in their way, enticing them each to her own lair.

At times a door unexpectedly opened at the end of a passage, through which one saw a half-naked woman wearing very short skirts and a very low-cut velvet bodice trimmed with gilt lace.

'Ah! lads, come here,' such a one would cry from a distance, or even ran out herself and catching hold of a sailor dragged him with all her strength towards her den. She stuck to him like a spider seizing a fly stronger than itself. The fellow resisted feebly and the others stopped to see the result, but Celestin Duclos shouted:

'Not there, don't go in there: come farther!'

The fellow obeyed, tearing himself from the woman by force, and the sailors went on, followed by the abuse of the enraged woman. At the noise of the encounter other women along the street rushed out and fell upon them, shouting the praises of their wares in hoarse voices, but the sailors went on farther and farther. Occasionally they met a soldier with jingling spurs or a solitary clerk or tradesman making his way to some accustomed haunt. In other side-streets shone other lamps of the same kind, but the sailors went farther and farther, tramping through the foul-smelling slush that oozed from the yards. At last Duclos stopped at a house of better appearance than the others, and led his comrades in.

II

THE sailors were sitting in the chief room of the establishment. Each of them had chosen a woman companion from whom he did not part the whole evening; such was the custom of the place. Three tables had been placed together, and first of all the sailors drank, each with his lass. Then they rose and went upstairs with them. Long and loud clattered their twenty feet in their thick boots on the wooden stairs before they had all tumbled through the narrow doors into their separate rooms. From there they came down again to drink, and then returned once more upstairs.

The carouse was kept up recklessly. The whole half-year's pay went in a four hours' debauch. By eleven o'clock they were all drunk, and with bloodshot eyes were shouting disconnected phrases not knowing what they said. They sang, shouted, beat with their fists on the table, or poured wine down their throats. Celestin Duclos was there among his comrades and with him sat a large, stout, red-cheeked woman. He had had as much to drink as the others, but was not yet quite drunk: some more or less connected thoughts still flickered through his brain. He grew tender, and tried to think of something to say to his lass, but the thoughts that came into his head vanished again at once and he was unable to remember or express them.

'Yes,' said he, laughing. 'Just so. . . . Just so. . . . And have you lived here long?'

'Six months,' replied the woman.

He nodded his head, as if to show his approval of this.

'And are you comfortable here?'

She thought a moment.

'I have got accustomed to it,' she said. 'One has to live somehow. It is not so bad as being in service or working in a laundry.'

He nodded his head approvingly, as if to commend her for this also.

'Were you born in these parts?' said he.

She shook her head.

'Do you come from far away?' he continued.

She nodded.

'Where from?'

She paused, as if to remember.

'I am from Perpignan,' said she.

'Yes, yes,' said he and ceased questioning her.

'And what are you – a sailor?' asked the woman in her turn.

'Yes, we are sailors.'

'And have you been on long voyages?'

'Yes, long enough! We have seen places of all sorts.'

'Have you been round the world?'

'Oh yes,' said he, 'not once only – we have been nearly twice round.'

She again paused, as if remembering something.

'I suppose you have met many ships?' said she.

'Of course we have.'

'Have you ever met the *Notre-Dame-des-Vents*? There is a ship of that name.'

He was surprised at her naming his vessel, and thought he would play a trick on her.

'Why, certainly,' said he; 'we met her only last week.'

'Is that the truth?' she said, growing pale.

'The solemn truth.'

'You are not telling me a lie?'

'So help me God,' swore he, 'I am telling the truth.'

'And did you not meet a man on board named Celestin Duclos?' asked she.

'Celestin Duclos?' he repeated, astonished and even alarmed. How did this woman know his name?

'Why! do you know him?' he asked.

It was evident that she too was alarmed.

'No, not I, but there is a woman here that knows him.'

'What woman? Here in this house?'

'No, but near here.'

'Tell me where?'

'Oh, not very far away.'

'Who is she?'

'Oh, just a woman – like myself.'

'What has she to do with him?'

'How should I know? Perhaps they come from the same parts.'

They looked searchingly into each other's eyes.

'I should like to see that woman,' he said.

'Why?' she asked. 'Have you anything to tell her?'

'I want to tell her . . .'

'To tell her – what?'

'That I have seen Celestin Duclos.'

'You have seen Celestin Duclos! Is he alive and well?'

'He is quite well. But what is that to you?'

She was silent, again collecting her thoughts. Then she said softly:

'What port is the *Notre-Dame-des-Vents* bound for?'

'What port? Why, Marseilles.'

'Is that true?' cried she.

'Quite true.'

'And you know Duclos?'

'I have already told you that I know him.'

She thought awhile.

'Yes, yes, it is well,' said she softly.

'What do you want with him?'

'If you should see him, tell him . . . No, better not!'

'What shall I tell him?'

'No, never mind.'

As he looked at her he became more and more agitated.

'Do you know him yourself?' asked he.

'No, I don't know him myself.'

'Then what does he matter to you?'

She did not answer, but jumping up ran to the counter, behind which the hostess sat. Taking a lemon, she cut it in half and squeezed the juice into a glass which she filled with water, and this she gave to Celestin.

'There – drink that!' she said, sitting down as before on his knees.

'What is this for?' he asked, taking the glass from her.

'To clear your head. Then I will tell you something. Drink it!'

He drank it, and wiped his lips with the back of his hand.

'Well, now tell me! I am attending.'

'But you must not let him know that you have seen me, nor tell him whom you heard it from.'

'Very well, I will not tell.'

'Swear it!'

He swore.

'So help you God!'

'So help me God!'

'Well then, tell him his father and mother are both dead and his brother also. A fever broke out and they all died in one and the same month.'

Duclos felt the blood rushing to his heart. For some minutes he sat in silence, not knowing what to say. Presently he uttered the words:

'Are you sure it is so?'

'Quite sure.'

'Who told you?'

She put her hands on his shoulders and looked him straight in the eyes.

'Swear you will not let it out!'

He swore it: 'So help me God!'

'I am his sister.'

'Françoise!' he shrieked.

She looked intently at him, and softly, softly moved her lips, hardly letting the words escape:

'So you are Celestin!'

They did not stir, but remained as though benumbed, gazing into each other's eyes.

Around them the others shouted with drunken voices. The ringing of glasses, the beating of hands and heels, and the piercing screams of women, intermingled with the singing and the shouting.

'How can it have happened?' said he, so gently that even she could hardly catch the words.

Her eyes suddenly filled with tears.

'They died,' she continued. 'All three in one month. What was I to do? I was left alone. The chemist, the doctor, the three funerals. . . . I had to sell everything to pay the debts. Nothing was left but the clothes I wore. I went as servant to Monsieur Cacheux. . . . Do you remember him? A lame man. I was only just fifteen. I was scarcely fourteen when you left home – and I went wrong with him. . . . You know how stupid we peasant girls are. Then I went as nurse in a notary's family – and it was the same with him. For a time he made me his mistress and I had a lodging of my own; but that did not last long. He left me, and for three days I was without food. No one would take me, so I came here like the rest of them.' And as she spoke the water flowed in streams from her eyes and nose, wetting her cheeks and trickling into her mouth.

'What have we done?' said he.

'I thought you were dead also. How could I have helped it?' whispered she through her tears.

'How was it you did not know me?' he answered, also in a whisper.

'I do not know. It was not my fault,' continued she, weeping yet more bitterly.

'How could I know you?' he said again. 'You were so different when I left home! But you should have known me!'

She threw up her hands in despair.

'Ah! I see so many of them – these men. They all look alike to me now!'

His heart contracted so painfully and so strongly that he wanted to cry aloud, as a little boy does when he is beaten.

He rose and held her at arm's length; then, seizing her head in his great sailor paws, he gazed intently into her face.

Little by little he recognized in her the small, slender, merry maiden he had left at home with those others whose eyes it had been her lot to close.

'Yes, you are Françoise! My sister!' he exclaimed. And suddenly sobs – the sobs of a strong man, sounding like the hiccups of a drunkard – rose in his throat. He let go of her head, and striking the table so that the glasses upset and broke to atoms, he cried out in a wild voice.

His comrades, astonished, turned towards him.

'See how he's swaggering,' said one.

'Stop that shouting,' said another.

'Eh, Duclos! What are you bawling about? Let's get upstairs again,' said a third, plucking Celestin by the sleeve with one hand while his other arm encircled a flushed, laughing, black-eyed lass, in a rose-coloured, low-cut, silk dress.

Duclos suddenly became quiet, and holding his breath looked at his comrades. Then, with the same strange and resolute expression with which he used to enter on a fight, he staggered up to the sailor who was embracing the girl, and struck down with his hand – dividing them apart.

'Away! Do you not see that she is your sister! Each of them is someone's sister. See, here is my sister, Françoise! Ha, ha...ha...' and he broke into sobs that almost sounded like laughter. Then he staggered, raised his hands, and fell with a crash to the floor, where he rolled about, striking the floor with his hands and feet and choking as though about to die.

'He must be put to bed,' said one of his comrades. 'We shall be having him taken up if we go out into the streets.'

So they lifted Celestin and dragged him upstairs to Françoise's room, where they laid him on her bed.

A TALK AMONG
LEISURED PEOPLE

AN INTRODUCTION TO THE STORY
THAT FOLLOWS

SOME guests assembled at a wealthy house one day happened to start a serious conversation about life.

They spoke of people present and absent, but failed to find anyone who was satisfied with his life.

Not only could no one boast of happiness, but not a single person considered that he was living as a Christian should do. All confessed that they were living worldly lives concerned only for themselves and their families, none of them thinking of their neighbours, still less of God.

So said all the guests, and all agreed in blaming themselves for living godless and unchristian lives.

'Then why do we live so?' exclaimed a youth. 'Why do we do what we ourselves disapprove of? Have we no power to change our way of life? We ourselves admit that we are ruined by our luxury, our effeminacy, our riches, and above all by our pride – our separation from our fellow-men. To be noble and rich we have to deprive ourselves of all that gives man joy. We crowd into towns, become effeminate, ruin our health, and in spite of all our amusements we die of ennui, and of regrets that our life is not what it should be.

'Why do we live so? Why do we spoil our lives and all the good that God gives us? I don't want to live in that old way! I will abandon the studies I have begun – they would only bring me to the same tormenting life of which we are all now complaining. I will renounce my property and go to the country and live among the poor. I will work with them, will learn to labour with my hands, and if my education is of any use to the poor I will share it with them, not through institutions and books but directly by living with them in a brotherly way.

469

'Yes, I have made up my mind,' he added, looking inquiringly at his father, who was also present.

'Your wish is a worthy one,' said his father, 'but thoughtless and ill-considered. It seems so easy to you only because you do not know life. There are many things that seem to us good, but the execution of what is good is complicated and difficult. It is hard enough to walk well on a beaten track, but it is harder still to lay out a new one. New paths are made only by men who are thoroughly mature and have mastered all that is attainable by man. It seems to you easy to make new paths of life only because you do not yet understand life. It is an outcome of thoughtlessness and youthful pride. We old folk are needed to moderate your impulsiveness and guide you by our experience, and you young folk should obey us in order to profit by that experience. Your active life lies before you. You are now growing up and developing. Finish your education, make yourself thoroughly conversant with things, get on to your own feet, have firm convictions of your own, and then start a new life if you feel you have strength to do so. But for the present you should obey those who are guiding you for your own good, and not try to open up new paths of life.'

The youth was silent and the older guests agreed with what the father had said.

'You are right,' said a middle-aged married man, turning to the youth's father. 'It is true that the lad, lacking experience of life, may blunder when seeking new paths of life and his decision cannot be a firm one. But you know we all agreed that our life is contrary to our conscience and does not give us happiness. So we cannot but recognize the justice of wishing to escape from it.

'The lad may mistake his fancy for a reasonable deduction, but I, who am no longer young, tell you for myself that as I listened to the talk this evening the same thought occurred to me. It is plain to me that the life I now live cannot give me peace of mind or happiness. Experience and reason alike show me that. Then what am I waiting for? We struggle from morning to night for our families, but it turns out that we and our families live ungodly lives and get more and more

sunk in sins. We work for our families, but our families are no
better off, because we are not doing the right thing for them.
And so I often think that it would be better if I changed my
whole way of life and did just what that young man proposed
to do: ceased to bother about my wife and children and began
to think about my soul. Not for nothing did Paul say: "He that
is married careth how he may please his wife, but he that is
unmarried careth how he may please the Lord." '

But before he had finished speaking his wife and all the
women present began to attack him.

'You ought to have thought about that before,' said an
elderly woman. 'You have put on the yoke, so you must
draw your load. Like that, everyone will say he wishes to go
off and save his soul when it seems hard to him to support and
feed his family. That is false and cowardly. No! A man should
be able to live in godly fashion with his family. Of course it
would be easy enough to save your own soul all by yourself.
But to behave like that would be to run contrary to Christ's
teaching. God bade us love others; but in that way you would
in His name offend others. No. A married man has his definite
obligations and he must not shirk them. It's different when
your family are already on their own feet. Then you may do as
you please for yourself, but no one has a right to force his
family.'

But the man who had spoken did not agree. 'I don't want to
abandon my family,' he said. 'All I say is that my family should
not be brought up in a worldly fashion, nor brought up to live
for their own pleasure, as we have just been saying, but should
be brought up from their early days to become accustomed to
privation, to labour, to the service of others, and above all to
live a brotherly life with all men. And for that we must
relinquish our riches and distinctions.'

'There is no need to upset others while you yourself do not
live a godly life,' exclaimed his wife irritably. 'You yourself
lived for your own pleasure when you were young, then why
do you want to torment your children and your family? Let
them grow up quietly, and later on let them do as they please
without coercion from you!'

Her husband was silent, but an elderly man who was there spoke up for him.

'Let us admit,' said he, 'that a married man, having accustomed his family to a certain comfort, cannot suddenly deprive them of it. It is true that if you have begun to educate your children it is better to finish it than to break up everything – especially as the children when grown up will choose the path they consider best for themselves. I agree that for a family man it is difficult and even impossible to change his way of life without sinning. But for us old men it is what God commands. Let me say for myself: I am now living without any obligations, and to tell the truth, simply for my belly. I eat, drink, rest, and am disgusting and revolting even to myself. So it is time for me to give up such a life, to give away my property, and at least before I die to live for a while as God bids a Christian live.'

But the others did not agree with the old man. His niece and godchild was present, to all of whose children he had stood sponsor and gave presents on holidays. His son was also there. They both protested.

'No,' said the son. 'You worked in your time, and it is time for you to rest and not trouble yourself. You have lived for sixty years with certain habits and must not change them now. You would only torment yourself in vain.'

'Yes, yes,' confirmed his niece. 'You would be in want and out of sorts, and would grumble and sin more than ever. God is merciful and will forgive all sinners – to say nothing of such a kind old uncle as you!'

'Yes, and why should you?' added another old man of the same age. 'You and I have perhaps only a couple of days to live, so why should we start new ways?'

'What a strange thing!' exclaimed one of the visitors who had hitherto been silent. 'What a strange thing! We all say that it would be good to live as God bids us and that we are living badly and suffer in body and soul, but as soon as it comes to practice it turns out that the children must not be upset and must be brought up not in godly fashion but in the old way. Young folk must not run counter to their parents' will and must live not in a godly fashion but in the old way. A married man must not upset his wife and children and must live not in a godly way but as of old. And there is no need for old men to begin anything: they are not accustomed to it and have only a couple of days left to live. So it seems that none of us may live rightly: we may only talk about it.'

WALK IN THE LIGHT
WHILE THERE IS LIGHT
A STORY OF EARLY CHRISTIAN TIMES

I

IT happened in the reign of the Roman Emperor Trajan a hundred years after the birth of Christ, at a time when disciples of Christ's disciples were still living and Christians held firmly to the Teacher's law, as is told in the Acts:

And the multitude of them that believed were of one heart and of one soul: neither said any of them that aught of the things which he possessed was his own; but they had all things in common. And with great power gave the apostles witness of the resurrection of the Lord Jesus: and great grace was upon them all. Neither was there any among them that lacked; for as many as were possessors of lands or houses sold them and brought the prices of the things that were sold, and laid them down at the apostles' feet: and distribution was made unto every man according as he had need (Acts iv. 32–5).

In those early times there lived in the province of Cilicia, in the city of Tarsus, a rich Syrian merchant, Juvenal by name, who dealt in precious stones. He was of poor and humble origin, but by industry and skill in his business had earned wealth and the respect of his fellow-citizens. He had travelled much in foreign countries, and though uneducated he had come to know and understand much, and the townsfolk respected him for his ability and probity. He professed the pagan Roman faith that was held by all respectable citizens of the Roman Empire, the ritual of which had been strictly enforced since the time of the Emperor Augustus and was still adhered to by the present Emperor Trajan. Cilicia was far from Rome, but was ruled by Roman governors, and all that was done in Rome was reflected in Cilicia, whose governors imitated their Emperor.

477

Juvenal remembered the stories he had heard in childhood of what Nero had done in Rome, and later on he saw how the emperors perished one after another, and being a clever man he understood that there was nothing sacred in the Roman religion but that it was all the work of human hands. But being a clear-headed man he understood that it would not be advantageous to struggle against the existing order of things, and that for his own tranquillity it was better to submit to it. The senselessness of the life all around him, and especially of what went on in Rome, where he repeatedly went on business, often however perplexed him. He had his doubts, he could not grasp it all, and he attributed this to his lack of learning.

He was married and had had four children, but three of them had died young and only one son, Julius, was left.

To him Juvenal devoted all his love and care. He particularly wished to educate his son so that that latter might not be tormented by such doubts about life as perplexed himself. When Julius had passed his fifteenth year his father entrusted him to a philosopher who had settled in their town and who received youths for their instruction. His father gave his son to this philosopher, together with his comrade Pamphilius, the son of a former slave whom Juvenal had freed.

The lads were friends, of the same age, and both handsome fellows. Both studied diligently and both were well conducted. Julius distinguished himself more in the study of the poets and in mathematics, but Pamphilius in the study of philosophy. A year before the completion of their studies, Pamphilius at school one day informed his teacher that his widowed mother was moving to the town of Daphne, and that he would have to abandon his studies.

The teacher was sorry to lose a pupil who was doing him credit, Juvenal too was sorry, but sorriest of all was Julius. But nothing would induce Pamphilius to remain, and after thanking his friends for their love and care, he took his leave.

Two years passed. Julius had finished his studies and during all that time had not once seen his friend.

One day however he met him in the street, invited him to his home, and began asking him how and where he was living.

Pamphilius told him that he and his mother were still living in the same place.

'We are not living alone,' said he, 'but among many friends with whom we have everything in common.'

'How "in common"?' inquired Julius.

'So that none of us considers anything his own.'

'Why do you do that?'

'We are Christians,' said Pamphilius.

'Is it possible?' exclaimed Julius. 'Why, I have heard that the Christians kill children and eat them! Is it possible that you take part in that?'

For to be a Christian in those days was the same thing as in our days to be an anarchist. As soon as a man was convicted of being a Christian he was immediately thrown into prison, and if he did not renounce his faith, was executed.

'Come and see,' replied Pamphilius. 'We do not do anything strange. We live simply, trying to do nothing bad.'

'But how can you live if you do not consider anything your own?'

'We manage to live. If we work for our brethren they do the same for us.'

'But if your brethren take your labour and do not give you theirs – how then?'

'There are none of that sort,' said Pamphilius. 'Such people like to live in luxury and will not come to us. Our life is simple and not luxurious.'

'But there are plenty of lazy people who would be glad to be fed for nothing.'

'There are such, and we receive them gladly. Lately a man of that kind came to us, a runaway slave. At first, it is true, he was lazy and led a bad life, but he soon changed his habits, and has now become a good brother.'

'But suppose he had not improved?'

'There are such, too, and our Elder, Cyril, says that we should treat these as our most valued brethren, and love them even more.'

'How can one love a good-for-nothing fellow?'

'One cannot help but love a man!'

'But how can you give to all whatever they ask?' queried Julius. 'If my father gave to all who ask he would very soon have nothing left.'

'I don't know about that,' replied Pamphilius. 'We have enough left for our needs, and if it happens that we have nothing to eat or to wear, we ask of others and they give to us. But that happens rarely. It only once happened to me to go to bed supperless, and then only because I was very tired and did not wish to go to ask for anything.'

'I don't know how you manage,' said Julius, 'but my father says that if you don't save what you have, and if you give to all who ask, you will yourself die of hunger.'

'We don't! Come and see. We live, and not only do not suffer want, but even have plenty to spare.'

'How is that?'

'Why, this way. We all profess one and the same faith, but the strength to fulfil it differs in each of us. One has more and another less of it. One has advanced much in the true path of life, while another is only just beginning it. In front of us all stands Christ with his life, and we all try to emulate him and see our welfare in that alone. Some of us, like the Elder Cyril and his wife Pelagia, are leaders, others stand behind them, others again are still farther behind, but we are all following the same path. Those in front already approach a fulfilment of Christ's law – self-renunciation and readiness to lose their life to save it. These desire nothing. They do not spare themselves, and in accord with Christ's law are ready to give the last of their possessions to those who ask. Others are feebler, they weaken and are sorry for themselves when they lack their customary clothing and food, and they do not give away everything. There are others who are still weaker – such as have only recently started on the path. These still live in the old way, keeping much for themselves, and only giving away their superfluities. And it is these hindmost people who give the largest material assistance to those in the van. Besides this, we are all of us entangled by our relationships with the pagans. One man's father is a pagan who has property and gives to his son. The son gives to those who ask, but then the father again gives to him. Another has a pagan mother who is sorry for her son and helps him. A third is the mother of pagan children, who take care of her and give her things, begging her not to give them away, and she takes what they give her out of love for them, but still gives to others. A fourth has a pagan wife and a fifth a pagan husband. So we are all entangled, and the foremost, who would gladly give away their all, are not able to do so. That is why our life does not prove too hard for those weak in the faith, and why it happens that we have much that is superfluous.'

To this Julius said:

'But if that is so, then you fail to observe Christ's teaching and only pretend to do so. If you do not give up everything there is no difference between you and us. To my mind if a man is a Christian he ought to fulfil Christ's whole law – give up everything and become a pauper.'

'That would be best of all,' said Pamphilius. 'Why do you not do it?'

'Yes, I will when I see you do it.'

'We don't want to do anything for show. And I don't advise you to come to us and renounce your present way of life for the sake of appearances. We act as we do not for appearances, but according to our faith.'

'What does "according to our faith" mean?'

'"According to our faith" means that salvation from the evils of the world, from death, is only to be found in a life according to the teaching of Christ. We are indifferent to what people may say of us. We act as we do not for men's approval, but because in this alone do we see life and welfare.'

'It is impossible not to live for oneself,' said Julius. 'The gods themselves have implanted it in us that we love ourselves more than others and seek pleasure for ourselves. And you do the same. You yourself say that some among you have pity on themselves. They will seek pleasures for themselves more and more, and will more and more abandon your faith and behave just as we do.'

'No,' said Pamphilius, 'our brethren are travelling another path and will not weaken but will grow ever stronger, just as a fire will never go out when more wood is laid on it. That is our faith.'

'I don't understand what this faith of yours is!'

'Our faith consists in this, that we understand life as Christ has explained it to us.'

'How is that?'

'Christ once told this parable. Certain men kept a vineyard and had to pay rent to its owner. That is, we men who live in the world must pay rent to God by doing His will. But these men, in accord with their worldly belief, considered that the vineyard was theirs and that they need pay no rent for it, but had only to enjoy its fruits. The owner sent a messenger to them to collect the rent, but they drove him away. Then the owner sent his son, but him they killed, thinking that after that no one would disturb them. That is the faith of the world by which all worldly people live who do not acknowledge that life is only given us that we may serve God. But Christ has taught us that this worldly belief – that it is better for man if he drives the messenger and the owner's son out of the vineyard and avoids paying the rent – is a false one, for there is no avoiding the fact that we must either pay the rent or be driven out of the garden. He has taught us that all the things we call pleasures – eating, drinking, and merry-making – cannot be pleasures if we devote our lives to them, but are pleasures only when we are seeking something else – to live a life in conformity with the will of God. Only then do these pleasures follow as a natural reward of the fulfilment of His will. To wish to take the pleasures without the labour of fulfilling God's will – to tear the pleasures away from duty – is the same as to tear up a flower and replant it without its roots. We believe this, and so we cannot follow error when we see the truth. Our faith is that the good of life is not in its pleasures but in the fulfilment of God's will, without any thought of present or future pleasures. And the longer we live the more we see that the pleasures and the good come in the wake of a fulfilment of God's will, as a wheel follows the shafts. Our Teacher said: "Come unto me, all ye that labour and are heavy laden, and I will give you rest. Take my yoke upon you, and learn of me, for I am meek and lowly in heart, and ye shall find rest unto your souls. For my yoke is easy and my burden is light."'

So spoke Pamphilius. Julius listened and his heart was touched, but what Pamphilius had said was not clear to him. At first it seemed to him that Pamphilius was deceiving him; but then he looked into his friend's kindly eyes and remembered his goodness, and it seemed to him that Pamphilius was deceiving himself.

Pamphilius invited Julius to come to see their way of life and, if it pleased him, to remain to live with them.

And Julius promised, but he did not go to see Pamphilius, and being absorbed by his own affairs he forgot about him.

II

JULIUS's father was wealthy, and as he loved his only son and was proud of him, he did not grudge him money. Julius lived the usual life of a rich young man, in idleness, luxury, and dissipated amusements, which have always been and still remain the same: wine, gambling, and loose women.

But the pleasures to which Julius abandoned himself demanded more and more money, and he began to find that he had not enough. On one occasion he asked his father for more than he usually gave him. His father gave what he asked, but reproved his son. Julius, feeling himself to blame, but unwilling to admit it, became angry and was rude to his father, as those who know they are to blame and do not wish to acknowledge it, always do.

The money Julius got from his father was very soon all spent. And just at that time it happened that he and a drunken companion became involved in a brawl and killed a man. The city prefect heard of this and would have had him arrested, but his father intervened and obtained his pardon. Julius now needed still more money for dissipation, and this time he borrowed it from a companion, promising to repay it. Moreover his mistress demanded a present: she had taken a fancy to a pearl necklace, and Julius knew that if he did not gratify her wish she would abandon him and attach herself to a rich man who had long been trying to entice her away.

Julius went to his mother and told her that he must have some money, and that he would kill himself if he could not get what he needed. He placed the blame for his being in such a position not on himself but on his father. He said: 'My father accustomed me to a life of luxury and then began to grudge me money. Had he given me at first and without reproaches what he gave me later, I should have arranged my life properly and should not have been in such difficulties, but as he never gave me enough I had to go to the money-lenders and they squeezed everything out of me, and I had nothing left on which to live the life natural to me as a rich young man, and was made to feel ashamed among my companions. But my father does not wish to understand anything of all this. He forgets that he was young once himself. He has brought me to this state, and now if he will not give me what I ask I shall kill myself.'

The mother, who spoilt her son, went to his father, and Juvenal called his son and began to upbraid both him and his mother. Julius answered his father rudely and Juvenal struck him. Julius seized his father's arm, at which Juvenal shouted to his slaves and bade them bind his son and lock him up.

Julius was left alone, and he cursed his father and his own life.

It seemed to him that the only way of escape from his present position was either by his own or his father's death.

Julius's mother suffered even more than he did. She did not try to understand who was to blame for all this. She only pitied her adored son. She went again to her husband to implore him to forgive the youth, but he would not listen to her, and reproached her for having spoilt their son. She in turn reproached him, and it ended by Juvenal beating his wife. Disregarding this, however, she went to her son and persuaded him to beg his father's pardon and yield to his wishes, in return for which she promised to take the money he needed from her husband by stealth, and give it him. Julius agreed, and then his mother again went to Juvenal and urged him to forgive his son. Juvenal scolded his wife and son for a long time, but at last decided that he would forgive Julius, on condition that he should abandon his dissolute life and marry the daughter of a rich merchant – a match Juvenal was very anxious to arrange.

'He will get money from me and also have his wife's dowry,' said Juvenal, 'and then let him settle down to a decent life. If he promises to obey my wishes, I will forgive him; but I will not give him anything at present, and the first time he transgresses I will hand him over to the prefect.'

Julius submitted to his father's conditions and was released. He promised to marry and to abandon his bad life, but he had no intention of doing so.

Life at home now became a hell for him. His father did not speak to him and quarrelled with his mother on his account, and his mother wept.

One day she called him into her apartments and secretly handed him a precious stone which she had taken from her husband's room.

'Go and sell it,' she said, 'not here but in another town, and then do what you have to do. I shall be able to conceal its loss for the present, and if it is discovered I will lay the blame on one of the slaves.'

Julius's heart was pierced by his mother's words. He was horrified at what she had done, and without taking the precious stone he left the house.

He did not himself know where he was going or with what aim. He walked on and on out of the town, feeling that he needed to be alone, and thinking over all that had happened to him and that awaited him. Going farther and farther away at last he reached the sacred grove of the goddess Diana. Coming to a secluded spot he began to think, and the first thought that occurred to him was to seek the goddess's aid. But he no longer believed in the gods, and knew that he could not expect aid from them. And if not from them, then from whom?

To think out his position for himself seemed to him too strange. All was darkness and confusion in his soul. But there was nothing else to be done. He had to listen to his conscience, and began to consider his life and his actions in the light of it.

And both appeared to him bad, and above all stupid. Why had he tormented himself like this? Why had he ruined his young life in such a way? It had brought him little happiness and much sorrow and unhappiness. But chiefly he felt himself alone. Formerly he had had a mother whom he loved, a father, and friends. Now there was no one. Nobody loved him! He was a burden to them all. He had been a cause of suffering to all who knew him. For his mother he was the cause of discord with his father. For his father he was the dissipator of the wealth collected by a lifetime of labour. For his friends he was a dangerous and disagreeable rival. They must all desire his death.

Passing his life in review he remembered Pamphilius and his last meeting with him, and how Pamphilius had invited him to go there, to the Christians. And it occurred to him not to return home, but to go straight to the Christians and remain with them.

But could his position be so desperate? he wondered. Again he recalled all that had happened to him, and again he was horrified at the idea that nobody loved him and that he loved no one. His mother, father, and friends did not care for him and must wish for his death. But did he himself love anyone? His friends? He felt that he loved none of them: they were all his rivals and would be pitiless to him now that he was in distress. His father? He was seized with horror when he put himself that question. He looked into his heart and found that not only did he not love his father, he even hated him for the restraint and insult he had put upon him. He hated him, and more than that he saw clearly that his father's death was necessary for his own happiness.

'Yes,' he said to himself. 'If I knew that no one would see it or ever know of it, what should I do if I could immediately, at one stroke, deprive him of life and free myself?'

And he answered his own question: 'I should kill him!' And he was horrified at that reply.

'My mother? I am sorry for her but I do not love her: it is all the same to me what becomes of her. All I need is her help. . . . I am a beast, and a wretched, hunted one at that. I only differ from a beast in that I can by my own will quit this false and evil life. I can do what a beast cannot do – I can kill myself. I hate my father. There is no one I love . . . neither my mother nor my friends . . . unless, perhaps, Pamphilius alone?'

And he again thought of him. He recalled their last meeting, their conversation, and Pamphilius's words that, according to their teaching, Christ had said: 'Come unto me all ye that labour and are heavy laden, and I will give you rest.' Could that be true?

He went on thinking, and remembering Pamphilius's gentle, fearless, and happy face, he wished to believe what Pamphilius had said.

'What indeed am I?' he said to himself. 'Who am I? A man seeking happiness. I sought it in my lusts and did not find it. And all who live as I did fail to find it. They are all evil and suffer. But there is a man who is always full of joy because he demands nothing. He says that there are many like him and that all men will be such if they follow their Master's teaching. What if this be true? True or not it attracts me and I will go there.'

So said Julius to himself, and he left the grove, having decided not to return home but to go to the village where the Christians lived.

III

JULIUS went along briskly and joyously, and the farther he went the more vividly did he imagine to himself the life of the Christians, recalling all that Pamphilius had said, and the happier he felt. The sun was already declining towards evening and he wished to rest, when he came upon a man seated by the roadside having a meal. He was a man of middle age with an intelligent face, and was sitting there eating olives and a flat cake. On seeing Julius he smiled and said:

'Greeting to you, young man! The way is still long. Sit down and rest.'

Julius thanked him and sat down.

'Where are you going?' asked the stranger.

'To the Christians,' said Julius, and by degrees he recounted to the unknown his whole life and his decision.

The stranger listened attentively and asked about some
details without himself expressing an opinion, but when Julius
had ended he packed the remaining food in his wallet, adjusted
his dress, and said:

'Young man, do not pursue your intention. You would be
making a mistake. I know life; you do not. I know the
Christians; you do not. Listen! I will review your life and
your thoughts, and when you have heard them from me,
you will take what decision seems to you wisest. You are
young, rich, handsome, strong, and the passions boil in your
veins. You wish to find a quiet refuge where they will not
agitate you and you would not suffer from their consequences.
And you think that you can find such a shelter among the
Christians.

'There is no such refuge, dear young man, because what
troubles you does not dwell in Cilicia or in Rome but in
yourself. In the quiet solitude of a village the same passions
will torment you, only a hundred times more strongly. The
deception of the Christians, or their delusion – for I do not
wish to judge them – consists in not wishing to recognize
human nature. Only an old man who has outlived all his
passions could fully carry out their teaching. But a man in
the vigour of life, or a youth like you who has not yet tested
life and tried himself, cannot submit to their law, because it is
based not on human nature but on idle speculations. If you go
to them you will suffer from what makes you suffer now, only
to a much greater extent. Now your passions lead you into
wrong paths, but having once mistaken your road you can
correct it. Now at any rate you have the satisfaction of desires
fulfilled – that is life. But among the Christians, forcibly
restraining your passions, you will err yet more and in a similar
way, and besides that suffering you will have the incessant
suffering of unsatisfied desires. Release the water from a dam
and it will irrigate the earth and the meadows and supply drink
for the animals, but confine it and it will burst its banks and
flow away as mud. So it is with the passions. The teaching of
the Christians (besides the belief in another life with which
they console themselves and of which I will not speak) – their

practical teaching is this: They do not approve of violence, do not recognize wars, or tribunals, or property, or the sciences and arts, or anything that makes life easy and pleasant.

'That might be well enough if all men were such as they describe their Teacher as having been. But that is not and cannot be so. Men are evil and subject to passions. That play of passions and the conflicts caused by them are what keep men in the social condition in which they live. The barbarians know no restraint, and for the satisfaction of his desires one such man would destroy the whole world if all men submitted as these Christians do. If the gods implanted in men the sentiments of anger, revenge, and even of vindictiveness against the wicked, they did so because these sentiments are necessary for human life. The Christians teach that these feelings are bad, and that without them men would be happy, and there would be no murders, executions, and wars. That is true, but it is like supposing that people would be happy if they did not eat food. There would then indeed be no greed or hunger, or any of the calamities that result from them. But that supposition would not change human nature. And if some two or three dozen people believed in it, and did actually refrain from food and die of hunger, it would still not alter human nature. The same is true of man's other passions: indignation, anger, revenge, even the love of women, of luxury, or of the pomp and grandeur characteristic of the gods and therefore unalterable characteristics of man too. Abolish man's nutrition and man will be destroyed. And similarly abolish the passions natural to man and mankind will be unable to exist. It is the same with ownership, which the Christians are supposed to reject. Look around you: every vineyard, every enclosure, every house, every ass, has been produced by man under conditions of ownership. Abandon the rights of property and not one vineyard will be tilled or one animal raised and tended. The Christians say that they have no property, but they enjoy the fruits of it. They say that they have all things in common and that everything is brought together into a common pool. But what they bring together they have received from people who owned property. They merely deceive others, or at best deceive themselves. You say that they themselves work to support themselves, but what they get by work would not support them if they did not avail themselves of what men who recognize ownership have produced. Even if they could support themselves it would be a bare subsistence, and there would be no place among them for the sciences or arts. They do not even recognize the use of our sciences and arts. Nor can it be otherwise. Their whole teaching tends to reduce them to a primitive condition of savagery – to an animal existence.

'They cannot serve humanity by our arts and sciences, and being ignorant of them they condemn them. Nor can they serve humanity in any of the ways which constitute man's peculiar prerogative and ally him to the gods. They have neither temples nor statues nor theatres nor museums. They say they do not need these things. The easiest way to avoid being ashamed of one's degradation is to scorn what is lofty, and that is what they do. They are atheists. They do not acknowledge the gods or their participation in human affairs. They believe only in the Father of their Teacher, whom they also call their Father, and the Teacher himself, who they think has revealed to them all the mysteries of life. Their teaching is a pitiful fraud! Consider just this. Our religion says: The world depends on the gods, the gods protect men, and in order to live well men must respect the gods, and must themselves search and think. In this way our life is guided on the one hand by the will of the gods, and on the other by the collective wisdom of mankind. We live, think, search, and thus advance towards the truth.

'But these Christians have neither the gods, nor their own will, nor the wisdom of humanity. They have only a blind faith in their crucified Teacher and in all that he said to them. Now consider which is the more trustworthy guide – the will of the gods and the free activity of collective human wisdom, or the compulsory, blind belief in the words of one man?'

Julius was struck by what the stranger said and particularly by his last words. Not only was his intention of going to the Christians shaken, but it now appeared to him strange that, under the influence of his misfortunes, he could ever have decided on such an insanity. But the question still remained of what he was to do now, and what exit to find from the difficult circumstances in which he was placed, and so, having explained his position, he asked the stranger's advice.

'It was just of that matter I now wished to speak to you,' replied the stranger. 'What are you to do? Your path – in as far as human wisdom is accessible to me – is clear. All your misfortunes have resulted from the passions natural to mankind. Passion has seduced you and led you so far that you have suffered. Such are the ordinary lessons of life. We should avail ourselves of them. You have learnt much and know what is bitter and what is sweet, you cannot now repeat those mistakes. Profit by your experience. What distresses you most is your enmity towards your father. That enmity is due to your position. Choose another and it will cease, or at least will not manifest itself so painfully. All your misfortunes are the result of the irregularity of your situation. You gave yourself up to youthful pleasures: that was natural and therefore good. But it was good only as long as it corresponded to your age. That time passed, but though you had grown to manhood you still devoted yourself to the frivolities of youth, and this was bad. You have reached an age when you should recognize that you are a man, a citizen, and should serve the State and work on its behalf. Your father wishes you to marry. His advice is wise. You have outlived one phase of life – your youth – and have reached another. All your troubles are indications of a period of transition. Recognize that youth has passed, boldly throw aside all that was natural to it but not natural for a man, and enter upon a new path. Marry, give up the amusements of youth, apply yourself to commerce, public affairs, the sciences and arts, and you will not only be reconciled to your father and friends, but will yourself find peace and happiness. You have reached manhood, and should marry and be a husband. So my chief advice is: accede to your father's wish and marry. If you are attracted by the seclusion you thought to find among the Christians, if you are inclined to philosophy and not towards an active life, you can with advantage devote yourself to it only after you have experienced the real meaning of life. But you will know that only as an independent citizen and the head of a family. If afterwards you still feel drawn to solitude, yield to that feeling. It will then be a true desire and not a mere flash of vexation such as it is now. Then go!'

These last words persuaded Julius more than anything else. He thanked the stranger and returned home.

His mother welcomed him with joy. His father too, on hearing of his intention to submit to his will and marry the girl he had chosen for him, was reconciled to his son.

IV

THREE months later the marriage of Julius with the beautiful Eulampia was celebrated. The young couple lived in a separate house belonging to Julius, and he took over a branch of his father's business which was transferred to him. He had now changed his way of life entirely.

One day he went on business to a neighbouring town, and there, while sitting in a shop, he saw Pamphilius passing by with a girl whom Julius did not know. They both carried heavy baskets of grapes which they were selling. On seeing his friend, Julius went out to him and asked him into the shop to have a talk.

The girl, seeing that Pamphilius wished to go with his friend but hesitated to leave her alone, hastened to assure him that she did not need his help, but would sit down with the grapes and wait for customers. Pamphilius thanked her, and he and Julius went into the shop.

Julius asked the shopkeeper, whom he knew, to let him take his friend into a private room at the back of the shop, and having received permission they went there.

The two friends questioned each other about their lives. Pamphilius was still living as before in the Christian community and had not married, and he assured his friend that his life had been growing happier and happier each year, each day, and each hour.

Julius told his friend what had happened to himself, and how he had actually been on his way to join the Christians when an encounter with a stranger cleared up for him the mistakes of the Christians and showed him what he ought to do, and how he had followed that advice and had married.

'Well, and are you happy now?' inquired Pamphilius. 'Have you found in marriage what the stranger promised you?'

'Happy?' said Julius. 'What is happiness? If you mean the complete satisfaction of my desires, then of course I am not happy. I am at present managing my business successfully, people begin to respect me, and in both these things I find some satisfaction. Though I see many men richer and more highly regarded than myself, I foresee the possibility of equalling or even surpassing them. That side of my life is full, but marriage, I will say frankly, does not satisfy me. More than that, I feel that it is just my marriage – which should have given me happiness – that has failed. The joy I at first experienced gradually diminished and at last vanished, and instead of happiness came sorrow. My wife is beautiful, clever, well-educated, and kind. At first I was perfectly happy. But now – not having a wife you will not have experienced this – differences arise, sometimes because she desires my attentions when I am indifferent to her, and sometimes for the contrary reason. Besides this, for passion novelty is essential. A woman less fascinating than my wife attracts me more when I first know her, but afterwards becomes still less attractive than my wife: I have experienced that. No, I have not found satisfaction in marriage. Yes, my friend,' Julius concluded, 'the philosophers are right. Life does not afford us what the soul desires. I have now experienced that in marriage. But the fact that life does not give the happiness that the soul desires does not prove that your deception can give it,' he added with a smile.

'In what do you see our "deception"?' asked Pamphilius.

'Your deception consists in this: that to deliver man from the evils connected with life, you reject all life – repudiate life itself. To avoid disenchantment you reject enchantment. You reject marriage itself.'

'We do not reject marriage,' said Pamphilius.

'Well, if you don't reject marriage, at any rate you reject love.'

'On the contrary, we reject everything except love. For us it is the basis of everything.'

'I do not understand you,' said Julius. 'As far as I have heard from others and from yourself, and judging by the fact that you are not yet married though you are the same age as myself, I conclude that your people do not marry. Those who are already married continue to be so, but the others do not form fresh marriages. You do not concern yourself about continuing the human race. And if you were the only people the human race would long ago have died out,' he concluded, repeating what he had often heard said.

'That is unjust,' replied Pamphilius. 'It is true that we do not set ourselves the aim of continuing the human race, and do not make it our concern in the way I have often heard your philosophers speak of it. We suppose that our Father has already provided for that. Our aim is simply to live in accord with His will. If it is His will that the human race should continue, it will do so, if not it will end. That is not our affair, nor our care. Our care is to live in accord with His will. And His will is expressed both in our teaching and in our revelation, in which it is said that a husband shall cleave unto his wife and they twain shall be one flesh.

'Marriage among us is not only not forbidden, but it is encouraged by our elders and teachers. The difference between marriage among us and marriage among you consists only in the fact that our law reveals to us that every lustful look at a woman is a sin, and so we and our women, instead of adorning ourselves to stimulate desire, try so to avoid it that the feeling of love between us as between brothers and sisters, may be stronger than the feeling of desire for a woman which you call love.'

'But all the same you cannot suppress admiration for beauty,' said Julius. 'I feel sure, for instance, that the beautiful girl with whom you were bringing the grapes evokes in you the feeling of desire – in spite of the dress which hides her charms.'

'I do not yet know,' said Pamphilius, blushing. 'I have not thought about her beauty. You are the first to speak to me of it. To me she is as a sister. But to continue what I was saying about the difference between our marriages and yours, that difference arises from the fact that among you lust, under the name of beauty and love, and the worship of the goddess Venus, is evoked and developed in people. With us on the contrary lust is considered, not as an evil – for God did not create evil – but as a good which begets evil when it is out of place: a temptation as we call it. And we try by all means to avoid it. And that is why I am not yet married, though very possibly I may marry to-morrow.'

'But what will decide that?'

'The will of God.'

'How will you know it?'

'If you never seek its indications you will never discern it, but if you constantly seek them they become clear, as divinations from sacrifices and birds are for you. And as you have your wise men who interpret for you the will of the gods by their wisdom and from the entrails of their sacrificed animals and by the flight of birds, so we too have our wise men who explain to us the will of the Father according to Christ's revelation and the promptings of their hearts and the thoughts of others, and chiefly by their love of men.'

'But all this is very indefinite,' retorted Julius. 'Who will indicate to you, for instance, when and whom to marry? When I was about to marry I had the choice of three girls. Those three were chosen from among others because they were beautiful and rich, and my father was agreeable to my marrying any one of them. Of the three I chose Eulampia because she was the most beautiful, and more attractive to me than the others. That is easily understood. But what will guide you in your choice?'

'To answer you,' said Pamphilius, 'I must first tell you that as by our teaching all men are equal in our Father's eyes, therefore they are also equal in our eyes both in their station and in their spiritual and bodily qualities, and consequently our choice (to use a word we consider meaningless) cannot in any way be limited. Anyone in the whole world may be the husband or wife of a Christian.'

'That makes it still more impossible to decide,' said Julius.

'I will tell you what our Elder said to me about the difference between the marriage of a Christian and a pagan. A pagan, such as yourself, chooses the wife who in his opinion will give him the greatest amount of personal enjoyment. In such circumstances the eye wanders and it is difficult to decide, especially as the enjoyment is to be in the future. But a Christian has no such choice to make, or rather, when choosing, his personal enjoyment occupies not the first but a secondary place. For a Christian the question is how not to infringe the will of God by his marriage.'

'But in what way can there be an infringement of God's will by marriage?'

'I might have forgotten the *Iliad* which we used to read and study together, but you who live among sages and poets cannot have forgotten it. What is the whole *Iliad*? It is a story of the infringement of God's will in relation to marriage. Menelaus and Paris and Helen; Achilles and Agamemnon and Chryseis – it is all a description of the terrible ills that flowed and still flow from such infringements.'

'But in what does the infringement consist?'

'In this: that a man loves a woman for the enjoyment he can get by connexion with her and not because she is a human being like himself. He marries her solely for his own enjoyment. Christian marriage is possible only when a man loves his fellow men, and when the object of his carnal love is first of all an object of this brotherly love. As a house can only be built rationally and durably when there is a foundation, and a picture can be painted only when something has been prepared on which to paint it, so carnal love is only legitimate, reasonable, and permanent when it is based on the respect and love of one human being for another. Only on that foundation can a reasonable Christian family life be established.'

'But still,' said Julius, 'I do not see why such a Christian marriage, as you call it, excludes the kind of love for a woman that Paris experienced. . . .'

'I do not say that Christian marriage does not admit of any exclusive feeling for one woman: on the contrary, only then is it reasonable and holy. But an exclusive love for one woman can arise only when the previously existent love for all men is not infringed.

'The exclusive love for one woman which the poets sing, considering it as good in itself without being based on the general love of man, has no right to be called love. It is animal lust and very often changes into hatred. The best examples of how such so-called love (*eros*) becomes bestial when it is not based on brotherly love for all men, are cases of the violation of the very woman the man is supposed to love, but who causes her to suffer and ruins her. In such violence there is evidently no brotherly love, for the man torments the one he loves. In un–Christian marriage there is often a concealed violence – as when a man who marries a girl who does not love him, or who loves another, compels her to suffer, and has no compassion for her, using her merely to satisfy his "love".'

'Granted that that is so,' said Julius, 'but if the maiden loves him there is no injustice and I don't see the difference between Christian and pagan marriage.'

'I do not know the details of your marriage,' replied Pamphilius, 'but I know that every marriage based on nothing but personal happiness cannot but result in discord, just as among animals, or men differing little from animals, the simple act of taking food cannot occur without quarrelling and strife. Each wants a nice morsel, and as there are not enough choice morsels for all, discord results. Even if it is not expressed openly it is still there secretly. The weak man desires a dainty morsel but knows that the strong man will not give it to him, and though he knows it is impossible to take it away directly from the strong man, he watches him with secret and envious malice and avails himself of the first opportunity to take it from him by guile. The same is true of pagan marriage, but there it is twice as bad because the object of desire is a human being, so that the enmity arises between husband and wife.'

'But how can married couples possibly love no one but each other? There will always be some man or woman who loves the one or the other, and then, in your opinion, marriage is impossible. So I see the justice of what is said of you – that you deny marriage. That is why you are not married and probably will not marry. It is not possible for a man to marry a woman without ever having aroused the feeling of love in some other woman, or for a girl to reach maturity without having aroused any man's feeling for herself. What ought Helen to have done?'

'Our Elder Cyril speaks thus about it: In the pagan world men, without thinking of loving their brethren – without cultivating that sentiment – think only of arousing in themselves passionate love for a woman, and they foster that passion in themselves. And so in their world Helen, and every woman like her, arouses the love of many men. Rivals fight one another and strive to surpass one another, as animals do to possess a female. And to a greater or lesser extent their marriage is an act of violence. In our community we not only do not think about the personal enjoyment a woman's beauty may afford, but we avoid all temptations which lead to this – which in the pagan world is regarded as a merit and an object of worship. We, on the contrary, think of those obligations of respect and love of our neighbour which we feel for all men, for the greatest beauty and the greatest deformity. We cultivate them with all our might, and so the feeling of brotherly love supplants the seduction of beauty, vanquishes it, and eliminates the discords arising from sexual intercourse. A Christian marries only when he knows that his union with the woman will not cause pain to anyone.'

'But is that possible?' rejoined Julius. 'Can men control their passions?'

'It is impossible if they are allowed free play, but we can prevent their awakening and being aroused. Take, for example, the relations of a father and his daughter, a mother and her son, or of brothers and sisters. However beautiful she may be, the mother is for her son an object of pure love and not of personal enjoyment. And it is the same with a daughter and her father, and a sister and her brother. Feelings of desire are not awakened. They would awaken only if the father learnt that she whom he considered to be his daughter was not his daughter, and similarly in the relation of a mother and son, and a brother and sister. But even then the sensation would be very feeble and easily suppressed, and it would be in the man's power to restrain it. The feeling of desire would be feeble because at its base would lie the sentiment of maternal, paternal, or fraternal love. Why do you not wish to believe that such a feeling towards all women – as mothers, sisters, and daughters – may be cultivated and confirmed in men, and that the feeling of conjugal love could grow up on the basis of that feeling? As the brother will only allow a feeling of love for her as a woman to arise in himself after he has learnt that she is not his sister, so also a Christian will only allow that feeling to arise in his soul when he feels that his love will cause pain to no one.'

'But suppose two men love the same girl?'

'Then one will sacrifice his happiness for that of the other.'

'But how if she loves one of them?'

'Then the one whom she loves less will sacrifice his feeling for her happiness.'

'And if she loves both of them and they both sacrifice themselves, she will not marry at all?'

'No, in that case the elders will look into the matter and advise so that there may be the greatest good for all with the greatest amount of love.'

'But you know that is not done! It is not done because it would be contrary to human nature.'

'Contrary to human nature? What human nature? A man is a human being besides being an animal, and while it is true that such a relation to a woman is not consonant with man's animal nature, it is consonant with his rational nature. When man uses his reason to serve his animal nature he becomes worse than an animal, and descends to violence and incest and to things no animal would do. But when he uses his reason to restrain his animal nature, then that animal nature serves his reason, and only then does he attain a happiness that satisfies him.'

V

'BUT tell me about yourself,' said Julius. 'I see you with that lovely girl, it seems that you live near her and help her. Is it possible that you do not wish to become her husband?'

'I do not think about it,' said Pamphilius. 'She is the daughter of a Christian widow. I serve them as others do. You ask whether I love her so that I wish to unite my life with hers? That question is hard for me to answer, but I will do so frankly. That thought has occurred to me but I dare not as yet entertain it, for there is another young man who loves her. That young man is a Christian and loves us both, and so I cannot do anything that would cause him pain. I live without thinking of it. I seek only one thing: to fulfil the law of love of man. That is the one thing needful. I shall marry when I see that it is necessary.'

'But it cannot be a matter of indifference to her mother to get a good industrious son-in-law. She will want you and not someone else.'

'No, it is a matter of indifference to her, because she knows that we are all ready to serve her, as we would anyone else, and that I should serve her neither more nor less whether I became her son-in-law or not. If it comes about that I marry her daughter, I shall accept it gladly, as I should do her marriage with someone else.'

'That is impossible!' exclaimed Julius. 'What is so terrible about you is that you deceive yourselves and so deceive others. What that stranger told me about you was correct. When I listen to you I involuntarily yield to the beauty of the life you describe, but when I reflect I see that it is all a deception leading to savagery, to a coarseness of life resembling that of the animals.'

'In what do you see this savagery?'

'In this, that supporting yourselves by labour, you can have neither leisure nor opportunity to occupy yourselves with the sciences and arts. Here you are in ragged garments, with coarsened hands and feet; and your companion, who could be a goddess of beauty, resembles a slave. You have neither songs to Apollo, nor temples, nor poetry, nor games – none of the things the gods have given for the adornment of man's life. To work, to work like slaves or like oxen, merely to feed coarsely – is not this a voluntary and impious renunciation of man's will and of human nature?'

'Again "human nature"!' said Pamphilius. 'But in what does this nature consist? In tormenting slaves to work beyond their strength, in killing one's brother-men and enslaving them, and making women into instruments of pleasure? All this is needed for that beauty of life which you consider natural for human beings. Is that man's nature? Or is it to live in love and concord with all men, feeling oneself a member of one universal brotherhood?

'You are much mistaken, too, if you think that we do not recognize the arts and sciences. We value highly all the capacities with which human nature is endowed, but we regard all man's inherent capacities as means for the attainment of one and the same end, to which we consecrate our lives, namely the fulfilment of God's will. We do not regard art and science as an amusement, of use only to while away the time of idle people. We demand of science and art, as of all human occupations, that in them should be realized that activity of love of God and of our neighbours which should be the aim of all Christian activities. We regard as true science only such knowledge as helps us to live a better life, and we esteem as art only what purifies our thoughts, elevates our souls, and strengthens the powers we need for a life of labour and love. Such knowledge we do not fail to develop in ourselves and in our children as far as we can, and to such art we willingly devote our leisure time. We read and study the works bequeathed to us by the wisdom of those who lived before us. We sing songs and paint pictures, and our poems and pictures brace our spirit and console us in moments of grief. That is why we cannot approve of the applications you make of the arts and sciences. Your learned men employ their mental capacities to devise new means of injuring men. They perfect methods of warfare, that is of murder. They contrive new methods of gain, by getting rich at the expense of others.

Your art serves for the erection and adornment of temples in honour of gods in whom the more educated among you have long ceased to believe, but whom you encourage others to believe in, in order by such deception the better to keep them in your power. You erect statues in honour of the most powerful and cruel of your tyrants, whom none respect but all fear. In your theatres performances are given extolling guilty love. Music serves for the delectation of your rich, who glut themselves with food and drink at their luxurious feasts. Painting is employed in houses of debauchery to depict scenes such as no sober man, or man not stupefied by animal passion, could look at without blushing. No, not for such ends have those higher capacities which distinguish him from the animals been given to man. They must not be employed for bodily gratification. Devoting our whole lives to the fulfilment of God's will, we employ our highest faculties especially in that service.'

'Yes,' said Julius. 'All that would be excellent if life were possible under such conditions, but one cannot live so. You deceive yourselves. You condemn our laws, our institutions, and our armies. You do not recognize the protection we afford. If it were not for the Roman legions could you live at peace? You profit by the protection of the State without acknowledging it. Some of your people, as you told me yourself, have even defended themselves. You do not recognize the right of private property, but you make use of it. Our people have it and give to you. You yourself do not give away your grapes, but sell them and buy other things. It is all a deception! If you did what you say that would be all right, but as it is you deceive yourselves and others!'

He spoke heatedly and said all that he had in his mind. Pamphilius waited in silence, and when Julius had finished, he said:

'You are wrong in thinking that we avail ourselves of your protection without acknowledging it. Our welfare consists in not requiring defence, and this no one can take from us. Even if material things which in your eyes constitute property pass through our hands, we do not regard them as our own, and we give them to anyone who needs them for their sustenance. We sell the grapes to those who wish to buy them, not for the sake of personal gain, but solely to acquire necessities for those who need them. If someone wished to take those grapes from us we should give them up without resistance. For the same reason we are not afraid of an incursion of the barbarians. If they began to take from us the product of our toil we should let them have it, and if they demanded that we should work for them, we should also do that gladly; and they would not merely have no reason to kill or ill-treat us, but it would conflict with their own interests to do so. They would soon understand and learn to love us, and we should have less to suffer from them than from the civilized people who now surround us and persecute us.

'You say that the things necessary for existence can only be produced under a system of private property. But consider who really produces the necessaries of life. To whose labour do we owe all these riches of which you are so proud? Were they produced by those who issued orders to their slaves and workmen without themselves moving a finger, and who now possess all the property; or were they produced by the poor slaves who carried out their masters' orders for their daily bread, and who now possess no property and have barely enough to supply their daily needs? And do you suppose that these slaves, who expend all their strength in executing orders often quite incomprehensible to them, would not work for themselves and for those they love and care for if they were allowed to do so – that is to say, if they might work for aims they clearly understood and approved of?

'You accuse us of not completely achieving what we strive for, and for taking advantage of violence and property even while we do not recognize them. If we are cheats, it is no use talking to us and we are worthy neither of anger nor of exposure, but only of contempt. And we willingly accept your contempt, for one of our precepts is the recognition of our insignificance. But if we sincerely strive towards what we profess, then your accusation of fraud is unjust. If we strive, as

I and my brethren do, to fulfil our Master's law and to live without violence and without private property – which is the result of violence – we do so not for external ends, riches or honours – we account these as nothing – but for something else. We seek happiness just as you do, only we have a different conception of what it is. You believe that happiness is to be found in wealth and honours, but we believe it is found in something else. Our belief shows us that happiness lies not in violence, but in submissiveness; not in wealth, but in giving everything up. And we, like plants striving towards the light, cannot help but press forward in the direction of our happiness. We do not accomplish all that we desire for our own welfare. That is true. But can it be otherwise? You strive to have the most beautiful wife and the largest fortune. But have you, or has anyone else, ever attained them? If an archer does not hit the mark will he cease to aim at it because he often fails? So it is with us. Our happiness, according to Christ's teaching, lies in love. We seek our happiness, but attain it far from fully and each in his own way.'

'Yes, but why do you disbelieve all human wisdom? Why have you turned away from it? Why do you believe only in your crucified Master? Your slavish submission to him – that is what repels me.'

'There again you are mistaken, and so is anyone who thinks that we hold our faith because we were bidden to do so by the man in whom we believe. On the contrary, those who with their whole soul seek a knowledge of the truth and communion with the Father – all those who seek for the good – involuntarily come to the path which Christ followed, and so cannot but see him before them, and follow him! All who love God will meet on that path, and you will, too! Our Master is the son of God and a mediator between God and men, not because someone has said so and we blindly believe it, but because all who seek God find His son before them on the path, and involuntarily come to understand, to see, and to know God, only through him.'

Julius did not reply, and they sat in silence for a long time.

'Are you happy?' he asked.

'I wish for nothing better. More than that, I generally experience a feeling of perplexity and am conscious of a kind of injustice that I am so tremendously happy,' said Pamphilius with a smile.

'Yes,' said Julius, 'perhaps I should be happier if I had not met that stranger and had come to you.'

'If you think so, what keeps you back?'

'How about my wife?'

'You say that she is inclined towards Christianity – so she might come with you.'

'Yes, but we have already begun a different kind of life. How can we break it up? As it has been begun we must live it out,' said Julius, picturing to himself the dissatisfaction of his father, his mother, his friends, and above all the effort that would have to be made to effect the change.

Just then the maiden, Pamphilius's companion, came to the door accompanied by a young man. Pamphilius went out to them, and in Julius's presence the young man explained that he had been sent by Cyril to buy some hides. The grapes were already sold and some wheat purchased. Pamphilius proposed that the young man should go with Magdalene and take the wheat home, while he would himself buy and bring home the hides. 'It will be better for you,' he said.

'No, Magdalene had better go with you,' said the young man, and went away.

Julius took Pamphilius into the shop of a tradesman he knew, and Pamphilius poured the wheat into bags, and having given Magdalene a small share to carry, took up his own heavy load, bid farewell to Julius, and left the town with the maiden. At the turning of the street he looked round and nodded to Julius with a smile. Then, with a still more joyous smile, he said something to Magdalene and they disappeared from view.

'Yes, I should have done better had I then gone to them,' thought Julius. And in his imagination two pictures alternated: the kindly bright faces of the lusty Pamphilius and the tall strong maiden as they carried the baskets on their heads; and then the domestic hearth from which he had come that morning and to which he must soon return, where his beautiful, but pampered and wearisome wife, who had become repulsive to him, would be lying on rugs and cushions, wearing bracelets and rich attire.

But Julius had no time to think of this. Some merchant companions of his came up to him, and they began their usual occupations, finishing up with dinner and drinking, and spending the night with women.

VI

TEN years passed. Julius had not met Pamphilius again, and the meeting with him had slowly passed from his memory, and the impression of him and of the Christian life wore off.

Julius's life ran its usual course. During these ten years his father had died and he had taken over the management of his whole business, which was a complicated one. There were the regular customers, salesmen in Africa, clerks, and debts to be collected and paid. Julius found himself involuntarily absorbed in it all and gave his whole time to it. Besides this, new cares presented themselves. He was elected to a public office, and this new occupation, which flattered his vanity, attracted him. In addition to his business affairs he now attended to public matters also, and being capable and a good speaker he began to distinguish himself among his fellows, and appeared likely to reach high public office. In his family life a considerable and unpleasant change had occurred during these ten years. Three children had been born to him, and this had separated him from his wife. In the first place she had lost much of her beauty and freshness, and in the second place she paid less attention to her husband. All her tenderness and endearments were devoted to her children. Though according to the pagan custom the children were handed over to wet-nurses and attendants, Julius often found them with their mother, or found her with them instead of in her own apartments. For the most part Julius found the children a burden, affording him more annoyance than pleasure.

Occupied with business and public affairs he had abandoned his former dissipated life, but considered that he needed some refined recreation after his labours. This, however, he did not find with his wife, the more so as during this time she had cultivated an acquaintance with her Christian slave-girl, had become more and more attracted by the new teaching, and had discarded from her life all the external, pagan things that had attracted Julius. Not finding what he wanted in his wife, Julius formed an intimacy with a woman of light conduct, and passed with her the leisure that remained after his business.

Had he been asked whether he was happy or unhappy during those years he would have been unable to answer.

He was so busy! From one affair or pleasure he passed to another affair or pleasure, but not one of them was such as fully to satisfy him or make him wish it to continue. Everything he did was of such a nature that the quicker he could free himself from it the better he was pleased, and his pleasures were all poisoned in some way, or the tedium of satiety mingled with them.

In this way he was living when something happened that came near to altering his whole manner of life. He took part in the races at the Olympic Games, and was driving his chariot successfully to the end of the course when he suddenly collided with another which was overtaking him. His wheel broke, and he was thrown out and broke his arm and two ribs. His injuries were serious, though they did not endanger his life, and he was taken home and had to keep to his bed for three months.

During these three months of severe physical suffering his mind worked, and he had leisure to think about his life as if it were someone else's. And his life presented itself to him in a gloomy light, the more so as during that time three unpleasant events occurred which much distressed him.

The first was that a slave, who had been his father's trusted servant, decamped with some precious jewels he had received in Africa, thus causing a heavy loss and a disorganization of Julius's affairs.

The second was that his mistress deserted him and found herself another protector.

The third and most unpleasant event for him, was that during his illness there was an election, and his opponent secured the position he had hoped to obtain.

All this, it seemed to Julius, came about because his chariot-wheel had swerved a finger-breadth to the left.

Lying alone on his couch he began involuntarily to reflect on the fact that his happiness depended on such insignificant happenings, and these thoughts led him on to others, and to the recollection of his former misfortunes – of his attempt to go to the Christians, and of Pamphilius, whom he had now not seen for ten years. These recollections were strengthened by conversations with his wife, who was often with him during his illness and told him everything she had learnt about Christianity from her slave-girl.

This slave-girl had at one time been in the same community with Pamphilius, and knew him. Julius wished to see her, and when she came to his couch questioned her about everything in detail, and especially about Pamphilius.

Pamphilius, the slave-girl said, was one of the best of the brethren, and was loved and esteemed by them all. He had married that same Magdalene whom Julius had seen ten years ago, and they already had several children.

'Yes, any man who does not believe that God has created men for happiness should go to see their life,' concluded the slave-girl.

Julius let the slave-girl go, and remained alone, thinking of what he had heard. It made him envious to compare Pamphilius's life with his own, and he did not wish to think about it.

To distract himself he took up a Greek manuscript which his wife had left by his couch, and began to read as follows:[1]

'There are two ways: one of life and the other of death. The way of life is this: First, thou shalt love God who has created thee; secondly, thou shalt love thy neighbour as thyself; and

1 The following text reproduces, in substance, the first part of *The Teaching of the Twelve Apostles* (The Didachē), a very early Christian manuscript discovered at Constantinople in 1875, which greatly interested Tolstoy.

thou shalt do to no one what thou wouldst not have him do to thee.

'Now this is the meaning of these words: Bless them that curse you, pray for your enemies and for those that persecute you. For what merit have you if you love only those who love you? Do not the heathen so? Love them that hate you, and you shall have no enemies. Put away from you all carnal and worldly desires. If a man smites you on the right cheek, turn to him the other also, and you shall be perfect. If a man compelleth thee to walk a mile with him, go with him two. If he taketh what belongeth to thee, demand it not again, for this thou shalt not do; if he taketh thy outer garment, give him thy shirt also. Give to everyone that asketh of thee, and demand nothing back, for the Father wishes that His abundant gifts should be received by all. Blessed is he who giveth according to the commandment!

'The second commandment of the teaching is this: Do not kill, do not commit adultery, do not be wanton, do not steal, do not employ sorcery, do not poison, do not covet thy neighbour's goods. Take no oath, do not bear false witness, speak no evil, do not remember injuries. Shun duplicity in thy thoughts and be not double-tongued. Let not thy words be false nor empty, but in accord with thy deeds. Be not covetous, nor rapacious, nor hypocritical, nor ill-tempered, nor proud. Have no evil intention against thy neighbour. Cherish no hatred of any man, but rebuke some, pray for others, and love some more than thine own soul.

'My child! Shun evil and all appearance of evil. Be not angry, for anger leadeth to murder. Be not jealous, nor quarrelsome, nor passionate, for of all these things cometh murder.

'My child! Be not lustful, for lust leadeth to wantonness, and be not foul-mouthed, for of this cometh adultery.

'My child! Be not untruthful, for lying leadeth to theft; neither be fond of money, nor vain, for of all these cometh theft also.

'My child! Do not repine, for that leadeth to blasphemy; neither be arrogant, nor a thinker of evil, for of all these things cometh blasphemy also. Be humble, for the meek shall inherit the earth. Be long-suffering, merciful, forgiving, humble, and kind, and take heed of the words that ye hear. Do not exalt thyself, and yield not thy soul to arrogance nor let thy soul cleave to the proud, but have converse with the humble and just. Accept as a blessing all that befalleth thee, knowing that nothing happens without God's will. . . .

'My child! Do not sow dissensions, but reconcile those that are at strife. Stretch not out thy hand to receive, nor hold it back from giving. Be not slow in giving, nor repine when giving, for thou shalt know the good Giver of rewards. Turn not away from the needy, but in everything have communion with thy brother, and call not anything thy own, for if ye are partakers in that which is incorruptible, how much more so in that which is corruptible. Teach thy children the fear of God from their youth. Deal not with thy slave in anger, lest he cease to fear God who is above you both, for He is no respecter of persons but calleth those whom the Spirit hath prepared.

'But this is the way of death: First of all it is wrathful and full of curses; here are murder, adultery, lust, wantonness, theft, idolatry, sorcery, poisoning, plundering, false witness, hypo-crisy, deceitfulness, insidiousness, pride, malice, arrogance, avarice, obscenity, envy, insolence, presumption, and vanity. Here are the persecutors of the righteous, haters of the truth, lovers of falsehood, who do not acknowledge the reward for righteousness nor cleave to what is good or to righteous judgements, who are vigilant not for what is good but for evil, from whom meekness and patience are far removed. Here are those that love vanity, who follow after rewards, who have no pity for their neighbours and do not labour for the oppressed or know their Creator. Here are the murderers of children, destroyers of God's image, who turn away from the needy. Here are the oppressors of the oppressed, defenders of the rich, unjust judges of the poor, sinners in all things. Beware, children, of all these!'

Long before he had read the manuscript to the end, Julius had entered with his whole soul into communion with those who had inspired it – as often happens to men who read a book (that is, another person's thoughts) with a sincere desire to

WALK IN THE LIGHT 511

discern the truth. He read on, guessing in advance what was coming, and not only agreed with the thoughts expressed in the book but seemed to be expressing them himself.

He experienced that ordinary, but mysterious and significant phenomenon, unnoticed by many people: of a man, supposed to be alive, becoming really alive on entering into communion with those accounted dead, and uniting and living one life with them.

Julius's soul united with him who had written and inspired those thoughts, and in the light of this communion he contemplated himself and his life. And it appeared to him to be all a terrible mistake. He had not lived, but had only destroyed in himself the possibility of living by all the cares and temptations of life.

'I do not wish to ruin my life. I want to live and to follow the path of life!' he said to himself.

He remembered all that Pamphilius had said to him in their former conversations, and it all now seemed so clear and unquestionable that he was surprised that he could have listened to the stranger and not have held to his intention of going to the Christians. He remembered also that the stranger had said to him: 'Go when you have had experience of life!'

'I have now had experience of life, and have found nothing in it!' thought Julius.

He also recalled the words of Pamphilius: that whenever he might go to the Christians, they would be glad to receive him.

'No, I have erred and suffered enough!' he said to himself. 'I will give up everything and go to them and live as it says here!'

He told his wife of his plan, and she was delighted with it. She was ready for everything. The only difficulty was to decide how to put the plan into execution. What was to be done with the children? Were they to be taken with them or left with their grandmother? How could they be taken? How, after the delicacy of their upbringing, could they be subjected to all the difficulties of a rough life? The slave-girl proposed to go with them, but the mother was afraid for the children, and said that it would be better to leave them with their grandmother and to go alone. And to this they agreed.

All was decided. Only Julius's illness delayed the execution of their plans.

VII

In that state of mind Julius fell asleep. In the morning he was told that a skilful physician was visiting the town and wished to see him, promising him speedy relief. Julius willingly consented to see him, and the physician proved to be none other than the stranger whom he had met when he started to join the Christians. Having examined his injuries the physician prescribed certain potions of herbs to strengthen him.

'Shall I be able to work with my hands?' inquired Julius.

'Oh yes! You will be able to write and to drive a chariot.'

'But hard work – digging?'

'I was not thinking of that,' said the physician, 'because it cannot be necessary for a man in your position.'

'On the contrary, it is just what is wanted,' said Julius, and he told the physician that since he had last seen him he had followed his advice and had experienced life; and that life had not given him what it promised, but on the contrary had disillusioned him, and that he now wished to carry out the intention he had then spoken of.

'They have evidently employed all their deceptions and have enchanted you so that in spite of your position and the responsibilities that rest upon you – especially in regard to your children – you still do not see their error.'

'Read that!' was all Julius said in reply, handing him the manuscript he had been reading.

The physician took the manuscript and looked at it.

'I know this,' he said. 'I know this deception, and am surprised that such a man as you should be caught by such a snare.'

'I don't understand you. Where is the snare?'

'It is all tested by life! These sophists and rebels against men and gods propose a way of life in which all men will be happy, and there will be no wars or executions, no poverty or depravity, no strife or anger. And they insist that this condition will come about when all men fulfil the law of Christ – not to quarrel, nor yield to lust, nor take oaths, nor do violence, nor take arms against another nation. But they deceive themselves and others by taking the end for the means.

'Their aim is not to quarrel, not to bind themselves by oaths, not to be wanton, and so forth, and this aim can only be attained by means of public life. But what they say is as if a teacher of archery should say: "You will hit the target when your arrow flies to it in a straight line." The problem is how to make it fly straight. And that result is attained in archery by having a taut bow-string, a flexible bow, and a straight arrow. It is the same in life. The best life, in which men have no need to quarrel, to be wanton, or to commit murder, is attained by having a taut bow-string (the rulers), a flexible bow (the power of government), and a straight arrow (the justice of the law). But they, under pretext of living a better life, destroy all that has improved or does improve it. They recognize neither government, nor the authorities, nor the laws.'

'But they say that if men fulfil the law of Christ, life will be better without rulers, authorities, and laws.'

'Yes, but what guarantee is there that men will fulfil it? None! They say: "You have experienced life under rulers and laws, and life has not been perfected. Try it now without rulers and laws and it will become perfect. You cannot deny this, for you have not tried it." But this is the obvious sophistry of these impious people. In saying that, is it not in effect as though a man should say to a farmer: "You sow your seed in the ground and cover it up, and yet the harvest is not what you would wish. I advise you to sow in the sea. It will be better like that – and you cannot deny my proposition, for you have not tried it"?'

'Yes, that is true,' said Julius, who was beginning to waver.

'But that is not all,' continued the physician. 'Let us assume the absurd and impossible. Let us assume that the principles of the Christian teaching can be poured into men like medicine, and that suddenly all men will begin to fulfil Christ's teaching, to love God and their fellows, and to fulfil his commandments. Even assuming all that, the path of life inculcated by them would still not stand examination. Life would come to an end and the race would die out. Their Teacher was a young vagabond, and such will his followers be, and according to our supposition such would the whole world become if it followed his teaching. Those living would last their time, but their children would not survive, or hardly one in ten would do so. According to their teaching all children should be alike to every mother and to every father, whether they are their own children or not. How will these children be looked after, when we see that all the devotion and all the love implanted in mothers hardly preserves their own children from perishing? What will happen when this devotion is replaced by a compassion shared by all children alike? Which child is to be taken and preserved? Who will sit up at night with a sick and malodorous child except its own mother? Nature has provided a protection for the child in its mother's love, but the Christians want to deprive it of that protection, and offer nothing in exchange! Who will train a son, who will penetrate into his soul like his father? Who will defend him from dangers? All this they reject! All life – that is, the continuation of the human race – is made away with.'

'That also is true,' said Julius, carried away by the physician's eloquence.

'Yes, my friend, have nothing to do with these ravings. Live rationally, especially now that you have such great and serious and pressing responsibilities. It is a matter of honour for you to fulfil them. You have reached the second period of your doubts, but go on and your doubts will vanish. Your first and evident duty is the education of your children, which you have neglected. You must train them to be worthy servants of their country. The existing political structure has given you everything you have, and you must serve it yourself and give it worthy servants in the persons of your children, on whom you will thereby also confer a benefit. Another obligation you have is the service of the community. You are mortified and discouraged by your accidental and temporary failure. But nothing is achieved without effort and struggle, and the joy of triumph is great only when the victory has been hardly won. Leave it to your wife to amuse herself with the babble of the Christian writers. You should be a man, and bring up your children to be men. Begin to live with the consciousness of duty, and all your doubts will fall away of themselves. They were caused by your illness. Fulfil your duty to the State by serving it and by preparing your children for its service. Set them on their feet, so that they may be able to take your place, and then peacefully abandon yourself to the life which attracts you. Till then you have no right to do so, and were you to do so you would encounter nothing but suffering.'

VIII

WHETHER it was the effect of the medicinal herbs or the advice given him by the wise physician, Julius speedily recovered, and his plans of adopting a Christian life now appeared to him like ravings.

After staying a few days the physician left the city. Soon afterwards Julius left his sick bed and began a new life in accord with the advice he had received. He engaged teachers for his children and supervised their studies himself. He spent his own time on public affairs and soon acquired great influence in the city.

So a year passed, and during that time Julius did not even think about the Christians. But at the end of the year a legate from the Roman Emperor arrived in Cilicia to suppress the Christian movement, and a trial was arranged to take place in Tarsus. Julius heard of the measures that were being undertaken against the Christians, but he paid no attention to them, not thinking that they related to the commune in which Pamphilius was living. But one day as he was walking in the forum to attend to his duties, a poorly dressed elderly man approached him whom he did not at first recognize. It was Pamphilius. He came up to Julius leading a child by the hand, and said:

'Greetings, friend! I have a great favour to ask of you, but now that the Christians are being persecuted I do not know whether you will wish to acknowledge me as your friend, or whether you will not be afraid of losing your post if you have anything to do with me.'

'I am not afraid of anyone,' replied Julius, 'and as a proof of it I ask you to come with me to my house. I will even neglect my business in the forum to have a talk with you and help you. Come with me. Whose child is that?'

'He is my son.'

'I need not have asked. I recognize your features in him, and I also recognize those light-blue eyes, and need not ask who your wife is. She is the lovely girl I saw you with several years ago.'

'You have guessed right,' replied Pamphilius. 'She became my wife soon after you saw us.'

On reaching the house, Julius called his wife and handed the boy over to her, and then led Pamphilius to his luxurious private room.

'You can speak freely here,' he said. 'No one will hear us.'

'I am not afraid of being heard,' replied Pamphilius. 'My request is not that the Christians who have been arrested should not be judged and executed, but only that they should be allowed to announce their faith in public.'

And Pamphilius told how the Christians who had been seized by the authorities had succeeded in sending word from their prison to the community telling of their condition. Cyril the Elder, knowing of Pamphilius's relations with Julius, had sent him to intercede for the Christians. They did not ask for mercy. They looked upon it as their vocation to testify to the truth of Christ's teaching, and they could do this equally well by suffering martyrdom as by a life of eighty years. They would accept either fate with equal indifference, and physical death, which must inevitably overtake them, was as welcome and void of terror now as it would be fifty years hence. But they wished by their death to serve their fellow-men, and therefore Pamphilius had been sent to ask that their trial and execution should be public.

Julius was surprised at Pamphilius's request, but promised to do all in his power to aid him.

'I have promised to help you,' he said, 'out of friendship, and because of the particular feeling of tenderness you have always aroused in me, but I must say that I consider your teaching most senseless and harmful. I can judge of this because some time ago, when I was ill, disappointed, and low-spirited, I myself once again shared your views and came very near to abandoning everything and joining your community. I know now on what your error is based, for I have myself experienced it. It is based on love of self, weakness of spirit, and sickly enervation. It is a creed for women, not for men.'

'But why?'

'Because, while you recognize the fact that discord lies in man's nature and that strife results therefrom, you do not wish to take part in that strife or to teach others to do so; and without taking your share of the burden you avail yourselves of the organization of the world, which is based on violence. Is that fair? Our world owes its existence to the fact that there have always been rulers. Those rulers took on themselves the trouble and all the responsibility of defending us from foreign and domestic foes, and in return for that we subjects submitted to them and rendered them honour, or helped them by serving the State. But you, out of pride, instead of taking your part in the affairs of the State and rising higher and higher in men's regard by your labours and to the extent of your deserts – you in your pride at once declare all men to be equal, in order that you may consider no one higher than yourself, but may reckon yourself equal to Caesar. That is what you yourself think and teach others to think. And for weak and idle people that is a great temptation! Every slave, instead of labouring, at once considers himself Caesar's equal. But you do more than this: you deny taxes, and slavery, and the courts, and executions, and war – everything that holds people together. If people listened to you, society would fall to pieces and we should return to primitive savagery.

'Living under a government you preach the destruction of government. But your very existence is dependent on that government. Without it you would not exist. You would all be slaves of the Scythians or the barbarians – the first people who happened to hear of your existence. You are like a tumour which destroys the body but can only nourish itself on the body. And a living body resists that tumour and over-comes it! We do the same with you, and cannot but do so. And in spite of my promise to help you obtain your wish, I look upon your teaching as most harmful and despicable: despicable because I consider it dishonourable and unjust to gnaw the breast that feeds you – to avail yourselves of the advantages of governmental order, and to destroy that order by which the State is maintained, without taking part in it!'

'If we really lived as you suppose there would be much justice in what you say,' replied Pamphilius. 'But you do not know our life, and have formed a false conception of it. The means of subsistence which we employ are obtainable without the aid of violence. It is difficult for you, with your luxurious habits, to realize on how little a man can live without priva-tion. A healthy man is so constituted that he can produce with his hands far more than he needs for his subsistence. Living together in a community we are able by our common work to feed without difficulty our children, our old people, and the sick and weak. You say of the rulers that they protect people from external and internal enemies – but we love our enemies, and so we have none. You assert that we Christians stir up in the slave a desire to be Caesar, but on the contrary, both by word and deed we profess one thing: patient humility and labour, the humblest of labour, that of a working man. We neither know nor understand anything about political matters. We only know one thing, and we know that with certainty, that our welfare lies solely in the good of others, and we seek that welfare. The welfare of all men lies in their union with one another, and union is attained not by violence but by love. The violence of a brigand inflicted on a traveller is as atrocious to us as the violence of an army to its prisoners, or of a judge to those who are executed, and we cannot intentionally parti-cipate in the one or the other. Nor can we profit by the labour of others enforced by violence. Violence is reflected on us, but our participation in violence consists not in inflicting it but in submissively enduring its infliction on ourselves.'

'Yes,' said Julius, 'you preach about love, but when one looks at the results it turns out to be quite another thing. It leads to barbarism and a reversion to savagery, murder, robbery, and violence, which according to your doctrine must not be repressed in any way.'

'No, that is not so,' said Pamphilius, 'and if you really examine the results of our teaching and of our lives carefully and impartially, you will see that not only do they not lead to murder, robbery, and violence, but on the contrary those crimes can only be opposed by the means we practise. Murder, robbery, and all evils, existed long before Christianity, and men have always contended with them, but unsuccessfully, because they employed means that we deplore, meeting violence by violence; and this never checks crime, but on the contrary provokes it by sowing hatred and exasperation.

'Look at the mighty Roman Empire. Nowhere else is such trouble taken about the laws as in Rome. Studying and perfecting the laws constitutes a special science. The laws are taught in the schools, discussed in the Senate, and reformed and administered by the most educated citizens. Legal justice is considered the highest virtue, and the office of Judge is held in peculiar respect. Yet in spite of this it is known that there is now no city in the world so steeped in crime and corruption as Rome. Remember Roman history: in olden times when the laws were very primitive the Roman people possessed many virtues, but in our days, despite the elaboration and administration of law, the morals of the citizens are becoming worse and worse. The number of crimes constantly increases, and they become more varied and more elaborate every day.

'Nor can it be otherwise. Crime and evil can be successfully opposed only by the Christian method of love, and not by the heathen methods of revenge, punishment, and violence. I am sure you would like men to abstain from evil voluntarily and not from fear of punishment. You would not wish men to be like prisoners who only refrain from crime because they are watched by their gaolers. But no laws or restrictions or punishments make men averse to doing evil or desirous of doing good. That can only be attained by destroying evil at its root, which is in the heart of man. That is what we aim at, while you only try to repress the outward manifestations of evil. You do not look for its source and do not know where it is, and so you can never find it.

'The commonest crimes – murder, robbery, and fraud – are the result of men's desire to increase their possessions, or even to obtain the necessaries of life which they have been unable to procure in any other way. Some of these crimes are punished by the law, but the most important and far-reaching in their consequences are perpetrated under the wing of the law, as, for instance, the huge commercial frauds and the innumerable ways in which the rich rob the poor. Those crimes which are punished by law may indeed to a certain extent be repressed – or rendered more difficult of execution – and the criminals for fear of punishment become more prudent and cunning and invent new forms of crime which the law does not punish. But by leading a Christian life a man preserves himself from all these crimes, which result on the one hand from the struggle for money and possessions, and on the other from the unequal concentration of riches in the hands of the few. Our one way of checking theft and murder is to keep for ourselves only as much as is indispensable for life, and to give to others all the superfluous products of our toil. We Christians do not lead men into temptation by the sight of accumulated wealth, for we rarely possess more than enough for our daily bread. A hungry man, driven to despair and ready to commit a crime for a piece of bread, if he comes to us will find all he wants without committing any crime, because that is what we live for – to share all we have with those who are cold and hungry. And the result is that one sort of evil-doer avoids us, while others turn to us, give up their criminal life, and are saved, and gradually become workers labouring for the good of all.

'Other crimes are prompted by the passions of jealousy, revenge, carnal love, anger and hatred. Such crimes cannot be suppressed by law. A man who commits them is in a brutal state of unbridled passion; he is incapable of reflecting on the consequences of his actions, opposition only exasperates him, and so the law is powerless to restrain these crimes. We how-ever believe that man can find satisfaction and the meaning of life only in the spirit, and that as long as he serves his passions he can never find happiness. We curb our passions by a life of love and labour, and develop in ourselves the power of the spirit, and the more deeply and widely our faith spreads the rarer will crime inevitably become.

'A third class of crime', Pamphilius continued, 'arises from the desire to help men. Some men − revolutionary conspirators − are anxious to alleviate the people's lot, and kill tyrants, imagining that they are thereby doing good to the majority of the people. The origin of such crimes is the belief that one can do good by committing evil. Such crimes, prompted by an idea, are not crushed out by legal punish-ments: on the contrary they are inflamed and evoked by them. In spite of their errors the men who commit them do so from a noble motive − a desire to serve mankind. They are sincere, they readily sacrifice themselves and do not shrink from danger. And so the fear of punishment does not stop them. On the contrary, danger stimulates them, and sufferings and executions exalt them to the dignity of heroes, gain sympathy for them, and incite others to follow their example. We see this in the history of all nations. But we Christians believe that evil will only pass away when men understand the misery that results from it both for themselves and for others. We know that brotherhood can only be attained when we are all brothers − that brotherhood without brothers is impossible.

'And though we see the errors of the revolutionary con-spirators, yet we appreciate their sincerity and unselfishness, and are attracted by the good that is in them.

'Which of us then is more successful in the struggle with crime and does more to suppress evil − we Christians, who prove by our life the happiness of a spiritual existence from which no evil results and whose means of influence are ex-ample and love; or you, whose rulers and judges pass sentences in accord with the dead letter of the law, ruin their victims, and drive them to the last extremity of exasperation?'

'When one listens to you,' said Julius, 'one almost begins to think that you may be right. But tell me, Pamphilius, why are people hostile to you? Why do they persecute you, hunt you down, and kill you? Why does your teaching of love lead to discord?'

'The reason of that lies not in us but outside us. Till now I have been speaking of crimes which are regarded as such both by the State and by us. These crimes constitute a form of violence which infringes the temporary laws of any State. But besides these there are other laws implanted in man – laws that are eternal, common to all men, and written in their hearts. We Christians obey these Divine, universal laws, and find their fullest, clearest, and most perfect realization in the words and life of our Master, and we regard as a crime any violence that transgresses the commands of Christ, because they express God's law. We consider that to avoid discord we must also obey the State laws of the country we live in, but we regard the law of God, which governs our conscience and reason, as supreme, and we can only obey those human laws which do not conflict with the Divine Law. "Render unto Caesar the things that are Caesar's, and unto God the things that are God's." Our struggle against crime is therefore both deeper and wider than the State's, for while we avoid transgressing the laws of the particular country we happen to live in, we seek above all not to infringe the will of God – the law common to all human nature. And because we regard the law of God as the highest law, men hate and fear us, for they consider some particular laws as supreme – the legislation of their own country, for instance, or even very often some custom of their own class. They are incapable of becoming, or unwilling to become, real human beings, in the sense of Christ's saying that "The truth shall make you free". They are content with their position as subjects of this or that State or as members of society, and so they naturally feel enmity towards those who see and proclaim the higher destiny of man. Incapable of understanding, or unwilling to understand, this higher destiny for themselves, they are unwilling to admit it for others. It was of such that Christ said: "Woe unto you,

Pharisees! for ye take away the key of knowledge: ye enter not in yourselves, and them that are entering in ye hinder." They are the authors of those persecutions which raise doubts in your mind.

'We have no enmity towards any man, not even towards those who persecute us, and our life brings harm and injury to no one. If men are irritated against us and even hate us, the reason can only be that our life is a thorn in their side, a constant condemnation of their own life which is founded on violence. We are unable to prevent this enmity against us, which does not proceed from us, for we cannot forget the truth we have understood, and cannot begin to live contrary to our conscience and our reason. Of this hostility which our belief provokes against us in others our Teacher said: "Think not that I come to bring peace upon earth. I come not to bring peace, but a sword!" Christ himself experienced this hostility, and he warned us, his pupils, of it more than once. He said: "The world hateth me, because its deeds are evil. If ye were of the world, the world would love you, but because ye are not of the world and I have delivered you from the world, therefore the world hateth you. The time cometh that whosoever killeth you will think that he doeth God service."

'But we, like Christ, fear not them that kill the body and then can do nothing more to us. Sufferings and the death of the flesh will not pass any man by, but we live in the light and therefore our life does not depend on the body. It is not we who suffer from the attacks upon us, but our persecutors and enemies, who suffer from the feeling of enmity and hatred they nurse like a serpent in their breasts. "And this is the condemnation, that light is come into the world, and men loved darkness rather than light, because their deeds were evil." There is no need to be disconcerted about this, for the truth will prevail. The sheep hear the voice of the shepherd and follow him, because they know his voice. And Christ's flock will not perish, but increase, drawing new sheep to itself from all the countries of the earth, for the Spirit bloweth where it listeth, and thou hearest the sound thereof but canst not tell whence it cometh nor whither it goeth.'

'Yes,' Julius interrupted him, 'but are there many among you who are sincere? You are often accused of only pretending to be martyrs and glad to die for the truth, but the truth is not on your side. You are proud madmen, destroying all the foundations of social life!'

Pamphilius made no reply, and looked sorrowfully at Julius.

IX

Just then Pamphilius's little son ran into the room and pressed close to his father's side.

Despite the caresses Julius's wife had bestowed upon him, he had run away from her to find his father. Pamphilius sighed, caressed the child, and got up to go, but Julius detained him, asking him to stay to dinner and have a further talk.

'It surprises me', he said, 'to see that you are married and have children. I cannot understand how you Christians can bring up a family while having no property. How can the mothers among you live at peace, knowing that their children are not provided for?'

'Why are our children less provided for than yours?'

'Because you have neither slaves nor property. My wife is much inclined to Christianity. She even at one time wished to give up our way of life, and I intended to go away with her. But she feared the insecurity and poverty she foresaw for the children, and I could not but agree with her. That was at the time of my illness. My whole way of life was repulsive to me just then and I wished to abandon it. But my wife's fears, and the explanation given me by the physician who was treating me, convinced me that though a Christian life as you live it may be right and possible for people who have no family, it is impossible for family people, or for mothers with children: that with your outlook life itself – the human race – would cease to exist. And it seems to me that that is quite correct. So your appearance with a son greatly surprised me.'

'Not only a son – there is also one at the breast and a three-year-old girl, who have remained at home.'

'But I don't understand it! Not so long ago I was ready to give up everything and become one of you. But I had children, and it was clear to me that, however good your life might be for myself, I had no right to sacrifice my children. So for their sake I remained here, living as before, that they might be brought up in the conditions in which I myself grew up and have lived.'

'It is strange how differently we look at things,' said Pamphilius. 'We say that if adults live in the worldly way it may be excused, for they are already spoilt, but for children it is terrible. To bring them up in worldly fashion and expose them to temptation! "Woe unto the world because of occasions of stumbling; for it must needs be that the occasions come; but woe to that man through whom the occasion cometh!" So says our Teacher, and I repeat it to you not as a retort, but because it is really true. The chief necessity for us to live as we do comes from the fact that there are children among us; those children of whom it is said: "Except ye become as little children ye shall not enter the kingdom of heaven."'

'But how can a Christian family manage to live without definite means of livelihood?'

'According to our belief there is only one means – that of loving work for men. Your method is violence. But that method may fail and be destroyed, as riches are destroyed, and then only work and the love of men is left. We consider that love is the basis of all, and should be firmly held to and increased. And when that is so, families live and prosper. No,' continued Pamphilius, 'if I doubted the truth of Christ's teaching, or hesitated to follow it, my doubts and hesitations would vanish when I thought of the fate of children brought up among the pagans in the conditions in which you and your children have been and are being brought up. Whatever arrangement of life some people may make, with palaces, slaves, and the imported produce of other lands, the life of the majority of men will remain as it should be. And the security for that life will always be the same – brotherly love and labour. We wish to exempt ourselves and our children from these conditions, and make men work for us by means of violence and not by love, and strange to say the more we apparently secure ourselves thereby, the more do we actually deprive ourselves of the true, natural, and reliable security – that of love. The greater a ruler's power the less he is loved. It is the same with the other security – labour. The more a man frees himself from labour and accustoms himself to luxury, the less capable of work he becomes and the more he deprives himself of true and reliable security. And yet when people have placed their children in these conditions they say they have "provided for them"! Take your son and mine and send the two of them to find their way anywhere, to transmit instructions, or to do some necessary thing, and you will see which of the two will do it better. Or offer them for education, and you will see which of the two would be accepted the more readily. No! Do not make that terrible statement that a Christian life is only possible for the childless. On the contrary it might be said that a pagan life may be pardonable only for those who have no children. "But woe unto him that shall cause one of these little ones to stumble."'

Julius was silent for some time.

'Yes,' he said at last. 'Perhaps you are right. But my children's education has been begun, they have the best teachers. Let them learn all we know – there can be no harm in that. There is time enough both for me and for them. They can come to you when they are grown up if they find it necessary. And I can do the same when I have set them on their feet and am left free.'

'Know the truth, and the truth shall make you free,' said Pamphilius. 'Christ gives perfect freedom at once: the world's teaching will never give it. Farewell!' And Pamphilius called his son and went away.

The Christians were condemned and executed publicly, and Julius saw Pamphilius with other Christians clearing away the bodies of the martyrs.

He saw him, but from fear of the higher authorities did not approach him or invite him to his house.

X

ANOTHER twenty years passed. Julius's wife died. His life flowed on in public activity and in efforts to obtain power, which sometimes seemed within his reach and sometimes eluded him. His wealth was great and continued to increase.

His sons had grown up; and the second, especially, began to lead an extravagant life. He made holes in the bottom of the bucket which held his father's wealth, and in proportion as that wealth increased so did the rapidity of the outflow through those holes. And here began for Julius a conflict with his sons such as he had had with his father – anger, hatred, and jealousy.

About this time a new Prefect was appointed and deprived Julius of favour. His former flatterers abandoned him, and he was in danger of banishment. He went to Rome to explain matters but was not received, and was ordered to return.

On reaching home he found his son carousing with dissolute companions. A report had spread in Cilicia that Julius was dead, and the son was celebrating his father's death! Julius lost control of himself and felled his son to the ground. He then retired to his wife's rooms. There he found a copy of the Gospels, and read:

'Come unto me, all ye that labour and are heavy laden, and I will give you rest. Take my yoke upon you, and learn of me; for I am meek and lowly in heart; and ye shall find rest unto your souls. For my yoke is easy, and my burden is light.'

'Yes,' thought Julius, 'he has long been calling me. I did not believe him but was refractory and wicked, and my yoke was heavy and my burden grievous.'

He sat there for a long time with the open Gospel on his knee, thinking over his whole past life and remembering all that Pamphilius had said to him at different times. At last he rose and went to his son. To his surprise he found him on his feet, and was inexpressibly glad to find that he had sustained no injury.

Without saying a word to his son Julius went out into the street and set off towards the Christian settlement. He walked all day, and in the evening stopped at a villager's for the night.

In the room which he entered lay a man, who got up at the sound of footsteps. It was his acquaintance the physician.

'No, this time you shall not dissuade me!' cried Julius. 'This is the third time I have started to go thither, and now I know that only there shall I find peace of mind.'

'Where?' asked the physician.

'Among the Christians.'

'Yes, perhaps you may find peace of mind, but you will not have fulfilled your duty. You lack manliness: misfortunes crush your spirit. Not so do true philosophers behave! Misfortunes are only the fire in which gold is tried. You have passed through a test. And now that you are wanted you run away! Now is the time to try people and yourself. You have acquired true wisdom and should employ it for the good of your country. What would happen to the people if all who have learnt to know men, their passions, and the conditions of life, were to bury their knowledge and experience in their search for peace of mind, instead of sharing them for the benefit of society? Your experience of life was gained among men and you ought to use it for their benefit.'

'But I have no wisdom at all! I am altogether sunk in error! My errors have not become wisdom because they are ancient, any more than water becomes wine because it is stale and foul.'

And seizing his cloak Julius hastily left the house and set out to walk farther, without staying to rest. By the close of another day he reached the Christian settlement.

They received him gladly, though they did not know that he was a friend of Pamphilius, whom they all loved and respected. At the refectory Pamphilius, seeing his friend, ran to him gladly and embraced him.

'At last I have come,' said Julius. 'Tell me what I am to do and I will obey you.'

'Don't trouble about that,' said Pamphilius. 'Come with me.' And he led Julius into the guest-house, and showing him a bed, said:

'When you have had time to observe our life you will see for yourself how you can best be of use to men. But I will show you something to do to-morrow to occupy your time for the present. We are gathering grapes in our vineyards. Go there and help. You will see yourself what you can do.'

Next morning Julius went into the vineyards. The first was of young vines which were loaded with clusters. Young people were plucking and gathering them. The places were all occupied and Julius, having walked about for some time, found no place for himself. He went on farther and came to an older vineyard where there was less fruit. But here also there was nothing for him to do; the gatherers were all working in pairs and there was no place for him. He went still farther and entered a very old, deserted vineyard. The vine-stocks were gnarled and crooked and Julius could see no grapes.

'There, that is like my life,' he said to himself. 'Had I come the first time, it would have been like the fruit in the first vineyard. Had I come when I started the second time, it would have been like the fruit in the second vineyard. But now here is my life – like these useless superannuated vines, only fit for fuel!' And Julius was terrified at what he had done, terrified at the punishment awaiting him for having uselessly wasted his life. And he became sad and said aloud:

'I am no longer good for anything and can now do nothing!' And he sat down and wept because he had wasted what he could never recover. Suddenly he heard the voice of an old man calling him:

'Work, brother!' said the voice.

Julius looked round and saw an old man, grey and bowed by age and scarcely able to move his feet. He was standing by the vines and gathering the few sweet bunches that still remained here and there. Julius went up to him.

'Work, dear brother! Work is joyous!' And the old man showed him where to look for bunches of the grapes that still remained. Julius began to look for them, and finding some, brought them and laid them in the old man's basket. And the old man said to him:

'Look, in what way are these bunches any worse than those they are gathering in the other vineyards? "Walk while ye have the light!" said our Teacher. "The will of Him that sent me is that every one who seeth the son, and believeth on him, may have everlasting life: and I will raise him up at the last day. For God sent not His son into the world to condemn the world; but that the world through him might be saved. He that believeth on him is not condemned, but he that believeth not is condemned already, because he hath not believed in the son, who is of one nature with God. And this is the condemnation, that light is come into the world, and men loved darkness rather than light, because their deeds were evil. For every one that doeth evil hateth the light, neither cometh to the light, lest his deeds should be reproved. But he that doeth truth cometh to the light, that his deeds may be made manifest, that they are wrought in God." My son, be not unhappy! We are all sons of God and His servants! We are all one army! Do you think that He has no servants besides you, and that if you had devoted yourself to His service with your whole strength you could have done all that He needs – all that is needful for the establishment of His kingdom? You say you would do twice, ten times, a hundred times, more than you did. But if you did ten thousand times ten thousand more than all men have done, what would that have been in the work of God? A mere nothing! God's work, like Himself, is infinite. God's work is you. Come to Him, and be not a labourer but a son, and you will become a partner of the infinite God and of His world. In God's sight there is neither small nor great, there is only what is straight and what is crooked. Enter into the straight path of life and you will be with God and your work will be neither small nor great, it will be God's work. Remember that in heaven there is more joy over one sinner than over a hundred just persons. The world's work – all that you have neglected to do – has only shown you your sin, and you have repented. And when you repented you found the straight path. Go forward and follow it, and do not think of the past nor of what is great or small. All men are equal in God's sight! There is one God and one life!'

And Julius was comforted, and from that day he lived and worked for the brethren according to his strength. And so he lived joyfully for another twenty years, and did not notice how death took his body.

THE COFFEE-HOUSE OF SURAT

(AFTER BERNARDIN DE SAINT-PIERRE)

IN the town of Surat, in India, was a coffee-house where many travellers and foreigners from all parts of the world met and conversed.

One day a learned Persian theologian visited this coffee-house. He was a man who had spent his life studying the nature of the Deity, and reading and writing books upon the subject. He had thought, read, and written so much about God, that eventually he lost his wits, became quite confused, and ceased even to believe in the existence of a God. The Shah, hearing of this, had banished him from Persia.

After having argued all his life about the First Cause, this unfortunate theologian had ended by quite perplexing himself, and instead of understanding that he had lost his own reason, he began to think that there was no higher Reason controlling the universe.

This man had an African slave who followed him everywhere. When the theologian entered the coffee-house, the slave remained outside, near the door, sitting on a stone in the glare of the sun, and driving away the flies that buzzed around him. The Persian having settled down on a divan in the coffee-house, ordered himself a cup of opium. When he had drunk it and the opium had begun to quicken the workings of his brain, he addressed his slave through the open door:

'Tell me, wretched slave,' said he, 'do you think there is a God, or not?'

'Of course there is,' said the slave, and immediately drew from under his girdle a small idol of wood.

'There,' said he, 'that is the God who has guarded me from the day of my birth. Everyone in our country worships the fetish tree, from the wood of which this God was made.'

This conversation between the theologian and his slave was listened to with surprise by the other guests in the coffee-house. They were astonished at the master's question, and yet more so at the slave's reply.

One of them, a Brahmin, on hearing the words spoken by the slave, turned to him and said:

'Miserable fool! Is it possible you believe that God can be carried under a man's girdle? There is one God – Brahma, and He is greater than the whole world, for He created it. Brahma is the One, the mighty God, and in His honour are built the temples on the Ganges' banks, where His true priests, the Brahmins, worship him. They know the true God, and none but they. A thousand score of years have passed, and yet through revolution after revolution these priests have held their sway, because Brahma, the one true God, has protected them.'

So spoke the Brahmin, thinking to convince everyone; but a Jewish broker who was present replied to him, and said:

'No! the temple of the true God is not in India. Neither does God protect the Brahmin caste. The true God is not the God of the Brahmins, but of Abraham, Isaac, and Jacob. None does He protect but His chosen people, the Israelites. From the commencement of the world, our nation has been beloved of Him, and ours alone. If we are now scattered over the whole earth, it is but to try us; for God has promised that He will one day gather His people together in Jerusalem. Then, with the Temple of Jerusalem – the wonder of the ancient world – restored to its splendour, shall Israel be established a ruler over all nations.'

So spoke the Jew, and burst into tears. He wished to say more, but an Italian missionary who was there interrupted him.

'What you are saying is untrue,' said he to the Jew. 'You attribute injustice to God. He cannot love your nation above the rest. Nay rather, even if it be true that of old He favoured the Israelites, it is now nineteen hundred years since they angered Him, and caused Him to destroy their nation and scatter them over the earth, so that their faith makes no converts and has died out except here and there. God shows preference to no nation, but calls all who wish to be saved to the bosom of the Catholic Church of Rome, the one outside whose borders no salvation can be found.'

So spoke the Italian. But a Protestant minister, who happened to be present, growing pale, turned to the Catholic missionary and exclaimed:

'How can you say that salvation belongs to your religion? Those only will be saved, who serve God according to the Gospel, in spirit and in truth, as bidden by the word of Christ.'

Then a Turk, an office-holder in the custom-house at Surat, who was sitting in the coffee-house smoking a pipe, turned with an air of superiority to both the Christians.

'Your belief in your Roman religion is vain,' said he. 'It was superseded twelve hundred years ago by the true faith; that of Mohammed! You cannot but observe how the true Mohammedan faith continues to spread both in Europe and Asia, and even in the enlightened country of China. You say yourselves that God has rejected the Jews; and, as a proof, you quote the fact that the Jews are humiliated and their faith does not spread. Confess then the truth of Mohammedanism, for it is triumphant and spreads far and wide. None will be saved but the followers of Mohammed, God's latest prophet; and of them, only the followers of Omar, and not of Ali, for the latter are false to the faith.'

To this the Persian theologian, who was of the sect of Ali, wished to reply; but by this time a great dispute had arisen among all the strangers of different faiths and creeds present. There were Abyssinian Christians, Lamas from Thibet, Ismailians and Fire-worshippers. They all argued about the nature of God, and how He should be worshipped. Each of them asserted that in his country alone was the true God known and rightly worshipped.

Everyone argued and shouted, except a Chinaman, a student of Confucius, who sat quietly in one corner of the coffee-house, not joining in the dispute. He sat there drinking tea and listening to what the others said, but did not speak himself.

The Turk noticed him sitting there, and appealed to him, saying:

'You can confirm what I say, my good Chinaman. You hold your peace, but if you spoke I know you would uphold my opinion. Traders from your country, who come to me for assistance, tell me that though many religions have been introduced into China, you Chinese consider Mohammedanism the best of all, and adopt it willingly. Confirm, then, my words, and tell us your opinion of the true God and of His prophet.'

'Yes, yes,' said the rest, turning to the Chinaman, 'let us hear what you think on the subject.'

The Chinaman, the student of Confucius, closed his eyes, and thought a while. Then he opened them again, and drawing his hands out of the wide sleeves of his garment, and folding them on his breast, he spoke as follows, in a calm and quiet voice.

Sirs, it seems to me that it is chiefly pride that prevents men agreeing with one another on matters of faith. If you care to listen to me, I will tell you a story which will explain this by an example.

I came here from China on an English steamer which had been round the world. We stopped for fresh water, and landed on the east coast of the island of Sumatra. It was midday, and some of us, having landed, sat in the shade of some coconut palms by the seashore, not far from a native village. We were a party of men of different nationalities.

As we sat there, a blind man approached us. We learnt afterwards that he had gone blind from gazing too long and too persistently at the sun, trying to find out what it is, in order to seize its light.

He strove a long time to accomplish this, constantly looking at the sun; but the only result was that his eyes were injured by its brightness, and he became blind.

Then he said to himself:

'The light of the sun is not a liquid; for if it were a liquid it would be possible to pour it from one vessel into another, and it would be moved, like water, by the wind. Neither is it fire; for if it were fire, water would extinguish it. Neither is light a spirit, for it is seen by the eye; nor is it matter, for it cannot be moved. Therefore, as the light of the sun is neither liquid, nor fire, nor spirit, nor matter, it is – nothing!'

So he argued, and, as a result of always looking at the sun and always thinking about it, he lost both his sight and his reason. And when he went quite blind, he became fully convinced that the sun did not exist.

With this blind man came a slave, who after placing his master in the shade of a coconut tree, picked up a coconut from the ground, and began making it into a night-light. He twisted a wick from the fibre of the coconut: squeezed oil from the nut into the shell, and soaked the wick in it.

As the slave sat doing this, the blind man sighed and said to him:

'Well, slave, was I not right when I told you there is no sun? Do you not see how dark it is? Yet people say there is a sun. . . . But if so, what is it?'

'I do not know what the sun is,' said the slave. 'That is no business of mine. But I know what light is. Here, I have made a night-light, by the help of which I can serve you and find anything I want in the hut.'

And the slave picked up the coconut shell, saying:

'This is my sun.'

A lame man with crutches, who was sitting near by, heard these words, and laughed:

'You have evidently been blind all your life,' said he to the blind man, 'not to know what the sun is. I will tell you what it is. The sun is a ball of fire, which rises every morning out of the sea and goes down again among the mountains of our island each evening. We have all seen this, and if you had had your eyesight you too would have seen it.'

A fisherman, who had been listening to the conversation, said:

'It is plain enough that you have never been beyond your own island. If you were not lame, and if you had been out as I have in a fishing-boat, you would know that the sun does not set among the mountains of our island, but as it rises from the ocean every morning so it sets again in the sea every night. What I am telling you is true, for I see it every day with my own eyes.'

Then an Indian who was of our party, interrupted him by saying:

'I am astonished that a reasonable man should talk such nonsense. How can a ball of fire possibly descend into the water and not be extinguished? The sun is not a ball of fire at all, it is the Deity named Deva, who rides for ever in a chariot round the golden mountain, Meru. Sometimes the evil serpents Ragu and Ketu attack Deva and swallow him: and then the earth is dark. But our priests pray that the Deity may be released, and then he is set free. Only such ignorant men as you, who have never been beyond their own island, can imagine that the sun shines for their country alone.'

Then the master of an Egyptian vessel, who was present, spoke in his turn.

'No,' said he, 'you also are wrong. The sun is not a Deity, and does not move only round India and its golden mountain. I have sailed much on the Black Sea, and along the coasts of Arabia, and have been to Madagascar and to the Philippines. The sun lights the whole earth, and not India alone. It does not circle round one mountain, but rises far in the east, beyond the Isles of Japan, and sets far, far away in the west, beyond the islands of England. That is why the Japanese call their country "Nippon", that is "the birth of the sun". I know this well, for I have myself seen much, and heard more from my grandfather, who sailed to the very ends of the sea.'

He would have gone on, but an English sailor from our ship interrupted him.

'There is no country', he said, 'where people know so much about the sun's movements as in England. The sun, as everyone in England knows, rises nowhere and sets nowhere. It is always moving round the earth. We can be sure of this for we have just been round the world ourselves, and nowhere knocked up against the sun. Wherever we went, the sun showed itself in the morning and hid itself at night, just as it does here.'

And the Englishman took a stick and, drawing circles on the sand, tried to explain how the sun moves in the heavens and goes round the world. But he was unable to explain it clearly, and pointing to the ship's pilot said:

'This man knows more about it than I do. He can explain it properly.'

The pilot, who was an intelligent man, had listened in silence to the talk till he was asked to speak. Now everyone turned to him, and he said:

'You are all misleading one another, and are yourselves deceived. The sun does not go round the earth, but the earth goes round the sun, revolving as it goes, and turning towards the sun in the course of each twenty-four hours, not only Japan, and the Philippines, and Sumatra where we now are, but Africa, and Europe, and America, and many lands besides. The sun does not shine for some one mountain, or for some one island, or for some one sea, nor even for one earth alone, but for other planets as well as our earth. If you would only look up at the heavens, instead of at the ground beneath your own feet, you might all understand this, and would then no longer suppose that the sun shines for you, or for your country alone.'

Thus spoke the wise pilot, who had voyaged much about the world, and had gazed much upon the heavens above.

'So on matters of faith,' continued the Chinaman, the student of Confucius, 'it is pride that causes error and discord among men. As with the sun, so it is with God. Each man wants to have a special God of his own, or at least a special God for his native land. Each nation wishes to confine in its own temples Him, whom the world cannot contain.

'Can any temple compare with that which God Himself has built to unite all men in one faith and one religion?

'All human temples are built on the model of this temple, which is God's own world. Every temple has its fonts, its vaulted roof, its lamps, its pictures or sculptures, its inscriptions, its books of the law, its offerings, its altars and its priests. But in what temple is there such a font as the ocean; such a vault as that of the heavens; such lamps as the sun, moon, and stars; or any figures to be compared with living, loving, mutually-helpful men? Where are there any records of God's goodness so easy to understand as the blessings which God has strewn abroad for man's happiness? Where is there any book of the law so clear to each man as that written in his heart? What sacrifices equal the self-denials which loving men and women make for one another? And what altar can be compared with the heart of a good man, on which God Himself accepts the sacrifice?

'The higher a man's conception of God, the better will he know Him. And the better he knows God, the nearer will he draw to Him, imitating His goodness, His mercy, and His love of man.

'Therefore, let him who sees the sun's whole light filling the world, refrain from blaming or despising the superstitious man, who in his own idol sees one ray of that same light. Let him not despise even the unbeliever who is blind and cannot see the sun at all.'

So spoke the Chinaman, the student of Confucius; and all who were present in the coffee-house were silent, and disputed no more as to whose faith was the best.

MASTER AND MAN

I

IT happened in the 'seventies in winter, on the day after St Nicholas's Day. There was a fête in the parish and the inn-keeper, Vasíli Andréevich Brekhunóv, a Second Guild merchant, being a church elder had to go to church, and had also to entertain his relatives and friends at home.

But when the last of them had gone he at once began to prepare to drive over to see a neighbouring proprietor about a grove which he had been bargaining over for a long time. He was now in a hurry to start, lest buyers from the town might forestall him in making a profitable purchase.

The youthful landowner was asking ten thousand rubles for the grove simply because Vasíli Andréevich was offering seven thousand. Seven thousand was, however, only a third of its real value. Vasíli Andréevich might perhaps have got it down to his own price, for the woods were in his district and he had a long-standing agreement with the other village dealers that no one should run up the price in another's district, but he had now learnt that some timber-dealers from town meant to bid for the Goryáchkin grove, and he resolved to go at once and get the matter settled. So as soon as the feast was over, he took seven hundred rubles from his strong box, added to them two thousand three hundred rubles of church money he had in his keeping, so as to make up the sum to three thousand; carefully counted the notes, and having put them into his pocket-book made haste to start.

Nikíta, the only one of Vasíli Andréevich's labourers who was not drunk that day, ran to harness the horse. Nikíta, though a habitual drunkard, was not drunk that day because since the last day before the fast, when he had drunk his coat and leather boots, he had sworn off drink and had kept his vow for two months, and was still keeping it despite the temptation of the vodka that had been drunk everywhere during the first two days of the feast.

Nikíta was a peasant of about fifty from a neighbouring village, 'not a manager' as the peasants said of him, meaning that he was not the thrifty head of a household but lived most of his time away from home as a labourer. He was valued everywhere for his industry, dexterity, and strength at work, and still more for his kindly and pleasant temper. But he never settled down anywhere for long because about twice a year, or even oftener, he had a drinking bout, and then besides spending all his clothes on drink he became turbulent and quarrelsome. Vasíli Andréevich himself had turned him away several times, but had afterwards taken him back again – valuing his honesty, his kindness to animals, and especially his cheapness. Vasíli Andréevich did not pay Nikíta the eighty rubles a year such a man was worth, but only about forty, which he gave him haphazard, in small sums, and even that mostly not in cash but in goods from his own shop and at high prices.

Nikíta's wife Martha, who had once been a handsome vigorous woman, managed the homestead with the help of her son and two daughters, and did not urge Nikíta to live at home: first because she had been living for some twenty years already with a cooper, a peasant from another village who lodged in their house; and secondly because though she managed her husband as she pleased when he was sober, she feared him like fire when he was drunk. Once when he had got drunk at home, Nikíta, probably to make up for his submissiveness when sober, broke open her box, took out her best clothes, snatched up an axe, and chopped all her under-garments and dresses to bits. All the wages Nikíta earned went to his wife, and he raised no objection to that. So now, two days before the holiday, Martha had been twice to see Vasíli Andréevich and had got from him wheat flour, tea, sugar, and a quart of vodka, the lot costing three rubles, and also five rubles in cash, for which she thanked him as for a special favour, though he owed Nikíta at least twenty rubles.

'What agreement did we ever draw up with you?' said Vasíli Andréevich to Nikíta. 'If you need anything, take it; you will work it off. I'm not like others to keep you waiting, and making up accounts and reckoning fines. We deal straightforwardly. You serve me and I don't neglect you.'

And when saying this Vasíli Andréevich was honestly convinced that he was Nikíta's benefactor, and he knew how to put it so plausibly that all those who depended on him for their money, beginning with Nikíta, confirmed him in the conviction that he was their benefactor and did not overreach them.

'Yes, I understand, Vasíli Andréevich. You know that I serve you and take as much pains as I would for my own father. I understand very well!' Nikíta would reply. He was quite aware that Vasíli Andréevich was cheating him, but at the same time he felt that it was useless to try to clear up his accounts with him or explain his side of the matter, and that as long as he had nowhere else to go he must accept what he could get.

Now, having heard his master's order to harness, he went as usual cheerfully and willingly to the shed, stepping briskly and easily on his rather turned-in feet; took down from a nail the heavy tasselled leather bridle, and jingling the rings of the bit went to the closed stable where the horse he was to harness was standing by himself.

'What, feeling lonely, feeling lonely, little silly?' said Nikíta in answer to the low whinny with which he was greeted by the good-tempered, medium-sized bay stallion, with a rather slanting crupper, who stood alone in the shed. 'Now then, now then, there's time enough. Let me water you first,' he went on, speaking to the horse just as to someone who understood the words he was using, and having whisked the dusty grooved back of the well-fed young stallion with the skirt of his coat, he put a bridle on his handsome head, straightened his ears and forelock, and having taken off his halter led him out to water.

Picking his way out of the dung-strewn stable, Mukhórty frisked, and making play with his hind leg pretended that he meant to kick Nikíta, who was running at a trot beside him to the pump.

'Now then, now then, you rascal!' Nikíta called out, well knowing how carefully Mukhórty threw out his hind leg just to touch his greasy sheepskin coat but not to strike him – a trick Nikíta much appreciated.

After a drink of the cold water the horse sighed, moving his strong wet lips, from the hairs of which transparent drops fell into the trough; then standing still as if in thought, he suddenly gave a loud snort.

'If you don't want any more, you needn't. But don't go asking for any later,' said Nikíta quite seriously and fully explaining his conduct to Mukhórty. Then he ran back to the shed pulling the playful young horse, who wanted to gambol all over the yard, by the rein.

There was no one else in the yard except a stranger, the cook's husband, who had come for the holiday.

'Go and ask which sledge is to be harnessed – the wide one or the small one – there's a good fellow!'

The cook's husband went into the house, which stood on an iron foundation and was iron-roofed, and soon returned saying that the little one was to be harnessed. By that time Nikíta had put the collar and brass-studded belly-band on Mukhórty and, carrying a light, painted shaft-bow in one hand, was leading the horse with the other up to two sledges that stood in the shed.

'All right, let it be the little one!' he said, backing the intelligent horse, which all the time kept pretending to bite him, into the shafts, and with the aid of the cook's husband he proceeded to harness. When everything was nearly ready and only the reins had to be adjusted, Nikíta sent the other man to the shed for some straw and to the barn for a drugget.

'There, that's all right! Now, now, don't bristle up!' said Nikíta, pressing down into the sledge the freshly threshed oat straw the cook's husband had brought. 'And now let's spread the sacking like this, and the drugget over it. There, like that it will be comfortable sitting,' he went on, suiting the action to the words and tucking the drugget all round over the straw to make a seat.

'Thank you, dear man. Things always go quicker with two working at it!' he added. And gathering up the leather reins fastened together by a brass ring, Nikíta took the driver's seat and started the impatient horse over the frozen manure which lay in the yard, towards the gate.

'Uncle Nikíta! I say, Uncle, Uncle!' a high-pitched voice shouted, and a seven-year-old boy in a black sheepskin coat, new white felt boots, and a warm cap, ran hurriedly out of the house into the yard. 'Take me with you!' he cried, fastening up his coat as he ran.

'All right, come along, darling!' said Nikíta, and stopping the sledge he picked up the master's pale thin little son, radiant with joy, and drove out into the road.

It was past two o'clock and the day was windy, dull, and cold, with more than twenty degrees Fahrenheit of frost. Half the sky was hidden by a lowering dark cloud. In the yard it was quiet, but in the street the wind was felt more keenly. The snow swept down from a neighbouring shed and whirled about in the corner near the bath-house.

Hardly had Nikíta driven out of the yard and turned the horse's head to the house, before Vasíli Andréevich emerged from the high porch in front of the house with a cigarette in his mouth and wearing a cloth-covered sheepskin coat tightly girdled low at his waist, and stepped onto the hard-trodden snow which squeaked under the leather soles of his felt boots, and stopped. Taking a last whiff of his cigarette he threw it down, stepped on it, and letting the smoke escape through his moustache and looking askance at the horse that was coming up, began to tuck in his sheepskin collar on both sides of his ruddy face, clean-shaven except for the moustache, so that his breath should not moisten the collar.

'See now! The young scamp is there already!' he exclaimed when he saw his little son in the sledge. Vasíli Andréevich was excited by the vodka he had drunk with his visitors, and so he was even more pleased than usual with everything that was his and all that he did. The sight of his son, whom he always thought of as his heir, now gave him great satisfaction. He looked at him, screwing up his eyes and showing his long teeth.

His wife – pregnant, thin and pale, with her head and shoulders wrapped in a shawl so that nothing of her face could be seen but her eyes – stood behind him in the vestibule to see him off.

'Now really, you ought to take Nikíta with you,' she said timidly, stepping out from the doorway.

Vasíli Andréevich did not answer. Her words evidently annoyed him and he frowned angrily and spat.

'You have money on you,' she continued in the same plaintive voice. 'What if the weather gets worse! Do take him, for goodness' sake!'

'Why? Don't I know the road that I must needs take a guide?' exclaimed Vasíli Andréevich, uttering every word very distinctly and compressing his lips unnaturally, as he usually did when speaking to buyers and sellers.

'Really you ought to take him. I beg you in God's name!' his wife repeated, wrapping her shawl more closely round her head.

'There, she sticks to it like a leech! . . . Where am I to take him?'

'I'm quite ready to go with you, Vasíli Andréevich,' said Nikíta cheerfully. 'But they must feed the horses while I am away,' he added, turning to his master's wife.

'I'll look after them, Nikíta dear. I'll tell Simon,' replied the mistress.

'Well, Vasíli Andréevich, am I to come with you?' said Nikíta, awaiting a decision.

'It seems I must humour my old woman. But if you're coming you'd better put on a warmer cloak,' said Vasíli Andréevich, smiling again as he winked at Nikíta's short sheepskin coat, which was torn under the arms and at the back, was greasy and out of shape, frayed to a fringe round the skirt, and had endured many things in its lifetime.

'Hey, dear man, come and hold the horse!' shouted Nikíta to the cook's husband, who was still in the yard.

'No, I will myself, I will myself!' shrieked the little boy, pulling his hands, red with cold, out of his pockets, and seizing the cold leather reins.

'Only don't be too long dressing yourself up. Look alive!' shouted Vasíli Andréevich, grinning at Nikíta.

'Only a moment, father, Vasíli Andréevich!' replied Nikíta, and running quickly with his in-turned toes in his felt boots with their soles patched with felt, he hurried across the yard and into the workmen's hut.

'Arínushka! Get my coat down from the stove. I'm going with the master,' he said, as he ran into the hut and took down his girdle from the nail on which it hung.

The workmen's cook, who had had a sleep after dinner and was now getting the samovar ready for her husband, turned cheerfully to Nikíta, and infected by his hurry began to move as quickly as he did, got down his miserable worn-out cloth coat from the stove where it was drying, and began hurriedly shaking it out and smoothing it down.

'There now, you'll have a chance of a holiday with your goodman,' said Nikíta, who from kind-hearted politeness always said something to anyone he was alone with.

Then, drawing his worn narrow girdle round him, he drew in his breath, pulling in his lean stomach still more, and girdled himself as tightly as he could over his sheepskin.

'There now,' he said, addressing himself no longer to the cook but the girdle, as he tucked the ends in at the waist, 'now you won't come undone!' And working his shoulders up and down to free his arms, he put the coat over his sheepskin, arched his back more strongly to ease his arms, poked himself under the armpits, and took down his leather-covered mittens from the shelf. 'Now we're all right!'

'You ought to wrap your feet up, Nikíta. Your boots are very bad.'

Nikíta stopped as if he had suddenly realized this.

'Yes, I ought to.... But they'll do like this. It isn't far!' and he ran out into the yard.

'Won't you be cold, Nikíta?' said the mistress as he came up to the sledge.

'Cold? No, I'm quite warm,' answered Nikíta as he pushed some straw up to the forepart of the sledge so that it should cover his feet, and stowed away the whip, which the good horse would not need, at the bottom of the sledge.

Vasíli Andréevich, who was wearing two fur-lined coats one over the other, was already in the sledge, his broad back filling nearly its whole rounded width, and taking the reins he immediately touched the horse. Nikíta jumped in just as the sledge started, and seated himself in front on the left side, with one leg hanging over the edge.

II

THE good stallion took the sledge along at a brisk pace over the smooth-frozen road through the village, the runners squeaking slightly as they went.

'Look at him hanging on there! Hand me the whip, Nikíta!' shouted Vasíli Andréevich, evidently enjoying the sight of his 'heir', who standing on the runners was hanging on at the back of the sledge. 'I'll give it you! Be off to mamma, you dog!'

The boy jumped down. The horse increased his amble and, suddenly changing foot, broke into a fast trot.

The Crosses, the village where Vasíli Andréevich lived, consisted of six houses. As soon as they had passed the black-smith's hut, the last in the village, they realized that the wind was much stronger than they had thought. The road could hardly be seen. The tracks left by the sledge-runners were immediately covered by snow and the road was only distinguished by the fact that it was higher than the rest of the ground. There was a whirl of snow over the fields and the line where sky and earth met could not be seen. The Telyátin forest, usually clearly visible, now only loomed up occasionally and dimly through the driving snowy dust. The wind came from the left, insistently blowing over to one side the mane on Mukhórty's sleek neck and carrying aside even his fluffy tail, which was tied in a simple knot. Nikíta's wide coat-collar, as he sat on the windy side, pressed close to his cheek and nose.

'This road doesn't give him a chance – it's too snowy,' said Vasíli Andréevich, who prided himself on his good horse. 'I once drove to Pashútino with him in half an hour.'

'What?' asked Nikíta, who could not hear on account of his collar.

'I say I once went to Pashútino in half an hour,' shouted Vasíli Andréevich.

'It goes without saying that he's a good horse,' replied Nikíta.

They were silent for awhile. But Vasíli Andréevich wished to talk.

'Well, did you tell your wife not to give the cooper any vodka?' he began in the same loud tone, quite convinced that Nikíta must feel flattered to be talking with so clever and important a person as himself, and he was so pleased with his jest that it did not enter his head that the remark might be unpleasant to Nikíta.

The wind again prevented Nikíta's hearing his master's words.

Vasíli Andréevich repeated the jest about the cooper in his loud, clear voice.

'That's their business, Vasíli Andréevich. I don't pry into their affairs. As long as she doesn't ill-treat our boy – God be with them.'

'That's so,' said Vasíli Andréevich. 'Well, and will you be buying a horse in spring?' he went on, changing the subject.

'Yes, I can't avoid it,' answered Nikíta, turning down his collar and leaning back towards his master.

The conversation now became interesting to him and he did not wish to lose a word.

'The lad's growing up. He must begin to plough for himself, but till now we've always had to hire someone,' he said.

'Well, why not have the lean-cruppered one. I won't charge much for it,' shouted Vasíli Andréevich, feeling animated, and consequently starting on his favourite occupation – that of horse-dealing – which absorbed all his mental powers.

'Or you might let me have fifteen rubles and I'll buy one at the horse-market,' said Nikíta, who knew that the horse Vasíli

Andréevich wanted to sell him would be dear at seven rubles, but that if he took it from him it would be charged at twenty-five, and then he would be unable to draw any money for half a year.

'It's a good horse. I think of your interest as of my own – according to conscience. Brekhunóv isn't a man to wrong anyone. Let the loss be mine. I'm not like others. Honestly!' he shouted in the voice in which he hypnotized his customers and dealers. 'It's a real good horse.'

'Quite so!' said Nikíta with a sigh, and convinced that there was nothing more to listen to, he again released his collar, which immediately covered his ear and face.

They drove on in silence for about half an hour. The wind blew sharply onto Nikíta's side and arm where his sheepskin was torn.

He huddled up and breathed into the collar which covered his mouth, and was not wholly cold.

'What do you think – shall we go through Karamýshevo or by the straight road?' asked Vasíli Andréevich.

The road through Karamýshevo was more frequented and was well marked with a double row of high stakes. The straight road was nearer but little used and had no stakes, or only poor ones covered with snow.

Nikíta thought awhile.

'Though Karamýshevo is farther, it is better going,' he said.

'But by the straight road, when once we get through the hollow by the forest, it's good going – sheltered,' said Vasíli Andréevich, who wished to go the nearest way.

'Just as you please,' said Nikíta, and again let go of his collar.

Vasíli Andréevich did as he had said, and having gone about half a verst came to a tall oak stake which had a few dry leaves still dangling on it, and there he turned to the left.

On turning they faced directly against the wind, and snow was beginning to fall. Vasíli Andréevich, who was driving, inflated his cheeks, blowing the breath out through his moustache. Nikíta dozed.

So they went on in silence for about ten minutes. Suddenly Vasíli Andréevich began saying something.

'Eh, what?' asked Nikíta, opening his eyes.

Vasíli Andréevich did not answer, but bent over, looking behind them and then ahead of the horse. The sweat had curled Mukhórty's coat between his legs and on his neck. He went at a walk.

'What is it?' Nikíta asked again.

'What is it? What is it?' Vasíli Andréevich mimicked him angrily. 'There are no stakes to be seen! We must have got off the road!'

'Well, pull up then, and I'll look for it,' said Nikíta, and jumping down lightly from the sledge and taking the whip from under the straw, he went off to the left from his own side of the sledge.

The snow was not deep that year, so that it was possible to walk anywhere, but still in places it was knee-deep and got into Nikíta's boots. He went about feeling the ground with his feet and the whip, but could not find the road anywhere.

'Well, how is it?' asked Vasíli Andréevich when Nikíta came back to the sledge.

'There is no road this side. I must go to the other side and try there,' said Nikíta.

'There's something there in front. Go and have a look.'

Nikíta went to what had appeared dark, but found that it was earth which the wind had blown from the bare fields of winter oats and had strewn over the snow, colouring it. Having searched to the right also, he returned to the sledge, brushed the snow from his coat, shook it out of his boots, and seated himself once more.

'We must go to the right,' he said decidedly. 'The wind was blowing on our left before, but now it is straight in my face. Drive to the right,' he repeated with decision.

Vasíli Andréevich took his advice and turned to the right, but still there was no road. They went on in that direction for some time. The wind was as fierce as ever and it was snowing lightly.

'It seems, Vasíli Andréevich, that we have gone quite astray,' Nikíta suddenly remarked, as if it were a pleasant thing. 'What is that?' he added, pointing to some potato bines that showed up from under the snow.

Vasíli Andréevich stopped the perspiring horse, whose deep sides were heaving heavily.

'What is it?'

'Why, we are on the Zakhárov lands. See where we've got to!'

'Nonsense!' retorted Vasíli Andréevich.

'It's not nonsense, Vasíli Andréevich. It's the truth,' replied Nikíta. 'You can feel that the sledge is going over a potato-field, and there are the heaps of bines which have been carted here. It's the Zakhárov factory land.'

'Dear me, how we have gone astray!' said Vasíli Andréevich. 'What are we to do now?'

'We must go straight on, that's all. We shall come out somewhere – if not at Zakhárova then at the proprietor's farm,' said Nikíta.

Vasíli Andréevich agreed, and drove as Nikíta had indicated. So they went on for a considerable time. At times they came onto bare fields and the sledge-runners rattled over frozen lumps of earth. Sometimes they got onto a winter-rye field, or a fallow field on which they could see stalks of worm-wood, and straws sticking up through the snow and swaying in the wind; sometimes they came onto deep and even white snow, above which nothing was to be seen.

The snow was falling from above and sometimes rose from below. The horse was evidently exhausted, his hair had all curled up from sweat and was covered with hoar-frost, and he went at a walk. Suddenly he stumbled and sat down in a ditch or water-course. Vasíli Andréevich wanted to stop, but Nikíta cried to him:

'Why stop? We've got in and must get out. Hey, pet! Hey, darling! Gee up, old fellow!' he shouted in a cheerful tone to the horse, jumping out of the sledge and himself getting stuck in the ditch.

The horse gave a start and quickly climbed out onto the frozen bank. It was evidently a ditch that had been dug there.

'Where are we now?' asked Vasíli Andréevich.

'We'll soon find out!' Nikíta replied. 'Go on, we'll get somewhere.'

'Why, this must be the Goryáchkin forest!' said Vasíli Andréevich, pointing to something dark that appeared amid the snow in front of them.

'We'll see what forest it is when we get there,' said Nikíta.

He saw that beside the black thing they had noticed, dry, oblong willow-leaves were fluttering, and so he knew it was not a forest but a settlement, but he did not wish to say so. And in fact they had not gone twenty-five yards beyond the ditch before something in front of them, evidently trees, showed up black, and they heard a new and melancholy sound. Nikíta had guessed right: it was not a wood, but a row of tall willows with a few leaves still fluttering on them here and there. They had evidently been planted along the ditch round a thresh-ing-floor. Coming up to the willows, which moaned sadly in the wind, the horse suddenly planted his forelegs above the height of the sledge, drew up his hind legs also, pulling the sledge onto higher ground, and turned to the left, no longer sinking up to his knees in snow. They were back on a road.

'Well, here we are, but heaven only knows where!' said Nikíta.

The horse kept straight along the road through the drifted snow, and before they had gone another hundred yards the straight line of the dark wattle wall of a barn showed up black before them, its roof heavily covered with snow which poured down from it. After passing the barn the road turned to the wind and they drove into a snow-drift. But ahead of them was a lane with houses on either side, so evidently the snow had been blown across the road and they had to drive through the drift. And so in fact it was. Having driven through the snow they came out into a street. At the end house of the village some frozen clothes hanging on a line – shirts, one red and one white, trousers, leg-bands, and a petticoat – fluttered wildly in the wind. The white shirt in particular struggled desperately, waving its sleeves about.

'There now, either a lazy woman or a dead one has not taken her clothes down before the holiday,' remarked Nikíta, looking at the fluttering shirts.

III

At the entrance to the street the wind still raged and the road was thickly covered with snow, but well within the village it was calm, warm, and cheerful. At one house a dog was barking, at another a woman, covering her head with her coat, came running from somewhere and entered the door of a hut, stopping on the threshold to have a look at the passing sledge. In the middle of the village girls could be heard singing. Here in the village there seemed to be less wind and snow, and the frost was less keen.

'Why, this is Gríshkino,' said Vasíli Andréevich.

'So it is,' responded Nikíta.

It really was Gríshkino, which meant that they had gone too far to the left and had travelled some six miles, not quite in the direction they aimed at, but towards their destination for all that.

From Gríshkino to Goryáchkin was about another four miles.

In the middle of the village they almost ran into a tall man walking down the middle of the street.

'Who are you?' shouted the man, stopping the horse, and recognizing Vasíli Andréevich he immediately took hold of the shaft, went along it hand over hand till he reached the sledge, and placed himself on the driver's seat.

He was Isáy, a peasant of Vasíli Andréevich's acquaintance, and well known as the principal horse-thief in the district.

'Ah, Vasíli Andréevich! Where are you off to?' said Isáy, enveloping Nikíta in the odour of the vodka he had drunk.

'We were going to Goryáchkin.'

'And look where you've got to! You should have gone through Molchánovka.'

'Should have, but didn't manage it,' said Vasíli Andréevich, holding in the horse.

'That's a good horse,' said Isáy, with a shrewd glance at Mukhórty, and with a practised hand he tightened the loosened knot high in the horse's bushy tail.

'Are you going to stay the night?'

'No, friend. I must get on.'

'Your business must be pressing. And who is this? Ah, Nikíta Stepánych!'

'Who else?' replied Nikíta. 'But I say, good friend, how are we to avoid going astray again?'

'Where can you go astray here? Turn back straight down the street and then when you come out keep straight on. Don't take to the left. You will come out onto the high road, and then turn to the right.'

'And where do we turn off the high road? As in summer, or the winter way?' asked Nikíta.

'The winter way. As soon as you turn off you'll see some bushes, and opposite them there is a way-mark – a large oak one with branches – and that's the way.'

Vasíli Andréevich turned the horse back and drove through the outskirts of the village.

'Why not stay the night?' Isáy shouted after them.

But Vasíli Andréevich did not answer and touched up the horse. Four miles of good road, two of which lay through the forest, seemed easy to manage, especially as the wind was apparently quieter and the snow had stopped.

Having driven along the trodden village street, darkened here and there by fresh manure, past the yard where the clothes hung out and where the white shirt had broken loose and was now attached only by one frozen sleeve, they again came within sound of the weird moan of the willows, and again emerged on the open fields. The storm, far from ceasing, seemed to have grown yet stronger. The road was completely covered with drifting snow, and only the stakes showed that they had not lost their way. But even the stakes ahead of them were not easy to see, since the wind blew in their faces.

Vasíli Andréevich screwed up his eyes, bent down his head, and looked out for the way-marks, but trusted mainly to the horse's sagacity, letting it take its own way. And the horse really did not lose the road but followed its windings, turning now to the right and now to the left and sensing it under his feet, so that though the snow fell thicker and the wind strengthened they still continued to see way-marks now to the left and now to the right of them.

So they travelled on for about ten minutes, when suddenly, through the slanting screen of wind-driven snow, something black showed up which moved in front of the horse.

This was another sledge with fellow-travellers. Mukhórty overtook them, and struck his hoofs against the back of the sledge in front of him.

'Pass on . . . hey there . . . get in front!' cried voices from the sledge.

Vasíli Andréevich swerved aside to pass the other sledge. In it sat three men and a woman, evidently visitors returning from a feast. One peasant was whacking the snow-covered croup of their little horse with a long switch, and the other two sitting in front waved their arms and shouted something. The woman, completely wrapped up and covered with snow, sat drowsing and bumping at the back.

'Who are you?' shouted Vasíli Andréevich.

'From A-a-a . . .' was all that could be heard.

'I say, where are you from?'

'From A-a-a-a!' one of the peasants shouted with all his might, but still it was impossible to make out who they were.

'Get along! Keep up!' shouted another, ceaselessly beating his horse with the switch.

'So you're from a feast, it seems?'

'Go on, go on! Faster, Simon! Get in front! Faster!'

The wings of the sledges bumped against one another, almost got jammed but managed to separate, and the peasants' sledge began to fall behind.

Their shaggy, big-bellied horse, all covered with snow, breathed heavily under the low shaft-bow and, evidently using the last of its strength, vainly endeavoured to escape from the switch, hobbling with its short legs through the deep snow which it threw up under itself.

Its muzzle, young-looking, with the nether lip drawn up like that of a fish, nostrils distended and ears pressed back from fear, kept up for a few seconds near Nikíta's shoulder and then began to fall behind.

'Just see what liquor does!' said Nikíta. 'They've tired that little horse to death. What pagans!'

For a few minutes they heard the panting of the tired little horse and the drunken shouting of the peasants. Then the panting and the shouts died away, and around them nothing could be heard but the whistling of the wind in their ears and now and then the squeak of their sledge-runners over a wind-swept part of the road.

This encounter cheered and enlivened Vasíli Andréevich, and he drove on more boldly without examining the way-marks, urging on the horse and trusting to him.

Nikíta had nothing to do, and as usual in such circumstances he drowsed, making up for much sleepless time. Suddenly the horse stopped and Nikíta nearly fell forward onto his nose.

'You know we're off the track again!' said Vasíli Andrée-vich.

'How's that?'

'Why, there are no way-marks to be seen. We must have got off the road again.'

'Well, if we've lost the road we must find it,' said Nikíta curtly, and getting out and stepping lightly on his pigeon-toed feet he started once more going about on the snow.

He walked about for a long time, now disappearing and now reappearing, and finally he came back.

'There is no road here. There may be farther on,' he said, getting into the sledge.

It was already growing dark. The snow-storm had not increased but had also not subsided.

'If we could only hear those peasants!' said Vasíli Andréevich.

'Well they haven't caught us up. We must have gone far astray. Or maybe they have lost their way too.'

'Where are we to go then?' asked Vasíli Andréevich.

'Why, we must let the horse take its own way,' said Nikíta. 'He will take us right. Let me have the reins.'

Vasíli Andréevich gave him the reins, the more willingly because his hands were beginning to feel frozen in his thick gloves.

Nikíta took the reins, but only held them, trying not to shake them and rejoicing at his favourite's sagacity. And indeed the clever horse, turning first one ear and then the other now to one side and then to the other, began to wheel round.

'The one thing he can't do is to talk,' Nikíta kept saying. 'See what he is doing! Go on, go on! You know best. That's it, that's it!'

The wind was now blowing from behind and it felt warmer.

'Yes, he's clever,' Nikíta continued, admiring the horse. 'A Kirgiz horse is strong but stupid. But this one – just see what he's doing with his ears! He doesn't need any telegraph. He can scent a mile off.'

Before another half-hour had passed they saw something dark ahead of them – a wood or a village – and stakes again appeared to the right. They had evidently come out onto the road.

'Why, that's Gríshkino again!' Nikíta suddenly exclaimed.

And indeed, there on their left was that same barn with the snow flying from it, and farther on the same line with the frozen washing, shirts and trousers, which still fluttered desperately in the wind.

Again they drove into the street and again it grew quiet, warm, and cheerful, and again they could see the manure-stained street and hear voices and songs and the barking of a dog. It was already so dark that there were lights in some of the windows.

Half-way through the village Vasíli Andréevich turned the horse towards a large double-fronted brick house and stopped at the porch.

Nikíta went to the lighted snow-covered window, in the rays of which flying snow-flakes glittered, and knocked at it with his whip.

'Who is there?' a voice replied to his knock.

'From Krestý, the Brekhunóvs, dear fellow,' answered Nikíta. 'Just come out for a minute.'

Someone moved from the window, and a minute or two later there was the sound of the passage door as it came unstuck, then the latch of the outside door clicked and a tall white-bearded peasant, with a sheepskin coat thrown over his white holiday shirt, pushed his way out holding the door firmly against the wind, followed by a lad in a red shirt and high leather boots.

'Is that you, Andréevich?' asked the old man.

'Yes, friend, we've gone astray,' said Vasíli Andréevich. 'We wanted to get to Goryáchkin but found ourselves here. We went a second time but lost our way again.'

'Just see how you have gone astray!' said the old man. 'Petrúshka, go and open the gate!' he added, turning to the lad in the red shirt.

'All right,' said the lad in a cheerful voice, and ran back into the passage.

'But we're not staying the night,' said Vasíli Andréevich.

'Where will you go in the night? You'd better stay!'

'I'd be glad to, but I must go on. It's business, and it can't be helped.'

'Well, warm yourself at least. The samovar is just ready.'

'Warm myself? Yes, I'll do that,' said Vasíli Andréevich. 'It won't get darker. The moon will rise and it will be lighter. Let's go in and warm ourselves, Nikíta.'

'Well, why not? Let us warm ourselves,' replied Nikíta, who was stiff with cold and anxious to warm his frozen limbs.

Vasíli Andréevich went into the room with the old man, and Nikíta drove through the gate opened for him by Petrúshka, by whose advice he backed the horse under the penthouse. The ground was covered with manure and the tall bow over the horse's head caught against the beam. The hens and the cock had already settled to roost there, and clucked peevishly, clinging to the beam with their claws. The disturbed sheep shied and rushed aside trampling the frozen manure with their hoofs. The dog yelped desperately with fright and anger and then burst out barking like a puppy at the stranger.

Nikíta talked to them all, excused himself to the fowls and assured them that he would not disturb them again, rebuked the sheep for being frightened without knowing why, and kept soothing the dog, while he tied up the horse.

'Now that will be all right,' he said, knocking the snow off his clothes. 'Just hear how he barks!' he added, turning to the dog. 'Be quiet, stupid! Be quiet. You are only troubling yourself for nothing. We're not thieves, we're friends. . . .'

'And these are, it's said, the three domestic counsellors,' remarked the lad, and with his strong arms he pushed under the pent-roof the sledge that had remained outside.

'Why counsellors?' asked Nikíta.

'That's what is printed in Paulson. A thief creeps to a house – the dog barks, that means, "Be on your guard!" The cock crows, that means, "Get up!" The cat licks herself – that means, "A welcome guest is coming. Get ready to receive him!"' said the lad with a smile.

Petrúshka could read and write and knew Paulson's primer, his only book, almost by heart, and he was fond of quoting sayings from it that he thought suited the occasion, especially when he had had something to drink, as to-day.

'That's so,' said Nikíta.

'You must be chilled through and through,' said Petrúshka.

'Yes, I am rather,' said Nikíta, and they went across the yard and the passage into the house.

IV

THE household to which Vasíli Andréevich had come was one of the richest in the village. The family had five allotments, besides renting other land. They had six horses, three cows, two calves, and some twenty sheep. There were twenty-two members belonging to the homestead: four married sons, six grandchildren (one of whom, Petrúshka, was married), two great-grandchildren, three orphans, and four daughters-in-law with their babies. It was one of the few homesteads that remained still undivided, but even here the dull internal work of disintegration which would inevitably lead to separation had already begun, starting as usual among the women. Two sons were living in Moscow as water-carriers, and one was in the army. At home now were the old man and his wife, their second son who managed the homestead, the eldest who had come from Moscow for the holiday, and all the women and children. Besides these members of the family there was a visitor, a neighbour who was godfather to one of the children.

Over the table in the room hung a lamp with a shade, which brightly lit up the tea-things, a bottle of vodka, and some refreshments, besides illuminating the brick walls, which in the far corner were hung with icons on both sides of which were pictures. At the head of the table sat Vasíli Andréevich in a black sheepskin coat, sucking his frozen moustache and observing the room and the people around him with his prominent hawk-like eyes. With him sat the old, bald, white-bearded master of the house in a white homespun shirt, and next him the son home from Moscow for the holi- day – a man with a sturdy back and powerful shoulders and clad in a thin print shirt – then the second son, also broad- shouldered, who acted as head of the house, and then a lean red-haired peasant – the neighbour.

Having had a drink of vodka and something to eat, they were about to take tea, and the samovar standing on the floor beside the brick oven was already humming. The children could be seen in the top bunks and on the top of the oven. A woman sat on a lower bunk with a cradle beside her. The old housewife, her face covered with wrinkles which wrinkled even her lips, was waiting on Vasíli Andréevich.

As Nikíta entered the house she was offering her guest a small tumbler of thick glass which she had just filled with vodka.

'Don't refuse, Vasíli Andréevich, you mustn't! Wish us a merry feast. Drink it, dear!' she said.

The sight and smell of vodka, especially now when he was chilled through and tired out, much disturbed Nikíta's mind. He frowned, and having shaken the snow off his cap and coat, stopped in front of the icons as if not seeing anyone, crossed himself three times, and bowed to the icons. Then, turning to the old master of the house and bowing first to him, then to all those at table, then to the women who stood by the oven, and muttering: 'A merry holiday!' he began taking off his outer things without looking at the table.

'Why, you're all covered with hoar-frost, old fellow!' said the eldest brother, looking at Nikíta's snow-covered face, eyes, and beard.

Nikíta took off his coat, shook it again, hung it up beside the oven, and came up to the table. He too was offered vodka. He went through a moment of painful hesitation and nearly took up the glass and emptied the clear fragrant liquid down his throat, but he glanced at Vasíli Andréevich, remembered his oath and the boots that he had sold for drink, recalled the cooper, remembered his son for whom he had promised to buy a horse by spring, sighed, and declined it.

'I don't drink, thank you kindly,' he said frowning, and sat down on a bench near the second window.

'How's that?' asked the eldest brother.

'I just don't drink,' replied Nikíta without lifting his eyes but looking askance at his scanty beard and moustache and getting the icicles out of them.

'It's not good for him,' said Vasíli Andréevich, munching a cracknel after emptying his glass.

'Well, then, have some tea,' said the kindly old hostess. 'You must be chilled through, good soul. Why are you women dawdling so with the samovar?'

'It is ready,' said one of the young women, and after flicking with her apron the top of the samovar which was now boiling over, she carried it with an effort to the table, raised it, and set it down with a thud.

Meanwhile Vasíli Andréevich was telling how he had lost his way, how they had come back twice to this same village, and how they had gone astray and had met some drunken peasants. Their hosts were surprised, explained where and why they had missed their way, said who the tipsy people they had met were, and told them how they ought to go.

'A little child could find the way to Molchánovka from here. All you have to do is to take the right turning from the high road. There's a bush you can see just there. But you didn't even get that far!' said the neighbour.

'You'd better stay the night. The women will make up beds for you,' said the old woman persuasively.

'You could go on in the morning and it would be pleasanter,' said the old man, confirming what his wife had said.

'I can't, friend. Business!' said Vasíli Andréevich. 'Lose an hour and you can't catch it up in a year,' he added, remembering the grove and the dealers who might snatch that deal from him. 'We shall get there, shan't we?' he said, turning to Nikíta.

Nikíta did not answer for some time, apparently still intent on thawing out his beard and moustache.

'If only we don't go astray again,' he replied gloomily.

He was gloomy because he passionately longed for some vodka, and the only thing that could assuage that longing was tea and he had not yet been offered any.

'But we have only to reach the turning and then we shan't go wrong. The road will be through the forest the whole way,' said Vasíli Andréevich.

'It's just as you please, Vasíli Andréevich. If we're to go, let us go,' said Nikíta, taking the glass of tea he was offered.

'We'll drink our tea and be off.'

Nikíta said nothing but only shook his head, and carefully pouring some tea into his saucer began warming his hands, the fingers of which were always swollen with hard work, over the steam. Then, biting off a tiny bit of sugar, he bowed to his hosts, said, 'Your health!' and drew in the steaming liquid.

'If somebody would see us as far as the turning,' said Vasíli Andréevich.

'Well, we can do that,' said the eldest son. 'Petrúshka will harness and go that far with you.'

'Well, then, put in the horse, lad, and I shall be thankful to you for it.'

'Oh, what for, dear man?' said the kindly old woman. 'We are heartily glad to do it.'

'Petrúshka, go and put in the mare,' said the eldest brother.

'All right,' replied Petrúshka with a smile, and promptly snatching his cap down from a nail he ran away to harness.

While the horse was being harnessed the talk returned to the point at which it had stopped when Vasíli Andréevich drove up to the window. The old man had been complaining to his neighbour, the village elder, about his third son who had not sent him anything for the holiday though he had sent a French shawl to his wife.

'The young people are getting out of hand,' said the old man.

'And how they do!' said the neighbour. 'There's no managing them! They know too much. There's Demóchkin now, who broke his father's arm. It's all from being too clever, it seems.'

Nikíta listened, watched their faces, and evidently would have liked to share in the conversation, but he was too busy drinking his tea and only nodded his head approvingly. He emptied one tumbler after another and grew warmer and warmer and more and more comfortable. The talk continued on the same subject for a long time – the harmfulness of a household dividing up – and it was clearly not an abstract discussion but concerned the question of a separation in that house; a separation demanded by the second son who sat there morosely silent.

It was evidently a sore subject and absorbed them all, but out of propriety they did not discuss their private affairs before strangers. At last, however, the old man could not restrain himself, and with tears in his eyes declared that he would not consent to a break-up of the family during his lifetime, that his house was prospering, thank God, but that if they separated they would all have to go begging.

'Just like the Matvéevs,' said the neighbour. 'They used to have a proper house, but now they've split up none of them has anything.'

'And that is what you want to happen to us,' said the old man, turning to his son.

The son made no reply and there was an awkward pause. The silence was broken by Petrúshka, who having harnessed the horse had returned to the hut a few minutes before this and had been listening all the time with a smile.

'There's a fable about that in Paulson,' he said. 'A father gave his sons a broom to break. At first they could not break it, but when they took it twig by twig they broke it easily. And it's the same here,' and he gave a broad smile. 'I'm ready!' he added.

'If you're ready, let's go,' said Vasíli Andréevich. 'And as to separating, don't you allow it, grandfather. You got everything together and you're the master. Go to the Justice of the Peace. He'll say how things should be done.'

'He carries on so, carries on so,' the old man continued in a whining tone. 'There's no doing anything with him. It's as if the devil possessed him.'

Nikíta having meanwhile finished his fifth tumbler of tea laid it on its side instead of turning it upside down, hoping to be offered a sixth glass. But there was no more water in the samovar, so the hostess did not fill it up for him. Besides, Vasíli Andréevich was putting his things on, so there was nothing for it but for Nikíta to get up too, put back into the sugar-basin the lump of sugar he had nibbled all round, wipe his perspiring face with the skirt of his sheepskin, and go to put on his overcoat.

Having put it on he sighed deeply, thanked his hosts, said good-bye, and went out of the warm bright room into the cold dark passage, through which the wind was howling and where snow was blowing through the cracks of the shaking door, and from there into the yard.

Petrúshka stood in his sheepskin in the middle of the yard by his horse, repeating some lines from Paulson's primer. He said with a smile:

> 'Storms with mist the sky conceal,
> Snowy circles wheeling wild.
> Now like savage beast 'twill howl,
> And now 'tis wailing like a child.'

Nikíta nodded approvingly as he arranged the reins.

The old man, seeing Vasíli Andréevich off, brought a lantern into the passage to show him a light, but it was blown out at once. And even in the yard it was evident that the snowstorm had become more violent.

'Well, this is weather!' thought Vasíli Andréevich. 'Perhaps we may not get there after all. But there is nothing to be done. Business! Besides, we have got ready, our host's horse has been harnessed, and we'll get there with God's help!'

Their aged host also thought they ought not to go, but he had already tried to persuade them to stay and had not been listened to.

'It's no use asking them again. Maybe my age makes me timid. They'll get there all right, and at least we shall get to bed in good time and without any fuss,' he thought.

Petrúshka did not think of danger. He knew the road and the whole district so well, and the lines about 'snowy circles wheeling wild' described what was happening outside so aptly that it cheered him up. Nikíta did not wish to go at all, but he had been accustomed not to have his own way and to serve others for so long that there was no one to hinder the departing travellers.

V

VASÍLI ANDRÉEVICH went over to his sledge, found it with difficulty in the darkness, climbed in and took the reins.

'Go on in front!' he cried.

Petrúshka kneeling in his low sledge started his horse. Mukhórty, who had been neighing for some time past, now scenting a mare ahead of him started after her, and they drove out into the street. They drove again through the outskirts of the village and along the same road, past the yard where the frozen linen had hung (which, however, was no longer to be seen), past the same barn, which was now snowed up almost to the roof and from which the snow was still endlessly pouring, past the same dismally moaning, whistling, and swaying willows, and again entered into the sea of blustering snow raging from above and below. The wind was so strong that when it blew from the side and the travellers steered against it, it tilted the sledges and turned the horses to one side. Petrúshka drove his good mare in front at a brisk trot and kept shouting lustily. Mukhórty pressed after her.

After travelling so for about ten minutes, Petrúshka turned round and shouted something. Neither Vasíli Andréevich nor Nikíta could hear anything because of the wind, but they guessed that they had arrived at the turning. In fact Petrúshka had turned to the right, and now the wind that had blown from the side blew straight in their faces, and through the snow they saw something dark on their right. It was the bush at the turning.

'Well now, God speed you!'

'Thank you, Petrúshka!'

'Storms with mist the sky conceal!' shouted Petrúshka as he disappeared.

'There's a poet for you!' muttered Vasíli Andréevich, pulling at the reins.

'Yes, a fine lad – a true peasant,' said Nikíta.

They drove on.

Nikíta, wrapping his coat closely about him and pressing his head down so close to his shoulders that his short beard covered his throat, sat silently, trying not to lose the warmth he had obtained while drinking tea in the house. Before him he saw the straight lines of the shafts which constantly deceived him into thinking they were a well-travelled road, and the horse's swaying crupper with his knotted tail blown to one side, and farther ahead the high shaft-bow and the swaying head and neck of the horse with its waving mane. Now and then he caught sight of a way-sign, so that he knew they were still on a road and that there was nothing for him to be concerned about.

Vasíli Andréevich drove on, leaving it to the horse to keep to the road. But Mukhórty, though he had had a breathing-space in the village, ran reluctantly, and seemed now and then to get off the road, so that Vasíli Andréevich had repeatedly to correct him.

'Here's a stake to the right, and another, and here's a third,' Vasíli Andréevich counted, 'and here in front is the forest,' thought he, as he looked at something dark in front of him. But what had seemed to him a forest was only a bush. They passed the bush and drove on for another hundred yards but there was no fourth way-mark nor any forest.

'We must reach the forest soon,' thought Vasíli Andréevich, and animated by the vodka and the tea he did not stop but shook the reins, and the good obedient horse responded, now ambling, now slowly trotting in the direction in which he was sent, though he knew that he was not going the right way. Ten minutes went by, but there was still no forest.

'There now, we must be astray again,' said Vasíli Andréevich, pulling up.

Nikíta silently got out of the sledge and holding his coat, which the wind now wrapped closely about him and now almost tore off, started to feel about in the snow, going first to one side and then to the other. Three or four times he was completely lost to sight. At last he returned and took the reins from Vasíli Andréevich's hand.

'We must go to the right,' he said sternly and peremptorily, as he turned the horse.

'Well, if it's to the right, go to the right,' said Vasíli Andréevich, yielding up the reins to Nikíta and thrusting his freezing hands into his sleeves.

Nikíta did not reply.

'Now then, friend, stir yourself!' he shouted to the horse, but in spite of the shake of the reins Mukhórty moved only at a walk.

The snow in places was up to his knees, and the sledge moved by fits and starts with his every movement.

Nikíta took the whip that hung over the front of the sledge and struck him once. The good horse, unused to the whip, sprang forward and moved at a trot, but immediately fell back into an amble and then to a walk. So they went on for five minutes. It was dark and the snow whirled from above and rose from below, so that sometimes the shaft-bow could not be seen. At times the sledge seemed to stand still and the field to run backwards. Suddenly the horse stopped abruptly, evidently aware of something close in front of him. Nikíta again sprang lightly out, throwing down the reins, and went ahead to see what had brought him to a standstill, but hardly had he made a step in front of the horse before his feet slipped and he went rolling down an incline.

'Whoa, whoa, whoa!' he said to himself as he fell, and he tried to stop his fall but could not, and only stopped when his feet plunged into a thick layer of snow that had drifted to the bottom of the hollow.

The fringe of a drift of snow that hung on the edge of the hollow, disturbed by Nikíta's fall, showered down on him and got inside his collar.

'What a thing to do!' said Nikíta reproachfully, addressing the drift and the hollow and shaking the snow from under his collar.

'Nikíta! Hey, Nikíta!' shouted Vasíli Andréevich from above.

But Nikíta did not reply. He was too occupied in shaking out the snow and searching for the whip he had dropped when rolling down the incline. Having found the whip he tried to climb straight up the bank where he had rolled down, but it was impossible to do so: he kept rolling down again, and so he had to go along at the foot of the hollow to find a way up. About seven yards farther on he managed with difficulty to crawl up the incline on all fours, then he followed the edge of the hollow back to the place where the horse should have been. He could not see either horse or sledge, but as he walked against the wind he heard Vasíli Andréevich's shouts and Mukhórty's neighing, calling him.

'I'm coming! I'm coming! What are you cackling for?' he muttered.

Only when he had come up to the sledge could he make out the horse, and Vasíli Andréevich standing beside it and looking gigantic.

'Where the devil did you vanish to? We must go back, if only to Gríshkino,' he began reproaching Nikíta.

'I'd be glad to get back, Vasíli Andréevich, but which way are we to go? There is such a ravine here that if we once get in it we shan't get out again. I got stuck so fast there myself that I could hardly get out.'

'What shall we do, then? We can't stay here! We must go somewhere!' said Vasíli Andréevich.

Nikíta said nothing. He seated himself in the sledge with his back to the wind, took off his boots, shook out the snow that had got into them, and taking some straw from the bottom of the sledge, carefully plugged with it a hole in his left boot.

Vasíli Andréevich remained silent, as though now leaving everything to Nikíta. Having put his boots on again, Nikíta drew his feet into the sledge, put on his mittens and took up the reins, and directed the horse along the side of the ravine. But they had not gone a hundred yards before the horse again stopped short. The ravine was in front of him again.

Nikíta again climbed out and again trudged about in the snow. He did this for a considerable time and at last appeared from the opposite side to that from which he had started.

'Vasíli Andréevich, are you alive?' he called out.

'Here!' replied Vasíli Andréevich. 'Well, what now?'

'I can't make anything out. It's too dark. There's nothing but ravines. We must drive against the wind again.'

They set off once more. Again Nikíta went stumbling through the snow, again he fell in, again climbed out and trudged about, and at last quite out of breath he sat down beside the sledge.

'Well, how now?' asked Vasíli Andréevich.

'Why, I am quite worn out and the horse won't go.'

'Then what's to be done?'

'Why, wait a minute.'

Nikíta went away again but soon returned.

'Follow me!' he said, going in front of the horse.

Vasíli Andréevich no longer gave orders but implicitly did what Nikíta told him.

'Here, follow me!' Nikíta shouted, stepping quickly to the right, and seizing the rein he led Mukhórty down towards a snow-drift.

At first the horse held back, then he jerked forward, hoping to leap the drift, but he had not the strength and sank into it up to his collar.

'Get out!' Nikíta called to Vasíli Andréevich who still sat in the sledge, and taking hold of one shaft he moved the sledge closer to the horse. 'It's hard, brother!' he said to Mukhórty, 'but it can't be helped. Make an effort! Now, now, just a little one!' he shouted.

The horse gave a tug, then another, but failed to clear himself and settled down again as if considering something.

'Now, brother, this won't do!' Nikíta admonished him. 'Now once more!'

Again Nikíta tugged at the shaft on his side, and Vasíli Andréevich did the same on the other.

Mukhórty lifted his head and then gave a sudden jerk.

'That's it! That's it!' cried Nikíta. 'Don't be afraid – you won't sink!'

One plunge, another, and a third, and at last Mukhórty was out of the snow-drift, and stood still, breathing heavily and shaking the snow off himself. Nikíta wished to lead him farther, but Vasíli Andréevich, in his two fur coats, was so out of breath that he could not walk farther and dropped into the sledge.

'Let me get my breath!' he said, unfastening the kerchief with which he had tied the collar of his fur coat at the village.

'It's all right here. You lie there,' said Nikíta. 'I will lead him along.' And with Vasíli Andréevich in the sledge he led the horse by the bridle about ten paces down and then up a slight rise, and stopped.

The place where Nikíta had stopped was not completely in the hollow where the snow sweeping down from the hillocks might have buried them altogether, but still it was partly sheltered from the wind by the side of the ravine. There were moments when the wind seemed to abate a little, but that did not last long and as if to make up for that respite the storm swept down with tenfold vigour and tore and whirled the more fiercely. Such a gust struck them at the moment when Vasíli Andréevich, having recovered his breath, got out of the sledge and went up to Nikíta to consult him as to what they should do. They both bent down involuntarily and waited till the violence of the squall should have passed. Mukhórty too laid back his ears and shook his head discontentedly. As soon as the violence of the blast had abated a little, Nikíta took off his mittens, stuck them into his belt, breathed on to his hands, and began to undo the straps of the shaft-bow.

'What's that you are doing there?' asked Vasíli Andréevich.

'Unharnessing. What else is there to do? I have no strength left,' said Nikíta as though excusing himself.

'Can't we drive somewhere?'

'No, we can't. We shall only kill the horse. Why, the poor beast is not himself now,' said Nikíta, pointing to the horse, which was standing submissively waiting for what might come, with his steep wet sides heaving heavily. 'We shall have to stay the night here,' he said, as if preparing to spend the night at an inn, and he proceeded to unfasten the collar-straps. The buckles came undone.

'But shan't we be frozen?' remarked Vasíli Andréevich.

'Well, if we are we can't help it,' said Nikíta.

VI

ALTHOUGH Vasíli Andréevich felt quite warm in his two fur coats, especially after struggling in the snow-drift, a cold shiver ran down his back on realizing that he must really spend the night where they were. To calm himself he sat down in the sledge and got out his cigarettes and matches.

Nikíta meanwhile unharnessed Mukhórty. He unstrapped the belly-band and the back-band, took away the reins, loosened the collar-strap, and removed the shaft-bow, talking to him all the time to encourage him.

'Now come out! Come out!' he said, leading him clear of the shafts. 'Now we'll tie you up here and I'll put down some straw and take off your bridle. When you've had a bite you'll feel more cheerful.'

But Mukhórty was restless and evidently not comforted by Nikíta's remarks. He stepped now on one foot and now on another, and pressed close against the sledge, turning his back to the wind and rubbing his head on Nikíta's sleeve. Then, as if not to pain Nikíta by refusing his offer of the straw he put before him, he hurriedly snatched a wisp out of the sledge, but immediately decided that it was now no time to think of straw and threw it down, and the wind instantly scattered it, carried it away, and covered it with snow.

'Now we will set up a signal,' said Nikíta, and turning the front of the sledge to the wind he tied the shafts together with a strap and set them up on end in front of the sledge. 'There now, when the snow covers us up, good folk will see the shafts and dig us out,' he said, slapping his mittens together and putting them on. 'That's what the old folk taught us!'

Vasíli Andréevich meanwhile had unfastened his coat, and holding its skirts up for shelter, struck one sulphur match after another on the steel box. But his hands trembled, and one match after another either did not kindle or was blown out by the wind just as he was lifting it to the cigarette. At last a match did burn up, and its flame lit up for a moment the fur of his coat, his hand with the gold ring on the bent forefinger, and the snow-sprinkled oat-straw that stuck out from under the drugget. The cigarette lighted, he eagerly took a whiff or two, inhaled the smoke, let it out through his moustache, and would have inhaled again, but the wind tore off the burning tobacco and whirled it away as it had done the straw.

But even these few puffs had cheered him.

'If we must spend the night here, we must!' he said with decision. 'Wait a bit, I'll arrange a flag as well,' he added, picking up the kerchief which he had thrown down in the sledge after taking it from round his collar, and drawing off his gloves and standing up on the front of the sledge and stretching himself to reach the strap, he tied the handkerchief to it with a tight knot.

The kerchief immediately began to flutter wildly, now clinging round the shaft, now suddenly streaming out, stretching and flapping.

'Just see what a fine flag!' said Vasíli Andréevich, admiring his handiwork and letting himself down into the sledge. 'We should be warmer together, but there's not room enough for two,' he added.

'I'll find a place,' said Nikíta. 'But I must cover up the horse first – he sweated so, poor thing. Let go!' he added, drawing the drugget from under Vasíli Andréevich.

Having got the drugget he folded it in two, and after taking off the breechband and pad, covered Mukhórty with it.

'Anyhow it will be warmer, silly!' he said, putting back the breechband and the pad on the horse over the drugget. Then having finished that business he returned to the sledge, and addressing Vasíli Andréevich, said: 'You won't need the sack-cloth, will you? And let me have some straw.'

And having taken these things from under Vasíli Andrée-vich, Nikíta went behind the sledge, dug out a hole for himself in the snow, put straw into it, wrapped his coat well round him, covered himself with the sackcloth, and pulling his cap well down seated himself on the straw he had spread, and leant against the wooden back of the sledge to shelter himself from the wind and the snow.

Vasíli Andréevich shook his head disapprovingly at what Nikíta was doing, as in general he disapproved of the peasants' stupidity and lack of education, and he began to settle himself down for the night.

He smoothed the remaining straw over the bottom of the sledge, putting more of it under his side, then he thrust his hands into his sleeves and settled down, sheltering his head in the corner of the sledge from the wind in front.

He did not wish to sleep. He lay and thought: thought ever of the one thing that constituted the sole aim, meaning, pleasure, and pride of his life – of how much money he had made and might still make, of how much other people he knew had made and possessed, and of how those others had made and were making it, and how he, like them, might still make much more. The purchase of the Goryáchkin grove was a matter of immense importance to him. By that one deal he hoped to make perhaps ten thousand rubles. He began men-tally to reckon the value of the wood he had inspected in autumn, and on five acres of which he had counted all the trees.

'The oaks will go for sledge-runners. The undergrowth will take care of itself, and there'll still be some thirty sázheens of fire-wood left on each desyatín,' said he to himself. 'That means there will be at least two hundred and twenty-five rubles' worth left on each desyatín. Fifty-six desyatíns means fifty-six hundreds, and fifty-six hundreds, and fifty-six tens, and another fifty-six tens, and then fifty-six fives....' He saw that it came out to more than twelve thousand rubles, but could not reckon it up exactly without a counting-frame. 'But I won't give ten thousand, anyhow. I'll give about eight thousand with a deduction on account of the glades. I'll grease the surveyor's palm – give him a hundred rubles, or a hundred and fifty, and he'll reckon that there are some five desyatíns of glade to be deducted. And he'll let it go for eight thousand. Three thousand cash down. That'll move him, no fear!' he thought, and he pressed his pocket-book with his forearm.

'God only knows how we missed the turning. The forest ought to be there, and a watchman's hut, and dogs barking. But the damned things don't bark when they're wanted.' He turned his collar down from his ear and listened, but as before only the whistling of the wind could be heard, the flapping and fluttering of the kerchief tied to the shafts, and the pelting of the snow against the woodwork of the sledge. He again covered up his ear.

'If I had known I would have stayed the night. Well, no matter, we'll get there to-morrow. It's only one day lost. And the others won't travel in such weather.' Then he remembered that on the 9th he had to receive payment from the butcher for his oxen. 'He meant to come himself, but he won't find me, and my wife won't know how to receive the money. She doesn't know the right way of doing things,' he thought, recalling how at their party the day before she had not known how to treat the police-officer who was their guest. 'Of course she's only a woman! Where could she have seen anything? In my father's time what was our house like? Just a rich peasant's house: just an oat-mill and an inn – that was the whole property. But what have I done in these fifteen years? A shop, two taverns, a flour-mill, a grain-store, two farms leased out, and a house with an iron-roofed barn,' he thought proudly. 'Not as it was in father's time! Who is talked of in the whole district now? Brekhunóv! And why? Because I stick to business. I take trouble, not like others who lie abed or waste their time on foolishness while I don't sleep of nights.

Blizzard or no blizzard I start out. So business gets done. They think money-making is a joke. No, take pains and rack your brains! You get overtaken out of doors at night, like this, or keep awake night after night till the thoughts whirling in your head make the pillow turn,' he meditated with pride. 'They think people get on through luck. After all, the Mirónovs are now millionaires. And why? Take pains and God gives. If only He grants me health!'

The thought that he might himself be a millionaire like Mirónov, who began with nothing, so excited Vasíli Andrée-vich that he felt the need of talking to somebody. But there was no one to talk to. . . . If only he could have reached Goryáchkin he would have talked to the landlord and shown him a thing or two.

'Just see how it blows! It will snow us up so deep that we shan't be able to get out in the morning!' he thought, listening to a gust of wind that blew against the front of the sledge, bending it and lashing the snow against it. He raised himself and looked round. All he could see through the whirling darkness was Mukhórty's dark head, his back covered by the fluttering drugget, and his thick knotted tail; while all round, in front and behind, was the same fluctuating whity darkness, sometimes seeming to get a little lighter and sometimes grow-ing denser still.

'A pity I listened to Nikíta,' he thought. 'We ought to have driven on. We should have come out somewhere, if only back to Gríshkino and stayed the night at Tarás's. As it is we must sit here all night. But what was I thinking about? Yes, that God gives to those who take trouble, but not to loafers, lie-abeds, or fools. I must have a smoke!'

He sat down again, got out his cigarette-case, and stretched himself flat on his stomach, screening the matches with the skirt of his coat. But the wind found its way in and put out match after match. At last he got one to burn and lit a cigarette. He was very glad that he had managed to do what he wanted, and though the wind smoked more of the cigarette than he did, he still got two or three puffs and felt more cheerful. He again leant back, wrapped himself up, started reflecting and remembering, and suddenly and quite unexpectedly lost consciousness and fell asleep.

Suddenly something seemed to give him a push and awoke him. Whether it was Mukhórty who had pulled some straw from under him, or whether something within him had startled him, at all events it woke him, and his heart began to beat faster and faster so that the sledge seemed to tremble under him. He opened his eyes. Everything around him was just as before. 'It looks lighter,' he thought. 'I expect it won't be long before dawn.' But he at once remembered that it was lighter because the moon had risen. He sat up and looked first at the horse. Mukhórty still stood with his back to the wind, shivering all over. One side of the drugget, which was completely covered with snow, had been blown back, the breeching had slipped down and the snow-covered head with its waving forelock and mane were now more visible. Vasíli Andréevich leant over the back of the sledge and looked behind. Nikíta still sat in the same position in which he had settled himself. The sacking with which he was covered, and his legs, were thickly covered with snow.

'If only that peasant doesn't freeze to death! His clothes are so wretched. I may be held responsible for him. What shiftless people they are – such a want of education,' thought Vasíli Andréevich, and he felt like taking the drugget off the horse and putting it over Nikíta, but it would be very cold to get out and move about and, moreover, the horse might freeze to death. 'Why did I bring him with me? It was all her stupidity!' he thought, recalling his unloved wife, and he rolled over into his old place at the front part of the sledge. 'My uncle once spent a whole night like this,' he reflected, 'and was all right.' But another case came at once to his mind. 'But when they dug Sebastian out he was dead – stiff like a frozen carcass. If I'd only stopped the night in Gríshkino all this would not have happened!'

And wrapping his coat carefully round him so that none of the warmth of the fur should be wasted but should warm him all over, neck, knees, and feet, he shut his eyes and tried to sleep again. But try as he would he could not get drowsy, on the contrary he felt wide awake and animated. Again he began counting his gains and the debts due to him, again he began bragging to himself and feeling pleased with himself and his position, but all this was continually disturbed by a stealthily approaching fear and by the unpleasant regret that he had not remained in Grishkino.

'How different it would be to be lying warm on a bench!' He turned over several times in his attempts to get into a more comfortable position more sheltered from the wind, he wrapped up his legs closer, shut his eyes, and lay still. But either his legs in their strong felt boots began to ache from being bent in one position, or the wind blew in somewhere, and after lying still for a short time he again began to recall the disturbing fact that he might now have been lying quietly in the warm hut at Grishkino. He again sat up, turned about, muffled himself up, and settled down once more.

Once he fancied that he heard a distant cock-crow. He felt glad, turned down his coat-collar and listened with strained attention, but in spite of all his efforts nothing could be heard but the wind whistling between the shafts, the flapping of the kerchief, and the snow pelting against the frame of the sledge.

Nikita sat just as he had done all the time, not moving and not even answering Vasíli Andréevich who had addressed him a couple of times. 'He doesn't care a bit – he's probably asleep!' thought Vasíli Andréevich with vexation, looking behind the sledge at Nikita who was covered with a thick layer of snow.

Vasíli Andréevich got up and lay down again some twenty times. It seemed to him that the night would never end. 'It must be getting near morning,' he thought, getting up and looking around. 'Let's have a look at my watch. It will be cold to unbutton, but if I only know that it's getting near morning I shall at any rate feel more cheerful. We could begin harnessing.'

In the depth of his heart Vasíli Andréevich knew that it could not yet be near morning, but he was growing more and more afraid, and wished both to get to know and yet to deceive himself. He carefully undid the fastening of his sheepskin, pushed in his hand, and felt about for a long time before he got to his waistcoat. With great difficulty he managed to draw out his silver watch with its enamelled flower design, and tried to make out the time. He could not see anything without a light. Again he went down on his knees and elbows as he had done when he lighted a cigarette, got out his matches, and proceeded to strike one. This time he went to work more carefully, and feeling with his fingers for a match with the largest head and the greatest amount of phosphorus, lit it at the first try. Bringing the face of the watch under the light he could hardly believe his eyes. . . . It was only ten minutes past twelve. Almost the whole night was still before him.

'Oh, how long the night is!' he thought, feeling a cold shudder run down his back, and having fastened his fur coats again and wrapped himself up, he snuggled into a corner of the sledge intending to wait patiently. Suddenly, above the monotonous roar of the wind, he clearly distinguished another new and living sound. It steadily strengthened, and having become quite clear diminished just as gradually. Beyond all doubt it was a wolf, and he was so near that the movement of his jaws as he changed his cry was brought down the wind. Vasíli Andréevich turned back the collar of his coat and listened attentively. Mukhórty too strained to listen, moving his ears, and when the wolf had ceased its howling he shifted from foot to foot and gave a warning snort. After this Vasíli Andréevich could not fall asleep again or even calm himself. The more he tried to think of his accounts, his business, his reputation, his worth and his wealth, the more and more was he mastered by fear; and regrets that he had not stayed the night at Gríshkino dominated and mingled in all his thoughts.

'Devil take the forest! Things were all right without it, thank God. Ah, if we had only put up for the night!' he said to himself. 'They say it's drunkards that freeze,' he thought, 'and I have had some drink.' And observing his sensations he noticed that he was beginning to shiver, without knowing whether it was from cold or from fear. He tried to wrap himself up and lie down as before, but could no longer do so. He could not stay in one position. He wanted to get up, to do something to master the gathering fear that was rising in him and against which he felt himself powerless. He again got out his cigarettes and matches, but only three matches were left and they were bad ones. The phosphorus rubbed off them all without lighting.

'The devil take you! Damned thing! Curse you!' he muttered, not knowing whom or what he was cursing, and he flung away the crushed cigarette. He was about to throw away the match-box too, but checked the movement of his hand and put the box in his pocket instead. He was seized with such unrest that he could no longer remain in one spot. He climbed out of the sledge and standing with his back to the wind began to shift his belt again, fastening it lower down in the waist and tightening it.

'What's the use of lying and waiting for death? Better mount the horse and get away!' The thought suddenly occurred to him. 'The horse will move when he has someone on his back. As for him,' he thought of Nikíta – 'it's all the same to him whether he lives or dies. What is his life worth? He won't grudge his life, but I have something to live for, thank God.'

He untied the horse, threw the reins over his neck and tried to mount, but his coats and boots were so heavy that he failed. Then he clambered up in the sledge and tried to mount from there, but the sledge tilted under his weight, and he failed again. At last he drew Mukhórty nearer to the sledge, cautiously balanced on one side of it, and managed to lie on his stomach across the horse's back. After lying like that for a while he shifted forward once and again, threw a leg over, and finally seated himself, supporting his feet on the loose breeching-straps. The shaking of the sledge awoke Nikíta. He raised himself, and it seemed to Vasíli Andréevich that he said something.

'Listen to such fools as you! Am I to die like this for nothing?' exclaimed Vasíli Andréevich. And tucking the loose skirts of his fur coat in under his knees, he turned the horse and rode away from the sledge in the direction in which he thought the forest and the forester's hut must be.

VII

FROM the time he had covered himself with the sackcloth and seated himself behind the sledge, Nikíta had not stirred.

Like all those who live in touch with nature and have known want, he was patient and could wait for hours, even days, without growing restless or irritable. He heard his master call him, but did not answer because he did not want to move or talk. Though he still felt some warmth from the tea he had drunk and from his energetic struggle when clambering about in the snow-drift, he knew that this warmth would not last long and that he had no strength left to warm himself again by moving about, for he felt as tired as a horse when it stops and refuses to go further in spite of the whip, and its master sees that it must be fed before it can work again. The foot in the boot with a hole in it had already grown numb, and he could no longer feel his big toe. Besides that, his whole body began to feel colder and colder.

The thought that he might, and very probably would, die that night occurred to him, but did not seem particularly unpleasant or dreadful. It did not seem particularly unpleasant, because his whole life had been not a continual holiday, but on the contrary an unceasing round of toil of which he was beginning to feel weary. And it did not seem particularly dreadful, because besides the masters he had served here, like Vasíli Andréevich, he always felt himself dependent on the Chief Master, who had sent him into this life, and he knew that when dying he would still be in that Master's power and would not be ill-used by Him. 'It seems a pity to give up what one is used to and accustomed to. But there's nothing to be done; I shall get used to the new things.'

'Sins?' he thought, and remembered his drunkenness, the money that had gone on drink, how he had offended his wife, his cursing, his neglect of church and of the fasts, and all the things the priest blamed him for at confession. 'Of course they are sins. But then, did I take them on of myself? That's evidently how God made me. Well, and the sins? Where am I to escape to?'

So at first he thought of what might happen to him that night, and then did not return to such thoughts but gave himself up to whatever recollections came into his head of themselves. Now he thought of Martha's arrival, of the drunkenness among the workers and his own renunciation of drink, then of their present journey and of Tarás's house and the talk about the breaking-up of the family, then of his own lad, and of Mukhórty now sheltered under the drugget, and then of his master who made the sledge creak as he tossed about in it. 'I expect you're sorry yourself that you started out, dear man,' he thought. 'It would seem hard to leave a life such as his! It's not like the likes of us.'

Then all these recollections began to grow confused and got mixed in his head, and he fell asleep.

But when Vasíli Andréevich, getting on the horse, jerked the sledge against the back of which Nikíta was leaning, and it shifted away and hit him in the back with one of its runners, he awoke and had to change his position whether he liked it or not. Straightening his legs with difficulty and shaking the snow off them he got up, and an agonizing cold immediately penetrated his whole body. On making out what was happening he called to Vasíli Andréevich to leave him the drugget which the horse no longer needed, so that he might wrap himself in it.

But Vasíli Andréevich did not stop, but disappeared amid the powdery snow.

Left alone, Nikíta considered for a moment what he should do. He felt that he had not the strength to go off in search of a house. It was no longer possible to sit down in his old place – it was by now all filled with snow. He felt that he could not get warmer in the sledge either, for there was nothing to cover himself with, and his coat and sheepskin no longer warmed him at all. He felt as cold as though he had nothing on but a shirt. He became frightened. 'Lord, heavenly Father!' he muttered, and was comforted by the consciousness that he was not alone but that there was One who heard him and would not abandon him. He gave a deep sigh, and keeping the sackcloth over his head he got inside the sledge and lay down in the place where his master had been.

But he could not get warm in the sledge either. At first he shivered all over, then the shivering ceased and little by little he began to lose consciousness. He did not know whether he was dying or falling asleep, but felt equally prepared for the one as for the other.

VIII

MEANWHILE Vasíli Andréevich, with his feet and the ends of the reins, urged the horse on in the direction in which for some reason he expected the forest and the forester's hut to be. The snow covered his eyes and the wind seemed intent on stopping him, but bending forward and constantly lapping his coat over and pushing it between himself and the cold harness pad which prevented him from sitting properly, he kept urging the horse on. Mukhórty ambled on obediently though with difficulty, in the direction in which he was driven.

Vasíli Andréevich rode for about five minutes straight ahead, as he thought, seeing nothing but the horse's head and the white waste, and hearing only the whistle of the wind about the horse's ears and his coat collar.

Suddenly a dark patch showed up in front of him. His heart beat with joy, and he rode towards the object, already seeing in imagination the walls of village houses. But the dark patch was not stationary, it kept moving; and it was not a village but some tall stalks of wormwood sticking up through the snow on the boundary between two fields, and desperately tossing about under the pressure of the wind which beat it all to one side and whistled through it. The sight of that wormwood tormented by the pitiless wind made Vasíli Andréevich shudder, he knew not why, and he hurriedly began urging the horse on, not noticing that when riding up to the wormwood he had quite changed his direction and was now heading the opposite way, though still imagining that he was riding towards where the hut should be. But the horse kept making towards the right, and Vasíli Andréevich kept guiding it to the left.

Again something dark appeared in front of him. Again he rejoiced, convinced that now it was certainly a village. But once more it was the same boundary line overgrown with wormwood, once more the same wormwood desperately tossed by the wind and carrying unreasoning terror to his heart. But its being the same wormwood was not all, for beside it there was a horse's track partly snowed over. Vasíli Andrée-vich stopped, stooped down and looked carefully. It was a horse-track only partially covered with snow, and could be none but his own horse's hoofprints. He had evidently gone round in a small circle. 'I shall perish like that!' he thought, and not to give way to his terror he urged on the horse still more, peering into the snowy darkness in which he saw only flitting and fitful points of light. Once he thought he heard the barking of dogs or the howling of wolves, but the sounds were so faint and indistinct that he did not know whether he heard them or merely imagined them, and he stopped and began to listen intently.

Suddenly some terrible, deafening cry resounded near his ears, and everything shivered and shook under him. He seized Mukhórty's neck, but that too was shaking all over and the terrible cry grew still more frightful. For some seconds Vasíli Andréevich could not collect himself or understand what was happening. It was only that Mukhórty, whether to encourage himself or to call for help, had neighed loudly and resonantly. 'Ugh, you wretch! How you frightened me, damn you!' thought Vasíli Andréevich. But even when he understood the cause of his terror he could not shake it off.

'I must calm myself and think things over,' he said to himself, but yet he could not stop, and continued to urge the horse on, without noticing that he was now going with the wind instead of against it. His body, especially between his legs where it touched the pad of the harness and was not covered by his overcoats, was getting painfully cold, especially when the horse walked slowly. His legs and arms trembled and his breathing came fast. He saw himself perishing amid this dread-ful snowy waste, and could see no means of escape.

Suddenly the horse under him tumbled into something and, sinking into a snow-drift, began to plunge and fell on his side. Vasíli Andréevich jumped off, and in so doing dragged to one side the breechband on which his foot was resting, and twisted round the pad to which he held as he dismounted. As soon as he had jumped off, the horse struggled to his feet, plunged forward, gave one leap and another, neighed again, and dragging the drugget and the breechband after him, disappeared, leaving Vasíli Andréevich alone in the snow-drift.

The latter pressed on after the horse, but the snow lay so deep and his coats were so heavy that, sinking above his knees at each step, he stopped breathless after taking not more than twenty steps. 'The copse, the oxen, the leasehold, the shop, the tavern, the house with the iron-roofed barn, and my heir,' thought he. 'How can I leave all that? What does this mean? It cannot be!' These thoughts flashed through his mind. Then he thought of the wormwood tossed by the wind, which he had twice ridden past, and he was seized with such terror that he did not believe in the reality of what was happening to him. 'Can this be a dream?' he thought, and tried to wake up but could not. It was real snow that lashed his face and covered him and chilled his right hand from which he had lost the glove, and this was a real desert in which he was now left alone like that wormwood, awaiting an inevitable, speedy, and meaningless death.

'Queen of Heaven! Holy Father Nicholas, teacher of temperance!' he thought, recalling the service of the day before and the holy icon with its black face and gilt frame, and the tapers which he sold to be set before that icon and which were almost immediately brought back to him scarcely burnt at all, and which he put away in the store-chest.[1] He began to pray to that same Nicholas the Wonder-Worker to save him, promising him a thanksgiving service and some candles. But he clearly and indubitably realized that the icon, its frame, the candles, the priest, and the thanksgiving service, though very important and necessary in church, could do nothing for him here, and that there was and could be no connexion between those candles and services and his present disastrous plight. 'I must not despair,' he thought. 'I must follow the horse's

---

1 As churchwarden Vasíli Andréevich sold the tapers the worshippers bought to set before the icons. These were collected at the end of the service, and could afterwards be resold to the advantage of the church revenue.

track before it is snowed under. He will lead me out, or I may even catch him. Only I must not hurry, or I shall stick fast and be more lost than ever.'

But in spite of his resolution to go quietly, he rushed forward and even ran, continually falling, getting up and falling again. The horse's track was already hardly visible in places where the snow did not lie deep. 'I am lost!' thought Vasíli Andréevich. 'I shall lose the track and not catch the horse.' But at that moment he saw something black. It was Mukhórty, and not only Mukhórty, but the sledge with the shafts and the kerchief. Mukhórty, with the sacking and the breechband twisted round to one side, was standing not in his former place but nearer to the shafts, shaking his head which the reins he was stepping on drew downwards. It turned out that Vasíli Andréevich had sunk in the same ravine Nikíta had previously fallen into, and that Mukhórty had been bringing him back to the sledge and he had got off his back no more than fifty paces from where the sledge was.

IX

HAVING stumbled back to the sledge Vasíli Andréevich caught hold of it and for a long time stood motionless, trying to calm himself and recover his breath. Nikíta was not in his former place, but something, already covered with snow, was lying in the sledge and Vasíli Andréevich concluded that this was Nikíta. His terror had now quite left him, and if he felt any fear it was lest the dreadful terror should return that he had experienced when on the horse and especially when he was left alone in the snow-drift. At any cost he had to avoid that terror, and to keep it away he must do something – occupy himself with something. And the first thing he did was to turn his back to the wind and open his fur coat. Then, as soon as he recovered his breath a little, he shook the snow out of his boots and out of his left-hand glove (the right-hand glove was hopelessly lost and by this time probably lying somewhere under a dozen inches of snow), then as was his custom when going out of his shop to buy grain from the peasants, he pulled his girdle

low down and tightened it and prepared for action. The
first thing that occurred to him was to free Mukhórty's leg
from the rein. Having done that, and tethered him to the iron
cramp at the front of the sledge where he had been before, he
was going round the horse's quarters to put the breechband
and pad straight and cover him with the cloth, but at that
moment he noticed that something was moving in the sledge
and Nikíta's head rose up out of the snow that covered it.
Nikíta, who was half frozen, rose with great difficulty and sat
up, moving his hand before his nose in a strange manner just as
if he were driving away flies. He waved his hand and said
something, and seemed to Vasíli Andréevich to be calling him.
Vasíli Andréevich left the cloth unadjusted and went up to the
sledge.

'What is it?' he asked. 'What are you saying?'

'I'm dy... ing, that's what,' said Nikíta brokenly and with
difficulty. 'Give what is owing to me to my lad, or to my wife,
no matter.'

'Why, are you really frozen?' asked Vasíli Andréevich.

'I feel it's my death. Forgive me for Christ's sake...' said
Nikíta in a tearful voice, continuing to wave his hand before
his face as if driving away flies.

Vasíli Andréevich stood silent and motionless for half a
minute. Then suddenly, with the same resolution with
which he used to strike hands when making a good purchase,
he took a step back and turning up his sleeves began raking the
snow off Nikíta and out of the sledge. Having done this he
hurriedly undid his girdle, opened out his fur coat, and having
pushed Nikíta down, lay down on top of him, covering him
not only with his fur coat but with the whole of his body,
which glowed with warmth. After pushing the skirts of his
coat between Nikíta and the sides of the sledge, and holding
down its hem with his knees, Vasíli Andréevich lay like that
face down, with his head pressed against the front of the
sledge. Here he no longer heard the horse's movements or
the whistling of the wind, but only Nikíta's breathing. At first
and for a long time Nikíta lay motionless, then he sighed
deeply and moved.

'There, and you say you are dying! Lie still and get warm, that's our way. . . .' began Vasíli Andréevich.

But to his great surprise he could say no more, for tears came to his eyes and his lower jaw began to quiver rapidly. He stopped speaking and only gulped down the risings in his throat. 'Seems I was badly frightened and have gone quite weak,' he thought. But this weakness was not only not unpleasant, but gave him a peculiar joy such as he had never felt before.

'That's our way!' he said to himself, experiencing a strange and solemn tenderness. He lay like that for a long time, wiping his eyes on the fur of his coat and tucking under his knee the right skirt, which the wind kept turning up.

But he longed so passionately to tell somebody of his joyful condition that he said: 'Nikíta!'

'It's comfortable, warm!' came a voice from beneath.

'There, you see, friend, I was going to perish. And you would have been frozen, and I should have. . . .'

But again his jaws began to quiver and his eyes to fill with tears, and he could say no more.

'Well, never mind,' he thought. 'I know about myself what I know.'

He remained silent and lay like that for a long time.

Nikíta kept him warm from below and his fur coats from above. Only his hands, with which he kept his coat-skirts down round Nikíta's sides, and his legs which the wind kept uncovering, began to freeze, especially his right hand which had no glove. But he did not think of his legs or of his hands but only of how to warm the peasant who was lying under him. He looked out several times at Mukhórty and could see that his back was uncovered and the drugget and breeching lying on the snow, and that he ought to get up and cover him, but he could not bring himself to leave Nikíta and disturb even for a moment the joyous condition he was in. He no longer felt any kind of terror.

'No fear, we shan't lose him this time!' he said to himself, referring to his getting the peasant warm with the same boastfulness with which he spoke of his buying and selling.

Vasíli Andréevich lay in that way for one hour, another, and a third, but he was unconscious of the passage of time. At first impressions of the snow-storm, the sledge-shafts, and the horse with the shaft-bow shaking before his eyes, kept passing through his mind, then he remembered Nikíta lying under him, then recollections of the festival, his wife, the police-officer, and the box of candles, began to mingle with these; then again Nikíta, this time lying under that box, then the peasants, customers and traders, and the white walls of his house with its iron roof with Nikíta lying underneath, presented themselves to his imagination. Afterwards all these impressions blended into one nothingness. As the colours of the rainbow unite into one white light, so all these different impressions mingled into one, and he fell asleep.

For a long time he slept without dreaming, but just before dawn the visions recommenced. It seemed to him that he was standing by the box of tapers and that Tíkhon's wife was asking for a five-kopek taper for the church fête. He wished to take one out and give it to her, but his hands would not lift being held tight in his pockets. He wanted to walk round the box but his feet would not move and his new clean goloshes had grown to the stone floor, and he could neither lift them nor get his feet out of the goloshes. Then the taper-box was no longer a box but a bed, and suddenly Vasíli Andréevich saw himself lying in his bed at home. He was lying in his bed and could not get up. Yet it was necessary for him to get up because Iván Matvéich, the police-officer, would soon call for him and he had to go with him – either to bargain for the forest or to put Mukhórty's breeching straight.

He asked his wife: 'Nikoláevna,[1] hasn't he come yet?' 'No, he hasn't,' she replied. He heard someone drive up to the front steps. 'It must be him.' 'No, he's gone past.' 'Nikoláevna! I say, Nikoláevna, isn't he here yet?' 'No.' He was still lying on his bed and could not get up, but was always waiting. And this waiting was uncanny and yet joyful. Then suddenly his joy was completed. He whom he was expecting came; not Iván

---

1 A familiar peasant use of the patronymic in place of the Christian name.

Matvéich the police-officer, but someone else – yet it was he whom he had been waiting for. He came and called him; and it was he who had called him and told him to lie down on Nikíta. And Vasíli Andréevich was glad that that one had come for him.

'I'm coming!' he cried joyfully, and that cry awoke him, but woke him up not at all the same person he had been when he fell asleep. He tried to get up but could not, tried to move his arm and could not, to move his leg and also could not, to turn his head and could not. He was surprised but not at all disturbed by this. He understood that this was death, and was not at all disturbed by that either. He remembered that Nikíta was lying under him and that he had got warm and was alive, and it seemed to him that he was Nikíta and Nikíta was he, and that his life was not in himself but in Nikíta. He strained his ears and heard Nikíta breathing and even slightly snoring. 'Nikíta is alive, so I too am alive!' he said to himself triumphantly.

And he remembered his money, his shop, his house, the buying and selling, and Mirónov's millions, and it was hard for him to understand why that man, called Vasíli Brekhunóv, had troubled himself with all those things with which he had been troubled.

'Well, it was because he did not know what the real thing was,' he thought, concerning that Vasíli Brekhunóv. 'He did not know, but now I know and know for sure. Now I know!' And again he heard the voice of the one who had called him before. 'I'm coming! Coming!' he responded gladly, and his whole being was filled with joyful emotion. He felt himself free and that nothing could hold him back any longer.

After that Vasíli Andréevich neither saw, heard, nor felt anything more in this world.

All around the snow still eddied. The same whirlwinds of snow circled about, covering the dead Vasíli Andréevich's fur coat, the shivering Mukhórty, the sledge, now scarcely to be seen, and Nikíta lying at the bottom of it, kept warm beneath his dead master.

Nikíta awoke before daybreak. He was aroused by the cold that had begun to creep down his back. He had dreamt that he was coming from the mill with a load of his master's flour and when crossing the stream had missed the bridge and let the cart get stuck. And he saw that he had crawled under the cart and was trying to lift it by arching his back. But strange to say the cart did not move, it stuck to his back and he could neither lift it nor get out from under it. It was crushing the whole of his loins. And how cold it felt! Evidently he must crawl out. 'Have done!' he exclaimed to whoever was pressing the cart down on him. 'Take out the sacks!' But the cart pressed down colder and colder, and then he heard a strange knocking, awoke completely, and remembered everything. The cold cart was his dead and frozen master lying upon him. And the knock was produced by Mukhórty, who had twice struck the sledge with his hoof.

'Andréeich! Eh, Andréeich!'[1] Nikíta called cautiously, beginning to realize the truth, and straightening his back. But Vasíli Andréevich did not answer and his stomach and legs were stiff and cold and heavy like iron weights.

'He must have died! May the Kingdom of Heaven be his!' thought Nikíta.

He turned his head, dug with his hand through the snow about him and opened his eyes. It was daylight; the wind was whistling as before between the shafts, and the snow was falling in the same way, except that it was no longer driving against the frame of the sledge but silently covered both sledge and horse deeper and deeper, and neither the horse's move-ments nor his breathing were any longer to be heard.

'He must have frozen too,' thought Nikíta of Mukhórty, and indeed those hoof knocks against the sledge, which had awakened Nikíta, were the last efforts the already numbed Mukhórty had made to keep on his feet before dying.

---

1 Again the characteristic peasant use of the patronymic without the Chris-tian name preceding it.

'O Lord God, it seems Thou art calling me too!' said Nikíta.
'Thy Holy Will be done. But it's uncanny. . . . Still, a man can't
die twice and must die once. If only it would come soon!'

And he again drew in his head, closed his eyes, and became
unconscious, fully convinced that now he was certainly and
finally dying.

*   *   *

It was not till noon that day that peasants dug Vasíli Andréevich and Nikíta out of the snow with their shovels, not more
than seventy yards from the road and less than half a mile from
the village.

The snow had hidden the sledge, but the shafts and the
kerchief tied to them were still visible. Mukhórty, buried up
to his belly in snow, with the breeching and drugget hanging
down, stood all white, his dead head pressed against his frozen
throat: icicles hung from his nostrils, his eyes were covered with
hoar-frost as though filled with tears, and he had grown so thin
in that one night that he was nothing but skin and bone.

Vasíli Andréevich was stiff as a frozen carcass, and when they
rolled him off Nikíta his legs remained apart and his arms
stretched out as they had been. His bulging hawk eyes were
frozen, and his open mouth under his clipped moustache was
full of snow. But Nikíta though chilled through was still alive.
When he had been brought to, he felt sure that he was already
dead and that what was taking place with him was no longer
happening in this world but in the next. When he heard the
peasants shouting as they dug him out and rolled the frozen
body of Vasíli Andréevich from off him, he was at first surprised that in the other world peasants should be shouting in
the same old way and had the same kind of body, and then
when he realized that he was still in this world he was sorry
rather than glad, especially when he found that the toes on
both his feet were frozen.

Nikíta lay in hospital for two months. They cut off three of
his toes, but the others recovered so that he was still able to
work and went on living for another twenty years, first as a
farm-labourer, then in his old age as a watchman. He died at

home as he had wished, only this year, under the icons with a lighted taper in his hands. Before he died he asked his wife's forgiveness and forgave her for the cooper. He also took leave of his son and grandchildren, and died sincerely glad that he was relieving his son and daughter-in-law of the burden of having to feed him, and that he was now really passing from this life of which he was weary into that other life which every year and every hour grew clearer and more desirable to him. Whether he is better or worse off there where he awoke after his death, whether he was disappointed or found there what he expected, we shall all soon learn.

TOO DEAR!

(TOLSTOY'S ADAPTATION OF A STORY BY
GUY DE MAUPASSANT)

NEAR the borders of France and Italy, on the shore of the Mediterranean Sea, lies a tiny little kingdom called Monaco. Many a small country town can boast more inhabitants than this kingdom, for there are only about seven thousand of them all told, and if all the land in the kingdom were divided there would not be an acre for each inhabitant. But in this toy kingdom there is a real kinglet; and he has a palace, and courtiers, and ministers, and a bishop, and generals, and an army.

It is not a large army, only sixty men in all, but still it is an army. There were also taxes in this kingdom, as elsewhere: a tax on tobacco, and on wine and spirits, and a poll-tax. But though the people there drink and smoke as people do in other countries, there are so few of them that the King would have been hard put to it to feed his courtiers and officials and to keep himself, if he had not found a new and special source of revenue. This special revenue comes from a gaming house, where people play roulette. People play, and whether they win or lose the keeper always gets a percentage on the turnover; and out of his profits he pays a large sum to the King. The reason he pays so much is that it is the only such gambling establishment left in Europe. Some of the little German Sovereigns used to keep gaming houses of the same kind, but some years ago they were forbidden to do so. The reason they were stopped was because these gaming houses did so much harm. A man would come and try his luck, then he would risk all he had and lose it, then he would even risk money that did not belong to him and lose that too, and then, in despair, he would drown or shoot himself. So the

Germans forbade their rulers to make money in this way; but there was no one to stop the King of Monaco, and he remained with a monopoly of the business.

So now everyone who wants to gamble goes to Monaco. Whether they win or lose, the King gains by it. 'You can't earn stone palaces by honest labour,' as the proverb says; and the Kinglet of Monaco knows it is a dirty business, but what is he to do? He has to live; and to draw a revenue from drink and from tobacco is also not a nice thing. So he lives and reigns, and rakes in the money, and holds his court with all the ceremony of a real king.

He has his coronation, his levées; he rewards, sentences, and pardons; and he also has his reviews, councils, laws, and courts of justice: just like other kings, only all on a smaller scale.

Now it happened a few years ago that a murder was committed in this toy King's domains. The people of that kingdom are peaceable, and such a thing had not happened before. The judges assembled with much ceremony and tried the case in the most judicial manner. There were judges, and prosecutors, and jurymen, and barristers. They argued and judged, and at last they condemned the criminal to have his head cut off as the law directs. So far so good. Next they submitted the sentence to the King. The King read the sentence and confirmed it. 'If the fellow must be executed, execute him.'

There was only one hitch in the matter; and that was that they had neither a guillotine for cutting heads off, nor an executioner. The Ministers considered the matter, and decided to address an inquiry to the French Government, asking whether the French could not lend them a machine and an expert to cut off the criminal's head; and if so, would the French kindly inform them what the cost would be. The letter was sent. A week later the reply came: a machine and an expert could be supplied, and the cost would be 16,000 francs. This was laid before the King. He thought it over. Sixteen thousand francs! 'The wretch is not worth the money,' said he. 'Can't it be done, somehow, cheaper? Why, 16,000 francs is more than two francs a head on the whole population. The people won't stand it, and it may cause a riot!'

So a Council was called to consider what could be done; and it was decided to send a similar inquiry to the King of Italy. The French Government is republican, and has no proper respect for kings; but the King of Italy was a brother monarch, and might be induced to do the thing cheaper. So the letter was written, and a prompt reply was received.

The Italian Government wrote that they would have pleasure in supplying both a machine and an expert; and the whole cost would be 12,000 francs, including travelling expenses. This was cheaper, but still it seemed too much. The rascal was really not worth the money. It would still mean nearly two francs more per head on the taxes. Another Council was called. They discussed and considered how it could be done with less expense. Could not one of the soldiers, perhaps, be got to do it in a rough and homely fashion? The General was called and was asked: 'Can't you find us a soldier who would cut the man's head off? In war they don't mind killing people. In fact, that is what they are trained for.' So the General talked it over with the soldiers to see whether one of them would not undertake the job. But none of the soldiers would do it. 'No,' they said, 'we don't know how to do it; it is not a thing we have been taught.'

What was to be done? Again the Ministers considered and reconsidered. They assembled a Commission, and a Committee, and a Sub-Committee, and at last they decided that the best thing would be to alter the death sentence to one of imprisonment for life. This would enable the King to show his mercy, and it would come cheaper.

The King agreed to this, and so the matter was arranged. The only hitch now was that there was no suitable prison for a man sentenced for life. There was a small lock-up where people were sometimes kept temporarily, but there was no strong prison fit for permanent use. However, they managed to find a place that would do, and they put the young fellow there and placed a guard over him. The guard had to watch the criminal, and had also to fetch his food from the palace kitchen.

The prisoner remained there month after month till a year had passed. But when a year had passed, the Kinglet, looking over the account of his income and expenditure one day, noticed a new item of expenditure. This was for the keep of the criminal; nor was it a small item either. There was a special guard, and there was also the man's food. It came to more than 600 francs a year. And the worst of it was that the fellow was still young and healthy, and might live for fifty years. When one came to reckon it up, the matter was serious. It would never do. So the King summoned his Ministers and said to them:

'You must find some cheaper way of dealing with this rascal. The present plan is too expensive.' And the Ministers met and considered and reconsidered, till one of them said: 'Gentlemen, in my opinion we must dismiss the guard.' 'But then,' rejoined another Minister, 'the fellow will run away.' 'Well,' said the first speaker, 'let him run away, and be hanged to him!' So they reported the result of their deliberations to the Kinglet, and he agreed with them. The guard was dismissed, and they waited to see what would happen. All that happened was that at dinner-time the criminal came out, and, not finding his guard, he went to the King's kitchen to fetch his own dinner. He took what was given him, returned to the prison, shut the door on himself, and stayed inside. Next day the same thing occurred. He went for his food at the proper time; but as for running away, he did not show the least sign of it! What was to be done? They considered the matter again.

'We shall have to tell him straight out,' said they, 'that we do not want to keep him.' So the Minister of Justice had him brought before him.

'Why do you not run away?' said the Minister. 'There is no guard to keep you. You can go where you like, and the King will not mind.'

'I daresay the King would not mind,' replied the man, 'but I have nowhere to go. What can I do? You have ruined my character by your sentence, and people will turn their backs on me. Besides, I have got out of the way of working. You have treated me badly. It is not fair. In the first place, when once you sentenced me to death you ought to have executed me; but you did not do it. That's one thing. I did not complain about that. Then you sentenced me to imprisonment for life and put a guard to bring me my food; but after a time you took him away again and I had to fetch my own food. Again I did not complain. But now you actually want me to go away! I can't agree to that. You may do as you like, but I won't go away!'

What was to be done? Once more the Council was summoned. What course could they adopt? The man would not go. They reflected and considered. The only way to get rid of him was to offer him a pension. And so they reported to the King. 'There is nothing else for it,' said they; 'we must get rid of him somehow.' The sum fixed was 600 francs, and this was announced to the prisoner.

'Well,' said he, 'I don't mind, so long as you undertake to pay it regularly. On that condition I am willing to go.'

So the matter was settled. He received one-third of his annuity in advance, and left the King's dominions. It was only a quarter of an hour by rail; and he emigrated, and settled just across the frontier, where he bought a bit of land, started market-gardening, and now lives comfortably. He always goes at the proper time to draw his pension. Having received it, he goes to the gaming tables, stakes two or three francs, sometimes wins and sometimes loses, and then returns home. He lives peaceably and well.

It is a good thing that he did not commit his crime in a country where they do not grudge expense to cut a man's head off, or to keeping him in prison for life.

HADJI MURÁD

A LIST OF TARTAR WORDS USED IN 'HADJI MURÁD'

THROUGHOUT this edition I have tried to avoid the use of Russian words, employing their English equivalents wherever possible. In the following story, however, Tolstoy makes use of a number of Tartar words which he does not translate. As there are generally no one- or two-word equivalents for them in English, it would be difficult to avoid following his example and retaining these Tartar words. I have therefore done so, and the reader should refer to the following alphabetical list when he encounters one of them that needs explanation.

AYLMER MAUDE.

Aoul   A Tartar village.

Bar   Have.

Beshmét   A Tartar undergarment with sleeves.

Búrka   A long round felt cape.

Dzhigít   The same as a *brave* among the Red Indians, but the word is inseparably connected with the idea of skilful horsemanship.

Ghazavát Holy War against the infidels.

Imám   The leader in the Holy War, uniting in himself supreme spiritual and temporal power.

Khansha   Khan's wife.

Kizyák   A fuel made of straw and manure.

Kunák   A sworn friend, an adopted brother.

Murid   A disciple or follower: 'One who desires' to find the way in Muridism.

Muridism Almost identical with Sufism.

Murshíd   'One who shows' the way in Muridism.

Naïb   A Tartar lieutenant or governor.

Pilau   An Oriental dish, prepared with rice and mutton or chicken.

Sáklya   A Caucasian house, clay-plastered and often built of earth.

Shariát   The written Mohammedan law.

Tarikát   'The Path' leading to the higher life.

Yok   No, not.

I

I WAS returning home by the fields. It was midsummer, the hay harvest was over and they were just beginning to reap the rye. At that season of the year there is a delightful variety of flowers – red, white, and pink scented tufty clover; milk-white ox-eye daisies with their bright yellow centres and pleasant spicy smell; yellow honey-scented rape blossoms; tall campanulas with white and lilac bells, tulip-shaped; creeping vetch; yellow, red, and pink scabious; faintly scented, neatly arranged purple plantains with blossoms slightly tinged with pink; cornflowers, the newly opened blossoms bright blue in the sunshine but growing paler and redder towards evening or when growing old; and delicate almond-scented dodder flowers that withered quickly. I gathered myself a large nosegay and was going home when I noticed in a ditch, in full bloom, a beautiful thistle plant of the crimson variety, which in our neighbourhood they call 'Tartar' and carefully avoid when mowing – or, if they do happen to cut it down, throw out from among the grass for fear of pricking their hands. Thinking to pick this thistle and put it in the centre of my nosegay, I climbed down into the ditch, and after driving away a velvety humble-bee that had pene-trated deep into one of the flowers and had there fallen sweetly asleep, I set to work to pluck the flower. But this proved a very difficult task. Not only did the stalk prick on every side – even through the handkerchief I wrapped round my hand – but it was so tough that I had to struggle with it for nearly five minutes, breaking the fibres one by one; and when I had at last plucked it, the stalk was all frayed and the flower itself no longer seemed so fresh and beautiful. Moreover, owing to its coarseness and stiffness, it did not seem in place among the delicate blossoms of my nosegay. I threw it away feeling sorry to have vainly destroyed a flower that looked beautiful in its proper place.

'But what energy and tenacity! With what determination it defended itself, and how dearly it sold its life!' thought I, remembering the effort it had cost me to pluck the flower. The way home led across black-earth fields that had just been ploughed up. I ascended the dusty path. The ploughed field belonged to a landed proprietor and was so large that on both sides and before me to the top of the hill nothing was visible but evenly furrowed and moist earth. The land was well tilled and nowhere was there a blade of grass or any kind of plant to be seen, it was all black. 'Ah, what a destructive creature is man.... How many different plant-lives he destroys to support his own existence!' thought I, involuntarily looking around for some living thing in this lifeless black field. In front of me to the right of the road I saw some kind of little clump, and drawing nearer I found it was the same kind of thistle as that which I had vainly plucked and thrown away. This 'Tartar' plant had three branches. One was broken and stuck out like the stump of a mutilated arm. Each of the other two bore a flower, once red but now blackened. One stalk was broken, and half of it hung down with a soiled flower at its tip. The other, though also soiled with black mud, still stood erect. Evidently a cartwheel had passed over the plant but it had risen again, and that was why, though erect, it stood twisted to one side, as if a piece of its body had been torn from it, its bowels drawn out, an arm torn off, and one of its eyes plucked out. Yet it stood firm and did not surrender to man who had destroyed all its brothers around it....

'What vitality!' I thought. 'Man has conquered everything and destroyed millions of plants, yet this one won't submit.' And I remembered a Caucasian episode of years ago, which I had partly seen myself, partly heard of from eye-witnesses, and in part imagined.

The episode, as it has taken shape in my memory and imagination, was as follows.

*   *   *

It happened towards the end of 1851.

On a cold November evening Hadji Murád rode into Makhmet, a hostile Chechen *aoul* that lay some fifteen miles from Russian territory and was filled with the scented smoke of burning *kizyák*. The strained chant of the muezzin had just ceased, and through the clear mountain air, impregnated with *kizyák* smoke, above the lowing of the cattle and the bleating of the sheep that were dispersing among the *sáklyas* (which were crowded together like the cells of a honeycomb), could be clearly heard the guttural voices of disputing men, and sounds of women's and children's voices rising from near the fountain below.

This Hadji Murád was Shamil's *naïb*, famous for his exploits, who used never to ride out without his banner and some dozens of *murids*, who caracoled and showed off before him. Now wrapped in hood and *búrka*, from under which protruded a rifle, he rode, a fugitive, with one *murid* only, trying to attract as little attention as possible and peering with his quick black eyes into the faces of those he met on his way.

When he entered the *aoul*, instead of riding up the road leading to the open square, he turned to the left into a narrow side-street, and on reaching the second *sáklya*, which was cut into the hill-side, he stopped and looked round. There was no one under the penthouse in front, but on the roof of the *sáklya* itself, behind the freshly plastered clay chimney, lay a man covered with a sheepskin. Hadji Murád touched him with the handle of his leather-plaited whip and clicked his tongue, and an old man, wearing a greasy old *beshmét* and a nightcap, rose from under the sheepskin. His moist red eyelids had no lashes, and he blinked to get them unstuck. Hadji Murád, repeating the customary 'Selaam aleikum!' uncovered his face. 'Aleikum, selaam!' said the old man, recognizing him, and smiling with his toothless mouth. And raising himself on his thin legs he began thrusting his feet into the wooden-heeled slippers that stood by the chimney. Then he leisurely slipped his arms into the sleeves of his crumpled sheepskin, and going to the ladder that leant against the roof he descended backwards. While he dressed and as he climbed down he kept shaking his head on its thin, shrivelled sunburnt neck and mumbling something with his toothless mouth. As soon as he reached the ground he hospitably seized Hadji Murád's bridle and right stirrup; but the strong active *murid* had quickly dismounted and, motioning the old man aside, took his place. Hadji Murád also dismounted, and walking with a slight limp, entered under the penthouse. A boy of fifteen, coming quickly out of the door, met him and wonderingly fixed his sparkling eyes, black as ripe sloes, on the new arrivals.

'Run to the mosque and call your father,' ordered the old man as he hurried forward to open the thin, creaking door into the *sáklya*.

As Hadji Murád entered the outer door, a slight, spare, middle-aged woman in a yellow smock, red *beshmét*, and wide blue trousers came through an inner door carrying cushions.

'May thy coming bring happiness!' said she, and bending nearly double began arranging the cushions along the front wall for the guest to sit on.

'May thy sons live!' answered Hadji Murád, taking off his *búrka*, his rifle, and his sword, and handing them to the old man who carefully hung the rifle and sword on a nail beside the weapons of the master of the house, which were suspended between two large basins that glittered against the clean clay-plastered and carefully whitewashed wall.

Hadji Murád adjusted the pistol at his back, came up to the cushions, and wrapping his Circassian coat closer round him, sat down. The old man squatted on his bare heels beside him, closed his eyes, and lifted his hands palms upwards. Hadji Murád did the same; then after repeating a prayer they both stroked their faces, passing their hands downwards till the palms joined at the end of their beards.

'*Ne habar?*' ('Is there anything new?') asked Hadji Murád, addressing the old man.

'*Habar yok*' ('Nothing new'), replied the old man, looking with his lifeless red eyes not at Hadji Murád's face but at his breast. 'I live at the apiary and have only to-day come to see my son.... He knows.'

Hadji Murád, understanding that the old man did not wish to say what he knew and what Hadji Murád wanted to know, slightly nodded his head and asked no more questions.

'There is no good news,' said the old man. 'The only news is that the hares keep discussing how to drive away the eagles, and the eagles tear first one and then another of them. The other day the Russian dogs burnt the hay in the Mitchit *aoul*.... May their faces be torn!' he added hoarsely and angrily.

Hadji Murád's *murid* entered the room, his strong legs striding softly over the earthen floor. Retaining only his dagger and pistol, he took off his *búrka*, rifle, and sword as Hadji Murád had done, and hung them up on the same nails as his leader's weapons.

'Who is he?' asked the old man, pointing to the newcomer.

'My *murid*. Eldár is his name,' said Hadji Murád.

'That is well,' said the old man, and motioned Eldár to a place on a piece of felt beside Hadji Murád. Eldár sat down, crossing his legs and fixing his fine ram-like eyes on the old man who, having now started talking, was telling how their brave fellows had caught two Russian soldiers the week before and had killed one and sent the other to Shamil in Vedén.

Hadji Murád heard him absently, looking at the door and listening to the sounds outside. Under the penthouse steps were heard, the door creaked, and Sado, the master of the house, came in. He was a man of about forty, with a small beard, long nose, and eyes as black, though not as glittering, as those of his fifteen-year-old son who had run to call him home and who now entered with his father and sat down by the door. The master of the house took off his wooden slippers at the door, and pushing his old and much-worn cap to the back of his head (which had remained unshaved so long that it was beginning to be overgrown with black hair), at once squatted down in front of Hadji Murád.

He too lifted his hands palms upwards, as the old man had done, repeated a prayer, and then stroked his face downwards. Only after that did he begin to speak. He told how an order had come from Shamil to seize Hadji Murád alive or dead, that

Shamil's envoys had left only the day before, that the people were afraid to disobey Shamil's orders, and that therefore it was necessary to be careful.

'In my house,' said Sado, 'no one shall injure my *kunák* while I live, but how will it be in the open fields? . . . We must think it over.'

Hadji Murád listened with attention and nodded approvingly. When Sado had finished he said:

'Very well. Now we must send a man with a letter to the Russians. My *murid* will go but he will need a guide.'

'I will send brother Bata,' said Sado. 'Go and call Bata,' he added, turning to his son.

The boy instantly bounded to his nimble feet as if he were on springs, and swinging his arms, rapidly left the *sáklya*. Some ten minutes later he returned with a sinewy, short-legged Chechen, burnt almost black by the sun, wearing a worn and tattered yellow Circassian coat with frayed sleeves, and crumpled black leggings.

Hadji Murád greeted the newcomer, and again without wasting a single word, immediately asked:

'Canst thou conduct my *murid* to the Russians?'

'I can,' gaily replied Bata. 'I can certainly do it. There is not another Chechen who would pass as I can. Another might agree to go and might promise anything, but would do nothing; but I can do it!'

'All right,' said Hadji Murád. 'Thou shalt receive three for thy trouble,' and he held up three fingers.

Bata nodded to show that he understood, and added that it was not money he prized, but that he was ready to serve Hadji Murád for the honour alone. Everyone in the mountains knew Hadji Murád, and how he slew the Russian swine.

'Very well. . . . A rope should be long but a speech short,' said Hadji Murád.

'Well then I'll hold my tongue,' said Bata.

'Where the river Argun bends by the cliff,' said Hadji Murád, 'there are two stacks in a glade in the forest – thou knowest?'

'I know.'

'There my four horsemen are waiting for me,' said Hadji Murád.

'Aye,' answered Bata, nodding.

'Ask for Khan Mahomá. He knows what to do and what to say. Canst thou lead him to the Russian commander, Prince Vorontsóv?'

'Yes, I'll take him.'

'Canst thou take him and bring him back again?'

'I can.'

'Then take him there and return to the wood. I shall be there too.'

'I will do it all,' said Bata, rising, and putting his hands on his heart he went out.

Hadji Murád turned to his host.

'A man must also be sent to Chekhi,' he began, and took hold of one of the cartridge pouches of his Circassian coat, but let his hand drop immediately and became silent on seeing two women enter the *sáklya*.

One was Sado's wife – the thin middle-aged woman who had arranged the cushions. The other was quite a young girl, wearing red trousers and a green *beshmét*. A necklace of silver coins covered the whole front of her dress, and at the end of the short but thick plait of hard black hair that hung between her thin shoulder-blades a silver ruble was suspended. Her eyes, as sloe-black as those of her father and brother, sparkled brightly in her young face which tried to be stern. She did not look at the visitors, but evidently felt their presence.

Sado's wife brought in a low round table on which stood tea, pancakes in butter, cheese, *churek* (that is, thinly rolled out bread), and honey. The girl carried a basin, a ewer, and a towel.

Sado and Hadji Murád kept silent as long as the women, with their coin ornaments tinkling, moved softly about in their red soft-soled slippers, setting out before the visitors the things they had brought. Eldár sat motionless as a statue, his ram-like eyes fixed on his crossed legs, all the time the women were in the *sáklya*. Only after they had gone and their soft footsteps could no longer be heard behind the door, did he give a sigh of relief.

Hadji Murád having pulled out a bullet from one of the cartridge-pouches of his Circassian coat, and having taken out a rolled-up note that lay beneath it, held it out, saying:

'To be handed to my son.'

'Where must the answer be sent?'

'To thee; and thou must forward it to me.'

'It shall be done,' said Sado, and placed the note in a cartridge-pocket of his own coat. Then he took up the metal ewer and moved the basin towards Hadji Murád.

Hadji Murád turned up the sleeves of his *beshmét* on his white muscular arms, held out his hands under the clear cold water which Sado poured from the ewer, and having wiped them on a clean unbleached towel, turned to the table. Eldár did the same. While the visitors ate, Sado sat opposite and thanked them several times for their visit. The boy sat by the door never taking his sparkling eyes off Hadji Murád's face, and smiled as if in confirmation of his father's words.

Though he had eaten nothing for more than twenty-four hours Hadji Murád ate only a little bread and cheese; then, drawing out a small knife from under his dagger, he spread some honey on a piece of bread.

'Our honey is good,' said the old man, evidently pleased to see Hadji Murád eating his honey. 'This year, above all other years, it is plentiful and good.'

'I thank thee,' said Hadji Murád and turned from the table. Eldár would have liked to go on eating but he followed his leader's example, and having moved away from the table, handed him the ewer and basin.

Sado knew that he was risking his life by receiving such a guest in his house, for after his quarrel with Shamil the latter had issued a proclamation to all the inhabitants of Chechnya forbidding them to receive Hadji Murád on pain of death. He knew that the inhabitants of the *aoul* might at any moment become aware of Hadji Murád's presence in his house and might demand his surrender. But this not only did not frighten Sado, it even gave him pleasure: he considered it his duty to protect his guest though it should cost him his life, and he was proud and pleased with himself because he was doing his duty.

'Whilst thou art in my house and my head is on my shoulders no one shall harm thee,' he repeated to Hadji Murád.

Hadji Murád looked into his glittering eyes and understanding that this was true, said with some solemnity –

'Mayest thou receive joy and life!'

Sado silently laid his hand on his heart in token of thanks for these kind words.

Having closed the shutters of the *sáklya* and laid some sticks in the fireplace, Sado, in an exceptionally bright and animated mood, left the room and went into that part of his *sáklya* where his family all lived. The women had not yet gone to sleep, and were talking about the dangerous visitors who were spending the night in their guest-chamber.

II

A T Vozdvízhensk, the advanced fort situated some ten miles from the *aoul* in which Hadji Murád was spending the night, three soldiers and a non-commissioned officer left the fort and went beyond the Shahgirínsk Gate. The soldiers, dressed as Caucasian soldiers used to be in those days, wore sheepskin coats and caps, and boots that reached above their knees, and they carried their cloaks tightly rolled up and fastened across their shoulders. Shouldering arms, they first went some five hundred paces along the road and then turned off it and went some twenty paces to the right – the dead leaves rustling under their boots – till they reached the blackened trunk of a broken plane tree just visible through the darkness. There they stopped. It was at this plane tree that an ambush party was usually placed.

The bright stars, that had seemed to be running along the tree-tops while the soldiers were walking through the forest, now stood still, shining brightly between the bare branches of the trees.

'A good job it's dry,' said the non-commissioned officer Panóv, bringing down his long gun and bayonet with a clang from his shoulder and placing it against the plane tree.

The three soldiers did the same.

'Sure enough I've lost it!' muttered Panóv crossly. 'Must have left it behind or I've dropped it on the way.'

'What are you looking for?' asked one of the soldiers in a bright, cheerful voice.

'The bowl of my pipe. Where the devil has it got to?'

'Have you got the stem?' asked the cheerful voice.

'Here it is.'

'Then why not stick it straight into the ground?'

'Not worth bothering!'

'We'll manage that in a minute.'

Smoking in ambush was forbidden, but this ambush hardly deserved the name. It was rather an outpost to prevent the mountaineers from bringing up a cannon unobserved and firing at the fort as they used to. Panóv did not consider it necessary to forgo the pleasure of smoking, and therefore accepted the cheerful soldier's offer. The latter took a knife from his pocket and made a small round hole in the ground. Having smoothed it, he adjusted the pipe-stem to it, then filled the hole with tobacco and pressed it down, and the pipe was ready. A sulphur match flared and for a moment lit up the broad-cheeked face of the soldier who lay on his stomach, the air whistled in the stem, and Panóv smelt the pleasant odour of burning tobacco.

'Fixed it up?' said he, rising to his feet.

'Why, of course!'

'What a smart chap you are, Avdéev! . . . As wise as a judge! Now then, lad.'

Avdéev rolled over on his side to make room for Panóv, letting smoke escape from his mouth.

Panóv lay down prone, and after wiping the mouthpiece with his sleeve, began to inhale.

When they had had their smoke the soldiers began to talk.

'They say the commander has had his fingers in the cash-box again,' remarked one of them in a lazy voice. 'He lost at cards, you see.'

'He'll pay it back again,' said Panóv.

'Of course he will! He's a good officer,' assented Avdéev.

'Good! good!' gloomily repeated the man who had started the conversation. 'In my opinion the company ought to speak to him. "If you've taken the money, tell us how much and when you'll repay it."'

'That will be as the company decides,' said Panóv, tearing himself away from the pipe.

'Of course. "The community is a strong man,"' assented Avdéev, quoting a proverb.

'There will be oats to buy and boots to get towards spring. The money will be wanted, and what shall we do if he's pocketed it?' insisted the dissatisfied one.

'I tell you it will be as the company wishes,' repeated Panóv. 'It's not the first time: he takes it and gives it back.'

In the Caucasus in those days each company chose men to manage its own commissariat. They received 6 rubles 50 kopeks[1] a month per man from the treasury, and catered for the company. They planted cabbages, made hay, had their own carts, and prided themselves on their well-fed horses. The company's money was kept in a chest of which the com-mander had the key, and it often happened that he borrowed from the chest. This had just happened again, and the soldiers were talking about it. The morose soldier, Nikítin, wished to demand an account from the commander, while Panóv and Avdéev considered that unnecessary.

After Panóv, Nikítin had a smoke, and then spreading his cloak on the ground sat down on it leaning against the trunk of the plane tree. The soldiers were silent. Far above their heads the crowns of the trees rustled in the wind and suddenly, above this incessant low rustling, rose the howling, whining, weep-ing, and chuckling of jackals.

---

1 About £1, for at that time the ruble was worth about three shillings.

'Just listen to those accursed creatures – how they cater-waul!'

'They're laughing at you because your mouth's all on one side,' remarked the high voice of the third soldier, an Ukrainian.

All was silent again, except for the wind that swayed the branches, now revealing and now hiding the stars.

'I say, Panóv,' suddenly asked the cheerful Avdéev, 'do you ever feel dull?'

'Dull, why?' replied Panóv reluctantly.

'Well, I do. . . . I feel so dull sometimes that I don't know what I might not be ready to do to myself.'

'There now!' was all Panóv replied.

'That time when I drank all the money it was from dullness. It took hold of me . . . took hold of me till I thought to myself, "I'll just get blind drunk!"'

'But sometimes drinking makes it still worse.'

'Yes, that's happened to me too. But what is a man to do with himself?'

'But what makes you feel so dull?'

'What, me? . . . Why, it's the longing for home.'

'Is yours a wealthy home then?'

'No; we weren't wealthy, but things went properly – we lived well.' And Avdéev began to relate what he had already told Panóv many times.

'You see, I went as a soldier of my own free will, instead of my brother,' he said. 'He has children. They were five in the family and I had only just married. Mother began begging me to go. So I thought, "Well, maybe they will remember what I've done." So I went to our proprietor . . . he was a good master and he said, "You're a fine fellow, go!" So I went instead of my brother.'

'Well, that was right,' said Panóv.

'And yet, will you believe me, Panóv, it's chiefly because of that that I feel so dull now? "Why did you go instead of your brother?" I say to myself. "He's living like a king now over there, while you have to suffer here"; and the more I think of it the worse I feel. . . . It seems just a piece of ill-luck!'

Avdéev was silent.

'Perhaps we'd better have another smoke,' said he after a pause.

'Well then, fix it up!'

But the soldiers were not to have their smoke. Hardly had Avdéev risen to fix the pipe-stem in its place when above the rustling of the trees they heard footsteps along the road. Panóv took his gun and pushed Nikítin with his foot.

Nikítin rose and picked up his cloak.

The third soldier, Bondarénko, rose also, and said:

'And I have dreamt such a dream, mates....'

'Sh!' said Avdéev, and the soldiers held their breath, listening. The footsteps of men in soft-soled boots were heard approaching. The fallen leaves and dry twigs could be heard rustling clearer and clearer through the darkness. Then came the peculiar guttural tones of Chechen voices. The soldiers could now not only hear men approaching, but could see two shadows passing through a clear space between the trees; one shadow taller than the other. When these shadows had come in line with the soldiers, Panóv, gun in hand, stepped out on to the road, followed by his comrades.

'Who goes there?' cried he.

'Me, friendly Chechen,' said the shorter one. This was Bata. 'Gun, *yok!*...sword, *yok!*' said he, pointing to himself. 'Prince, want!'

The taller one stood silent beside his comrade. He too was unarmed.

'He means he's a scout, and wants the Colonel,' explained Panóv to his comrades.

'Prince Vorontsóv...much want! Big business!' said Bata.

'All right, all right! We'll take you to him,' said Panóv. 'I say, you'd better take them,' said he to Avdéev, 'you and Bondarénko; and when you've given them up to the officer on duty come back again. Mind,' he added, 'be careful to make them keep in front of you!'

'And what of this?' said Avdéev, moving his gun and bayonet as though stabbing someone. 'I'd just give a dig, and let the steam out of him!'

'What'll he be worth when you've stuck him?' remarked Bondarénko.

'Now, march!'

When the steps of the two soldiers conducting the scouts could no longer be heard, Panóv and Nikítin returned to their post.

'What the devil brings them here at night?' said Nikítin.

'Seems it's necessary,' said Panóv. 'But it's getting chilly,' he added, and unrolling his cloak he put it on and sat down by the tree.

About two hours later Avdéev and Bondarénko returned.

'Well, have you handed them over?'

'Yes. They weren't yet asleep at the colonel's – they were taken straight in to him. And do you know, mates, those shaven-headed lads are fine!' continued Avdéev. 'Yes, really. What a talk I had with them!'

'Of course you'd talk,' remarked Nikítin disapprovingly.

'Really they're just like Russians. One of them is married. "Molly," says I, "*bar?*" "*Bar*," he says. Bondarénko, didn't I say "*bar?*" "Many *bar?*" "A couple," says he. A couple! Such a good talk we had! Such nice fellows!'

'Nice, indeed!' said Nikítin. 'If you met him alone he'd soon let the guts out of you.'

'It will be getting light before long,' said Panóv.

'Yes, the stars are beginning to go out,' said Avdéev, sitting down and making himself comfortable.

And the soldiers were silent again.

III

THE windows of the barracks and the soldiers' houses had long been dark in the fort; but there were still lights in the windows of the best house.

In it lived Prince Simon Mikhaílovich Vorontsóv, Commander of the Kurín Regiment, an Imperial Aide-de-Camp and son of the Commander-in-Chief. Vorontsóv's wife, Márya Vasílevna, a famous Petersburg beauty, was with him and they lived in this little Caucasian fort more luxuriously than anyone had ever lived there before. To Vorontsóv, and even more to his wife, it seemed that they were not only living a very modest life, but one full of privations, while to the inhabitants of the place their luxury was surprising and extraordinary.

Just now, at midnight, the host and hostess sat playing cards with their visitors, at a card-table lit by four candles, in the spacious drawing-room with its carpeted floor and rich curtains drawn across the windows. Vorontsóv, who had a long face and wore the insignia and gold cords of an aide-de-camp, was partnered by a shaggy young man of gloomy appearance, a graduate of Petersburg University whom Princess Vorontsóv had lately had sent to the Caucasus to be tutor to her little son (born of her first marriage). Against them played two officers: one a broad, red-faced man, Poltorátsky, a company commander who had exchanged out of the Guards; and the other the regimental adjutant, who sat very straight on his chair with a cold expression on his handsome face.

Princess Márya Vasílevna, a large-built, large-eyed, black-browed beauty, sat beside Poltorátsky – her crinoline touching his legs – and looked over his cards. In her words, her looks, her smile, her perfume, and in every movement of her body, there was something that reduced Poltorátsky to obliviousness of everything except the consciousness of her nearness, and he made blunder after blunder, trying his partner's temper more and more.

'No . . . that's too bad! You've wasted an ace again,' said the regimental adjutant, flushing all over as Poltorátsky threw out an ace.

Poltorátsky turned his kindly, wide-set black eyes towards the dissatisfied adjutant uncomprehendingly, as though just aroused from sleep.

'Do forgive him!' said Márya Vasílevna, smiling. 'There, you see! Didn't I tell you so?' she went on, turning to Poltorátsky.

'But that's not at all what you said,' replied Poltorátsky, smiling.

'Wasn't it?' she queried, with an answering smile, which excited and delighted Poltorátsky to such a degree that he blushed crimson and seizing the cards began to shuffle.

'It isn't your turn to deal,' said the adjutant sternly, and with his white ringed hand he began to deal himself, as though he wished to get rid of the cards as quickly as possible.

The prince's valet entered the drawing-room and announced that the officer on duty wanted to speak to him.

'Excuse me, gentlemen,' said the prince, speaking Russian with an English accent. 'Will you take my place, Márya?'

'Do you all agree?' asked the princess, rising quickly and lightly to her full height, rustling her silks, and smiling the radiant smile of a happy woman.

'I always agree to everything,' replied the adjutant, very pleased that the princess – who could not play at all – was now going to play against him.

Poltorátsky only spread out his hands and smiled.

The rubber was nearly finished when the prince returned to the drawing-room, animated and obviously very pleased.

'Do you know what I propose?'

'What?'

'That we have some champagne.'

'I am always ready for that,' said Poltorátsky.

'Why not? We shall be delighted!' said the adjutant.

'Bring some, Vasíli!' said the prince.

'What did they want you for?' asked Márya Vasílevna.

'It was the officer on duty and another man.'

'Who? What about?' asked Márya Vasílevna quickly.

'I mustn't say,' said Vorontsóv, shrugging his shoulders.

'You mustn't say!' repeated Márya Vasílevna. 'We'll see about that.'

When the champagne was brought each of the visitors drank a glass, and having finished the game and settled the scores they began to take their leave.

'Is it your company that's ordered to the forest to-morrow?' the prince asked Poltorátsky as they said good-bye.

'Yes, mine ... why?'

'Then we shall meet to-morrow,' said the prince, smiling slightly.

'Very pleased,' replied Poltorátsky, not quite understanding what Vorontsóv was saying to him and preoccupied only by the thought that he would in a minute be pressing Márya Vasílevna's hand.

Márya Vasílevna, according to her wont, not only pressed his hand firmly but shook it vigorously, and again reminding him of his mistake in playing diamonds, she gave him what he took to be a delightful, affectionate, and meaning smile.

Poltorátsky went home in an ecstatic condition only to be understood by people like himself who, having grown up and been educated in society, meet a woman belonging to their own circle after months of isolated military life, and moreover a woman like Princess Vorontsóv.

When he reached the little house in which he and his comrade lived he pushed the door, but it was locked. He knocked, with no result. He felt vexed, and began kicking the door and banging it with his sword. Then he heard a sound of footsteps and Vovílo – a domestic serf of his – undid the cabin-hook which fastened the door.

'What do you mean by locking yourself in, blockhead?'

'But how is it possible, sir . . . ?'

'You're tipsy again! I'll show you "how it is possible!" ' and Poltorátsky was about to strike Vovílo but changed his mind. 'Oh, go to the devil! . . . Light a candle.'

'In a minute.'

Vovílo was really tipsy. He had been drinking at the name-day party of the ordnance-sergeant, Iván Petróvich. On returning home he began comparing his life with that of the latter. Iván Petróvich had a salary, was married, and hoped in a year's time to get his discharge.

Vovílo had been taken 'up' when a boy – that is, he had been taken into his owner's household service – and now although he was already over forty he was not married, but lived a campaigning life with his harum-scarum young master. He was a good master, who seldom struck him, but what kind of a life was it? 'He promised to free me when we return from the Caucasus, but where am I to go with my freedom? . . . It's a dog's life!' thought Vovílo, and he felt so sleepy that, afraid lest someone should come in and steal something, he fastened the hook of the door and fell asleep.

* * *

Poltorátsky entered the bedroom which he shared with his comrade Tíkhonov.

'Well, have you lost?' asked Tíkhonov, waking up.

'No, as it happens, I haven't. I've won seventeen rubles, and we drank a bottle of Cliquot!'

'And you've looked at Márya Vasílevna?'

'Yes, and I've looked at Márya Vasílevna,' repeated Poltorátsky.

'It will soon be time to get up,' said Tíkhonov. 'We are to start at six.'

'Vovílo!' shouted Poltorátsky, 'see that you wake me up properly to-morrow at five!'

'How can I wake you if you fight?'

'I tell you you're to wake me! Do you hear?'

'All right.' Vovílo went out, taking Poltorátsky's boots and clothes with him. Poltorátsky got into bed and smoked a cigarette and put out his candle, smiling the while. In the dark he saw before him the smiling face of Márya Vasílevna.

* * *

The Vorontsóvs did not go to bed at once. When the visitors had left, Márya Vasílevna went up to her husband and standing in front of him, said severely –

'*Eh bien! Vous allez me dire ce que c'est.*'

'*Mais, ma chère . . .*'

'*Pas de "ma chère"! C'était un émissaire, n'est-ce pas?*'

'*Quand même, je ne puis pas vous le dire.*'

'*Vous ne pouvez pas? Alors, c'est moi qui vais vous le dire!*'

'*Vous?*'[1]

[1] 'Well now! You're going to tell me what it is.'
'But, my dear....'
'Don't "my dear" me! It was an emissary, wasn't it?'
'Supposing it was, still I must not tell you.'
'You must not? Well then, I will tell you!'
'You?'

'It was Hadji Murád, wasn't it?' said Márya Vasílevna, who had for some days past heard of the negotiations and thought that Hadji Murád himself had been to see her husband. Vorontsóv could not altogether deny this, but disappointed her by saying that it was not Hadji Murád himself but only an emissary to announce that Hadji Murád would come to meet him next day at the spot where a wood-cutting expedition had been arranged.

In the monotonous life of the fortress the young Vorontsóvs – both husband and wife – were glad of this occurrence, and it was already past two o'clock when, after speaking of the pleasure the news would give his father, they went to bed.

IV

AFTER the three sleepless nights he had passed flying from the *murids* Shamil had sent to capture him, Hadji Murád fell asleep as soon as Sado, having bid him good-night, had gone out of the *sáklya*. He slept fully dressed with his head on his hand, his elbow sinking deep into the red down-cushions his host had arranged for him.

At a little distance, by the wall, slept Eldár. He lay on his back, his strong young limbs stretched out so that his high chest, with the black cartridge-pouches sewn into the front of his white Circassian coat, was higher than his freshly shaven, blue-gleaming head, which had rolled off the pillow and was thrown back. His upper lip, on which a little soft down was just appearing, pouted like a child's, now contracting and now expanding, as though he were sipping something. Like Hadji Murád he slept with pistol and dagger in his belt. The sticks in the grate burnt low, and a night-light in a niche in the wall gleamed faintly.

In the middle of the night the floor of the guest-chamber creaked, and Hadji Murád immediately rose, putting his hand to his pistol. Sado entered, treading softly on the earthen floor.

'What is it?' asked Hadji Murád, as if he had not been asleep at all.

'We must think,' replied Sado, squatting down in front of him. 'A woman from her roof saw you arrive and told her husband, and now the whole *aoul* knows. A neighbour has just been to tell my wife that the Elders have assembled in the mosque and want to detain you.'

'I must be off!' said Hadji Murád.

'The horses are saddled,' said Sado, quickly leaving the *sáklya*.

'Eldár!' whispered Hadji Murád. And Eldár, hearing his name, and above all his master's voice, leapt to his feet, setting his cap straight as he did so.

Hadji Murád put on his weapons and then his *búrka*. Eldár did the same, and they both went silently out of the *sáklya* into the penthouse. The black-eyed boy brought their horses. Hearing the clatter of hoofs on the hard-beaten road, someone stuck his head out of the door of a neighbouring *sáklya*, and a man ran up the hill towards the mosque, clattering with his wooden shoes. There was no moon, but the stars shone brightly in the black sky so that the outlines of the *sáklya* roofs could be seen in the darkness, the mosque with its minarets in the upper part of the village rising above the other buildings. From the mosque came a hum of voices.

Quickly seizing his gun, Hadji Murád placed his foot in the narrow stirrup, and silently and easily throwing his body across, swung himself on to the high cushion of the saddle.

'May God reward you!' he said, addressing his host while his right foot felt instinctively for the stirrup, and with his whip he lightly touched the lad who held his horse, as a sign that he should let go. The boy stepped aside, and the horse, as if it knew what it had to do, started at a brisk pace down the lane towards the principal street. Eldár rode behind him. Sado in his sheepskin followed, almost running, swinging his arms and crossing now to one side and now to the other of the narrow side-street. At the place where the streets met, first one moving shadow and then another appeared in the road.

'Stop . . . who's that? Stop!' shouted a voice, and several men blocked the path.

Instead of stopping, Hadji Murád drew his pistol from his belt and increasing his speed rode straight at those who blocked the way. They separated, and without looking round he started down the road at a swift canter. Eldár followed him at a sharp trot. Two shots cracked behind them and two bullets whistled past without hitting either Hadji Murád or Eldár. Hadji Murád continued riding at the same pace, but having gone some three hundred yards he stopped his slightly panting horse and listened.

In front of him, lower down, gurgled rapidly running water. Behind him in the *aoul* cocks crowed, answering one another. Above these sounds he heard behind him the approaching tramp of horses and the voices of several men. Hadji Murád touched his horse and rode on at an even pace. Those behind him galloped and soon overtook him. They were some twenty mounted men, inhabitants of the *aoul*, who had decided to detain Hadji Murád or at least to make a show of detaining him in order to justify themselves in Shamil's eyes. When they came near enough to be seen in the darkness, Hadji Murád stopped, let go his bridle, and with an accustomed movement of his left hand unbuttoned the cover of his rifle, which he drew forth with his right. Eldár did the same.

'What do you want?' cried Hadji Murád. 'Do you wish to take me?... Take me, then!' and he raised his rifle. The men from the *aoul* stopped, and Hadji Murád, rifle in hand, rode down into the ravine. The mounted men followed him but did not draw any nearer. When Hadji Murád had crossed to the other side of the ravine the men shouted to him that he should hear what they had to say. In reply he fired his rifle and put his horse to a gallop. When he reined it in his pursuers were no longer within hearing and the crowing of the cocks could also no longer be heard; only the murmur of the water in the forest sounded more distinctly and now and then came the cry of an owl. The black wall of the forest appeared quite close. It was in this forest that his *murids* awaited him.

On reaching it Hadji Murád paused, and drawing much air into his lungs he whistled and then listened silently. The next minute he was answered by a similar whistle from the forest. Hadji Murád turned from the road and entered it. When he had gone about a hundred paces he saw among the trunks of the trees a bonfire, the shadows of some men sitting round it, and, half lit-up by the firelight, a hobbled horse which was saddled. Four men were seated by the fire.

One of them rose quickly, and coming up to Hadji Murád took hold of his bridle and stirrup. This was Hadji Murád's sworn brother who managed his household affairs for him.

'Put out the fire,' said Hadji Murád, dismounting.

The men began scattering the pile and trampling on the burning branches.

'Has Bata been here?' asked Hadji Murád, moving towards a *búrka* that was spread on the ground.

'Yes, he went away long ago with Khan Mahomá.'

'Which way did they go?'

'That way,' answered Khanéfi pointing in the opposite direction to that from which Hadji Murád had come.

'All right,' said Hadji Murád, and unslinging his rifle he began to load it.

'We must take care – I have been pursued,' he said to a man who was putting out the fire.

This was Gamzálo, a Chechen. Gamzálo approached the *búrka*, took up a rifle that lay on it wrapped in its cover, and without a word went to that side of the glade from which Hadji Murád had come.

When Eldár had dismounted he took Hadji Murád's horse, and having reined up both horses' heads high, tied them to two trees. Then he shouldered his rifle as Gamzálo had done and went to the other side of the glade. The bonfire was extinguished, the forest no longer looked as black as before, but in the sky the stars still shone, though faintly.

Lifting his eyes to the stars and seeing that the Pleiades had already risen half-way up the sky, Hadji Murád calculated that it must be long past midnight and that his nightly prayer was long overdue. He asked Khanéfi for a ewer (they always carried one in their packs), and putting on his *búrka* went to the water.

Having taken off his shoes and performed his ablutions, Hadji Murád stepped onto the *búrka* with bare feet and then squatted down on his calves, and having first placed his fingers in his ears and closed his eyes, he turned to the south and recited the usual prayer.

When he had finished he returned to the place where the saddle-bags lay, and sitting down on the *búrka* he leant his elbows on his knees and bowed his head and fell into deep thought.

Hadji Murád always had great faith in his own fortune. When planning anything he always felt in advance firmly convinced of success, and fate smiled on him. It had been so, with a few rare exceptions, during the whole course of his stormy military life; and so he hoped it would be now. He pictured to himself how – with the army Vorontsóv would place at his disposal – he would march against Shamil and take him prisoner, and revenge himself on him; and how the Russian Tsar would reward him and how he would again rule not only over Avaria, but over the whole of Chechnya, which would submit to him. With these thoughts he unwittingly fell asleep.

He dreamt how he and his brave followers rushed at Shamil with songs and with the cry, 'Hadji Murád is coming!' and how they seized him and his wives and how he heard the wives crying and sobbing. He woke up. The song, *Lya-il-allysha*, and the cry, 'Hadji Murád is coming!' and the weeping of Shamil's wives, was the howling, weeping, and laughter of jackals that awoke him. Hadji Murád lifted his head, glanced at the sky which, seen between the trunks of the trees, was already growing light in the east, and inquired after Khan Mahomá of a *murid* who sat at some distance from him. On hearing that Khan Mahomá had not yet returned, Hadji Murád again bowed his head and at once fell asleep.

He was awakened by the merry voice of Khan Mahomá returning from his mission with Bata. Khan Mahomá at once sat down beside Hadji Murád and told him how the soldiers had met them and had led them to the prince himself, and how pleased the prince was and how he promised to meet them in the morning where the Russians would be felling trees beyond the Mitchík in the Shalín glade. Bata interrupted his fellow-envoy to add details of his own.

Hadji Murád asked particularly for the words with which Vorontsóv had answered his offer to go over to the Russians, and Khan Mahomá and Bata replied with one voice that the prince promised to receive Hadji Murád as a guest, and to act so that it should be well for him.

Then Hadji Murád questioned them about the road, and when Khan Mahomá assured him that he knew the way well and would conduct him straight to the spot, Hadji Murád took out some money and gave Bata the promised three rubles. Then he ordered his men to take out of the saddle-bags his gold-ornamented weapons and his turban, and to clean themselves up so as to look well when they arrived among the Russians.

While they cleaned their weapons, harness, and horses, the stars faded away, it became quite light, and an early morning breeze sprang up.

V

EARLY in the morning, while it was still dark, two companies carrying axes and commanded by Poltorátsky marched six miles beyond the Shahgirínsk Gate, and having thrown out a line of sharpshooters set to work to fell trees as soon as the day broke. Towards eight o'clock the mist which had mingled with the perfumed smoke of the hissing and crackling damp green branches on the bonfires began to rise and the wood-fellers – who till then had not seen five paces off but had only heard one another – began to see both the bonfires and the road through the forest, blocked with fallen trees. The sun now appeared like a bright spot in the fog and now again was hidden.

In the glade, some way from the road, Poltorátsky, his subaltern Tíkhonov, two officers of the Third Company, and Baron Freze, an ex-officer of the Guards and a fellow-student of Poltorátsky's at the Cadet College, who had been reduced to the ranks for fighting a duel, were sitting on drums. Bits of paper that had contained food, cigarette stumps, and empty bottles, lay scattered around them. The officers had had some vodka and were now eating, and drinking porter. A drummer was uncorking their third bottle.

Poltorátsky, although he had not had enough sleep, was in that peculiar state of elation and kindly careless gaiety which he always felt when he found himself among his soldiers and with his comrades where there was a possibility of danger.

The officers were carrying on an animated conversation, the subject of which was the latest news: the death of General Sleptsóv. None of them saw in this death that most important moment of a life, its termination and return to the source whence it sprang – they saw in it only the valour of a gallant officer who rushed at the mountaineers sword in hand and hacked them desperately.

Though all of them – and especially those who had been in action – knew and could not help knowing that in those days in the Caucasus, and in fact anywhere and at any time, such hand-to-hand hacking as is always imagined and described never occurs (or if hacking with swords and bayonets ever does occur, it is only those who are running away that get hacked), that fiction of hand-to-hand fighting endowed them with the calm pride and cheerfulness with which they sat on the drums – some with a jaunty air, others on the contrary in a very modest pose, and drank and joked without troubling about death, which might overtake them at any moment as it had overtaken Sleptsóv. And in the midst of their talk, as if to confirm their expectations, they heard to the left of the road the pleasant stirring sound of a rifle-shot; and a bullet, merrily whistling somewhere in the misty air, flew past and crashed into a tree.

'Hullo!' exclaimed Poltorátsky in a merry voice; 'why that's at our line. . . . There now, Kóstya,' and he turned to Freze, 'now's your chance. Go back to the company. I will lead the whole company to support the cordon and we'll arrange a battle that will be simply delightful . . . and then we'll make a report.'

Freze jumped to his feet and went at a quick pace towards the smoke-enveloped spot where he had left his company.

Poltorátsky's little Kabardá dapple-bay was brought to him, and he mounted and drew up his company and led it in the direction whence the shots were fired. The outposts stood on the skirts of the forest in front of the bare descending slope of a ravine. The wind was blowing in the direction of the forest, and not only was it possible to see the slope of the ravine, but the opposite side of it was also distinctly visible. When Poltorátsky rode up to the line the sun came out from behind the mist, and on the other side of the ravine, by the outskirts of a young forest, a few horsemen could be seen at a distance of a quarter of a mile. These were the Chechens who had pursued Hadji Murád and wanted to see him meet the Russians. One of them fired at the line. Several soldiers fired back. The Chechens retreated and the firing ceased.

But when Poltorátsky and his company came up he nevertheless gave orders to fire, and scarcely had the word been passed than along the whole line of sharpshooters the incessant, merry, stirring rattle of our rifles began, accompanied by pretty dissolving cloudlets of smoke. The soldiers, pleased to have some distraction, hastened to load and fired shot after shot. The Chechens evidently caught the feeling of excitement, and leaping forward one after another fired a few shots at our men. One of these shots wounded a soldier. It was that same Avdéev who had lain in ambush the night before.

When his comrades approached him he was lying prone, holding his wounded stomach with both hands, and rocking himself with a rhythmic motion moaned softly. He belonged to Poltorátsky's company, and Poltorátsky, seeing a group of soldiers collected, rode up to them.

'What is it, lad? Been hit?' said Poltorátsky. 'Where?'

Avdéev did not answer.

'I was just going to load, your honour, when I heard a click,' said a soldier who had been with Avdéev; 'and I look and see he's dropped his gun.'

'Tut, tut, tut!' Poltorátsky clicked his tongue. 'Does it hurt much, Avdéev?'

'It doesn't hurt but it stops me walking. A drop of vodka now, your honour!'

Some vodka (or rather the spirit drunk by the soldiers in the Caucasus) was found, and Panóv, severely frowning, brought Avdéev a can-lid full. Avdéev tried to drink it but immediately handed back the lid.

'My soul turns against it,' he said. 'Drink it yourself.'

Panóv drank up the spirit.

Avdéev raised himself but sank back at once. They spread out a cloak and laid him on it.

'Your honour, the Colonel is coming,' said the sergeant-major to Poltorátsky.

'All right. Then will you see to him?' said Poltorátsky, and flourishing his whip he rode at a fast trot to meet Vorontsóv.

Vorontsóv was riding his thoroughbred English chestnut gelding, and was accompanied by the adjutant, a Cossack, and a Chechen interpreter.

'What's happening here?' asked Vorontsóv.

'Why, a skirmishing party attacked our advanced line,' Poltorátsky answered.

'Come, come – you arranged the whole thing yourself!'

'Oh no, Prince, not I,' said Poltorátsky with a smile; 'they pushed forward of their own accord.'

'I hear a soldier has been wounded?'

'Yes, it's a great pity. He's a good soldier.'

'Seriously?'

'Seriously, I believe . . . in the stomach.'

'And do you know where I am going?' Vorontsóv asked.

'I don't.'

'Can't you guess?'

'No.'

'Hadji Murád has surrendered and we are now going to meet him.'

'You don't mean to say so?'

'His envoy came to me yesterday,' said Vorontsóv, with difficulty repressing a smile of pleasure. 'He will be waiting for me at the Shalín glade in a few minutes. Place sharpshooters as far as the glade, and then come and join me.'

'I understand,' said Poltorátsky, lifting his hand to his cap, and rode back to his company. He led the sharpshooters to the right himself, and ordered the sergeant-major to do the same on the left side.

The wounded Avdéev had meanwhile been taken back to the fort by some of the soldiers.

On his way back to rejoin Vorontsóv, Poltorátsky noticed behind him several horsemen who were overtaking him. In front on a white-maned horse rode a man of imposing appearance. He wore a turban and carried weapons with gold ornaments. This man was Hadji Murád. He approached Poltorátsky and said something to him in Tartar. Raising his eyebrows, Poltorátsky made a gesture with his arms to show that he did not understand, and smiled. Hadji Murád gave him smile for smile, and that smile struck Poltorátsky by its childlike kindliness. Poltorátsky had never expected to see the terrible mountain chief look like that. He had expected to see a morose, hard-featured man, and here was a vivacious person whose smile was so kindly that Poltorátsky felt as if he were an old acquaintance. He had only one peculiarity: his eyes, set wide apart, which gazed from under their black brows calmly, attentively, and penetratingly into the eyes of others.

Hadji Murád's suite consisted of five men, among them Khan Mahomá, who had been to see Prince Vorontsóv that night. He was a rosy, round-faced fellow with black lashless eyes and a beaming expression, full of the joy of life. Then there was the Avar Khanéfi, a thick-set, hairy man, whose eyebrows met. He was in charge of all Hadji Murád's property and led a stud-bred horse which carried tightly packed saddlebags. Two men of the suite were particularly striking. The first was a Lesghian: a youth, broad-shouldered but with a waist as slim as a woman's, beautiful ram-like eyes, and the beginnings of a brown beard. This was Eldár. The other, Gamzálo, was a Chechen with a short red beard and no eyebrows or eyelashes; he was blind in one eye and had a scar across his nose and face. Poltorátsky pointed out Vorontsóv, who had just appeared on the road. Hadji Murád rode to meet him, and putting his right hand on his heart said something in Tartar and stopped. The Chechen interpreter translated.

'He says, "I surrender myself to the will of the Russian Tsar. I wish to serve him," he says. "I wished to do so long ago but Shamil would not let me."'

Having heard what the interpreter said, Vorontsóv stretched out his hand in its wash-leather glove to Hadji Murád. Hadji Murád looked at it hesitatingly for a moment and then pressed it firmly, again saying something and looking first at the interpreter and then at Vorontsóv.

'He says he did not wish to surrender to anyone but you, as you are the son of the Sirdar and he respects you much.'

Vorontsóv nodded to express his thanks. Hadji Murád again said something, pointing to his suite.

'He says that these men, his henchmen, will serve the Russians as well as he.'

Vorontsóv turned towards them and nodded to them too. The merry, black-eyed, lashless Chechen, Khan Mahomá, also nodded and said something which was probably amusing, for the hairy Avar drew his lips into a smile, showing his ivory-white teeth. But the red-haired Gamzálo's one red eye just glanced at Vorontsóv and then was again fixed on the ears of his horse.

When Vorontsóv and Hadji Murád with their retinues rode back to the fort, the soldiers released from the lines gathered in groups and made their own comments.

'What a lot of men that damned fellow has destroyed! And now see what a fuss they will make of him!'

'Naturally. He was Shamil's right hand, and now – no fear!'

'Still there's no denying it! he's a fine fellow – a regular *dzhigít!*'

'And the red one! He squints at you like a beast!'

'Ugh! He must be a hound!'

They had all specially noticed the red one. Where the wood-felling was going on the soldiers nearest to the road ran out to look. Their officer shouted to them, but Vorontsóv stopped him.

'Let them have a look at their old friend.'

'You know who that is?' he added, turning to the nearest soldier, and speaking the words slowly with his English accent.

'No, your Excellency.'

'Hadji Murád. . . . Heard of him?'

'How could we help it, your Excellency? We've beaten him many a time!'

'Yes, and we've had it hot from him too.'

'Yes, that's true, your Excellency,' answered the soldier, pleased to be talking with his chief.

Hadji Murád understood that they were speaking about him, and smiled brightly with his eyes.

Vorontsóv returned to the fort in a very cheerful mood.

VI

YOUNG Vorontsóv was much pleased that it was he, and no one else, who had succeeded in winning over and receiving Hadji Murád – next to Shamil Russia's chief and most active enemy. There was only one unpleasant thing about it: General Meller-Zakomélsky was in command of the army at Vozd-vízhensk, and the whole affair ought to have been carried out through him. As Vorontsóv had done everything himself without reporting it there might be some unpleasantness, and this thought rather interfered with his satisfaction. On reaching his house he entrusted Hadji Murád's henchmen to the regimental adjutant and himself showed Hadji Murád into the house.

Princess Márya Vasílevna, elegantly dressed and smiling, and her little son, a handsome curly-headed child of six, met Hadji Murád in the drawing-room. The latter placed his hands on his heart, and through the interpreter – who had entered with him – said with solemnity that he regarded himself as the prince's *kunák*, since the prince had brought him into his own house; and that a *kunák*'s whole family was as sacred as the *kunák* himself.

Hadji Murád's appearance and manners pleased Márya Vasílevna, and the fact that he flushed when she held out her large white hand to him inclined her still more in his favour.

She invited him to sit down, and having asked him whether he drank coffee, had some served. He, however, declined it when it came. He understood a little Russian but could not speak it. When something was said which he could not understand he smiled, and his smile pleased Márya Vasílevna just as it had pleased Poltorátsky. The curly-haired, keen-eyed little boy (whom his mother called Búlka) standing beside her did not take his eyes off Hadji Murád, whom he had always heard spoken of as a great warrior.

Leaving Hadji Murád with his wife, Vorontsóv went to his office to do what was necessary about reporting the fact of Hadji Murád's having come over to the Russians. When he had written a report to the general in command of the left flank – General Kozlóvsky – at Grózny, and a letter to his father, Vorontsóv hurried home, afraid that his wife might be vexed with him for forcing on her this terrible stranger, who had to be treated in such a way that he should not take offence, and yet not too kindly. But his fears were needless. Hadji Murád was sitting in an arm-chair with little Búlka, Vorontsóv's stepson, on his knee, and with bent head was listening attentively to the interpreter who was translating to him the words of the laughing Márya Vasílevna. Márya Vasílevna was telling him that if every time a kunák admired anything of his he made him a present of it, he would soon have to go about like Adam....

When the prince entered, Hadji Murád rose at once and, surprising and offending Búlka by putting him off his knee, changed the playful expression of his face to a stern and serious one. He only sat down again when Vorontsóv had himself taken a seat.

Continuing the conversation he answered Márya Vasílevna by telling her that it was a law among his people that anything your kunák admired must be presented to him.

'Thy son, kunák!' he said in Russian, patting the curly head of the boy who had again climbed on his knee.

'He is delightful, your brigand!' said Márya Vasílevna to her husband in French. 'Búlka has been admiring his dagger, and he has given it to him.'

Búlka showed the dagger to his father. '*C'est un objet de prix!*'[1] added she.

'*Il faudra trouver l'occasion de lui faire cadeau,*'[2] said Vorontsóv.

Hadji Murád, his eyes turned down, sat stroking the boy's curly hair and saying: '*Dzhigít, dzhigít!*'

'A beautiful, beautiful dagger,' said Vorontsóv, half drawing out the sharpened blade which had a ridge down the centre. 'I thank thee!'

'Ask him what I can do for him,' he said to the interpreter.

The interpreter translated, and Hadji Murád at once replied that he wanted nothing but that he begged to be taken to a place where he could say his prayers.

Vorontsóv called his valet and told him to do what Hadji Murád desired.

As soon as Hadji Murád was alone in the room allotted to him his face altered. The pleased expression, now kindly and now stately, vanished, and a look of anxiety showed itself. Vorontsóv had received him far better than Hadji Murád had expected. But the better the reception the less did Hadji Murád trust Vorontsóv and his officers. He feared everything: that he might be seized, chained, and sent to Siberia, or simply killed; and therefore he was on his guard. He asked Eldár, when the latter entered his room, where his *murids* had been put and whether their arms had been taken from them, and where the horses were. Eldár reported that the horses were in the prince's stables; that the men had been placed in a barn; that they retained their arms, and that the interpreter was giving them food and tea.

Hadji Murád shook his head in doubt, and after undressing said his prayers and told Eldár to bring him his silver dagger. He then dressed, and having fastened his belt sat down on the divan with his legs tucked under him, to await what might befall him.

At four in the afternoon the interpreter came to call him to dine with the prince.

1 'It is a thing of value.'
2 'We must find an opportunity to make him a present.'

At dinner he hardly ate anything except some *pilau*, to which he helped himself from the very part of the dish from which Márya Vasílevna had helped herself.

'He is afraid we shall poison him,' Márya Vasílevna remarked to her husband. 'He has helped himself from the place where I took my helping.' Then instantly turning to Hadji Murád she asked him through the interpreter when he would pray again. Hadji Murád lifted five fingers and pointed to the sun. 'Then it will soon be time,' and Vorontsóv drew out his watch and pressed a spring. The watch struck four and one quarter. This evidently surprised Hadji Murád, and he asked to hear it again and to be allowed to look at the watch.

'*Voilà l'occasion! Donnez-lui la montre,*'[1] said the princess to her husband.

Vorontsóv at once offered the watch to Hadji Murád.

The latter placed his hand on his breast and took the watch. He touched the spring several times, listened, and nodded his head approvingly.

After dinner, Meller-Zakomélsky's aide-de-camp was announced.

The aide-de-camp informed the prince that the general, having heard of Hadji Murád's arrival, was highly displeased that this had not been reported to him, and required Hadji Murád to be brought to him without delay. Vorontsóv replied that the general's command should be obeyed, and through the interpreter informed Hadji Murád of these orders and asked him to go to Meller with him.

When Márya Vasílevna heard what the aide-de-camp had come about, she at once understood that unpleasantness might arise between her husband and the general, and in spite of all her husband's attempts to dissuade her, decided to go with him and Hadji Murád.

'*Vous feriez bien mieux de rester – c'est mon affaire, non pas la vôtre. . . .*'

[1] 'This is the opportunity! Give him the watch.'

'*Vous ne pouvez pas m'empêcher d'aller voir madame la générale!*'[1]

'You could go some other time.'

'But I wish to go now!'

There was no help for it, so Vorontsóv agreed, and they all three went.

When they entered, Meller with sombre politeness conducted Márya Vasílevna to his wife and told his aide-de-camp to show Hadji Murád into the waiting-room and not let him out till further orders.

'Please . . .' he said to Vorontsóv, opening the door of his study and letting the prince enter before him.

Having entered the study he stopped in front of Vorontsóv and, without offering him a seat, said:

'I am in command here and therefore all negotiations with the enemy have to be carried on through me! Why did you not report to me that Hadji Murád had come over?'

'An emissary came to me and announced his wish to capitulate only to me,' replied Vorontsóv growing pale with excitement, expecting some rude expression from the angry general and at the same time becoming infected with his anger.

'I ask you why I was not informed?'

'I intended to inform you, Baron, but . . .'

'You are not to address me as "Baron", but as "Your Excellency"!' And here the baron's pent-up irritation suddenly broke out and he uttered all that had long been boiling in his soul.

'I have not served my sovereign twenty-seven years in order that men who began their service yesterday, relying on family connexions, should give orders under my very nose about matters that do not concern them!'

'Your Excellency, I request you not to say things that are incorrect!' interrupted Vorontsóv.

'I am saying what is correct, and I won't allow . . .' said the general, still more irritably.

---

[1] 'You would do much better to remain at home . . . this is my business, and not yours.'

'You cannot prevent my going to see the general's wife!'

But at that moment Márya Vasílevna entered, rustling with her skirts and followed by a modest-looking little lady, Meller-Zakomélsky's wife.

'Come, come, Baron! Simon did not wish to displease you,' began Márya Vasílevna.

'I am not speaking about that, Princess. . . .'

'Well, well, let's forget it all! . . . You know, "A bad peace is better than a good quarrel!" . . . Oh dear, what am I saying?' and she laughed.

The angry general capitulated to the enchanting laugh of the beauty. A smile hovered under his moustache.

'I confess I was wrong,' said Vorontsóv, 'but —'

'And I too got rather carried away,' said Meller, and held out his hand to the prince.

Peace was re-established, and it was decided to leave Hadji Murád with the general for the present, and then to send him to the commander of the left flank.

Hadji Murád sat in the next room and though he did not understand what was said, he understood what it was necessary for him to understand – namely, that they were quarrelling about him, that his desertion of Shamil was a matter of immense importance to the Russians, and that therefore not only would they not exile or kill him, but that he would be able to demand much from them. He also understood that though Meller-Zakomélsky was the commanding-officer, he had not as much influence as his subordinate Vorontsóv, and that Vorontsóv was important and Meller-Zakomélsky un-important; and therefore when Meller-Zakomélsky sent for him and began to question him, Hadji Murád bore himself proudly and ceremoniously, saying that he had come from the mountains to serve the White Tsar and would give account only to his Sirdar, meaning the commander-in-chief, Prince Vorontsóv senior, in Tiflis.

VII

THE wounded Avdéev was taken to the hospital – a small wooden building roofed with boards at the entrance of the fort

– and was placed on one of the empty beds in the common ward. There were four patients in the ward: one ill with typhus and in high fever; another, pale, with dark shadows under his eyes, who had ague, was just expecting another attack and yawned continually; and two more who had been wounded in a raid three weeks before: one in the hand – he was up – and the other in the shoulder. The latter was sitting on a bed. All of them except the typhus patient surrounded and questioned the newcomer and those who had brought him.

'Sometimes they fire as if they were spilling peas over you, and nothing happens . . . and this time only about five shots were fired,' related one of the bearers.

'Each man gets what fate sends!'

'Oh!' groaned Avdéev loudly, trying to master his pain when they began to place him on the bed; but he stopped groaning when he was on it, and only frowned and moved his feet continually. He held his hands over his wound and looked fixedly before him.

The doctor came, and gave orders to turn the wounded man over to see whether the bullet had passed out behind.

'What's this?' the doctor asked, pointing to the large white scars that crossed one another on the patient's back and loins.

'That was done long ago, your honour!' replied Avdéev with a groan.

They were scars left by the flogging Avdéev had received for the money he drank.

Avdéev was again turned over, and the doctor probed in his stomach for a long time and found the bullet, but failed to extract it. He put a dressing on the wound, and having stuck plaster over it went away. During the whole time the doctor was probing and bandaging the wound Avdéev lay with clenched teeth and closed eyes, but when the doctor had gone he opened them and looked around as though amazed. His eyes were turned on the other patients and on the surgeon's orderly, though he seemed to see not them but something else that surprised him.

His friends Panóv and Serógin came in, but Avdéev continued to lie in the same position looking before him with surprise. It was long before he recognized his comrades, though his eyes gazed straight at them.

'I say, Peter, have you no message to send home?' said Panóv.

Avdéev did not answer, though he was looking Panóv in the face.

'I say, haven't you any orders to send home?' again repeated Panóv, touching Avdéev's cold, large-boned hand.

Avdéev seemed to come to.

'Ah! . . . Panóv!'

'Yes, I'm here . . . I've come! Have you nothing for home? Serógin would write a letter.'

'Serógin . . .' said Avdéev moving his eyes with difficulty towards Serógin, 'will you write? . . . Well then, write so: "Your son," say, "Peter, has given orders that you should live long.[1] He envied his brother" . . . I told you about that to-day . . . "and now he is himself glad. Don't worry him. . . . Let him live. God grant it him. I am glad!" Write that.'

Having said this he was silent for some time with his eyes fixed on Panóv.

'And did you find your pipe?' he suddenly asked.

Panóv did not reply.

'Your pipe . . . your pipe! I mean, have you found it?' Avdéev repeated.

'It was in my bag.'

'That's right! . . . Well, and now give me a candle to hold . . . I am going to die,' said Avdéev.

Just then Poltorátsky came in to inquire after his soldier.

'How goes it, my lad! Badly?' said he.

Avdéev closed his eyes and shook his head negatively. His broad-cheeked face was pale and stern. He did not reply, but again said to Panóv:

'Bring a candle. . . . I am going to die.'

A wax taper was placed in his hand but his fingers would not bend, so it was placed between them and held up for him.

---

1 A popular expression, meaning that the sender of the message is already dead.

Poltorátsky went away, and five minutes later the orderly put his ear to Avdéev's heart and said that all was over.

Avdéev's death was described in the following manner in the report sent to Tiflis:

'*23rd Nov.* – Two companies of the Kurín regiment advanced from the fort on a wood-felling expedition. At mid-day a considerable number of mountaineers suddenly attacked the wood-fellers. The sharpshooters began to retreat, but the 2nd Company charged with the bayonet and overthrew the mountaineers. In this affair two privates were slightly wounded and one killed. The mountaineers lost about a hundred men killed and wounded.'

VIII

ON the day Peter Avdéev died in the hospital at Vozdvízhensk, his old father with the wife of the brother in whose stead he had enlisted, and that brother's daughter – who was already approaching womanhood and almost of age to get married – were threshing oats on the hard-frozen threshing-floor.

There had been a heavy fall of snow the previous night, followed towards morning by a severe frost. The old man woke when the cocks were crowing for the third time, and seeing the bright moonlight through the frozen window-panes got down from the stove, put on his boots, his sheepskin coat and cap, and went out to the threshing-floor. Having worked there for a couple of hours he returned to the hut and awoke his son and the women. When the woman and the girl came to the threshing-floor they found it ready swept, with a wooden shovel sticking in the dry white snow, beside which were birch brooms with the twigs upwards and two rows of oat-sheaves laid ears to ears in a long line the whole length of the clean threshing-floor. They chose their flails and started threshing, keeping time with their triple blows. The old man struck powerfully with his heavy flail, breaking the straw, the girl struck the ears from above with measured blows, and the daughter-in-law turned the oats over with her flail.

The moon had set, dawn was breaking, and they were finishing the line of sheaves when Akím, the eldest son, in his sheepskin and cap, joined the threshers.

'What are you lazing about for?' shouted his father to him, pausing in his work and leaning on his flail.

'The horses had to be seen to.'

'"Horses seen to!"' the father repeated, mimicking him. 'The old woman will look after them. . . . Take your flail! You're getting too fat, you drunkard!'

'Have you been standing me treat?' muttered the son.

'What?' said the old man, frowning sternly and missing a stroke.

The son silently took a flail and they began threshing with four flails.

'Trak, tapatam . . . trak, tapatam . . . trak . . .' came down the old man's heavy flail after the three others.

'Why, you've got a nape like a goodly gentleman! . . . Look here, my trousers have hardly anything to hang on!' said the old man, omitting his stroke and only swinging his flail in the air so as not to get out of time.

They had finished the row, and the women began removing the straw with rakes.

'Peter was a fool to go in your stead. They'd have knocked the nonsense out of you in the army, and he was worth five of such as you at home!'

'That's enough, father,' said the daughter-in-law, as she threw aside the binders that had come off the sheaves.

'Yes, feed the six of you and get no work out of a single one! Peter used to work for two. He was not like . . .'

Along the trodden path from the house came the old man's wife, the frozen snow creaking under the new bark shoes she wore over her tightly wound woollen leg-bands. The men were shovelling the unwinnowed grain into heaps, the woman and the girl sweeping up what remained.

'The Elder has been and orders everybody to go and work for the master, carting bricks,' said the old woman. 'I've got breakfast ready. . . . Come along, won't you?'

'All right. . . . Harness the roan and go,' said the old man to Akím, 'and you'd better look out that you don't get me into trouble as you did the other day! . . . I can't help regretting Peter!'

'When he was at home you used to scold him,' retorted Akím. 'Now he's away you keep nagging at me.'

'That shows you deserve it,' said his mother in the same angry tones. 'You'll never be Peter's equal.'

'Oh, all right,' said the son.

'"All right," indeed! You've drunk the meal, and now you say "all right!"'

'Let bygones be bygones!' said the daughter-in-law.

The disagreements between father and son had begun long ago – almost from the time Peter went as a soldier. Even then the old man felt that he had parted with an eagle for a cuckoo. It is true that it was right – as the old man understood it – for a childless man to go in place of a family man. Akím had four children and Peter had none; but Peter was a worker like his father, skilful, observant, strong, enduring, and above all industrious. He was always at work. If he happened to pass by where people were working he lent a helping hand as his father would have done, and took a turn or two with the scythe, or loaded a cart, or felled a tree, or chopped some wood. The old man regretted his going away, but there was no help for it. Conscription in those days was like death. A soldier was a severed branch, and to think about him at home was to tear one's heart uselessly. Only occasionally, to prick his elder son, did the father mention him, as he had done that day. But his mother often thought of her younger son, and for a long time – more than a year now – she had been asking her husband to send Peter a little money, but the old man had made no response.

The Kúrenkovs were a well-to-do family and the old man had some savings hidden away, but he would on no account have consented to touch what he had laid by. Now however the old woman having heard him mention their younger son, made up her mind to ask him again to send him at least a ruble after selling the oats. This she did. As soon as the young people had gone to work for the proprietor and the old folk were left alone together, she persuaded him to send Peter a ruble out of the oats-money.

So when ninety-six bushels of the winnowed oats had been packed onto three sledges lined with sacking carefully pinned together at the top with wooden skewers, she gave her husband a letter the church clerk had written at her dictation, and the old man promised when he got to town to enclose a ruble and send it off to the right address.

The old man, dressed in a new sheepskin with a homespun cloak over it, his legs wrapped round with warm white woollen leg-bands, took the letter, placed it in his wallet, said a prayer, got into the front sledge, and drove to town. His grandson drove in the last sledge. When he reached town the old man asked the inn-keeper to read the letter to him, and listened to it attentively and approvingly.

In her letter Peter's mother first sent him her blessing, then greetings from everybody and the news of his godfather's death, and at the end she added that Aksínya (Peter's wife) had not wished to stay with them but had gone into service, where they heard she was living honestly and well. Then came a reference to the present of a ruble, and finally a message which the old woman, yielding to her sorrow, had dictated with tears in her eyes and the church clerk had taken down exactly, word for word:

'One thing more, my darling child, my sweet dove, my own Peterkin! I have wept my eyes out lamenting for thee, thou light of my eyes. To whom hast thou left me?...' At this point the old woman had sobbed and wept, and said: 'That will do!' So the words stood in the letter; but it was not fated that Peter should receive the news of his wife's having left home, nor the present of the ruble, nor his mother's last words. The letter with the money in it came back with the announcement that Peter had been killed in the war, 'defending his Tsar, his Fatherland, and the Orthodox Faith'. That is how the army clerk expressed it.

The old woman, when this news reached her, wept for as long as she could spare time, and then set to work again. The very next Sunday she went to church and had a requiem chanted and Peter's name entered among those for whose souls prayers were to be said, and she distributed bits of holy bread to all the good people in memory of Peter, the servant of God.

Aksínya, his widow, also lamented loudly when she heard of the death of her beloved husband with whom she had lived but one short year. She regretted her husband and her own ruined life, and in her lamentations mentioned Peter's brown locks and his love, and the sadness of her life with her little orphaned Vánka, and bitterly reproached Peter for having had pity on his brother but none on her – obliged to wander among strangers!

But in the depth of her soul Aksínya was glad of her husband's death. She was pregnant a second time by the shopman with whom she was living, and no one would now have a right to scold her, and the shopman could marry her as he had said he would when he was persuading her to yield.

IX

MICHAEL Semënovich Vorontsóv, being the son of the Russian Ambassador, had been educated in England and possessed a European education quite exceptional among the higher Russian officials of his day. He was ambitious, gentle and kind in his manner with inferiors, and a finished courtier with superiors. He did not understand life without power and submission. He had obtained all the highest ranks and decorations and was looked upon as a clever commander, and even as the conqueror of Napoleon at Krásnoe.[1]

In 1852 he was over seventy, but young for his age, he moved briskly, and above all was in full possession of a facile, refined, and agreeable intellect which he used to maintain his power and strengthen and increase his popularity. He possessed large means – his own and his wife's (who had been a Countess Branítski) – and received an enormous salary as Viceroy, and he spent a great part of his means on building a palace and laying out a garden on the south coast of the Crimea.

1 A town thirty miles south-west of Smolensk, at which, in November 1812, the rear-guard of Napoleon's army was defeated during the retreat from Moscow. It is mentioned in *War and Peace*.

On the evening of December the 4th, 1852, a courier's troyka drew up before his palace in Tiflis. An officer, tired and black with dust, sent by General Kozlóvski with the news of Hadji Murád's surrender to the Russians, entered the wide porch, stretching the stiffened muscles of his legs as he passed the sentinel. It was six o'clock, and Vorontsóv was just going in to dinner when he was informed of the courier's arrival. He received him at once, and was therefore a few minutes late for dinner.

When he entered the drawing-room the thirty persons invited to dine, who were sitting beside Princess Elizabeth Ksavérevna Vorontsóva, or standing in groups by the windows, turned their faces towards him. Vorontsóv was dressed in his usual black military coat, with shoulder-straps but no epaulettes, and wore the White Cross of the Order of St George at his neck.

His clean-shaven, foxlike face wore a pleasant smile as, screwing up his eyes, he surveyed the assembly. Entering with quick soft steps he apologized to the ladies for being late, greeted the men, and approaching Princess Manana Orbelyáni – a tall, fine, handsome woman of Oriental type about forty-five years of age – he offered her his arm to take her in to dinner. Princess Elizabeth Ksavérevna Vorontsóva gave her arm to a red-haired general with bristly moustaches who was visiting Tiflis. A Georgian prince offered his arm to Princess Vorontsóva's friend, Countess Choiseuil. Doctor Andréevsky, the aide-de-camp, and others, with ladies or without, followed these first couples. Footmen in livery and knee-breeches drew back and replaced the guests' chairs when they sat down, while the major-domo ceremoniously ladled out steaming soup from a silver tureen.

Vorontsóv took his place in the centre of one side of the long table, and his wife sat opposite, with the general on her right. On the prince's right sat his lady, the beautiful Orbelyáni; and on his left was a graceful, dark, red-cheeked Georgian woman, glittering with jewels and incessantly smiling.

'*Excellentes, chère amie!*'[1] replied Vorontsóv to his wife's inquiry about what news the courier had brought him. '*Simon a eu de la chance!*'[2] And he began to tell aloud, so that everyone could hear, the striking news (for him alone not quite unexpected, because negotiations had long been going on) that Hadji Murád, the bravest and most famous of Shamil's officers, had come over to the Russians and would in a day or two be brought to Tiflis.

Everybody – even the young aides-de-camp and officials who sat at the far ends of the table and who had been quietly laughing at something among themselves – became silent and listened.

'And you, General, have you ever met this Hadji Murád?' asked the princess of her neighbour, the carroty general with the bristly moustaches, when the prince had finished speaking.

'More than once, Princess.'

And the general went on to tell how Hadji Murád, after the mountaineers had captured Gergebel in 1843, had fallen upon General Pahlen's detachment and killed Colonel Zolotúkhin almost before their very eyes.

Vorontsóv listened to the general and smiled amiably, evidently pleased that the latter had joined in the conversation. But suddenly his face assumed an absent-minded and depressed expression.

The general, having started talking, had begun to tell of his second encounter with Hadji Murád.

'Why, it was he, if your Excellency will please remember,' said the general, 'who arranged the ambush that attacked the rescue party in the "Biscuit" expedition.'

'Where?' asked Vorontsóv, screwing up his eyes.

What the brave general spoke of as the 'rescue' was the affair in the unfortunate Dargo campaign in which a whole detachment, including Prince Vorontsóv who commanded it, would certainly have perished had it not been rescued by the arrival of fresh troops. Everyone knew that the whole Dargo campaign

1 'Excellent, my dear!'
2 'Simon has had good luck.'

under Vorontsóv's command — in which the Russians lost many killed and wounded and several cannon — had been a shameful affair, and therefore if anyone mentioned it in Vorontsóv's presence they did so only in the aspect in which Vorontsóv had reported it to the Tsar — as a brilliant achievement of the Russian army. But the word 'rescue' plainly indicated that it was not a brilliant victory but a blunder costing many lives. Everybody understood this and some pretended not to notice the meaning of the general's words, others nervously waited to see what would follow, while a few exchanged glances and smiled. Only the carroty general with the bristly moustaches noticed nothing, and carried away by his narrative quietly replied:

'At the rescue, your Excellency.'

Having started on his favourite theme, the general recounted circumstantially how Hadji Murád had so cleverly cut the detachment in two that if the rescue party had not arrived (he seemed to be particularly fond of repeating the word 'rescue') not a man in the division would have escaped, because . . . He did not finish his story, for Manana Orbelyáni having understood what was happening, interrupted him by asking if he had found comfortable quarters in Tiflis. The general, surprised, glanced at everybody all round and saw his aides-de-camp from the end of the table looking fixedly and significantly at him, and he suddenly understood! Without replying to the princess's question, he frowned, became silent, and began hurriedly swallowing the delicacy that lay on his plate, the appearance and taste of which both completely mystified him.

Everybody felt uncomfortable, but the awkwardness of the situation was relieved by the Georgian prince — a very stupid man but an extraordinarily refined and artful flatterer and courtier — who sat on the other side of Princess Vorontsóva. Without seeming to have noticed anything he began to relate how Hadji Murád had carried off the widow of Akhmet Khan of Mekhtulí.

'He came into the village at night, seized what he wanted, and galloped off again with the whole party.'

'Why did he want that particular woman?' asked the princess.

'Oh, he was her husband's enemy, and pursued him but could never once succeed in meeting him right up to the time of his death, so he revenged himself on the widow.'

The princess translated this into French for her old friend Countess Choiseuil, who sat next to the Georgian prince.

'*Quelle horreur!*'[1] said the countess, closing her eyes and shaking her head.

'Oh no!' said Vorontsóv, smiling. 'I have been told that he treated his captive with chivalrous respect and afterwards released her.'

'Yes, for a ransom!'

'Well, of course. But all the same he acted honourably.'

These words of Vorontsóv's set the tone for the further conversation. The courtiers understood that the more importance was attributed to Hadji Murád the better the prince would be pleased.

'The man's audacity is amazing. A remarkable man!'

'Why, in 1849 he dashed into Temir Khan Shurá and plundered the shops in broad daylight.'

An Armenian sitting at the end of the table, who had been in Temir Khan Shurá at the time, related the particulars of that exploit of Hadji Murád's.

In fact, Hadji Murád was the sole topic of conversation during the whole dinner.

Everybody in succession praised his courage, his ability, and his magnanimity. Someone mentioned his having ordered twenty-six prisoners to be killed, but that too was met by the usual rejoinder, 'What's to be done? *À la guerre, comme à la guerre!*'[2]

'He is a great man.'

'Had he been born in Europe he might have been another Napoleon,' said the stupid Georgian prince with a gift of flattery.

---

1 'How horrible!'
2 'War is war.'

He knew that every mention of Napoleon was pleasant to Vorontsóv, who wore the White Cross at his neck as a reward for having defeated him.

'Well, not Napoleon perhaps, but a gallant cavalry general if you like,' said Vorontsóv.

'If not Napoleon, then Murat.'

'And his name is Hadji *Murád!*'

'Hadji Murád has surrendered and now there'll be an end to Shamil too,' someone remarked.

'They feel that now' (this 'now' meant under Vorontsóv) 'they can't hold out,' remarked another.

'*Tout cela est grâce à vous!*'[1] said Manana Orbelyáni.

Prince Vorontsóv tried to moderate the waves of flattery which began to flow over him. Still, it was pleasant, and in the best of spirits he led his lady back into the drawing-room.

After dinner, when coffee was being served in the drawing-room, the prince was particularly amiable to everybody, and going up to the general with the red bristly moustaches he tried to appear not to have noticed his blunder.

Having made a round of the visitors he sat down to the card-table. He only played the old-fashioned game of ombre. His partners were the Georgian prince, an Armenian general (who had learnt the game of ombre from Prince Vorontsóv's valet), and Doctor Andréevsky, a man remarkable for the great influence he exercised.

Placing beside him his gold snuff-box with a portrait of Alexander I on the lid, the prince tore open a pack of highly glazed cards and was going to spread them out, when his Italian valet, Giovanni, brought him a letter on a silver tray.

'Another courier, your Excellency.'

Vorontsóv laid down the cards, excused himself, opened the letter, and began to read.

The letter was from his son, who described Hadji Murád's surrender and his own encounter with Meller-Zakomélsky.

The princess came up and inquired what their son had written.

1 'All this is thanks to you!'

'It's all about the same matter. . . . *Il a eu quelques désagréments avec le commandant de la place. Simon a eu tort.*[1] . . . But "All's well that ends well",' he added in English, handing the letter to his wife; and turning to his respectfully waiting partners he asked them to draw cards.

When the first round had been dealt Vorontsóv did what he was in the habit of doing when in a particularly pleasant mood: with his white, wrinkled old hand he took out a pinch of French snuff, carried it to his nose, and released it.

X

WHEN Hadji Murád appeared at the prince's palace next day, the waiting-room was already full of people. Yesterday's general with the bristly moustaches was there in full uniform with all his decorations, having come to take leave. There was the commander of a regiment who was in danger of being court-martialled for misappropriating commissariat money, and there was a rich Armenian (patronized by Doctor Andréevsky) who wanted to obtain from the Government a renewal of his monopoly for the sale of vodka. There, dressed in black, was the widow of an officer who had been killed in action. She had come to ask for a pension, or for free education for her children. There was a ruined Georgian prince in a magnificent Georgian costume who was trying to obtain for himself some confiscated church property. There was an official with a large roll of paper containing a new plan for subjugating the Caucasus. There was also a Khan who had come solely to be able to tell his people at home that he had called on the prince.

They all waited their turn and were one by one shown into the prince's cabinet and out again by the aide-de-camp, a handsome, fair-haired youth.

When Hadji Murád entered the waiting-room with his brisk though limping step all eyes were turned towards him and he heard his name whispered from various parts of the room.

[1] 'He has had some unpleasantness with the commandant of the place. Simon was in the wrong.'

He was dressed in a long white Circassian coat over a brown *beshmét* trimmed round the collar with fine silver lace. He wore black leggings and soft shoes of the same colour which were stretched over his instep as tight as gloves. On his head he wore a high cap draped turban-fashion – that same turban for which, on the denunciation of Akhmet Khan, he had been arrested by General Klügenau and which had been the cause of his going over to Shamil.

He stepped briskly across the parquet floor of the waiting-room, his whole slender figure swaying slightly in consequence of his lameness in one leg which was shorter than the other. His eyes, set far apart, looked calmly before him and seemed to see no one.

The handsome aide-de-camp, having greeted him, asked him to take a seat while he went to announce him to the prince, but Hadji Murád declined to sit down and, putting his hand on his dagger, stood with one foot advanced, looking round contemptuously at all those present.

The prince's interpreter, Prince Tarkhánov, approached Hadji Murád and spoke to him. Hadji Murád answered abruptly and unwillingly. A Kumýk prince, who was there to lodge a complaint against a police official, came out of the prince's room, and then the aide-de-camp called Hadji Murád, led him to the door of the cabinet, and showed him in.

The Commander-in-Chief received Hadji Murád standing beside his table, and his old white face did not wear yesterday's smile but was rather stern and solemn.

On entering the large room with its enormous table and great windows with green venetian blinds, Hadji Murád placed his small sunburnt hands on his chest just where the front of his white coat overlapped, and lowering his eyes began, without hurrying, to speak distinctly and respectfully, using the Kumýk dialect which he spoke well.

'I place myself under the powerful protection of the great Tsar and of yourself,' said he, 'and promise to serve the White Tsar in faith and truth to the last drop of my blood, and I hope to be useful to you in the war with Shamil who is my enemy and yours.'

Having heard the interpreter out, Vorontsóv glanced at Hadji Murád and Hadji Murád glanced at Vorontsóv.

The eyes of the two men met, and expressed to each other much that could not have been put into words and that was not at all what the interpreter said. Without words they told each other the whole truth. Vorontsóv's eyes said that he did not believe a single word Hadji Murád was saying, and that he knew he was and always would be an enemy to everything Russian and had surrendered only because he was obliged to. Hadji Murád understood this and yet continued to give assurances of his fidelity. His eyes said, 'That old man ought to be thinking of his death and not of war, but though he is old he is cunning, and I must be careful.' Vorontsóv understood this also, but nevertheless spoke to Hadji Murád in the way he considered necessary for the success of the war.

'Tell him', said Vorontsóv, 'that our sovereign is as merciful as he is mighty and will probably at my request pardon him and take him into his service. . . . Have you told him?' he asked, looking at Hadji Murád. . . . 'Until I receive my master's gracious decision, tell him I take it on myself to receive him and make his sojourn among us pleasant.'

Hadji Murád again pressed his hands to the centre of his chest and began to say something with animation.

'He says', the interpreter translated, 'that formerly, when he governed Avaria in 1839, he served the Russians faithfully and would never have deserted them had not his enemy, Akhmet Khan, wishing to ruin him, calumniated him to General Klügenau.'

'I know, I know,' said Vorontsóv (though if he had ever known he had long forgotten it). 'I know,' he repeated, sitting down and motioning Hadji Murád to the divan that stood beside the wall. But Hadji Murád did not sit down. Shrugging his powerful shoulders as a sign that he could not bring himself to sit in the presence of so important a man, he went on, addressing the interpreter:

'Akhmet Khan and Shamil are both my enemies. Tell the prince that Akhmet Khan is dead and I cannot revenge myself on him, but Shamil lives and I will not die without taking vengeance on him,' said he, knitting his brows and tightly closing his mouth.

'Yes, yes; but how does he want to revenge himself on Shamil?' said Vorontsóv quietly to the interpreter. 'And tell him he may sit down.'

Hadji Murád again declined to sit down, and in answer to the question replied that his object in coming over to the Russians was to help them to destroy Shamil.

'Very well, very well,' said Vorontsóv; 'but what exactly does he wish to do? . . . Sit down, sit down!'

Hadji Murád sat down, and said that if only they would send him to the Lesghian line and would give him an army, he would guarantee to raise the whole of Daghestan and Shamil would then be unable to hold out.

'That would be excellent. . . . I'll think it over,' said Vorontsóv.

The interpreter translated Vorontsóv's words to Hadji Murád.

Hadji Murád pondered.

'Tell the Sirdar one thing more,' Hadji Murád began again, 'that my family are in the hands of my enemy, and that as long as they are in the mountains I am bound and cannot serve him. Shamil would kill my wife and my mother and my children if I went openly against him. Let the prince first exchange my family for the prisoners he has, and then I will destroy Shamil or die!'

'All right, all right,' said Vorontsóv. 'I will think it over. . . . Now let him go to the chief of the staff and explain to him in detail his position, intentions, and wishes.'

Thus ended the first interview between Hadji Murád and Vorontsóv.

That evening an Italian opera was performed at the new theatre, which was decorated in Oriental style. Vorontsóv was in his box when the striking figure of the limping Hadji Murád wearing a turban appeared in the stalls. He came in with Lóris-Mélikov,[1] Vorontsóv's aide-de-camp, in whose charge he was placed, and took a seat in the front row. Having sat through the first act with Oriental Mohammedan dignity, expressing no pleasure but only obvious indifference, he rose and looking calmly round at the audience went out, drawing to himself everybody's attention.

The next day was Monday and there was the usual evening party at the Vorontsóvs'. In the large brightly lighted hall a band was playing, hidden among trees. Young women and women not very young wearing dresses that displayed their bare necks, arms, and breasts, turned round and round in the embrace of men in bright uniforms. At the buffet, footmen in red swallow-tail coats and wearing shoes and knee-breeches, poured out champagne and served sweetmeats to the ladies. The 'Sirdar's' wife also, in spite of her age, went about half-dressed among the visitors smiling affably, and through the interpreter said a few amiable words to Hadji Murád who glanced at the visitors with the same indifference he had shown yesterday in the theatre. After the hostess, other half-naked women came up to him and all of them stood shame-lessly before him and smilingly asked him the same question: How he liked what he saw? Vorontsóv himself, wearing gold epaulettes and gold shoulder-knots with his white cross and ribbon at his neck, came up and asked him the same question, evidently feeling sure, like all the others, that Hadji Murád could not help being pleased at what he saw. Hadji Murád replied to Vorontsóv as he had replied to them all, that among his people nothing of the kind was done, without expressing an opinion as to whether it was good or bad that it was so.

Here at the ball Hadji Murád tried to speak to Vorontsóv about buying out his family, but Vorontsóv, pretending that he had not heard him, walked away, and Lóris-Mélikov after-wards told Hadji Murád that this was not the place to talk about business.

---

1 Count Michael Tariélovich Lóris-Mélikov, who afterwards became Min-ister of the Interior and framed the Liberal ukase which was signed by Alexander II the day that he was assassinated.

When it struck eleven Hadji Murád, having made sure of the time by the watch the Vorontsóvs had given him, asked Lóris-Mélikov whether he might now leave. Lóris-Mélikov said he might, though it would be better to stay. In spite of this Hadji Murád did not stay, but drove in the phaeton placed at his disposal to the quarters that had been assigned to him.

XI

ON the fifth day of Hadji Murád's stay in Tiflis Lóris-Mélikov, the Viceroy's aide-de-camp, came to see him at the latter's command.

'My head and my hands are glad to serve the Sirdar,' said Hadji Murád with his usual diplomatic expression, bowing his head and putting his hands to his chest. 'Command me!' said he, looking amiably into Lóris-Mélikov's face.

Lóris-Mélikov sat down in an arm-chair placed by the table and Hadji Murád sank onto a low divan opposite and, resting his hands on his knees, bowed his head and listened attentively to what the other said to him.

Lóris-Mélikov, who spoke Tartar fluently, told him that though the prince knew about his past life, he yet wanted to hear the whole story from himself.

'Tell it me, and I will write it down and translate it into Russian and the prince will send it to the Emperor.'

Hadji Murád remained silent for a while (he never interrupted anyone but always waited to see whether his collocutor had not something more to say), then he raised his head, shook back his cap, and smiled the peculiar childlike smile that had captivated Márya Vasílevna.

'I can do that,' said he, evidently flattered by the thought that his story would be read by the Emperor.

'Thou must tell me' (in Tartar nobody is addressed as 'you') 'everything, deliberately from the beginning,' said Lóris-Mélikov drawing a notebook from his pocket.

'I can do that, only there is much – very much – to tell! Many events have happened!' said Hadji Murád.

'If thou canst not do it all in one day thou wilt finish it another time,' said Lóris-Mélikov.

'Shall I begin at the beginning?'

'Yes, at the very beginning...where thou wast born and where thou didst live.'

Hadji Murád's head sank and he sat in that position for a long time. Then he took a stick that lay beside the divan, drew a little knife with an ivory gold-inlaid handle, sharp as a razor, from under his dagger, and started whittling the stick with it and speaking at the same time.

'Write: Born in Tselméss, a small *aoul*, "the size of an ass's head", as we in the mountains say,' he began. 'Not far from it, about two cannon-shots, lies Khunzákh where the Khans lived. Our family was closely connected with them.

'My mother, when my eldest brother Osman was born, nursed the eldest Khan, Abu Nutsal Khan. Then she nursed the second son of the Khan, Umma Khan, and reared him; but Akhmet my second brother died, and when I was born and the Khansha bore Bulách Khan, my mother would not go as wet-nurse again. My father ordered her to, but she would not. She said: "I should again kill my own son, and I will not go." Then my father, who was passionate, struck her with a dagger and would have killed her had they not rescued her from him. So she did not give me up, and later on she composed a song...but I need not tell that.'

'Yes, you must tell everything. It is necessary,' said Lóris-Mélikov.

Hadji Murád grew thoughtful. He remembered how his mother had laid him to sleep beside her under a fur coat on the roof of the *sáklya*, and he had asked her to show him the place in her side where the scar of her wound was still visible.

He repeated the song, which he remembered:

'My white bosom was pierced by the blade of bright steel,
But I laid my bright sun, my dear boy, close upon it
Till his body was bathed in the stream of my blood.

And the wound healed without aid of herbs or of grass.
As I feared not death, so my boy will ne'er fear it.'

'My mother is now in Shamil's hands,' he added, 'and she must be rescued.'

He remembered the fountain below the hill, when holding on to his mother's *sharováry* (loose Turkish trousers) he had gone with her for water. He remembered how she had shaved his head for the first time, and how the reflection of his round bluish head in the shining brass vessel that hung on the wall had astonished him. He remembered a lean dog that had licked his face. He remembered the strange smell of the *lepéshki* (a kind of flat cake) his mother had given him – a smell of smoke and of sour milk. He remembered how his mother had carried him in a basket on her back to visit his grandfather at the farmstead. He remembered his wrinkled grandfather with his grey hairs, and how he had hammered silver with his sinewy hands.

'Well, so my mother did not go as nurse,' he said with a jerk of his head, 'and the Khansha took another nurse but still remained fond of my mother, and my mother used to take us children to the Khansha's palace, and we played with her children and she was fond of us.

'There were three young Khans: Abu Nutsal Khan my brother Osman's foster-brother; Umma Khan my own sworn brother; and Bulách Khan the youngest – whom Shamil threw over the precipice. But that happened later.

'I was about sixteen when *murids* began to visit the *aouls*. They beat the stones with wooden scimitars and cried, "Mussulmans, *Ghazavát!*" The Chechens all went over to Muridism and the Avars began to go over too. I was then living in the palace like a brother of the Khans. I could do as I liked, and I became rich. I had horses and weapons and money. I lived for pleasure and had no care, and went on like that till the time when Kazi-Mulla, the Imám, was killed and Hamzád succeeded him. Hamzád sent envoys to the Khans to say that if they did not join the *Ghazavát* he would destroy Khunzákh.

'This needed consideration. The Khans feared the Russians, but were also afraid to join in the Holy War. The old Khansha sent me with her second son, Umma Khan, to Tiflis to ask the Russian Commander-in-Chief for help against Hamzád. The Commander-in-Chief at Tiflis was Baron Rosen. He did not receive either me or Umma Khan. He sent word that he would help us, but did nothing. Only his officers came riding to us and played cards with Umma Khan. They made him drunk with wine and took him to bad places, and he lost all he had to them at cards. His body was as strong as a bull's and he was as brave as a lion, but his soul was weak as water. He would have gambled away his last horses and weapons if I had not made him come away.

'After visiting Tiflis my ideas changed and I advised the old Khansha and the Khans to join the *Ghazavát*. . . .'

'What made you change your mind?' asked Lóris-Mélikov. 'Were you not pleased with the Russians?'

Hadji Murád paused.

'No, I was not pleased,' he answered decidedly, closing his eyes. 'And there was also another reason why I wished to join the *Ghazavát*.'

'What was that?'

'Why, near Tselméss the Khan and I encountered three *murids*, two of whom escaped but the third one I shot with my pistol.

'He was still alive when I approached to take his weapons. He looked up at me, and said, "Thou hast killed me . . . I am happy; but thou art a Mussulman, young and strong. Join the *Ghazavát!* God wills it!"'

'And did you join it?'

'I did not, but it made me think,' said Hadji Murád, and he went on with his tale.

'When Hamzád approached Khunzákh we sent our Elders to him to say that we would agree to join the *Ghazavát* if the Imám would send a learned man to explain it to us. Hamzád had our Elders' moustaches shaved off, their nostrils pierced, and cakes hung to their noses, and in that condition he sent them back to us.

'The Elders brought word that Hamzád was ready to send a sheik to teach us the *Ghazavát*, but only if the Khansha sent him her youngest son as a hostage. She took him at his word and sent her youngest son, Bulách Khan. Hamzád received him well and sent to invite the two elder brothers also. He sent word that he wished to serve the Khans as his father had served their father.... The Khansha was a weak, stupid, and conceited woman, as all women are when they are not under control. She was afraid to send away both sons and sent only Umma Khan. I went with him. We were met by *murids* about a mile before we arrived and they sang and shot and caracoled around us, and when we drew near, Hamzád came out of his tent and went up to Umma Khan's stirrup and received him as a Khan. He said, "I have not done any harm to thy family and do not wish to do any. Only do not kill me and do not prevent my bringing the people over to the *Ghazavát*, and I will serve you with my whole army as my father served your father! Let me live in your house and I will help you·with my advice, and you shall do as you like!"

'Umma Khan was slow of speech. He did not know how to reply and remained silent. Then I said that if this was so, let Hamzád come to Khunzákh and the Khansha and the Khans would receive him with honour.... But I was not allowed to finish – and here I first encountered Shamil, who was beside the Imám. He said to me, "Thou hast not been asked.... It was the Khan!"

'I was silent, and Hamzád led Umma Khan into his tent. Afterwards Hamzád called me and ordered me to go to Khunzákh with his envoys. I went. The envoys began persuading the Khansha to send her eldest son also to Hamzád. I saw there was treachery and told her not to send him; but a woman has as much sense in her head as an egg has hair. She ordered her son to go. Abu Nutsal Khan did not wish to. Then she said, "I see thou art afraid!" Like a bee she knew where to sting him most painfully. Abu Nutsal Khan flushed and did not speak to her any more, but ordered his horse to be saddled. I went with him.

'Hamzád met us with even greater honour than he had shown Umma Khan. He himself rode out two rifle-shot lengths down the hill to meet us. A large party of horsemen with their banners followed him, and they too sang, shot, and caracoled.

'When we reached the camp, Hamzád led the Khan into his tent and I remained with the horses. . . .

'I was some way down the hill when I heard shots fired in Hamzád's tent. I ran there and saw Umma Khan lying prone in a pool of blood, and Abu Nutsal was fighting the *murids*. One of his cheeks had been hacked off and hung down. He supported it with one hand and with the other stabbed with his dagger at all who came near him. I saw him strike down Hamzád's brother and aim a blow at another man, but then the *murids* fired at him and he fell.'

Hadji Murád stopped and his sunburnt face flushed a dark red and his eyes became bloodshot.

'I was seized with fear and ran away.'

'Really? . . . I thought thou never wast afraid,' said Lóris-Mélikov.

'Never after that. . . . Since then I have always remembered that shame, and when I recalled it I feared nothing!'

XII

'But enough! It is time for me to pray,' said Hadji Murád drawing from an inner breast-pocket of his Circassian coat Vorontsóv's repeater watch and carefully pressing the spring. The repeater struck twelve and a quarter. Hadji Murád listened with his head on one side, repressing a childlike smile.

'*Kunák* Vorontsóv's present,' he said, smiling.

'It is a good watch,' said Lóris-Mélikov. 'Well then, go thou and pray, and I will wait.'

'*Yakshí*. Very well,' said Hadji Murád and went to his bedroom.

Left by himself, Lóris-Mélikov wrote down in his notebook the chief things Hadji Murád had related, and then lighting a cigarette began to pace up and down the room. On reaching the door opposite the bedroom he heard animated voices speaking rapidly in Tartar. He guessed that the speakers were Hadji Murád's *murids*, and opening the door he went in to them.

The room was impregnated with that special leathery acid smell peculiar to the mountaineers. On a *búrka* spread out on the floor sat the one-eyed, red-haired Gamzálo, in a tattered greasy *beshmét*, plaiting a bridle. He was saying something excitedly, speaking in a hoarse voice, but when Lóris-Mélikov entered he immediately became silent and continued his work without paying any attention to him.

In front of Gamzálo stood the merry Khan Mahomá showing his white teeth, his black lashless eyes glittering, and saying something over and over again. The handsome Eldár, his sleeves turned up on his strong arms, was polishing the girths of a saddle suspended from a nail. Khanéfi, the principal worker and manager of the household, was not there, he was cooking their dinner in the kitchen.

'What were you disputing about?' asked Lóris-Mélikov after greeting them.

'Why, he keeps on praising Shamil,' said Khan Mahomá giving his hand to Lóris-Mélikov. 'He says Shamil is a great man, learned, holy, and a *dzhigít*.'

'How is it that he has left him and still praises him?'

'He has left him and still praises him,' repeated Khan Mahomá, his teeth showing and his eyes glittering.

'And does he really consider him a saint?' asked Lóris-Mélikov.

'If he were not a saint the people would not listen to him,' said Gamzálo rapidly.

'Shamil is no saint, but Mansúr was!' replied Khan Mahomá. 'He was a real saint. When he was Imám the people were quite different. He used to ride through the *aouls* and the people used to come out and kiss the hem of his coat and confess their sins and vow to do no evil. Then all the people – so the old men say – lived like saints: not drinking, nor smoking, nor neglecting their prayers, and forgiving one another their sins even when blood had been spilt. If anyone then found money or anything, he tied it to a stake and set it up by the roadside. In those days God gave the people success in everything – not as now.'

'In the mountains they don't smoke or drink now,' said Gamzálo.

'Your Shamil is a *lamorey*,' said Khan Mahomá, winking at Lóris-Mélikov. (*Lamorey* was a contemptuous term for a mountaineer.)

'Yes, *lamorey* means mountaineer,' replied Gamzálo. 'It is in the mountains that the eagles dwell.'

'Smart fellow! Well hit!' said Khan Mahomá with a grin, pleased at his adversary's apt retort.

Seeing the silver cigarette-case in Lóris-Mélikov's hand, Khan Mahomá asked for a cigarette, and when Lóris-Mélikov remarked that they were forbidden to smoke, he winked with one eye and jerking his head in the direction of Hadji Murád's bedroom replied that they could do it as long as they were not seen. He at once began smoking – not inhaling – and pouting his red lips awkwardly as he blew out the smoke.

'That is wrong!' said Gamzálo severely, and left the room. Khan Mahomá winked in his direction, and while smoking asked Lóris-Mélikov where he could best buy a silk *beshmét* and a white cap.

'Why, hast thou so much money?'

'I have enough,' replied Khan Mahomá with a wink.

'Ask him where he got the money,' said Eldár, turning his handsome smiling face towards Lóris-Mélikov.

'Oh, I won it!' said Khan Mahomá quickly, and related how while walking in Tiflis the day before he had come upon a group of men – Russians and Armenians – playing at *orlyánka* (a kind of heads-and-tails). The stake was a large one: three gold pieces and much silver. Khan Mahomá at once saw what the game consisted in, and jingling the coppers he had in his pocket he went up to the players and said he would stake the whole amount.

'How couldst thou do it? Hadst thou so much?' asked Lóris-Mélikov.

'I had only twelve kopeks,' said Khan Mahomá, grinning.

'But if thou hadst lost?'

'Why, this!' said Khan Mahomá pointing to his pistol.

'Wouldst thou have given that?'

'Give it indeed! I should have run away, and if anyone had tried to stop me I should have killed him – that's all!'

'Well, and didst thou win?'

'Aye, I won it all and went away!'

Lóris-Mélikov quite understood what sort of men Khan Mahomá and Eldár were. Khan Mahomá was a merry fellow, careless and ready for any spree. He did not know what to do with his superfluous vitality. He was always gay and reckless, and played with his own and other people's lives. For the sake of that sport with life he had now come over to the Russians, and for the same sport he might go back to Shamil to-morrow.

Eldár was also quite easy to understand. He was a man entirely devoted to his *murshíd*; calm, strong, and firm.

The red-haired Gamzálo was the only one Lóris-Mélikov did not understand. He saw that that man was not only loyal to Shamil but felt an insuperable aversion, contempt, repugnance, and hatred for all Russians, and Lóris-Mélikov could therefore not understand why he had come over to them. It occurred to him that, as some of the higher officials suspected, Hadji Murád's surrender and his tales of hatred of Shamil might be false, and that perhaps he had surrendered only to spy out the Russians' weak spots that, after escaping back to the mountains, he might be able to direct his forces accordingly. Gamzálo's whole person strengthened this suspicion.

'The others, and Hadji Murád himself, know how to hide their intentions, but this one betrays them by his open hatred,' thought he.

Lóris-Mélikov tried to speak to him. He asked whether he did not feel dull. 'No, I don't!' he growled hoarsely without stopping his work, and glancing at his questioner out of the corner of his one eye. He replied to all Lóris-Mélikov's other questions in a similar manner.

While Lóris-Mélikov was in the room Hadji Murád's fourth *murid* came in, the Avar Khanéfi; a man with a hairy face and neck and an arched chest as rough as if it were overgrown with moss. He was strong and a hard worker, always engrossed in his duties, and like Eldár unquestioningly obedient to his master.

When he entered the room to fetch some rice, Lóris-Mélikov stopped him and asked where he came from and how long he had been with Hadji Murád.

'Five years,' replied Khanéfi. 'I come from the same *aoul* as he. My father killed his uncle and they wished to kill me,' he said calmly, looking from under his joined eyebrows straight into Lóris-Mélikov's face. 'Then I asked them to adopt me as a brother.'

'What do you mean by "adopt as a brother"?'

'I did not shave my head nor cut my nails for two months, and then I came to them. They let me in to Patimát, his mother, and she gave me the breast and I became his brother.'

Hadji Murád's voice could be heard from the next room and Eldár, immediately answering his call, promptly wiped his hands and went with large strides into the drawing-room.

'He asks thee to come,' said he, coming back.

Lóris-Mélikov gave another cigarette to the merry Khan Mahomá and went into the drawing-room.

XIII

WHEN Lóris-Mélikov entered the drawing-room Hadji Murád received him with a bright face.

'Well, shall I continue?' he asked, sitting down comfortably on the divan.

'Yes, certainly,' said Lóris-Mélikov. 'I have been in to have a talk with thy henchmen. . . . One is a jolly fellow!' he added.

'Yes, Khan Mahomá is a frivolous fellow,' said Hadji Murád. 'I liked the young handsome one.'

'Ah, that's Eldár. He's young but firm – made of iron!'

They were silent for a while.

'So I am to go on?'

'Yes, yes!'

'I told thee how the Khans were killed. . . . Well, having killed them Hamzád rode into Khunzákh and took up his quarters in their palace. The Khansha was the only one of the family left alive. Hamzád sent for her. She reproached him, so he winked to his *murid* Aseldár, who struck her from behind and killed her.'

'Why did he kill her?' asked Lóris-Mélikov.

'What could he do? . . . Where the forelegs have gone the hind legs must follow! He killed off the whole family. Shamil killed the youngest son – threw him over a precipice. . . .

'Then the whole of Avaria surrendered to Hamzád. But my brother and I would not surrender. We wanted his blood for the blood of the Khans. We pretended to yield, but our only thought was how to get his blood. We consulted our grandfather and decided to await the time when he would come out of his palace, and then to kill him from an ambush. Someone overheard us and told Hamzád, who sent for grandfather and said, "Mind, if it be true that thy grandsons are planning evil against me, thou and they shall hang from one rafter. I do God's work and cannot be hindered. . . . Go, and remember what I have said!"

'Our grandfather came home and told us.

'Then we decided not to wait but to do the deed on the first day of the feast in the mosque. Our comrades would not take part in it but my brother and I remained firm.

'We took two pistols each, put on our *búrkas*, and went to the mosque. Hamzád entered the mosque with thirty *murids*. They all had drawn swords in their hands. Aseldár, his favourite *murid* (the one who had cut off the Khansha's head), saw us, shouted to us to take off our *búrkas*, and came towards me. I had my dagger in my hand and I killed him with it and rushed at Hamzád; but my brother Osman had already shot him. He was still alive and rushed at my brother dagger in hand, but I gave him a finishing blow on the head. There were thirty *murids* and we were only two. They killed my brother Osman, but I kept them at bay, leapt through the window, and escaped.

'When it was known that Hamzád had been killed all the people rose. The *murids* fled and those of them who did not flee were killed.'

Hadji Murád paused, and breathed heavily.

'That was very good,' he continued, 'but afterwards everything was spoilt.

'Shamil succeeded Hamzád. He sent envoys to me to say that I should join him in attacking the Russians, and that if I refused he would destroy Khunzákh and kill me.

'I answered that I would not join him and would not let him come to me. . . .'

'Why didst thou not go with him?' asked Lóris-Mélikov.

Hadji Murád frowned and did not reply at once.

'I could not. The blood of my brother Osman and of Abu Nutsal Khan was on his hands. I did not go to him. General Rosen sent me an officer's commission and ordered me to govern Avaria. All this would have been well but that Rosen appointed as Khan of Kazi-Kumúkh, first Mahómet-Murza, and afterwards Akhmet Khan, who hated me. He had been trying to get the Khansha's daughter, Sultanetta, in marriage for his son, but she would not give her to him, and he believed me to be the cause of this. . . . Yes, Akhmet Khan hated me and sent his henchmen to kill me, but I escaped from them. Then he spoke ill of me to General Klügenau. He said that I told the Avars not to supply wood to the Russian soldiers, and he also said that I had donned a turban – this one' (Hadji Murád touched his turban) 'and that this meant that I had gone over to Shamil. The general did not believe him and gave orders that I should not be touched. But when the general went to Tiflis, Akhmet Khan did as he pleased. He sent a company of soldiers to seize me, put me in chains, and tied me to a cannon.

'So they kept me six days,' he continued. 'On the seventh day they untied me and started to take me to Temir-Khan-Shurá. Forty soldiers with loaded guns had me in charge. My hands were tied and I knew that they had orders to kill me if I tried to escape.

'As we approached Mansokha the path became narrow, and on the right was an abyss about a hundred and twenty yards deep. I went to the right – to the very edge. A soldier wanted to stop me, but I jumped down and pulled him with me. He was killed outright but I, as you see, remained alive.

'Ribs, head, arms, and leg – all were broken! I tried to crawl but grew giddy and fell asleep. I awoke wet with blood. A shepherd saw me and called some people who carried me to an *aoul*. My ribs and head healed, and my leg too, only it has remained short,' and Hadji Murád stretched out his crooked leg. 'It still serves me, however, and that is well,' said he.

'The people heard the news and began coming to me. I recovered and went to Tselméss. The Avars again called on me to rule over them,' he went on, with tranquil, confident pride, 'and I agreed.'

He rose quickly and taking a portfolio out of a saddle-bag, drew out two discoloured letters and handed one of them to Lóris-Mélikov. They were from General Klügenau. Lóris-Mélikov read the first letter, which was as follows:

'Lieutenant Hadji Murád, thou hast served under me and I was satisfied with thee and considered thee a good man.

'Recently Akhmet Khan informed me that thou art a traitor, that thou hast donned a turban and hast intercourse with Shamil, and that thou hast taught the people to disobey the Russian Government. I ordered thee to be arrested and brought before me but thou fleddst. I do not know whether this is for thy good or not, as I do not know whether thou art guilty or not.

'Now hear me. If thy conscience is pure, if thou art not guilty in anything towards the great Tsar, come to me, fear no one. I am thy defender. The Khan can do nothing to thee, he is himself under my command, so thou hast nothing to fear.'

Klügenau added that he always kept his word and was just, and he again exhorted Hadji Murád to appear before him.

When Lóris-Mélikov had read this letter Hadji Murád, before handing him the second one, told him what he had written in reply to the first.

'I wrote that I wore a turban not for Shamil's sake but for my soul's salvation; that I neither wished nor could go over to

Shamil, because he had caused the death of my father, my brothers, and my relations; but that I could not join the Russians because I had been dishonoured by them. (In Khunzákh, a scoundrel had spat on me while I was bound, and I could not join your people until that man was killed.) But above all I feared that liar, Akhmet Khan.

'Then the general sent me this letter,' said Hadji Murád, handing Lóris-Mélikov the other discoloured paper.

'Thou hast answered my first letter and I thank thee,' read Lóris-Mélikov. 'Thou writest that thou art not afraid to return but that the insult done thee by a certain giaour prevents it, but I assure thee that the Russian law is just and that thou shalt see him who dared to offend thee punished before thine eyes. I have already given orders to investigate the matter.

'Hear me, Hadji Murád! I have a right to be displeased with thee for not trusting me and my honour, but I forgive thee, for I know how suspicious mountaineers are in general. If thy conscience is pure, if thou hast put on a turban only for thy soul's salvation, then thou art right and mayst look me and the Russian Government boldly in the eye. He who dishonoured thee shall, I assure thee, be punished and *thy property shall be restored to thee*, and thou shalt see and know what Russian law is. Moreover we Russians look at things differently, and thou hast not sunk in our eyes because some scoundrel has dishonoured thee.

'I myself have consented to the Chimrints wearing turbans, and I regard their actions in the right light, and therefore I repeat that thou hast nothing to fear. Come to me with the man by whom I am sending thee this letter. He is faithful to me and is not the slave of thy enemies, but is the friend of a man who enjoys the special favour of the Government.'

Further on Klügenau again tried to persuade Hadji Murád to come over to him.

'I did not believe him,' said Hadji Murád when Lóris-Mélikov had finished reading, 'and did not go to Klügenau. The chief thing for me was to revenge myself on Akhmet Khan, and that I could not do through the Russians. Then Akhmet Khan surrounded Tselméss and wanted to take me or kill me. I had too few men and could not drive him off, and just then came an envoy with a letter from Shamil promising to help me to defeat and kill Akhmet Khan and making me ruler over the whole of Avaria. I considered the matter for a long time and then went over to Shamil, and from that time I have fought the Russians continually.'

Here Hadji Murád related all his military exploits, of which there were very many and some of which were already familiar to Lóris-Mélikov. All his campaigns and raids had been remarkable for the extraordinary rapidity of his movements and the boldness of his attacks, which were always crowned with success.

'There never was any friendship between me and Shamil,' said Hadji Murád at the end of his story, 'but he feared me and needed me. But it so happened that I was asked who should be Imám after Shamil, and I replied: "He will be Imám whose sword is sharpest!"

'This was told to Shamil and he wanted to get rid of me. He sent me into Tabasarán. I went, and captured a thousand sheep and three hundred horses, but he said I had not done the right thing and dismissed me from being *Naïb*, and ordered me to send him all the money. I sent him a thousand gold pieces. He sent his *murids* and they took from me all my property. He demanded that I should go to him, but I knew he wanted to kill me and I did not go. Then he sent to take me. I resisted and went over to Vorontsóv. Only I did not take my family. My mother, my wives, and my son are in his hands. Tell the Sirdar that as long as my family is in Shamil's power I can do nothing.'

'I will tell him,' said Lóris-Mélikov.

'Take pains, try hard! . . . What is mine is thine, only help me with the prince! I am tied up and the end of the rope is in Shamil's hands,' said Hadji Murád concluding his story.

XIV

ON the 20th of December Vorontsóv wrote to Chernyshóv, the Minister of War. The letter was in French:

'I did not write to you by the last post, dear Prince, as I wished first to decide what we should do with Hadji Murád, and for the last two or three days I have not been feeling quite well.

'In my last letter I informed you of Hadji Murád's arrival here. He reached Tiflis on the 8th, and next day I made his acquaintance, and during the following seven or eight days have spoken to him and considered what use we can make of him in the future, and especially what we are to do with him at present, for he is much concerned about the fate of his family, and with every appearance of perfect frankness says that while they are in Shamil's hands he is paralysed and cannot render us any service or show his gratitude for the friendly reception and forgiveness we have extended to him.

'His uncertainty about those dear to him makes him restless, and the persons I have appointed to live with him assure me that he does not sleep at night, eats hardly anything, prays continually, and asks only to be allowed to ride out accompanied by several Cossacks – the sole recreation and exercise possible for him and made necessary to him by lifelong habit. Every day he comes to me to know whether I have any news of his family, and to ask me to have all the prisoners in our hands collected and offered to Shamil in exchange for them. He would also give a little money. There are people who would let him have some for the purpose. He keeps repeating to me: "Save my family and then give me a chance to serve thee" (preferably, in his opinion, on the Lesghian line), "and if within a month I do not render you great service, punish me as you think fit." I reply that to me all this appears very just, and that many among us would even not trust him so long as his family remain in the mountains and are not in our hands as hostages, and that I will do everything possible to collect the prisoners on our frontier, that I have no power under our laws to give him money for the ransom of his family in addition to the sum he may himself be able to raise, but that I may perhaps find some other means of helping him. After that I told him frankly that in my opinion Shamil would not in any case give up the family, and that Shamil might tell him so straight out and promise him a full pardon and his former posts, and might threaten if Hadji Murád did not return, to kill his mother, his wives, and his six children. I asked him whether he could say frankly what he would do if he received such an announcement from Shamil. He lifted his eyes and arms to heaven, and said that everything is in God's hands, but that he would never surrender to his foe, for he is certain Shamil would not forgive him and he would therefore not have long to live. As to the destruction of his family, he did not think Shamil would act so rashly: firstly, to avoid making him a yet more desperate and dangerous foe, and secondly, because there were many people, and even very influential people, in Daghestan, who would dissuade Shamil from such a course. Finally, he repeated several times that whatever God might decree for him in the future, he was at present interested in nothing but his family's ransom, and he implored me in God's name to help him and allow him to return to the neighbourhood of the Chechnya, where he could, with the help and consent of our commanders, have some intercourse with his family and regular news of their condition and of the best means to liberate them. He said that many people, and even some *Naïbs* in that part of the enemy's territory, were more or less attached to him, and that among the whole of the population already subjugated by Russia or neutral it would be easy with our help to establish relations very useful for the attainment of the aim which gives him no peace day or night, and the attainment of which would set him at ease and make it possible for him to act for our good and win our confidence.

'He asks to be sent back to Grózny with a convoy of twenty or thirty picked Cossacks who would serve him as a protection against foes and us as a guarantee of his good faith.

'You will understand, dear Prince, that I have been much perplexed by all this, for do what I will a great responsibility rests on me. It would be in the highest degree rash to trust him entirely, yet in order to deprive him of all means of escape we should have to lock him up, and in my opinion that would be both unjust and impolitic. A measure of that kind, the news of which would soon spread over the whole of Daghestan, would do us great harm by keeping back those who are now inclined more or less openly to oppose Shamil (and there are many such), and who are keenly watching to see how we treat the Imám's bravest and most adventurous officer now that he has found himself obliged to place himself in our hands. If we treat Hadji Murád as a prisoner all the good effect of the situation will be lost. Therefore I think that I could not act otherwise than as I have done, though at the same time I feel that I may be accused of having made a great mistake if Hadji Murád should take it into his head to escape again. In the service, and especially in a complicated situation such as this, it is difficult, not to say impossible, to follow any one straight path without risking mistakes and without accepting responsibility, but once a path seems to be the right one I must follow it, happen what may.

'I beg of you, dear Prince, to submit this to his Majesty the Emperor for his consideration; and I shall be happy if it pleases our most august monarch to approve my action.

'All that I have written above I have also written to Generals Zavodóvsky and Kozlóvsky, to guide the latter when communicating direct with Hadji Murád whom I have warned not to act or go anywhere without Kozlóvsky's consent. I also told him that it would be all the better for us if he rode out with our convoy, as otherwise Shamil might spread a rumour that we were keeping him prisoner, but at the same time I made him promise never to go to Vozdvízhensk, because my son, to whom he first surrendered and whom he looks upon as his *kunák* (friend), is not the commander of that place and some unpleasant misunderstanding might easily arise. In any case Vozdvízhensk lies too near a thickly populated hostile settlement, while for the intercourse with his friends which he desires, Grózny is in all respects suitable.

'Besides the twenty chosen Cossacks who at his own request are to keep close to him, I am also sending Captain Lóris-Mélikov – a worthy, excellent, and highly intelligent officer who speaks Tartar, and knows Hadji Murád well and apparently enjoys his full confidence. During the ten days that Hadji

Murád has spent here, he has, however, lived in the same house with Lieutenant-Colonel Prince Tarkhánov, who is in command of the Shoushín District and is here on business connected with the service. He is a truly worthy man whom I trust entirely. He also has won Hadji Murád's confidence, and through him alone — as he speaks Tartar perfectly — we have discussed the most delicate and secret matters. I have consulted Tarkhánov about Hadji Murád, and he fully agrees with me that it was necessary either to act as I have done, or to put Hadji Murád in prison and guard him in the strictest manner (for if we once treat him badly he will not be easy to hold), or else to remove him from the country altogether. But these two last measures would not only destroy all the advantage accruing to us from Hadji Murád's quarrel with Shamil, but would inevitably check any growth of the present insubordination, and possible future revolt, of the people against Shamil's power. Prince Tarkhánov tells me he himself has no doubt of Hadji Murád's truthfulness, and that Hadji Murád is convinced that Shamil will never forgive him but would have him executed in spite of any promise of forgiveness. The only thing Tarkhánov has noticed in his intercourse with Hadji Murád that might cause any anxiety, is his attachment to his religion. Tarkhánov does not deny that Shamil might influence Hadji Murád from that side. But as I have already said, he will never persuade Hadji Murád that he will not take his life sooner or later should the latter return to him.

'This, dear Prince, is all I have to tell you about this episode in our affairs here.'

XV

THE report was dispatched from Tiflis on the 24th of December 1851, and on New Year's Eve a courier, having overdriven a dozen horses and beaten a dozen drivers till they bled, delivered it to Prince Chernyshóv who at that time was Minister of War; and on the 1st of January 1852 Chernyshóv took Vorontsóv's report, among other papers, to the Emperor Nicholas.

Chernyshóv disliked Vorontsóv because of the general respect in which the latter was held and because of his immense wealth, and also because Vorontsóv was a real aristocrat while Chernyshóv, after all, was a *parvenu*, but especially because the Emperor was particularly well disposed towards Vorontsóv. Therefore at every opportunity Chernyshóv tried to injure Vorontsóv.

When he had last presented a report about Caucasian affairs he had succeeded in arousing Nicholas's displeasure against Vorontsóv because – through the carelessness of those in command – almost the whole of a small Caucasian detachment had been destroyed by the mountaineers. He now intended to present the steps taken by Vorontsóv in relation to Hadji Murád in an unfavourable light. He wished to suggest to the Emperor that Vorontsóv always protected and even indulged the natives to the detriment of the Russians, and that he had acted unwisely in allowing Hadji Murád to remain in the Caucasus for there was every reason to suspect that he had only come over to spy on our means of defence, and that it would therefore be better to transport him to Central Russia and make use of him only after his family had been rescued from the mountaineers and it had become possible to convince ourselves of his loyalty.

Chernyshóv's plan did not succeed merely because on that New Year's Day Nicholas was in particularly bad spirits, and out of perversity would not have accepted any suggestion whatever from anyone, least of all from Chernyshóv whom he only tolerated – regarding him as indispensable for the time being but looking upon him as a blackguard, for Nicholas knew of his endeavours at the trial of the Decembrists[1] to secure the conviction of Zacháry Chernyshóv, and of his attempt to obtain Zacháry's property for himself. So thanks to Nicholas's ill temper Hadji Murád remained in the Caucasus, and his circumstances were not changed as they

---

1 The military conspirators who tried to secure a Constitution for Russia in 1825, on the accession of Nicholas I.

might have been had Chernyshóv presented his report at
another time.

* * *

It was half-past nine o'clock Mwhen through the mist of the
cold morning (the thermometer showed 13 degrees below zero
Fahrenheit) Chernyshóv's fat, bearded coachman, sitting on
the box of a small sledge (like the one Nicholas drove about in)
with a sharp-angled, cushion-shaped azure velvet cap on his
head, drew up at the entrance of the Winter Palace and gave a
friendly nod to his chum, Prince Dolgorúky's coachman – who
having brought his master to the palace had himself long been
waiting outside, in his big coat with the thickly wadded skirts,
sitting on the reins and rubbing his numbed hands together.
Chernyshóv had on a long cloak with a large cape and a fluffy
collar of silver beaver, and a regulation three-cornered hat with
cocks' feathers. He threw back the bearskin apron of the sledge
and carefully disengaged his chilled feet, on which he had no
over-shoes (he prided himself on never wearing any). Clanking
his spurs with an air of bravado he ascended the carpeted
steps and passed through the hall door which was respectfully
opened for him by the porter, and entered the hall. Having
thrown off his cloak which an old Court lackey hurried
forward to take, he went to a mirror and carefully removed
the hat from his curled wig. Looking at himself in the mirror, he
arranged the hair on his temples and the tuft above his forehead
with an accustomed movement of his old hands, and adjusted
his cross, the shoulder-knots of his uniform, and his large-
initialled epaulettes, and then went up the gently ascending
carpeted stairs, his not very reliable old legs feebly mounting
the shallow steps. Passing the Court lackeys in gala livery
who stood obsequiously bowing, Chernyshóv entered the
waiting-room. He was respectfully met by a newly appointed
aide-de-camp of the Emperor's in a shining new uniform with
epaulettes and shoulder-knots, whose face was still fresh and
rosy and who had a small black moustache, and the hair on his
temples brushed towards his eyes in the same way as the
Emperor.

Prince Vasíli Dolgorúky, Assistant-Minister of War, with an expression of *ennui* on his dull face – which was ornamented with similar whiskers, moustaches, and temple tufts brushed forward like Nicholas's – greeted him.

'*L'empereur?*' said Chernyshóv, addressing the aide-de-camp and looking inquiringly towards the door leading to the cabinet.

'*Sa majesté vient de rentrer,*'[1] replied the aide-de-camp, evidently enjoying the sound of his own voice, and stepping so softly and steadily that had a tumbler of water been placed on his head none of it would have been spilt, he approached the door and disappeared, his whole body evincing reverence for the spot he was about to visit.

Dolgorúky meanwhile opened his portfolio to see that it contained the necessary papers, while Chernyshóv, frowning, paced up and down to restore the circulation in his numbed feet, and thought over what he was about to report to the Emperor. He was near the door of the cabinet when it opened again and the aide-de-camp, even more radiant and respectful than before, came out and with a gesture invited the minister and his assistant to enter.

The Winter Palace had been rebuilt after a fire some considerable time before this, but Nicholas was still occupying rooms in the upper storey. The cabinet in which he received the reports of his ministers and other high officials was a very lofty apartment with four large windows. A big portrait of the Emperor Alexander I hung on the front side of the room. Two bureaux stood between the windows, and several chairs were ranged along the walls. In the middle of the room was an enormous writing-table, with an arm-chair before it for Nicholas, and other chairs for those to whom he gave audience.

Nicholas sat at the table in a black coat with shoulder-straps but no epaulettes, his enormous body – with his overgrown stomach tightly laced in – was thrown back, and he gazed at the newcomers with fixed, lifeless eyes. His long pale face,

1 'His Majesty has just returned.'

with its enormous receding forehead between the tufts of hair
which were brushed forward and skilfully joined to the wig
that covered his bald patch, was specially cold and stony that
day. His eyes, always dim, looked duller than usual, the compressed lips under his upturned moustaches, the high collar
which supported his chin, and his fat freshly shaven cheeks on
which symmetrical sausage-shaped bits of whiskers had been
left, gave his face a dissatisfied and even irate expression. His
bad mood was caused by fatigue, due to the fact that he had
been to a masquerade the night before, and while walking
about as was his wont in his Horse Guards' uniform with a bird
on the helmet, among the public which crowded round and
timidly made way for his enormous, self-assured figure, he
had again met the mask who at the previous masquerade had
aroused his senile sensuality by her whiteness, her beautiful
figure, and her tender voice. At that former masquerade she
had disappeared after promising to meet him at the next one.

At yesterday's masquerade she had come up to him, and this
time he had not let her go, but had led her to the box specially
kept ready for that purpose, where he could be alone with her.
Having arrived in silence at the door of the box Nicholas
looked round to find the attendant, but he was not there. He
frowned and pushed the door open himself, letting the lady
enter first.

'*Il y a quelqu'un!*'[1] said the mask, stopping short.

And the box actually was occupied. On the small velvet-
covered sofa, close together, sat an Uhlan officer and a pretty,
fair curly-haired young woman in a domino, who had
removed her mask. On catching sight of the angry figure of
Nicholas drawn up to its full height, she quickly replaced her
mask, but the Uhlan officer, rigid with fear, gazed at Nicholas
with fixed eyes without rising from the sofa.

Used as he was to the terror he inspired in others, that terror
always pleased Nicholas, and by way of contrast he sometimes
liked to astound those plunged in terror by addressing kindly
words to them. He did so on this occasion.

---

1 'There's someone there!'

'Well, friend,' said he to the officer, 'you are younger than I and might give up your place to me!'

The officer jumped to his feet, and growing first pale and then red and bending almost double, he followed his partner silently out of the box, leaving Nicholas alone with his lady.

She proved to be a pretty, twenty-year-old virgin, the daughter of a Swedish governess. She told Nicholas how when quite a child she had fallen in love with him from his portraits; how she adored him and had made up her mind to attract his attention at any cost. Now she had succeeded and wanted nothing more – so she said.

The girl was taken to the place where Nicholas usually had rendezvous with women, and there he spent more than an hour with her.

When he returned to his room that night and lay on the hard narrow bed about which he prided himself, and covered himself with the cloak which he considered to be (and spoke of as being) as famous as Napoleon's hat, it was a long time before he could fall asleep. He thought now of the frightened and elated expression on that girl's fair face, and now of the full, powerful shoulders of his established mistress, Nelídova, and he compared the two. That profligacy in a married man was a bad thing did not once enter his head, and he would have been greatly surprised had anyone censured him for it. Yet though convinced that he had acted rightly, some kind of unpleasant after-taste remained, and to stifle that feeling he dwelt on a thought that always tranquillized him – the thought of his own greatness.

Though he had fallen asleep so late, he rose before eight, and after attending to his toilet in the usual way – rubbing his big well-fed body all over with ice – and saying his prayers (repeating those he had been used to from childhood – the prayer to the Virgin, the Apostles' Creed, and the Lord's Prayer, without attaching any kind of meaning to the words he uttered), he went out through the smaller portico of the palace onto the embankment in his military cloak and cap.

On the embankment he met a student in the uniform of the School of Jurisprudence, who was as enormous as himself. On recognizing the uniform of that school, which he disliked for its freedom of thought, Nicholas frowned, but the stature of the student and the painstaking manner in which he drew himself up and saluted, ostentatiously sticking out his elbow, mollified his displeasure.

'Your name?' said he.

'Polosátov, your Imperial Majesty.'

'... fine fellow!'

The student continued to stand with his hand lifted to his hat. Nicholas stopped.

'Do you wish to enter the army?'

'Not at all, your Imperial Majesty.'

'Blockhead!' And Nicholas turned away and continued his walk, and began uttering aloud the first words that came into his head.

'Kopervine ... Kopervine —' he repeated several times (it was the name of yesterday's girl). 'Horrid ... horrid —' He did not think of what he was saying, but stifled his feelings by listening to the words.

'Yes, what would Russia be without me?' said he, feeling his former dissatisfaction returning. 'What would – not Russia alone but Europe be, without me?' and calling to mind the weakness and stupidity of his brother-in-law the King of Prussia, he shook his head.

As he was returning to the small portico, he saw the carriage of Helena Pávlovna,[1] with a red-liveried footman, approaching the Saltykóv entrance of the palace.

Helena Pávlovna was to him the personification of that futile class of people who discussed not merely science and poetry, but even the ways of governing men: imagining that they could govern themselves better than he, Nicholas, governed them! He knew that however much he crushed such people they reappeared again and again, and he recalled his brother, Michael Pávlovich, who had died not long before. A feeling of sadness and vexation came over him and with a

1 Widow of Nicholas's brother Michael: a clever, well-educated woman, interested in science, art, and public affairs.

dark frown he again began whispering the first words that came into his head, which he only ceased doing when he re-entered the palace.

On reaching his apartments he smoothed his whiskers and the hair on his temples and the wig on his bald patch, and twisted his moustaches upwards in front of the mirror, and then went straight to the cabinet in which he received reports.

He first received Chernyshóv, who at once saw by his face, and especially by his eyes, that Nicholas was in a particularly bad humour that day, and knowing about the adventure of the night before he understood the cause. Having coldly greeted him and invited him to sit down, Nicholas fixed on him a lifeless gaze. The first matter Chernyshóv reported upon was a case of embezzlement by commissariat officials which had just been discovered; the next was the movement of troops on the Prussian frontier; then came a list of rewards to be given at the New Year to some people omitted from a former list; then Vorontsóv's report about Hadji Murád; and lastly some unpleasant business concerning an attempt by a student of the Academy of Medicine on the life of a professor.

Nicholas heard the report of the embezzlement silently with compressed lips, his large white hand – with one ring on the fourth finger – stroking some sheets of paper, and his eyes steadily fixed on Chernyshóv's forehead and on the tuft of hair above it.

Nicholas was convinced that everybody stole. He knew he would have to punish the commissariat officials now, and decided to send them all to serve in the ranks, but he also knew that this would not prevent those who succeeded them from acting in the same way. It was a characteristic of officials to steal, but it was his duty to punish them for doing so, and tired as he was of that duty he conscientiously performed it.

'It seems there is only one honest man in Russia!' said he.

Chernyshóv at once understood that this one honest man was Nicholas himself, and smiled approvingly.

'It looks like it, your Imperial Majesty,' said he.

'Leave it – I will give a decision,' said Nicholas, taking the document and putting it on the left side of the table.

Then Chernyshóv reported about the rewards to be given and about moving the army on the Prussian frontier.

Nicholas looked over the list and struck out some names, and then briefly and firmly gave orders to move two divisions to the Prussian frontier. He could not forgive the King of Prussia for granting a Constitution to his people after the events of 1848, and therefore while expressing most friendly feelings to his brother-in-law in letters and conversation, he considered it necessary to keep an army near the frontier in case of need. He might want to use these troops to defend his brother-in-law's throne if the people of Prussia rebelled (Nicholas saw a readiness for rebellion everywhere) as he had used troops to suppress the rising in Hungary a few years previously. They were also of use to give more weight and influence to such advice as he gave to the King of Prussia.

'Yes – what would Russia be like now if it were not for me?' he again thought.

'Well, what else is there?' said he.

'A courier from the Caucasus,' said Chernyshóv, and he reported what Vorontsóv had written about Hadji Murád's surrender.

'Well, well!' said Nicholas. 'It's a good beginning!'

'Evidently the plan devised by your Majesty begins to bear fruit,' said Chernyshóv.

This approval of his strategic talents was particularly pleasant to Nicholas because, though he prided himself upon them, at the bottom of his heart he knew that they did not really exist, and he now desired to hear more detailed praise of himself.

'How do you mean?' he asked.

'I mean that if your Majesty's plans had been adopted before, and we had moved forward slowly and steadily, cutting down forests and destroying the supplies of food, the Caucasus would have been subjugated long ago. I attribute Hadji Murád's surrender entirely to his having come to the conclusion that they can hold out no longer.'

'True,' said Nicholas.

Although the plan of a gradual advance into the enemy's territory by means of felling forests and destroying the food supplies was Ermólov's and Velyamínov's plan, and was quite contrary to Nicholas's own plan of seizing Shamil's place of residence and destroying that nest of robbers – which was the plan on which the Dargo expedition in 1845 (that cost so many lives) had been undertaken – Nicholas nevertheless attributed to himself also the plan of a slow advance and a systematic felling of forests and devastation of the country. It would seem that to believe the plan of a slow movement by felling forests and destroying food supplies to have been his own would have necessitated hiding the fact that he had insisted on quite contrary operations in 1845. But he did not hide it and was proud of the plan of the 1845 expedition as well as of the plan of a slow advance – though the two were obviously contrary to one another. Continual brazen flattery from everybody round him in the teeth of obvious facts had brought him to such a state that he no longer saw his own inconsistencies or measured his actions and words by reality, logic, or even simple common sense; but was quite convinced that all his orders, however senseless, unjust, and mutually contradictory they might be, became reasonable, just, and mutually accordant simply because he gave them. His decision in the case next reported to him – that of the student of the Academy of Medicine – was of that senseless kind.

The case was as follows: A young man who had twice failed in his examinations was being examined a third time, and when the examiner again would not pass him, the young man whose nerves were deranged, considering this to be an injustice, seized a pen-knife from the table in a paroxysm of fury, and rushing at the professor inflicted on him several trifling wounds.

'What's his name?' asked Nicholas.

'Bzhezóvski.'

'A Pole?'

'Of Polish descent and a Roman Catholic,' answered Chernyshóv.

Nicholas frowned. He had done much evil to the Poles. To justify that evil he had to feel certain that all Poles were rascals, and he considered them to be such and hated them in proportion to the evil he had done them.

'Wait a little,' he said, closing his eyes and bowing his head.

Chernyshóv, having more than once heard Nicholas say so, knew that when the Emperor had to take a decision it was only necessary for him to concentrate his attention for a few moments and the spirit moved him, and the best possible decision presented itself as though an inner voice had told him what to do. He was now thinking how most fully to satisfy the feeling of hatred against the Poles which this incident had stirred up within him, and the inner voice suggested the following decision. He took the report and in his large handwriting wrote on its margin with three orthographical mistakes:

'*Diserves deth, but, thank God, we have no capitle punishment, and it is not for me to introduce it. Make him run the gauntlet of a thousand men twelve times. – Nicholas.*'

He signed, adding his unnaturally huge flourish.

Nicholas knew that twelve thousand strokes with the regulation rods were not only certain death with torture, but were a superfluous cruelty, for five thousand strokes were sufficient to kill the strongest man. But it pleased him to be ruthlessly cruel and it also pleased him to think that we have abolished capital punishment in Russia.

Having written his decision about the student, he pushed it across to Chernyshóv.

'There,' he said, 'read it.'

Chernyshóv read it, and bowed his head as a sign of respectful amazement at the wisdom of the decision.

'Yes, and let all the students be present on the drill-ground at the punishment,' added Nicholas.

'It will do them good! I will abolish this revolutionary spirit and will tear it up by the roots!' he thought.

'It shall be done,' replied Chernyshóv; and after a short pause he straightened the tuft on his forehead and returned to the Caucasian report.

'What do you command me to write in reply to Prince Vorontsóv's dispatch?'

'To keep firmly to my system of destroying the dwellings and food supplies in Chechnya and to harass them by raids,' answered Nicholas.

'And what are your Majesty's commands with reference to Hadji Murád?' asked Chernyshóv.

'Why, Vorontsóv writes that he wants to make use of him in the Caucasus.'

'Is it not dangerous?' said Chernyshóv, avoiding Nicholas's gaze. 'Prince Vorontsóv is too confiding, I am afraid.'

'And you – what do you think?' asked Nicholas sharply, detecting Chernyshóv's intention of presenting Vorontsóv's decision in an unfavourable light.

'Well, I should have thought it would be safer to deport him to Central Russia.'

'You would have thought!' said Nicholas ironically. 'But I don't think so, and agree with Vorontsóv. Write to him accordingly.'

'It shall be done,' said Chernyshóv, rising and bowing himself out.

Dolgorúky also bowed himself out, having during the whole audience only uttered a few words (in reply to a question from Nicholas) about the movement of the army.

After Chernyshóv, Nicholas received Bíbikov, General-Governor of the Western Provinces. Having expressed his approval of the measures taken by Bíbikov against the mutinous peasants who did not wish to accept the Orthodox Faith, he ordered him to have all those who did not submit tried by court-martial. That was equivalent to sentencing them to run the gauntlet. He also ordered the editor of a newspaper to be sent to serve in the ranks of the army for publishing information about the transfer of several thousand State peasants to the Imperial estates.

'I do this because I consider it necessary,' said Nicholas, 'and I will not allow it to be discussed.'

Bíbikov saw the cruelty of the order concerning the Uniate[1] peasants and the injustice of transferring State peasants (the only free peasants in Russia in those days) to the Crown, which meant making them serfs of the Imperial family. But it was impossible to express dissent. Not to agree with Nicholas's decisions would have meant the loss of that brilliant position which it had cost Bíbikov forty years to attain and which he now enjoyed; and he therefore submissively bowed his dark head (already touched with grey) to indicate his submission and his readiness to fulfil the cruel, insensate, and dishonest supreme will.

Having dismissed Bíbikov, Nicholas stretched himself, with a sense of duty well fulfilled, glanced at the clock, and went to get ready to go out. Having put on a uniform with epaulettes, orders, and a ribbon, he went out into the reception hall where more than a hundred persons – men in uniforms and women in elegant low-necked dresses, all standing in the places assigned to them – awaited his arrival with agitation.

He came out to them with a lifeless look in his eyes, his chest expanded, his stomach bulging out above and below its bandages, and feeling everybody's gaze tremulously and obsequiously fixed upon him he assumed an even more triumphant air. When his eyes met those of people he knew, remembering who was who, he stopped and addressed a few words to them sometimes in Russian and sometimes in French, and transfixing them with his cold glassy eye listened to what they said.

Having received all the New Year congratulations he passed on to church, where God, through His servants the priests, greeted and praised Nicholas just as worldly people did; and weary as he was of these greetings and praises Nicholas duly accepted them. All this was as it should be, because the welfare and happiness of the whole world depended on him, and wearied though he was he would still not refuse the universe his assistance.

When at the end of the service the magnificently arrayed deacon, his long hair crimped and carefully combed, began the

1 The Uniates acknowledge the Pope of Rome, though in other respects they are in accord with the Orthodox Russo-Greek Church.

chant *Many Years*, which was heartily caught up by the splendid choir, Nicholas looked round and noticed Nelídova, with her fine shoulders, standing by a window, and he decided the comparison with yesterday's girl in her favour.

After Mass he went to the Empress and spent a few minutes in the bosom of his family, joking with the children and his wife. Then passing through the Hermitage,[1] he visited the Minister of the Court, Volkónski, and among other things ordered him to pay out of a special fund a yearly pension to the mother of yesterday's girl. From there he went for his customary drive.

Dinner that day was served in the Pompeian Hall. Besides the younger sons of Nicholas and Michael there were also invited Baron Lieven, Count Rzhévski, Dolgorúky, the Prussian Ambassador, and the King of Prussia's aide-de-camp.

While waiting for the appearance of the Emperor and Empress an interesting conversation took place between Baron Lieven and the Prussian Ambassador concerning the disquieting news from Poland.

'*La Pologne et le Caucase, ce sont les deux cautères de la Russie,*' said Lieven. '*Il nous faut cent mille hommes à peu près, dans chacun de ces deux pays.*'[2]

The Ambassador expressed a fictitious surprise that it should be so.

'*Vous dites, la Pologne* —' began the Ambassador.

'*Oh, oui, c'était un coup de maître de Metternich de nous en avoir laissé l'embarras....*'[3]

At this point the Empress, with her trembling head and fixed smile, entered followed by Nicholas.

At dinner Nicholas spoke of Hadji Murád's surrender and said that the war in the Caucasus must now soon come to an end in consequence of the measures he was taking to limit the

1 A celebrated museum and picture gallery in St Petersburg, adjoining the Winter Palace.
2 'Poland and the Caucasus are Russia's two sores. We need about 100,000 men in each of those two countries.'
3 'You say that Poland —' 'Oh yes, it was a masterstroke of Metternich's to leave us the bother of it....'

scope of the mountaineers by felling their forests and by his system of erecting a series of small forts.

The Ambassador, having exchanged a rapid glance with the aide-de-camp – to whom he had only that morning spoken about Nicholas's unfortunate weakness for considering himself a great strategist – warmly praised this plan which once more demonstrated Nicholas's great strategic ability.

After dinner Nicholas drove to the ballet where hundreds of women marched round in tights and scanty clothing. One of them specially attracted him, and he had the German ballet-master sent for and gave orders that a diamond ring should be presented to him.

The next day when Chernyshóv came with his report, Nicholas again confirmed his order to Vorontsóv – that now that Hadji Murád had surrendered, the Chechens should be more actively harassed than ever and the cordon round them tightened.

Chernyshóv wrote in that sense to Vorontsóv; and another courier, overdriving more horses and bruising the faces of more drivers, galloped to Tiflis.

XVI

IN obedience to this command of Nicholas a raid was imme-diately made in Chechnya that same month, January 1852.

The detachment ordered for the raid consisted of four infantry battalions, two companies of Cossacks, and eight guns. The column marched along the road; and on both sides of it in a continuous line, now mounting, now descend-ing, marched *Jägers* in high boots, sheepskin coats, and tall caps, with rifles on their shoulders and cartridges in their belts.

As usual when marching through a hostile country, silence was observed as far as possible. Only occasionally the guns jingled jolting across a ditch, or an artillery horse snorted or neighed, not understanding that silence was ordered, or an angry commander shouted in a hoarse subdued voice to his subordinates that the line was spreading out too much or marching too near or too far from the column. Only once was the silence broken, when from a bramble patch between the line and the column a gazelle with a white breast and grey back jumped out followed by a buck of the same colour with small backward-curving horns. Doubling up their forelegs at each big bound they took, the beautiful timid creatures came so close to the column that some of the soldiers rushed after them laughing and shouting, intending to bayonet them, but the gazelles turned back, slipped through the line of *Jägers*, and pursued by a few horsemen and the company's dogs, fled like birds to the mountains.

It was still winter, but towards noon, when the column (which had started early in the morning) had gone three miles, the sun had risen high enough and was powerful enough to make the men quite hot, and its rays were so bright that it was painful to look at the shining steel of the bayonets or at the reflections – like little suns – on the brass of the cannons.

The clear and rapid stream the detachment had just crossed lay behind, and in front were tilled fields and meadows in shallow valleys. Farther in front were the dark mysterious forest-clad hills with crags rising beyond them, and farther still on the lofty horizon were the ever-beautiful ever-changing snowy peaks that played with the light like diamonds.

At the head of the 5th Company, Butler, a tall handsome officer who had recently exchanged from the Guards, marched along in a black coat and tall cap, shouldering his sword. He was filled with a buoyant sense of the joy of living, the danger of death, a wish for action, and the consciousness of being part of an immense whole directed by a single will. This was his second time of going into action and he thought how in a moment they would be fired at, and he would not only not stoop when the shells flew overhead, or heed the whistle of the bullets, but would carry his head even more erect than before and would look round at his comrades and the soldiers with smiling eyes, and begin to talk in a perfectly calm voice about quite other matters.

The detachment turned off the good road onto a little-used one that crossed a stubbly maize field, and they were drawing near the forest when, with an ominous whistle, a shell flew past amid the baggage wagons – they could not see whence – and tore up the ground in the field by the roadside.

'It's beginning,' said Butler with a bright smile to a comrade who was walking beside him.

And so it was. After the shell a thick crowd of mounted Chechens appeared with their banners from under the shelter of the forest. In the midst of the crowd could be seen a large green banner, and an old and very far-sighted sergeant-major informed the short-sighted Butler that Shamil himself must be there. The horsemen came down the hill and appeared to the right, at the highest part of the valley nearest the detachment, and began to descend. A little general in a thick black coat and tall cap rode up to Butler's company on his ambler, and ordered him to the right to encounter the descending horsemen. Butler quickly led his company in the direction indicated, but before he reached the valley he heard two cannon shots behind him. He looked round: two clouds of grey smoke had risen above two cannon and were spreading along the valley. The mountaineers' horsemen – who had evidently not expected to meet artillery – retired. Butler's company began firing at them and the whole ravine was filled with the smoke of powder. Only higher up above the ravine could the mountaineers be seen hurriedly retreating, though still firing back at the Cossacks who pursued them. The company followed the mountaineers farther, and on the slope of a second ravine came in view of an *aoul*.

Following the Cossacks, Butler and his company entered the *aoul* at a run, to find it deserted. The soldiers were ordered to burn the corn and the hay as well as the *sáklyas*, and the whole *aoul* was soon filled with pungent smoke amid which the soldiers rushed about dragging out of the *sáklyas* what they could find, and above all catching and shooting the fowls the mountaineers had not been able to take away with them.

The officers sat down at some distance beyond the smoke, and lunched and drank. The sergeant-major brought them some honeycombs on a board. There was no sign of any Chechens and early in the afternoon the order was given to retreat. The companies formed into a column behind the *aoul* and Butler happened to be in the rear-guard. As soon as they started Chechens appeared, following and firing at the detachment, but they ceased this pursuit as soon as they came out into an open space.

Not one of Butler's company had been wounded, and he returned in a most happy and energetic mood. When after fording the same stream it had crossed in the morning, the detachment spread over the maize fields and the meadows, the singers[1] of each company came forward and songs filled the air.

'Very diff'rent, very diff'rent, *Jägers* are, *Jägers* are!' sang Butler's singers, and his horse stepped merrily to the music. Trezórka, the shaggy grey dog belonging to the company, ran in front, with his tail curled up with an air of responsibility like a commander. Butler felt buoyant, calm, and joyful. War presented itself to him as consisting only in his exposing himself to danger and to possible death, thereby gaining rewards and the respect of his comrades here, as well as of his friends in Russia. Strange to say, his imagination never pictured the other aspect of war: the death and wounds of the soldiers, officers, and mountaineers. To retain his poetic conception he even unconsciously avoided looking at the dead and wounded. So that day when we had three dead and twelve wounded, he passed by a corpse lying on its back and did not stop to look, seeing only with one eye the strange position of the waxen hand and a dark red spot on the head. The hillsmen appeared to him only as mounted *dzhigíts* from whom he had to defend himself.

'You see, my dear sir,' said his major in an interval between two songs, 'it's not as it is with you in Petersburg – "Eyes right! Eyes left!" Here we have done our job, and now we go home and Másha will set a pie and some nice cabbage soup before us. That's life – don't you think so? – Now then! *As the Dawn was Breaking!*' He called for his favourite song.

There was no wind, the air was fresh and clear and so transparent that the snow hills nearly a hundred miles away seemed quite near, and in the intervals between the songs the

---

1 Each regiment had a choir of singers.

regular sound of the footsteps and the jingle of the guns was heard as a background on which each song began and ended. The song that was being sung in Butler's company was composed by a cadet in honour of the regiment, and went to a dance tune. The chorus was: 'Very diff'rent, very diff'rent, *Jägers* are, *Jägers* are!'

Butler rode beside the officer next in rank above him, Major Petróv, with whom he lived, and he felt he could not be thankful enough to have exchanged from the Guards and come to the Caucasus. His chief reason for exchanging was that he had lost all he had at cards and was afraid that if he remained there he would be unable to resist playing though he had nothing more to lose. Now all that was over, his life was quite changed and was such a pleasant and brave one! He forgot that he was ruined, and forgot his unpaid debts. The Caucasus, the war, the soldiers, the officers – those tipsy, brave, good-natured fellows – and Major Petróv himself, all seemed so delightful that sometimes it appeared too good to be true that he was not in Petersburg – in a room filled with tobacco-smoke, turning down the corners of cards[1] and gambling, hating the holder of the bank and feeling a dull pain in his head – but was really here in this glorious region among these brave Caucasians.

The major and the daughter of a surgeon's orderly, formerly known as Másha, but now generally called by the more respectful name of Márya Dmítrievna, lived together as man and wife. Márya Dmítrievna was a handsome, fair-haired, very freckled, childless woman of thirty. Whatever her past may have been she was now the major's faithful companion and looked after him like a nurse – a very necessary matter, since he often drank himself into oblivion.

When they reached the fort everything happened as the major had foreseen. Márya Dmítrievna gave him and Butler, and two other officers of the detachment who had been invited, a nourishing and tasty dinner, and the major ate and

---

1 A way of doubling one's stake at the game of *shtos*.

drank till he was unable to speak, and then went off to his room to sleep.

Butler, having drunk rather more chikhír wine than was good for him, went to his bedroom, tired but contented, and hardly had time to undress before he fell into a sound, dreamless, and unbroken sleep with his hand under his handsome curly head.

XVII

THE *aoul* which had been destroyed was that in which Hadji Murád had spent the night before he went over to the Russians. Sado and his family had left the *aoul* on the approach of the Russian detachment, and when he returned he found his *sáklya* in ruins – the roof fallen in, the door and the posts supporting the penthouse burned, and the interior filthy. His son, the handsome bright-eyed boy who had gazed with such ecstasy at Hadji Murád, was brought dead to the mosque on a horse covered with a *búrka*: he had been stabbed in the back with a bayonet. The dignified woman who had served Hadji Murád when he was at the house now stood over her son's body, her smock torn in front, her withered old breasts exposed, her hair down, and she dug her nails into her face till it bled, and wailed incessantly. Sado, taking a pick-axe and spade, had gone with his relatives to dig a grave for his son. The old grandfather sat by the wall of the ruined *sáklya* cutting a stick and gazing stolidly in front of him. He had only just returned from the apiary. The two stacks of hay there had been burnt, the apricot and cherry trees he had planted and reared were broken and scorched, and worse still all the beehives and bees had been burnt. The wailing of the women and the little children, who cried with their mothers, mingled with the lowing of the hungry cattle for whom there was no food. The bigger children, instead of playing, followed their elders with frightened eyes. The fountain was polluted, evidently on purpose, so that the water could not be used. The mosque was polluted in the same way, and the Mullah and his assistants were cleaning it out. No one spoke of hatred of the Russians.

The feeling experienced by all the Chechens, from the youngest to the oldest, was stronger than hate. It was not hatred, for they did not regard those Russian dogs as human beings, but it was such repulsion, disgust, and perplexity at the senseless cruelty of these creatures, that the desire to exterminate them – like the desire to exterminate rats, poisonous spiders, or wolves – was as natural an instinct as that of self-preservation.

The inhabitants of the *aoul* were confronted by the choice of remaining there and restoring with frightful effort what had been produced with such labour and had been so lightly and senselessly destroyed, facing every moment the possibility of a repetition of what had happened; or to submit to the Russians – contrary to their religion and despite the repulsion and contempt they felt for them. The old men prayed, and unanimously decided to send envoys to Shamil asking him for help. Then they immediately set to work to restore what had been destroyed.

XVIII

ON the morning after the raid, not very early, Butler left the house by the back porch meaning to take a stroll and a breath of fresh air before breakfast, which he usually had with Petróv. The sun had already risen above the hills and it was painful to look at the brightly lit-up white walls of the houses on the right side of the street. But then as always it was cheerful and soothing to look to the left, at the dark receding and ascending forest-clad hills and at the dim line of snow peaks, which as usual pretended to be clouds. Butler looked at these mountains, inhaling deep breaths and rejoicing that he was alive, that it was just he that was alive, and that he lived in this beautiful place.

He was also rather pleased that he had behaved so well in yesterday's affair both during the advance and especially during the retreat when things were pretty hot; he was also pleased to remember how Másha (or Márya Dmítrievna), Petróv's mistress, had treated them at dinner on their return after the raid, and how she had been particularly nice and simple with everybody, but specially kind – as he thought – to him.

Márya Dmítrievna with her thick plait of hair, her broad shoulders, her high bosom, and the radiant smile on her kindly freckled face, involuntarily attracted Butler, who was a healthy young bachelor. It sometimes even seemed to him that she wanted him, but he considered that that would be doing his good-natured simple-hearted comrade a wrong, and he maintained a simple, respectful attitude towards her and was pleased with himself for doing so.

He was thinking of this when his meditations were disturbed by the tramp of many horses' hoofs along the dusty road in front of him, as if several men were riding that way. He looked up and saw at the end of the street a group of horsemen coming towards him at a walk. In front of a score of Cossacks rode two men: one in a white Circassian coat with a tall turban on his head, the other an officer in the Russian service, dark, with an aquiline nose, and much silver on his uniform and weapons. The man with the turban rode a fine chestnut horse with mane and tail of a lighter shade, a small head, and beautiful eyes. The officer's was a large, handsome Karabákh horse. Butler, a lover of horses, immediately recognized the great strength of the first horse and stopped to learn who these people were.

The officer addressed him. 'This the house of commanding officer?' he asked, his foreign accent and his words betraying his foreign origin.

Butler replied that it was. 'And who is that?' he added, coming nearer to the officer and indicating the man with the turban.

'That Hadji Murád. He come here to stay with the commander,' said the officer.

Butler knew about Hadji Murád and about his having come over to the Russians, but he had not at all expected to see him here in this little fort. Hadji Murád gave him a friendly look.

'Good day, *kotkildy*,' said Butler, repeating the Tartar greeting he had learnt.

'*Saubul!*' ('Be well!') replied Hadji Murád, nodding. He rode up to Butler and held out his hand, from two fingers of which hung his whip.

'Are you the chief?' he asked.

'No, the chief is in here. I will go and call him,' said Butler addressing the officer, and he went up the steps and pushed the door. But the door of the visitors' entrance, as Márya Dmítrievna called it, was locked, and as it still remained closed after he had knocked, Butler went round to the back door. He called his orderly but received no reply, and finding neither of the two orderlies he went into the kitchen, where Márya Dmítrievna – flushed, with a kerchief tied round her head and her sleeves rolled up on her plump white arms – was rolling pastry, white as her hands, and cutting it into small pieces to make pies of.

'Where have the orderlies gone to?' asked Butler.

'Gone to drink,' replied Márya Dmítrievna. 'What do you want?'

'To have the front door opened. You have a whole horde of mountaineers in front of your house. Hadji Murád has come!'

'Invent something else!' said Márya Dmítrievna, smiling.

'I am not joking, he is really waiting by the porch!'

'Is it really true?' said she.

'Why should I wish to deceive you? Go and see, he's just at the porch!'

'Dear me, here's a go!' said Márya Dmítrievna pulling down her sleeves and putting up her hand to feel whether the hair-pins in her thick plait were all in order. 'Then I will go and wake Iván Matvéich.'

'No, I'll go myself. And you Bondarénko, go and open the door,' said he to Petróv's orderly who had just appeared.

'Well, so much the better!' said Márya Dmítrievna and returned to her work.

When he heard that Hadji Murád had come to his house, Iván Matvéich Petróv, the major, who had already heard that Hadji Murád was in Grózny, was not at all surprised. Sitting up in bed he rolled a cigarette, lit it, and began to dress, loudly clearing his throat and grumbling at the authorities who had sent 'that devil' to him.

When he was ready he told his orderly to bring him some medicine. The orderly knew that 'medicine' meant vodka, and brought some.

'There is nothing so bad as mixing,' muttered the major when he had drunk the vodka and taken a bite of rye bread. 'Yesterday I drank a little chikhír and now I have a headache. . . . Well, I'm ready,' he added, and went to the parlour, into which Butler had already shown Hadji Murád and the officer who accompanied him.

The officer handed the major orders from the commander of the left flank to the effect that he should receive Hadji Murád and should allow him to have intercourse with the mountaineers through spies, but was on no account to allow him to leave the fort without a convoy of Cossacks.

Having read the order the major looked intently at Hadji Murád and again scrutinized the paper. After passing his eyes several times from one to the other in this manner, he at last fixed them on Hadji Murád and said:

'*Yakshí, Bek; yakshí*!' '('Very well, sir, very well!')' 'Let him stay here, and tell him I have orders not to let him out – and what is commanded is sacred! Well, Butler, where do you think we'd better lodge him? Shall we put him in the office?'

Butler had not time to answer before Márya Dmítrievna – who had come from the kitchen and was standing in the doorway – said to the major:

'Why? Keep him here! We will give him the guest-chamber and the storeroom. Then at any rate he will be within sight,' said she, glancing at Hadji Murád; but meeting his eyes she turned quickly away.

'Do you know, I think Márya Dmítrievna is right,' said Butler.

'Now then, now then, get away! Women have no business here,' said the major frowning.

During the whole of this discussion Hadji Murád sat with his hand on the hilt of his dagger and a faint smile of contempt on his lips. He said it was all the same to him where he lodged, and that he wanted nothing but what the Sirdar had permitted – namely, to have communication with the mountaineers, and that he therefore wished they should be allowed to come to him.

The major said this should be done, and asked Butler to entertain the visitors till something could be got for them to eat and their rooms prepared. Meantime he himself would go across to the office to write what was necessary and to give some orders.

Hadji Murád's relations with his new acquaintances were at once very clearly defined. From the first he was repelled by and contemptuous of the major, to whom he always behaved very haughtily. Márya Dmítrievna, who prepared and served up his food, pleased him particularly. He liked her simplicity and especially the – to him – foreign type of her beauty, and he was influenced by the attraction she felt towards him and unconsciously conveyed. He tried not to look at her or speak to her, but his eyes involuntarily turned towards her and followed her movements. With Butler, from their first acquaintance, he immediately made friends and talked much and willingly with him, questioning him about his life, telling him of his own, communicating to him the news the spies brought him of his family's condition, and even consulting him as to how he ought to act.

The news he received through the spies was not good. During the first four days of his stay in the fort they came to see him twice and both times brought bad news.

XIX

HADJI MURÁD's family had been removed to Vedenó soon after his desertion to the Russians, and were there kept under guard awaiting Shamil's decision. The women – his old mother Patimát and his two wives with their five little children – were kept under guard in the *sáklya* of the officer Ibrahim Raschid, while Hadji Murád's son Yusúf, a youth of eighteen, was put in prison – that is, into a pit more than seven feet deep, together with seven criminals, who like himself were awaiting a decision as to their fate.

The decision was delayed because Shamil was away on a campaign against the Russians.

On January 6, 1852, he returned to Vedenó after a battle, in which according to the Russians he had been vanquished and had fled to Vedenó; but in which according to him and all the *murids* he had been victorious and had repulsed the Russians. In this battle he himself fired his rifle – a thing he seldom did – and drawing his sword would have charged straight at the Russians had not the *murids* who accompanied him held him back. Two of them were killed on the spot at his side.

It was noon when Shamil, surrounded by a party of *murids* who caracoled around him firing their rifles and pistols and continually singing *Lya illyah il Allah!* rode up to his place of residence.

All the inhabitants of the large *aoul* were in the street or on their roofs to meet their ruler, and as a sign of triumph they also fired off rifles and pistols. Shamil rode a white Arab steed which pulled at its bit as it approached the house. The horse had no gold or silver ornaments, its equipment was of the simplest – a delicately worked red leather bridle with a stripe down the middle, metal cup-shaped stirrups, and a red saddle-cloth showing a little from under the saddle. The Imám wore a brown cloth cloak lined with black fur showing at the neck and sleeves, and was tightly girded round his long thin waist with a black strap which held a dagger. On his head he wore a tall cap with flat crown and black tassel, and round it was wound a white turban, one end of which hung down on his neck. He wore green slippers, and black leggings trimmed with plain braid.

He wore nothing bright – no gold or silver – and his tall, erect, powerful figure, clothed in garments without any orna-ments, surrounded by *murids* with gold and silver on their clothes and weapons, produced on the people just the impres-sion and influence he desired and knew how to produce. His pale face framed by a closely trimmed reddish beard, with his small eyes always screwed up, was as immovable as though hewn out of stone. As he rode through the *aoul* he felt the gaze of a thousand eyes turned eagerly on him, but he himself looked at no one.

Hadji Murád's wives had come out into the penthouse with the rest of the inmates of the *sáklya* to see the Imám's entry. Only Patimát, Hadji Murád's old mother, did not go out but remained sitting on the floor of the *sáklya* with her grey hair down, her long arms encircling her thin knees, blinking with her fiery black eyes as she watched the dying embers in the fireplace. Like her son she had always hated Shamil, and now she hated him more than ever and had no wish to see him. Neither did Hadji Murád's son see Shamil's triumphal entry. Sitting in the dark and fetid pit he heard the firing and singing, and endured tortures such as can only be felt by the young who are full of vitality and deprived of freedom. He only saw his unfortunate, dirty, and exhausted fellow-prisoners – embittered and for the most part filled with hatred of one another. He now passionately envied those who, enjoying fresh air and light and freedom, caracoled on fiery steeds around their chief, shooting and heartily singing: *Lya illyah il Allah!*

When he had crossed the *aoul* Shamil rode into the large courtyard adjoining the inner court where his seraglio was. Two armed Lesghians met him at the open gates of this outer court, which was crowded with people. Some had come from distant parts about their own affairs, some had come with petitions, and some had been summoned by Shamil to be tried and sentenced. As the Imám rode in, they all respectfully saluted him with their hands on their breasts, some of them kneeling down and remaining on their knees while he rode across the court from the outer to the inner gates. Though he recognized among the people who waited in the court many whom he disliked, and many tedious petitioners who wanted his attention, Shamil passed them all with the same immovable, stony expression on his face, and having entered the inner court dismounted at the penthouse in front of his apartment, to the left of the gate. He was worn out, mentally rather than physically, by the strain of the campaign, for in spite of the public declaration that he had been victorious he knew very well that his campaign had been unsuccessful, that many Chechen *aouls* had been burnt down and ruined, and that the unstable and fickle Chechens were wavering and those nearest the border line were ready to go over to the Russians.

All this had to be dealt with, and it oppressed him, for at that moment he did not wish to think at all. He only desired one thing: rest and the delights of family life, and the caresses of his favourite wife, the black-eyed quick-footed eighteen-year-old Aminal, who at that very moment was close at hand behind the fence that divided the inner court and separated the men's from the women's quarters (Shamil felt sure she was there with his other wives, looking through a chink in the fence while he dismounted). But not only was it impossible for him to go to her, he could not even lie down on his feather cushions and rest from his fatigues; he had first of all to perform the midday rites for which he had just then not the least inclination, but which as the religious leader of the people he could not omit, and which moreover were as necessary to him himself as his daily food. So he performed his ablutions and said his prayers and summoned those who were waiting for him.

The first to enter was Jemal Eddin, his father-in-law and teacher, a tall grey-haired good-looking old man with a beard white as snow and a rosy red face. He said a prayer and began questioning Shamil about the incidents of the campaign and telling him what had happened in the mountains during his absence.

Among events of many kinds – murders connected with blood-feuds, cattle-stealing, people accused of disobeying the Tarikát (smoking and drinking wine) – Jemal Eddin related how Hadji Murád had sent men to bring his family over to the Russians, but that this had been detected and the family had been brought to Vedenó where they were kept under guard and awaited the Imám's decision. In the next room, the guest-chamber, the Elders were assembled to discuss all these affairs, and Jemal Eddin advised Shamil to finish with them and let them go that same day, as they had already been waiting three days for him.

After eating his dinner – served to him in his room by Zeidát, a dark, sharp-nosed, disagreeable-looking woman whom he did not love but who was his eldest wife – Shamil passed into the guest-chamber.

The six old men who made up his council – white, grey, or red-bearded, with tall caps on their heads, some with turbans and some without, wearing new *beshméts* and Circassian coats girdled with straps on which their daggers were suspended – rose to greet him on his entrance. Shamil towered a head above them all. On entering the room he, as well as all the others, lifted his hands, palms upwards, closed his eyes and recited a prayer, and then stroked his face downwards with both hands, uniting them at the end of his beard. Having done this they all sat down, Shamil on a larger cushion than the others, and discussed the various cases before them.

In the case of the criminals the decisions were given according to the Shariát: two were sentenced to have a hand cut off for stealing, one man to be beheaded for murder, and three were pardoned. Then they came to the principal business: how to stop the Chechens from going over to the Russians. To counteract that tendency Jemal Eddin drew up the following proclamation:

'I wish you eternal peace with God the Almighty!

'I hear that the Russians flatter you and invite you to surrender to them. Do not believe what they say, and do not surrender but endure. If ye be not rewarded for it in this life ye shall receive your reward in the life to come. Remember what happened before when they took your arms from you! If God had not brought you to reason then, in 1840, ye would now be soldiers, and your wives would be dishonoured and would no longer wear trousers.

'Judge of the future by the past. It is better to die in enmity with the Russians than to live with the Unbelievers. Endure for a little while and I will come with the Koran and the sword and will lead you against the enemy. But now I strictly command you not only to entertain no intention, but not even a thought, of submitting to the Russians!'

Shamil approved this proclamation, signed it, and had it sent out.

After this business they considered Hadji Murád's case. This was of the utmost importance to Shamil. Although he did not wish to admit it, he knew that if Hadji Murád with his agility, boldness, and courage, had been with him, what had now happened in Chechnya would not have occurred. It would therefore be well to make it up with Hadji Murád and have the benefit of his services again. But as this was not possible it would never do to allow him to help the Russians, and therefore he must be enticed back and killed. They might accomplish this either by sending a man to Tiflis who would kill him there, or by inducing him to come back and then killing him. The only means of doing the latter was by making use of his family and especially his son, whom Shamil knew he loved passionately. Therefore they must act through the son.

When the councillors had talked all this over, Shamil closed his eyes and sat silent.

The councillors knew that this meant that he was listening to the voice of the Prophet, who spoke to him and told him what to do.

After five minutes of solemn silence Shamil opened his eyes, and narrowing them more than usual, said:

'Bring Hadji Murád's son to me.'

'He is here,' replied Jemal Eddin, and in fact Yusúf, Hadji Murád's son, thin, pale, tattered, and evil-smelling, but still handsome in face and figure, with black eyes that burnt like his grandmother Patimát's, was already standing by the gate of the outside court waiting to be called in.

Yusúf did not share his father's feelings towards Shamil. He did not know all that had happened in the past, or if he knew it, not having lived through it he still did not understand why his father was so obstinately hostile to Shamil. To him who wanted only one thing – to continue living the easy, loose life that, as the *naïb*'s son, he had led in Khunzákh – it seemed quite unnecessary to be at enmity with Shamil. Out of defiance and a spirit of contradiction to his father he particularly admired Shamil, and shared the ecstatic adoration with which he was regarded in the mountains. With a peculiar feeling of tremulous veneration for the Imám he now entered the guest-chamber. As he stopped by the door he met the steady gaze of Shamil's half-closed eyes. He paused for a moment, and then approached Shamil and kissed his large, long-fingered hand.

'Thou art Hadji Murád's son?'

'I am, Imám.'

'Thou knowest what he has done?'

'I know, Imám, and deplore it.'

'Canst thou write?'

'I was preparing myself to be a Mullah — '

'Then write to thy father that if he will return to me now, before the Feast of Bairam, I will forgive him and everything shall be as it was before; but if not, and if he remains with the Russians' – and Shamil frowned sternly – 'I will give thy grandmother, thy mother, and the rest to the different *aouls*, and thee I will behead!'

Not a muscle of Yusúf's face stirred, and he bowed his head to show that he understood Shamil's words.

'Write that and give it to my messenger.'

Shamil ceased speaking, and looked at Yusúf for a long time in silence.

'Write that I have had pity on thee and will not kill thee, but will put out thine eyes as I do to all traitors! ... Go!'

While in Shamil's presence Yusúf appeared calm, but when he had been led out of the guest-chamber he rushed at his attendant, snatched the man's dagger from its sheath and tried to stab himself, but he was seized by the arms, bound, and led back to the pit.

That evening at dusk after he had finished his evening prayers, Shamil put on a white fur-lined cloak and passed out to the other side of the fence where his wives lived, and went straight to Aminal's room, but he did not find her there. She was with the older wives. Then Shamil, trying to remain unseen, hid behind the door and stood waiting for her. But Aminal was angry with him because he had given some silk stuff to Zeidát and not to her. She saw him come out and go into her room looking for her, and she purposely kept away. She stood a long time at the door of Zeidát's room, laughing softly at Shamil's white figure that kept going in and out of her room.

Having waited for her in vain, Shamil returned to his own apartments when it was already time for the midnight prayers.

XX

HADJI Murád had been a week in the major's house at the fort. Although Márya Dmítrievna quarrelled with the shaggy Khanéfi (Hadji Murád had only brought two of his *murids*, Khanéfi and Eldár, with him) and had turned him out of her kitchen – for which he nearly killed her – she evidently felt a particular respect and sympathy for Hadji Murád. She now no longer served him his dinner, having handed that duty over to Eldár, but she seized every opportunity of seeing him and rendering him service. She always took the liveliest interest in the negotiations about his family, knew how many wives and children he had, and their ages, and each time a spy came to see him she inquired as best she could into the results of the negotiations.

Butler during that week had become quite friendly with Hadji Murád. Sometimes the latter came to Butler's room, sometimes Butler went to Hadji Murád's: sometimes they conversed by the help of the interpreter, and sometimes they got on as best they could with signs and especially with smiles.

Hadji Murád had evidently taken a fancy to Butler, as could be gathered from Eldár's relations with the latter. When Butler entered Hadji Murád's room Eldár met him with a pleased smile showing his glittering teeth, and hurried to put down a cushion for him to sit on and to relieve him of his sword if he was wearing one.

Butler also got to know, and became friendly with, the shaggy Khanéfi, Hadji Murád's sworn brother. Khanéfi knew many mountain songs and sang them well, and to please Butler, Hadji Murád often made Khanéfi sing, choosing the songs he considered best. Khanéfi had a high tenor voice and sang with extraordinary clearness and expression. One of the songs Hadji

Murád specially liked impressed Butler by its solemnly mournful tone and he asked the interpreter to translate it.

The subject of the song was the very blood-feud that had existed between Khanéfi and Hadji Murád. It ran as follows:

'The earth will dry on my grave,
      Mother, my Mother!
   And thou wilt forget me!
And over me rank grass will wave,
      Father, my Father!
   Nor wilt thou regret me
When tears cease thy dark eyes to lave,
      Sister, dear Sister!
   No more will grief fret thee!

'But thou, my Brother the elder, wilt never forget,
      With vengeance denied me!
And thou, my Brother the younger, wilt ever regret,
      Till thou liest beside me!

'Hotly thou camest, O death-bearing ball that I spurned,
      For thou wast my slave!
And thou, black earth, that battle-steed trampled and churned,
      Wilt cover my grave!

'Cold art Thou, O Death, yet I was thy Lord and thy Master!
My body sinks fast to the earth, my soul to Heaven flies faster.'

Hadji Murád always listened to this song with closed eyes and when it ended on a long gradually dying note he always remarked in Russian –

'Good song! Wise song!'

After Hadji Murád's arrival and his intimacy with him and his *murids*, the poetry of the stirring mountain life took a still stronger hold on Butler. He procured for himself a *beshmét* and a Circassian coat and leggings, and imagined himself a mountaineer living the life those people lived.

On the day of Hadji Murád's departure the major invited several officers to see him off. They were sitting, some at the table where Márya Dmítrievna was pouring out tea, some at another table on which stood vodka, chikhír, and light refreshments, when Hadji Murád dressed for the journey came limping into the room with soft, rapid footsteps.

They all rose and shook hands with him. The major offered him a seat on the divan, but Hadji Murád thanked him and sat down on a chair by the window.

The silence that followed his entrance did not at all abash him. He looked attentively at all the faces and fixed an indifferent gaze on the tea-table with the samovar and refreshments. Petróvsky, a lively officer who now met Hadji Murád for the first time, asked him through the interpreter whether he liked Tiflis.

'*Alya!*' he replied.

'He says "Yes",' translated the interpreter.

'What did he like there?'

Hadji Murád said something in reply.

'He liked the theatre best of all.'

'And how did he like the ball at the house of the commander-in-chief?'

Hadji Murád frowned. 'Every nation has its own customs! Our women do not dress in such a way,' said he, glancing at Márya Dmítrievna.

'Well, didn't he like it?'

'We have a proverb,' said Hadji Murád to the interpreter, '"The dog gave meat to the ass and the ass gave hay to the dog, and both went hungry,"' and he smiled. 'Its own customs seem good to each nation.'

The conversation went no farther. Some of the officers took tea, some other refreshments. Hadji Murád accepted the tumbler of tea offered him and put it down before him.

'Won't you have cream and a bun?' asked Márya Dmítrievna, offering them to him.

Hadji Murád bowed his head.

'Well, I suppose it is good-bye!' said Butler, touching his knee. 'When shall we meet again?'

'Good-bye, good-bye!' said Hadji Murád, in Russian, with a smile. '*Kunák bulug.* Strong *kunák* to thee! Time – *ayda* – go!' and he jerked his head in the direction in which he had to go.

Eldár appeared in the doorway carrying something large and white across his shoulder and a sword in his hand. Hadji Murád beckoned to him and he crossed the room with big strides and handed him a white *búrka* and the sword. Hadji Murád rose, took the *búrka*, threw it over his arm, and saying something to the interpreter handed it to Márya Dmítrievna.

'He says thou hast praised the *búrka*, so accept it,' said the interpreter.

'Oh, why?' said Márya Dmítrievna blushing.

'It is necessary. Like Adam,' said Hadji Murád.

'Well, thank you,' said Márya Dmítrievna, taking the *búrka*. 'God grant that you rescue your son,' she added. '*Ulan yakshi*. Tell him that I wish him success in releasing his son.'

Hadji Murád glanced at Márya Dmítrievna and nodded his head approvingly. Then he took the sword from Eldár and handed it to the major. The major took it and said to the interpreter, 'Tell him to take my chestnut gelding. I have nothing else to give him.'

Hadji Murád waved his hand in front of his face to show that he did not want anything and would not accept it. Then, pointing first to the mountains and then to his heart, he went out.

All the household followed him as far as the door, while the officers who remained inside the room drew the sword from its scabbard, examined its blade, and decided that it was a real Gurda.[1]

Butler accompanied Hadji Murád to the porch, and then came a very unexpected incident which might have ended fatally for Hadji Murád had it not been for his quick observation, determination, and agility.

The inhabitants of the Kumúkh *aoul*, Tash-Kichu, which was friendly to the Russians, respected Hadji Murád greatly and had often come to the fort merely to look at the famous *naïb*. They had sent messengers to him three days previously to ask him to visit their mosque on the Friday. But the Kumúkh princes who lived in Tash-Kichu hated Hadji Murád because there was a blood-feud between them, and on hearing of this

---

1 A highly prized quality of blade.

invitation they announced to the people that they would not allow him to enter the mosque. The people became excited and a fight occurred between them and the princes' supporters. The Russian authorities pacified the mountaineers and sent word to Hadji Murád not to go to the mosque.

Hadji Murád did not go and everyone supposed that the matter was settled.

But at the very moment of his departure, when he came out into the porch before which the horses stood waiting, Arslán Khan, one of the Kumúkh princes and an acquaintance of Butler and the major, rode up to the house.

When he saw Hadji Murád he snatched a pistol from his belt and took aim, but before he could fire, Hadji Murád in spite of his lameness rushed down from the porch like a cat towards Arslán Khan who missed him.

Seizing Arslán Khan's horse by the bridle with one hand, Hadji Murád drew his dagger with the other and shouted something to him in Tartar.

Butler and Eldár both ran at once towards the enemies and caught them by the arms. The major, who had heard the shot, also came out.

'What do you mean by it, Arslán – starting such a nasty business on my premises?' said he, when he heard what had happened. 'It's not right, friend! "To the foe in the field you need not yield!" – but to start this kind of slaughter in front of my house —'

Arslán Khan, a little man with black moustaches, got off his horse pale and trembling, looked angrily at Hadji Murád, and went into the house with the major. Hadji Murád, breathing heavily and smiling, returned to the horses.

'Why did he want to kill him?' Butler asked the interpreter.

'He says it is a law of theirs,' the interpreter translated Hadji Murád's reply. 'Arslán must avenge a relation's blood and so he tried to kill him.'

'And supposing he overtakes him on the road?' asked Butler.

Hadji Murád smiled.

'Well, if he kills me it will prove that such is Allah's will. . . . Good-bye,' he said again in Russian, taking his

horse by the withers. Glancing round at everybody who had
come out to see him off, his eyes rested kindly on Márya
Dmítrievna.

'Good-bye, my lass,' said he to her. 'I thank you.'

'God help you – God help you to rescue your family!'
repeated Márya Dmítrievna.

He did not understand her words, but felt her sympathy for
him and nodded to her.

'Mind, don't forget your *kunák*,' said Butler.

'Tell him I am his true friend and will never forget him,'
answered Hadji Murád to the interpreter, and in spite of his
short leg he swung himself lightly and quickly into the high
saddle, barely touching the stirrup, and automatically feeling
for his dagger and adjusting his sword. Then, with that peculiarly proud look with which only a Caucasian hill-man sits his
horse – as though he were one with it – he rode away from the
major's house. Khanéfi and Eldár also mounted and having
taken a friendly leave of their hosts and of the officers, rode off
at a trot, following their *murshíd*.

As usual after a departure, those who remained behind
began to discuss those who had left.

'Plucky fellow! He rushed at Arslán Khan like a wolf! His
face quite changed!'

'But he'll be up to tricks – he's a terrible rogue, I should say,'
remarked Petróvsky.

'It's a pity there aren't more Russian rogues of such a kind!'
suddenly put in Márya Dmítrievna with vexation. 'He has
lived a week with us and we have seen nothing but good
from him. He is courteous, wise, and just,' she added.

'How did you find that out?'

'No matter, I did find it out!'

'She's quite smitten, and that's a fact!' said the major, who
had just entered the room.

'Well, and if I am smitten? What's that to you? Why run
him down if he's a good man? Though he's a Tartar he's still a
good man!'

'Quite true, Márya Dmítrievna,' said Butler, 'and you're
quite right to take his part!'

XXI

LIFE in our advanced forts in the Chechen lines went on as usual. Since the events last narrated there had been two alarms when the companies were called out and militiamen galloped about; but both times the mountaineers who had caused the excitement got away, and once at Vozdvízhensk they killed a Cossack and succeeded in carrying off eight Cossack horses that were being watered. There had been no further raids since the one in which the *aoul* was destroyed, but an expedition on a large scale was expected in consequence of the appointment of a new commander of the left flank, Prince Baryátinsky. He was an old friend of the Viceroy's and had been in command of the Kabardá Regiment. On his arrival at Grózny as commander of the whole left flank he at once mustered a detachment to continue to carry out the Tsar's commands as communicated by Chernyshóv to Vorontsóv. The detachment mustered at Vozdvízhensk left the fort and took up a position towards Kurín, where the troops were encamped and were felling the forest. Young Vorontsóv lived in a splendid cloth tent, and his wife, Márya Vasílevna, often came to the camp and stayed the night. Baryátinsky's relations with Márya Vasílevna were no secret to anyone, and the officers who were not in the aristocratic set and the soldiers abused her in coarse terms – for her presence in camp caused them to be told off to lie in ambush at night. The mountaineers were in the habit of bringing guns within range and firing shells at the camp. The shells generally missed their aim and therefore at ordinary times no special measures were taken to prevent such firing, but now men were placed in ambush to hinder the mountaineers from injuring or frightening Márya Vasílevna with their cannon. To have to be always lying in ambush at night to save a lady from being frightened, offended and annoyed them, and therefore the soldiers, as well as the officers not admitted to the higher society, called Márya Vasílevna bad names.

Having obtained leave of absence from his fort, Butler came to the camp to visit some old messmates from the cadet corps and fellow officers of the Kurín regiment who were serving as

adjutants and orderly officers. When he first arrived he had a
very good time. He put up in Poltorátsky's tent and there met
many acquaintances who gave him a hearty welcome. He also
called on Vorontsóv, whom he knew slightly, having once
served in the same regiment with him. Vorontsóv received
him very kindly, introduced him to Prince Baryátinsky, and
invited him to the farewell dinner he was giving in honour of
General Kozlóvsky, who until Baryátinsky's arrival had been in
command of the left flank.

The dinner was magnificent. Special tents were erected in a
line, and along the whole length of them a table was spread as
for a dinner-party, with dinner-services and bottles. Everything recalled life in the Guards in Petersburg. Dinner was
served at two o'clock. Kozlóvsky sat in the middle on one side,
Baryátinsky on the other. At Kozlóvsky's right and left hand sat
the Vorontsóvs, husband and wife. All along the table on both
sides sat the officers of the Kabardá and Kurín regiments.
Butler sat next to Poltorátsky and they both chatted merrily
and drank with the officers around them. When the roast was
served and the orderlies had gone round and filled the champagne glasses, Poltorátsky said to Butler, with real anxiety:

'Our Kozlóvsky will disgrace himself!'

'Why?'

'Why, he'll have to make a speech, and what good is he at
that? . . . It's not as easy as capturing entrenchments under fire!
And with a lady beside him too, and these aristocrats!'

'Really it's painful to look at him,' said the officers to one
another. And now the solemn moment had arrived. Baryátinsky rose and lifting his glass, addressed a short speech to
Kozlóvsky. When he had finished, Kozlóvsky – who always
had a trick of using the word 'how' superfluously – rose and
stammeringly began:

'In compliance with the august will of his Majesty I am
leaving you – parting from you, gentlemen,' said he. 'But
consider me as always remaining among you. The truth of
the proverb, how "One man in the field is no warrior", is well
known to you, gentlemen. . . . Therefore, how every reward
I have received . . . how all the benefits showered on me by the

great generosity of our sovereign the Emperor . . . how all my position – how my good name . . . how everything decidedly . . . how . . .' (here his voice trembled) '. . . how I am indebted to you for it, to you alone, my friends!' The wrinkled face puckered up still more, he gave a sob and tears came into his eyes. 'How from my heart I offer you my sincerest, heartfelt gratitude!'

Kozlóvsky could not go on but turned round and began to embrace the officers. The princess hid her face in her handkerchief. The prince blinked, with his mouth drawn awry. Many of the officers' eyes grew moist and Butler, who had hardly known Kozlóvsky, could also not restrain his tears. He liked all this very much.

Then followed other toasts. Healths were drunk to Baryátinsky, Vorontsóv, the officers, and the soldiers, and the visitors left the table intoxicated with wine and with the military elation to which they were always so prone. The weather was wonderful, sunny and calm, and the air fresh and bracing. Bonfires crackled and songs resounded on all sides. It might have been thought that everybody was celebrating some joyful event. Butler went to Poltorátsky's in the happiest, most emotional mood. Several officers had gathered there and a card-table was set. An adjutant started a bank with a hundred rubles. Two or three times Butler left the tent with his hand gripping the purse in his trousers-pocket, but at last he could resist the temptation no longer, and despite the promise he had given to his brother and to himself not to play, he began to do so. Before an hour was past, very red, perspiring, and soiled with chalk, he was sitting with both elbows on the table and writing on it – under cards bent for 'corners' and 'transports'[1] – the figures of his stakes. He had already lost so much that he was afraid to count up what was scored against him. But he knew without counting that all the pay he could draw in advance, added to the value of his horse, would not suffice to pay what the adjutant, a stranger to him, had written down

1 These expressions relate to the game of *shtos* and have been explained in *Two Hussars*.

against him. He would still have gone on playing, but the adjutant sternly laid down the cards he held in his large clean hands and added up the chalked figures of the score of Butler's losses. Butler, in confusion, began to make excuses for being unable to pay the whole of his debt at once, and said he would send it from home. When he said this he noticed that everybody pitied him and that they all – even Poltorátsky – avoided meeting his eye. That was his last evening there. He reflected that he need only have refrained from playing and gone to the Vorontsóvs who had invited him, and all would have been well, but now it was not only not well – it was terrible.

Having taken leave of his comrades and acquaintances he rode home and went to bed, and slept for eighteen hours as people usually sleep after losing heavily. From the fact that he asked her to lend him fifty kopeks to tip the Cossack who had escorted him, and from his sorrowful looks and short answers, Márya Dmítrievna guessed that he had lost at cards and she reproached the major for having given him leave of absence.

When he woke up at noon next day and remembered the situation he was in he longed again to plunge into the oblivion from which he had just emerged, but it was impossible. Steps had to be taken to repay the four hundred and seventy rubles he owed to the stranger. The first step he took was to write to his brother, confessing his sin and imploring him, for the last time, to lend him five hundred rubles on the security of the mill they still owned in common. Then he wrote to a stingy relative asking her to lend him five hundred rubles at whatever rate of interest she liked. Finally he went to the major, knowing that he – or rather Márya Dmítrievna – had some money, and asked him to lend him five hundred rubles.

'I'd let you have them at once,' said the major, 'but Másha won't! These women are so close-fisted – who the devil can understand them? . . . And yet you must get out of it somehow, devil take him! . . . Hasn't that brute the canteen-keeper got something?'

But it was no use trying to borrow from the canteen-keeper, so Butler's salvation could only come from his brother or his stingy relative.

XXII

NOT having attained his aim in Chechnya, Hadji Murád returned to Tiflis and went every day to Vorontsóv's, and whenever he could obtain audience he implored the Viceroy to gather together the mountaineer prisoners and exchange them for his family. He said that unless that were done his hands were tied and he could not serve the Russians and destroy Shamil as he desired to do. Vorontsóv vaguely promised to do what he could, but put it off, saying that he would decide when General Argutínski reached Tiflis and he could talk the matter over with him.

Then Hadji Murád asked Vorontsóv to allow him to go to live for a while in Nukhá, a small town in Transcaucasia where he thought he could better carry on negotiations about his family with Shamil and with the people who were attached to himself. Moreover Nukhá, being a Mohammedan town, had a mosque where he could more conveniently perform the rites of prayer demanded by the Mohammedan law. Vorontsóv wrote to Petersburg about it but meanwhile gave Hadji Murád permission to go to Nukhá.

For Vorontsóv and the authorities in Petersburg, as well as for most Russians acquainted with Hadji Murád's history, the whole episode presented itself as a lucky turn in the Caucasian war, or simply as an interesting event. For Hadji Murád it was a terrible crisis in his life – especially latterly. He had escaped from the mountains partly to save himself and partly out of hatred of Shamil, and difficult as this flight had been he had attained his object, and for a time was glad of his success and really devised a plan to attack Shamil, but the rescue of his family – which he had thought would be easy to arrange – had proved more difficult than he expected.

Shamil had seized the family and kept them prisoners, threatening to hand the women over to the different *aouls* and to blind or kill the son. Now Hadji Murád had gone to Nukhá intending to try by the aid of his adherents in Daghestan to rescue his family from Shamil by force or by cunning. The last spy who had come to see him in Nukhá informed him that the Avars, who were devoted to him, were preparing to capture his family and themselves bring them over to the Russians, but that there were not enough of them and they could not risk making the attempt in Vedenó, where the family was at present imprisoned, but could do so only if the family were moved from Vedenó to some other place – in which case they promised to rescue them on the way.

Hadji Murád sent word to his friends that he would give three thousand rubles for the liberation of his family.

At Nukhá a small house of five rooms was assigned to Hadji Murád near the mosque and the Khan's palace. The officers in charge of him, his interpreter, and his henchmen, stayed in the same house. Hadji Murád's life was spent in the expectation and reception of messengers from the mountains and in rides he was allowed to take in the neighbourhood.

On 24th April, returning from one of these rides, Hadji Murád learnt that during his absence an official sent by Vorontsóv had arrived from Tiflis. In spite of his longing to know what message the official had brought him he went to his bedroom and repeated his noonday prayer before going into the room where the officer in charge and the official were waiting. This room served him both as drawing- and reception-room. The official who had come from Tiflis, Councillor Kiríllov, informed Hadji Murád of Vorontsóv's wish that he should come to Tiflis on the 12th to meet General Argutínski.

'*Yakshi!*' said Hadji Murád angrily. The councillor did not please him. 'Have you brought money?'

'I have,' answered Kiríllov.

'For two weeks now,' said Hadji Murád, holding up first both hands and then four fingers. 'Give here!'

'We'll give it you at once,' said the official, getting his purse out of his travelling-bag. 'What does he want with the money?' he went on in Russian, thinking that Hadji Murád would not understand. But Hadji Murád had understood, and glanced angrily at him. While getting out the money the councillor, wishing to begin a conversation with Hadji Murád in order to have something to tell Prince Vorontsóv on his return, asked through the interpreter whether he was not feeling dull there. Hadji Murád glanced contemptuously out of the corner of his eye at the fat, unarmed little man dressed as a civilian, and did not reply. The interpreter repeated the question.

'Tell him that I cannot talk with him! Let him give me the money!' and having said this, Hadji Murád sat down at the table ready to count it.

Hadji Murád had an allowance of five gold pieces a day, and when Kiríllov had got out the money and arranged it in seven piles of ten gold pieces each and pushed them towards Hadji Murád, the latter poured the gold into the sleeve of his Circassian coat, rose, quite unexpectedly smacked Councillor Kiríllov on his bald pate, and turned to go.

The councillor jumped up and ordered the interpreter to tell Hadji Murád that he must not dare to behave like that to him who held a rank equal to that of colonel! The officer in charge confirmed this, but Hadji Murád only nodded to signify that he knew, and left the room.

'What is one to do with him?' said the officer in charge. 'He'll stick his dagger into you, that's all! One cannot talk with those devils! I see that he is getting exasperated.'

As soon as it began to grow dusk two spies with hoods covering their faces up to their eyes, came to him from the hills. The officer in charge led them to Hadji Murád's room. One of them was a fleshy, swarthy Tavlinian, the other a thin old man. The news they brought was not cheering. Hadji Murád's friends who had undertaken to rescue his family now definitely refused to do so, being afraid of Shamil, who threatened to punish with most terrible tortures anyone who helped Hadji Murád. Having heard the messengers he sat with his elbows on his crossed legs, and bowing his turbaned head remained silent a long time.

He was thinking and thinking resolutely. He knew that he was now considering the matter for the last time and that it was necessary to come to a decision. At last he raised his head, gave each of the messengers a gold piece, and said: 'Go!'

'What answer will there be?'

'The answer will be as God pleases.... Go!'

The messengers rose and went away, and Hadji Murád continued to sit on the carpet leaning his elbows on his knees. He sat thus a long time and pondered.

'What am I to do? To take Shamil at his word and return to him?' he thought. 'He is a fox and will deceive me. Even if he did not deceive me it would still be impossible to submit to that red liar. It is impossible . . . because now that I have been with the Russians he will not trust me,' thought Hadji Murád; and he remembered a Tavlinian fable about a falcon who had been caught and lived among men and afterwards returned to his own kind in the hills. He returned, wearing jesses with bells, and the other falcons would not receive him. 'Fly back to where they hung those silver bells on thee!' said they. 'We have no bells and no jesses.' The falcon did not want to leave his home and remained, but the other falcons did not wish to let him stay there and pecked him to death.

'And they would peck me to death in the same way,' thought Hadji Murád. 'Shall I remain here and conquer Caucasia for the Russian Tsar and earn renown, titles, riches?'

'That could be done,' thought he, recalling his interviews with Vorontsóv and the flattering things the prince had said; 'but I must decide at once, or Shamil will destroy my family.'

That night he remained awake, thinking.

XXIII

BY midnight his decision had been formed. He had decided that he must fly to the mountains, and break into Vedenó with the Avars still devoted to him, and either die or rescue his family. Whether after rescuing them he would return to the Russians or escape to Khunzákh and fight Shamil, he had not made up his mind. All he knew was that first of all he must escape from the Russians into the mountains, and he at once began to carry out his plan.

He drew his black wadded *beshmét* from under his pillow and went into his henchmen's room. They lived on the other side of the hall. As soon as he entered the hall, the outer door of which stood open, he was at once enveloped by the dewy freshness of the moonlit night and his ears were filled by the whistling and trilling of several nightingales in the garden by the house.

Having crossed the hall he opened the door of his henchmen's room. There was no light there, but the moon in its first quarter shone in at the window. A table and two chairs were standing on one side of the room, and four of his henchmen were lying on carpets or on *búrkas* on the floor. Khanéfi slept outside with the horses. Gamzálo heard the door creak, rose, turned round, and saw him. On recognizing him he lay down again, but Eldár, who lay beside him, jumped up and began putting on his *beshmét*, expecting his master's orders. Khan Mahomá and Bata slept on. Hadji Murád put down the *beshmét* he had brought on the table, which it hit with a dull sound, caused by the gold sewn up in it.

'Sew these in too,' said Hadji Murád, handing Eldár the gold pieces he had received that day. Eldár took them and at once went into the moonlight, drew a small knife from under his dagger and started unstitching the lining of the *beshmét*. Gamzálo raised himself and sat up with his legs crossed.

'And you, Gamzálo, tell the men to examine the rifles and pistols and get the ammunition ready. To-morrow we shall go far,' said Hadji Murád.

'We have bullets and powder, everything shall be ready,' replied Gamzálo, and roared out something incomprehensible. He understood why Hadji Murád had ordered the rifles to be loaded. From the first he had desired only one thing – to slay and stab as many Russians as possible and to escape to the hills – and this desire had increased day by day. Now at last he saw that Hadji Murád also wanted this and he was satisfied.

When Hadji Murád went away Gamzálo roused his comrades, and all four spent the rest of the night examining their rifles, pistols, flints, and accoutrements; replacing what was damaged, sprinkling fresh powder onto the pans, and stoppering with bullets wrapped in oiled rags packets filled with the right amount of powder for each charge, sharpening their swords and daggers and greasing the blades with tallow.

Before daybreak Hadji Murád again came out into the hall to get water for his ablutions. The songs of the nightingales that had burst into ecstasy at dawn were now even louder and more incessant, while from his henchmen's room, where the daggers were being sharpened, came the regular screech and rasp of iron against stone.

Hadji Murád got himself some water from a tub, and was already at his own door when above the sound of the grinding he heard from his *murids'* room the high tones of Khanéfi's voice singing a familiar song. He stopped to listen. The song told of how a *dzhigít*, Hamzád, with his brave followers captured a herd of white horses from the Russians, and how a Russian prince followed him beyond the Térek and surrounded him with an army as large as a forest; and then the song went on to tell how Hamzád killed the horses, entrenched his men behind this gory bulwark, and fought the Russians as long as they had bullets in their rifles, daggers in their belts, and blood in their veins. But before he died Hamzád saw some birds flying in the sky and cried to them:

'Fly on, ye winged ones, fly to our homes!
Tell ye our mothers, tell ye our sisters,
Tell the white maidens, that fighting we died
For Ghazavát! Tell them our bodies
Never will lie and rest in a tomb!
Wolves will devour and tear them to pieces,
Ravens and vultures will pluck out our eyes.'

With that the song ended, and at the last words, sung to a mournful air, the merry Bata's vigorous voice joined in with a loud shout of '*Lya-il-lyakha-il Allakh!*' finishing with a shrill shriek. Then all was quiet again, except for the *tchuk, tchuk, tchuk, tchuk* and whistling of the nightingales from the garden and from behind the door the even grinding, and now and then the whiz, of iron sliding quickly along the whetstone.

Hadji Murád was so full of thought that he did not notice how he tilted his jug till the water began to pour out. He shook his head at himself and re-entered his room. After performing his morning ablutions he examined his weapons and sat down on his bed. There was nothing more for him to do. To be allowed to ride out he would have to get permission from the officer in charge, but it was not yet daylight and the officer was still asleep.

Khanéfi's song reminded him of the song his mother had composed just after he was born – the song addressed to his father that Hadji Murád had repeated to Lóris-Mélikov.

And he seemed to see his mother before him – not wrinkled and grey-haired, with gaps between her teeth, as he had lately left her, but young and handsome, and strong enough to carry him in a basket on her back across the mountains to her father's when he was a heavy five-year-old boy.

And the recollection of himself as a little child reminded him of his beloved son, Yusúf, whose head he himself had shaved for the first time; and now this Yusúf was a handsome young *dzhigít*. He pictured him as he was when last he saw him on the day he left Tselméss. Yusúf brought him his horse and asked to be allowed to accompany him. He was ready dressed and armed, and led his own horse by the bridle, and his rosy handsome young face and the whole of his tall slender figure (he was taller than his father) breathed of daring, youth, and the joy of life. The breadth of his shoulders, though he was so young, the very wide youthful hips, the long slender waist, the strength of his long arms, and the power, flexibility, and agility of all his movements had always rejoiced Hadji Murád, who admired his son.

'Thou hadst better stay. Thou wilt be alone at home now. Take care of thy mother and thy grandmother,' said Hadji Murád. And he remembered the spirited and proud look and the flush of pleasure with which Yusúf had replied that as long as he lived no one should injure his mother or grandmother. All the same, Yusúf had mounted and accompanied his father as far as the stream. There he turned back, and since then Hadji Murád had not seen his wife, his mother, or his son. And it was this son whose eyes Shamil threatened to put out! Of what would be done to his wife Hadji Murád did not wish to think.

These thoughts so excited him that he could not sit still any longer. He jumped up and went limping quickly to the door, opened it, and called Eldár. The sun had not yet risen, but it was already quite light. The nightingales were still singing.

'Go and tell the officer that I want to go out riding, and saddle the horses,' said he.

XXIV

BUTLER'S only consolation all this time was the poetry of warfare, to which he gave himself up not only during his hours of service but also in private life. Dressed in his Circassian costume, he rode and swaggered about, and twice went into ambush with Bogdanóvich, though neither time did they discover or kill anyone. This closeness to and friendship with Bogdanóvich, famed for his courage, seemed pleasant and warlike to Butler. He had paid his debt, having borrowed the money off a Jew at an enormous rate of interest – that is to say, he had postponed his difficulties but had not solved them. He tried not to think of his position, and to find oblivion not only in the poetry of warfare but also in wine. He drank more and more every day, and day by day grew morally weaker. He was now no longer the chaste Joseph he had been towards Márya Dmítrievna, but on the contrary began courting her grossly, meeting to his surprise with a strong and decided repulse which put him to shame.

At the end of April there arrived at the fort a detachment with which Baryátinsky intended to effect an advance right through Chechnya, which had till then been considered impassable. In that detachment were two companies of the Kabardá regiment, and according to Caucasian custom these were treated as guests by the Kurín companies. The soldiers were lodged in the barracks, and were treated not only to supper, consisting of buckwheat-porridge and beef, but also to vodka. The officers shared the quarters of the Kurín officers, and as usual those in residence gave the new-comers a dinner at which the regimental singers performed and which ended up with a drinking-bout. Major Petróv, very drunk and no longer red but ashy pale, sat astride a chair and, drawing his sword, hacked at imaginary foes, alternately swearing and laughing, now embracing someone and now dancing to the tune of his favourite song.

> 'Shamil, he began to riot
> In the days gone by;
> Try, ry, rataty,
> In the years gone by!'

Butler was there too. He tried to see the poetry of warfare in this also, but in the depth of his soul he was sorry for the major. To stop him, however, was quite impossible; and Butler, feeling that the fumes were mounting to his own head, quietly left the room and went home.

The moon lit up the white houses and the stones on the road. It was so light that every pebble, every straw, every little heap of dust was visible. As he approached the house he met Márya Dmítrievna with a shawl over her head and neck. After the rebuff she had given him Butler had avoided her, feeling rather ashamed, but now in the moonlight and after the wine he had drunk he was pleased to meet her and wished to make up to her again.

'Where are you off to?' he asked.

'Why, to see after my old man,' she answered pleasantly. Her rejection of Butler's advances was quite sincere and decided, but she did not like his avoiding her as he had done lately.

'Why bother about him? He'll soon come back.'

'But will he?'

'If he doesn't they'll bring him.'

'Just so. . . . That's not right, you know! . . . But you think I'd better not go?'

'Yes, I do. We'd better go home.'

Márya Dmítrievna turned back and walked beside him. The moon shone so brightly that a halo seemed to move along the road round the shadows of their heads. Butler was looking at this halo and making up his mind to tell her that he liked her as much as ever, but he did not know how to begin. She waited for him to speak, and they walked on in silence almost to the house, when some horsemen appeared from round the corner. These were an officer with an escort.

'Who's that coming now?' said Márya Dmítrievna, stepping aside. The moon was behind the rider so that she did not recognize him until he had almost come up to them. It was Peter Nikoláevich Kámenev, an officer who had formerly served with the major and whom Márya Dmítrievna therefore knew.

'Is that you, Peter Nikoláevich?' said she, addressing him.

'It's me,' said Kámenev. 'Ah, Butler, how d'you do? . . . Not asleep yet? Having a walk with Márya Dmítrievna! You'd better look out or the major will give it you. . . . Where is he?'

'Why, there. . . . Listen!' replied Márya Dmítrievna pointing in the direction whence came the sounds of a *tulumbas*[1] and songs. 'They're on the spree.'

'Why? Are your people having a spree on their own?'

'No; some officers have come from Hasav-Yurt, and they are being entertained.'

'Ah, that's good! I shall be in time. . . . I just want the major for a moment.'

'On business?' asked Butler.

'Yes, just a little business matter.'

'Good or bad?'

'It all depends. . . . Good for us but bad for some people,' and Kámenev laughed.

By this time they had reached the major's house.

'Chikhirév,' shouted Kámenev to one of his Cossacks, 'come here!'

A Don Cossack rode up from among the others. He was dressed in the ordinary Don Cossack uniform with high boots and a mantle, and carried saddle-bags behind.

'Well, take the thing out,' said Kámenev, dismounting.

The Cossack also dismounted, and took a sack out of his saddle-bag. Kámenev took the sack from him and inserted his hand.

1 *Tulumbas*, a sort of kettledrum.

'Well, shall I show you a novelty? You won't be frightened, Márya Dmítrievna?'

'Why should I be frightened?' she replied.

'Here it is!' said Kámenev taking out a man's head and holding it up in the light of the moon. 'Do you recognize it?'

It was a shaven head with salient brows, black short-cut beard and moustaches, one eye open and the other half-closed. The shaven skull was cleft, but not right through, and there was congealed blood in the nose. The neck was wrapped in a blood-stained towel. Notwithstanding the many wounds on the head, the blue lips still bore a kindly childlike expression.

Márya Dmítrievna looked at it, and without a word turned away and went quickly into the house.

Butler could not tear his eyes from the terrible head. It was the head of that very Hadji Murád with whom he had so recently spent his evenings in such friendly intercourse.

'What does this mean? Who has killed him?' he asked.

'He wanted to give us the slip, but was caught,' said Kámenev, and he gave the head back to the Cossack and went into the house with Butler.

'He died like a hero,' he added.

'But however did it all happen?'

'Just wait a bit. When the major comes I'll tell you all about it. That's what I am sent for. I take it round to all the forts and *aouls* and show it.'

The major was sent for, and came back accompanied by two other officers as drunk as himself, and began embracing Kámenev.

'And I have brought you Hadji Murád's head,' said Kámenev.

'No?... Killed?'

'Yes; wanted to escape.'

'I always said he would bamboozle them!... And where is it? The head, I mean.... Let's see it.'

The Cossack was called, and brought in the bag with the head. It was taken out and the major looked long at it with drunken eyes.

'All the same, he was a fine fellow,' said he. 'Let me kiss him!'

'Yes, it's true. It was a valiant head,' said one of the officers.

When they had all looked at it, it was returned to the Cossack who put it in his bag, trying to let it bump against the floor as gently as possible.

'I say, Kámenev, what speech do you make when you show the head?' asked an officer.

'No! . . . Let me kiss him. He gave me a sword!' shouted the major.

Butler went out into the porch.

Márya Dmítrievna was sitting on the second step. She looked round at Butler and at once turned angrily away again.

'What's the matter, Márya Dmítrievna?' asked he.

'You're all cut-throats! . . . I hate it! You're cut-throats, really,' and she got up.

'It might happen to anyone,' remarked Butler, not knowing what to say. 'That's war.'

'War? War, indeed! . . . Cut-throats and nothing else. A dead body should be given back to the earth, and they're grinning at it there! . . . Cut-throats, really,' she repeated, as she descended the steps and entered the house by the back door.

Butler returned to the room and asked Kámenev to tell them in detail how the thing had happened.

And Kámenev told them.

This is what had happened.

XXV

HADJI MURÁD was allowed to go out riding in the neighbour-hood of the town, but never without a convoy of Cossacks. There was only half a troop of them altogether in Nukhá, ten of whom were employed by the officers, so that if ten were sent out with Hadji Murád (according to the orders received) the same men would have had to go every other day. Therefore after ten had been sent out the first day, it was decided to send only five in future and Hadji Murád was asked not to take all his henchmen with him. But on April the 25th he rode out with all five. When he mounted, the commander, noticing that all five henchmen were going with him, told him that he was forbidden to take them all, but Hadji Murád pretended not to hear, touched his horse, and the commander did not insist.

With the Cossacks rode a non-commissioned officer, Nazárov, who had received the Cross of St George for bravery. He was a young, healthy, brown-haired lad, as fresh as a rose. He was the eldest of a poor family belonging to the sect of Old Believers, had grown up without a father, and had maintained his old mother, three sisters, and two brothers.

'Mind, Nazárov, keep close to him!' shouted the commander.

'All right, your honour!' answered Nazárov, and rising in his stirrups and adjusting the rifle that hung at his back he started his fine large roan gelding at a trot. Four Cossacks followed him: Ferapóntov, tall and thin, a regular thief and plunderer (it was he who had sold gunpowder to Gamzálo); Ignátov, a sturdy peasant who boasted of his strength, though he was no longer young and had nearly completed his service; Míshkin, a weakly lad at whom everybody laughed; and the young fair-haired Petrakóv, his mother's only son, always amiable and jolly.

The morning had been misty, but it cleared up later on and the opening foliage, the young virgin grass, the sprouting corn, and the ripples of the rapid river just visible to the left of the road, all glittered in the sunshine.

Hadji Murád rode slowly along followed by the Cossacks and by his henchmen. They rode out along the road beyond the fort at a walk. They met women carrying baskets on their heads, soldiers driving carts, and creaking wagons drawn by buffaloes. When he had gone about a mile and a half Hadji Murád touched up his white Kabardá horse, which started at an amble that obliged the henchmen and Cossacks to ride at a quick trot to keep up with him.

'Ah, he's got a fine horse under him,' said Ferapóntov. 'If only he were still an enemy I'd soon bring him down.'

'Yes, mate. Three hundred rubles were offered for that horse in Tiflis.'

'But I can get ahead of him on mine,' said Nazárov.

'You get ahead? A likely thing!'

Hadji Murád kept increasing his pace.

'Hey, *kunák*, you mustn't do that. Steady!' cried Nazárov, starting to overtake Hadji Murád.

Hadji Murád looked round, said nothing, and continued to ride at the same pace.

'Mind, they're up to something, the devils!' said Ignátov. 'See how they are tearing along.'

So they rode for the best part of a mile in the direction of the mountains.

'I tell you it won't do!' shouted Nazárov.

Hadji Murád did not answer or look round, but only increased his pace to a gallop.

'Humbug! You won't get away!' shouted Nazárov, stung to the quick. He gave his big roan gelding a cut with his whip and, rising in his stirrups and bending forward, flew full speed in pursuit of Hadji Murád.

The sky was so bright, the air so clear, and life played so joyously in Nazárov's soul as, becoming one with his fine strong horse, he flew along the smooth road behind Hadji Murád, that the possibility of anything sad or dreadful happening never occurred to him. He rejoiced that with every step he was gaining on Hadji Murád.

Hadji Murád judged by the approaching tramp of the big horse behind him that he would soon be overtaken, and seizing his pistol with his right hand, with his left he began slightly to rein in his Kabardá horse which was excited by hearing the tramp of hoofs behind it.

'You mustn't, I tell you!' shouted Nazárov, almost level with Hadji Murád and stretching out his hand to seize the latter's bridle. But before he reached it a shot was fired. 'What are you doing?' he screamed, clutching at his breast. 'At them, lads!' and he reeled and fell forward on his saddle-bow.

But the mountaineers were beforehand in taking to their weapons, and fired their pistols at the Cossacks and hewed at them with their swords.

Nazárov hung on the neck of his horse, which careered round his comrades. The horse under Ignátov fell, crushing his leg, and two of the mountaineers, without dismounting, drew their swords and hacked at his head and arms. Petrakóv was about to rush to his comrade's rescue when two shots – one in his back and the other in his side – stung him, and he fell from his horse like a sack.

Míshkin turned round and galloped off towards the fortress. Khanéfi and Bata rushed after him, but he was already too far away and they could not catch him. When they saw that they could not overtake him they returned to the others.

Petrakóv lay on his back, his stomach ripped open, his young face turned to the sky, and while dying he gasped for breath like a fish.

Gamzálo having finished off Ignátov with his sword, gave a cut to Nazárov too and threw him from his horse. Bata took their cartridge-pouches from the slain. Khanéfi wished to take Nazárov's horse, but Hadji Murád called out to him to leave it, and dashed forward along the road. His *murids* galloped after him, driving away Nazárov's horse that tried to follow them. They were already among rice-fields more than six miles from Nukhá when a shot was fired from the tower of that place to give the alarm.

* * *

'O good Lord! O God! my God! What have they done?' cried the commander of the fort seizing his head with his hands when he heard of Hadji Murád's escape. 'They've done for me! They've let him escape, the villains!' cried he, listening to Míshkin's account.

An alarm was raised everywhere and not only the Cossacks of the place were sent after the fugitives but also all the militia that could be mustered from the pro-Russian *aouls*. A thousand rubles reward was offered for the capture of Hadji Murád alive or dead, and two hours after he and his followers had escaped from the Cossacks more than two hundred mounted men were following the officer in charge at a gallop to find and capture the runaways.

After riding some miles along the high road Hadji Murád checked his panting horse, which, wet with sweat, had turned from white to grey.

To the right of the road could be seen the *sáklyas* and minarets of the *aoul* Benerdzhík, on the left lay some fields, and beyond them the river. Although the way to the mountains lay to the right, Hadji Murád turned to the left, in the opposite direction, assuming that his pursuers would be sure to go to the right, while he, abandoning the road, would cross the Alazán and come out onto the high road on the other side where no one would expect him – ride along it to the forest, and then after recrossing the river make his way to the mountains.

Having come to this conclusion he turned to the left; but it proved impossible to reach the river. The rice-field which had to be crossed had just been flooded, as is always done in spring, and had become a bog in which the horses' legs sank above their pasterns. Hadji Murád and his henchmen turned now to the left, now to the right, hoping to find drier ground; but the field they were in had been equally flooded all over and was now saturated with water. The horses drew their feet out of the sticky mud into which they sank, with a pop like that of a cork drawn from a bottle, and stopped, panting, after every few steps. They struggled in this way so long that it began to grow dusk and they had still not reached the river. To their left lay a patch of higher ground overgrown with shrubs and Hadji Murád decided to ride in among these clumps and remain there till night to rest their exhausted horses and let them graze. The men themselves ate some bread and cheese they had brought with them. At last night came on and the moon that had been shining at first, hid behind the hill and it became dark. There were a great many nightingales in that neighbourhood and there were two of them in these shrubs. As long as Hadji Murád and his men were making a noise among the bushes the nightingales had been silent, but when they became still the birds again began to call to one another and to sing.

Hadji Murád, awake to all the sounds of night, listened to them involuntarily, and their trills reminded him of the song about Hamzád which he had heard the night before when he went to get water. He might now at any moment find himself in the position in which Hamzád had been. He fancied that it would be so, and suddenly his soul became serious. He spread out his *búrka* and performed his ablutions, and scarcely had he finished before a sound was heard approaching their shelter. It was the sound of many horses' feet plashing through the bog.

The keen-sighted Bata ran out to one edge of the clump, and peering through the darkness saw black shadows, which were men on foot and on horseback. Khanéfi discerned a similar crowd on the other side. It was Kargánov, the military commander of the district, with his militia.

'Well, then, we shall fight like Hamzád,' thought Hadji Murád.

When the alarm was given, Kargánov with a troop of militiamen and Cossacks had rushed off in pursuit of Hadji Murád, but had been unable to find any trace of him. He had already lost hope and was returning home when, towards evening, he met an old man and asked him if he had seen any horsemen about. The old man replied that he had. He had seen six horsemen floundering in the rice-field, and then had seen them enter the clump where he himself was getting wood. Kargánov turned back, taking the old man with him, and seeing the hobbled horses he made sure that Hadji Murád was there. In the night he surrounded the clump and waited till morning to take Hadji Murád alive or dead.

Having understood that he was surrounded, and having discovered an old ditch among the shrubs, Hadji Murád decided to entrench himself in it and to resist as long as strength and ammunition lasted. He told his comrades this, and ordered them to throw up a bank in front of the ditch, and his henchmen at once set to work to cut down branches, dig up the earth with their daggers, and make an entrenchment. Hadji Murád himself worked with them.

As soon as it began to grow light the commander of the militia troop rode up to the clump and shouted:

'Hey! Hadji Murád, surrender! We are many and you are few!'

In reply came the report of a rifle, a cloudlet of smoke rose from the ditch and a bullet hit the militiaman's horse, which staggered under him and began to fall. The rifles of the militiamen who stood at the outskirt of the clump of shrubs began cracking in their turn, and their bullets whistled and hummed, cutting off leaves and twigs and striking the embankment, but not the men entrenched behind it. Only Gamzálo's horse, that had strayed from the others, was hit in the head by a bullet. It did not fall, but breaking its hobbles and rushing among the bushes it ran to the other horses, pressing close to them and watering the young grass with its blood. Hadji Murád and his men fired only when any of the militiamen came forward, and rarely missed their aim. Three militiamen were wounded, and the others, far from making up their minds to rush the entrenchment, retreated farther and farther back, only firing from a distance and at random.

So it continued for more than an hour. The sun had risen to about half the height of the trees, and Hadji Murád was already thinking of leaping on his horse and trying to make his way to the river, when the shouts were heard of many men who had just arrived. These were Hadji Aga of Mekhtulí with his followers. There were about two hundred of them. Hadji Aga had once been Hadji Murád's *kunák* and had lived with him in the mountains, but he had afterwards gone over to the Russians. With him was Akhmet Khan, the son of Hadji Murád's old enemy.

Like Kargánov, Hadji Aga began by calling to Hadji Murád to surrender, and Hadji Murád answered as before with a shot.

'Swords out, my men!' cried Hadji Aga, drawing his own; and a hundred voices were raised by men who rushed shrieking in among the shrubs.

The militiamen ran in among the shrubs, but from behind the entrenchment came the crack of one shot after another. Some three men fell, and the attackers stopped at the outskirts of the clump and also began firing. As they fired they gradually approached the entrenchment, running across from behind one shrub to another. Some succeeded in getting across, others fell under the bullets of Hadji Murád or of his men. Hadji

Murád fired without missing; Gamzálo too rarely wasted a
shot, and shrieked with joy every time he saw that his bullet
had hit its aim. Khan Mahomá sat at the edge of the ditch
singing '*Il lyakha il Allakh!*' and fired leisurely, but often
missed. Eldár's whole body trembled with impatience to rush
dagger in hand at the enemy, and he fired often and at random,
constantly looking round at Hadji Murád and stretching out
beyond the entrenchment. The shaggy Khanéfi, with his
sleeves rolled up, did the duty of a servant even here. He loaded
the guns which Hadji Murád and Khan Mahomá passed to him,
carefully driving home with a ramrod the bullets wrapped in
greasy rags, and pouring dry powder out of the powder-flask
onto the pans. Bata did not remain in the ditch as the others did,
but kept running to the horses, driving them away to a safer
place and, shrieking incessantly, fired without using a prop for
his gun. He was the first to be wounded. A bullet entered his
neck and he sat down spitting blood and swearing. Then Hadji
Murád was wounded, the bullet piercing his shoulder. He tore
some cotton wool from the lining of his *beshmét*, plugged the
wound with it, and went on firing.

'Let us fly at them with our swords!' said Eldár for the third
time, and he looked out from behind the bank of earth ready
to rush at the enemy; but at that instant a bullet struck him and
he reeled and fell backwards onto Hadji Murád's leg. Hadji
Murád glanced at him. His eyes, beautiful like those of a ram,
gazed intently and seriously at Hadji Murád. His mouth, the
upper lip pouting like a child's, twitched without opening.
Hadji Murád drew his leg away from under him and continued
firing.

Khanéfi bent over the dead Eldár and began taking the
unused ammunition out of the cartridge-cases of his coat.

Khan Mahomá meanwhile continued to sing, loading
leisurely and firing. The enemy ran from shrub to shrub,
hallooing and shrieking and drawing ever nearer and nearer.

Another bullet hit Hadji Murád in the left side. He lay down
in the ditch and again pulled some cotton wool out of his
beshmét and plugged the wound. This wound in the side was
fatal and he felt that he was dying. Memories and pictures

succeeded one another with extraordinary rapidity in his imagination. Now he saw the powerful Abu Nutsal Khan, dagger in hand and holding up his severed cheek he rushed at his foe; then he saw the weak, bloodless old Vorontsóv with his cunning white face, and heard his soft voice; then he saw his son Yusúf, his wife Sofiát, and then the pale, red-bearded face of his enemy Shamil with its half-closed eyes. All these images passed through his mind without evoking any feeling within him – neither pity nor anger nor any kind of desire: everything seemed so insignificant in comparison with what was beginning, or had already begun, within him.

Yet his strong body continued the thing that he had commenced. Gathering together his last strength he rose from behind the bank, fired his pistol at a man who was just running towards him, and hit him. The man fell. Then Hadji Murád got quite out of the ditch, and limping heavily went dagger in hand straight at the foe.

Some shots cracked and he reeled and fell. Several militiamen with triumphant shrieks rushed towards the fallen body. But the body that seemed to be dead suddenly moved. First the uncovered, bleeding, shaven head rose; then the body with hands holding to the trunk of a tree. He seemed so terrible, that those who were running towards him stopped short. But suddenly a shudder passed through him, he staggered away from the tree and fell on his face, stretched out at full length like a thistle that had been mown down, and he moved no more.

He did not move, but still he felt.

When Hadji Aga, who was the first to reach him, struck him on the head with a large dagger, it seemed to Hadji Murád that someone was striking him with a hammer and he could not understand who was doing it or why. That was his last consciousness of any connexion with his body. He felt nothing more and his enemies kicked and hacked at what had no longer anything in common with him.

Hadji Aga placed his foot on the back of the corpse and with two blows cut off the head, and carefully – not to soil his shoes with blood – rolled it away with his foot. Crimson blood spurted from the arteries of the neck, and black blood flowed from the head, soaking the grass.

Kargánov and Hadji Aga and Akhmet Khan and all the militiamen gathered together – like sportsmen round a slaughtered animal – near the bodies of Hadji Murád and his men (Khanéfi, Khan Mahomá, and Gamzálo they bound), and amid the powder-smoke which hung over the bushes they triumphed in their victory.

The nightingales, that had hushed their songs while the firing lasted, now started their trills once more: first one quite close, then others in the distance.

* * *

It was of this death that I was reminded by the crushed thistle in the midst of the ploughed field.

STORIES GIVEN TO AID
THE PERSECUTED JEWS

ESARHADDON, KING OF ASSYRIA[1]

THE Assyrian King, Esarhaddon, had conquered the kingdom of King Lailie, had destroyed and burnt the towns, taken all the inhabitants captive to his own country, slaughtered the warriors, beheaded some chieftains and impaled or flayed others, and had confined King Lailie himself in a cage.

As he lay on his bed one night, King Esarhaddon was thinking how he should execute Lailie, when suddenly he heard a rustling near his bed, and opening his eyes saw an old man with a long grey beard and mild eyes.

'You wish to execute Lailie?' asked the old man.

'Yes,' answered the King. 'But I cannot make up my mind how to do it.'

'But you are Lailie,' said the old man.

'That's not true,' replied the King. 'Lailie is Lailie, and I am I.'

'You and Lailie are one,' said the old man. 'You only imagine you are not Lailie, and that Lailie is not you.'

'What do you mean by that?' said the King. 'Here am I, lying on a soft bed; around me are obedient men-slaves

---

1 In this story Tolstoy has used the names of real people. Esarhaddon (or Assur-akhi-iddina) is mentioned three times in the Bible (2 Kings xix. 37; Isaiah xxxvii. 38, and Ezra iv. 2), and is also alluded to in 2 Chron. xxxiii. 11, as, 'the King of Assyria, which took Manasseh in chains, and bound him with fetters, and carried him to Babylon'. His son, Assur-bani-pal, whom he promoted to power before his own death, is once mentioned in the Bible, under the name of Asnappar (Ezra iv. 10). Of Lailie history does not tell us much; but in Ernest A. Budge's *History of Esarhaddon* we read: 'A King, called Lailie, asked that the gods which Esarhaddon had captured from him might be restored. His request was granted, and Esarhaddon said, "I spoke to him of brotherhood, and entrusted to him the sovereignty of the districts of Bazu."'

and women-slaves, and to-morrow I shall feast with my friends as I did to-day; whereas Lailie is sitting like a bird in a cage, and to-morrow he will be impaled, and with his tongue hanging out will struggle till he dies, and his body will be torn in pieces by dogs.'

'You cannot destroy his life,' said the old man.

'And how about the fourteen thousand warriors I killed, with whose bodies I built a mound?' said the King. 'I am alive, but they no longer exist. Does not that prove that I can destroy life?'

'How do you know they no longer exist?'

'Because I no longer see them. And, above all, they were tormented, but I was not. It was ill for them, but well for me.'

'That, also, only seems so to you. You tortured yourself, but not them.'

'I do not understand,' said the King.

'Do you wish to understand?'

'Yes, I do.'

'Then come here,' said the old man, pointing to a large font full of water.

The King rose and approached the font.

'Strip, and enter the font.'

Esarhaddon did as the old man bade him.

'As soon as I begin to pour this water over you,' said the old man, filling a pitcher with the water, 'dip down your head.'

The old man tilted the pitcher over the King's head, and the King bent his head till it was under water.

And as soon as King Esarhaddon was under the water, he felt that he was no longer Esarhaddon, but someone else. And, feeling himself to be that other man, he saw himself lying on a rich bed, beside a beautiful woman. He had never seen her before, but he knew she was his wife. The woman raised herself and said to him:

'Dear husband, Lailie! You were wearied by yesterday's work and have slept longer than usual, and I have guarded your rest, and have not roused you. But now the Princes await you in the Great Hall. Dress and go out to them.'

And Esarhaddon – understanding from these words that he was Lailie, and not feeling at all surprised at this, but only wondering that he did not know it before – rose, dressed, and went into the Great Hall where the Princes awaited him.

The Princes greeted Lailie, their King, bowing to the ground, and then they rose, and at his word sat down before him; and the eldest of the Princes began to speak, saying that it was impossible longer to endure the insults of the wicked King Esarhaddon, and that they must make war on him. But Lailie disagreed, and gave orders that envoys should be sent to remonstrate with King Esarhaddon; and he dismissed the Princes from the audience. Afterwards he appointed men of note to act as ambassadors, and impressed on them what they were to say to King Esarhaddon. Having finished this business, Esarhaddon – feeling himself to be Lailie – rode out to hunt wild asses. The hunt was successful. He killed two wild asses himself, and, having returned home, feasted with his friends, and witnessed a dance of slave girls. The next day he went to the Court, where he was awaited by petitioners, suitors, and prisoners brought for trial; and there as usual he decided the cases submitted to him. Having finished this business, he again rode out to his favourite amusement: the hunt. And again he was successful: this time killing with his own hand an old lioness, and capturing her two cubs. After the hunt he again feasted with his friends, and was entertained with music and dances, and the night he spent with the wife whom he loved.

So, dividing his time between kingly duties and pleasures, he lived for days and weeks, awaiting the return of the ambassadors he had sent to that King Esarhaddon who used to be himself. Not till a month had passed did the ambassadors return, and they returned with their noses and ears cut off.

King Esarhaddon had ordered them to tell Lailie that what had been done to them – the ambassadors – would be done to King Lailie himself also, unless he sent immediately a tribute of silver, gold, and cypress-wood, and came himself to pay homage to King Esarhaddon.

Lailie, formerly Esarhaddon, again assembled the Princes, and took counsel with them as to what he should do. They all with one accord said that war must be made against Esarhaddon, without waiting for him to attack them. The King agreed; and taking his place at the head of the army, started on the campaign. The campaign lasts seven days. Each day the King rode round the army to rouse the courage of his warriors. On the eighth day his army met that of Esarhaddon in a broad valley through which a river flowed. Lailie's army fought bravely, but Lailie, formerly Esarhaddon, saw the enemy swarming down from the mountains like ants, over-running the valley and overwhelming his army; and, in his chariot, he flung himself into the midst of the battle, hewing and felling the enemy. But the warriors of Lailie were but as hundreds, while those of Esarhaddon were as thousands; and Lailie felt himself wounded and taken prisoner. Nine days he journeyed with other captives, bound, and guarded by the warriors of Esarhaddon. On the tenth day he reached Nineveh, and was placed in a cage. Lailie suffered not so much from hunger and from his wound as from shame and impotent rage. He felt how powerless he was to avenge himself on his enemy for all he was suffering. All he could do was to deprive his enemies of the pleasure of seeing his sufferings; and he firmly resolved to endure courageously, without a murmur, all they could do to him. For twenty days he sat in his cage, awaiting execution. He saw his relatives and friends led out to death; he heard the groans of those who were executed: some had their hands and feet cut off, others were flayed alive, but he showed neither disquietude, nor pity, nor fear. He saw the wife he loved, bound, and led by two black eunuchs. He knew she was being taken as a slave to Esarhaddon. That, too, he bore without a murmur. But one of the guards placed to watch him said, 'I pity you, Lailie; you were a king, but what are you now?' And hearing these words, Lailie remembered all he had lost. He clutched the bars of his cage, and, wishing to kill himself, beat his head against them. But he had not the strength to do so; and, groaning in despair, he fell upon the floor of his cage.

At last two executioners opened his cage door, and having strapped his arms tight behind him, led him to the place of execution, which was soaked with blood. Lailie saw a sharp stake dripping with blood, from which the corpse of one of his friends had just been torn, and he understood that this had been done that the stake might serve for his own execution. They stripped Lailie of his clothes. He was startled at the leanness of his once strong, handsome body. The two executioners seized that body by its lean thighs; they lifted him up and were about to let him fall upon the stake.

'This is death, destruction!' thought Lailie, and, forgetful of his resolve to remain bravely calm to the end, he sobbed and prayed for mercy. But no one listened to him.

'But this cannot be,' thought he. 'Surely I am asleep. It is a dream.' And he made an effort to rouse himself, and did indeed awake, to find himself neither Esarhaddon nor Lailie – but some kind of an animal. He was astonished that he was an animal, and astonished, also, at not having known this before.

He was grazing in a valley, tearing the tender grass with his teeth, and brushing away flies with his long tail. Around him was frolicking a long-legged, dark-grey ass-colt, striped down its back. Kicking up its hind legs, the colt galloped full speed to Esarhaddon, and poking him under the stomach with its smooth little muzzle, searched for the teat, and, finding it, quieted down, swallowing regularly. Esarhaddon understood that he was a she-ass, the colt's mother, and this neither surprised nor grieved him, but rather gave him pleasure. He experienced a glad feeling of simultaneous life in himself and in his offspring.

But suddenly something flew near with a whistling sound and hit him in the side, and with its sharp point entered his skin and flesh. Feeling a burning pain, Esarhaddon – who was at the same time the ass – tore the udder from the colt's teeth, and laying back his ears galloped to the herd from which he had strayed. The colt kept up with him, galloping by his side. They had already nearly reached the herd, which had started off, when another arrow in full flight struck the colt's neck. It pierced the skin and quivered in its flesh. The colt sobbed piteously and fell upon its knees. Esarhaddon could not abandon it, and remained standing over it. The colt rose, tottered on its long, thin legs, and again fell. A fearful two-legged being – a man – ran up and cut its throat.

'This cannot be; it is still a dream!' thought Esarhaddon, and made a last effort to awake. 'Surely I am not Lailie, nor the ass, but Esarhaddon!'

He cried out, and at the same instant lifted his head out of the font. . . . The old man was standing by him, pouring over his head the last drops from the pitcher.

'Oh, how terribly I have suffered! And for how long!' said Esarhaddon.

'Long?' replied the old man. 'You have only dipped your head under water and lifted it again; see, the water is not yet all out of the pitcher. Do you now understand?'

Esarhaddon did not reply, but only looked at the old man with terror.

'Do you now understand', continued the old man, 'that Lailie is you, and the warriors you put to death were you also? And not the warriors only, but the animals which you slew when hunting and ate at your feasts, were also you. You thought life dwelt in you alone, but I have drawn aside the veil of delusion, and have let you see that by doing evil to others you have done it to yourself also. Life is one in them all, and yours is but a portion of this same common life. And only in that one part of life that is yours, can you make life better or worse – increasing or decreasing it. You can only improve life in yourself by destroying the barriers that divide your life from that of others, and by considering others as yourself, and loving them. By so doing you increase your share of life. You injure your life when you think of it as the only life, and try to add to its welfare at the expense of other lives. By so doing you only lessen it. To destroy the life that dwells in others is beyond your power. The life of those you have slain has vanished from your eyes, but is not destroyed. You thought to lengthen your own life and to shorten theirs, but you cannot do this. Life knows neither time nor space. The life of a moment, and the life of a thousand years: your life, and the life of all the visible and invisible beings in the world, are equal. To destroy life, or to alter it, is impossible; for life is the one thing that exists. All else, but seems to us to be.'

Having said this the old man vanished.

Next morning King Esarhaddon gave orders that Lailie and all the prisoners should be set at liberty, and that the executions should cease.

On the third day he called his son Assur-bani-pal, and gave the kingdom over into his hands; and he himself went into the desert to think over all he had learnt. Afterwards he went about as a wanderer through the towns and villages, preaching to the people that all life is one, and that when men wish to harm others, they really do evil to themselves.

WORK, DEATH AND SICKNESS

A LEGEND

THIS is a legend current among the South American Indians.

God, say they, at first made men so that they had no need to work: they needed neither houses, nor clothes, nor food, and they all lived till they were a hundred, and did not know what illness was.

When, after some time, God looked to see how people were living, he saw that instead of being happy in their life, they had quarrelled with one another, and, each caring for himself, had brought matters to such a pass that far from enjoying life, they cursed it.

Then God said to himself: 'This comes of their living separately, each for himself.' And to change this state of things, God so arranged matters that it became impossible for people to live without working. To avoid suffering from cold and hunger, they were now obliged to build dwellings, and to dig the ground, and to grow and gather fruits and grain.

'Work will bring them together,' thought God. 'They cannot make their tools, prepare and transport their timber, build their houses, sow and gather their harvests, spin and weave, and make their clothes, each one alone by himself.

'It will make them understand that the more heartily they work together, the more they will have and the better they will live; and this will unite them.'

Time passed on, and again God came to see how men were living, and whether they were now happy.

But he found them living worse than before. They worked together (that they could not help doing), but not all together, being broken up into little groups. And each group tried to

748

snatch work from other groups, and they hindered one another, wasting time and strength in their struggles, so that things went ill with them all.

Having seen that this, too, was not well, God decided so to arrange things that man should not know the time of his death, but might die at any moment; and he announced this to them.

'Knowing that each of them may die at any moment,' thought God, 'they will not, by grasping at gains that may last so short a time, spoil the hours of life allotted to them.'

But it turned out otherwise. When God returned to see how people were living, he saw that their life was as bad as ever.

Those who were strongest, availing themselves of the fact that men might die at any time, subdued those who were weaker, killing some and threatening others with death. And it came about that the strongest and their descendants did no work, and suffered from the weariness of idleness, while those who were weaker had to work beyond their strength, and suffered from lack of rest. Each set of men feared and hated the other. And the life of man became yet more unhappy.

Having seen all this, God, to mend matters, decided to make use of one last means; he sent all kinds of sickness among men. God thought that when all men were exposed to sickness they would understand that those who are well should have pity on those who are sick, and should help them, that when they themselves fall ill, those who are well might in turn help them.

And again God went away; but when He came back to see how men lived now that they were subject to sicknesses, he saw that their life was worse even than before. The very sickness that in God's purpose should have united men, had divided them more than ever. Those men who were strong enough to make others work, forced them also to wait on them in times of sickness; but they did not, in their turn, look after others who were ill. And those who were forced to work for others and to look after them when sick, were so worn with work that they had no time to look after their own sick, but left them without attendance. That the sight of sick folk might not disturb the pleasures of the wealthy, houses were arranged in which these poor people suffered and died, far from those whose sympathy might have cheered them, and in the arms of hired people who nursed them without compassion, or even with disgust. Moreover, people considered many of the illnesses infectious, and, fearing to catch them, not only avoided the sick, but even separated themselves from those who attended the sick.

Then God said to Himself: 'If even this means will not bring men to understand wherein their happiness lies, let them be taught by suffering.' And God left men to themselves.

And, left to themselves, men lived long before they understood that they all ought to, and might be, happy. Only in the very latest times have a few of them begun to understand that work ought not to be a bugbear to some and like galley-slavery for others, but should be a common and happy occupation, uniting all men. They have begun to understand that with death constantly threatening each of us, the only reasonable business of every man is to spend the years, months, hours, and minutes, allotted him – in unity and love. They have begun to understand that sickness, far from dividing men, should, on the contrary, give opportunity for loving union with one another.

THREE QUESTIONS

I T once occurred to a certain king, that if he always knew the right time to begin everything; if he knew who were the right people to listen to, and whom to avoid; and, above all, if he always knew what was the most important thing to do, he would never fail in anything he might undertake.

And this thought having occurred to him, he had it proclaimed throughout his kingdom that he would give a great reward to anyone who would teach him what was the right time for every action, and who were the most necessary people, and how he might know what was the most important thing to do.

And learned men came to the King, but they all answered his questions differently.

In reply to the first question, some said that to know the right time for every action, one must draw up in advance, a table of days, months and years, and must live strictly according to it. Only thus, said they, could everything be done at its proper time. Others declared that it was impossible to decide beforehand the right time for every action; but that, not letting oneself be absorbed in idle pastimes, one should always attend to all that was going on, and then do what was most needful. Others, again, said that however attentive the King might be to what was going on, it was impossible for one man to decide correctly the right time for every action, but that he should have a Council of wise men, who would help him to fix the proper time for everything.

But then again others said there were some things which could not wait to be laid before a Council, but about which one had at once to decide whether to undertake them or not.

But in order to decide that, one must know beforehand what was going to happen. It is only magicians who know that; and, therefore, in order to know the right time for every action, one must consult magicians.

Equally various were the answers to the second question. Some said, the people the King most needed were his councillors; others, the priests; others, the doctors; while some said the warriors were the most necessary.

To the third question, as to what was the most important occupation: some replied that the most important thing in the world was science. Others said it was skill in warfare; and others, again, that it was religious worship.

All the answers being different, the King agreed with none of them, and gave the reward to none. But still wishing to find the right answers to his questions, he decided to consult a hermit, widely renowned for his wisdom.

The hermit lived in a wood which he never quitted, and he received none but common folk. So the King put on simple clothes, and before reaching the hermit's cell dismounted from his horse, and, leaving his bodyguard behind, went on alone.

When the King approached, the hermit was digging the ground in front of his hut. Seeing the King, he greeted him and went on digging. The hermit was frail and weak, and each time he stuck his spade into the ground and turned a little earth, he breathed heavily.

The King went up to him and said: 'I have come to you, wise hermit, to ask you to answer three questions: How can I learn to do the right thing at the right time? Who are the people I most need, and to whom should I, therefore, pay more attention than to the rest? And, what affairs are the most important, and need my first attention?'

The hermit listened to the King, but answered nothing. He just spat on his hand and recommenced digging.

'You are tired,' said the King, 'let me take the spade and work awhile for you.'

'Thanks!' said the hermit, and, giving the spade to the King, he sat down on the ground.

When he had dug two beds, the King stopped and repeated his questions. The hermit again gave no answer, but rose, stretched out his hand for the spade, and said:

'Now rest awhile – and let me work a bit.'

But the King did not give him the spade, and continued to dig. One hour passed, and another. The sun began to sink behind the trees, and the King at last stuck the spade into the ground, and said:

'I came to you, wise man, for an answer to my questions. If you can give me none, tell me so, and I will return home.'

'Here comes someone running,' said the hermit, 'let us see who it is.'

The King turned round, and saw a bearded man come running out of the wood. The man held his hands pressed against his stomach, and blood was flowing from under them. When he reached the King, he fell fainting on the ground moaning feebly. The King and the hermit unfastened the man's clothing. There was a large wound in his stomach. The King washed it as best he could, and bandaged it with his handkerchief and with a towel the hermit had. But the blood would not stop flowing, and the King again and again removed the bandage soaked with warm blood, and washed and rebandaged the wound. When at last the blood ceased flowing, the man revived and asked for something to drink. The King brought fresh water and gave it to him. Meanwhile the sun had set, and it had become cool. So the King, with the hermit's help, carried the wounded man into the hut and laid him on the bed. Lying on the bed the man closed his eyes and was quiet; but the King was so tired with his walk and with the work he had done, that he crouched down on the threshold, and also fell asleep – so soundly that he slept all through the short summer night. When he awoke in the morning, it was long before he could remember where he was, or who was the strange bearded man lying on the bed and gazing intently at him with shining eyes.

'Forgive me!' said the bearded man in a weak voice, when he saw that the King was awake and was looking at him.

'I do not know you, and have nothing to forgive you for,' said the King.

'You do not know me, but I know you. I am that enemy of yours who swore to revenge himself on you, because you executed his brother and seized his property. I knew you had gone alone to see the hermit, and I resolved to kill you on your way back. But the day passed and you did not return. So I came out from my ambush to find you, and I came upon your bodyguard, and they recognized me, and wounded me. I escaped from them, but should have bled to death had you not dressed my wound. I wished to kill you, and you have saved my life. Now, if I live, and if you wish it, I will serve you as your most faithful slave, and will bid my sons do the same. Forgive me!'

The King was very glad to have made peace with his enemy so easily, and to have gained him for a friend, and he not only forgave him, but said he would send his servants and his own physician to attend him, and promised to restore his property.

Having taken leave of the wounded man, the King went out into the porch and looked around for the hermit. Before going away he wished once more to beg an answer to the questions he had put. The hermit was outside, on his knees, sowing seeds in the beds that had been dug the day before.

The King approached him, and said:

'For the last time, I pray you to answer my questions, wise man.'

'You have already been answered!' said the hermit still crouching on his thin legs, and looking up at the King, who stood before him.

'How answered? What do you mean?' asked the King.

'Do you not see?' replied the hermit. 'If you had not pitied my weakness yesterday, and had not dug these beds for me, but had gone your way, that man would have attacked you, and you would have repented of not having stayed with me. So the most important time was when you were digging the beds; and I was the most important man; and to do me good was your most important business. Afterwards, when that man ran to us, the most important time was when you were attending to him, for if you had not bound up his wounds he would have died without having made peace with you. So he was the most important man, and what you did for him was your most important business. Remember then: there is only one time that is important – Now! It is the most important time because it is the only time when we have any power. The most necessary man is he with whom you are, for no man knows whether he will ever have dealings with anyone else: and the most important affair is, to do him good, because for that purpose alone was man sent into this life!'

FËDOR KUZMÍCH

[Posthumous notes of the hermit, Fëdor Kuzmích, who died in Siberia in a hut belonging to Khrómov, the merchant, near the town of Tomsk, on the 20th January 1864]

DURING the lifetime of the hermit Fëdor Kuzmích, who appeared in Siberia in 1836 and lived there in different parts for twenty-seven years, strange rumours were rife that he – concealing his real name and rank – was none other than Alexander I. After his death these rumours became more definite and widespread. That he really was Alexander I was believed during the reign of Alexander III not only by the people, but also in Court circles and even by members of the Imperial family. Among others, the historian Schilder, who wrote a history of Alexander's reign, believed it.

These rumours were occasioned by the following facts: first, Alexander died quite unexpectedly without any previous serious illness; secondly, he died far from his family in the out-of-the-way town of Taganróg.[1] Thirdly, those who saw him placed in his coffin said he had so changed as to be unrecognizable, and he was therefore covered up and not shown to anyone. Fourthly, Alexander had repeatedly said and written – especially of late years – that he only desired to be free from his position and retire from the world. Fifthly – a little-known fact – in the official report describing his body it is mentioned that his back and loins were purple-brown and red, which the Emperor's pampered body would certainly not have been.

The reasons why Kuzmích was suspected of being Alexander I in hiding were, in the first place, that the hermit resembled the Emperor in height, figure, and countenance so much that those who had seen Alexander and his portraits (a palace footman, for instance, who recognized Kuzmích as

1 A trading port on the Sea of Azov.

Alexander) noticed a striking resemblance between the two. They were of the same age and had the same characteristic stoop. Secondly, Kuzmích, who gave himself out as a tramp who had forgotten his parentage, knew foreign languages and by his dignified affability showed himself to be a man accustomed to the highest position. Thirdly, the hermit never disclosed his name or calling to anyone, yet by expressions that escaped him involuntarily, betrayed himself as one who had once ranked above everybody else. Fourthly, shortly before his death he destroyed some papers of which a single sheet remained with strange ciphers and the initials A. P.[1] Fifthly, notwithstanding his great piety the hermit never went to confession, and when a bishop who visited him tried to persuade him to fulfil that Christian duty, he replied, 'If I did not tell the truth about myself at confession the heavens would be amazed, but if I told who I am the earth would be amazed.'

All these guesses and doubts ceased to be doubts and became certainties as a result of the finding of Kuzmích's diary. This diary is here given. It begins as follows:

God bless my invaluable friend Iván Grigórevich[2] for this delightful retreat. I do not deserve his kindness and God's mercy. Here I am at peace. Fewer people come and I am alone with my guilty memories and with God. I will try to avail myself of the solitude to give a close description of my life. It may be of use to others.

I was born and spent forty-seven years of my life amid most terrible temptations. I not only did not resist them but revelled in them, was tempted and tempted others, sinned and caused others to sin. But God turned his eyes on me, and the whole vileness of my life, which I had tried to justify to myself by

---

1 Presumably standing for 'Alexander Pávlovich' (Alexander, son of Paul).
2 Iván Grigórevich Latýshev – a peasant of the village of Krasnorechínsk, whom Fëdor Kuzmích met and became acquainted with in 1839, and who, after the latter had lived in various places, built him a cell in a wood away from the road, on a hill above a cliff. In this cell Kuzmích began his diary. L. T.

laying the blame on others, revealed itself to me at last in its full horror. And God helped me to liberate myself, not from evil – I am still full of it though I struggle against it – but from participation in it. What mental sufferings I endured and what went on in my soul when I understood my whole sinfulness and the necessity of atonement – not a belief in atonement, but real atonement for sins by my own suffering – I will describe in due course. At present I will only describe my actions: how I managed to escape from my position, leaving in place of my body the corpse of a soldier I had tormented to death; and I will begin the description of my life from its very commencement.

My flight occurred in this way:

In Taganróg I lived in the same mad way in which I had been living for the last twenty-four years. I – the greatest of criminals, the murderer of my father, the murderer of hundreds of thousands of men in wars I had occasioned, an abominable debauchee and a miscreant – believed what people told me about myself and considered myself the saviour of Europe, a benefactor of mankind, an exceptionally perfect man, *un heureux hasard*,[1] as I once expressed it to Madame de Staël. I considered myself such, but God had not quite forsaken me and the never-sleeping voice of conscience troubled me unceasingly. Nothing pleased me, everyone was to blame. I alone was good and no one understood it. I turned to God, prayed to the Orthodox God with Fóti,[2] then to the Roman Catholic God, then to the Protestant God with Parrot,[3] then to the God of the Illuminati with Krüdener;[4] but even to God I only turned in the sight of men, that they might admire me. I despised everybody, and yet the opinion of the peoples despised was the only thing important to me; I lived and

1 'A fortunate accident.'
2 Fóti (1792–1838). An archimandrite who enjoyed much influence in court circles.
3 G. F. von Parrot (1767–1852), Member of the Russian Academy of Science. His letters to Alexander I were published in 1894–5.
4 Baroness B. J. Krüdener (1764–1824), pietist and authoress, at one time a friend of Alexander I.

acted for its sake alone. It was terrible for me to be alone. Still more terrible was it to be with her – my wife, narrow-minded, deceitful, capricious, malicious, consumptive, and full of pretence. She poisoned my life more than anything else. We were supposed to be spending a second honeymoon, but it was a hell in forms of respectability – false and terrible.

Once I felt particularly wretched. I had received a letter from Arakchéev[1] the evening before about the assassination of his mistress. He described to me his desperate grief. Strange to say, his continual subtle flattery, and not only flattery but real dog-like devotion – which had begun while my father was alive and when we both swore allegiance to him in secret from my grandmother[2] – that dog-like devotion of his made me love him, if indeed latterly I loved any man – and though to use the word love of such a monster is wrong. Another thing that bound me to him was his not having taken part in the murder of my father, as many others did who became hateful to me just because they were my accomplices in that crime, but he not only took no part in it but was devoted both to my father and to me; of that later, however.

I slept badly. Strange to say, the murder of that beauty – the spiteful Nastásya (she was extraordinarily voluptuously beautiful) – aroused desire in me, and I could not sleep all night. The fact that my consumptive, abhorrent, and undesired wife lay in the next room but one vexed and tormented me still more. The memory of Márya,[3] who deserted me for an insignificant diplomat, also tormented me. It seemed that both my father and I were fated to be jealous of a Gagárin.[4] But I am again letting myself be carried away by reminiscences. I did not sleep all night. Dawn began to break. I drew the curtain, put on my white dressing-gown, and called my valet. All were still asleep.

1 The exceedingly harsh Minister to whom Alexander entrusted the government when he himself began to cease to exercise power.
2 The grandmother was Catherine the Great. The father was her half-mad son, afterwards the Emperor Paul, who was assassinated.
3 Márya Antónovna Narýshkina, at one time Alexander I's mistress.
4 The Princes Gagárin are a famous Russian family.

I donned a frock-coat, a civilian overcoat and cap, and went out past the sentinels and into the street.

The sun was just rising over the sea. It was a cool autumn morning, and in the fresh air I immediately felt better and my sombre thoughts vanished. I walked towards the sun-flecked sea. Before reaching the green-coloured house at the corner I heard the sounds of drums and flutes from the square. I listened, and realized that someone was being made to run the gauntlet. I, who had so often sanctioned that form of punishment, had never seen it executed. And strange to say – evidently at the devil's instigation – the thought of the murdered, voluptuously beautiful Nastásya and of the soldier's body being lashed by rods, merged into one stimulating sensation. I remembered the men of the Semënov Regiment and the military exiles, hundreds of whom were flogged to death in this way, and the strange idea of witnessing that spectacle suddenly occurred to me. As I was in civilian clothes this was possible.

The nearer I drew the clearer came the rattling of the drums and the sound of the flutes. Being short-sighted I could not see clearly without my lorgnette, but could already make out the rows of soldiers and a tall, white-backed figure moving between them. When I got among the crowd that stood behind the rows watching the spectacle, I drew out my lorgnette and was able to see all that was being done. A tall, round-shouldered man, his bare arms tied to a bayonet, and his bare back here and there already growing red with blood, was advancing between rows of soldiers who held rods. That man was I: he was my double. The same height, the same round shoulders, the same bald head, the same whiskers without a moustache, the same cheek-bones, the same mouth and blue eyes; but his mouth did not smile; it kept opening and twisting as he screamed at the blows, and his eyes, now closing and now opening, were not tender and caressing but started terribly from his head.

When I had looked well at this man I recognized him. It was Struménski, a left-flank non-commissioned officer of the 3rd Company of the Semënov Regiment, at one time well known to all the Guards on account of his likeness to me. They used jokingly to call him Alexander II.

I knew that he had been transferred to garrison-duty with other rioters of the Semënov Regiment, and I guessed that here, in garrison, he had done something – probably deserted – had been recaptured, and was now being punished. I learnt later that this was so.

I stood as one spellbound, watching how the unfortunate man moved and how they flogged him, and I felt that something was going on within me. But I suddenly noticed that the people standing beside me, the spectators, were looking at me, and that some drew back from me while others approached. I had evidently been recognized. Having realized this I turned to hurry home. The drums still beat and the flutes played – so the tortures were still going on. My chief feeling was that I ought to approve of what was being done to this double of mine; or if not approve at least acknowledge that it was the proper thing to do, but I could not. Yet I felt that if I did not admit it to be necessary and right, I should have to admit that my whole life and all my actions were bad, and should have to do what I had long wished to: abandon everything, go away, and disappear.

I struggled against this feeling that seized me: now admitting that the thing was right – a melancholy necessity – and now admitting that I ought myself to have been in the place of that wretched man. But strangely enough I felt no pity for him, and instead of stopping the torture I went home, fearing only lest I should be recognized.

Soon the sounds of the drums ceased, and on reaching home I seemed to have shaken off the feeling that had come over me. There I drank tea and received a report from Volkónski.[1] Then came the usual lunch, the usual burdensome and insincere relations with my wife; then Diebitsch[2] with a report confirming information we had had of a secret society. In due

1 Field-Marshal Prince P. M. Volkónski, Minister of the Palace.
2 General Count Diebitsch, a German by birth, Chief of the Russian General Staff. He constantly accompanied Alexander I.

time, when I write the whole story of my life, I will, God willing, recount it all in detail; but now I will only say that I received that report too with outward composure. But this lasted only till after dinner, when I went to my study, lay down on the couch, and immediately fell asleep.

I had hardly been asleep five minutes when a shock passing through my whole body seemed to awake me, and I heard the rattling of the drums, the flutes, the sound of the blows, the screams of Struménski, and saw him or myself – I could not tell which of us was I; I saw his look of suffering and the gloomy faces of the soldiers and officers. This delusion did not last long. I jumped up, buttoned my coat, put on my hat and sword, and went out, saying I was going for a walk.

I knew where the military hospital was and went straight to it. My appearance as usual caused a commotion. The head doctor and the head of the staff came running up breathless. I said I wished to go through the wards. In the second ward I saw Struménski's bald head. He was lying prone with his head on his arms, moaning pitifully. 'He has been punished for trying to desert,' I was told.

I said 'Ah!' and made my usual gesture of approval at what I heard, and I walked on.

Next day I sent to inquire how Struménski was, and was told that he had received the sacrament and was dying.

It was my brother Michael's name-day,[1] and there was to be a parade and a special service. I said I was unwell after my journey through the Crimea, and I did not attend the Mass. Diebitsch returned, and again reported about the plot in the Second Army, reminding me of what Count Witte had told me before my visit to the Crimea, and of the report of the non-commissioned officer Sherwood.

Only while listening to the report of Diebitsch, who attached such immense importance to all these attempted conspiracies, did I suddenly feel the full significance and strength of the change that had taken place within me. They were conspiring in order to alter our system of government

1 The day of his patron-saint, which is kept like an English birthday.

and introduce a Constitution – the very thing that I had wanted to do twenty years back. I had made and unmade Constitutions in Europe, and what and who is any the better for it? And above all who was I that I should do it? All external life, all arrangements of external affairs and all participation in them – had I not participated in them and rearranged the life of the peoples of Europe? – seemed unimportant, unnecessary, and not at all my business. I suddenly realized that none of it was my business, that my business was with myself – my soul. All my old desires to abdicate – formerly ostentatious, with a wish to reveal the grandeur of my soul and to astonish people and make them regret me – now returned with fresh force and complete sincerity. I no longer thought of what other people would think, but only of myself, my soul. It was as if my whole life, a brilliant one in the worldly sense, had been lived only that I might return to that youthful desire – evoked by repentance – to abandon everything; but to abandon it without vanity, without thought of human fame, only for my own soul's sake and for God. Then it had been a vague desire, now it was the impossibility of continuing to live as I had done.

But how? Not so as to astonish people and to be praised, but on the contrary, to go away with suffering and with no one's knowledge. And this thought so pleased and delighted me that I began to think of how to accomplish it. I employed all the powers of my mind and all my characteristic cunning to effect it. But the execution of my intention was surprisingly easier than I had expected. My plan was to pretend to be ill and dying, and having persuaded and bribed a doctor to have the dying Struménski put in my place, to go away, to fly – concealing my identity from everyone.

It was as if everything happened expressly for the success of my project. On the 9th,[1] as if on purpose, I fell ill with intermittent fever. I was ill for about a week, during which my intention became stronger and stronger and I considered my plan thoroughly. On the 16th I got up feeling well.

1 9th November 1825 o.s. = 21st November, n.s.

That day I shaved as usual, and being deep in thought, cut myself badly near the chin. I lost much blood and, feeling faint, fell down. People came running and lifted me. I saw at once that this would help the execution of my plan, and though I felt quite well I pretended to be very weak, went to bed, and had Dr Vimier's assistant called. Vimier would not have agreed to any deception, but I hoped to be able to bribe this young man. I disclosed my intention and plan to him, and offered him eighty thousand rubles if he would do what I demanded. My plan was this: Struménski, as I had learnt that morning, was near death and not expected to live beyond the evening. I went to bed and, pretending to be vexed with everybody, would not let anyone in except the physician I had bribed. That night he was to bring Struménski's body in a bath, put it in my place, and announce my sudden death. Strange to say, everything happened as we had planned, and on the 17th of November[1] I was a free man. Struménski's body, in its closed coffin, was buried with the greatest pomp, and my brother Nicholas ascended the throne, having banished the conspirators to forced labour in Siberia. I afterwards met some of them there. I experienced sufferings trifling in comparison with my crimes, and the greatest and quite undeserved happiness of which I will speak in due course.

Now, on the brink of the grave, at the age of seventy-two, having understood the vanity of my former life and the significance of the life I have lived and am living as a wanderer, I will try to tell the story of my former life.

MY LIFE

12th December, 1849. Siberian Forest-swamp near Krasnorechínsk

T O-D A Y is my birthday, I am seventy-two. Seventy-two years ago I was born in Petersburg in the Winter Palace, in the

---

1 Officially Alexander I died on 19th November, o.s. = 1st December, n.s. Whether Tolstoy had some reason for making it the 17th I do not know.

apartments of my mother the Empress, then the Grand Duchess Mária Fëdorovna.

I slept pretty well last night. After yesterday's indisposition I feel rather better again. The chief thing is that the spiritual torpor I was in has passed, and I can again communicate with God with my whole soul. Last night I prayed in the dark. I was clearly conscious of my position in the world. My whole life is something required by Him who sent me here, and I can do what He requires or not just as I please. By doing what He requires I conduce towards the welfare of the whole world. By not doing it I deprive myself of welfare – not of all welfare, but of the welfare that might be mine; but I do not deprive the world of the welfare destined for it. What I ought to have done will be done by others, so that His will may be accomplished. That is what my free will consists in. But if He knows what will be, if everything is ordained by Him, is there any freedom? I don't know. Here thought reaches its limits and prayer begins, the simple prayer of childhood and old age. 'Father, not my will but Thine be done.' Simply: 'Lord forgive and have mercy. Yes, Lord forgive and have mercy, and forgive and have mercy. I cannot express it in words but Thou knowest the heart. Thou Thyself dwellest therein.'

I fell soundly asleep. As usual, from the weakness of old age, I woke five or six times and dreamt I was bathing in the sea and swimming. The water was greenish and beautiful, and I was surprised that it held me up so high that I did not sink at all. Some men and women were on the shore hindering me from getting out, for I was naked. The meaning of this dream is that the vigour of my body still hinders me, but that the exit is near at hand.

I rose before daybreak and struck a flint, but for a long time could not light the tinder. I put on my elk-skin dressing-gown and went out. Behind the snow-clad larches and pines glowed a rosy-orange sky. I brought in the firewood I chopped yesterday, lit the stove, and chopped some more wood. It grew lighter. I ate some moistened rusks. The stove had grown hot and I closed the damper and sat down to write.

I was born just seventy-two years ago, on the 12th of December, 1777, in Petersburg, in the Winter Palace. By my grandmother's wish I was named Alexander, to betoken, as she told me herself, my becoming as great a man as Alexander the Great and as holy as Alexander Névski. I was christened a week later in the large Palace Church. I was carried on a brocade pillow by the Duchess of Courland. My coverlet was held up by officials of the highest rank. The Empress was my godmother, and the Emperor of Austria and the King of Prussia were my godfathers. The room allotted to me had been arranged to my grandmother's plan. (I don't remember it at all, but know of it from hearsay.) In the middle of that spacious room with its three large windows between four pillars, a velvet canopy was fastened to the ceiling with silk hangings descending to the ground. Under the canopy was placed an iron cot with a leather mattress, a small pillow, and a light English blanket. Beyond the hangings was a railing nearly five feet high, to prevent visitors from approaching too near. There was no other furniture in the room, except a bed behind the canopy for my wet-nurse. Every detail of my physical nurture was thought out by my grandmother. Rocking me to sleep was forbidden; I was swaddled in a special way; I wore no socks; was bathed first in warm and then in cold water, and had special clothing without seams or ribbons, but which could all be put on at once. As soon as I could crawl I was placed on the carpet and left to my own devices. I have been told that at first my grandmother herself used often to come and sit on the carpet to play with me. I don't remember anything of this, nor do I remember my wet-nurse at that time.

She was Avdótya Petróvna, the wife of an assistant gardener from Tsárskoe Seló. I did not remember her then. But I met her once when I was eighteen and she came up to me in the garden at Tsárskoe Seló. That was the good period of my life, the early days of my friendship with Adam Czartorýski, when I was sincerely disgusted at what was going on at both the courts – that of my unfortunate father and of my grandmother, who had then become hateful to me. I was still a human being then, and not even a bad one, having good intentions. I was walking in the park with Adam when a well-dressed woman with an unusually kind, pleasant, smiling, and excited face came down a side-path. She approached me quickly, fell on her knees, seized my hand, and began kissing it.

'My dear, your Highness! Now, God has granted —'

'Who are you?'

'Your nurse, Avdótya — Dunyásha — I nursed you eleven months. God grants me to see you again.'

I raised her with difficulty, asked where she lived, and promised to go to see her. The delightful home life in her clean little house, her sweet daughter, my foster-sister — a genuine Russian beauty engaged to one of the Court grooms — my nurse's husband, the gardener, just as smiling as his wife, and their crowd of smiling children seemed to light up the darkness around me. 'Here is true life, real happiness!' thought I. 'It is all so simple, so clear. No intrigues, jealousies, or quarrels.'

It was this amiable Dunyásha who nursed me. My head nurse was Sophia Ivánovna Benkendorf, a German; and the second nurse was an Englishwoman named Hessler. Sophia Ivánovna Benkendorf was a stout, white-skinned, straight-nosed woman, of majestic appearance when giving orders in the nursery but surprisingly servile in grandmother's presence — bowing and curtseying low to her who was a head shorter than herself. She was very obsequious to me and yet severe. Sometimes she was a queen, in her broad skirts and with her majestic straight-nosed face, and then suddenly she became an affected young hussy.

Praskóvya Ivánovna Hessler,[1] my English nurse, was a long-faced, red-haired, serious Englishwoman; but when she smiled her whole face beamed so that one could not help smiling with her. I liked her tidiness, her equanimity, her cleanliness, and her gentle firmness. It seemed as if she knew something

---

1 It was customary in Russia for people of other nationalities to adopt a Russian Christian name and patronymic, so in this case Miss Hessler assumed the names Praskóvya Ivánovna.

nobody else knew – neither my mother, nor my father, nor even my grandmother herself.

My mother I first recollect as a strange, sad, supernatural and charming vision. Handsome, elegant, glittering with diamonds, silks, and laces, and with her round, white arms bare, she would enter my room, and with a strange, melancholy expression on her face, alien to me and having no reference to me, would caress me, take me up in her strong beautiful arms, lift me to her still more beautiful face, and shaking back her thick, scented hair, would kiss me and cry, and once she even let me slip from her arms and fell down in a faint.

It is strange, but whether by my grandmother's influence, or as a result of my mother's behaviour to me, or because with a child's quick instinct I was aware of the intrigues that centred around me, it so happened that I had no simple feeling, or indeed any feeling, of love for my mother. I felt something strained in her treatment of me. She seemed to be parading herself through me, oblivious of me, and I felt it. So it really was. My grandmother took me from my parents entirely into her own hands, in order to pass the crown on to me and to disinherit her son, my unfortunate father, whom she hated. Of course I knew nothing about this till long after; but from my earliest consciousness, without understanding the reason, I was aware of being the object of some enmity and competition – a tool in some intrigue – and I was sensible of a coldness and indifference to myself, to my childish soul which desired no crown, but only simple love which was lacking. There was my mother, always sad in my presence. Once when she was speaking German to Sophia Ivánovna about something, she burst out crying and almost ran out of the room on hearing grandmother's footsteps. There was my father, who sometimes came to our room, and to whom, later on, my brother and I used to be taken; but at the sight of me my unfortunate father expressed his dissatisfaction and suppressed anger to a greater extent and more decidedly than my mother.

I remember being taken with my brother Constantine to his part of the palace. This was when he was starting on his journey abroad in 1781. He suddenly pushed me aside with his hand and jumped up from his arm-chair with a terrible look in his eyes, and in a choking voice said something about me and my grandmother. I did not understand what it was, but remember the words, *Après '62 tout est possible.*[1] I became frightened and began to cry. My mother took me on her arm and began kissing me, and then carried me to him. He hurriedly gave me his blessing and ran out of the room clattering with his high heels. Long afterwards I came to understand the meaning of that outburst. He and my mother were starting to travel as *Comte et Comtesse du Nord* – my grandmother wished them to do so – and he was afraid that during their absence he would be deprived of his right to the throne and I should be appointed heir. . . . Oh, my God, my God! He prized what ruined both him and me physically and spiritually – and I, unfortunate that I was, also prized it!

Someone has come knocking, saying: 'In the name of the Father and of the Son.' I have answered 'Amen'. I will now put my writing away and go and open the door. God willing, I will continue to-morrow.

13th December –
   I slept little and had bad dreams. Some unpleasant and weak woman was clinging to me, and though I was not afraid of her or of sinning, I was afraid my wife would see it and reproach me again. Seventy-two, and I am not free yet. When awake one can deceive oneself, but a dream gives a true valuation of the state one has attained to. I also dreamt – and this again shows the low level of morality on which I stand – that someone had brought me here some sweetmeats wrapped in moss – some unusual kind of sweetmeats – and we picked them out of the moss and divided them. But after the division some sweetmeats were left over and I began picking them out for myself; and just then a black-eyed and unpleasant boy, something like the Sultan of Turkey's son, stretched out

---

1 'After '62 everything is possible.' The Emperor Peter III, Catherine's husband, had been dethroned by a conspiracy and murdered, in July 1762.

towards the sweets and took them in his hand, and I pushed him away, though I knew that it is much more natural for a child to eat sweets than for me to do so. I did not let him have them, and knowing that this was wrong felt ill will towards him.

And strangely enough a similar thing really happened to me to-day. Márya Martemyánovna came. Yesterday a messenger from her had knocked at my door asking if she might call. I said she might. These visits are trying to me, but I knew that a refusal would hurt her. So she came to-day. The runners of her sledge could be heard in the distance squeaking over the snow. And when she entered in her fur cloak and several shawls, she brought in some bags of eatables (dumplings, Lenten oil, and apples), and so much cold air that I had to put on my dressing-gown. She came to ask my advice: whether to let her daughter marry a rich widower who is wooing her. Their belief in my sagacity is very trying to me, and all I say to correct it is attributed to my humility. I said what I always say: that chastity is better than marriage, but, as St Paul says, it is better to marry than to burn. With her came her son-in-law Nikanór Ivánovich – the one who invited me to come and live in his house and who has since unceasingly pestered me with his visits.

Nikanór Ivánovich is a great trial to me. I cannot overcome my antipathy and aversion for him. 'O Lord, grant me to see my own iniquities and not to judge my brother-man.' But I see all his faults, discern them with the penetration of malignity, see all his weaknesses, and cannot conquer my antipathy for him – my brother-man, who like myself proceeds from God.

What do such feelings mean? I have experienced them more than once in my long life. My two strongest aversions were for Louis XVIII, with his big stomach, hooked nose, repulsive white hands, and his self-confidence, insolence, and obtuseness – there, I cannot keep from abusing him – and the other antipathy is for this Nikanór Ivánovich who tormented me for two hours yesterday. Everything about him, from the sound of his voice to his hair and his nails, evokes repulsion in me, and to explain my gloominess to Márya Martemyánovna I told her a lie, saying that I was not well. After they had gone I prayed, and after the prayer I grew calm. I thank Thee, O Lord, that the one and only thing I need is in my own power. I remembered that Nikanór Ivánovich had been an infant and that he would die. I recalled the same with reference to Louis XVIII, knowing him to be already dead, and I regretted that Nikanór Ivánovich was no longer here that I might express my goodwill to him.

Márya Martemyánovna brought me some candles so that I can write in the evenings. I went out. To the left the bright stars have disappeared in a wonderful aurora borealis. How beautiful, how beautiful! But now I will continue.

My father and mother had gone abroad, and I and my brother Constantine, born two years after me, were in our grandmother's complete control for the whole of their absence. My brother had been named Constantine to denote that he was to become Emperor of Constantinople.

Children love everybody and especially those who love and caress them. My grandmother caressed and praised me, and I loved her in spite of the smell, repulsive to me, which always hung about her, notwithstanding her perfumes, and was especially noticeable when she took me on her lap. Her hands too were unpleasant to me – clean, yellowish, shrivelled, slippery, and shiny, with fingers bent inwards and with long nails from which the skin had been pushed back unnaturally far. Her eyes were dull, weary, almost lifeless, and this together with her smiling, toothless mouth, created a painful though not exactly repulsive impression. I attributed that expression of her eyes – which I now remember with loathing – to her exertions on behalf of her people, as it was explained to me, and I pitied her for that languid expression. Once or twice I saw Potëmkin[1] – a one-eyed, squinting, enormous, dark, perspiring, and dirty man who was terrible. He seemed to me particularly terrible because he alone was not afraid of grandmother, but spoke

[1] Field-Marshal Count G. A. Potëmkin (1739–91). For a long time the most influential of Catherine's favourites.

loud in her presence in his bellowing voice, and boldly caressed and teased me, though addressing me as 'your Highness'.

Among those I saw with her in my early childhood was Lanskóy.[1] He was always with her and everybody noticed him and paid court to him. My grandmother especially looked at him continually. Of course I did not then understand what it meant, and Lanskóy pleased me very much. I liked his curls, his handsome thighs in tightly stretched elk-skin breeches, his well-shaped calves, his merry careless smile, and the diamonds that glittered all over him.

It was a very merry time. We were taken to Tsárskoe Seló, where we boated, dug in the garden, went for walks, and rode on horseback. Constantine, plump, red-haired, *un petit Bacchus*, as grandmother called him, amused everybody by his tricks, his boldness, and his devices. He mimicked everybody, including Sophia Ivánovna and even grandmother herself.

The most important event of that time was Sophia Ivánovna Bénkendorf's death. It happened one evening at Tsárskoe Seló, in grandmother's presence. Sophia Ivánovna had just brought us in after dinner and was smilingly saying something, when her face suddenly became grave, she reeled, leant against the door, slipped, and fell heavily. People came running in and we were taken away. But next day we learnt that she was dead. I cried for a long time and was depressed and not myself. Everybody thought I was crying about Sophia Ivánovna, but it was not for her that I cried, but that people should die – that death should exist. I could not understand and could not believe that it was the fate of everybody. I remember that in my childish, five-year-old soul the questions, What is death? and, What is life which ends in death? then arose in their full significance – those chief questions which confront all mankind and to which the wise seek and find replies, and which the frivolous try to thrust aside and forget. I did what was natural for a child, especially in the world in which I lived: I put the question aside, forgot about death, lived as if it did not exist, and have now lived till it has become terrible to me.

1 Count A. D. Lanskóy (1754–84), a General and a favourite of Catherine II.

Another important event connected with Sophia Ivánovna's death was our being transferred to the charge of a man, and Nicholas Ivánovich Saltykóv being appointed our tutor – not the Saltykóv who in all probability was our grandfather, but Nicholas Ivánovich who was in service at my father's court; a little man with a huge head and a stupid face with a continual grimace, which my little brother Constantine imitated wonderfully. Being entrusted to a man grieved me, because it meant parting from my nurse, dear Praskóvya Ivánovna.

Those who have not the misfortune to be born in a royal family must, I think, find it difficult to realize how distorted is the view of people and of our relation towards them which is instilled into us and was instilled into me. Instead of the feeling of dependence on grown-up and older persons natural to a child, instead of gratitude for all the blessings which we enjoyed, we were led to believe that we were some kind of exceptional beings who not only ought to be supplied with all the good things a human being can have, but by a word or a smile could not only more than pay for all those blessings, but could also reward people and make them happy. It is true that we were expected to treat people politely, but with my childish instinct I realized that this was only for show, and was done not for the sake of the people to whom we had to be polite but for our own sake, so that our grandeur should be still more noticeable.

One fête-day we were driving along the Névski Prospect in an enormous landau: we two brothers and Nicholas Ivánovich Saltykóv. We sat in the chief seats. Two powdered footmen in red liveries stood behind. It was a bright spring day. I wore an unbuttoned uniform with a white waistcoat and the blue St Andrew's ribbon across it. Constantine was dressed in the same way; on our heads we wore plumed hats which we continually raised as we bowed. The people everywhere stopped and bowed; some of them ran after us. '*On vous salue*,'[1] Nicholas Ivánovich kept repeating. '*A droite*.'[2]

1 'They are bowing to you.'
2 'On the right.'

We went past the guard-house and the guards ran out. Those I always noticed, for I loved soldiers and military exercises from my childhood. We were told, especially by grandmother – the very one who believed it least of all – that all men are equal and that we ought to remember this, but I knew that those who said so did not believe it.

I remember once how Sásha Golítzin, who was playing with me at barricades, accidentally knocked me and hurt me.

'How dare you!'

'I did not mean to. What does it matter?'

I felt the blood rush to my heart with vexation and anger. I complained to Nicholas Ivánovich and was not ashamed when Golítzin begged my pardon.

That is enough for to-day. My candle has burnt low and I have yet to chop sticks, my axe is blunt and I have nothing to sharpen it on, besides which I don't know how to.

16th December –

I have not written for three days. I was not well. I have been reading the Gospels but could not arouse in myself that under-standing of them, that communion with God, which I experi-enced before. I used often to think that man cannot help having desires. I always had and still have desires. First I wished to conquer Napoleon, I wished to give peace to Europe, I wished to be released from my crown: and all my wishes were either fulfilled and as soon as that happened ceased to attract me, or became impossible of fulfilment and I ceased to wish for them. But while my wishes were being fulfilled or becoming impossible, new wishes arose, and so it went on and goes on to the end. I wished for the winter – it has come; I wished for solitude – and have almost attained it; now I wish to describe my life, and to do it in the best way possible, that it may be of use to others. And whether this wish is fulfilled or not, new wishes will awaken. Life consists in that. And it occurs to me that if the whole of life consists in the birth of wishes and the joy of life lies in their fulfilment, is there no wish which would be natural to man, to every human being, always, and would always be fulfilled or rather would be approaching fulfilment? And it has become clear to me that this would be so for a man who desired death. His whole life would be an approach to the fulfilment of that wish and the wish would certainly be fulfilled.

At first this seemed strange to me. But having considered it I suddenly saw that it really is so; that this alone, this approach to death, is the only reasonable wish a man can have. A wish not for death itself, but for the movement of life which leads to death. That movement consists in a release from passions and temptations of that spiritual element which dwells in every man. I feel this now, having freed myself from most of the things that used to hide from me what is essential in my soul – its oneness with God: used to hide God. I arrived at it unconsciously. But if I placed my welfare first (and this is not only possible, but is what ought to be) and considered my highest welfare to lie in liberation from passions and an approach towards God, then everything that brought me nearer to death – old age, and illness – would be a fulfilment of my one great desire. That is so, and I feel it when I am well. But when I have indigestion, as was the case yesterday and the day before, I cannot awaken that feeling, and though I do not resist death I am unable to wish to draw nearer to it.

Well, such a condition is one of spiritual sleep. One has to wait quietly. I will now go on from where I left off. What I write about my childhood I recount mainly from hearsay, and often what was told me about myself gets mixed up with what I experienced; so that I sometimes do not know what I myself experienced and what I heard from others.

My whole life from my birth to my present old age makes me think of a place enveloped in a thick mist, or even of the battlefield at Dresden: everything is hidden, nothing visible, and suddenly here and there little islands open out, *des éclaircies*[1] in which one sees people and objects unconnected with anything else and surrounded on all sides by an impenetrable curtain. Such are my childish recollections. For the time of

1 Clearings.

my childhood these *éclaircies* very very rarely open out amid the
sea of mist or smoke, afterwards they occur more and more
frequently; but even now I have times that leave no memories
behind. In childhood there are very few memories, and the
farther back the fewer there are.

I have spoken of the clearings that belong to my early life:
Sophia Bénkendorf's death, the good-bye to my parents, and
Constantine's mimicking, but several other memories of that
period open out now as I think of the past. For instance, I don't
at all remember when Kóstya[1] appeared and we began to live
together; but I well remember how once when I was seven
and he five we went to bed after service on Christmas eve and
taking advantage of the fact that everybody had left our room,
we got into one bed together. Kóstya in his little shirt climbed
over to me and we began playing a merry game which consisted in slapping one another on our bare bodies; and we
laughed till our stomachs ached and were very happy, when
suddenly Nicholas Ivánovich, with his huge powdered head,
entered wearing his embroidered coat and his orders, and
rushed towards us with staring eyes, in horror which I could
not at all explain to myself, and separated us and angrily
promised to punish us and to tell our grandmother.

Another occurrence I well remember happened rather late –
when I was about nine; it was an encounter in grandmother's
room, and almost in our presence, between Alexéy Grigórevich Orlóv[2] and Potëmkin. It was not long before grandmother's journey to the Crimea and our first journey to
Moscow. Nicholas Ivánovich had taken us as usual to see
grandmother. The large room, the ceiling of which was ornamented with stucco-work and paintings, was full of people.
Grandmother's hair had already been done. It was combed
back from the forehead and very skilfully arranged on the
temples. She sat at her dressing-table in a white powder-
mantle. Her maid stood behind her adjusting her hair. She

---

1 A pet name for Constantine.
2 Count Alexéy Grigórevich Orlóv, a General and Admiral. He had
strangled Peter III with his own hands.

looked at us with a smile, continuing her conversation with a big, tall, and stout General decorated with the ribbon of St Andrew, who had a terrible scar across his cheek from mouth to ear. This was Orlóv, '*Le balafré*'.[1] It was there I saw him for the first time. Grandmother's Anderson hare-hounds were beside her, and my pet Mimi jumped up from her skirt and leaping at me put its feet on my shoulders and licked my face. We came up to grandmother and kissed her white, plump hand. She turned it round and her bent fingers caught my face and caressed me. In spite of her perfumes I was aware of her disagreeable smell. She went on looking at Balafré and speaking to him.

'A fine fellow,' she said, with her strong German accent, pointing to me, 'you had not seen him before.'

'They are both fine fellows,' said the count, kissing my hand and Constantine's.

'It's all right, it's all right,' she said to her maid who was putting her cap on for her. That maid was Márya Stepánovna, painted red and white, a kind-hearted woman who always caressed me.

'*Où est ma tabatière?*'[2]

Lanskóy came up and handed her an open snuff-box. Grandmother took a pinch and looked at her jester Matrëna Danílovna, who was approaching her. . . .

(*The story breaks off here, and was left in this unfinished state when Tolstoy died.*)

1 'The gash'.
2 'Where is my snuff-box?'

APPENDIX I
TWO EARLY STORIES

PREFACE

TOLSTOY was not only a prolific writer, but a writer given to producing numerous plot outlines, drafts and re-drafts, and unfinished sections of works which either never came to fruition or were re-absorbed into the making of other stories or novels. The ninety volumes of the Russian-language Jubilee Edition (1928–58) contain, as well as Tolstoy's letters and diaries, a great quantity of this type of material, much of it of interest only to specialists. The two texts printed below, apparently not translated into English before, are included in the present edition both because they are documents of some biographical and literary value, and because readers of biographies and critical studies of Tolstoy in English may well come across references to them.

The first and much better-known of the two, *A History of Yesterday*, is a fragment written in a few days in late March 1851, some four weeks before Lev Tolstoy left with his brother Nikolai for the Caucasus, where (from November 1851 to July 1852) he was to write the fourth, final draft of his first published work, *Childhood*. *Childhood* looks like a thinly disguised autobiography, but is actually a complex blend of borrowed experiences, personal recollections and fiction. In *A History of Yesterday*, on the other hand, Tolstoy has, in Eikhenbaum's words, 'not yet severed the umbilical cord which connects the story to his diaries'. *A History of Yesterday* is much nearer to autobiography, or rather to Tolstoy's diaries, of which there are surviving volumes for parts of 1847 and 1850, most of 1851 and nearly all of 1852.

A. N. Wilson points out the very close relationship between the opening section of the story and the diary's record of the evening of 24 March 1851, which Tolstoy spent playing cards at the Moscow house of his cousin Alexander Volkonsky, and flirting with Alexander's wife, Louisa Ivanovna. The story's account of this social evening, with a minute dissection of the narrator's thoughts and his conversation (spoken and implied) with his hostess, is followed by a description of his journey home. This includes a short essay on cab-drivers and their characteristics: the populist note and the details of verbal abuse and Russian nicknames are strongly reminiscent of Gogol's *Dead Souls* (1842). Having brought his bachelor narrator home, Tolstoy plunges him into a long and typically heavy-footed disquisition on the diary or journal form itself, and its usefulness – or its futility – as a tool of moral self-improvement. This is the first in a long line of similar meditations in Tolstoy's fiction, though by no means the first in his own diaries. It leads in turn to a detailed account of the processes of falling asleep, dreaming and waking up. The account of the experience is far more entertaining than the leaden analysis which follows: Proust's treatment of very similar material sixty years later yielded a far more beautiful result. The text concludes with a much shorter fragment 'written on another day', a day which seems to bear no relation whatever to the *Yesterday* of the title, about the narrator's projected journey down the Volga to Astrakhan, on the Caspian Sea. Even this small fragment again partially reflects Tolstoy's own life experience: he and Nikolai accomplished a three-week section of their journey to the Caucasus on a boat which took them down the Volga, not from Moscow but from Saratov to Astrakhan. (It is characteristic of Tolstoy's endless and economical recycling of the raw material of experience that a similar journey down the Volga is undertaken by the Polish exiles escaping from Siberia in the late story *What For?*)

Important as the autobiographical element in *A History of Yesterday* is, scholars have emphasized the decisive literary influence which led Tolstoy to write it in the first place – his passionate enthusiasm for Sterne's *A Sentimental Journey* (1768), which he read early in 1851 and partially translated into Russian. Some critics have enthused about the daring originality of Tolstoy's early foray into 'stream of consciousness' writing: D. S. Mirsky invokes the names of Proust and Joyce. But a version of the 'stream of consciousness' convention is already present in Sterne, and A. N. Wilson argues that 'far from being proto-Modernist, the fragment actually suggests (with its debts and allusions to Sterne and Rousseau) a world of literary modes and models which, by the standards of Western Europe, were at least half a century out of date'. R. F. Christian lists the many unmistakably Sternian fingerprints in this story – including frequent dashes (and parentheses) – and notes its paradoxical Shandean failure ever to get as far as telling us about what happened 'yesterday'. He concludes: 'The occasional diary-like entries and the passage on the subject of diaries are evidence also that Tolstoy's own writing habits no less than his reading tastes are reflected in this early story which, like much of his juvenilia, is related less to contemporary life than to literature.'

The other early story included here for the first time in English is much less well-known. *A Christmas Night* dates from 1853, the year when Tolstoy's second published story, *The Raid*, appeared, and in which he was working on *Boyhood*, the second part of his trilogy, while serving with the army in the Caucasus. Henri Troyat refers to this story (under the title *A Holy Night*) as the earliest of several texts, autobiographical as well as fictional, dealing with sexual initiation and sexual disgust. There is no suggestion, however, that *A Christmas Night* is a piece of barely-concealed journal writing in the manner of *A History of Yesterday*. *A Christmas Night* is a more conventionally literary piece, close to the mainstream of nineteenth-century novel fiction. This time the narrative is almost entirely in the 'omniscient' third person mode, and is far closer to Balzac than to Sterne, especially in its melodramatic treatment of romantic love and in the substantial ball scene which reads like an admiring pastiche of *Le Père Goriot*.

The text of *A Christmas Night* is incomplete, with two

chapter headings indicated but not fleshed out, and the surviving manuscript is a mixture of a first rough draft, and a second 'fair copy' draft which extends almost to the end of Chapter III. As a result there are some incoherences in the treatment and the development of the minor characters, as well as a hesitation about the name of the hero – initially Alexandre, but in the second draft Seriozha Ivin. (In this translation 'Seriozha' is used throughout.) As in *A History of Yesterday*, the ms. contains a number of deleted but still decipherable passages, indicated in the present edition of both stories by pointed brackets.

Despite these imperfections, *A Christmas Night* is a complete and coherent story as it stands. It has a clear plot line, plenty of observation of human behaviour at carefully contrasted different social levels (an echo perhaps of the literary *physiologies* which came into fashion in the mid-1840s in imitation of French models), some passages of lyrical nature description which would be equally at home in *Youth*, and the perennial Tolstoyan theme of the moral superiority of the country over the city. The only undigested element (which Tolstoy would surely have excised, had he ever prepared this piece for publication) is the digression on gypsy music towards the end, which may be of some historical and even musicological interest but radically disrupts the narrative flow. This apart, if *A History of Yesterday* shows the young Tolstoy's mastery of the Sternean sentimental manner, *A Christmas Night*, coming only two years later, demonstrates that he was also capable of producing a convincing Russian equivalent of the French romantic fiction of the 1830s and 1840s.

A HISTORY OF
YESTERDAY

I AM writing a history of yesterday, not because yesterday was in any way remarkable, or could even be called remarkable, but because I have long desired to tell the story of the intimate side of a single day. God alone knows how many varied and interesting impressions, and thoughts aroused by those impressions (obscure and ill-defined but nonetheless intelligible to our own soul) occur in the course of a single day. If it were possible to recount them in such a way as to make it easy for me to read my own self, and for others to read me as I really am, the result would be a really instructive and absorbing book – a book indeed for which the world could not provide enough ink for the writing, or printers for the publishing of it. ⟨From whatever angle you look into the human soul, you find everywhere the same boundlessness, and speculations arise to which there is no end, from which there is no way out, and which I find alarming.⟩—But to business.—

Yesterday I got up late, at a quarter to ten, and that was simply because I had gone to bed after midnight the night before. (I long ago set myself the rule of not going to bed later than twelve o'clock, but all the same I find myself doing so some three times each week); however there are certain circumstances in which I would class this not as a crime but rather as a minor lapse: such circumstances are of many kinds, and how it was yesterday I shall now explain.

Here I must beg your indulgence for recounting things which occurred the day *before* yesterday, but as you are well aware, novelists are given to writing whole histories about their heroes' immediate forebears.

I was playing cards, but certainly not from any passionate liking for cards, however it may appear. As regards the love of card-playing, it is rather like the case of those people who dance the polka just because they enjoy the exercise. Jean-Jacques Rousseau, among the many suggestions he made which no one agreed with, advocated playing with a cup-and-ball [bilboquet] in society in order to give one's hands something to do; but that does not go far enough, for in society the head too needs to be occupied, or at least it needs some sort of activity about which people can either talk or remain silent.—In our country such an activity has in fact been devised – card-playing.—Persons born in the last century complain that 'there is no conversation whatever to be had nowadays'. I do not know what people were like in the last century (it seems to me, though, that they have always been pretty much the same); however, genuine conversation is never a real possibility. Conversation merely as a pastime is the stupidest of inventions. It is not because of intellectual inadequacy that there is no conversation, but because of egoism. Everyone wants to speak about himself or about what concerns him; and if one person talks and the other listens, that is not conversation, but lecturing. And even if two people agree to concentrate on the same topic, it only takes the addition of a third person for the whole thing to be ruined: he intervenes, they must do their best to accommodate him, and the conversation goes to the devil.

There are also conversations where two people are interested in the same thing and nobody interferes with them, yet here the situation is even worse. Each of them talks about the same thing, but from his own point of view, measuring everything by his own yardstick, and the longer the conversation goes on, the farther each of them gets from the other, until each realizes that he has ceased to converse, but is preaching with a freedom no one else could equal, setting himself up as an example, and the other person is not really listening, but doing likewise. Have you ever engaged in rolling Easter eggs during Holy Week? You set in motion two identical hard-boiled eggs along the same strip of bast matting, but each egg has in fact a slight irregularity in its side. They may start rolling in the same direction, but then each egg begins to roll in a direction dictated by its own tiny irregularity. In conversation, as in egg-rolling, there are the *shlyupiks*[1] which roll noisily and not very far, and there are the sharp-ended ones which get carried away goodness knows where; but there are no two eggs, *shlyupiks* apart, which are likely to roll in exactly the same direction. Each one has its own particular irregularity.

I am not referring to those conversations which occur because it would be improper not to say something, in the same way that it would be improper not to wear a necktie. One party is thinking: 'You realize of course that it is no matter to me what I talk about, but I have to do so'; and the other is thinking: 'Talk on, talk on, you poor fellow, – I accept that it is necessary.' This is not conversation, but rather – like black tail-coats, visiting cards and gloves – a matter of propriety.

That is why I say that card-playing is an excellent invention. During the game it is possible to converse a little and flatter one's self-esteem, to let fall some charming little *mot*, without being obliged to continue in the same vein, as one would have to do in a society where there was nothing but conversation available.

It is essential to keep back your final volley of wit for the last circle of acquaintances you encounter that evening, just as you are taking your hat: this is the moment to squander all the reserves you have been holding on to. Like a horse in the final straight going all out to win. Otherwise you will appear feeble and colourless; and I have noticed that people who are not merely clever, but capable of shining in society, have failed because they have misjudged the level of their remarks. If you say something in the heat of the moment before anyone has had time to get tired of you, and then,

1 Literally a soft old mushroom: metaphorically, something battered and knocked about, as here a hard-boiled egg which has been rolled too many times to roll smoothly, and in *Anna Karenina*, Part 7, Ch. 3, a veteran clubman.

feeling bored, you do not wish to converse further, that is how you will be seen as you depart: the final impression is the one which will stick, and people will say 'How difficult he is . . .' But when a card-game is going on no such thing can happen. One is allowed to remain silent without being censured for it.

Besides, if women (young women) are playing, there begins to be something better to aim at – to spend two or three hours in close proximity to the right woman.—And of course if the right woman simply happens to be there, then that is already satisfaction enough.

So there I was playing cards, sitting now on her right, now on her left, now opposite her, and wherever I sat it was all wonderful.

This mode of entertainment went on until a quarter to twelve. Three rubbers had been completed. Why does this woman love me? – how I should like to be able to write that! but I must write instead – Why does this woman love to put me in embarrassing situations? And that apart, I am already hardly in command of myself when I am in her presence: at one moment it seems to me that my hands are really dirty, at another that I am sitting awkwardly, at another that I am tormented by a pimple on my cheek precisely on the side where she can see it.

However, I feel that none of this is her fault – I never feel quite myself when I am with people whom I either dislike or love very much. Why should this be? It is surely because one wants to show one person that one does not like them, and to show another that one loves them, but to show what one wants to show is very difficult. In my case it always comes out the wrong way round: you wish to appear chilly, but then you feel you are overdoing it, and you make yourself too affable; and although being with people you really and truly love is delightful, the idea that they may think you love them in a dishonourable way confounds you, and you end up making your manner curt and abrupt.

She is the woman for me because she possesses those sweet qualities which compel me to love them, or better still, to

love her, for I do love her; but not because she would be
capable of giving herself to a lover. That thought does not
enter my head. She has the unpleasing habit of billing and
cooing with her husband in the presence of others, but that
is no business of mine; it would be all the same to me if she
were to choose to kiss the stove or the table – she is simply
playing with her husband, as a swallow might play with a
wisp of fluff, because she has a kindly soul and this makes
her cheerful.—

She is a coquette; no, not a coquette, but she does enjoy
being liked, and turning men's heads. I would not call her a
coquette, because either the word itself is bad, or the conno-
tations attached to it are bad. People apply the term
'coquetry' to the display of bare flesh, or falseness in love –
this is not coquetry, but insolent and ill-bred behaviour.—
No, but the desire to please and to turn heads is a fine and
attractive thing, it harms no one, because there are no Wer-
thers here, and it gives her and others innocent pleasure. Here
am I, for example, utterly content that she pleases me and
desiring nothing further. And then there is intelligent
coquetry and stupid coquetry: the intelligent sort is when the
coquetry is unobtrusive and there is no villain to be caught
red-handed; the stupid sort is just the opposite, where nothing is concealed. And this is how it finds expression: 'I may
not be particularly beautiful in myself, but just look what
pretty feet I have! Just look: do you see? Well, do you like
them?'—Your feet are perhaps pretty, but I did not take any
notice of your feet, because you deliberately made a display
of them.—Intelligent coquetry says: 'It is all one and the same
to me whether you look at me or you don't, but I feel warm,
so I have taken off my hat.'—I look at you all the time.—'And
why should I mind?' Hers is the innocent and intelligent sort.

I glanced at my watch and got up. It is astonishing: except
when I am speaking to her I have never seen her glance
resting on me, and yet she sees my every movement.—'Oh,
what a lovely rose-tinted watch-face he has!'—I was greatly
offended that anyone should comment on my Bréguet time-
piece being rose-coloured, in the same way that I should be

annoyed to be told that I was wearing a pink waistcoat. I must have looked visibly embarrassed, because when I said that it was actually an extremely fine watch, she in her turn looked embarrassed. No doubt she regretted having said something which put me in an awkward position. We both realized the absurdity of it, and smiled. A stupid thing, but we were sharing in it.—I adore these secret relationships which express themselves by an unobtrusive little smile and by the expression of the eyes, and which cannot be openly declared. It is not that one of us has suddenly understood the other, but each understands that the other understands that he or she is understood, etc., etc.

Whether she wanted to put an end to this conversation which I found so pleasant, or to watch me refuse to stay, or to know whether I would refuse, or simply to go on playing, – the fact was that she glanced at the numbers written on the card table, ran the chalk across its surface, drew some kind of figure unrecognized in mathematics or in painting, looked first at her husband and then from him to me, and said: 'Let us play three more rubbers.' I was so absorbed in watching, not these movements but the whole phenomenon known as *charme*, which it is impossible to describe, that my imagination was far, far away and my mind was unable to clothe my words in any appropriate form; I simply said 'No, I cannot.' No sooner had I managed to say this, than I started to regret it, – that is to say, not all of me, but just one part of me.—There is no action which some little part of the soul would not condemn; on the other hand there is always some part to be found which will say approvingly: What does it matter if you get to bed after twelve, and anyway, how do you know if you will ever have such a successful evening again? Evidently this part of me spoke up most eloquently and persuasively (though I am unable to convey just what it said), for I became alarmed and began to seek for excuses.—In the first place, there won't be much enjoyment in it, I said to myself: you don't really like her at all and you are in an awkward position; and then you have already said that you can't stay, and you have lost face . . .

'Comme il est aimable, ce jeune homme.' [2]

This sentence, following straight after mine, interrupted my reflections.—I began to apologize for not being able to stay, but as this required no thought, I went on arguing with myself: How I love her referring to me in the third person. In German it's rude, but I should love it, even in German. And why can't she find a suitable form of address for me? It's obvious that she is uncomfortable calling me by my Christian name, or by my surname and title. Can it possibly be because I . . . 'Do stay and have some supper,' said her husband. Since I was busy pondering the matter of third person forms of address, I failed to notice that my body, having made the politest possible excuses for being unable to stay, had put down my hat again and sunk calmly into an armchair. It was evident that the intellectual side of me was taking no part in this folly. I began to feel extremely vexed, and was just starting to take myself to task when I was diverted by a most agreeable development. She was sketching something with great attention, what it was I could not see, then she raised the piece of chalk slightly higher than neces- sary and put it down on the table. Then, resting her arms on the sofa she was sitting on and shifting herself from one side to the other, she drew herself up against the back of the sofa and raised her charming little head – her head with the delicately curving profile of her face and her dark, half- closed yet animated eyes, her slender and so, so sharp little nose, and a mouth that, with her eyes, composed a unity and at every moment seemed to convey something quite new. How could one say what, at that instant, it expressed? There was pensiveness, mockery, fragility, the desire not to laugh, self-importance, capriciousness, intelligence, stupid- ity, passion, apathy, and who knows what else in that expres- sion.—A few moments later her husband went out, no doubt to order supper to be served.

When I am left alone with her I always become nervous and clumsy. As I follow with my eyes the people leaving the

2 How pleasant he is, this young man.

room I feel as ill at ease as in the fifth figure of the quadrille,
when I see my partner crossing to the far side, condemning
me to be left alone. I am sure Napoleon did not feel so
wretched when the Saxons went over to the enemy at
Waterloo, as I did in my early youth when I contemplated
this cruel manoeuvre. The tactic I use in dancing the quadrille, I now use in this situation too: I try to give the
impression that I have not noticed I am alone. Now even
the conversation which had begun before his exit had come
to a halt; I repeated the last words I had spoken, adding only:
'So it had to be,' and she repeated her previous words, adding
'Yes'. But alongside this there began at once a second,
inaudible conversation.

She: 'I know why you are repeating what you have already
said: you feel embarrassed to be alone with me, and you can
see I am embarrassed too – so to appear interested you had
to say something. I am grateful to you for your consideration,
but you might have said something a bit more intelligent.'—
I: 'That is true, your remark is accurate, but I don't know
why you should feel embarrassed; can you be thinking that
if you are alone with me I may start saying the kind of things
which you would find unacceptable? Just to prove to you
how ready I am to sacrifice my own satisfactions for your
benefit, however delightful our present conversation may be
to me, I shall now start to speak aloud. Or perhaps you
would like to start.' *She:* 'Well then, let us do so!'

I was still composing my mouth to say something of the
kind which allows one to be thinking one thing while
conversing about something else, when she launched into a
conversation out loud which gave the impression that it
might go on for some time; but in this sort of situation
even the most significant topics fall flat, because that *other*
conversation is still going on. Having produced a sentence
each, we fell silent, attempted once more to speak, then
lapsed again into silence. *The other conversation:*—*I:* 'No, it is
quite impossible to converse. Since I can see that you are
embarrassed, it would be preferable if your husband came
back.' *She (aloud):* 'Boy, where is Ivan Ivanovich? Go and

ask him to come here.' If anyone did not believe that such secret conversations do exist, I hope this example will convince them.

'I am very glad we are alone now,' I continued in the same mode. 'I have already remarked to you that you often upset me by your lack of trust in me. If I accidentally touch your foot with mine, you at once hasten to apologize, and do not give me time to apologize first, while I, having made sure that it was your foot I touched, wanted simply to apologize. I cannot keep up with you in these matters, yet you still think that I lack delicacy.'

Her husband came back. We sat down to supper and chatted, and I returned home at half-past midnight.

In the sledge

It is spring now, the twenty-fifth of March. The night is still and clear; the new moon has come into view from behind the red roof of the big white house opposite; the snow has mostly melted.

'Let's be off, driver! . . .'

My night-service sledge was the only one waiting near the house porch and Dmitry had evidently heard me coming out without waiting for any shouted summons from the footman, for the smacking noise he made with his lips was audible, as though he were kissing someone in the darkness: a sound which I suppose was meant to tell the little horse to pull the sledge off the stone roadway, on which the runners screeched and scraped unpleasantly. At length the sledge drew up. The obliging footman took my elbow and guided me towards the seat; had he not supported me I should have jumped straight into the sledge, but now, so as not to offend him, I made my way more cautiously and broke through the layer of thin ice on a puddle, wetting my feet. 'Thank you, my man.'—'Dmitry, is it freezing?'—'As well as you could wish for, sir; at this time of the year you still get a good light frost any night, sir.'

—How stupid! Why am I asking him?—No, that's not

true, there's nothing stupid about it: you have an urge to talk, to make contact with people, because you are in a cheerful mood. So why am I cheerful? If I had got into the sledge at any time in the past half-hour I would not have started chatting. It is because you spoke really rather well before taking your leave, and because her husband came out to see you off and said 'When shall we be seeing one another again?' And because as soon as the footman caught sight of you he immediately roused himself, and for all that his breath smelt strongly of parsley, he attended to you with such enthusiasm. I once gave him fifty copecks. In all our memories the central part gets lost, but the first and last impressions remain, especially the last. Hence the delightful custom whereby the master of the house sees a guest to the door where, generally standing there with his legs twined together in semi-embarrassment, he cannot avoid saying something kind to his guest: no matter how short the acquaintance may have been, this rule cannot be neglected. Thus, for example, 'When shall we be seeing each other again?' means nothing, but the guest out of self-esteem translates it so: *when* means 'Please let it be soon'; *we* means 'my wife and I, for my wife too greatly enjoys seeing you'; *again* means 'We have only just finished spending this evening together, but in your company no one could possibly be bored'; *be seeing one another* means 'Please do us the pleasure once more'. And the guest departs with an agreeable impression. It is likewise essential, particularly in less well organized houses where not all the servants, especially the doorman (he is a most important person because he provides one's first and last impressions) are courteous, to give them some money. They meet you and they see you off just as if you were one of the household, and their obligingness, which may well be the result of a fifty-copeck piece, can be translated so:—'Everyone here likes you and respects you, and so we try, just as we oblige our masters, to oblige you too.' Perhaps it is only the footman himself who does really like and respect you, but all the same it is very pleasant. What harm is there if you should be mistaken? If there were no such thing as illusion, that would not mean that . . .

'If he hasn't gone clean out of his wits! . . . De-evil take him! . . .'

Dmitry and I had been driving very gently and very carefully along some boulevard or other, keeping to the thin covering of ice on the right-hand side of the carriageway, when some 'wood demon' (as Dmitry afterwards referred to him) with a carriage and pair had run into us. We extricated ourselves, and when we were already a dozen or so paces safely distant from them Dmitry said: 'See there, the wood demon doesn't know his right from his left!'

Do not assume that Dmitry was a timid fellow or slow to respond. No, quite the reverse: although short in stature and beardless (but still with a moustache) he was deeply conscious of his own worth, and scrupulous in carrying out his duties. The cause of his apparent weakness in this instance was twofold. First, Dmitry was accustomed to driving carriages which inspired respect, whereas now we were travelling in an insignificant little sledge behind a small horse in extremely long shafts, so that even with the length of the whip it was quite hard to reach the animal, and the horse in question was pathetically unsteady in the hind legs and liable to call forth ridicule from passers-by who saw it: so that this incident was particularly awkward for Dmitry, sufficiently so to cancel out his customary feeling of dignity. Second, my question 'Is it freezing?' probably reminded him of the same sort of question I would ask when going out with him on hunting trips in the autumn. He is a sportsman, and a sportsman has plenty of material for daydreaming – which may even make him forget to curse appropriately a driver who does not keep to the right. Among coachmen as with everyone else, that man is in the right who shouts at the other driver first and with the greater conviction. There are exceptions: for example, a poor droshky-driver cannot possibly shout at a carriage, and a man on his own, even if he is a bit of a dandy, is hard put to it to shout at a team of four horses; in fact everything turns on the nature of the particular circumstances, and chiefly on the personality of the coachman and the direction he is travelling in. In Tula I once witnessed a striking example of the effect one man can produce on others by sheer audacity.

It was a Shrove Tuesday and everyone was out driving: sledges and pairs, four-in-hands, carriages, trotters, ladies in silk coats – all parading in a row along Kiev Street – hordes of pedestrians too. Suddenly there was a shout from a street which crossed the main one at right-angles: 'Hey, hold him there, hold that horse back! Hey, give way there!' in a thoroughly self-confident tone. Involuntarily the pedestrians stood aside and the fours all reined in. What do you think? A ragged cabman standing upright on a ramshackle sledge drawn by a wretched jade and brandishing the reins above his head, was forcing his way through by dint of shouting, to the opposite side of the street, while nobody realized what was going on. Even the policemen on duty were bursting out laughing when they saw it.

Although Dmitry is a man ready to take a chance and one who enjoys a bit of cursing, he has a good heart and is kind to animals. He uses the whip not as a means of compulsion, but of correction, that is to say, he does not urge the horse on with the whip: for him this would be quite incompatible with the dignity of a city coachman; but if a trotter should refuse to stand at a house entrance, he will 'give him a touch or two'. I had occasion to see this presently: turning out of one street into another, our little horse was having difficulty in pulling us round, and from the agitated movements of Dmitry's back and arms and the smacking noises he was making with his lips, it was clear to me that he was in a difficult position. Would he resort to the whip? It was against his habit to do so. But what if the horse should just stop still? He could not tolerate that, even though here there was no cause to worry about some joker who might say 'Suppose you tried giving him something to eat?' This seems to me a demonstration of the fact that Dmitry acts more from an awareness of principle than from vanity.

I reflected further on the great variety of relations between coachmen themselves, their mentality, their resourcefulness and their pride. No doubt when many coachmen are gathered together in one place they recognize one another, including those drivers they have been in collisions with, and they progress from hostile to peaceable relations. All human beings in this world are of interest, and particularly fascinating are the attitudes and relationships of those classes to which we do not ourselves belong.

When the two carriages involved in an incident are travelling in the same direction, any disagreement is usually more protracted: the man who has given offence tries to drive off or to drop back, and the other driver may manage to show that the first driver was in the wrong, and to gain the upper hand; however, when both parties are travelling the same way the advantage is on the side of the driver whose horses are swifter. All these attitudes are readily applicable to the relations one encounters in everyday life as a whole. I am equally intrigued by the attitudes of gentlemen to one another and to coachmen, in encounters of this sort.— 'Where d'you think you're rushing off to, you load of rubbish?' When this condemnation is addressed to the whole carriage, the passenger cannot help trying to appear serious, or merry, or carefree – in a word, to appear different from what he was the moment before: he would plainly be only too pleased if the whole thing had happened the other way round. I have observed that gentlemen with moustaches are particularly sensitive to insults hurled at their own carriages.—

—'Who goes there?'

This was the shout of a policeman, a man I had happened to see only that morning being insulted by another coachman. Near the house entrance just opposite this very policeman's box there had been a carriage standing. The splendid red-bearded coachman had tucked the reins under him, and propping his elbows on his knees, was warming his back in the sun, evidently with great enjoyment, for his eyes were almost closed. Across the road from him the policeman was pacing up and down the area in front of his sentry-box and with the end of his halberd was straightening a plank which bridged a puddle in front of his platform. Suddenly he looked displeased, perhaps because there was a carriage standing there, or because he felt envious of the coachman sunning himself so happily, or just because he wanted a bit of a chat: he walked along his little platform, glanced up the side-street, and then with a thump of his halberd on the plank, began: 'Hey, you, what are you waiting there for? You're blocking up the road.' The coachman opened his left eye a crack, looked at the policeman, and shut it again.—'Move along, do you hear?' No sign of any attention whatever.— 'So you can't hear me, eh? Get off the road, I tell you!' The policeman, seeing that he was not getting any response, walked along his platform and took another look up the side-street, clearly getting ready to say something that would really strike home. At that moment the coachman sat up, adjusted the reins, and turning with sleepy eyes towards the policeman, said: 'What are you gawping at? They didn't stick a rifle in your hands, you old fool, but you bellow just the same!'

—'Get moving!'

The coachman roused himself and got moving.

I glanced at the policeman: he was muttering something and gave me an angry look. He evidently did not like my listening to him and looking at him. I know that there is no more effective way of offending a man than by making it obvious that you have noticed him but that you have no intention of speaking to him; and so I was embarrassed, and feeling sorry for the policeman went on my way.

Another thing I like about Dmitry is his ability to give someone the right name straight off: I find this most amusing. 'Give way, fur hat,—Let's have some service there, beardy, Give way, you toboggan, Give way, laundress, Give way, horse-doctor,—Give way, you *fine figure*, Give way, Monsieur'. It is amazing how a Russian manages to find the right abusive term for another man whom he is seeing for the very first time, and not just for the person, but for his social status: the petty bourgeois is 'cat-dealer', as if the lower middle classes go about purloining cats; a footman is 'flunkey, dish-licker'; a peasant is, why I do not know,

'Ryurik'; a coachman is 'cart-driver', and so forth – there are too many of these terms to count. If a Russian gets into a squabble with someone he has just seen for the first time, he immediately bestows on him a nickname which will cut him to the quick: crooknose, cross-eyed devil, rubber-lipped rogue, snubnose. One needs to experience it to know how truly and accurately these names always hit the right tender spot. I shall never forget an insult which I received in my absence. A certain Russian man said of me: 'Oh, he's an old gap-tooth!' It must be admitted that my teeth are indeed exceptionally bad, decayed, and widely-spaced.—

At home

I arrived home. Dmitry jumped down to open the main gates, and so did I, to try to get through the wicket gate before he could get through the others. This is how it always happens: I hurry to get in because that is my custom, and he hurries to bring me right up to the house steps, because that is his custom.—For some time I could get no reply to my ringing of the door-bell; inside, the tallow candle was in serious need of snuffing and Prov, my little old manservant, was asleep. While I was ringing this is what I was thinking: Why do I dislike coming home, wherever and in whatever circumstances I happen to be living? Why do I dislike seeing the same old Prov in the same place, the same candle, the same stains on the wallpaper, the same pictures, so that I even begin to feel quite depressed?—

I am particularly tired of the wallpaper and the pictures, because they purport to give you variety, yet you only need to look at them for two days for them to be worse than a blank wall. This disagreeable feeling on getting home must be due to the fact that I was not designed to be living as a bachelor at the age of twenty-two. How much better it would be if I could ask Prov (who has jumped up, and with a great clatter of his boots, no doubt to show that he has been alert and listening for me for ages, is opening the door): 'Is the mistress asleep?' 'Not at all, sir, she is reading a book.'

How much better it would be: I should clasp her dear head in my hands and hold it for a moment, and look at her and kiss her, and look at her again and kiss her again; and I should not feel at all gloomy about returning home. But as things are, the one question I can ask Prov, to show him I have noticed that he never goes to sleep while I am out, is: 'Did anyone call?' 'No one.' Whenever this sort of question is put to him Prov invariably answers in a pathetic tone, and every time I feel like saying to him: 'Oh why do you speak in that pathetic tone of voice? I am delighted that no one has called.' But I restrain myself: Prov might take offence, and he is a man worthy of some consideration.—

In the evening I usually write my diary, and a journal after the style of Benjamin Franklin, and do my daily accounts. On this particular day I had not spent anything, because there was not even a single half-copeck in my purse, thus there was nothing to write in my account book.—

The diary and the journal are another matter: I really ought to write in them, but it is late, so I put it off until the morrow.—

I have often chanced to hear the remark: 'He is an empty fellow, he leads an aimless life'; and I too have often used these words and still do, not to echo someone else's opinion but because I feel in my soul that this is a bad thing, and that one ought to have an *aim* in life.

But how do you set about being 'a whole man, with an aim in living'? To set yourself such an aim is quite impossible.—I have attempted it so many times, and it has never worked out. You must not so much try to invent an aim, as to find one which conforms to your own personal leanings, one which was already in existence, and which you have but to recognize. It seems to me that I have actually found an aim of that kind: the all-round cultivation and development of my abilities. One of the principal and most widely acknow-ledged means to that end is the keeping of a diary and a *Franklin* journal.—In the diary I confess every day all the wrong things I have done. In the journal my weaknesses are listed in columns – laziness, lying, gluttony, indecisiveness, showing off, sensuality, insufficient *fierté*, and other such mean and petty passions: I then transfer all my transgressions from the diary to this journal by putting little crosses in the appropriate columns.

I began to get undressed and thought: 'Where is this all-round cultivation and development of your abilities, where are your virtues, and is this route really going to lead you to virtue? Where is this journal getting you? It serves you only as an index of your weaknesses, which are unending, and getting more numerous every day; and even if you did succeed in eliminating them you would not attain to virtue by this means. You are merely deceiving yourself, and amusing yourself with all this like a child with a plaything. Could it ever be sufficient for an artist just to know what things not to do, in order to be an artist? Can it be possible negatively, simply by refraining from harmful actions, to achieve anything worthwhile? It is not enough for the peasant farmer to weed his field, he must also plough it and sow it. Make yourself some rules of virtue and follow them.'—All this was said by that part of my mind which specializes in being critical.

I fell to thinking. Can it be enough to destroy the cause of evil, that good may then exist? Good is something positive, not negative. From that it follows clearly and demonstrably that good is positive and evil is negative; evil is capable of destroying, but good is not. There is always some good in our souls, and the soul itself is good; but evil is implanted in us. If there is no evil present, the good will develop. The comparison with the peasant farmer will not do; he has to sow and plough his land, but in his own soul the good is already sown. The artist needs to practise, and he will attain the creation of art, provided he does not adopt negative principles, but he must avoid arbitrariness. For practice in virtue, there is no need of exercises: the exercise is life itself.

Cold is the absence of warmth. Darkness is the absence of light. Evil is the absence of good. Why does man love warmth, light and good? Because they are natural. There is an origin of warmth, light and good – the sun, God; but there is no sun of cold and darkness, no God of evil. We see the light and the rays of light, we seek their cause and we say that the sun exists: our proof is both the light and heat, and the law of gravity. This is in the physical world. In the moral world we see the good, see its rays, and we see that there is the same law of attraction of the good towards something higher which is its source – God.——

Remove the rough outer crust from a diamond, and inside there will be – brightness; discard the envelope of human weaknesses, and you will have – virtue. But can it be only those trivialities and weaknesses you record in your journal which are preventing you from being good? Are there not also some great passions? And how is it that this host of weaknesses increases with every day that passes?: now *self-deception*, now *cowardice*, etc., and that there is never any lasting improvement, and in many instances no way forward? (It is once again the part of me devoted to criticism which has observed all this.) True, all these weaknesses I have noted down can be reduced to three types, but since all of them can be found at many different levels, their combinations may be countless. The three categories are: (1) pride, (2) weakness of will, (3) lack of intelligence. But it is impossible to attribute all these weaknesses individually to one of the three types, for they arise from combinations of them. The first two types have diminished, but the last, as a separate element, can only make progress over time. For example, today I told a lie, quite clearly without any apparent reason: I was called to dinner and I declined to come, then said that I could not because I was due to have a lesson.——What sort of a lesson?——English (whereas in fact it was a gymnastics lesson). The causes were: (1) lack of intelligence, in that I suddenly failed to see how stupid it is to lie; (2) lack of resolution, in that I did not explain why; (3) a silly kind of pride, in supposing that English might be a more suitable excuse than gymnastics.

Can virtue really consist in freeing yourself from the weaknesses which are harmful to you in life, so that virtue would seem to be identical with selflessness?——Not so. Virtue brings happiness, because happiness brings virtue.—Every time I write something honestly in my diary, I feel no vexation with myself for my weaknesses: it seems to me that if I have owned up to having them, then they are no longer there.

A pleasant thought. I said my prayers and got into bed. I pray better at night than in the morning. I have a better understanding of what I am saying, and even of what I feel; at the end of the day I am not anxious for myself, but in the morning I am – there is so much ahead of me in the coming day. What a wonderful thing is sleep in all its stages: getting ready for it, going to sleep, sleep itself. As soon as I had lain down I thought: What delight to escape into this growing warmth and presently to forget myself entirely; but hardly had I begun to fall asleep than I recollected that it was pleasant to fall asleep, and woke up again. All the pleasures of the body are destroyed by consciousness of them. One must avoid being conscious: but I was conscious that I was conscious, and so it went on and on, and I could not sleep. Oh, the vexation of it! What did God give us consciousness for, when it serves merely as a barrier to living? He did so because our moral pleasures, unlike the physical ones, are felt more deeply when we are conscious of them. Reasoning in this fashion I turned over on to my other side, and the bedclothes fell off. What an unpleasant sensation it is to lose your bedclothes in the dark. One always feels: someone or something may come and grab me, or lay a cold or a hot hand on my uncovered leg. I hastened to cover myself up, tucked the blanket under me on both sides, hid my head in the covers, and began to fall asleep, thinking to myself as follows.

⟨'Morpheus, take me into your embrace.' Morpheus is a god whose devotee I would most gladly be. Do you recall that young lady who was so offended when someone said to her: '*Quand je suis passé chez vous, vous étiez encore dans les bras de Morphée*'?[3] She thought that Morpheus [Morfei] was

3 When I called to see you, you were still in the arms of Morpheus.

some man called Andrei Malafei. What a ridiculous name!
. . . But it's a wonderful expression: *dans les bras*; I can imagine
so vividly and gracefully the position *dans les bras* – and
particularly vividly the *bras* themselves – arms bare to the
shoulder with little dimples and little folds, and a white
nightdress indiscreetly open.—How lovely women's arms
are, specially if there is just one little dimple! I stretched
myself out in bed. Do you remember, St Thomas[4] was always
telling us it was bad form to stretch. Just like Diedrichs. The
two of them were riding along together. The sport was
excellent and just behind them I was riding along too, tally-
hoing to my dog Angel, and my other dog Raider was
catching enough game for them all, it was a regular slaughter.
And wasn't Seriozha furious!—He was with his sister.—
What a charmer Masha is – and what a wife she'd make for
someone! Morpheus would make a fine old hunter, if he
could cope with a bit of bareback riding, and he might even
find you a wife into the bargain.—Phew, just look how St
Thomas is bowling along there – and there's the young lady
charging along behind them all; it's no use just stretching
out, though it is really nice *dans les bras*. At this point I must
have fallen asleep properly.—I dreamt that I was trying to
catch up with the lady, when suddenly there was a mountain
in front of us and I was pushing her, pushing her up it with
my hands – but she fell down to the bottom (I had pushed
my pillow off the bed), and I rode home to dinner. It was
not ready: why not? Vasily started to throw his weight about
and to bluster (which made the lady of the house who was
on the other side of the partition ask to know what all the
noise was about, so the chambermaid explained – I could
hear it all, because that too was part of my dream). Vasily
came in and everyone was trying to ask him why the dinner
wasn't ready, but they could see – Vasily was wearing a
camisole, and a ribbon across his shoulder. I felt scared, and
fell to my knees weeping and kissing his feet; I enjoyed this

4 Prosper de St Thomas: Tolstoy's boyhood tutor, the model for St Jérôme
in *Boyhood*.

just as much as if I had been kissing *her* feet – in fact more so. Vasily ignored me and asked: 'Is it loaded?' Diedrichs, the pastry-cook from Tula, replied 'Ready!'—Very well, fire!—And they fired a volley (the shutter banged).—and then there we were walking down Polskaya Street, Vasily and I, but it was no longer Vasily but *she*. Suddenly, horrors! I noticed that my trousers were so short that my bare knees were showing. I cannot describe how awful I felt (my bare knees had come out of the bedclothes); in my dream I spent a long time trying to cover them up and at last succeeded. But there was more to come: now we were going down Polskaya Street again and the Queen of Württemberg was there; but suddenly I was dancing a Ukrainian *kazachok*. Why? Because I couldn't help it. At length someone brought me an overcoat and a pair of boots; but now it was even worse – there were no trousers at all. Of course none of this could be happening in reality: I was most likely asleep and dreaming. I woke up.—And began to drop off again, thinking, then ran out of thoughts and began to see pictures in my imagination, and my imaginings were quite coherent, picturesque even, but then my imagination itself went to sleep, and all that remained were obscure and confused notions; and then my body too fell asleep. A dream is always composed of first and last impressions.⟩

It seemed to me that now, underneath this blanket, nothing and no one could possibly get at me.—Sleep is a state of our existence in which we completely lose the consciousness of ourselves; but since a man falls asleep by degrees, he also loses consciousness by degrees.—Consciousness is another name for what we call our soul; but the word *soul* denotes something which is a unity, whereas there are as many consciousnesses as there are different elements which make up a human being. As I see it there are three of these: (1) the mind, (2) the emotions, (3) the body. (1) is the highest of the three, and this type of consciousness is confined to developed human beings – brute beasts and brutish humans do not possess it; this is the first element to fall asleep. (2) The consciousness of emotion is also the property of human beings alone, and it goes to sleep after the first sort of consciousness. (3) The consciousness of the body goes to sleep last of all, and almost never completely. This gradualness of falling asleep is not to be found in animals, nor in human beings who become unconscious as a result of some powerful shock, or of drunkenness. The consciousness of being asleep is liable to wake us up again at once.

Our remembrance of the time we spend asleep is not derived from the same source as our remembrance of real life – from memory, the capacity to recall our impressions – but from the capacity to group our impressions together. At the moment of waking we bring together all the impressions we have had while going to sleep and while sleeping (a man is hardly ever completely asleep) into a unity under the influence of the particular impression which contributed to our waking up – and waking up, like going to sleep, proceeds by degrees, from the lowest level to the highest.—This operation takes place so swiftly that it is hard to be completely aware of it, and being accustomed as we are to the sequential nature of things and to the mould of time in which life reveals itself to us, we accept this aggregate of impressions as the remembrance of the time we have spent asleep.—How are you to explain the fact that you may have a long dream which ends with precisely that circumstance which has woken you up? You dream that you are going out hunting, you load your rifle, spring the game, take aim and fire; and the noise you took for the gunshot was actually the water carafe which you have upset on to the floor in your sleep. Or again, you arrive at your friend N.'s house and you are waiting to see him; at length a servant appears and announces that N. has just come in; but in the real world it is your own servant who is talking to you in order to wake you up. In recognizing the truth of this, God forbid that you should believe in all those dreams related to you by people who have invariably seen something in them, and what is more, something both meaningful and important.

These people, from their habit of drawing conclusions from dreams on the basis of guesses, have provided themselves with a particular form to which they reduce everything: they make up any deficiencies from their own imagination, and reject anything which refuses to fit into the given form. For example, a mother will tell you how she dreamed that she saw her daughter flying off into the heavens and saying 'Goodbye, dearest Mamma, I shall pray for you!' Whereas she actually dreamed that her daughter was climbing on to the house roof, not saying anything, and that this daughter, as she climbed higher and higher, suddenly turned into Ivan the cook and said 'You can't climb up here.'

And perhaps by the power of habit, what they relate has actually taken that shape in their imagination: if so, that is further evidence for my theory of dreams ...

If you want to confirm it, try the experiment on yourself: recall the thoughts and imaginings you had while going to sleep and waking up, and if anyone else saw you asleep and can tell you all the circumstances which may have affected you, you will then be able to understand why you had that particular dream and not some other. There are so many of these circumstances, depending on people's bodily constitution, on their digestion, and on other physical causes, that they are past enumerating. Yet there is a saying that when we dream that we are flying or swimming, it means that we are growing. If you can observe what makes you dream on one occasion that you are swimming, and on another flying, and if you are able to recall it all, you will quite easily arrive at an explanation.

If my dream had been dreamt by one of those people who, as I have said, are accustomed to interpreting dreams, this is how the account of it (by a lady) might have run: 'I dreamt that St Thomas was running and running for a very long time, and I seemed to be asking him "Why are you running?" and he said to me "I am looking for a bride."'— So you see, either he is getting married, or I shall soon be receiving a letter from him ...'

Note also that in memories there is no gradation of time. If you are able to recall your dream, then you know you have already dreamt it. ⟨I awoke in the morning and began to recall what I had been dreaming about. It seemed that my brother and I were out hunting and had brought to bay a lady of exemplary virtue in a thicket. No; before that, before we had gone out hunting, I dreamt that St Thomas came to ask me to forgive him.⟩

At night you almost always wake up several times, but it is only the two lower levels of consciousness which are fully awake – the body and the feelings. After this the feelings and the body fall asleep again, and the impressions they have accumulated during the period of wakefulness combine with the general impression of the dream, in no particular order or sequence.—If the third, highest level of consciousness has woken too, and then you fall asleep again, your dream will already be divided into two halves.—

Another day. (On the Volga)

I had taken it into my head to travel down the Volga from Saratov to Astrakhan.

In the first place, I had thought it would be better, should the season turn out to be unpropitious, to extend my journey, but not to go jolting on by road for another seven hundred versts; besides, the picturesque banks of the Volga, my daydreams, the perils of the journey – all these things are agreeable and might prove to have a beneficial effect on me. I imagined myself to be a poet, thought about those characters and heroes whom I liked and tried to put myself in their place, – in a word, I thought as I always think when I am embarking on anything new: now at last real life is about to begin, and everything up to this point has been a sort of feeble preface not worth bothering with. I realize of course that this is all nonsense. How many times have I observed that I remain exactly the same, and am no more a poet when I am on the Volga than when I am on the Voronka,[5] yet I still go on believing, seeking, hoping for

5 A local stream neat Tolstoy's home at Yasnaya Polyana.

something. I still cannot help thinking when I am pondering whether to undertake something or not: 'Suppose you don't do this thing, you don't visit that place — that is where happiness was lying in wait for you, and you will have missed it for ever.' I always think: 'Look, it is going to start without me.'—This may be absurd, but it is what decided me to go down the Volga to Astrakhan. At first I was afraid, and ashamed to be taking action for such ridiculous reasons, but so far as I can judge in looking at my past life, the grounds for my actions have always been no less ridiculous. I do not know how it is for other people, but I have grown accustomed to this state of affairs, and for me the words *trivial*, *ridiculous*, have ceased to have any meaning. So where are these *powerful*, *serious* reasons for acting?

I went down to the Moscow ferry and began to stroll along beside the boats and the barges. 'Well, are all these boats engaged? Is there one that is free?' I enquired of the crowd of barge-haulers standing about near the foreshore. 'And what does your worship require?' asked an old man with a long beard, in a grey homespun coat and a lambswool hat.—'A boat to take me to Astrakhan.' 'Right you are, sir, it can be done!'—

A CHRISTMAS NIGHT

I

ON one of the clear, frosty twelve nights of Christmas in January of the year 18—, a cab drawn by a pair of lean and broken-down horses was rolling at a jerky trot down the Kuznetsky Most, in Moscow.

Only the lofty dark-blue sky scattered with stars hurtling through space, the hoarfrosted beard of the cabman as he snatched a breath, the air stinging your face and the crunch of the wheels on the frosty snow – only these things would have reminded you of those cold yet poetic Christmases which from childhood on have become associated in our minds with a confusion of feelings – affection for the cherished traditions of older times and the folk customs of the simple, uneducated people, but also the expectation that something mysterious, something extraordinary is about to happen ...

Here there are no great white drifts of powdery snow heaped up against doors, fences and windows, no narrow paths beaten between the drifts, no tall black trees with rime-covered branches, no infinite expanses of dazzling white fields lit by a bright winter moon, none of the magical silence of an inexpressibly lovely night in the countryside. Here in the city the tall, oppressively regular buildings block out the horizon and weary the eye with their monotony; the steady urban rumble of wheels never ceases, and inspires in the soul a kind of nagging, intolerable anguish; a patchy, dung-strewn layer of snow lies on the streets, illuminated here and there by lamplight falling from the wide window of a shop, or by a dim streetlight against which a grimy-looking policeman has placed his stepladder and is trying to

817

adjust the light. The whole scene makes a sharp and dismal contrast with the endless, sparkling covering of snow which we associate with a Christmas night. God's world, man's world.

The cab drew up before a brightly lit shop. Out of it jumped a fine, well-proportioned young fellow – of about eighteen, to judge by his appearance – wearing a round hat and an overcoat with a beaver fur collar which partly revealed a white evening tie; ringing the bell, he hurriedly entered the shop.

'*Une paire de gants, je vous prie,*'[1] he replied to the interrogative '*Bonsoir Monsieur?*' with which he was greeted by a skinny Frenchwoman seated at a writing-desk.

'*Vot' numéro?*'[2]

'*Six et demie,*'[3] he replied, showing her a small, almost femininely delicate hand.

The young man seemed to be in a great hurry to get somewhere: he paced up and down the shop, then started to put on the gloves so carelessly that he managed to split one pair. With a childish movement of annoyance which was also an indication of the energy within him, he flung the offending glove on the floor and began to stretch another one.

'Is that you, my boy?' said a pleasant-sounding, confident voice from the next room. 'Come in here.'

At the sound of the voice, and especially at the appellation 'my boy', the young man realized that this was an acquaintance of his, and went into the adjoining room.

His friend was a tall, unusually thin man of about thirty, with ginger side-whiskers extending from mid-cheek to the corners of his mouth and the sharp upturned points of his collar. He had a long, fleshless nose, tranquil, rather deep-set blue eyes expressive of intelligence and humour, and exceptionally thin, pale lips which, except when opening in

1 A pair of gloves, please.
2 Your size?
3 Six and a half.

an appealing smile to reveal a set of fine white teeth, had about them an air of firmness and resolution.

He was sitting, his long legs stretched out, in front of a large pier-glass in which he seemed to be regarding with pleasure the reflection of the young man's handsome face, and giving Monsieur Charles every opportunity to display his coiffeuring skills. The latter, expertly twirling a pair of curling-tongs in his pomaded hands, shouted for Ernest, who came and took them from him so that he could, in his own words, give '*un coup de peigne à la plus estimable de ses pratiques*'.[4]

'Well, is it a ball you are off to, dear boy?'

'Yes, Prince; and you?'

'I too have to go out, – as you see,' he added, indicating his white waistcoat and tie, but still in such a gloomy tone of voice that the young man asked with surprise whether he was in fact unwilling to go, and if so, what he would prefer to spend the evening doing.

'Sleeping,' he replied calmly and without the least affectation.

'That I cannot believe!'

'Neither would I have believed it, ten years ago: in those days I was ready to gallop three hundred versts by post-chaise and go without sleep for ten nights just to attend one ball; but of course I was young then, and accustomed to falling in love at every ball, and, even more important – I was cheerful then: because I knew that I was good-looking and whichever way they turned me round no one would see a bald patch or a hairpiece or a false tooth ...

'And who is it you are running after, my boy?' he added, standing in front of the mirror and straightening his shirt collar.

This question, delivered in such a straightforward conversational tone, appeared to take the young man by surprise and to throw him into such confusion that, blushing and stammering, he was scarcely able to get out the words: 'I'm

4 Give this most distinguished of his clients a touch of the comb.

not ... running after ... I mean I've never ... run after ... anyone.'

'Forgive me. I had forgotten that at your time of life you don't pursue women, you fall in love with them, so do at least tell me, – who are you in love with?'

'You know, Prince,' said the young man with a smile, 'that I really have no idea what it means to pursue someone, to *faire la cour* ...'[5]

'Then I will proceed to explain to you. You know what it means to be in love?'

'Yes, I know.'

'Well, to pursue a woman means doing the exact opposite of what you would do if you were in love with her – expressing your feelings little by little, trying to make her fall in love with you. You really have to do the opposite of what you do in a relationship with some *sweet little débardeur*[6] with whom you are in love.'

The young man blushed once more.

'I was talking to your cousin about you only this morning, and she revealed your secret to me. Why haven't you got yourself presented to her yet?'

'I have not had an opportunity.'

'How can there possibly have been no opportunity? No, it would be truer to say that you haven't been able to make up your mind to do it; I realize that true love, especially if it is first love, is always bashful. That is no good at all.'

'My cousin promised me not long ago that she would introduce me to her,' said the young man, with a shy, childlike smile.

'No, no, you must allow *me* to introduce you, my dear boy. Believe me, I would do it far better than your cousin would – you see, I shall do it with my own special lightness of touch,' he added as he put on his overcoat and his hat. 'Let us go together.'

5 Pay court to.
6 *Débardeur*. Literally 'a longshoreman' – a popular fancy-dress costume in the nineteenth century.

'To be sucessful with women,' he went on in a didactic manner as he headed towards the door, ignoring both Monsieur Charles' bow and the smile of the *demoiselle de comptoir*[7] who was listening to what he was saying. 'To be successful with women you need to be enterprising, and to be enterprising you need to be successful with women, particularly in the case of a first love; and to be successful in first love you need to be enterprising. You see, it is a *cercle vicieux*.'[8]

II

The young man's name was Seriozha Ivin. He was a first-rate fellow with a soul as yet unshadowed by the consciousness of mistakes made in life, and thus full of radiant fantasies and noble motives. Having completed his course at the —— College when still a child in mind and body, he had come to Moscow to be with his mother, a deeply gentle woman born in the last century who loved him as any mother does her only son in whom she takes great pride.

Once in Moscow he almost unwittingly and imperceptibly came to feel at ease in the genial, one might even say familial atmosphere of Muscovite society, in which people of an acknowledged pedigree, whatever their outward qualities, are accepted in all respects as kith and kin; and this with particular confidence and enthusiasm when, like Ivin, they do not carry with them any sort of unknown past. It is hard to say whether this was a piece of good fortune for him or not. From one point of view Moscow society gave him many genuine pleasures, and to be able to enjoy oneself at this period of one's early manhood when every gratifying experience makes its impression on the youthful spirit and sets the fresh strings of happiness vibrating – this is already a great blessing. From the contrary point of view, however, Moscow society developed in him that dreadful moral infection which establishes itself in every department of the soul

7 Shop girl.
8 Vicious circle.

and which is known by the name of vanity. Not that purely
social vanity which is never content with the circle in which
it lives, and is constantly seeking and attaining some new
one in which it will feel awkward and ill at ease. Moscow
society is notably indulgent and agreeable, in that its judgements of people are kindly and independent: once a man
finds himself accepted in it, then he is accepted everywhere
and considered by everyone in the same light, and there is
nothing further for him to aspire to: live as you wish and as
it pleases you. No, Seriozha's vanity, despite the fact that he
was a clever and energetic young fellow, was the vanity of
youth. Absurdly enough, he who was among the best
dancers in Moscow dreamed of how he might get into the
tedious social set of G.O. on the cheap, and how he, innocent and bashful as a young girl, could gain an entrée to the
scandalous evening parties given by Madame Z., and strike
up an intimacy with the debauched and corrupt bachelor
Dolgov. Beautiful dreams of love and friendship, and ridiculous dreams of vanity and the power of youthful attraction
filled his imagination and became strangely mingled within
him.

At the various balls held that winter, which were the first
in his experience, he several times encountered Countess
Schöfing, whom Prince Kornakov (who gave nicknames to
all and sundry) referred to as *the sweet little débardeur*. Once,
when he found himself dancing opposite her, Seriozha's eyes
had met the ingenuously curious gaze of the Countess and
this gaze of hers had so struck him and given him such
delight that he could not understand why he was not already
head over heels in love with her, and it filled him, heaven
knows why, with such trepidation that he began to regard
her as some sort of exceptional, higher being with whom he
was unworthy to have anything in common, and for this
reason he had several times avoided the chance of being
presented to her.

Countess Schöfing united in herself all those elements
calculated to inspire love, especially in a young boy such as
Seriozha. She was unusually attractive, attractive both as a

woman and as a child: enchanting shoulders and bosom, a shapely, supple waist endowed with a fluid grace of movement; and an utterly childlike little face which breathed meekness and good-humour. Apart from all this she possessed the allure of a woman whose position is at the very top of the best society; and nothing lends a woman greater charm than to have the reputation of being a charming woman. Countess Schöfing had a further magic shared by very few, the magic of simplicity – not simplicity the opposite of affectation, but rather that endearing naïve simplicity so rarely encountered, which gives a most attractive quality of originality to a society woman. Every question she asked, she asked simply, and replied likewise to all questions which were put to her; she expressed everything which came into her charming, clever little head, and everything came out with extraordinary niceness. She was one of those uncommon women who are loved by all, even by those who ought to have been envious of her.

The strange thing was that such a woman should have given her hand with no regrets to Count Schöfing. But of course she could not know that beyond those sweet compliments paid her by her husband there existed other forms of speech; that beyond the merits of dancing excellently, being a devoted civil servant, and being the favourite of all respectable old ladies – merits which Count Schöfing possessed in the highest degree – there existed other merits; that beyond this decorous sociable and social life which her husband arranged for her, there existed another life in which it was possible to find love and happiness. That aside, one must be fair to Count Schöfing and acknowledge that he was in all respects the best of husbands: even Natalya Apollonovna herself was heard to say in her best nasal French accent, '*C'est un excellent parti, ma chère.*'[9] What more could she have desired? All the young men she had so far met in society were so similar to her *Jean*, and indeed were no better than he was; so that falling in love never entered her head –

9 He is an excellent match, my dear.

she imagined that she loved her husband – and her life had turned out so well. She loved dancing, and she danced; she loved to charm people, and she charmed them; she loved all her good friends, and everyone loved her in return.

III

Why bother to record all the details of the ball? Who does not remember the strange, striking impression produced on him by the blinding brightness of a thousand lights illuminating things from all sides at once and casting no shadow: the shine of diamonds, eyes, flowers, silk, velvet, bare shoulders, black evening coats, white waistcoats, satin slippers, multi-coloured uniforms and liveries; the scent of flowers and women's perfumes; the noise of hundreds of feet and voices, muffled by the captivating, intoxicating music of waltzes and polkas; and the continual, almost fantastic intermingling of all these elements? Who does not remember how impossible it was to separate one detail from another, how all these impressions blended together, leaving only one predominant feeling – of merriment, in which everything seemed so gay and light and joyful, and the heart beat fast with delight; or its opposite, in which everything seemed dreadfully heavy and oppressive, and full of sadness?

And the feelings aroused in our two friends by this ball were indeed utterly different, one from the other.

Such was Seriozha's agitation that one could almost see how fast and strongly his heart was beating beneath his white waistcoat; and for some reason he appeared short of breath as he made his way in the wake of Prince Kornakov through the diverse and seething crowd of guests both known and unknown, to approach the mistress of the house. His excitement grew still more intense when he drew near to the spacious ballroom, from which the strains of a waltz could now more clearly be heard. Inside the ballroom itself everything was noisier, brighter, hotter and more crowded than it had been in the first room. He scanned the crowd in search of Countess Schöfing and the light-blue dress in which he had seen her at the previous ball. (This impression was so vivid in his memory that he was incapable of imagining her in any other dress.) There was a blue dress over there – but that hair was not hers: it was horrible red hair, and what ugly shoulders and coarse features: how could he have been so mistaken? There is a woman in blue dancing the waltz: wasn't that her? But the waltzing couple drew level with him – and what a disappointment! Certainly this woman was by no means unattractive, but to Seriozha she seemed uglier than sin, so hard was it for any beauty to stand comparison with the image of his love which his imagination had built up with all the magical power of memory. Could she really not be here yet? How tedious and empty was this ball! What boring faces all these people had! And whatever had brought them all here? But over there was a small group of people, different from all the others: there were not many in this circle, but how many onlookers there seemed to be, gazing enviously from the outside but unable to get into it. Strange that these spectators, for all the strength of their desire, apparently could not step across the boundary into this magic circle. But Seriozha pushes his way through into the space in the centre. There are more of his acquaintances there, some smiling at him from a distance, some shaking his hand: but who is this in the white gown with a simple green headdress, standing next to Prince Kornakov, her head with its light-brown hair thrown back, looking naïvely into his eyes as she talks to him? It is she! The poetry-filled image of a woman in a blue dress which has haunted him since the last ball changes in an instant into an image which seems to him even more alluring and full of life – the image of this woman in white with her green headdress. But why does he suddenly feel ill at ease? He is not quite sure whether to hold his hat in his left hand or his right, and he looks anxiously round in search of his cousin or some good friend with whom to strike up a conversation and so hide his confusion; but alas, all the faces surrounding him are the faces of strangers and in their expression he seems to read the words '*Comme le petit Ivine est ridicule.'* [10] Thank heavens, there is his cousin beckoning to him, and he goes across to dance with her.

Prince Kornakov, on the other hand, made his way quite calmly through the first room, bowing to the gentlemen and ladies he knew, entered the great ballroom and joined the little circle of the elect, just as if he had been walking into his own room and with the same foreknowledge of what to expect as a civil servant who arrives at his Department and makes for his familiar corner and his own particular chair. He knows each one of them so well, and they him, that he is able to have some striking, interesting or amusing remark ready for each person, and on a subject which will appeal to them. In almost every case he offers a promising opening gambit, some little witticism, a few generalized recollections. ⟨For him nothing can come as a surprise: he is too decent a man, living in too decent a society, to encounter any sort of unpleasantness; and he has long since outgrown the habit of expecting to derive any pleasure from a ball.⟩ Not only does he not feel awkward or ill at ease, like Seriozha, as he walks through the three reception rooms thronged with guests, but he finds it intolerable to see all these familiar individuals whom he has long since appraised at their true value, and who would never revise their opinion of him, no matter what he did; yet he still cannot avoid going up to them and talking to them as if by some strange habit, saying things of no interest to either party, which they have in any case already heard and said on several previous occasions. So this is what he does; nevertheless it is boredom which is the predominant feeling in his soul.

Even his observations of men and women – the sole interest for a man like the Prince who takes no direct part in the ball as a card-player or a dancer – even these cannot afford him anything new or arresting. If he goes up to the groups of chatterers in the reception rooms, they are all composed of the same people and the frame of their conversation is always the same. Here is Madame D., a lady with a

10 How absurd young Ivin is.

reputation for being a Moscow beauty, and indeed her dress, her face, her shoulders are all lovely beyond reproach; but there is something tediously impassive in her look and her continual smile, and her beauty produces in him a reaction of irritation. Deep down he finds D. the most intolerable woman in the world yet he still pursues her, simply because she is the first lady of Moscow society. Next to her, as always, is a group of hangers-on: young M., who is said to be a thoroughly bad character – but on the other hand he is exceptionally witty and agreeable; also with her is the Petersburg dandy F., dedicated to looking down disdainfully on Moscow society, with the result that no one can stand him ... And here is the delightful Moscow aristocrat Annette Z., who, goodness knows why, has been failing to marry for such a long time; and consequently, somewhere here too is her last hope, a baron with a monocle and appallingly bad French who has been intending for a whole year past to marry her, but naturally will not get round to doing so. Here is the small, swarthy adjutant with a large nose who is convinced that the essence of civility in this modern age is to spout obscenities, and who is now splitting his sides as he relates something to the elderly but emancipated maiden lady G. Here is the stout old lady R., whose behaviour has been unseemly for so long that it has ceased to be original and has become simply disgusting; yet around her there still revolve an officer of hussars and a young student who imagine, poor things, that this will elevate them in the eyes of society. And if Prince Kornakov goes over to the card tables he will find the same tables in the same place they have occupied these five years or more, with the same people sitting at them. Even their particular ways of shuffling the cards, dealing, taking tricks and exchanging little jokes about gambling have all long since become familiar to him. Here is the old general who invariably loses heavily, however angry he gets and however much he shouts for the whole room to hear, but in particular the dried-up little man who sits opposite him in silence, hunched over the table and granting him an occasional sullen look from under his

eyebrows. Here too is a young man who hopes to prove, by
the fact of playing cards, that he has been doing this kind of
thing for years. And here are the three high-born old ladies
who have won two copecks each from their unlucky fellow-
player, and the poor man is about to give up all the money
he has in his pocket to pay them.

Kornakov approaches the tables with the intention of
acquiring some winnings; some of the players fail to notice
him, some shake his hand without looking round, a few
invite him to join them for a while ... Should he go into
the rooms where the dancing is in progress? There he can
see five or six students whirling round, a couple of newly
arrived Guards officers, and the eternal striplings, young in
years but already veterans of the Moscow parquet – Negi-
chev, Gubkov, Tamarin; and two or three ageing Moscow
lions who have already given up dancing in favour of paying
compliments, but who are now either summoning up the
courage to ask a lady to dance, or asking her with the sort
of expression that seems to say 'Look, what a gay dog I am.'

Also in the circle of gentlemen one can see as ever those
unknown and unmoving figures in dress coats who simply
stand and look; heaven alone knows what has made them
come – only occasionally is there a movement among them
as some bold spirit emerges, walks modestly or perhaps too
boldly across the empty space in the centre and invites a lady
– possibly the only one he knows – to dance, executes a few
turns of the waltz with her, though she is clearly finding it
an unpleasant experience, and returns to hide again behind
the wall of standing gentlemen. Usually in Moscow society
the men fall into two categories – the inexperienced young-
sters who gaze at the social whirl with excessive seriousness;
and the social lions well past their prime who look on, or
appear to look on, with an exaggerated degree of disdain.

Some pathetic fellows, not knowing anyone, who have
been invited only through the machinations of the hostess's
female relatives, sit around the walls of the ballroom, mortified with anger that despite their elegant turn-out which has
cost them as much as a month's earnings, no lady is willing

to dance with them.— So the tale goes on, and the fact is that Prince Kornakov finds it all too drearily familiar. Although during his time in society many old people have departed and many young ones have entered the social arena, the attitudes, conversations and activities of these people have remained exactly the same. The physical arrangements of the ball, down to the buffet, the supper, the music, the furnishing of the rooms, are all so familiar to the Prince that he sometimes feels an unbearable repugnance at being faced with the same old thing for the twentieth time. Prince Kornakov was one of those wealthy middle-aged bachelors for whom social life has become the most inevitable and tedious of obligations: inevitable, because having in his early youth effortlessly achieved a leading place in this society, his self-esteem has never permitted him to try out his talents in any other, unknown path of life, or even to admit the possibility that some other mode of life might exist; tedious, because he was too intelligent not to have perceived long ago all the emptiness of the social relations of people who are not bound together by any common interest or noble feeling, but who assume that the purpose of life can be found in the artificial maintenance of these same endless social relations. His soul was constantly filled with unconscious sadness for a past squandered to no purpose and a future which promised nothing, but his ennui did not find expression in anguish or repentance, but in irritability and social gossip – sometimes trenchant, sometimes vacuous, but always intelligent and distinguished by its originality. He took so little part in the doings of society, regarding it with such indifference, as if *à vol d'oiseau*,[11] that he was incapable of coming into conflict with anybody; so that no one liked him and no one disliked him, but everyone regarded him with the special respect accorded to those men who *constitute society*.

11 From a bird's eye view.

IV

Passion

'*Encore un tour, je t'en prie*,'[12] said Seriozha to his cousin as he clasped her slender waist and, flushed of face, lightly and gracefully sailed into the waltz for the tenth circuit of the ballroom.

'No, that is enough, I am already tired,' replied his charming cousin with a smile, disengaging his hand from her shoulder.

Seriozha was obliged to stop, and to stop right by the doorway where Prince Kornakov was leaning casually with his customary expression of self-satisfied composure, saying something to the charming little Countess Schöfing.

'Here he is in person,' he said with a glance in Seriozha's direction. 'Do come and join us,' he added, at the same time bowing respectfully to the pretty cousin. 'The Countess would like you to be presented to her.'

'I have wanted for a very long time to have this honour,' said Seriozha with every appearance of youthful confusion, and bowed.

'But there was really no need to wait until now to say so,' replied the Countess, looking at him with an ingenuous smile.

Seriozha did not answer but, growing redder and redder, racked his brains to think of something to say other than banalities.

Prince Kornakov seemed to be regarding the young man's genuine embarrassment with great pleasure, but observing that his embarrassment was continuing, and despite the Countess's social experience, was even beginning to affect her too, he said:

'*Accordez-vous un tour de valse, Madame la Comtesse?*'[13] The Countess, aware that he had not danced for a long time, looked at him in surprise.

12 Just one more turn, please.
13 Would you consent to a little waltz, Countess?

'*Pas à moi, Madame la Comtesse; je me sens trop laid et trop vieux pour prétendre à cet honneur.*'[14]

'You will forgive me, my dear boy, for taking on myself the role of your interpreter,' he added to Seriozha. Seriozha bowed. The Countess stood up and faced him, silently crooked her pretty arm and raised it to shoulder level, but just as Seriozha had put his arm round her the music stopped, and they stood there until the musicians, seeing the signs the Prince was making to them, again struck up the waltz. Seriozha would never forget those few seconds in which he twice took hold of and twice relinquished his lady's waist.

Seriozha could not feel his feet gliding over the parquet: it seemed to him that he was being transported farther and farther away from the many-coloured crowd all around him. All his vital energies were concentrated in his sense of hearing, which made him obey the sounds of the music, now causing him to moderate the vigour of his movements, now to whirl round faster and faster as he felt the Countess's waist conforming so wonderfully to his every movement that it seemed to be melting into him, becoming one with him; concentrated too in his gaze, which with an inexplicable blend of delight and dread rested at one moment on the Countess's white shoulder, and at the next on her radiant blue eyes covered with the lightest film of moisture which lent them an indescribable expression of languor and passion.

'Just look there, if you please – what could be finer than that young couple?' said Prince Kornakov, turning to Seriozha's cousin. 'You know what a passion I have for bringing attractive young people together.'

'Yes, now *Serge* does look really happy.'

'And not only *Serge* – I am sure the Countess too finds it far more agreeable to be dancing with him than with an old man like me.'

'You obviously want me to tell you that you are not yet "an old man".'

---

14 Not for myself, Countess; I feel that I am too ugly and too old to claim that honour.

'Whatever can you take me for? I am well aware that I am not yet old: but I am something worse than that – I am bored, I am played out, just like all these gentlemen here, though they are utterly incapable of realizing it; but in the first place Seriozha is a novelty for me, and in the second place it seems to me that no woman could imagine or desire a better man than he is. Just look, what a delight to see!' he went on, looking at them with a smile of satisfaction. 'And how adorable she is! I really am quite in love with them both . . .'

'I shall of course warn Liza at once.' (Liza was the Countess's name.)

'No, I have of course long ago apologized to the Countess for not having fallen in love with her – and she knows that it is only because I am quite incapable of falling in love; but I am in love with them both – the pair of them.'

Prince Kornakov was not the only one to admire Seriozha and Countess Schöfing as they waltzed round the floor: all who were not dancing could not help following the couple with their eyes – some with pure delight at the sight of something lovely, others with envy and annoyance.

Seriozha was so deeply stirred by the combined impressions of dancing, music and love, that when Countess Schöfing asked him to escort her back to her seat, and having thanked him with a smile took her hand from his shoulder, he suddenly felt an almost irresistible desire to seize the opportunity of the moment, and to kiss her.

[V]

[*Innocence*]

VI

Love

The whole ball passed for the infatuated Seriozha like a wonderful and captivating dream, the sort of dream one passionately wishes to be real. The Countess had only the sixth quadrille left unclaimed, and she danced it with him. Their conversation was of the kind usual at balls; but for Seriozha every word possessed a special meaning, as did every smile and glance and movement. During another quadrille an acknowledged admirer of the Countess's, one D., sat down near them. Seriozha for some reason interpreted this as a sign that D. took him for a mere boy, and was filled with the most hostile feelings towards him; but the Countess was particularly charming and kind to her new acquaintance, speaking in the most cursory manner to D., then at once turning to Seriozha with a smile and a look which clearly expressed her pleasure. There are no two things which are so intimately connected, yet frequently destructive of one another, as are love and self-love. But at this moment these two passions were combined to turn Seriozha's head completely and utterly. In the mazurka the Countess chose him twice and he chose her twice. During one of the figures she handed him her bouquet. Seriozha pulled out a sprig from it and hid it in his glove. The Countess saw him do it, and smiled.

The Countess was not able to stay for supper. Seriozha accompanied her as far as the steps.

'I hope we shall see you at our house,' she said, giving him her hand.

'And when may I come?'

'At any time.'

'At any time?!' he repeated in a voice filled with emotion, and involuntarily squeezed the delicate little hand which lay so trustfully in his. The Countess blushed, her hand quivered – was she trying to reply to his pressure, or to free her hand? Heaven knows – a shy smile trembling on her rosy little mouth, she walked away down the steps.

Seriozha was inexpressibly happy. The emotion of love, aroused in his youthful soul for the first time, could not confine itself to one object, but overflowed on to all human beings and everything around him. Everyone seemed to him so kind, so loving and so worthy of being loved. He stopped on the staircase, took the torn-off sprig out of his glove, and with a rapture which brought the tears to his eyes, pressed it several times to his lips.

'Well, and are you pleased with your *charming débardeur*?' asked Prince Kornakov.

'Oh, how grateful I am to you! I have never been so happy,' he answered ardently, pressing the Prince's hand.

VII

And she could be happy too

On arriving home the Countess enquired out of habit about the Count. He had not yet returned. For the first time she felt pleased that he was not there. She wanted for a few hours at least to set a distance between herself and the reality which seemed to her now, after this evening, oppressive, and to spend a short while alone with her dreams. And her dreams were delightful.

Seriozha was so unlike all the men who had hitherto surrounded her that he could not fail to catch her attention. His movements, his voice, his look, all bore the special stamp of youth, of openness and warmth of spirit. The type of the innocent boy who has yet to experience the upsurge of the passions and of sensual enjoyments, a type which ought to be such a normal one among people who have not strayed from the law of nature but which is, alas, so rarely met with among them, proved to be for the Countess, who had spent her whole life in this unnatural sphere called society, a most fascinating and delightful novelty.

In my opinion the Countess looked even better in her white house-coat and cap than she had done in her ball gown. Reclining with her feet upon the double bed and leaning her elbows on the pillow, she gazed into the pale light of the lamp. A half-sad smile still lingered on her lovely little mouth.

'Liza, may I come in?' asked the Count's voice from the other side of the door.

'Please do,' she answered without changing her position.

'Did you enjoy yourself this evening, my dear?' enquired the Count, kissing her.

'Yes, I did.'

'Then why are you looking so sad, Liza – you aren't angry with me, are you?'

The Countess remained silent and her lips started to tremble, like the lips of a child about to cry.

'I'm sure you are in fact angry with me – on account of my gambling. Well, you can set your mind at rest, my dearest: tonight I have just won back everything, and I shall not play again . . .

'What is the matter?' he asked again, gently kissing her hands: ⟨for he had noticed the tears which had suddenly started to her eyes.⟩

The Countess made no reply but the tears trickled from her eyes. However much the Count caressed her and questioned her, she would not tell him why she was weeping; but she cried more and more bitterly.

Let her alone, you man without heart, without conscience. She is weeping precisely because you are caressing her and because you have the right to do so; and because the comforting fancies which filled her imagination have been dissipated like vapour by the touch of reality – the reality to which she was so indifferent until this evening, but which now has become repulsive and frightful to her from the moment when she realized the possibility of genuine love, and happiness.

VIII

We meet a universally respected nobleman

'What, are you bored, my dear boy?' said Prince Kornakov to Seriozha, who was wandering from room to room with a strange expression of indifference and agitation, taking no part in the dancing or the conversations.

'Yes,' he replied with a smile, 'I would like to leave.'

'Let us go to my house then – *nous causerons*.'[15]

'I trust you are not staying here for supper, Kornakov?' asked a man passing by. He was a tall, stout man of about forty with a puffy, decidedly unattractive yet pleasingly impudent face, who passed through the crowd with a firm and confident step and now paused in the doorway, his hat in his hand.

'Have you finished your card game already?'

'I managed to get that over before suppertime, thank God, and now I am fleeing from a deadly mayonnaise with Russian truffles, a tainted sturgeon, and other suchlike attractions,' he shouted to practically the whole ballroom.

'Where are you going for supper?'

'Either to Trakhmanov's, if he's not asleep yet, or to the Novotroitsky inn. Why don't you come with us? Atalov here is going too.'

'Well, shall we go, Ivin?' said Prince Kornakov. 'By the way, are you acquainted?' he added, addressing the stout man.

Seriozha shook his head.

'This is Sergei Ivin, Marya Ivanovna's son,' said the Prince.

'Delighted,' said the stout gentleman without looking at him and proffering a podgy hand as he continued to make for the exit.

'Come along quickly now.'

I presume that no one requires a detailed description of the type of this stout gentleman, who was in fact called N. N. Dolgov. Every one of my readers, even if he does not know him, has probably seen him or heard of N.N.: it should therefore be enough to supply a few essential features, for this person to spring to life in the reader's imagination in all the fullness of his base and worthless nature. So, at least, it seems to me. Wealth, aristocratic birth, social sophistication, great and varied talents – all vitiated or disfigured by idleness and vice. A cynical mind which questions everything without limits, and resolves every question to the advantage of the lowest passions. A complete lack of conscience, shame,

15 We will have a chat.

and any notion of morality in one's pleasures. The blatant egoism of vice. A gift for coarse and harsh language. Sensuality, gluttony and drunkenness; contempt for everyone, himself excepted. A view of things from two aspects only – the satisfaction they can give him, and their defects. And two principal traits: a useless, aimless, thoroughly idle life, and the most vile depravity, which he not only does not bother to conceal, but flaunts openly with great satisfaction. People say that he is a wicked man; but always and everywhere he is respected, and people are proud to be linked with him; he is aware of this, and laughs, and despises them all the more. And how could he fail also to despise what is known as virtue, when all his life he has trampled on it, yet for all that is happy after his fashion – that is to say, his passions are gratified and people respect him.

Seriozha was in an exceptionally good humour. The presence of Prince Kornakov, whom he liked very much and who for some reason had a strong influence on him, gave him great satisfaction. And making the acquaintance of someone as notable as the stout gentleman tickled his vanity most pleasantly. At first the stout gentleman paid little attention to Seriozha, but when the Cossack waiter he had summoned on arriving at the Novotroitsky brought the pasties and wine he had ordered he grew more cordial, and noticing the young man's relaxed mood he began chatting to him (there is nothing men of Dolgov's stamp dislike more than shyness), patting him on the shoulder, and clinking glasses with him.

The thoughts and feelings of a young man in love are so powerfully focused on a single object that he has no time to observe and analyse the people he encounters; and of course nothing so much inhibits growing freedom and familiarity in social relations as the tendency, particularly in young men, not to accept people for what they seem to be, but to try to discover their inner, secret thoughts and motives. That evening Seriozha was in fact conscious of a powerful desire to be witty and amiable, and of the ability to be so without the slightest effort on his part.

Getting to know the retired General, a boon companion of Dolgov's, which had at one time been a fantasy of his vanity, now ceased to give him any great satisfaction. On the contrary, he had the impression that he himself was bestowing honour and satisfaction on this General by speaking to him at all, since instead of speaking to the General he could have been speaking to *her*, or at least thinking about her. Until now he had never ventured to call Kornakov 'thou', although Kornakov frequently addressed him in the second person singular, but this evening he took the plunge, and using this intimate form of address gave him extraordinary pleasure. The Countess's caressing look and her smile had given him a greater feeling of self-reliance than intelligence, academic distinction, good looks or constant praise could ever have done: in a single hour they had transformed him from boy to man. He suddenly felt within himself all those manly qualities which he had been only too well aware that he lacked: firmness, decision, courage, and a proud conviction of his own worth. An attentive observer might even have detected a change in his outward appearance that evening. His step had become more confident and freer, his body looked more upright, his arms no longer gave the impression that he was unsure what to do with them, his head was held higher, the childish softness and vagueness of his features was gone, the muscles of his brow and cheeks were more distinct, and his smile was bolder and firmer.

IX

Revelry

In a small and elegant back room of the Novotroitsky inn used only by patrons who were particularly well-known, our four acquaintances were sitting at a long table on which supper had been eaten.

'You know who I want to drink to,' said Seriozha to Prince Kornakov, pouring out a glass and raising it to his lips. Seriozha's face was very red and his eyes had an oily, unnatural appearance.

'Let us drink,' replied Kornakov, his usual bored and impassive expression transformed by an affectionate smile.

This toast to an unnamed person was repeated several times. The General had taken off his tie and was lying on a divan with a bottle of cognac, a glass and some cheese beside him. His face was somewhat redder and puffier than usual and from his impudent and half screwed-up eyes it was evident that he was enjoying himself.

'This is what I really like,' he said, looking at Seriozha who was seated opposite him emptying one glass after another. 'There was a time when I used to drink champagne, as you do. I would drink a whole bottle at supper at a ball, and then whatever happened I would dance and be even more charming than before.'

'No, I have no regrets for those days,' said N.N., leaning on his elbow and looking with a melancholy expression into Kornakov's agreeably animated eyes. 'I can still put away as many glasses as you could wish, but what of that? The only sad thing is that the time is long past when, like him, I would drink some lady's health, and I would sooner have died than refuse to drink to anyone when I was dead set on reaching *le fond de la bouteille*,[16] for I really believed that I would end up marrying the woman whose health I drank from this *fond de la bouteille*. Oh, if only I could have married all the women to whom I've dedicated that last drop, how many wonderful wives I would have had! Ah yes, what wonderful wives – if you only knew, Seriozha . . .' – and he waved his hand in the air. 'Well, and here is your *fond de la bouteille*,' he said, pouring out the last of the wine for him . . . 'But what am I saying? You shouldn't be doing this . . .' – and he gave him a cheerful and affectionate smile.

'Oh, don't remind me. I had forgotten all about the things I should not be doing, and I don't want to think about them, I feel so content here and now.' And his eyes shone with the pure delight of a young man throwing himself fearlessly into his first passionate love.

16 The bottom of the bottle.

'Well, what about this, how delightful he is!' said N.N., turning to the General. 'You can't imagine how much he reminds me of myself. *Débouchons-le tout à fait.*'[17]

'Yes,' said the General, 'you know ⟨I was thinking about taking the company along to visit the gypsies, and now I'm in the mood, let's go.⟩ *Allons au b . . . ,*[18] and we'll take him with us.'

Five minutes later Seriozha was sitting in N.N.'s evening sledge; the fresh, frosty air stung his face, and in front of him he could see the driver's burly back, as dim streetlights and the walls of houses sped past on both sides.

Daydreams

'Here I am in the country where I was born and spent my childhood, at Semyonovskoye, so full of dear and wonderful memories. It is an evening in spring, and I am in the garden, in the spot my late mother was so fond of beside the pond in the birch-tree walk, and I am not alone – with me is my wife, in a white dress, her hair swept up simply on her lovely head; and this wife of mine is the woman I love – the woman I love as I have never loved anyone before, more than anything in the world, more than myself even. The moon, sailing peacefully across a sky covered with transparent clouds, is brightly reflected, together with the clouds it illumines, in the mirror-like surface of the unruffled pond, and it lights up the green banks overgrown with yellowish sedge, the light-coloured logs of the little dam, the willow branches hanging above it, the dark-green foliage of the blossoming lilacs and bird-cherries which fill the pure air with a joyful spring fragrance, the leaves of the dogroses which crowd the flowerbeds between the winding paths, the long, leafy, motionless branches of the tall birches and the delicate greenery of the lime trees standing in their straight, dark avenues. From the far side of the pond the loud song

17 Let's take his cork out once and for all.
18 Let's go to the b . . . [brothel].

of the nightingale can be heard in the overgrown thicket of trees, and the music is reflected even more sonorously from the still surface of the water. I am holding the soft hand of the woman I love, and gazing into her wonderful wide eyes whose look has such a comforting effect on my soul, and she smiles and squeezes my hand in return – she is happy too!'

How stupid are these comforting dreams. Stupid because of their impossibility, comforting because of the poetic feeling with which they are filled. Granted, they will not, cannot indeed, come true; but why not let oneself be carried away by them if this fantasy is a source of such pure and lofty delight? It never occurred to Seriozha at that moment to ask himself the question: how could this woman become his wife when she was married already, and even if that were possible, would it be a good thing, the right thing? And if it were to be so, how then would he set about arranging his life? Beyond these few minutes of love and passion he was quite unable to picture this other life. True love experiences in itself such a range of sacred, innocent, powerful, invigorating, liberating feelings, that for true love neither crimes nor obstacles, nor the whole of the prosaic side of life, have any real existence.

Suddenly the sleigh came to a halt, and this interruption of the regular lulling motion roused him from his reverie. On his left he could see a snow-covered open space quite large for the city, with a few bare trees, and on his right the entrance porch of a low, rather crooked, drab little house with closed shutters.

'What, are we outside the town?' he enquired of the driver.

'Not at all, this is Patriarch's Ponds if you want to know, and that's right next to Kozikhi.'

N.N. and the cheery General were already standing by the entrance. The latter was alternately kicking the cracked and shaky-looking house door with his foot, and tugging at a rusty piece of bent wire which hung from the lintel, shouting quite loudly as he did so: 'Hey, you girls in there! Open up, girls!' At length a rustling sound was heard – the

noise of uncertain, cautious slippered footsteps, there was a
glimmer of light behind the shutters, and the door opened.
On the threshold appeared a bent old woman in a fox-fur
coat which she had thrown on over a white nightshirt,
holding a guttering tallow candle in her wrinkled hands.
From a first glance at her sharp, forceful, wrinkled features,
her glittering dark eyes, the jet-black hair streaked with grey
sticking out from beneath her kerchief, and the swarthy
brick-like hue of her skin, it could be seen beyond a doubt
that she was a gypsy. She held up the candle to the faces of
N.N. and the General, and at once recognized them, apparently with delight.

'Ah, goodness gracious, good Lord! Mikhail Nikolayevich,
my little father,' she began in her harsh voice, with that
particular accent which is peculiar to gypsies. 'What a joy to
see you, sun of our lives that you are! Aiee, and you too,
N.N., it's such a long time since you paid us a visit: won't
the girls be glad to see you! We humbly bid you come in,
and we'll have some dancing for you!'

'Are your people at home, then?'

'Yes, yes, all at home, they'll come running, my golden
one. Come in, come in.'

'*Entrons*,'[19] said N.N., and all four of them, without
removing their hats and overcoats, entered a small, low-
ceilinged dirty room which, its untidiness apart, resembled
the sort of room normally to be found in the houses of
lower-middle-class folk: it was furnished with little mirrors
in pretty frames, a tattered wooden-backed divan, and dirty-
looking veneered chairs and tables.

Young men are easily carried away and are capable of being
seduced even by something sordid, providing the seduction
occurs under the influence of men whom they respect.
Seriozha had already forgotten his dreams and was looking
at this unfamiliar décor with the curiosity of a man watching
some kind of chemical experiment being demonstrated. He
observed impatiently what was before him, waiting to see

19 Let's go in.

what would come of it all; and his opinion was that it would be something most enjoyable.

On the divan a young gypsy man lay asleep. He had long, dark, curly hair, slanting, almost sinister eyes, and large white teeth. In a moment he had sprung up, pulled on some clothes and spoken a few words to the old woman in the resonant gypsy tongue; he then began smilingly to greet the guests.

'Who is the leader of the troupe here now?' enquired N.N. 'I haven't been here for some time.'

'Ivan Matvyeich,' answered the gypsy.

'Vanka?'

'Yes, that's right, sir.'

'And who is your chief singer?'

'Tanya leads the singing, and Marya Vasilyevna too.'

'Ah, Masha, that pretty little thing who used to live at Bryantsovo? She's really back here again, is she?'

'Yes indeed, sir,' replied the gypsy, smiling. 'And she sometimes joins in the dancing too.'

'Just you go and fetch her, then, and bring us some champagne.'

The young man accepted the money which was offered him and hurried out. The old General, as befitted a seasoned patron of the gypsies, sat astride a table and struck up a conversation with the old woman about all the old gypsy men and women who used to be at the encampment in times gone by. He knew the lineage of each and every one of them. The Guards officer explained how there were no real women to be found in Moscow, yet it was out of the question to go and enjoy oneself among the gypsies because their living conditions were simply so dirty that they would put off any decent man. On the other hand, getting them to come to you was another matter entirely. N.N. told him that gypsies at home were, on the contrary, a thoroughly good thing, but they needed understanding, etc., etc. Seriozha listened attentively to what was being said, and although he remained silent, in his heart he was thoroughly on the side of N.N. and found so much in his surroundings novel and attractive that he realized he was certain to experience something special and agreeable. Now and again the door leading to the porch opened, letting in a blast of cold air, and the gypsies who made up the choir came in two by two. The men were dressed in light-blue coats of knee length which fitted tightly round their shapely waists, and wide trousers tucked into their boots, and all of them had long curly hair. The women wore fox-fur coats lined with satin and had bright silken shawls over their heads, and dresses which, though not fashionable, looked quite elegant and expensive. The young gypsy came back with the champagne, announcing that Masha would be here presently, and proposing to start the dancing without her. He said something to the leader of the band, a small, slender, handsome fellow in a pleated coat with lace trimmings, who put one foot on the windowsill and began tuning his guitar. The leader said something testily in reply; several old women joined in the discussion, which gradually grew louder and finally turned into a general shouting match; the old women, with fire in their eyes, waved their arms and shouted in the most piercing voices, and the men and a few other old women showed that they did not intend to be left out. In their arguing, which was incomprehensible to the guests, one frequently repeated word could be made out: Maka, Maka. A very pretty young girl called Steshka, whom the leader recommended as their new singer, was sitting with downcast eyes, the only one not to join in the conversation. The General realized what the trouble was. The young gypsy who had gone for the champagne had misled them in promising that Maka (i.e. Masha) would come, and the others wanted Steshka to lead the singing. The question at issue was whether or not she should receive an extra half-share of the proceeds for her services.

'Hey there, girls,' the General shouted, 'listen, listen,' but no one paid him the slightest attention. Finally he somehow got them to hear him out.

'If Maka is not coming,' he said, 'then you should say so.'

'On my honour,' said the leader, 'Steshka will sing just as well as she would: you should just hear how she sings "Night time" – there's no other gypsy girl to touch her, she has all the style of Tanyusha – you'll see. All our people here know I am speaking the truth,' he added, knowing that this would gratify the General. 'Please be so good as to hear her.'

The gypsy women raised their various voices to appeal to the General in similar terms.

'Well all right, all right, so please get on with it.'

'What song do you wish to hear?' asked the leader, standing, guitar in hand, before the half-circle of seated gypsies.

'Follow the usual order, of course, start with "You can hear".' The gypsy pushed the guitar into the right position with his knee and played a chord, and the choir launched smoothly and simultaneously into 'Just as you can he-e-ear . . .'

'Stop, stop,' cried the General, 'there is something missing still. We must all have a drink.'

All the gentlemen drank a glass of bad lukewarm champagne each. The General approached the gypsies, told one of the women, a former notable beauty who was still quite young, to stand up, sat down in her seat and planted her firmly on his knees. The choir once more struck up 'Just as you can hear'. At first the singing was smooth, but then it grew livelier and livelier, and finally it sounded as only gypsies singing their own songs can make it sound – full of extraordinary energy and inimitable art. Suddenly and unexpectedly the choir stopped singing. Again came an introductory chord, and the same melody was repeated by a sweetly tender, resonant solo voice, with remarkably original decorations and intonation, and the solo voice, in just the same way the choir had done, grew ever more powerful and animated, until at length it returned the melody discreetly and smoothly to the whole choir, who took it up again.

There was a time when no kind of music in all Russia was more beloved than the music of the gypsies, and when the gypsies used to sing the good old Russian folksongs such as 'Not alone' and 'You can hear', 'Youth', 'Farewell' and others, and when it was not considered eccentric to listen to the gypsies and to prefer them to the Italian singers. Nowadays the gypsies sing vaudeville ballads like 'Two maids', 'Vanka and Tanka', and so forth, for a public which gathers round them in city arcades. To love gypsy music, perhaps even to describe their singing as music, may appear absurd. It is a sad thing that this music has so fallen from favour. In our country gypsy music once formed a unique bridge between folk music and classical art music. Why should it be that in Italy every *lazzarone*[20] can appreciate a Donizetti or a Rossini aria and derive pleasure from it, whereas in Russia a merchant or a tradesman or suchlike, hearing something from *The Tomb of Askold* or *A Life for the Tsar*,[21] can only admire the decorations? And I am not referring here to the kind of Italian music for which not even a hundredth part of Russian concert-goers has any feeling, but to so-called popular operas. Whereas every Russian will be able to appreciate a gypsy song because its roots are in folk music. But people will tell me that this music does not obey the rules. No one is obliged to believe me, but I will say what I have experienced for myself, and those who like gypsy music will believe me, and those who are willing to try the experiment will also be convinced.

At one time I was very fond of gypsy music and of German music too, and I devoted myself to the study of both. A certain very good musician who was a friend of mine, German by his musical tendency as well as by his origins, was always falling out with me because gypsy choral singing contained unpardonable musical irregularities (though like everyone else he found the solos quite superlative), and he wanted to prove this to me. I composed reasonably well; he, very well indeed. We persuaded a gypsy choir to sing through a particular song some ten times and we both noted down every vocal line. On comparing our two scores we actually discovered passages in parallel fifths; but I still refused to give

20 Street idler, beggar.
21 *The Tomb of Askold*, *A Life for the Tsar*: popular Russian operas by Verstovsky (1799–1862) and Glinka (1804–57).

in and retorted that we might have written down the actual sounds correctly, but we could not grasp the precise tempi, and that the sequence of fifths he had pointed out to me was nothing other than an imitation at the fifth – something resembling a fugue, and very successfully worked out at that. We set about writing down the music yet again, and R. was completely convinced of what I had been saying. It should be said that each time we noted down the music something new emerged – the movement of the harmony was the same, but sometimes the chords were more condensed, and sometimes in place of a single note there was repetition of the preceding motif – an imitation in fact. But to make them sing each part separately was out of the question: they were all singing the top line, and each time the choir began to sing each one was effectively improvising.

I trust that those readers who have no interest in gypsy music will pardon this digression; I felt that it was out of place here, but my love for this unorthodox yet truly popular music which has always given me so much pleasure, got the upper hand.

While the choir were singing the first ballad the General listened attentively, sometimes smiling and screwing up his eyes, sometimes frowning and shaking his head in disapproval; then he stopped listening altogether and fell to conversing with Lyubasha, who at one moment was flashing her pearly teeth in a smile as she spoke to him, and the next calling comments and directions to the choir in her powerful alto voice as she glanced severely to left and right among the girl singers and gestured to them with her hands. The Guards officer took a seat near to the pretty Steshka, and turning to N.N., kept repeating *'Charmant, délicieux!'*[22] or offering her advice with no great success. This clearly displeased the gypsy girls and set them whispering to one another: one of them even nudged his arm and said 'Master, if you please.' N.N. had put his feet up on the divan and was holding a whispered conversation with a pretty dancer named

22 Charming, delightful!

Malushka. Seriozha, his waistcoat unbuttoned, was standing in front of the choir, evidently listening to them with delight. He was also aware that the young gypsy girls were throwing him glances, smiling and whispering among themselves, and he realized that they were not mocking but admiring him, which made him feel that he was a very attractive young fellow. But all of a sudden the General rose to his feet and said to N.N., '*Non, cela ne va pas sans Mashka, ce choeur ne vaut rien, n'est-ce pas?*'[23] N.N., who had appeared sleepy and apathetic since leaving the ball, agreed with him. The General handed the poor old woman some money but did not order them to sing anything in his honour, as was the custom.

'*Partons.*'[24] N.N., yawning, replied '*Partons*'. The Guards officer alone wanted to argue, but they paid him no attention. They all put on their fur coats and went out.

'I can't think of going to sleep now,' said the General as he invited N.N. to take a seat in his conveyance. '*Allons au b . . .*'[25]

'*Ich mache alles mit,*'[26] said N.N., and once more the two carriages and the sledge sped along the dark and silent streets. Seriozha felt only that his head was spinning and rested it against the padded wall of the carriage as he attempted to set his muddled thoughts in order, and he was not listening when the General said to him in a thoroughly calm and sober voice: '*Si ma femme savait que je bamboche avec vous . . .*'[27]

The carriage stopped. Seriozha, the General, N.N. and the Guards officer walked up a reasonably neat and well-lit flight of steps into a clean entrance hall where a footman took their overcoats, and from there they entered a brightly lit room furnished somewhat strangely, but with pretentions to luxury. In this room there was music playing and a few men and ladies were dancing. Some other ladies in low-necked dresses were sitting around the walls. Our friends

23 No, it's no good without Mashka, this choir is quite useless, isn't it?
24 Let us be going.
25 Let's go to the b[rothel].
26 I'll do whatever you are doing.
27 If wife did but know that I was out on the spree with you . . .

walked past them and came into another room. Several of the ladies followed them. They were given some more champagne. Seriozha was at first surprised by the strange manner in which his companions addressed these ladies, and still more surprised by the strange language, resembling German, which these ladies used with each other. Seriozha drank several more glasses of wine. N.N., who was sitting on a divan next to one of these women, beckoned him over. Seriozha went up to them and was struck, not so much by the beauty of this woman (she was in fact unusually good-looking) as by her unusual resemblance to the Countess. The same eyes, the same smile, only her expression was different – now too shy, now too pert. Finding himself alongside her, Seriozha spoke to her. Later he had only the vaguest recollection of the content of this conversation. Yet he did recall that the story of the *Lady of the Camellias*[28] was running with all its poetic fascination through his fevered imagination; he remembered N.N. calling her *la Dame aux Camélias* and saying that he had never seen a more beautiful woman, except for her hands; and that the *Dame aux Camélias* herself did not speak, but kept smiling at him from time to time, so that Seriozha began to be irritated by the sight of that smile; but the vapours of the wine had gone too powerfully to his young and unaccustomed head.

He remembered further that N.N. said something in her ear and at once moved away to join another group which had formed round the General and the Guards officer, and that this woman took him by the hand, and that they went off somewhere together.—

An hour later on the steps of this same house all four companions were taking leave of one another. Seriozha, making no reply to N.N.'s '*Adieu*', sat down in his carriage and burst out crying like a child. He was remembering the emotion of innocent love which had filled his breast with elation and vague longings, and realizing that for him the time of such love was now irrevocably past. And why was

28 *La Dame aux Camélias* (1848), by Dumas *fils*.

the General so full of cheer as he drove N.N. home in his carriage, and the latter jokingly remarked 'Le jeune a perdu son pucelage?[29] Yes, I do so enjoy bringing attractive young people together.'

Who is to blame? Surely not Seriozha, for having given himself up to the influence of men whom he liked, and to a natural desire? Certainly he is to blame; but who will cast the first stone at him? Is N.N. to blame, then, and the General too? Is it actually the essential function of men like these to do evil, to serve as tempters, that thereby goodness may take on a greater value? But you too are to blame, for tolerating such men, and not merely for tolerating them, but for choosing them as your leaders.—

Why? Who is to blame?

And how sad it is that two such excellent human beings, so wonderfully suited to one another and having only just become aware that this is so, should have their love ruined. They may perhaps still encounter someone else in times to come, and even fall in love, but what sort of a love will it be? Better that they should spend their whole life repenting, than that they should stifle this memory which they hold within themselves, and supplant with a guilty love, this true love which they have tasted, if only for one moment.

29 The lad has lost his maidenhead, eh?

APPENDIX II
FOUR LATE STORIES

not included in the Centenary Edition

PREFACE

TOLSTOY'S late stories have had a troubled critical history. In July 1883 Turgenev, then on his deathbed, sent Tolstoy the last letter he ever wrote, begging him to 'return to literary work'. Tolstoy's first published fictions after *Anna Karenina* and the moral and religious crisis which seemed to have ended his literary career were the cluster of 'popular tales', including *Where Love is, God is*, which appeared in 1885. It is doubtful whether Turgenev would have felt that this was 'literature' as he understood the word. The following year, with the appearance of *The Death of Ivan Ilych*, many of Tolstoy's admirers felt, in the words of one critic, that 'his train had come out of the tunnel', and this story was not the last to be greeted as a masterpiece on the level of the two great novels: *Hadji Murad* (ten drafts, 1896–1904) has long enjoyed a similarly high valuation. Yet *Hadji Murad* was written with a guilty conscience by a man who felt that it was a betrayal of his new-found moral principles, and of the new aesthetic which he was to state at length in *What is Art?*

This new aesthetic was to be based on simplicity, clarity and moral 'infectiousness' – that is, effectiveness in influencing the reader's outlook for good. From the point of view of the later Tolstoy, a simple moral fable which could be readily understood by a newly literate peasant was of far greater value than *Anna Karenina*, whose moral confusion and structural sophistication now seemed reprehensible. Not many later critics have agreed with the later Tolstoy, but estimates of how much of his post-1880 writing is valuable have varied widely, from the view that none of it beyond *Resurrection* and a very few stories is worth reading, to the view that anything Tolstoy wrote, even a child's reading book, must be of some value because it is by Tolstoy. The Centenary Edition (1928–37) of translations by Aylmer Maude (1858–1938) and his wife Louise included a selection of short tales in the folk idiom and a number of simple moral fables but did not attempt to be exhaustive. It excluded, along with most of the 'reading book material', a good many more substantial stories published posthumously, and the opportunity has now been taken to include a selection of these in the present edition.

In his essay on *Hadji Murad* A. D. P. Briggs, referring to the brutal raid on the Chechen village carried out on the orders of Nicholas I, writes: 'This is not only good story-telling, it is as effective a condemnation of cruel government and militarism as a trunkful of anarchist and pacifist pamphlets.' The same could be said of at least three of the stories printed below, and it neatly encapsulates the impossibility of separating the 'literature' from the 'pamphlet' in Tolstoy's late stories, which are consciously propaganda (literally: 'things to be propagated') as well as pieces of literary art.

After the Ball (1903) is a prime example: its *raison d'être* is the harrowing description of an army deserter being made to run the gauntlet, a punishment which was effectively a death sentence (although officially capital punishment did not exist in Russia at the time of Nicholas I). This description, and the effect the sight has on the man who witnessed it, provides the moral explosive charge of the story, but it is enclosed within an apparently anodyne story of rapturous young love. The narrator recalls his youthful passion for Varenka, the daughter of a distinguished army colonel ('with white, curled moustaches *à la* Nicholas I') who is almost as captivating on the dance floor as his lovely daughter, and the account of the ball at which father and daughter dance together is intoxicating in its exuberance – calculatedly so, of course, for early the next morning it is Varenka's father whom the narrator sees as the officer in charge of the punishment battalion, urging on the soldiers to strike harder and ordering fresh sticks. The story is an elegant theorem: its

QED, the brutality of the militaristic state and the disgust it should provoke in all humane people.

What For? (1906), though longer and more complex, is connected to *After the Ball* by a similar scene of brutal punishment, and to *Hadji Murad* by the scene in Chapter XV of that story where Tolstoy depicts the Tsar's loathing for the Poles and shows him sentencing a Polish exile to death by running the gauntlet. *What For?* is, like *Hadji Murad*, a miniature historical novel, if on a more modest scale. It ends with another bitter attack on Nicholas I, whose reign was the high-water mark of Russian militarism and chauvinism, but even in the days of Nicholas II this story would not have been considered publishable: it undermines the whole edifice of Great Russian patriotism and raises uncomfortable thoughts about political freedom by telling the story of the Polish insurrection of 1830 from an exclusively Polish point of view – a deeply shocking act in Russian eyes. If the result is somewhat simplistic, reading in places like an adventure story for school children, with a relatively happy ending, this is very likely in keeping with Tolstoy's design for a story which would entertain but also educate, to be read by young people – or by adults for whom literacy was only a recently won achievement.

The most ambitious by far of these four stories is *The Forged Coupon*. The idea of the story seems to have been in Tolstoy's mind for quite a long time: it is mentioned in a list of titles in 1895, and was 'half finished in rough' early in 1904. These dates place it in the same creative era as *Hadji Murad*. While this story is more clearly didactic than *Hadji Murad*, and less elegantly shaped, it shares with its more famous brother the honour of being Tolstoy's last exercise in the epic genre – if 'epic' can look forward to the linear, moralistic story-telling of Brecht, as well as back to *War and Peace*, *The Cossacks* and Homer.

The Forged Coupon, like *Resurrection*, is a story tracing the consequences of an evil action. Its moral message is close to the heart of Christianity (whether Tolstoy's version or any other): our actions are infectious, for good as well as for evil, and we are all responsible for one another. *Resurrection* pursues this theme in a single story line developed at great length. *The Forged Coupon*, in a much smaller space, attempts something more ambitious: to follow the ramifications of a simple act of dishonesty as they affect the lives of more and more characters in a variety of places and at many social levels. *The Forged Coupon* pushes at the limits of the reader's capacity to remember multiple groups of characters, but in doing so it achieves a remarkably wide panoramic view of Russian society from convict to Tsar, and something like a God's-eye view of human behaviour.

In Part One, Chapter VIII the narrator hints at 'something far more serious than anything merely human eyes could perceive' having happened: Tolstoy, the master of detailed observation and psychological analysis, is now pursuing God-like omniscience into the moral sphere. This involves a strong conviction not only of the power of darkness, but of the power of light. The central point of the story is the brutal murder of the saintly Mariya Semyonovna, and Part One ends with her killer Stepan, overcome with weariness and vodka, collapsing in a ditch where he lies until two days later. It is on the third day that he rises again, not yet to a redeemed life, but to the Tolstoyan equivalent of purgatory. Mariya Semyonovna's death haunts her killer and ultimately brings about Stepan's moral regeneration, and the salvation of others with whom he comes into contact, so that he comes nearest to being the hero of the story – if it had one. Despite the contrived nature of its structure, *The Forged Coupon*, like almost everything Tolstoy wrote, retains his extraordinary ability to make us feel that this is all part of real life, and as in many of his fictions the 'open', indeterminate ending seems a confirmation of this: life continues, the truth marches on, and despite the suffering and squalor there is hope.

Tolstoy coined his own term, *oproshchéniye* (from *prostói* – simple), to denote the process of simplifying down to embrace a way of life closer to that of the peasantry and the soil, and there are characters in *The Forged Coupon* who exemplify this process in action. The technique of the story, however, remains complex and sophisticated, even though its language is low-key throughout and in places approaches the speech of the common people. *Alyosha Gorshok* (1905) takes this linguistic process of simplifying down much further, and narrates the life (and since this is Tolstoy, the death) of a peasant character in the sort of language which he himself would have used – had he been articulate enough to tell his own story, which he certainly is not. *Alyosha Gorshok* is, for Tolstoy, an extreme example of laconicism, which has been justly compared to Chekhov. There are only two named characters in the story – Alyosha (or Alyoshka when he is very young, and when people are talking down to him) and the cook Ustinya, and all the material details are the humdrum details of daily life which would be much the same anywhere for the lower classes in Russia. Thus Alyosha becomes a semi-anonymous representative figure, and also a late example of the well-known Holy Fool, who smiles, obeys orders and 'dies well'. Yet the cryptic nature of the story gives no real clue to whether Tolstoy sees Alyosha as a hero, or merely as a victim, and the final impression is one of tragic waste, together with a mute, smouldering anger at the social system of which Alyosha is a victim. Despite everything, however, the economy of means and the implied sympathy produce a result which is both beautiful and moving. Would Turgenev have approved?

*

I should like to express my sincere gratitude to the following people for their help in the translation of these and the two preceding stories: to Gillian Squire of the London University School of Slavonic and East European Studies Library, for her assistance in tracing texts; and to Ignat Avsey, Leonid Feygin, Prince Andrei Golitsyn, Dmitry Usenko, Susan Wilkins and Helen Wozniak, for their invaluable advice on matters of fact and language.

N. J. Cooper
April 2000

AFTER THE BALL

'WHAT you are saying is, that a man is incapable of deciding for himself what is good and what is bad, that everything depends on the environment, that man is the victim of his environment. But as I see it, everything really depends on chance. Listen, I will tell you about something that happened to me personally . . .'

These words were spoken by our universally respected Ivan Vasilyevich at the end of a discussion we had been having about whether, in order to achieve individual perfection in life, it was first necessary to alter the conditions in which people live. In fact no one had actually argued that it is impossible to decide for oneself what is good and what is bad, but Ivan Vasilyevich had a curious way of answering questions of his own which had arisen in the course of discussion, and using these thoughts of his as a pretext for telling us about episodes which had occurred in his own life. He would frequently lose sight of the reason which had originally set off his narrative, and get carried away by the story, all the more so since he was an exceptionally sincere and truthful story-teller.

And so it was on this particular occasion.

'I will tell you about something that happened to me personally. My whole life has been like this – not influenced at all by environment, but by something else altogether.'

'By what, then?' we asked him.

'Well, it's a long story. It will take some telling if you are really going to understand.'

'Then please go on, and tell us.'

Ivan Vasilyevich reflected for a moment, then nodded his head.

'Yes,' he said, 'my whole life was changed by what happened one night, or rather one morning.'

'So what was it?'

'The thing was, I had fallen deeply in love. I had been in love many times before, but this time my feelings were something far stronger. It's a long time ago now; she even has married daughters of her own. Her family name was B——, yes, Varenka B——' (here Ivan Vasilyevich mentioned the family name). 'Even at fifty she was still an outstanding beauty. But when she was young, at eighteen, she was absolutely enchanting: tall, shapely, graceful, and imposing – yes, really imposing. She always held herself very erect, as though it was not in her nature to do otherwise, with her head thrown slightly back, and this, together with her beauty and her tall stature, and despite her thinness, boniness even, gave her a sort of regal air which might have been intimidating, had it not been for the charming, always joyful smile of her mouth and her wonderful shining eyes, and the general effect of her lovely, youthful being.'

'What a picture Ivan Vasilyevich is painting for us!'

'Well, describe her as I may, it is impossible by describing her to make you see her as she really was. But that is not the point. The events I want to tell you about took place in the 1840s. At that time I was a student at a provincial university. Whether it was a good thing or a bad thing I have no idea, but in those days our university contained no intellectual groups, no theories whatever; we were simply young men and we lived as young men typically do – studying, and enjoying ourselves too. I was a very jolly, lively young fellow, and well off into the bargain. I was the owner of a really spirited horse, an ambler; I used to go tobogganing with the young ladies (skating having not yet come into fashion); and I was much given to celebrating with my companions (in those days we never drank anything but champagne; and if there was no money we didn't drink at all – we never drank vodka instead, as they do nowadays). And my chief delight was going to evening parties and balls. I was a good dancer, and not at all bad-looking.'

'Come now, there's no need to be quite so modest,' put in one of the ladies in our company. 'We are quite familiar with your daguerreotype portrait. It isn't true to say that you were not bad-looking – you were handsome.'

'That is as may be, but that is not the point either. What matters is that just as my love for her was reaching its peak, on the last day of Shrovetide, I attended a ball at the house of the district marshal of the nobility, a genial old man who was wealthy, well known for his hospitality, and a chamberlain at court. His wife, as good-natured as he was, received the guests wearing a puce-coloured velvet gown, a diamond ferronnière on her forehead, and with her ageing, puffy shoulders and bosom on display, as in those portraits of the Empress Elizaveta Petrovna. It was a splendid ball: a beautiful ballroom with galleries for the musicians, and an orchestra, well known at that time, which was made up of serfs belonging to a landowner who was an amateur musician, and a veritable ocean of champagne. Although I was fond of champagne I didn't drink any, for I was already drunk without wine, drunk with love; but I still danced to the point of exhaustion – quadrilles, waltzes, polkas; and as far as possible of course, I danced them with Varenka. She was wearing a white dress with a pink sash, white kid gloves reaching almost to her slender, pointed elbows, and white satin shoes. The mazurka was filched from me by a most unpleasant engineer by the name of Anisimov – even today I cannot forgive him – who had asked her for this dance almost the moment she arrived, whereas I came in late, having called at the hairdresser's to collect my gloves. So I did not dance the mazurka with her, but with a German girl whom I had been pursuing some time before. But I'm afraid I treated her quite rudely that evening – not talking to her, not looking at her: I had eyes only for that tall, shapely figure in the white dress with the pink sash, her flushed, radiant face with its dimples, and her gentle, affectionate eyes. I wasn't the only one either: everybody looked at her and admired her, men and women alike, though she eclipsed them all. It was impossible not to admire her.

'By decree, so to speak, I danced the mazurka with someone else, but in fact I danced practically all the rest of the time with her. Without the least sign of embarrassment she would walk the whole length of the ballroom and come up to me, and I would jump up from my seat without waiting to be asked, and she would thank me with a smile for my quick-wittedness. When we were led before her so that she could choose a partner, and she was unable to guess the particular "quality" I was supposed to be representing, she was obliged to give her hand to some other young man, but she shrugged her slender shoulders and smiled at me as a sign of her regret and as a consolation.

'When the figures of the mazurka were being danced to a waltz I danced with her for quite a long time and she, breathless and smiling, said to me "*encore*". And I waltzed on and on with her until I was hardly aware of my body at all . . .'

'What do you mean, you were hardly aware of your body? I should think you were well aware of it when you had your arm round her waist; and not just your body, but hers as well,' said one of the guests.

Ivan Vasilyevich suddenly blushed, and replied with annoyance, almost shouting: 'Yes, that's modern young people for you. You don't see anything except the body. In our day it was not like that. The more deeply I was in love, the more disembodied she became for me. Nowadays you look at women's feet, their ankles, and more besides: you mentally undress the women you are in love with; but for me, as Alphonse Karr would say – he was a good writer, too – the object of my love was always clad in robes of bronze. Not only did we not undress them in our minds, we did our best to cover their nakedness, like the virtuous son of Noah in the Bible. But of course you wouldn't understand that . . .'

'Don't bother with him. What happened next?' said one of us.

'Yes. So there I was dancing with her, and losing all sense of time. The musicians were by now pretty desperately tired, you know how it is towards the end of a ball, and they kept on repeating the same section of a mazurka, and the mothers and fathers had already got up from the card tables and were waiting for supper to be served, and the manservants were running about faster than ever, carrying things. It was gone two o'clock. I had to make the most of those last minutes. Yet again I asked her to dance, and for the hundredth time we floated down the ballroom.

' "So may I have the quadrille after supper?" I asked as I led her back to her seat.

' "Of course, if they don't take me home before then," she said, smiling.

' "I won't allow it," I said.

' "Hand me my fan," she said.

' "It makes me sad even to do that," I said as I returned her simple white fan to her.

' "Well, here you are, just so that you won't grieve," she said, plucking a feather from the fan and giving it to me.

'I took the feather, and could only by a look express my delight and gratitude. I was not only happy and content, I was in a state of bliss, full of goodwill to all; I was no longer myself, but some unearthly being who had no knowledge of evil and was capable only of doing good. I hid away the feather in my glove and stood there, without the strength to walk away from her.

' "Look, they are trying to get papa to dance," she said to me, pointing to the tall, stately figure of her father, a colonel in silver epaulettes, standing in the doorway with the hostess and some other ladies.

' "Varenka, come over here," we heard the hostess, with her diamond ferronnière and Empress Elizaveta shoulders, calling in a loud voice.

'Varenka went across to the doorway, and I followed.

' "Do persuade your father to take a turn with you, *ma chère*. Come, Pyotr Vladislavich, do please dance with her," said the hostess to the Colonel.

'Varenka's father was a very handsome, stately, tall and youthful-looking elderly man. His face had a high colour, he had white, curled moustaches *à la* Nicholas I, with white side-whiskers curving down to meet them, and his hair was

combed forward over his temples; and the same joyful smile
as his daughter's played in his brilliant eyes and around his
lips. He was splendidly built, his broad chest thrust out in
the military manner and adorned with just the right quantity
of medals, his shoulders powerful, his legs long and well-
shaped. He was a military commander with all the bearing
of a veteran of the time of Nicholas I.

'As we approached the doorway the Colonel was making
excuses, saying that he had quite forgotten the art of dancing;
nevertheless he smiled, reached across with his right hand to
draw his sword from its scabbard and handed it to an obliging
young man; and putting a suede glove on his right hand –
"all according to regulations" as he said with a smile – he
took his daughter's hand and made a quarter turn, waiting
for the music to strike up.

'As soon as the music of the mazurka began, he stamped
one foot smartly on the floor and advanced the other, and
his tall, bulky figure began, now gently and smoothly, now
noisily and energetically with a clicking of soles and of one
boot against the other, to move around the ballroom. The
graceful figure of Varenka sailed along beside him, imperceptibly shortening or lengthening the steps of her little feet
in their white satin shoes. The whole room followed the
couple's every movement. I gazed at them not just with
admiration, but with a feeling of rapturous tenderness. I was
particularly moved by the sight of his boots, fastened with
little straps – good calf-skin boots, not the fashionable
pointed sort but old-fashioned boots with square toes and
without built-up heels. They were clearly the work of some
battalion cobbler. "To bring out his beloved daughter and
show her off he doesn't buy fashionable boots, he puts on
his everyday home-made ones," I thought, and those four-
square toecaps continued to move me. It was obvious that
he had once been an excellent dancer, but now he was stout
and his legs were not supple enough for all the quick and
elegant dance steps he was attempting to execute. All the
same, he completed two accomplished circuits of the floor.

'And when he swiftly parted his feet and brought them

together again and, although somewhat heavily, dropped on one knee, and she, smiling as she smoothed down her skirt where he had caught it, described a smooth circle round him, everyone burst into loud applause. Rising again with some effort to his feet, he tenderly and affectionately clasped his daughter's head between his hands and, kissing her on the forehead, led her across to me, assuming that I was dancing with her. I told him that I was not her escort.

' "Well, never mind, you dance this one with her," he said with a kindly smile as he put his sword back into its scabbard.

'Just as a single drop poured from a bottle is followed by all the liquid contained inside gushing out in great streams, so my love for Varenka released the entire capacity for love which I had in my soul. At that moment I embraced the whole world in my love. I loved the hostess with her ferronnière and her Imperial bosom, I loved her husband, her guests, her footmen, even Anisimov the engineer who was regarding me with dislike. And for her father with his home-cobbled boots and the same tender smile as his daughter's, for him I felt at that moment a sort of rapturous affection.

'The mazurka came to an end and the host and hostess invited their guests to sit down to supper, but Colonel B—— declined, saying that he had to be up early in the morning, and took his leave of them. I was terrified that Varenka too would be taken away, but she and her mother stayed on.

'When supper was over I danced the promised quadrille with her. And although it seemed to me that I was already infinitely happy, my happiness kept on growing and growing. We neither of us mentioned love; I did not ask her, or indeed ask myself, whether she loved me. It was sufficient for me that I loved her. My only fear was that something might come and spoil my happiness.

'When I had got home, undressed, and thought about going to sleep, I realized that sleep was quite out of the question. In my hand was the feather from her fan and one of her gloves, which she had given me on leaving just as I was helping first her mother and then her into their carriage. I gazed at these objects, and without closing my eyes saw her standing there before me just as she had looked at the moment when, faced with a choice between two partners, she had been trying to guess the quality I represented, and I had heard her lovely voice say "*Pride*? Yes?" – and she had joyfully given me her hand; or when at supper she was sipping from her goblet of champagne and had given me a sideways look with her caressing eyes. But most of all I saw her with her father, smoothly circling round him, then surveying the admiring spectators proudly and joyfully, both on her own account and on his. And I could not help including them both in a single feeling of tender affection.

'At that time I was living with my brother, who has since died. My brother in general had no time for society life and did not go to balls, and now he was preparing for his final examinations and leading a very regular life. He was asleep. I looked at his head buried in the pillow, half-hidden beneath the flannel blanket, and felt affectionately sorry for him – sorry that he neither knew nor shared the happiness I was experiencing. Our household serf Petrusha came in with a candle to help me undress, but I sent him away. The sight of my brother's sleepy face and tousled hair seemed to me deeply touching. Trying not to make a noise, I tiptoed to my room and sat down on the bed. No, I was too happy, I could not possibly sleep. What was more I felt too warm in the heated rooms, and without taking off my uniform I went quietly into the hallway, put on my overcoat, opened the front door and went out into the street.

'It was after 4 A.M. when I had left the ball, and what with the journey home and the time spent in the house, two hours had gone by, so that now, when I went out, it was already light. It was regular Shrovetide weather: it was foggy, the snow, saturated with water, was thawing on the roads, and water dripped from every roof. At that time the B——s lived at the far end of the town next to a large meadow, one end of which was used as a public pleasure-ground and the other was the site of an institute for young ladies. I walked along the deserted lane where our house stood and emerged into the main street, where I began to meet people on foot and draymen with loads of firewood on their sledges, which grazed the underlying surface of the roadway with their runners. And the horses rhythmically swaying their sopping wet heads under the glistening shaft-bows, and the cab-drivers with bast matting on their backs trudging along in enormous boots beside their vehicles, and the houses on each side of the street looming tall in the fog – all this seemed to me extraordinarily precious and filled with meaning.

'When I came out on to the field where their house was situated I saw at the far end, towards the pleasure-ground, something large and black, and I heard the sounds of fife and drum coming to me from that direction. All this time my mind was still full of music, and now and again I could still hear the melody of the mazurka. But this music was of quite a different kind – harsh and unpleasant.

' "Whatever is it?" I wondered as I made my way along the slippery path which had been beaten across the middle of the field, towards the place the sounds were coming from. When I had gone some hundred yards I managed to make out through the fog a crowd of dark figures. They were obviously soldiers. "Most likely a training exercise," I thought, and I went closer, walking just behind a blacksmith in a greasy sheepskin jacket and an apron, who was carrying something. Some soldiers in black uniforms were standing quite still in two rows facing one another, their rifles at the rest position. Behind them were some drummers, and a fife-player who kept on playing the same shrill and unpleasant tune over and over without a break.

' "What are they up to?" I asked the blacksmith, who had stopped beside me.

' "They're thrashing a Tatar for trying to desert," said the blacksmith angrily, his eyes fixed on a point at the far end of the ranks of men. I too looked in that direction and saw between the rows a fearful sight coming towards me. What was approaching was a man stripped to the waist and lashed to the rifles of two soldiers, who were leading him along. Alongside them walked a tall officer in a greatcoat and peaked cap, whose figure looked to me familiar. His whole body twitching, his feet slapping on the thawing snow, the man who was being punished moved towards me under a hail of blows which poured down on him from both sides, now throwing himself backwards – whereupon the NCOs leading him along on their rifles would thrust him forward, now plunging forward – whereupon the NCOs pulled him back, preventing him from falling. And keeping pace with them, walking with a firm, slightly quivering step, came the tall officer. It was her father, with his rubicund face and his white moustaches and side-whiskers.

'At each stroke the man being punished, as if in astonishment, turned his face contorted with suffering to the side from which the blow came, and baring his white teeth, kept repeating the same few words. Only when he had got quite close to me could I make out what these words were. He was repeating, in more of a sob than a voice: "Have mercy on me, lads. Have mercy, lads." But the lads did not have mercy on him, and as the procession drew level with me I saw the soldier standing opposite me step decisively forward, brandish his stick vigorously in the air and bring it whistling down on to the Tatar's back. The Tatar jerked forward but the NCOs restrained him, and another similar blow fell on him from the other side, followed by another from this side, another from that . . . The tall Colonel kept alongside: looking now down at his feet, now at the man being punished, he was drawing the air deeply into his lungs, blowing out his cheeks, then slowly letting it out through his protruding lips. When the procession had passed the place where I was standing, I caught between the ranks of soldiers a glimpse of the man's back. It was such a lurid, wet, red and unnatural-looking sight that I could not believe I was looking at a human body.

' "Jesus Christ" – said the blacksmith standing beside me.

'The procession was now moving away from us. The blows kept on falling from both sides on the stumbling,

contorted man, the drums kept on beating and the fife
shrilling, and the tall, stately figure of the Colonel kept on
walking with the same firm step beside the man who was
being punished. All at once the Colonel stopped and quickly
approached one of the soldiers.

' "I'll teach you to miss the mark," I heard his wrathful
voice saying. "Going to miss it, are you? Are you?"

'And I saw his powerful suede-gloved hand strike a puny,
terrified soldier full in the face for having failed to bring
down his stick hard enough on the Tatar's bleeding back.

' "Give them some fresh sticks!" he shouted, looking
round, and as he did so catching sight of me. He pretended
not to recognize me, and frowning angrily and menacingly
he turned hastily away.

'I was filled with such a pitch of shame that not knowing
where to look, as though I had been apprehended in some
shameful act, I lowered my eyes and hurried off home as fast
as I could. All the way I had in my ears the beating of the
drums and the shrilling of the fife, and I could still hear the
words "Have mercy on me, lads", followed by the self-
confident, angry voice of the Colonel shouting "Going to
miss it, are you? Are you?" And meanwhile I felt in my heart
an almost physical anguish, rising to the point of nausea, so
that several times I had to stop and I thought I was going to
vomit up all the horror with which this spectacle had filled
me. I do not remember how I reached home and got into
bed. But as soon as I began to fall asleep I heard and saw it
all again, and I leapt out of bed.

' "It's obvious that he knows something which I don't,"
I thought with reference to the Colonel. "If only I knew
what he knows, then I should understand what I have just
seen, and it would not upset me like this." But however
much I thought, I could not imagine what it was the Colonel
knew, and it was not until that evening that I managed to
fall asleep, and then only after I had been to visit a friend of
mine and we had got completely drunk.

'Well then, do you suppose I decided there and then that
what I had seen was something evil? Not at all. "If it was

carried out with such conviction and everyone involved recognized that it was necessary, then they must certainly have known something I did not know," I thought to myself, and I tried to discover what it was. But however much I tried, discover it I could not. And since I was unable to discover it, I was unable to go into the army as I had earlier intended, and not only did I not serve in the army, but I did not enter government service of any kind, and as you see, I ended up not doing anything very much.'

'Well, we know about that, how you ended up not doing anything much,' said one of us. 'But just tell us this: how many men would end up the same way if there were not men like you to give them the example?'

'Now that is plain nonsense,' said Ivan Vasilyevich with genuine irritation.

'Well, and what happened about that love of yours?' we all wanted to know.

'My love? From that day on my love went into a decline. Whenever she fell into a pensive mood, as she frequently did, with that smile on her face, I would immediately remember the Colonel on the square, and I would feel somehow awkward and sickened, so I began to see her less often. And so my love for her gradually dwindled away to nothing. That is how it just is with some affairs, and it is things like that which can alter the whole direction of a man's life. But you say . . .' he concluded.

THE FORGED
COUPON

Part One

I

FYODOR MIKHAILOVICH SMOKOVNIKOV, the head of a government department, a man of incorruptible integrity and proud of it, a liberal of a gloomy cast of mind, and not only a free-thinker but a hater of any and every manifestation of religious feeling, which he regarded as a relic of primitive superstition, had returned home from his department in an extremely vexed state of mind. The governor had sent him an utterly stupid memorandum from which it could have been inferred that Fyodor Mikhailovich had acted dishonestly. Fyodor Mikhailovich, furious at the suggestion, had lost no time in composing a biting and caustic reply.

Having got home, Fyodor Mikhailovich had the feeling that everything was happening to thwart him.

It was five minutes to five. He was expecting dinner to be served at once, but the dinner was not ready. Fyodor Mikhailovich banged the door and went off to his study. Someone knocked at the door. 'Who the devil is it now?' he thought, and called out:

'Who is it now?'

Into the room came Fyodor Mikhailovich's fifteen-year-old son, a grammar-school boy in the fifth year.

'What brings you here?'

'It's the first of the month today.'

'So, is it money you're after?'

By an established agreement, on the first day of each month the father gave his son an allowance of three roubles to spend on hobbies and amusements. Fyodor Mikhailovich frowned, reached for his wallet and fished out from it a two-and-a-half-rouble bond coupon,[1] then got out the purse in which he kept his small change and counted out a further fifty copecks. His son remained silent and did not take the money.

'Please, Papa, can you let me have an advance?'

'What?'

'I wouldn't ask you, but I borrowed some money on my word of honour, I promised to pay it back. As a man of honour I can't just ... I only need another three roubles, honestly. I won't ask you ... at least, I don't mean I won't ask you, it's simply that ... Please, Papa.'

'You have already been told that –'

'Yes, Papa, I know, but it's just for this once, really ...'

'You receive an allowance of three roubles, and it is always too little. When I was your age I didn't even get fifty copecks.'

'But all my friends get more than I do now. Petrov and Ivanitsky actually have fifty roubles a month.'

'And I tell you that if that is the way you are going to behave, then you will end up as a swindler. That is all I have to say on the matter.'

'And what if it is? You'll never look at things from my point of view: it means I shall have to look like an absolute cad. It's all very well for you.'

'Get out of here, you good-for-nothing, get out!'

Fyodor Mikhailovich jumped up from his chair and rushed at his son.

'Get out. What you need is a good hiding.'

His son was both frightened and bitterly resentful, but his resentment outweighed his fear, and bowing his head he made hurriedly for the door. Fyodor Mikhailovich had no intention of hitting him, but he was enjoying his own anger and he continued shouting and cursing at his son as the latter made his retreat.

When the maid came to say that the dinner was ready to serve, Fyodor Mikhailovich stood up.

---

1 A detachable voucher issued with government bonds and exchangeable for interest payments.

'At last,' he said. 'I've quite lost my appetite now.' And he walked scowling into the dining-room.

At the dinner table his wife struck up a conversation but his growled reply was so curt and irritable that she fell silent. His son too did not look up from his plate and said nothing. They ate their meal in silence, then silently got up from the table and went their separate ways.

After dinner the schoolboy went back to his own room, took the coupon and the small change out of his pocket and threw them on the desk table. Then he took off his school uniform and put on a jacket. For some time he pored over a battered Latin grammar, then he shut the door and fastened it on the hook, swept the money off the desk top and into a drawer, took some cigarette papers out of the drawer, filled one with tobacco, plugged the cardboard mouthpiece with some cotton wool, and started to smoke.

He spent a further two hours or so sitting over his grammar and his exercise books but without taking anything in, then he stood up and began pacing to and fro across the room, stamping his heels and recalling everything that had passed between him and his father. His father's abusive words, and above all the spiteful expression on his father's face, came back to him just as if he was hearing and seeing it now. 'Good-for-nothing. What you need is a good hiding.' And the more he remembered, the more furious with his father he became. He remembered his father saying to him 'I can see how you will end up – as a swindler. Don't say I didn't warn you' – and – 'You'll end up as a swindler if you go on like this.' 'It's all right for him,' he thought, 'he's forgotten what it was like when he was young. And what are these crimes I have committed? Just going to the theatre, and running out of money, and borrowing some from Petya Grushetsky. What's so dreadful about that? Anybody else would have been sympathetic and asked me all about it, but all he does is rage at me and think of nobody but himself. Whenever he doesn't get what he wants he shouts the house down, but I, I am a swindler. No, my father he may be, but I don't love him. I don't know whether all fathers are the same as he is, but I don't love him.'

The maid knocked at his door. She had brought him a note.

'They said you were to reply at once.'

The note read: 'This is the third time I am having to ask you to return the six roubles you borrowed from me, but you keep trying to get out of it. That is not how honourable men behave. I ask you to send the money at once by the bearer of this note. I am extremely hard up myself. Surely you can get it? Your – depending whether you pay me or you don't – contemptuous or respectful friend, Grushetsky.'

'Well, what do you make of that? What a swine. He can't wait for a bit. I shall just have to have another try.'

Mitya went to see his mother. This was his last hope. His mother was a kind-hearted woman who found it hard to refuse him anything, and she might indeed have helped him, but just now she was anxious about the illness of her youngest child, two-year-old Petya. She was annoyed with Mitya for coming in and making a noise, and she turned down his request on the spot.

He muttered something under his breath and started to walk out of the room. Feeling sorry for her son, she called him back.

'Just a minute, Mitya,' she said. 'I haven't any money at the moment but I can get some tomorrow.'

But Mitya was still seething with bitter anger against his father.

'What's the use of telling me "tomorrow", when I need it right away? You may as well know that I am going to see a friend to ask him for it.'

He went out, banging the door.

'There's nothing else to be done. He'll tell me where I can go to pawn my watch,' he thought, feeling for the watch which he had in his pocket.

Mitya took the coupon and the change out of the desk drawer, put on his overcoat and set off to see his friend Makhin.

II

Makhin too was a schoolboy, but a sophisticated one. He played cards and knew women, and he always had money. He lived with his aunt. Mitya was aware that Makhin was a bad character, but when he was with him he automatically deferred to Makhin's authority. Makhin was at home, getting ready to go out to the theatre: his scruffy little room smelt of scented soap and eau de Cologne.

'It's the last straw, my friend,' said Makhin when Mitya had told him his woeful story, shown him the coupon and the fifty copecks, and explained that he was in need of nine roubles. 'You could actually pawn your watch, but there is an even better way,' said Makhin, winking his eye.

'What sort of a better way?'

'It's really very simple.' Makhin took the coupon. 'You just need to put in a figure one in front of the 2 r.50, and it will read 12 r.50.'

'But are there coupons for that amount?'

'Naturally there are, on thousand-rouble bonds. I passed off one myself once.'

'But surely it's not possible?'

'Well, shall we have a go?' said Makhin, taking a pen and smoothing out the coupon with a finger of his left hand.

'But it can't be right.'

'Oh, what nonsense.'

'He was quite right,' thought Mitya, remembering again the bad things his father had said about him: a swindler. 'I'll be a swindler now.' He looked Makhin in the face. Makhin was looking at him and smiling quietly.

'Well then, shall we have a go?'

'All right, go ahead.'

Makhin painstakingly traced out a figure one.

'Right, now we'll go to a shop. The one on the corner there that sells photographic supplies. I happen to need a frame, to go round this person here.'

He produced a mounted photograph of a young woman with large eyes, luxuriant hair and a magnificent bosom.

'A real peach, eh?'

'Yes, yes, absolutely. But all the same ...'

'It's very simple. Let's go.'

Makhin put his coat on and the two of them went out together.

III

The bell over the door to the photographic shop gave a tinkle. The schoolboys entered and looked round the empty shop with its shelves of photographic supplies and glass display cases on the counters. From the door at the back of the shop emerged a plain-looking woman with a kindly face who took up her position behind the counter and asked them what they required.

'A nice little picture-frame, Madame.'

'At what sort of price?' asked the lady, swiftly and expertly running her mittened hands with their swollen finger joints over the various types of frames. 'These are priced at fifty copecks, these are a little dearer. And this one here is very nice, a new style – it costs one rouble twenty.'

'Very well, I'll take that one. But couldn't you knock it down a bit? I'll give you a rouble for it.'

'All the prices here are fixed,' said the lady with dignity.

'All right, as you wish,' said Makhin, putting the coupon down on the top of the display case. 'Please give me the frame and my change, and as quickly as you can, please. We don't want to be late for the theatre.'

'You have plenty of time yet,' said the lady, and she began examining the coupon with her shortsighted eyes.

'It'll look charming in that frame, won't it, eh?' said Makhin, turning to Mitya.

'Haven't you got any other money?' asked the saleslady.

'That's just the problem. I haven't. My father gave it to me, and I need to get it changed.'

'And do you really not have a rouble and twenty copecks on you?'

'I do have fifty copecks. But what's the matter, are you afraid we are going to swindle you with forged money?'

'No, I didn't say that.'

'Well, let me have it back please. We'll find somewhere else to change it.'

'So how much do I have to give you?'

'Let's see now, it should come to eleven something.'

The saleslady flicked the beads on her abacus, unlocked the bureau which served as a till, took out a ten-rouble note, and rummaging among the small change assembled a further six twenty-copeck and two five-copeck pieces.

'Would you kindly wrap it up for me please?' said Makhin, unhurriedly taking the money.

'Right away.'

The saleslady wrapped up the frame and tied the package with string.

Mitya only began to breathe easily once more when the entrance bell had tinkled behind them and they had emergd into the street.

'Well now, here's ten roubles for you, and let me take the rest. I'll give it back.'

And Makhin went off to the theatre, leaving Mitya to go and see Grushetsky and settle up with him.

IV

An hour after the boys had left the shop the owner returned home and started to count the takings.

'Oh, you stupid, muddling woman! What a fool you are!' he shouted at his wife as soon as he saw the coupon and immediately spotted the forgery. 'And why on earth have you been accepting coupons at all?'

'But I've been there when you have accepted them yourself, Zhenya, and they were twelve-rouble coupons just like this one,' said his wife, who was growing confused and angry and was on the point of bursting into tears. 'I don't know myself how they managed to take me in, those schoolboys.

He was a handsome young man too, he really looked so *comme il faut*.'[2]

'And you're a simpleton *comme il faut*,' shouted her husband abusively as he went on counting the contents of the till. 'I accept a coupon when I know and can see clearly what is written on it. But you no doubt spend your whole life gazing at the ugly mugs of schoolboys.'

His wife could take no more of this, and she too lost her temper.

'There's a man for you! Always blaming other people – and when you go and lose fifty-four roubles at cards, that's a mere nothing!'

'I – that's a different matter altogether.'

'I'm not talking to you any longer,' said his wife, and she went off to her room and began to recall how her family had been against her becoming the wife of this man who was socially so much her inferior, and how she had herself insisted on the marriage; she recalled her child who had died, and her husband's indifference at this loss, and she felt such hatred of her husband that she thought how glad she would be if he were to die. But when she had thought that she became alarmed at her own feelings and hastened to get dressed and go out. When her husband got back to their apartment she had already left. Without waiting for him she had put on her coat and driven by herself to the house of a teacher of French, an acquaintance of theirs, who had invited them to a social gathering that evening.

V

At the house of the French teacher, a Russian Pole, there was a formal tea party with sweet pastries, after which the guests sat down at several tables to play vint.[3]

The photographic-shop owner's wife was at a table with the host, an army officer and an elderly deaf lady in a wig who was the widow of a music-shop owner, and a passionate

2 Gentlemanly, respectable.
3 A card game resembling bridge.

and very good card-player. The play was going in favour of the photographic supplier's wife: she made two slams. Beside her was a plate containing grapes and a pear, and she was now in a thoroughly cheerful mood.

'Why isn't Yevgeny Mikhailovich here yet?' asked the hostess from another table. 'We were counting on him for our fifth hand.'

'I expect he's got tied up in doing the accounts,' said Yevgeny Mikhailovich's wife. 'This is the day when he settles the accounts for the groceries and the firewood.'

And remembering the scene with her husband she frowned, and her hands in their mittens trembled from the resentment she felt towards him.

'Well, talk of the devil,' said the host, turning towards Yevgeny Mikhailovich, who had just walked in. 'What kept you?'

'Oh, various kinds of business,' replied Yevgeny Mikhailovich in a jovial voice, rubbing his hands together. And to his wife's surprise, he came over to her and said:

'You know that coupon – I managed to get rid of it.'

'Really?'

'Yes, I gave it to a peasant for some firewood.'

And with great indignation Yevgeny Mikhailovich told everybody the story – with additional details supplied by his wife – of how some unscrupulous schoolboys had managed to dupe his wife.

'Well now, let's get on with the main business,' he said, sitting down at the table when his turn arrived and shuffling the cards.

VI

Yevgeny Mikhailovich had indeed managed to get rid of the coupon to a muzhik named Ivan Mironov in payment for some firewood.

Ivan Mironov's trade involved buying up single *sazhens*[4]

4 *Sazhen*: a measure equivalent to 2.13 metres (here cubic).

of firewood from the timber warehouses and delivering them to the townspeople; but he would divide the *sazhen* of wood into five parts, each of which he sold at the price a quarter-load would fetch in the woodyards. Early in the morning of this day which proved so ill-fated for him, Ivan Mironov had carted out an eighth-load intending to sell it, but he drove about until evening looking in vain for a customer. He continually came across experienced townsfolk who knew all about the tricks played by muzhik firewood-vendors and refused to believe his assurances that he had brought in this firewood from the country. He was getting really hungry and felt chilled to the marrow in his worn sheepskin jacket and his tattered cloth under-coat; by evening the temperature had dropped to twenty degrees of frost; and his little horse, which he had been driving pitilessly because he was at the point of selling it to the knacker, came to a complete stand-still. So that Ivan Mironov was even ready to consider selling off the firewood at a loss, when he encountered Yevgeny Mikhailovich who had popped out to the tobacconist's and was now on his way home.

'Do you want some firewood, master? I'll let you have it cheap. My horse won't go any further.'

'And where are you from, then?'

'From the country, sir. My own firewood it is, and good and dry too.'

'We know your sort. Well, so what are you asking for it?' Ivan Mironov named an absurdly high sum, then started progressively to reduce it, and finally let the firewood go for his usual price.

'Just for you, master, seeing as it's not too far to deliver it,' he said.

Yevgeny Mikhailovich did not waste too much time bargaining since he was pleased at the thought that he would now be able to pass on the coupon. Somehow or other, hauling on the shafts of the cart himself, Ivan Mironov managed to drag the load into the courtyard of the house and personally unloaded it into the woodshed. There was no yardman about. At first Ivan Mironov was reluctant to accept the coupon, but Yevgeny Mikhailovich was so persuasive and looked to be such an important gentleman, that he agreed to take it.

Entering the maids' quarters from the back porch, Ivan Mironov crossed himself, wiped the melting icicles from his beard, and turning back the flap of his sheepskin jacket, drew out a small leather purse and took from it eight roubles and fifty copecks in change. He handed over the money, and the coupon he rolled up in a piece of paper and put away in his purse.

Having thanked the gentleman in a manner befitting his rank, Ivan Mironov induced his wretched, doomed, frost-covered horse to get his legs moving, not by the whip but by the use of the whip handle, and drove the empty cart away in the direction of the tavern.

Once inside the tavern Ivan Mironov ordered himself eight copecks' worth of vodka and tea, and when he had warmed himself up and even begun to perspire a little and was in a really cheerful state of mind, he fell to chatting with the yardman who was sitting at the same table. He soon warmed to the conversation and told the yardman all about himself: how he came from the village of Vasilyevskoye twelve versts from the town, how he had taken his share of the family goods and left his father and brothers, and was now living with his wife and two sons, the elder of whom was attending a trade school and so wasn't yet able to help him financially. He told him how he was staying in lodgings here in town and that tomorrow he was going to the knacker to sell his old hack, and he would see, but if it worked out all right he might buy himself a new horse. He told him how he had managed to put by some twenty-five roubles, and half the money was in the form of a coupon. He took out the coupon and showed it to the yardman. The yardman could not read or write but he said that he had changed money like that for the tenants and that it was good money, but there were forgeries about, and for that reason he advised him to be on the safe side and to get it changed here at the tavern bar. Ivan Mironov handed the coupon to the waiter and told him to bring back the cash to him, but the waiter did not bring back the money: instead the bald, shiny-faced tavern manager came over, holding the coupon in his pudgy hand.

'Your money's no good,' he said, pointing at the coupon but not returning it.

'That's good money – a gentleman gave it me.'

'This money is not good, it's counterfeit.'

'Well, if it's counterfeit, give it back to me.'

'No, my man, people like you need to be taught a lesson. You and your swindling friends have been tampering with it.'

'Let me have my money, what right have you got to do this?'

'Sidor, call the police,' said the barman to the waiter.

Ivan Mironov was drunk, and being drunk he was starting to get worked up. He seized the manager by the collar and shouted:

'Give it back, and I'll go and see the gentleman. I know where to find him.'

The manager struggled free of Ivan Mironov's grasp, tearing his shirt in the process.

'Ah, if that's how you want it – hold him!'

The waiter grabbed Ivan Mironov and at that moment the policeman appeared. Taking charge of the situation he listened to their explanations, then quickly brought things to a conclusion.

'Down to the station with you.'

The policeman put the coupon into his own wallet and led Ivan Mironov and his horse off to the police station.

VII

Ivan Mironov spent the night in the cells at the police station along with drunks and thieves. It was not until almost noon the next day that he was summoned to appear before the local police officer. The officer questioned him and then sent him along with the constable to see the proprietor of the photographic shop. Ivan Mironov was able to remember the name of the street and the number of the house.

When the policeman had summoned the gentleman to the door and confronted him with the coupon and Ivan Mironov, who confirmed that this was the very gentleman who had given him the coupon, Yevgeny Mikhailovich put on an expression first of astonishment, and then of stern disapproval.

'Whatever are you talking about? You must be out of your mind. This is the first time I have ever set eyes on him.'

'Master, it's a sin to say that, remember we've all got to die,' said Ivan Mironov.

'What's the matter with him? You must have been dreaming. It was someone else you sold your firewood to,' said Yevgeny Mikhailovich. 'Anyway, wait there and I'll go and ask my wife if she bought any firewood yesterday.'

Yevgeny Mikhailovich went away and at once called the yardman to him. The yardman, Vasily, was a good-looking, unusually strong and nimble fellow, cheery in nature and something of a dandy. Yevgeny Mikhailovich told him that if anyone asked him where the last lot of firewood had come from he should say that they had got it from the woodyard and that they never bought firewood from muzhiks.

'There's a muzhik here claiming that I gave him a forged coupon. He's a muddle-headed peasant, but you're a man of understanding. So you tell him that we only ever buy our firewood from the woodyard. Oh, and I've been meaning for some time to give you this towards a new jacket,' added Yevgeny Mikhailovich, and he gave the yardman five roubles.

Vasily took the money, his eyes darting from the banknote to Yevgeny Mikhailovich's face, tossed back his hair and gave a slight smile.

'Everyone knows the common people are slow-witted. It's lack of education. Don't you worry, sir. I shall know well enough what to say.'

However tearfully Ivan Mironov begged Yevgeny Mikhailovich to acknowledge that the coupon was his, and the yardman to confirm what he was saying, both Yevgeny

Mikhailovich and the yardman stuck to their line: they had never bought firewood off carts. And the policeman took Ivan Mironov back to the police station where he was charged with forging a coupon.

Only by following the advice of his cellmate, a drunken clerk, and by slipping the local police officer a five-rouble note, did Ivan Mironov succeed in getting out of detention, minus his coupon and with just seven roubles instead of the twenty-five he had had the day before. Ivan Mironov used three of the seven roubles to get drunk, and with a face full of utter dejection and dead drunk he drove home to his wife.

His wife was pregnant and nearing her time, and she was feeling ill. She began swearing at her husband, he shoved her away, and she started hitting him. He did not retaliate, but lay belly down on the plank bed and wept loudly.

Only the next morning did his wife discover what had happened, and believing what her husband said, spent a long time cursing that brigand of a gentleman who had deceived her Ivan. And Ivan, who had now sobered up, remembered the advice of the factory-hand he had been drinking with the previous evening, and decided to go and find an *ablocate* and lodge a complaint.

VIII

The advocate took on the case, not so much for any money he might make from it, but rather because he believed Ivan Mironov and was indignant at the way this muzhik had been so shamelessly defrauded.

Both parties were present at the hearing, and Vasily the yardman was the sole witness. At the hearing it all came out as it had done before. Ivan Mironov referred to God and to the fact that we shall all die. Yevgeny Mikhailovich, although uncomfortably aware of the unpleasantness and the danger of what he was doing, could not now alter his testimony, and he continued with an outwardly calm appearance to deny everything.

Vasily the yardman received a further ten roubles and went

on asserting with a calm smile that he had never before so much as set eyes on Ivan Mironov. And when he was called to take the oath, although he quailed inwardly, he maintained a calm exterior as he repeated the words of the oath after the old priest specially brought in for this function, swearing on the cross and the Holy Gospel that he would tell the whole truth and nothing but the truth.

The proceedings ended with the judge dismissing the case brought by Ivan Mironov and decreeing that he was liable for court costs of five roubles, which Yevgeny Mikhailovich magnanimously paid on his behalf. Discharging Ivan Mironov, the judge admonished him to be more careful in future about making accusations against respectable people and said that he should be duly grateful that the court costs had been met for him and that he was not being prosecuted for slander, which could have led to his spending three months or more in prison.

'We humbly thank you, sir,' said Ivan Mironov, and shaking his head and sighing he left the courtroom.

It seemed as if the whole affair had ended well for Yevgeny Mikhailovich and for Vasily the yardman. But that was only how it looked. Something had actually happened which no one could see, something far more serious than anything merely human eyes could perceive.

It was more than two years now since Vasily had left his village and come to live in the town. With each year that passed he sent his father less and less of his earnings, and he did not get round to sending for his wife to come and join him, since he felt no need of her. Here in the town he had as many women as he could wish for, and not the sort of women who were anything like his old hag of a wife. With each year that passed Vasily forgot more and more the rules and standards of country life and became increasingly at home with the ways of the town. Back there in the country everything had been crude, dreary, impoverished and messy, but here everything was civilized, well-kept, clean and luxurious, as it ought to be. And he became more and more convinced that the country people lacked any understanding of life, like the beasts of the forest, whereas here – these people were real human beings. He read books by good authors, novels, and he went to theatrical performances at the People's House.[5] In his home village you would never see anything like that, not even in your dreams. In his village the old men would say: 'Live with your wife according to the law, work hard, don't eat too much and don't get above yourself'; but here people were clever, educated – and that meant they understood the real laws of life – and lived for their own pleasure. And it was all wonderful. Before the court case with the coupon Vasily had still not believed that the upper classes had no law governing the way they lived. He had always thought they must have some such law, although he did not know what it was. But this court hearing over the coupon, and most of all, his own perjury, which despite his fears had brought him no unpleasant repercussions but had actually earned him an extra ten roubles, convinced him that there were no laws at all, and that a man should simply live for his own pleasure. And so he did, and so he went on doing. To begin with he merely took a little extra profit on the purchases he made for the tenants, but this was not enough to meet all his expenses, so he began, whenever he could, to pilfer money and valuables from the tenants' apartments, and he even stole Yevgeny Mikhailovich's wallet. Yevgeny Mikhailovich, certain of Vasily's guilt, did not start proceedings against him, but gave him the sack.

Vasily had no desire to return home, but went on living in Moscow with his mistress while he looked for work. He found a low-paid job as a yardman to a small shopkeeper. Vasily started in the job, but the next month he was caught stealing sacks. His employer did not lodge an official complaint, but beat Vasily and threw him out. After this incident he was unable to find another job, his money was running out and he was getting short of clothes, so that in the end he was left with a single tattered coat, a pair of trousers and some down-at-heel shoes. His mistress abandoned him. But

5 An educational and cultural centre for working people.

Vasily did not lose his bright and cheery disposition, and he waited until it was spring again, and then set off on foot for his home village.

IX

Pyotr Nikolayevich Sventitsky, a short stocky man who wore dark glasses (he had trouble with his eyes and was in danger of losing his sight altogether), got up as usual before daybreak, and after drinking a glass of tea, put on his knee-length sheepskin coat trimmed with lambskin and set off to make the rounds of his property.

Pyotr Nikolayevich had been a customs officer and in that profession he had saved up the sum of eighteen thousand roubles. He had retired some twelve years earlier, not quite of his own volition, and had bought the small estate of a young landowner who had squandered his fortune. Pyotr Nikolayevich had married when he was still in government service. His wife, the poor orphaned daughter of an old aristocratic family, was a sturdy, plump and attractive woman who had borne him no children. Pyotr Nikolayevich was a man thorough and persistent in all his dealings. Although he knew nothing about farming (he was the son of a minor Polish nobleman) he went into it so efficiently that in ten years his ramshackle estate of three hundred *desyatins*[6] had become a model of its kind. All the structures he put up, from the house itself to the barn and the shelter for the fire-hose, were solid and reliable, covered with sheet-iron and regularly repainted. In the equipment shed there was an orderly array of carts, wooden and metal ploughs, and harrows. All the harnesses were kept well greased. The horses were of a modest size and almost always from his own stud, with light-brown coats and black mane and tail, sturdy and well-fed animals, matched in pairs. The threshing-machine operated in its own covered barn, the feed was stored in a special shed, and the manure slurry flowed away into a

6 One *desyatin* = 1.09 hectares or 2.7 acres.

properly paved pit. The cows too were bred on the estate, not particularly large, but good milkers. The pigs were of an English breed. There was a poultry-yard with hens of particularly good egg-laying strains. The fruit trees in the orchard were kept coated with grease and systematically replaced with new plants. Everything that could be seen was businesslike, clean, reliable and meticulous. Pyotr Nikolayevich took great delight in his estate and was proud of the fact that he had achieved all this not by treating his peasants oppressively, but on the contrary, by observing the strictest fairness in his dealings with them. Even in the society of the local nobility he maintained a moderate position that was more liberal than conservative, and invariably defended the common people to the advocates of serfdom. Treat them well, and they'll treat you well in return. True, he did not tolerate blunders and mistakes on the part of the men who worked for him and he would occasionally be seen in person urging them to greater efforts; he demanded hard work, but on the other hand the lodging and the victuals provided were of the very best, the wages were always paid on time, and on festival days he treated his men to vodka.

Stepping carefully over the melting snow – this was in February – Pyotr Nikolayevich made his way past the farm-hands' stable towards the large hut in which the farm-hands lived. It was still dark, all the darker because of the fog, but in the windows of the living-hut some light could be seen. The farm-hands were just getting up. He was intending to hurry them along: according to the work schedule six of them were to take a cart over to the copse and collect the last loads of firewood.

'What's this then?' he wondered, seeing the door of the stable wide open.

'Hey, who's in there?'

No one answered. Pyotr Nikolayevich went into the stable.

'Who's in there, I say?'

There was still no answer. It was dark in the stable, the ground beneath his feet was soft and there was a smell of manure. To the right of the doorway was a stall which should have been occupied by a pair of young chestnut horses. Pyotr Nikolayevich stretched out his hand – but the stall was empty. He felt in front of him with his foot. Perhaps the horses might be lying down. His foot encountered nothing but empty space. 'Where can they have taken them?' he thought. Could they have been taken out to be harnessed up? No, the sleigh was still there outside. He went outside again and called loudly: 'Hey, Stepan.'

Stepan was the head farm-hand. He was just emerging from the living-hut.

'Hello there!' Stepan called back cheerfully. 'Is that you, Pyotr Nikolaich? The lads are on their way.'

'Why have you left the stable door open?'

'The stable? I've no idea. Hey, Proshka, bring us a lantern here.' Proshka came running up with a lantern. They all went into the stable. Stepan realized at once what had occurred.

'We've had thieves here, Pyotr Nikolaich. The lock's been broken.'

'That can't be, surely.'

'They've taken them, the scoundrels. Mashka's gone, so is Hawk. No, he's over here. But Dapple isn't here. And neither is Beauty.'

Three horses were missing. Pyotr Nikolayevich did not say anything. He was frowning and breathing heavily.

'Ah, if I could get my hands on them ... Who was on watch?'

'Pyetka. Pyetka fell asleep.'

Pyotr Nikolayevich reported the theft to the police, to the district police superintendent and to the head of the zemstvo,[7] and he sent out his own men to look for the horses. But they were not found.

'Filthy peasants!' said Pyotr Nikolayevich, 'Doing this to me. Haven't I been good to them? Just you wait. Bandits they are, the lot of them. From now on you're going to get different treatment from me.'

7 An elected district council which functioned in Russia from 1864 to 1917.

X

But the horses – three chestnuts – had already been taken to outlying places. Mashka they sold to some gypsies for eighteen roubles; the second horse, Dapple, was exchanged for a peasant's horse in a village forty versts away; and Beauty they simply rode until he dropped, then slaughtered him. They sold his hide for three roubles. The leader of this enterprise was Ivan Mironov. He had worked for Pyotr Nikolayevich in the past, knew his way round the estate, and had decided to get some of his money back. And had consequently thought up the whole plan.

After his misfortune with the forged coupon Ivan Mironov embarked on a long drinking bout and would have drunk away everything he possessed if his wife had not hidden from him the horse collars, his clothes, and anything else he might have sold to buy vodka. All the time he was on his binge Ivan Mironov was thinking incessantly not just about the individual who had wronged him, but about all the masters, some of them worse than others, who only lived by what they could filch from the likes of him. On one occasion Ivan Mironov was drinking with some peasants who came from a place near Podolsk. And as they travelled along the road the muzhiks told him about how they had driven off some horses belonging to another muzhik. Ivan Mironov began ticking off those horse-thieves for committing such an offence against another muzhik. 'It's a sin,' he said. 'To a muzhik his horse is just like a brother, yet you go and deprive him of it. If you want to steal horses, then steal them from the masters. That's all those sons of bitches deserve anyway.' The further they went the more they talked, and the muzhiks from Podolsk said that if you wanted to steal horses from the gentry you had to be clever about it. You needed to know all about the lie of the land, and if you hadn't got someone on the inside, it couldn't be done. Then Ivan Mironov remembered about Sventitsky, on whose estate he had once lived and worked, and he remembered how Sventitsky had held back a rouble and a half from his wages to pay for a broken kingpin, and he remembered too the chestnut horses he had worked with on the farm.

Ivan Mironov went and saw Sventitsky on the pretext of looking for work, but in reality he was there to see how things were and find out all he could. Having done that, and discovered that there was no night-watchman and that the horses were kept in separate loose-boxes in the stable, he called in the horse-thieves and saw the whole business through.

After splitting the proceeds with the muzhiks from Podolsk Ivan Mironov returned to his village with five roubles. At home there was no work for him to do: he had no horse. And from that time on Ivan Mironov took to associating with horse-thieves and gypsies.

XI

Pyotr Nikolayevich Sventitsky did everything in his power to find the horse-thieves. He knew that the raid could not have been carried out without the help of one of his employees. And so he began to regard his farm-hands with suspicion and to enquire which of the farm-workers had not been sleeping at the farm on the night in question. He was told that Proshka Nikolayev had not spent that night at the farm. Proshka was a young fellow who had just returned from doing his military service, a good-looking, nimble fellow whom Pyotr Nikolayevich used to take with him on outings to serve as a coachman. The district superintendent of police was a friend of Pyotr Nikolayevich's, and he was also acquainted with the chief constable, the marshal of the nobility, the leader of the zemstvo and the investigating magistrate. All these persons regularly came to his name-day celebrations and were familiar with his delicious fruit liqueurs and his pickled mushrooms – white mushrooms, honey agarics and milk agarics. They all sympathized with him and attempted to offer him their help.

'There you are, and you are the one who is always defending the muzhiks,' said the district superintendent. 'I was telling the truth when I told you they were worse than wild animals. You can't do a thing with them unless you use the knout and the rod. So you say it was this Proshka, the one who rides out with you as coachman, do you?'

'Yes, he's the one.'

'Have him brought in here, please.'

Proshka was summoned and they began to question him.

'Where were you that night?'

Proshka tossed his hair back and flashed them a glance.

'At home.'

'What do you mean, "at home"? All the farm-hands say you were not there.'

'As you please, sir.'

'We're not talking about what I please. So where were you?'

'At home.'

'Very well, then. Constable, take this man to the district station.'

'As you please, sir.'

So Proshka still refused to say where he had been on the night of the raid, but the reason for his obstinacy was that he had spent the night with his girlfriend Parasha and he had promised not to give her away, so he did not do so. But there was no evidence. Proshka was released again. However, Pyotr Nikolayevich was sure that the raid had been wholly the work of this Prokofy Nikolayev, and from that time on he began to hate him. One day when Pyotr Nikolayevich had taken him out with him as coachman, he sent him off to the posting station to fetch the horses some fodder. Proshka, as was his custom, bought two measures of oats at a coaching inn. He fed one-and-a-half measures to the horses and exchanged the remaining half-measure for vodka. Pyotr Nikolayevich found out about this and informed the local justice of the peace. The justice of the peace sentenced Proshka to three months in gaol. Prokofy was a man with a good opinion of himself. He considered himself superior to others and was proud of it. Being in prison was a humiliating experience for him. He could no longer give himself airs among his fellow men, and he fell at once into a gloomy state of mind.

Proshka returned home from gaol embittered, not so much against Pyotr Nikolayevich, as against the world in general. As everyone said, after his time in prison Prokofy lost heart, and he took to drinking, was soon caught stealing clothes from a tradesman's wife, and again landed up in gaol.

Meanwhile all that Pyotr Nikolayevich could discover about the horses was that someone had come across the hide of a chestnut gelding, and Pyotr Nikolayevich identified it as Beauty's. And the impunity of these thieves came to exasperate Pyotr Nikolayevich more and more. Now he could not set eyes on muzhiks or even talk about them without being filled with anger, and whenever he had the chance he came down on them as hard as possible.

XII

Although, once he had passed on the coupon, Yevgeny Mikhailovich had stopped thinking about it, his wife Mariya Vasilyevna was unable to forgive either herself for having been duped, or her husband for the cruel things he had said to her, or – and this was the main thing – those two young villains for having taken her in so cleverly.

From the day of the deception onwards she began to look very closely at any grammar-school boys she encountered. Once she actually met Makhin but did not recognize him because he saw her first and contorted his features so effectively that it completely altered his face. But when two weeks later she came face to face with Mitya Smokovnikov on the pavement, she recognized him at once. She let him go by, then turned on her heel and walked after him. On reaching the flat where he lived she made enquiries and found out whose son he was, and the next day she went to the grammar school, where in the entrance hall she met Mikhail Vvedensky, the scripture teacher. He enquired what he could do for her. She replied that she wanted to see the headmaster.

'Unfortunately the headmaster is not here – he is unwell; but perhaps I can help you, or take a message for him.'

Mariya Vasilyevna decided to tell the scripture teacher everything.

Father Vvedensky was a widower, a graduate from the theological academy, and a man of considerable self-esteem. The previous year he had come across Smokovnikov senior at a society meeting in the course of a discussion about religious belief, in which Smokovnikov had soundly trounced him on all points and exposed him to ridicule. As a result Vvedensky had resolved to keep a watchful eye on the son, and having detected in him the same indifference to the Divine Law that his unbelieving father had displayed, he began to persecute him, and even failed him in an examination.

Having found out from Mariya Vasilyevna about young Smokovnikov's escapade, Vvedensky could not help feeling a certain satisfaction, seeing in this incident a confirmation of his own prejudices concerning those immoral people who lacked the guidance of the Church, and he decided to make use of the incident in order, as he tried to assure himself, to reveal the dangers threatening all those who abandoned the Church and her ways – but in the depths of his soul he simply wanted to get his own back on a proud and self-confident atheist.

'Yes, it is very sad, very sad,' said Father Vvedensky, stroking the smooth edges of his pectoral cross. 'I am so glad you have entrusted this matter to me: as a servant of the Church I shall naturally try to make sure that the young man is not left without moral guidance, but I shall also do my best to make his edification as gentle as possible.'

'Yes, I shall act in a way which befits my calling,' said Father Vvedensky to himself, thinking that he had now quite forgotten the father's hostility towards him and that he desired nothing but the moral good and salvation of the boy.

Next day during the scripture lesson Father Mikhail told his pupils all about the episode of the forged coupon and informed them that it was a grammar-school pupil who had been responsible for it.

'It was a vile, shameful act,' he said, 'but concealing it is even worse. If it was one of you who did this – which I cannot believe – then it would be better for him to own up to it than to hide his guilt.'

As he said this he was staring straight at Mitya Smokovnikov. Mitya went red and started to sweat, then he burst into tears and ran from the classroom.

When Mitya's mother heard about these events she persuaded her son to tell her the whole truth and then hurried off to the photographic supply shop. She paid back the twelve roubles fifty to the proprietor's wife and induced her to keep quiet about the schoolboy's name. She then instructed her son to deny everything, and on no account to make any confession to his father.

And indeed, when Fyodor Mikhailovich heard what had happened at the grammar school, and when his son on being questioned denied it all, he went to see the headmaster and explained the whole matter to him, saying that the scripture teacher's conduct had been deeply reprehensible and that he did not intend to let things rest there. The headmaster called in the scripture teacher and a heated exchange took place between him and Fyodor Mikhailovich.

'A stupid woman attempted to pin something on my son and then retracted her accusation, and you could find nothing better to do than to slander the honour of a thoroughly upright boy.'

'I did not slander him, and I will not permit you to speak to me in such a tone. You are forgetting my vocation.'

'I don't give a fig for your vocation.'

'Your deluded opinions, sir,' said the scripture teacher, his chin quivering so that his scanty little beard trembled in sympathy, 'your deluded opinions are well known to the whole town.'

'Gentlemen, Father,' said the headmaster, attempting to pacify the two disputants. But to pacify them was impossible.

'My holy vocation makes it my duty to concern myself with the moral and religious upbringing of the young.'

'Enough of this pretence. Do you think I don't know that you haven't a grain of genuine religious faith in you?'

'I consider it beneath me to continue talking to such a

gentleman as you,' declared Father Mikhail, who had been
particularly offended by Smokovnikov's last remark, since he
knew that it was accurate. He had gone through the whole
course at the theological academy and consequently had
long since ceased to believe in what he professed and what
he preached; in fact he believed only that everyone ought
to make themselves believe those things which he had made
himself believe.

Smokovnikov was not so much infuriated by the scripture
teacher's behaviour, as by discovering this striking example
of the clerical influence which was beginning to manifest
itself throughout our society, and he told everyone about
the incident.

Father Vvedensky on the other hand, seeing in it a demonstration of the nihilism and atheism which had taken hold
not only of the younger generation but of the older one as
well, became more and more convinced of the necessity of
combating them. The more he condemned the unbelief of
Smokovnikov and his kind, the more convinced he became
of the firm and unshakable character of his own faith, and
the less need he felt to test his faith or to reconcile it with
his actual way of living. His faith, acknowledged by the
world around him, was for him his principal weapon in his
fight against those who denied it.

These thoughts, called forth by his clash with Smokovnikov, together with the disagreeable events at the grammar
school which followed in its wake – namely, a reprimand
and a caution from the school authorities – impelled him to
take a decision which had been tantalizing him for a long
time, since the death of his wife, in fact: to take monastic
vows and thus opt for a career already followed by several of
his fellow-students at the academy, one of whom was already
a member of the hierarchy, another the superior of a monastery, and expected soon to be made a bishop.

Towards the end of the academic year Vvedensky left the
grammar school, took his monastic vows and the new name
of Misail, and was very soon given the rectorship of a
seminary in a town on the Volga.

XIII

Meanwhile Vasily the yardman had set out on the highroad to the south.

By day he walked, and at night the local policeman would show him to the usual quarters provided for wanderers. Wherever he went people gave him bread, and sometimes even asked him in to have supper with them. In one village in the Oryol province where he was spending the night he was told that a merchant who had leased an orchard from the landowner was looking for fit young fellows as night-watchmen. Vasily was tired of living as a beggar but he did not want to go back to his village, so he went to see the merchant with the orchard and got himself taken on as a night-watchman at a wage of five roubles per month.

Vasily found life in his watchman's hut very pleasant, particularly when the sweet apples had begun to ripen and the other watchmen brought in huge trusses of fresh straw gathered from under the threshing-machine in the master's shed. He would lie the whole day long on the fresh, fragrant straw beside the still more fragrant piles of spring and winter windfall apples, just keeping an eye open to make sure the children were not pilfering the apples still on the trees, and whistling and singing songs. Singing songs Vasily was really good at. He had a fine voice. The women and girls would come up from the village to get some apples. Vasily would laugh and joke with them a bit and gave more or less apples in exchange for eggs or a few copecks to whichever of them took his fancy – and then lie down again, only getting up to have his breakfast or his dinner or his supper.

Vasily possessed only one shirt, a pink cotton one full of holes, and he had nothing to put on his feet, but his body was strong and healthy, and when the porridge pot was taken off the fire Vasily would eat enough for three, so that the old man who was the chief watchman was always amazed at him. Vasily did not sleep at night and would whistle or call out to keep himself awake, and he could see a long way in the dark, like a cat. One night some big boys from the village climbed into the trees to shake the apples down. Vasily crept up and went for them; they did their best to beat him off but he sent them all flying, and took one of them back to the hut and handed him over to the master.

Vasily's first hut was at the far end of the orchard, but the second, where he lived for the sweet apple harvest, was only forty yards from the master's house. And in this hut Vasily enjoyed himself even more. All day long Vasily could see the gentlemen and the young ladies playing games, going out for drives or walks, and in the evenings and at night playing the piano or the violin, singing or dancing. He would see the students and the young ladies sitting in the windows snuggling up to one another, and then some of them would go for walks in the dark avenues of lime trees, where the moonlight only came through in streaks and patches. He would see the servants hurrying about with food and drink, he would see how the cooks, the laundresses, the stewards, the gardeners, the coachmen – all of them worked just to keep the masters supplied with food and drink and amusement. Sometimes the young gentlefolk would drop in to see him in his hut, and he would choose the finest apples, the ripe and rosy ones, to give to them, and the young ladies would bite into them there and then with a crunching noise, and praise the apples and say something – Vasily knew it was about him – in French, and get him to sing for them.

Vasily greatly admired this way of life, remembering the kind of life he had led in Moscow, and the thought that the beginning and the end of everything was to have money came more and more often into his head.

And Vasily began to think more and more about what he could do to get hold of some more money right away. He started to recall how he had made the odd profit before and he decided that that wasn't the way to go about it, just helping yourself to whatever was lying about; he needed to work out things in advance, to see what was what, and do a clean job leaving no evidence behind. Towards Christmas time they picked the last of the winter apples. The boss had made a good profit and he paid off all the watchmen, including Vasily, and thanked them.

Vasily put on the coat and the hat the young master had given him, but he did not go home, for the thought of that brutish, peasant life filled him with disgust – instead he went back to the town with the hard-drinking ex-conscripts who had worked alongside him as watchmen. Once back in the town he decided to break into and burgle the shop owned by his former employer who had beaten him and thrown him out without his wages. He knew the layout of the place and where the money was kept. He got one of the ex-soldiers to stand guard outside, and he himself smashed a window opening on to the yard, climbed in and took all the money. The thing was carried out skilfully, and no traces were found. Vasily got away with three hundred and seventy roubles. He gave a hundred to his assistant and went off with the rest to another town, where he went on a binge with his comrades and girlfriends.

XIV

Meanwhile Ivan Mironov had become an accomplished, daring and successful horse-thief. His wife Afimya, who used to nag him on account of what she called his 'botched schemes', was now well pleased with her husband and even quite proud of him, for he was the owner of a sheepskin coat with a hood, and she had a shawl and a new fur coat.

Everyone in the village and surrounding district knew that there was never a horse-theft in which he was not somehow involved, but they were afraid to give evidence against him, and even when some suspicion did fall on him he invariably emerged without a stain on his character. His most recent theft had been from the night-grazing ground at Kolotovka. As far as possible Ivan Mironov liked to choose who to steal from, and he got particular satisfaction when his victims were landowners and merchants. But stealing from landowners and merchants was more difficult. And so when landowners' and merchants' horses were not accessible he would steal peasants' horses instead. Thus he stole from the night-grazing at Kolotovka as many horses as he could get hold of. This job, however, was carried out not by him, but by a skilful young fellow called Gerasim whom he had persuaded to do it. The muzhiks did not discover that their horses were gone until daybreak, and then they rushed off along all possible roads to look for them. The horses were in fact already hidden in a ravine in the middle of the state forest. Ivan Mironov planned to keep them there until the following night, then to make off with them to a yardman he knew in a place forty versts away. Ivan Mironov visited Gerasim in the forest and brought him some pie and vodka, returning home by a forest path on which he hoped not to meet anybody. Unfortunately for him he came up against a forest guard.

'Been out after mushrooms, have you?' asked the guard.

'Yes, but I haven't found any today,' replied Ivan Mironov, pointing to the bast basket which he had brought with him in case of need.

'That's right, it's not the mushroom season,' said the guard, 'but there'll be some coming up in Lent.' And he went on his way.

The forest guard realized that there was something suspicious here. There was no reason for Ivan Mironov to be out walking in the state forest early in the morning. The guard turned back and started to circle round through the trees. On getting near to the ravine he heard the sound of horses snorting and he crept up very quietly to the place the sound was coming from. The ground in the ravine was trampled by horses' hooves and it was all over horse droppings. A little further on Gerasim was sitting eating something, and there were two horses standing tethered to a tree.

The guard ran back to the village and fetched the village elder, the constable and two witnesses. They approached the place where Gerasim was sitting from three directions, and seized him. Gerasim made no attempt to protest his innocence, but being drunk he at once confessed to everything. He told them that Ivan Mironov had got him drunk and talked him into doing the job, and had promised to come to the forest today to fetch the horses. The muzhiks left the horse and Gerasim where they were in the forest and set an ambush for Ivan Mironov. As soon as night had fallen they heard a whistle. Gerasim whistled back in reply. As soon as Ivan Mironov started to come down the slope they rushed at him, captured him and led him back to their village.

The next morning a crowd assembled in front of the elder's hut. Ivan Mironov was brought out and they began to interrogate him. Stepan Pelageyushkin, a tall, stooping, long-armed muzhik with a beaky nose and a dour expression, was the first to ask him a question. Stepan was an independent peasant who had completed his military service. He had not long since moved out of his father's house and was starting to do quite well, when his horse had been stolen from him. By working for a year in the mines Stepan managed to set himself up with two horses. Both of these had now been stolen.

'Tell me where my horses are,' began Stepan, pale with anger and glaring now at the ground, now straight into Ivan's face.

Ivan Mironov denied all knowledge of them. Then Stepan struck him in the face and broke his nose, from which the blood started to trickle.

'Tell me, or I'll kill you!'

Ivan Mironov bent his head but said nothing. Stepan struck him again with his long arm – once, then a second time. Ivan still did not speak, just swung his head from side to side.

'Come, all of you – beat him!' shouted the village elder. And they all began to beat him. Ivan Mironov fell silently to the ground, then cried out: 'You barbarians, you devils, beat me to death then. I'm not scared of you.'

Then Stepan took hold of a stone from a pile he had ready, and he smashed Ivan Mironov's head in.

XV

Ivan Mironov's murderers were brought to justice. Stepan Pelageyushkin was among them. The charge brought against him was particularly grave because they had all testified that he was the one who had smashed Ivan Mironov's head in with a stone. At his trial Stepan did not try to conceal anything, but explained how when his last pair of horses had been stolen he had reported it at the police station, and they could probably have tracked the horses down with the help of the gypsies, but the district police officer had not even seen him, and had made no effort to organize a search.

'What were we supposed to do with a man of his sort? He'd ruined us.'

'So why didn't the others beat him? Why just you?' asked the prosecutor.

'That's not true. They all beat him, the village community decided to do away with him. I was just the one who finished him off. Why make him suffer more than necessary?'

The judges were struck by Stepan's utterly calm expression as he described what he had done and how they had beaten Ivan Mironov to death and how he had finished him off.

Stepan did not indeed see anything very dreadful in this murder. When he was on his military service he had happened to be one of the firing-squad when a soldier was executed, and then, as also now at the murder of Ivan Mironov, he had seen nothing dreadful in it. If you killed a man, you killed a man. It's his turn today, tomorrow it may be mine.

Stepan's sentence was a light one: a year in prison. His peasant's clothes were taken away from him and put in the prison stores with a number attached to them, and they made him put on a prison overall and some slippers.

Stepan had never had much respect for the authorities, but now he was utterly convinced that everyone in authority, all the masters – apart from the Tsar, who pitied the common people and treated them justly – were all of them robbers, sucking the life-blood of the people. The stories told by the exiles and the hard-labour convicts he met in prison confirmed his view of things. One had been sentenced to exile with hard labour for having denounced the thievery of the local authorities, another for striking an official who was trying unlawfully to seize the property of some peasants, and a third, for forging banknotes. The gentry and the merchants, whatever they did, could get away with it, whereas the muzhiks who had nothing got sent off to prison to feed the lice on account of any little thing whatever.

Stepan's wife came to visit him from time to time in prison. With him away from home things had already been bad enough, but now she was ruined and destitute, and was reduced to begging with the children. The calamities afflicting his wife made Stepan even more bitter. His behaviour was vicious towards everyone he came into contact with in prison, and on one occasion he almost killed one of the cooks with an axe, for which he got an extra year on his sentence. During the course of that year he heard that his wife had died and his household no longer existed . . .

When Stepan had served his time he was summoned to the prison stores, and the clothes he had arrived in were taken down from a little shelf and given back to him.

'Where am I to go now?' he asked the quartermaster-sergeant as he put on his own clothes again.

'Home, of course.'

'I haven't got a home. I reckon I shall just have to go on the road. And rob people.'

'If you start robbing people, you'll soon be back in here again.'

'Well, what will be, will be.'

And Stepan went on his way. Despite what he had said, he set off in the direction of his home. He had nowhere else to go.

On his way there he happened to stop for the night at a coaching inn with a pothouse attached, which he knew.

The inn was kept by a fat tradesman from Vladimir. He knew Stepan. And he knew that Stepan had got himself into prison through bad luck. So he let him stay the night.

This rich tradesman had run off with the wife of a peasant neighbour and was living with her as his wife and business partner.

Stepan knew all about this episode – how the tradesman had offended the muzhik in his honour, and how this wretched woman had walked out on her husband and had grown obese with good eating; and now there she was, sitting all fat and sweaty over her tea – and was kind enough to invite Stepan to have some with her. There were no other travellers staying at the inn. Stepan was allowed to sleep the night in the kitchen. Matryona cleared away all the dishes and went off to the maid's room. Stepan lay down on top of the stove, but he could not get to sleep, and kept snapping under his body the pieces of kindling which had been put there to dry. He could not get out of his head the image of the tradesman's fat paunch bulging out of the waist of his cotton shirt, faded with washing and re-washing. The idea kept coming into his head of taking a knife and slashing that paunch wide open and letting out the fatty intestines. And of doing the same to the woman too. One moment he was saying to himself: 'Come on now, devil take them, I shall be out of here tomorrow,' and the next moment he would remember Ivan Mironov and start thinking again about the tradesman's paunch and Matryona's white, sweaty throat. If he was going to kill one, he might as well kill them both. The cock crew for the second time. If he was going to do it, it had better be now, before it got light. He had noticed a knife the evening before, and an axe. He climbed down from the stove, picked up the axe and the knife and went out of the kitchen. Just as he had got out of the room he heard the click of the latch on another door. The tradesman opened the door and came out. Stepan had not meant to do it like this. He couldn't use the knife in this situation, so he swung the axe up and brought it down, splitting the man's head open. The tradesman collapsed against the lintel of the door and fell to the ground.

Stepan went into the maid's room. Matryona jumped up and stood there by the bed in her nightshirt. Stepan killed her too with the same axe. Then he lit a candle, took the money from the cash desk, and made off.

XVI

In the chief town of a country district, in a house set somewhat apart from the other buildings, lived an old man who had been a civil servant in the days before he had taken to drink, his two daughters, and a son-in-law. The married daughter was also given to drinking and led a disreputable life, but the elder daughter Mariya Semyonovna, a thin, wrinkled woman of fifty whose husband had died, was their sole support on her pension of two hundred and fifty roubles a year. The whole family lived on this money. Mariya Semyonovna also did all the housework. She looked after her weak, drunken old father and her sister's baby, cooked and did the washing. And as is always the case in such situations, all three of them loaded all their wants and needs on to her, all three of them shouted abuse at her, and the son-in-law would even beat her when he was in a drunken state. She endured it all meekly and silently, and again, as is always the case, the more things she was expected to do, the more she managed to carry out. She even gave aid to the poor, to her own cost, giving away her clothing, and she helped to look after the sick.

On one occasion Mariya Semyonovna had a village tailor, a cripple who had lost one leg, staying in the house to do some work for her. He was altering her old father's coat and re-covering her sheepskin jacket with cloth for her to wear to market in the winter.

The crippled tailor was an intelligent and perceptive man who had met with a great variety of people in the course of his work, and because of his disability had to spend most of his time sitting down, which disposed him to do a lot of thinking. After living for a week in Mariya Semyonovna's household he was lost in wonderment for the life she led. Once she came into the kitchen where he was sewing, to wash some towels, and she chatted with him about his life, and how his brother had taken his share of the property and gone off to live on his own.

'I thought it would be better like that, but I'm still as poor as ever.'

'It's better not to change things, but to go on living as you've always lived,' said Mariya Semyonovna.

'That's what amazes me so much about you, Mariya Semyonovna, that you're always bustling about here and there worrying about other people's needs. But as I see it, you get precious little good back from them in return.'

Mariya Semyonovna did not answer.

'You must have decided that it's like it says in the holy books, that you'll get your reward in the next world.'

'We don't know about that,' said Mariya Semyonovna, 'but I'm sure it's better to live in that way.'

'And is that what it says in the holy books?'

'Yes, that's what it says,' she replied, and she read him the Sermon on the Mount from the Gospels. The tailor fell to thinking. And when he had been paid off and he had returned home he still kept thinking about what he had seen in Mariya Semyonovna's house, and about what she had said to him and read to him.

XVII

Pyotr Nikolayevich Sventitsky's attitude towards the common people had changed completely, and so had their attitude towards him. Before a year was out they had felled twenty-seven of his oak trees and burned down the barn and the threshing-floor, which were not insured. Pyotr Nikolayevich decided that it was impossible to go on living among these people.

About this time the Livyentsov family were seeking a steward to look after their estates, and the marshal of the nobility had recommended Pyotr Nikolayevich as being the best farmer in the district. The Livyentsov estates although enormous in size were not yielding any profit, and the peasants were helping themselves to everything they could.

Pyotr Nikolayevich undertook to set everything to rights, and after letting his own estate to a tenant he set off with his wife to go and live on the Livyentsovs' land in the far-off Volga province.

Pyotr Nikolayevich had always been a lover of law and order, and now he was more unwilling than ever to tolerate these wild, uncivilized peasants who were illegally taking possession of property which did not belong to them. He was glad to have this chance to teach them a lesson and he set about his task with severity. One peasant he had imprisoned for the theft of forest timber, another he flogged with his own hand for not giving way to him on the road and failing to take off his hat. Concerning the meadows, about which there was a dispute, since the peasants regarded them as theirs, Pyotr Nikolayevich announced that if anyone let their cattle on to them, then he would have the animals impounded.

Spring came, and the peasants, as they had done in previous years, let their livestock out on to the manorial meadows. Pyotr Nikolayevich called all his farm-hands together and gave the order to drive the cattle and sheep into the manor farmyard. The muzhiks were out ploughing, so the farmhands, despite the women's shrieks of protest, were able to drive the animals in. On getting back from their work the muzhiks gathered together and came across to the manor farmyard to demand that their livestock should be given back to them. Pyotr Nikolayevich came out to meet them carrying a rifle across his shoulders (he had just returned from making his tour of inspection on horseback) and informed them that he would only return their livestock to them on payment of a fine of fifty copecks per horned beast and ten copecks per sheep. The muzhiks began shouting that the meadows were theirs anyway, and had belonged to their fathers and their grandfathers before them, and that he had no right to go seizing other people's stock.

'Give us our cattle back, or it'll be the worse for you,' said one old man, going up to Pyotr Nikolayevich.

'It'll be the worse for me, will it?' cried Pyotr Nikolayevich, his face all pale, advancing on the old man.

'Give them back if you don't want to get hurt. Parasite.'

'What?' shouted Pyotr Nikolayevich, and he struck the old man in the face.

'You won't dare fight us. Come on lads, take the cattle by force.'

The crowd surged forward. Pyotr Nikolayevich made as if to get out of the way, but they did not let him. He tried to force his way through. His rifle went off by accident, killing one of the peasants. A general riot broke out. Pyotr Nikolayevich was crushed to death. And five minutes later his mutilated body was dragged away and thrown into a ravine.

The murderers were brought before a military tribunal, and two of them were sentenced to death by hanging.

XVIII

In the village where the tailor came from five wealthy peasants had leased from the landowner for eleven hundred roubles a hundred and five *desyatins* of rich arable land as black as tar and distributed it among the other muzhiks in parcels costing eighteen or fifteen roubles each. None of the allotments of land went for under twelve roubles. So that they made themselves a good profit. The muzhiks who had leased the land each took five *desyatins*, and this land cost them nothing at all. One of these five muzhiks died, and the others invited the crippled tailor to come in with them as a partner.

When the tenants began to divide up the land, the tailor did not join in drinking vodka with them, and when the discussion turned to the question of who should get how much land, the tailor said that they should allocate it equally, and without taking money they didn't need from the tenants, but only what they could afford.

'What do you mean?'

'If we don't do it like this, we are not acting like Christians. The other way may be all right for the masters, but we are Christian people. We should do things God's way. That's the law of Christ.'

'So where is this law written down, then?'

'In the holy book, in the Gospels. Why don't you come over to my place on Sunday, so we can talk about it?'

When Sunday came not all the peasants went to the tailor's house, but three of them did, and he started to read to them.

He read five chapters from the Gospel of Matthew, and then they started to discuss it. They all listened, but only one of them, Ivan Chuyev, really took it in. And he took it in to such an extent that he began trying to live his whole life according to God's way. And his family too began to live like that. He refused to take the extra land and kept only his proper share.

People began coming regularly to the tailor's house and to Ivan's house, and they began to understand, then they really grasped it, and they gave up smoking, and drinking, and swearing and using foul language, and they started helping one another. They also gave up going to church, and they took their household ikons back to the priest. In the end seventeen households, comprising sixty-five people, were involved. The village priest was alarmed and he reported the matter to the bishop. The bishop considered what he should do, and he decided to send to the village Father Misail, who had formerly been a scripture teacher in a grammar school.

XIX

The bishop invited Father Misail to sit down and began telling him about the strange new developments in his diocese.

'It is all the result of spiritual weakness and ignorance. Now you are a man of learning. I want you to go down there and call the people together and get the matter cleared up.'

'With your grace's blessing, I shall certainly try,' said Father Misail. He was glad to have this commission. Any situation in which he could demonstrate the strength of his faith gave him satisfaction. And in converting others he always managed to persuade himself even more thoroughly that he himself really believed.

'Please do your best, I am deeply troubled about my little flock,' said the bishop, unhurriedly accepting in his pudgy white hands the glass of tea which a lay brother had brought him.

'Why have you brought only one sort of jam? Go and get another,' he said to the lay brother. 'I really am deeply, deeply concerned about this matter,' he continued, addressing Misail.

Misail was glad of this opportunity to show his mettle. However, being a man of modest means he requested his travel expenses in advance, and since he feared that there might be some resistance from the uncouth peasantry, he requested that the governor of the province should be asked to send an instruction to the local police to give him every assistance, should the need arise.

The bishop set up all the arrangements, and Misail, having with the help of the lay brother and the cook assembled the hamper and provisions so necessary for a journey to the back of beyond, set off for his appointed destination. As he started out on this official mission Misail was agreeably aware of the importance of the job he was engaged in, and also of the easing of any doubts he might have had concerning his own faith: he was, on the contrary, fully confident of its authenticity.

His thoughts were centred not on the essence of his faith – this he took to be axiomatic – but on the refutation of these objections which were being made to its outward forms.

XX

The village priest and his wife received Father Misail with great respect, and the day after his arrival they called all the people together in the church. Misail, wearing a brand-new silk cassock and a pectoral cross, his hair well combed, advanced to the ambo;[8] beside him stood the priest, a little further away the deacons and the choristers, and at the side-doors a few policemen had been stationed. The sectarians had also made their appearance, dressed in dirty, rough sheepskin coats.

After the set prayers were over Father Misail delivered a sermon in which he exhorted those who had fallen away to return to the bosom of Holy Mother Church, threatening them with the pains of hell and promising full absolution to all who repented.

The sectarians did not say anything, but when questioned they did reply.

To the question, why they had fallen away from the Church, they replied that in the church people worshipped wooden gods made by human hands, whereas not only was this not laid down in Holy Scripture, but in the prophecies it said just the opposite. When Father Misail asked Chuyev whether it was true that they referred to the holy ikons as 'boards', Chuyev replied: 'That's right – just you take any ikon you like and turn it round, and you'll see for yourself.' When they were asked why they did not recognize the priesthood, they replied that in Scripture it was written 'freely have ye received, freely give', but priests would only dispense their grace in return for money. To all Misail's attempts to support his position by reference to Holy Scripture, the tailor and Chuyev retorted calmly but firmly, referring to the same Scripture, of which they had a thorough grasp. Misail grew angry and threatened them with the secular authorities. To this the sectarians replied that Scripture said 'If they have persecuted me, they will also persecute you.'

The encounter was inconclusive and the whole thing would have ended quietly, but the next day at mass Father Misail preached a sermon about the pernicious influence of those who distort the truth, and how they deserved all kinds

8 The raised platform from which the Scriptures were read and sermons preached.

of retribution; and some of the peasants as they came out of the church started talking about how it would be good to teach the godless ones a lesson so that they wouldn't go on confusing the people. And that very day, while Father Misail was enjoying some appetizers of salmon and white fish with the rural dean and an inspector who had arrived from the local town, a disorder broke out in the village. The Orthodox folk had gathered together in a crowd in front of Chuyev's hut and were waiting for those inside to come out so that they could give them a good hiding. There were about twenty of the sectarians in there, both men and women. Father Misail's sermon, followed by this assemblage of the Orthodox and their threatening shouts had aroused in the sectarians a fierceness which had not been there before. Evening had come and it was time for the peasant women to milk the cows, but the Orthodox believers continued to stand there and wait, and when a young lad came out they started hitting him and drove him back into the house.

The sectarians were discussing what they ought to do, but they were unable to agree among themselves.

The tailor said that they should put up with whatever happened to them and not try to defend themselves. Chuyev, however, said that if they just put up with it they might all end up getting slaughtered, and he seized a poker and went out into the village street. The Orthodox believers hurled themselves upon him.

'All right then, let it be according to the Law of Moses,' he shouted, and he started hitting the Orthodox believers with the poker, putting out one man's eye in the process. The rest of the sectarians slipped out of the hut and returned to their homes.

Chuyev was put on trial for heresy and blasphemy, and sentenced to exile.

Father Misail, however, received an award and was made an archimandrite.

XXI

Two years before these events took place, a healthy attractive young woman of oriental looks named Turchaninova had come from the Don Cossack territory to St Petersburg to study at the university. In Petersburg she met a student named Tyurin, the son of a zemstvo leader in the Simbirsk province, and fell in love with him, but her love for him was not of the usual womanly type, involving the desire to become his wife and the mother of his children, but a comradely love which drew its strength above all from a shared anger and detestation against the existing social order and the people who represented it, and from a consciousness of their own intellectual, educational and moral superiority to those people.

  She was a gifted student, well able to memorize the contents of lectures and to pass examinations without much effort, and in addition she devoured enormous quantities of the most recently published books. She was sure that her vocation lay not in bearing and bringing up children – in fact she regarded such a vocation with disgust and contempt – but in destroying the present order of things which fettered the fine potential of the common people, and in pointing out to men and women the new path of life revealed to her by the most recent European writers. Full in figure, pale of skin, rosy-cheeked and attractive, with dark flashing eyes and a thick plait of dark hair, she aroused in men feelings which she had no desire to arouse and could not possibly share, utterly absorbed as she was by her task of agitation and argument. But all the same she found it pleasant to arouse such feelings, and for that reason although she did not deliberately dress to show herself off, neither did she neglect her appearance. She enjoyed being attractive, and indeed it gave her the chance of showing how much she looked down on that which other women held to be so important. In her views on the possible means of struggle against the existing order she went further than most of her associates, her friend Tyurin among them, and took it as read that all methods in the struggle were valid and to be used, up to and including murder. Yet Katya Turchaninova the revolutionary was still at heart a kind and unselfish woman, forever spontaneously putting the interests, enjoyment and well-being of other people before her own, and always glad of the chance to do something to make someone else happy, whether it was a child, an old person, or an animal.

Turchaninova spent the summer vacation period in a district town in the Volga province staying with a friend of hers who was a village schoolmistress. Tyurin was living in the same district, in his father's house. The three young people, and the local doctor too, met together frequently, lent each other books, argued, and fed one another's shared sense of social indignation. The Tyurins' property adjoined the Livyentsov estate where Pyotr Nikolayevich Sventitsky was now working as the steward. As soon as Pyotr Nikolayevich had arrived there and set about restoring order, young Tyurin, noting that the Livyentsovs' peasants had a spirit of independence and a firm resolve to stand up for their rights, began to take an interest in them and often walked over to the village to talk to the peasants, explaining to them the principles of socialism in general and of the nationalization of the land in particular.

When Pyotr Nikolayevich was murdered and the court case began, the trial gave the group of revolutionaries in the district town a powerful cause for agitation, and they denounced it outspokenly. Tyurin's visits to the village and his conversations with the peasants were referred to in the court proceedings. Tyurin's house was searched and some revolutionary pamphlets discovered, and he was arrested and taken away to Petersburg.

Turchaninova travelled to Petersburg after him and went to the prison to try to see him, but they would not permit her to see him on just any day, but only on a public visiting-day, and even then she was only allowed to talk to Tyurin through a double iron grille. This visit strengthened her feelings of moral outrage still further. Her indignation finally reached its climax when she was faced with a young and handsome officer of the gendarmes who was obviously ready to grant her some concessions, provided she would agree to certain proposals of his. This incident drove her to the highest pitch of fury and hatred against all representatives of authority. She went to the chief of police in order to lodge a complaint. The chief of police echoed the words of the gendarme: that there was nothing they could do, and that the matter was under the jurisdiction of the Minister. She sent in a written memorandum to the Minister requesting an interview; it was refused. Then she decided that a desperate act was called for, and she bought a revolver.

XXII

The Minister was receiving visitors at his usual hour. After passing over three petitioners and talking for a while with a provincial governor, he went up to a pretty dark-eyed young woman in black who was standing there holding a piece of paper in her left hand. A lecherous glint appeared in the Minister's eyes at the sight of this charming petitioner, but remembering his position the Minister adopted a serious expression.

'And what can I do for you?' he asked, advancing towards her.

She made no reply, but swiftly drew out the revolver from beneath her cape, aimed it at the Minister's chest and fired, but she missed.

The Minister made a grab at her arm but she stepped back away from him and fired a second shot. The Minister fled. The young woman was immediately seized and held. She was shaking and unable to speak. Then suddenly she burst into hysterical laughter. The Minister had not even been wounded.

The woman was Turchaninova. She was sent to a special detention prison pending the investigation of her case. Meanwhile the Minister, who had received congratulations and commiserations from persons in the very highest places and even from the Sovereign himself, appointed a commission to investigate the conspiracy which had led to this attempt on his life.

There was of course no conspiracy whatever; but the officials of both the secret and civil police forces went assiduously to work to search out all the threads of the non-existent conspiracy, conscientiously justifying their salaries and their expenditure. Rising early in the morning when it was still dark, they conducted search after search, transcribed papers and books, perused diaries and private letters, and wrote out extracts from them in beautiful handwriting on the finest paper. They questioned Turchaninova any number of times and set up confrontations with witnesses in their efforts to get her to reveal the names of her accomplices.

The Minister was a kindly man at heart and felt very sorry for this healthy, attractive Cossack girl, but he told himself that he carried grave responsibilities to the state which he was bound to discharge, however painful this might prove to be. And when a former colleague of his, a court chamberlain who knew the Tyurin family, met him at a court ball and began to ask him about Tyurin and Turchaninova, the Minister shrugged his shoulders, crinkling the red sash he was wearing across his white waistcoat, and said:

'*Je ne demanderais pas mieux que de lâcher cette pauvre fillette, mais vous savez – le devoir.*'[9]

And meanwhile Turchaninova was sitting in her detention cell, exchanging occasional furtive tapped messages with her fellow-prisoners and reading the books she was given, but sometimes she would fall into a mood of fury and despair, beating on the walls with her fists, screaming and laughing.

XXIII

One day when Mariya Semyonovna had been to the local treasury office to draw her pension and was on her way home, she met a teacher whom she knew.

9 I should like nothing better than to release the poor little girl, but you know how it is – one must stick to one's duty.

'Good day, Mariya Semyonovna, have you been to collect your pay then?' he called out to her from the opposite side of the road.

'Yes, I have,' replied Mariya Semyonovna. 'It will do to plug a few gaps at least.'

'Well, you should have plenty to plug the gaps and still have some left over,' said the teacher, and he said goodbye to her and went on his way.

'Goodbye,' said Mariya Semyonovna, and as she was looking back at the teacher she walked straight into a tall man with extremely long arms and a stern face. As she came near to the house where she lived she was surprised to see this same long-armed man again. He watched her go into the house, stood there for a while, then turned and walked off.

At first Mariya Semyonovna felt alarmed, then her alarm turned to a sort of melancholy. But by the time she had gone inside and distributed little gifts to her old father and her little scrofulous nephew Fedya, and petted the little dog Trezorka, who yelped with delight, she was feeling cheerful again, and handing over the money to her father she got on with the housework, to which there never seemed to be an end.

The man she had bumped into was Stepan.

After leaving the coaching inn where he had murdered the innkeeper Stepan had not gone back to the town. And strange to say, not only did the memory of the innkeeper's murder not distress him, but he actually found himself returning to it in his mind several times each day. It gave him pleasure to think that he was capable of doing the deed so cleanly and skilfully that no one would ever find him out or prevent him from doing the same thing again, to other people. As he sat in a tavern drinking his tea and his vodka he kept scrutinizing the people around him with the same thought always in mind: how he could set about murdering them. To find himself a bed for the night he went to the house of a man who came from his own district, a drayman. The drayman was out. He said he would wait and sat down to chat with the man's wife. Then, when she turned her back on him to tend the stove, it occurred to him that he could kill her. Surprised at himself, he shook his head, but then he took his knife from the top of his boot, threw her to the floor and cut her throat. The children started screaming, so he killed them too, and left the town at once that same day. Once out of the town he went into a village inn, where he stopped and had a good night's sleep.

The next day he walked back to the district town, and overheard Mariya Semyonovna's conversation with the teacher while he was walking down the street. He was frightened by the way she had stared at him, nevertheless he decided to break into her house and take the money which she had drawn. When night came he broke the lock and went upstairs into a bedroom. The first person to hear him was the younger, married daughter. She cried out. Stepan immediately cut her throat. The son-in-law woke up and grappled with him. He got hold of Stepan by the throat and struggled with him for quite some time, but Stepan was too strong for him. Having finished off the son-in-law Stepan, now in a state of some agitation and excited by the struggle, went behind a partition. On the other side of the partition Mariya Semyonovna was lying in bed. She raised herself on the bed and looked at Stepan with gentle, frightened eyes and crossed herself. Once again her look frightened Stepan. He lowered his gaze.

'Where's the money?' he asked without looking up.

She did not answer.

'Where's the money?' said Stepan, showing her the knife.

'What are you doing? You can't do this,' she said.

'Oh yes I can, and I will.'

Stepan moved nearer, intending to seize her arms so that she could not stop him doing what he intended to do, but she did not raise her hands, did not resist, but simply pressed her hands to her bosom, sighed heavily and repeated:

'Oh, what a great sin. What are you doing? Have pity on yourself. You think you are destroying others, but it's your own soul you are destroying. Oh, oh!' she screamed.

Stepan could not stand her voice or the look on her face

any longer, and he slashed the knife right across her throat. – 'I haven't got time to waste chatting with you.' – She slumped back on to the pillows and began to wheeze, soaking one of the pillows with her blood. He turned away and walked through the bedrooms, collecting things as he went. When he had gathered up everything he wanted Stepan lit a cigarette, sat down for a moment, brushed down his clothes and then went out. He had thought he would get away with this murder just as easily as he had done with the previous ones, but even before he had reached the place where he planned to stay the night he suddenly felt so weary that he could hardly move a limb. He lay down in a ditch and stayed there for the rest of that night, the whole of the next day and the night that followed.

Part Two

I

As he lay there in the ditch Stepan kept seeing before him Mariya Semyonovna's thin, meek, terrified face and hearing her voice: 'You can't do this,' her peculiar lisping, pathetic voice kept on repeating. And Stepan kept reliving over again everything he had done to her. He began to feel really frightened, and he shut his eyes, swaying his shaggy head from side to side in an attempt to shake these thoughts and memories out of it. And for a moment he managed to free himself from his memories, but in their place appeared first one black devil, then another, and after them still other black devils with red eyes, all pulling hideous faces and all saying the same thing: 'You did away with her – now do away with yourself, or we won't give you any peace.' And he would open his eyes and once again see her and hear her voice, and he was filled with pity for her, and with fear and loathing towards himself. And he would shut his eyes again, and again the black devils would be there.

Towards the evening of the second day he got to his feet and walked to the tavern nearby. Reaching the tavern with

a great effort, he began drinking. Yet however much he
drank, he was quite unable to get drunk. He sat silently at a
table, downing one glass after another. Then into the tavern
walked the village constable.

'And who might you be then?' enquired the constable.

'I'm the one who cut all those people's throats at the
Dobrotvorovs' house the other night.'

They bound him, and after holding him for a day at the
district police station, sent him off to the main town of the
province. The warden of the prison, recognizing him as a
former prisoner and a trouble-maker who had now done
something really bad, gave him a stern reception.

'You'd best get it into your head that you won't be pulling
any tricks with me in charge,' said the warden in a hoarse
wheezing voice, frowning and sticking out his lower jaw.
'And if I see you trying anything, I'll have you flogged. And
you won't be escaping from this prison.'

'Why would I be escaping?' answered Stepan, looking at
the ground. 'I gave myself up of my own accord.'

'That's enough back-chat from you. And when a superior
is talking to you, look him in the eye,' shouted the warden,
giving him a punch on the jaw.

At that moment Stepan was again seeing Mariya
Semyonovna and hearing her voice. He heard nothing of
what the warden had just been saying.

'What?' he asked, coming to his senses as he felt the blow
on his chin.

'Come on, come on now – forward march, and none of
your funny business.'

The warden was expecting Stepan to get violent, to hatch
schemes with other prisoners, and to try and make a break
for it. But there was nothing of that kind. Whenever the
guard or the warden himself looked through the peephole
in his cell door, Stepan would be sitting there on a sack
stuffed with straw, his head propped up in his hands, whispering something to himself. When being questioned by the
investigator he also behaved quite differently from the other
prisoners: he seemed absent-minded, as if he did not hear

the questions, and when he did grasp them he was so truthful in his answers that the investigator, accustomed as he was to contending with the ingenuity and cunning of accused prisoners, felt rather like a man climbing a staircase in the dark, who lifts his foot to find the next step, which turns out not to be there. Stepan gave a full account of all the murders he had committed, screwing up his brow and staring at a fixed point in space, and speaking in the simplest, most businesslike manner as he tried to recall all the details: 'He came out barefoot,' said Stepan, talking about the first murder, 'and he stood there in the doorway, and so I slashed him just the once and he started to wheeze, and I got straight on with it and dealt with his old woman.' And so he went on. When the public prosecutor made his round of the cells Stepan was asked if he had any complaints or if he needed anything. He answered that there was nothing he needed and that he wasn't being mistreated. The prosecutor walked a few steps down the stinking corridor, then stopped and asked the warden, who was accompanying him, how this prisoner was behaving.

'It's a most extraordinary thing,' replied the warden, gratified that Stepan had praised the way he was being treated. 'He's been with us for over a month now, and his behaviour is exemplary. I am just concerned that he may be thinking up something. He's a fearless fellow, and he's exceptionally strong.'

II

During his first month in prison Stepan was constantly tormented by the same thing: he could see the grey walls of his cell and hear the prison noises – the hum of voices on the common cell in the floor below him, the guard's footsteps in the corridor, the clangs that marked the passing of the hours – but at the same time he could see *her*, and that meek expression of hers which had already got the better of him when he had met her in the street, and the scraggy, wrinkled throat which he had slashed; and he could hear her touching, pitiful, lisping voice saying: '*You think you're destroying others, but it's your own soul you're destroying. You can't do this.*' Then the voice would fall silent, and those three would appear – the black devils. And they kept on appearing just the same, whether his eyes were open or shut. When his eyes were shut they looked more distinct. When Stepan opened his eyes the devils would blend into the doorways and the walls and vanish for a while, but then they came at him again, from in front of him and from both sides, making dreadful faces and repeating: 'Do away with yourself, do away with yourself. You could make a noose, you could start a fire.' And then Stepan would start to shake, and to repeat all the prayers he could remember – the Hail Mary and the Our Father – and at first that seemed to help him. As he recited the prayers he would start to recall his past life: his father and mother, his village, the dog Wolfcub, his grandad asleep on top of the stove, the upturned benches on which he had gone sledging with the other lads; and then he would recall the girls and their songs, and the horses, how they had been stolen and how they had managed to catch the horse-thief, and how he had finished the thief off with a stone. And he would recall his first term in prison and his release, and he would recall the fat innkeeper and the drayman's wife and the children, and then once again he would recall *her*. And he would feel hot all over, and throw off his prison robe, leap up from his plank-bed and start pacing rapidly up and down his cramped cell like a wild animal in a cage, making a rapid turn each time he came up against the damp, oozing walls. And again he would start to recite his prayers, but the prayers were beginning to lose their effect.

One long autumn evening, when the wind was whistling and howling in the chimney-flues and he had had enough of pacing up and down his cell, he sat down on his bunk, and realizing that he could not go on struggling any longer, that the devils were too strong for him, he gave in to them. For some time he had had his eye on the stove-pipe. If he could wind some thin cord or some thin strips of cloth round it, it ought to hold. But he would need to go about it cleverly. So he set to work, and for two days he worked away to get some strips of linen from the palliasse he slept on (when the guard came in he covered the bunk with his dressing-gown). He tied the strips together with knots, double ones so that they would hold the weight of his body without pulling away. While he was busy with this task his torments abated. When everything was ready he made a noose, placed it round his neck, climbed up on to the bed and hanged himself. But his tongue had only just begun to protrude when the strips of cloth gave way, and he fell to the floor. Hearing the noise, the guard came running in. They summoned the medical orderly and took him off to the hospital. By the next day he was quite recovered, and was discharged from the hospital and placed not in a solitary cell, but in a communal one.

In the communal cell he lived as one of twenty inmates, but he lived there just as if he had been alone, seeing nobody, talking to nobody, and suffering the same mental torments as before. It was particularly bad for him when everyone else was sleeping and he could not, and as before he kept seeing *her* and hearing her voice, and then again the black devils would appear, with their dreadful eyes, mocking him.

Again, as before, he recited his prayers, and as before they were of no use.

On one occasion when, after he had said his prayers, she again appeared to him, he started to pray to her, to her little soul, praying that it would let him go, that it would forgive him. And when towards morning he collapsed on to his flattened straw palliasse, he fell fast asleep, and in his sleep he dreamt that she came towards him with her scraggy, wrinkled throat, all cut open.

'Please, will you forgive me?'

She looked at him with her meek look, and said nothing.

'Will you forgive me?'

And three times in the same way he begged her to forgive him. But she still said nothing. And then he woke up. From that time on he began to feel better: it was as though he had come to himself, and he looked round him, and for the first time he began to make friends with his cell-mates and to talk to them.

III

One of the prisoners in Stepan's communal cell was Vasily, who had again been caught stealing and had been sentenced to exile; another was Chuyev, who had likewise been sentenced to forcible resettlement. Vasily spent his time either singing songs in his splendid voice or telling his cell-mates the story of his adventures. Chuyev, on the other hand, was always working, or sewing away at some item of clothing or underwear, or reading the Gospels or the Psalms.

To Stepan's question as to why he was being exiled, Chuyev replied that it was because of his true faith in Christ and because the false priests could not bear to hear the spirit speaking through people such as he, who lived according to the Gospel, and thus showed up the priests for what they were. And when Stepan asked Chuyev what this Gospel law was, Chuyev explained to him how they had found out about this true faith from a one-legged tailor when they were sharing out some land.

'All right then, so what happens if you commit evil deeds?' asked Stepan.

'It tells you all about that.' And Chuyev proceeded to read to him:

' "When the Son of man shall come in his glory, and all the holy angels with him, then shall he sit upon the throne of his glory. And before him shall be gathered all nations; and he shall separate them one from another, as a shepherd divideth his sheep from the goats, and he shall set the sheep on his right hand, but the goats on the left. Then shall the King say unto them on his right hand, 'Come, ye blessed of my Father, inherit the kingdom prepared for you from the foundation of the world: for I was an hungred, and ye gave me meat; I was thirsty, and ye gave me drink; I was a stranger, and ye took me in; naked, and ye clothed me; I was sick, and ye visited me; I was in prison, and ye came unto me.' Then shall the righteous answer him, saying, 'Lord, when saw we thee an hungred, and fed thee? or thirsty, and gave thee drink? When saw we thee a stranger, and took thee in? or naked, and clothed thee? Or when saw we thee sick, or in prison, and came unto thee?' And the King shall answer and say unto them: 'Verily I say unto you, inasmuch as ye have done it unto one of the least of these my brethren, ye have done it unto me.' Then shall he say also unto them on the left hand: 'Depart from me, ye cursed, into everlasting fire, prepared for the devil and his angels: for I was an hungred, and ye gave me no meat; I was thirsty, and ye gave me no drink; I was a stranger, and ye took me not in; naked, and ye clothed me not; sick, and in prison, and ye visited me not.' Then shall they also answer him, saying: 'Lord, when saw we thee an hungred, or athirst, or a stranger, or naked, or sick, or in prison, and did not minister unto thee?' Then shall he answer them, saying: 'Verily I say unto you: inasmuch as ye did it not to one of the least of these, ye did it not to me.' And these shall go away into the everlasting punishment, but the righteous into life eternal."' (Matthew XXV, 31–46)

Vasily, who had been sitting on the floor opposite Chuyev and listening to him reading, nodded his handsome head approvingly.

'That's right,' he declared firmly, ' "Go," he says, "ye accursed ones into everlasting punishment, you never fed anyone, you just stuffed your own bellies." That's just what they deserve. Here, let me have the book and I'll read some myself,' he added, wanting to show off his reading skills.

'But does it say there won't be any forgiveness?' asked Stepan, lowering his shaggy head and waiting quietly to listen to the reading.

'Just you wait a bit and hold your noise,' said Chuyev to Vasily, who was still going on about the rich not feeding the poor stranger and not visiting anybody in prison. 'Just wait, will you,' repeated Chuyev, leafing through the Gospels. Finding the place he was looking for, Chuyev smoothed out the pages with his large, powerful hand, grown quite white from his time in prison.

' "And there were also two other, malefactors, led with him" – with Christ, that is,' began Chuyev, ' "to be put to death. And when they were come to the place, which is called the Skull, there they crucified him, and the male-factors, one on the right hand, and the other on the left.

' "Then said Jesus: 'Father, forgive them, for they know not what they do' . . . And the people stood beholding. And the rulers also with them derided him, saying: 'He saved others, let him save himself, if he be the Christ, the chosen of God.' And the soldiers also mocked him, coming to him and offering him vinegar, and saying: 'If thou be the king of the Jews, save thyself.' And a superscription also was written over him in letters of Greek, and Latin, and Hebrew: 'This is the king of the Jews.' And one of the malefactors which were hanged railed on him, saying: 'If thou be Christ, save thyself and us.' But the other answering, rebuked him, say-ing: 'Dost thou not fear God, seeing thou art in the same condemnation? And we indeed justly, for we receive the due reward for our deeds; but this man hath done nothing amiss.' And he said unto Jesus: 'Lord, remember me when thou comest into thy kingdom.' And Jesus said unto him: 'Verily I say unto thee: today shalt thou be with me in paradise.' " ' (Luke XXIII, 32–43)

Stepan said nothing, but sat deep in thought as though listening, although in fact he heard nothing more of what Chuyev was reading.

'So that is what the true faith is all about,' he thought. 'It's only the ones who have given food and drink to the poor and visited the prisoners who will be saved, and those who didn't do those things will go to hell. All the same, the thief only repented when he was already on the cross, and he still went to heaven.' He saw no contradiction in this; on the contrary, the one thing seemed to confirm the other: that the merciful would go to heaven, and the unmerciful to hell – that meant that everyone had better be merciful, and the fact that Christ forgave the thief meant that Christ him-self was merciful. All this was quite new to Stepan; he was merely surprised that it had remained hidden from him until now. And he spent all his spare time with Chuyev, asking questions and listening to his replies. And as he listened he began to understand. He realized that the overall meaning of this teaching was that men were brothers, and ought to love and pity each other, and then it would be well with all of them. As he listened, he perceived as something forgotten, yet familiar, everything that confirmed the overall meaning of this teaching, and he allowed everything that did not confirm it to slip past his ears, attributing it to his own lack of understanding.

And from that time onwards Stepan became a different man.

IV

Even before this happened Stepan Pelageyushkin had been a docile prisoner, but now the warden, the orderlies and his fellow-prisoners were all amazed at the change which had come over him. Without being ordered, and even when it was not his turn, he carried out all the most arduous duties, among them the cleaning out of the night-bucket. Yet despite his submissiveness his cell-mates respected and feared him, knowing his force of will and his great physical strength, especially after an incident in which two vagrants attacked him and he fought them off, breaking the arm of one of them in the process. These vagrants had set out to beat a well-heeled young prisoner at cards and had taken from him everything he owned. Stepan had stood up for him and managed to get back from them the money they had won. The vagrants had started cursing him, and then tried to beat him up, but he had overpowered them both. When the warden tried to find out the cause of the quarrel, the vagrants had maintained that it was Pelageyushkin who had set upon them both. Stepan made no attempt to justify himself, but meekly accepted his punishment, which consisted of three days in the punishment block, followed by transfer to a solitary cell.

He found it hard to be in solitary confinement because it

separated him from Chuyev and the Gospels; moreover, he was afraid that his visions of the woman he had killed and the black devils might start again. But his hallucinations did not return. His entire soul was now full of a new and joyful spirit. He would even have been glad of his isolation, if only he had been able to read and if he had possessed a copy of the Gospels. That the authorities would have provided him with, but he could not read.

As a boy he had begun to learn to read in the old-fashioned way, spelling out the letters – *az, buki, vyedi*[10] – but not being very bright he got no further than the alphabet, was quite unable at that stage to grasp how words were strung together, and so remained illiterate. Now, however, he determined to do the job properly, and asked the orderly for a copy of the New Testament. The orderly brought him one and he set to work. He was able to recognize the letters, but he could make no progress towards putting them together. However much he racked his brains to understand how words could be composed out of individual letters, he could make nothing of it. He could not sleep at night, could not stop thinking about his problem, and lost his appetite for food, falling so low in spirits that he had a bad infestation of lice and could not get rid of them.

'Well then, have you still not got there?' the orderly asked him one day.

'No, I haven't.'

'But you know the Our Father, don't you?'

'Of course I know it.'

'So, just try reading that. Look, here it is' – and the orderly showed him the Lord's Prayer in the New Testament.

Stepan started to recite the Our Father, fitting the letters he knew to the sounds he knew. And suddenly the mystery of the combining of letters was opened to him, and he began to read. It was a tremendous joy to him. From that day he

10 The traditional names for a, b, v – the first letters of the Russian alphabet. Tolstoy promoted a more phonetic method of learning, and wrote several reading books.

began reading, and the sense which emerged little by little from the painfully assembled words took on an even greater significance for him.

His isolation no longer weighed upon Stepan, it was a cause of rejoicing to him. He was entirely preoccupied with his task, and was not at all pleased when, to make room for some newly admitted politicals, he was moved back into the communal cell.

V

Now it was often not Chuyev, but Stepan who read the Gospels aloud in the cell, and although some of the prisoners sang bawdy songs, others listened to his reading and to the conversations which took place about what he had read. Two men in particular always listened to him attentively and in silence: one was the executioner Makhorkin who was doing hard labour for murder; the other was Vasily, who had been caught stealing and was being held in the same prison, awaiting trial. Makhorkin had twice fulfilled his duties as executioner during his stay in the prison, on both occasions in other towns where no one could be found to carry out the sentences the judges had imposed. The peasants who had murdered Pyotr Nikolayevich Sventitsky had been tried by a military tribunal and two of them had been condemned to death by hanging.

Makhorkin had been required to go to Penza to carry out his functions there. On previous occasions of this kind he had at once written to the governor – he was unusually good at reading and writing – explaining that he had been commanded to go to Penza to carry out his duties and requesting the provincial chief to grant him the appropriate daily subsistence allowance; but this time he declared, to the astonishment of the prison director, that he would not go, and that never again would he be carrying out the duty of executioner.

'And have you forgotten the whip?' shouted the warden.

'The whip is the whip right enough, but killing's against the law.'

'So you've been picking up ideas from Pelageyushkin, have you? Quite the prison prophet he's become. Well, just you wait.'

VI

Meanwhile Makhin, the grammar-school boy who had showed his friend how to forge the coupon, had left school and completed his course at the university Faculty of Law. Thanks to his success with women, including the former mistress of an elderly government minister who was a friend of his, he had while still quite a young man been made an examining magistrate. He was a dishonest man with considerable debts, a seducer of women and a gambler at cards, but he was a clever, quick-witted man with a retentive memory, and effective in his handling of legal cases.

He was examining magistrate in the district where Stepan Pelageyushkin was being tried. He had already been surprised during the first examination by Stepan's simple, accurate and level-headed replies to his questions. Makhin was almost unconsciously aware that this man standing before him shaven-headed and in shackles, who was brought here and guarded and would be taken away to be locked up again by two soldiers, this man was somehow perfectly free and existed on a moral level which he, Makhin, could not possibly attain. For this reason, as he examined the man he was obliged to keep on pulling himself together and urging himself on, so as not to get confused and to lose his way. He was struck by the manner in which Stepan spoke of the things he had done as of something which had happened long ago and which had been carried out not by him at all, but by another person.

'And you didn't feel sorry for them at all?' asked Makhin.

'No, I didn't feel sorry. I didn't understand at that time.'

'Well, and how do you feel towards them now?' Stepan smiled sadly.

'Now, you could roast me alive, but I wouldn't do such a thing again.'

'And why is that?'

'Because I've come to see that all men are brothers.'

'All right, so I am your brother, am I?'

'Of course you are.'

'What, I am your brother, though I am condemning you to penal servitude?'

'That's only because you don't understand.'

'And what don't I understand?'

'You can't understand, if you are passing judgement on me.'

'Well, let us get on. So where did you go after that? . . .'

Makhin was struck most of all by what he learned from the prison warden about Pelageyushkin's influence on the executioner Makhorkin who, at the risk of corporal punishment, had refused to carry out his official duties.

VII

At an evening party at the house of the Yeropkins, where there were two marriageable daughters both of whom Makhin was courting, after the singing of romances (at which the highly musical Makhin distinguished himself as second singer and as accompanist), Makhin was giving a faithful, detailed account – his memory was excellent – and a quite impartial account, of the strange criminal who had brought about the conversion of the executioner. Makhin was able to remember and describe everything so well, precisely because he was always utterly impartial towards the people he had to deal with. He did not and could not enter into the spiritual state of other people, and for this reason he was extremely good at recalling everything that had happened to them and all that they had done or said.

But Pelageyushkin had aroused his interest. He made no attempt to put himself in Stepan's place but he could not help wondering 'What is going on in his mind?' and although he came to no conclusions he felt that this was something of interest, and so he was giving a thorough account of the whole case at this soirée: the executioner's repudiation of his duties, the warden's stories about Pelageyushkin's strange behaviour, his reading of the Gospels, and the powerful influence he exerted on his fellow-prisoners.

Makhin's story intrigued everyone present, but it was of particular interest to the Yeropkins' younger daughter Liza, who was eighteen years old, had just completed her studies at a young ladies' academy, and was beginning to realize the darkness and narrowness of the thoroughly false environment in which she had been brought up – she was like a swimmer who had burst through the surface of the water and was eagerly gulping in the fresh air of life. She started to question Makhin about the details of the case and about how and why such a transformation had come upon Pelageyushkin, and Makhin told her what he had learned from Pelageyushkin about his most recent murder, and how the meekness and docility of this extraordinarily good-hearted woman with no fear of death, whom he had murdered, had vanquished him and opened his eyes, and how his reading of the Gospels had then completed the process.

For a long time that night Liza Yeropkina could not get to sleep. For some months already a struggle had been going on within her between the life of fashionable society, in which her sister had been trying to involve her, and her attraction towards Makhin, which was mingled with a desire to reform him. And now it was this latter impulse which gained the upper hand. She had already heard something of the woman who had been murdered. Now, however, after that dreadful death and what Makhin had told her based on Pelageyushkin's account of it, she knew the whole story of Mariya Semyonovna in detail and she was deeply moved by all that she had learned about her.

Liza felt an overwhelming desire to be a woman of the sort that Mariya Semyonovna had been. She was rich and she was afraid Makhin might be courting her simply for her money. And so she decided that she would give away the property she owned, and she confided her idea to Makhin.

Makhin was glad to have this opportunity of showing his disinterestedness, and he told Liza that he did not love her for her money, and this decision of hers, which seemed to him so magnanimous, moved him deeply. Meanwhile a struggle had begun between Liza and her mother (the estate had come to her from her father), who would not permit her to give her property away. Makhin gave Liza all the help he could. And the more he pursued this course of action, the more he began to understand this new world of spiritual aspirations which had formerly seemed to him so strange and alien, and which he now saw in Liza.

VIII

In the communal cell everything had grown quiet. Stepan was lying in his place on the plank-bed, not yet asleep. Vasily went over to him, and tugging at his foot, gave him a wink as a sign that he should get up and come across to where he was standing. Stepan slipped down from the plank-bed and went up to Vasily.

'Well now, brother,' said Vasily, 'I want you to help me, if you will.'

'What sort of help do you need?'

'I'm thinking of escaping.'

And Vasily explained that he had made all the necessary preparations for an escape attempt.

'Tomorrow I'm going to stir up some trouble with them' – he pointed at the prisoners lying asleep. 'They'll complain about me to the orderlies. I'll be transferred to the cells upstairs and once I'm there I know what to do. But I'll be relying on you to give me a hand to get out of the mortuary.'

'I can do that. But where will you go?'

'I'll go wherever I feel like going. I reckon there's no lack of bad characters out there.'

'That's true, brother, but it's not for us to judge them.'

'What I mean is, I'm no murderer, am I? I've never done in a single soul, and what's a bit of stealing? What's so wrong about that? Aren't they always robbing poor devils like you and me?'

'That's their affair. They'll answer for it.'

'So are we just meant to stand there and watch them get on with it? Like, I cleaned out a church once. What harm did that do anybody? What I've got in mind now isn't to rob some measly little shop. I'm going to go for some big money, and then give it away to them as need it.'

At that moment one of the prisoners sat up on the plank-bed and began listening to what they were saying. Stepan and Vasily went their separate ways.

The next day Vasily did what he had planned to do. He began complaining about the bread, saying that it was not properly cooked, and he urged the other prisoners to call the warden in and lodge an official complaint. The warden arrived and shouted abuse at them, and on discovering that Vasily was the one behind the whole thing he gave orders that he should be put into solitary confinement in one of the cells on the floor above.

That was exactly what Vasily needed.

IX

Vasily was thoroughly familiar with the upstairs cell into which they had put him. He knew how the floor was constructed and as soon as he got in there he set about taking it up. When he had managed to worm his way under the floorboards he prised apart the panels which formed the ceiling of the room below and jumped down, into the mortuary. That day there was only one dead body lying on the mortuary table. In the mortuary they kept the sacks used for making the prisoners' palliasses. Vasily was aware of this and he was counting on it. The padlock on the door had been taken off and the hasp pushed inside. Vasily opened the door and went into the room at the end of the corridor, where a new latrine was being built. In the latrine there was a hole leading from the second floor down to the lowest one, the basement. Groping his way back to the door, Vasily went into the mortuary again, removed the shroud from the corpse, which felt icy cold (he touched it with his hand in taking the shroud off it), then took some sacks and tied them and the shroud together to form a rope, and lowered his rope down the latrine hole; then he made the rope fast round a cross-beam and climbed down it. The rope was not long enough to reach the floor. Just how much too short it was he did not know, but there was nothing for it, so he hung down as far as he could, then jumped.

He hurt his legs, but he could still walk. In the basement there were two windows. They were big enough for him to crawl through, but they were fitted with iron gratings. He had to get one of them out, but what with? Vasily began to fumble about. On the floor of the basement there were some sections of timber. He found one which had a pointed end and began using it to lever out the bricks which held the grating in place. He worked away at it for a long time. The cocks had crowed for the second time, but the grating still held. At last one side of it came loose. Vasily inserted his piece of timber into the gap and pushed hard on it; the whole grating came away, but a brick fell out and crashed to the floor. The sentries might have heard. Vasily froze. All was quiet. He climbed up into the window aperture, and out. To make his escape he still had to get over the prison wall. In one corner of the yard there stood a lean-to shed. He would have to climb on to the roof of this shed, and from there on to the top of the wall. He would need to take a piece of the timber with him, otherwise he would not be able to get on to the roof. Vasily crawled back through the window. He crawled out once more with a length of timber and froze, listening to find out where the sentry was. As far as he could judge the sentry was walking along the far side of the square yard. Vasily approached the lean-to, placed the timber against it and started to climb up. The timber slipped, and fell to the ground. Vasily was in stockinged feet, with no shoes. He took off his socks so as to get a grip with his feet, put the timber in place once more, sprang on to it and managed to get his hand over the roof guttering. 'O Lord, don't let it come away, let it hold.' He gripped the guttering, then got one knee on to the roof. The sentry was coming. Vasily lay flat and froze. The sentry did not notice anything and continued on his way. Vasily leapt to his feet. The iron roof clattered beneath his feet. One more step, a second, and there was the wall in front of him. He could reach out and touch it. One hand, then the other, then he stretched up, and he was on the top of the wall. If only he didn't smash himself to bits now, jumping down. Vasily turned round, hung by both arms, stretched out as far as he could, and let go one hand, then the other. 'Lord be praised!' – he was on the ground. And the ground was soft. His legs were undamaged and he ran off.

When he reached his house at the edge of the town Malanya opened the door to him, and he crawled under the warm patchwork quilt which was impregnated with the smell of sweat.

X

Pyotr Nikolayevich's sturdy, attractive wife, ever placid, childless, plump, like a barren cow, watched from the window as the peasants murdered her husband and dragged his body away somewhere into the fields. The sensation of terror which Natalya Ivanovna (such was the name of Sventitsky's widow) experienced at the sight of this slaughter was – as is always the case – so powerful that it stifled all her other emotions. However, when the crowd of peasants had gone out of sight behind the garden fence and the hubbub of their voices had died away, and the barefooted girl Malanya, who worked for them, came running in wide-eyed as if to announce some glad tidings, with the news that they had murdered Pyotr Nikolayevich and thrown his body into the ravine, Natalya Ivanovna's initial feeling of terror began to be mingled with something different: a feeling of joy at her liberation from the despot, eyes hidden behind his tinted spectacles, who had kept her in slavery these past nineteen years. She was horrified at this feeling and did not even acknowledge it to herself, but tried all the more not to let anyone else know about it. When they washed his yellow, mutilated, hairy corpse and dressed it and placed it in the coffin she was overcome with horror, and she wept and sobbed. When the examining magistrate responsible for serious crimes came down and questioned her as a witness, she saw before her, right there in the investigator's office, the two peasants now in fetters who had been identified as the principal culprits. One of them was quite an old man, with a long, wavy white beard and a calm, sternly handsome face; the other looked like a gypsy, a youngish man with shining dark eyes and curly, tousled hair. She testified that as far as she knew these were the very same men who had been the first to seize Pyotr Nikolayevich by the arms, and despite the fact that the gypsy-like peasant turned his flashing eyes under his contorted brow directly upon her and said reproachfully 'It's a sin, lady! Ah, we shall all have to die one day' – in spite of that she felt no pity whatever for them. On the contrary, as the investigation went on there arose within her a feeling of hostility and a desire to revenge herself on her husband's murderers.

But when a month later the case, which had been transferred to a military tribunal, ended with eight men being condemned to penal servitude and the two men – the white-bearded old man and the dark-skinned 'gypsy lad', as they called him – being sentenced to be hanged, she experienced a most disagreeable feeling. But this disagreeable feeling of doubt was now quickly dissipated under the influence of the solemn ritual of the courtroom. If the higher authorities considered this to be necessary, then it must all be for the best.

The executions were to be carried out in the village. And returning from mass one Sunday in her new dress and new shoes, Malanya informed her mistress that they were putting up a gallows, that an executioner was expected to arrive from Moscow by Wednesday, and that the two men's relatives were wailing without ceasing, so that you could hear them all over the village.

Natalya Ivanovna stayed indoors so as not to see the gallows or the local people, and her only wish was that what must be done should soon be over. She thought solely of herself, and not at all about the condemned men and their families.

XI

On the Tuesday Natalya Ivanovna received a visit from the district superintendent, a friend of hers. Natalya Ivanovna entertained him with vodka and mushrooms she had pickled herself. The district superintendent drank his vodka and enjoyed some of the snacks, and then informed her that the executions would not be taking place tomorrow.

'What? How is that?'

'It's an extraordinary story. They have been unable to supply an executioner. There was one in Moscow but he, so my son tells me, got to reading the Gospels, and now he says that he can't kill anybody. He himself was condemned to hard labour for murder, but now all of a sudden – he can't kill someone even if it's legal. They told him he would be flogged. Flog me, he says, but I still can't do it.'

Natalya Ivanovna suddenly went red, and actually began to perspire because of what she was thinking.

'But would it be impossible to pardon them now?'

'How can they be pardoned when they have been sentenced by the court? Only the Tsar can grant pardons.'

'But how would the Tsar ever find out about them?'

'They have the right to appeal for mercy.'

'But it's on my account that they're being executed,' said Natalya Ivanovna, who was not very intelligent. 'And I forgive them.'

The district superintendent burst out laughing.

'Well then, why don't you lodge an appeal?'

'Can I do that?'

'Certainly you can.'

'But won't it be too late to get it to him now?'

'You could send it by telegram.'

'To the Tsar?'

'Of course, you can send a telegram even to the Tsar.'

The discovery that the executioner had refused to do his duty and was ready to suffer rather than kill anybody brought about a sudden upheaval in Natalya Ivanovna's soul, and the feeling of sympathy and horror which had come close to breaking out on several occasions, now burst its way into the open and took possession of her.

'Filipp Vasilyevich my dear, please write the telegram for me. I want to ask the Tsar to show mercy to them.'

The district superintendent shook his head. 'What if we were to get into trouble over this?'

'But I'll be the one responsible. I won't say anything about you at all.'

'What a kind woman she is,' thought the district superintendent, 'a good-hearted woman. If only my wife was like that, it would be heaven – quite different from the way things are.'

And so the district superintendent composed a telegram to the Tsar: 'To His Imperial Majesty the Sovereign Emperor. Your Imperial Majesty's loyal subject, widow of the Collegiate Assessor Pyotr Nikolayevich Sventitsky who was murdered by peasants, prostrating herself at Your Imperial Majesty's sacred feet' (the district superintendent was particularly pleased with this bit of the telegram he had composed) 'begs You to have mercy on the men condemned to death, the peasants so-and-so and so-and-so, of such-and-such a province, region, district and village.'

The district superintendent sent off the telegram in person, and Natalya Ivanovna's soul was filled with joy and happiness. It seemed to her that if she, the widow of the murdered man, was ready to forgive and to ask for mercy, then the Tsar could not fail to show mercy too.

XII

Liza Yeropkina was living on a plateau of continuous exaltation. The further she travelled along the Christian way of life which had been revealed to her, the more certain was she that this way was the true one, and the more jubilant did her soul become.

Now she had two immediate objectives in view. The first was to convert Makhin, or rather, as she expressed it to herself, to return him to his true self, to his own good and beautiful nature. She loved him, and by the light of her love she was able to perceive the divine element in his soul, common to all human beings, yet she saw in this fundamental element of life shared by all men and women a goodness, a tenderness and a distinction which were his alone. Her other objective was to cease to be rich. She had wanted to get free of her property in order to put Makhin to the test, but beyond that she desired to do this for her own sake, for the sake of her soul – and she wanted to do it according to the principles of the Gospel. She started the process by planning to give away her land, but she was thwarted in putting this idea into practice first by her father, and then even more so by the flood of suppliants who applied to her in person or in writing. Then she decided to turn to an elder, a man well known for the holiness of his life, and to ask him to take her money and to use it in whatever way he thought fitting. On hearing of this her father was very angry, and in a furious exchange he called her a madwoman and a psychopath, and announced his intention of taking steps to protect her from herself, as a person of unsound mind.

Her father's irritable, exasperated tone of voice affected her powerfully and she lost control of herself, bursting into angry tears and calling him a despot, and even a monster of selfishness.

She asked her father's forgiveness and he said that he was not angry with her, but she could see that he was hurt and that inwardly he had not really forgiven her. She was unwilling to talk to Makhin about any of this. Her sister was jealous of her attachment to Makhin and had become quite estranged from her. Thus Liza had no one to share her feelings with, no one she could confide in.

'God is the one I should be confiding in,' she told herself, and as it was now Lent she decided that she would observe the Lenten fast and make her confession, telling her confessor everything and asking his advice about what she should do next.

Not far from the city there was a monastery where the elder lived who had become famous for his way of life, his teaching, his prophecies, and the healings which were attributed to him.

The elder had received a letter from Yeropkin senior, warning him of his daughter's visit and of her abnormal, hysterical state and expressing his confidence that the elder would put her back on the right path – the path of the golden mean and the good Christian life lived in harmony with the existing order of things.

Tired out from his regular session of receiving visitors, the elder nonetheless agreed to see Liza and gently counselled her to behave with moderation and to submit to the existing circumstances of her life, and to her parents. Liza said nothing, merely blushed and perspired, but when he had finished she began to speak meekly, with tears in her eyes, about the words of Christ who had said 'Leave thy father and thy mother, and follow me'; then, becoming more and more animated, she began to explain to him her whole conception of what Christianity really meant. At first the elder smiled slightly and brought out some conventional points of teaching, but then he fell silent and began to sigh, repeating to himself 'O Lord, O Lord'.

'Very well then, come to me tomorrow and make your confession,' he said, blessing her with his wrinkled hand.

The next day he heard her confession, and without continuing their conversation of the previous day, sent her away, having briefly refused to take upon himself the disposal of her property.

This young woman's purity, her utter devotion to the will of God, her fervour, impressed the elder deeply. He had long wanted to renounce the world, but the monastery needed his activities, which were a source of income for the community. And he had accepted this, although he was vaguely aware of the falsity of his position. People were turning him into a saint, a miracle-worker, but in reality he was a weak man carried along by the current of his own success. And the soul of this young woman which had just been opened to him had revealed to him the truth about his own soul. And he had seen just how far he was from what he wanted to be and from the goal towards which his heart was drawing him.

Soon after Liza's visit he withdrew to his cell, and it was only after three weeks had gone by that he emerged again into the church to conduct a service; and after the service he preached a sermon in which he reproached himself and denounced the wickedness of the world and called it to repentance.

He took to delivering a sermon every two weeks. And more and more people came to hear these sermons. And his fame as a preacher spread further and further. There was something special, bold and sincere in his sermons. And this was why he had such a powerful effect upon other people.

XIII

Meanwhile Vasily had been carrying out his plans as he had intended. One night he and some companions got into the house of a rich man named Krasnopuzov. He knew that Krasnopuzov was a miser and a man of depraved character, and he broke into his writing-desk and stole thirty thousand roubles in cash. And Vasily did with it as he pleased. He actually stopped drinking, and gave money to poor girls so that they could get married. He financed weddings, paid off people's debts, and lay low himself. His only concern was how best to distribute the money. He even gave some to the police. And they stopped looking for him.

His heart rejoiced. And when eventually despite everything he was arrested, he laughed and boasted at his trial, saying that when it was in paunchy old Krasnopuzov's possession the money had never done any good, in fact the owner didn't know how much he'd got, 'Whereas I put the stuff into circulation and helped good folk with it'.

And his defence was so cheerful and good-hearted that the jury almost acquitted him. He was sentenced to be exiled.

He thanked the court and gave advance warning that he intended to escape.

XIV

The telegram which Sventitsky's widow sent to the Tsar produced no effect whatever. The committee which dealt with petitions decided initially that they would not even report it to the Tsar, but then one day when the Tsar was at luncheon and the conversation turned to the Sventitsky case, the chairman of the petitions committee who was at table with the sovereign informed him about the telegram they had received from the wife of the murdered man.

'*C'est très gentil de sa part*,'[11] remarked one of the ladies of the Imperial family.

The Tsar merely sighed, shrugged his shoulders beneath their epaulettes and said 'The law is the law.' And he held up his glass, into which a chamber-footman poured some sparkling Moselle. Everyone tried to look as though they were impressed by the wisdom of the sovereign's remark. And nothing further was said about the telegram. And the two peasants – the old man and the young man – were hanged with the assistance of a Tatar executioner, a cruel and bestial murderer who had been summoned from Kazan especially for the purpose.

The old man's wife wanted to dress her husband's body in a white shirt, white foot-cloths and new shoes, but she was not allowed to do so and both men were buried in a single grave outside the fence of the cemetery.

*

11 It is extremely nice of her.

'Princess Sofya Vladimirovna was telling me that he is a most wonderful preacher,' said the Tsar's mother, the Dowager Empress one day to her son. '*Faites-le venir. Il peut prêcher à la cathédrale.*'[12]

'No, it would be better to have him preach to us here,' said the Tsar, and he gave orders that the elder Isidor should be invited to come to the court.

All the generals and highest officials were assembled in the court chapel. A new and unusual preacher was something of an event.

A small grey-haired, thin old man came out and cast his eye over them all. 'In the name of the Father, and of the Son, and of the Holy Ghost,' he said, and began his sermon.

To begin with all was well, but the further it went, the worse it became. '*Il devenait de plus en plus aggressif,*'[13] as the Empress put it immediately afterwards. He fulminated against everyone and everything. He referred to the death penalty. He said that the need for the death penalty was a symptom of bad government. Could it really be permissible, in a Christian country, to kill people?

They all looked at one another, all of them concerned exclusively about the impropriety of the sermon and about how disagreeable it was for the sovereign, but no one said anything out loud. When Isidor had said 'Amen' the Metropolitan went up to him and asked him to come and have a word with him in private.

After his talk with the Metropolitan and the Chief Procurator of the Synod the old man was sent straight back to a monastery – not to his own monastery, but to the one at Suzdal, where the Father Superior and commandant of the prison was Father Misail.

XV

They all pretended that there had been nothing disagreeable about Father Isidor's sermon, and no one made any mention

12 Have him sent for. He can preach at the cathedral.
13 He grew more and more aggressive.

of it. Even the Tsar felt that the elder's words had left no impression in his mind, nevertheless on two occasions later that day his thoughts turned to the execution of the two peasants and to the telegram sent by Sventitsky's widow appealing for their pardon. That afternoon there was a parade, followed by a drive to an outdoor fête, then a reception for ministers, then dinner, and in the evening the theatre. As usual the Tsar fell asleep the moment his head touched the pillow. That night he was wakened by a terrible dream: in a field stood a gallows with corpses dangling from it, and the corpses were sticking out their tongues, and the tongues protruded further and further. And someone was shouting 'This is your doing, this is your doing.' The Tsar woke up sweating and started to think. For the first time ever he started to think about the responsibility which lay upon him, and all the things the little old man had said came back to him ...

But he could see the human being within himself only as if from a great distance, and he was unable to yield to the simple demands of the human being within him because of all the other demands coming at him from all sides as Tsar; and to acknowledge the demands of the human being within as taking precedence over those of the Tsar – that was beyond his strength.

XVI

After serving his second term in prison Prokofy [Proshka], that lively, proud, dandified young fellow, had come out an utterly broken man. When he was sober he simply sat about doing nothing, and however much his father shouted and swore at him, he went on living an idle life consuming the family's bread, and furthermore whenever he got the chance he would steal things and take them off to the tavern to get drunk on the proceeds. He lounged about, coughing, hawking and spitting. The doctor whom he went to consult listened to Prokofy's chest and shook his head.

'What you need, my lad, is what you haven't got.'

'I know that, it's what I've always needed.'

'You need to drink plenty of milk, and you mustn't smoke.'

'But it's Lent now, and anyway we don't have a cow.'

One night that spring he could not get to sleep the whole night, he felt rotten and he was longing for a drink. There was nothing in the house for him to get his hands on and sell. He put on his fur hat and went out. He walked down the street until he came to where the clergy lived. Outside the deacon's house there was a harrow standing propped up against the wattle fence. Prokofy went over, slung the harrow up on to his back and walked off with it to Petrovna at the inn. 'Maybe she'll give me just a little bottle of vodka for it.' He had not gone far before the deacon came out on to the porch of his house. It was now fully light, and he could see Prokofy making off with his harrow.

'Hey, what are you up to?'

The deacon's servants came out, seized Prokofy and threw him in the lock-up. The Justice of the Peace sentenced him to eleven months in prison.

Autumn came round. Prokofy was now transferred to the prison hospital. He was coughing all the time, fit to tear his lungs out. And he could not get warm. Those other patients must have been in better shape than he was, because they were not shivering. Prokofy, though, kept on shivering day and night. The warden was trying to economize on firewood and did not heat the prison hospital until November each year. Prokofy suffered physical agonies, but what he suffered spiritually was worse than anything. Everything seemed to him disgusting and he hated everybody: the deacon, the warden who refused to heat the hospital, the orderly, and the patient next to him who had a red, swollen lip. He also conceived a deep hatred for the new convict who was brought in to join them. This convict was Stepan. He had developed a severe inflammation of the head and had been transferred to the hospital and placed in a bed alongside Prokofy. To begin with Prokofy detested him, but later he became so fond of Stepan that his main aim in life was to have a chance of talking to him. It was only after talking to him that the pain in Prokofy's heart was ever eased.

Stepan was constantly telling the other patients about the most recent murder he had committed and about the effect it had had on him.

'She didn't scream or anything like that,' he would tell them, 'she just said "Here you are, cut my throat. It's not me you should feel sorry for, it's yourself."'

'Yes, I know that well enough, it's a terrible thing to do a person in. I once cut a sheep's throat, and I didn't feel too good about it myself. And here am I that's never killed anybody, but they've gone and done for me, the swine. I've never killed anybody . . .'

'Well and good, that'll be counted in your favour.'

'And where will that be then?'

'What do you mean, where? What about God then?'

'God? You don't see much of him about, do you? I don't believe all that stuff, friend. The way I see it is, you just die and the grass grows over you. And that's all about it.'

'How can you think that? I've done in that many, but she, she was kind-hearted, never did anything but help people. All right then, do you think it will be the same for me as it'll be for her? No, just you wait and see . . .'

'So you think that when you die, your soul goes on?'

'That's it. I reckon that's the truth.'

Dying was a hard process for Prokofy as he lay there gasping for breath. But when his last hour came he suddenly felt easier. He called Stepan over to him.

'Well, brother, goodbye. I can see it's time for me to die now. I was really scared, but it's all right now. I'd just like it to be quick.'

And Prokofy died in the prison hospital.

XVII

Meanwhile Yevgeny Mikhailovich's business affairs were going from bad to worse. His shop was mortgaged. Trade refused to pick up. Another shop had opened in the town and the interest on his mortage was due. He had to take out another loan to pay the interest. And in the end he was obliged to put up the shop and all the contents for sale. Yevgeny Mikhailovich and his wife rushed hither and thither but nowhere could they find the four hundred roubles they needed in order to save their business.

They had faint hopes of the merchant Krasnopuzov, whose mistress was friendly with Yevgeny Mikhailovich's wife. But now it was all over town that an enormous sum of money had been stolen from Krasnopuzov. People said that it amounted to half a million.

'And who do you think stole it?' Yevgeny Mikhailovich's wife was saying. 'Vasily, the one who used to be our yardman. They say he's throwing the money about all over the place, and the police have been bribed to take no notice.'

'He never was any good,' said Yevgeny Mikhailovich. 'Look how ready he was to perjure himself that time. I'd never have thought it of him.'

'They say he actually came round to our place one day. The cook said it was him. She says he paid the dowries for fourteen poor girls to get married.'

'Well, no doubt they're making it up.'

Just at that moment a strange-looking elderly man in a woollen jacket came into the shop.

'What do you want?'

'I've got a letter for you.'

'Who is it from?'

'It says on it.'

'I presume they will want a reply. Just wait a moment, please.'

'I can't.'

And the strange-looking man handed over the envelope and hurriedly departed.

'Extraordinary!'

Yevgeny Mikhailovich tore open the bulging envelope and could hardly believe his eyes: inside there were hundred-rouble notes. Four of them. What on earth was this? And there was a semi-literate letter addressed to Yevgeny

Mikhailovich. It read: 'In the Gospel it says to retern good
for evil. You did me a lot of evil with that cupon and I
offended that peasant to but now I am sorry for you. So take
these 4 Cathrines and remember your yardman Vasily.'

'This is absolutely amazing,' said Yevgeny Mikhailovich,
to his wife and to himself. And whenever he subsequently
remembered it or spoke of it to his wife, the tears would
come into his eyes and her heart would be filled with joy.

XVIII

In the prison at Suzdal there were fourteen clergymen who
were there primarily for having deviated from Orthodox
teaching; and this was where Isidor too had been sent.
Father Misail admitted Isidor in accordance with the written
instructions he had received and, without interviewing him,
gave the order that he should be placed in a solitary cell, as
befitted a serious offender. In the third week of Isidor's stay
in the prison Father Misail was making the rounds of the
inmates. Going into Isidor's cell, he asked whether there was
anything he needed.

'There is a great deal that I need, but I cannot talk about
it in the presence of other people. Please allow me the
opportunity to speak to you on your own.'

They looked at one another, and Father Misail realized
that he had nothing to fear from this man. He ordered that
Isidor should be brought to his cell in the monastery, and as
soon as they were left alone he said:

'Well, tell me what you have to say.'

Isidor fell to his knees.

'Brother!' said Isidor, 'what are you doing? Have mercy
on yourself. There cannot be a villain alive worse than you,
you have profaned everything that is holy . . .'

*

A month later Father Misail sent in applications for the
release, on the grounds of repentance, not only of Isidor,
but of seven of the other prisoners, together with a request

that he himself should be allowed to withdraw from the world in another monastery.

XIX

Ten years went by.

Mitya Smokovnikov had long since graduated from the technical institute and was now working as an engineer on a large salary in the Siberian gold-mines. He was due to go on a prospecting trip in a certain area. The mine director recommended that he should take with him the convict Stepan Pelageyushkin.

'But why should I take a convict with me? Won't that be dangerous?'

'There's nothing dangerous about him. He's a holy man. Ask anyone you like.'

'So why is he here?'

The director smiled.

'He murdered six people, but he's a holy man. I'll vouch for him absolutely.'

And so Mitya agreed to take Stepan, now bald, thin and weather-beaten, and they set off together.

On the journey Stepan looked after everybody's needs as far as he could, and he looked after Mitya Smokovnikov as if Mitya had been his own offspring; and as they travelled on he told Smokovnikov his whole story. And he told him how, and why, and on what lines he was living now.

And it was a very strange thing. Mitya Smokovnikov, who until that time had lived only to eat and drink, to play cards, and to enjoy wine and women, fell to thinking for the first time about his own life. And these thoughts of his would not leave him, in fact they started an upheaval in his soul which spread out wider and wider. He was offered a job which would have brought him great benefits. He turned it down and decided to settle for what he had, to buy an estate, to get married, and to serve the common people as best he could.

XX

And so he did. But first he went to see his father, with
whom his relations were strained on account of his father's
new wife and family. Now, however, he had decided to
make things up with his father. And so he did. And his father
was quite astonished, and ridiculed him at first, but then he
stopped criticizing his son and recalled the many, many
occasions when he had been at fault with regard to him.

ALYOSHA GORSHOK

ALYOSHKA was the youngest boy in his family. People started calling him 'Gorshok' because his mother once sent him to fetch some water for the deacon's wife, and he tripped up and smashed the pot [*gorshók*] he was carrying it in. His mother beat him, and the children took to mocking him by calling him 'Pot'. So 'Alyoshka Gorshok' – Alyoshka the Pot – became his nickname.

Alyoshka was a thin boy with lop-ears (his ears stuck out just like wings) and he had a big nose. The other children would taunt him by saying 'Alyoshka's got a nose like a dog on a hillock.' There was a school in the village, but Alyoshka never managed to learn reading and writing, in fact he had no time to study. His elder brother was living in a merchant's household in the town, and from his earliest childhood Alyoshka began helping his father. At the age of six he was already minding the sheep and cows on the common pasture with his sister who was not much older, and when he had got a little bigger he started minding the horses, by day and by night. From his twelfth year he was ploughing, and driving the cart. He was not particularly strong, but he had the knack of doing things. And he was always cheerful. The other children made fun of him, but he would just keep quiet, or laugh. If his father cursed at him, he kept quiet and listened. And when the cursing was over he would smile, and get on with the job in hand.

Alyosha was nineteen years old when his brother was taken away to be a soldier. And his father sent Alyosha to take his brother's place as a yardman at the merchant's house. Alyosha was given his brother's old boots, his father's cap

959

and a coat, and went off on a cart to the town. Alyosha himself was not too delighted with his outfit, but the merchant was quite displeased at the look of him.

'I reckoned I was going to get something like a man in place of Semyon,' said the merchant, giving Alyosha the once over, 'but this is a proper little milksop you've brought me. Whatever use is he going to be?'

'He can do anything you want – he can harness up, and fetch and carry anywhere, and he's a glutton for work. He may look like a yard of wattle fencing, but in fact he's a wiry young chap.'

'Well, I can see what he looks like, but I'll give him a try.'

'And the best thing about him is, he doesn't answer back. He's really keen to work.'

'There's no getting round you. All right, you can leave him with me.'

So Alyosha came to live at the merchant's house.

The merchant's family was a small one: the master's wife, his old mother, an elder son with only a basic education, married, who helped his father in the business, and another son who was a scholar – after leaving the grammar school he had gone to the university, but he had been expelled from there and was now living at home; and there was a daughter, a young schoolgirl.

To begin with Alyosha was not happy there – for he was a real country bumpkin, poorly dressed and without manners, and he called everyone 'thou'; but they soon got used to him. He worked even harder than his brother had done. He really was meek and didn't answer back: they sent him on all kinds of errands and he did everything willingly and quickly, and switched over from one task to the next with no break whatever. And as it had been at home, so too in the merchant's house, all manner of work fell on Alyosha's shoulders. The master's wife, the master's mother, the master's daughter and the master's son, the steward, the cook, they all sent him running hither and thither and told him to do this, that and the other. You would never hear anything but 'Run and fetch this, lad', or 'Alyosha, you sort it out', or 'You did remember to do that, didn't you Alyosha?' or 'Look here, Alyosha, don't forget this'. And Alyosha ran, and sorted out, and looked, and didn't forget, and managed to do it all, and all the time he never stopped smiling.

He soon wore his brother's boots to pieces and the master told him off for going about with his boots full of holes and his bare toes sticking out, and gave orders for some new boots to be bought for him at the bazaar. The boots were brand new and Alyosha was delighted with them, but his legs were still the same old pair, and towards evening they ached from all this running about, and he would get cross with them. Alyosha was afraid that his father, when he came to get his money, might take offence if the merchant was to deduct part of his wages in payment for the boots.

In winter Alyosha would get up before it was light, chop the firewood, sweep the yard, give the horse and the cow their fodder and water them. Then he would heat up the stoves, clean the master's boots and brush his clothes, and take out the samovars and clean them; then either the steward would call him to help get out the wares, or the cook would order him to knead the dough and scour the saucepans. Then he would be sent into town, sometimes with a note for somebody, sometimes to take something to the master's daughter at the grammar school, sometimes to fetch lamp-oil for the old lady.

'Wherever did you get to, you wretch?' now one of them, now another would say to him. 'Why go yourself? Alyosha will run and get it. Alyoshka! Here, Alyoshka!' And Alyosha would come running.

He ate his breakfast as he went along, and rarely managed to have his dinner with the others. The cook swore at him for not bringing everything that was needed, but then felt sorry for him all the same and left him something hot for his dinner or his supper. There was a particularly large amount of work for him on high days and holidays and on the days leading up to them. And Alyosha took special pleasure in the feastdays, because on feastdays they would give him tips, not much, of course – not above sixty copecks all told – but still, it was his own money. He was able to spend it as he wished. His actual wages he never set eyes on. His father would arrive and receive the money from the merchant, merely reprimanding Alyoshka for getting his boots looking worn so quickly.

When he had collected two roubles' worth of this 'tea-money', he bought, on the cook's advice, a fine knitted jacket, and when he put it on he was unable to stop grinning from sheer pleasure.

Alyosha spoke little, and when he did speak it was always short and fragmentary. And when he was ordered to do something, or asked whether he could do such and such a thing, he always replied without the slightest hesitation 'I can do that', and at once threw himself into the task, and did it.

Of prayers, he knew none at all. Whatever his mother had taught him he had forgotten, but he still prayed morning and evening – he prayed with his hands, by crossing himself.

Alyosha's life went on in this way for a year and a half, and then in the second half of the second year, something happened to him which was the most remarkable event in his life. This event had to do with his astonishing discovery that apart from the relationships between human beings which arise from their mutual needs, there are other, quite special relationships: not the ones which cause a person to brush the boots, to bring home some shopping, or to harness the horse, but the sort of relationship in which a man, although he is not needed at all by the other person, feels the need to devote himself to that other person, to be nice to them; and he discovered that he, Alyosha, was just such a man. He got to know about all this through the cook, Ustinya. Little Ustinya had been an orphan, and a hard-working child just like Alyosha. She began to feel sorry for Alyosha and Alyosha felt for the first time that he, he himself and not his services, was actually needed by another human being. When his mother had shown him that she was sorry for him, he had not really noticed it; it seemed to him that this was how things must be, that it was all one and the same, just as if he had been feeling sorry for himself. But now all of a sudden he realized that Ustinya was quite separate from him, but she did feel sorry for him and would leave him some buttery porridge at the bottom of the pot, and while he ate it she would rest her chin on her arm, the sleeve rolled up to her elbow, and watch him. And he would glance at her, and she would laugh, and then he would laugh too.

All this was so new and strange to him that at first it quite frightened Alyosha. He felt it was preventing him from carrying out his duties as he used to do. But all the same he felt glad, and when he looked at his trousers which Ustinya had darned, he shook his head and smiled. Often when he was working or as he walked along, he would think of Ustinya and say 'Oh yes, Ustinya!' Ustinya helped him where she could, and he helped her. She told him all about her past life, how she had lost her parents, how her aunt took her in, then sent her to the town, how the merchant's son had tried to talk her into doing something stupid, and how she had put him in his place. She loved talking, and he loved listening to her. He had heard that in towns it often happened that peasant workmen ended up marrying cooks. And on one occasion she asked him whether his family would soon be marrying him off. He said he didn't know, and that he wasn't keen to take a country girl for a wife.

'Well then, who have you got your eye set on?' she said.

'Ah, I'd like to marry you, of course. Would you be willing to marry me?'

'Just look at him, he may be only Alyosha the Pot, just a pot, but see how he's contrived to speak out and say what he wanted,' she said, giving him a whack on the back with the towel she was holding. 'And why shouldn't I marry you indeed?'

At Shrovetide the old man came to town to collect his money. The merchant's wife had heard how Alexei had hit on the idea that he was going to marry Ustinya, and she did not like it. 'She'll go and get pregnant, and what use will she be with a child?' she said to her husband.

The master paid over the money to Alexei's father.

'Well then, and how is the boy behaving himself?' asked the peasant. 'I told you he was a meek one.'

'Meek or not meek, he's thought up a thoroughly stupid scheme. He's got it into his head that he's going to marry the cook. But I'm not going to start employing married people. That sort of thing doesn't suit us.'

'He's a fool, nothing but a fool. Look what he's thought up here,' said the father. 'You wouldn't credit it. I'll tell him straight out he's got to give up this notion.'

Going into the kitchen, the father sat down at the table to wait for his son. Alyosha was out running errands, and he was panting when he came in.

'I thought you were a sensible lad. But now what's this you've gone and thought up?' said the father.

'I haven't thought up anything.'

'What do you mean, you haven't thought up anything? You've decided you want to get married. I'll marry you off when the time's right, and I'll marry you off to the right person, and not to some town slut.'

The father went on talking for some time. Alyosha stood there and sighed. When his father had finished talking, Alyosha smiled.

'So I'm to give the whole thing up.'

'That's right.'

When his father had gone and he was left alone with Ustinya, he said to her (she had been listening behind the door while the father was talking to his son):

'Our plan wasn't right, it didn't work out. Did you hear him? He got real angry; he won't allow it.'

She said nothing, but burst into tears and buried her face in her apron.

Alyosha made a clicking noise with his tongue.

'It's no use going against it. It's clear we must just give the whole thing up.'

That evening, when the merchant's wife ordered him to close the shutters, she said to him:

'Well then, did you listen to your father, and have you given up your silly notions?'

'Stands to reason I've given them up,' replied Alyosha; and he laughed, then immediately burst into tears.

*

From that time on Alyosha said nothing more to Ustinya about marriage, and he went on living as he had before.

One day in Lent the steward sent him to clear the snow off the roof. He had climbed up on to the roof, and had got it clear and was just starting to pull away the frozen snow from the gutters, when his feet slipped, and he fell off the roof, holding the shovel. Unfortunately he landed not on the snow, but on the iron-covered entrance gate of the yard. Ustinya came running up, as did the master's daughter.

'Are you hurt, Alyosha?'

'I reckon you could say that again. But not to worry.'

He tried to stand up, but could not, and he began to smile. They carried him into the yardman's lodge. The doctor's assistant arrived. He examined Alyosha and asked him where it hurt.

'It hurts all over, but it's not too bad. But the master's going to be upset. And they ought to send word to my old man.'

Alyosha lay in bed for two days and nights, and on the third day they sent for the priest.

'And what if you should be going to die?' asked Ustinya.

'What if I am? We don't go on living for ever, do we? You've got to go sometime,' said Alyosha quickly, in his usual tone of voice. 'Thank you, Ustinya, for having pity on me. But it was really better that they didn't let me get married, it wouldn't have been any good. And now we're on friendly terms, you and me.'

He accompanied the priest's prayers only with his hands and in his heart. But in his heart was the knowledge that life here on earth is good if you do what you are told and don't offend people, and there too it will be good.

He did not say very much. He just asked for something to drink, and as he drank it he looked as if he was surprised at something.

He looked surprised, stretched himself out, and died.

WHAT FOR?

A story from the time of the Polish insurrections

I

In the spring of 1830 Pan Jaczewski, who was living on his ancestral estate of Rozanka, received a visit from his late brother's only son, the young Josif Migurski. Jaczewski was an old man of sixty-five with a wide forehead, broad shoulders and a broad chest and long white whiskers on his brick-red face, and he was a patriot from the time of the Second Partition of Poland. As a young man he had served alongside Migurski the elder under the banner of Kosciuszko and he detested with all the strength of his patriotic soul the 'whore of the Apocalypse', as he called her, the Empress Catherine II, and her loathsome, traitorous lover Poniatowski, and he likewise believed in the restoration of the Commonwealth of Poland and Lithuania,[1] just as he believed at night that the sun would rise again by the next morning. In 1812 he had commanded a regiment in the army of Napoleon, whom he worshipped. Napoleon's downfall grieved him but he did not abandon the hope of a restoration of the Polish kingdom, were it only a mutilated one. The opening of the Sejm[2] in Warsaw by Alexander I revived his hopes, but the Holy Alliance and the triumph of the general reaction across the whole of Europe, and the petty tyranny of the Grand Duke Constantine put off indefinitely any realization of his cherished longings ... After 1825 Jaczewski made his home in the country, spending his time without interruption at Rozanka and occupying himself with farming, hunting, and the reading of newspapers and letters, by which means he

1 The Rzecz Pospolita, instituted in 1569 by King Sigismund II Augustus, last of the Jagellon dynasty.
2 Representative assembly, Diet.

969

continued ardently to follow political events in his homeland. He had taken as his second wife a beautiful but impoverished woman from the *szlachta*,[3] and the marriage was not a happy one. He neither loved nor respected this second wife of his: he felt her to be an encumbrance and treated her harshly and rudely, as if her were punishing her for his own mistake in remarrying. He had no children by his second wife. From the first marriage there were two daughters: the elder, Wanda, a stately beauty who was aware of the value of her attractions and was bored by country life; and the younger, Albina, her father's darling, a lively, bony little girl with curly blonde hair and, like her father, large widely-spaced sparkling blue eyes.

Albina was fifteen years old at the time of Josif Migurski's visit. Migurski had in fact stayed with the Jaczewskis before as a student, in Vilna where they spent the winters, and had paid court to Wanda, but now he was coming to visit them in the country for the first time as a grown up and independent young man. The arrival of young Migurski was agreeable to all the inhabitants of Rozanka. For old Juzio Migurski it was agreeable because it reminded him of his friend, Josif's father, of the time when they were both young, and of how they had talked together with great passion and the rosiest hopes about the current revolutionary ferment – and not only in Poland but also abroad, whence he had just returned. To Pani Jaczewska it was agreeable because when there were guests present old Jaczewski restrained himself and did not scold her for everything in his usual manner. To Wanda it was agreeable because she was sure that Migurski had come for her sake and that he intended to propose to her: she was preparing to accept, but she intended, as she expressed it to herself, to '*lui tenir la dragée haute*'.[4] Albina was glad because everyone else was glad. Wanda was not the only one convinced that Migurski had come with the

3 Polish aristocracy.
4 Literally: 'to hold the sweetmeat high' – i.e. to put him through his paces first.

intention of asking for her hand. The entire household, from old Jaczewski down to nanny Ludwika, thought so, although nobody said anything.

And they were correct. Migurski had arrived with that intention, but at the end of a week he left again, somehow confused and downcast, without having made any proposal. They were all surprised by this unexpected departure and no one, with the exception of Albina, understood the reason for it. Albina knew that the cause of his strange departure was she herself.

The whole time he had been at Rozanka she had noticed that Migurski seemed particularly animated and cheerful only when he was with her. He treated her like a child, joking with her and teasing her, but with her feminine intuition she sensed that underneath this treatment of her there lay not the attitude of an adult towards a child, but that of a man towards a woman. She could see this in the admiring expression and affectionate smile with which he greeted her whenever she came into the room and took his leave of her when she left. She had no clear awareness of what was happening, but his attitude towards her made her feel happy, and she unconsciously did her best to please him. In fact anything she could possibly have done would have pleased him. And so when he was present she did everything with a special kind of excitement. He was pleased when she ran races with her beautiful greyhound and it jumped up and licked her flushed, radiant face; he was pleased when at the slightest pretext she broke into loud and infectious laughter; he was pleased when, continuing her merry laughter in the expression of her eyes, she put on a serious face to listen to the Catholic priest's boring homily; he was pleased when, with exceptional accuracy and humour, she mimicked first her old nanny, then a drunken neighbour, and then Migurski himself, switching in an instant from the depiction of one to the depiction of the next. Most of all he was pleased by her enthusiastic *joie de vivre*. It was just as though she had only just realized the full charm of life and was hastening to enjoy it to the utmost. He liked this special *joie de vivre* of

LEO TOLSTOY

hers, and this *joie de vivre* was aroused and heightened especially when she was aware that it was delightful to him. And
so it was that Albina alone was aware why Migurski, who
had come to propose to Wanda, had gone away without
doing so. Although she could not have brought herself to
tell anybody and did not confess it directly even to herself,
in the depths of her soul she knew that he had wanted to
fall in love with her sister, but had actually fallen in love
with her, Albina. Albina was greatly astonished at this, counting herself totally insignificant in comparison with the clever,
well-educated and beautiful Wanda, but she could not help
knowing that it was so and she could not help rejoicing in
the fact, because she herself had come to love Migurski with
all the strength of her soul, to love him as people only love
for the first, the only time in their lives.

II

At the end of the summer the newspapers brought the news
of the July Revolution in Paris. After that news began to
arrive of impending disorders in Warsaw. With a mixture of
fear and hope Jaczewski awaited with every post news of
the assassination of Constantine and the beginning of a
revolution. At last in November the news arrived at Rozanka
– first of the attack on the Belvedere Palace and the flight of
the Grand Duke Constantine Pavlovich; then that the Sejm
had pronounced that the Romanov dynasty had been
deprived of the Polish throne and that Chlopicki had
been proclaimed dictator and the Polish people were once
more free.

The insurrection had not yet reached Rozanka, but all the
inhabitants followed its progress, awaiting its arrival in their
home region and making ready for it. Old Jaczewski corresponded with an acquaintance of long ago who was one of
the leaders of the insurrection, received a number of secretive
Jewish commercial agents not on economic but on revolutionary business, and prepared to join the insurrection when
the time should be right. Pani Jaczewska concerned herself

as always, but now more than ever, with her husband's material comforts, and by that very fact managed to irritate him more and more. Wanda sent off her diamonds to a girlfriend in Warsaw so that the money obtained for them could be given to the revolutionary committee. Albina was interested only in what Migurski was doing. She learned via her father that he had enlisted in Dwernicki's detachment and she tried to find out all she could about that particular detachment. Migurski wrote twice: the first time to inform them that he had joined the army; and the second time, in mid-February, an enthusiastic letter about the Polish victory at the battle of Stoczek, where they had captured six Russian guns and some prisoners.

'*Zwyciestwo polaków i kleska moskali! Wiwat!*'[5] – he wrote at the conclusion of his letter. Albina was in raptures. She scrutinized the map, trying to work out when and where the decisively defeated Muscovites must be, and she went pale and trembled as her father slowly unsealed the packets brought from the post office. On one occasion her step-mother chanced to go into Albina's room and came upon her standing before the mirror wearing trousers and a *konfederatka*.[6] Albina was getting ready to run away from home in male attire to join the Polish army. Her stepmother went and told her father. Her father summoned Albina to him, and concealing the sympathy, even admiration, he felt for her, delivered a stern rebuke, demanding that she should banish from her head any stupid ideas about taking part in the war. 'A woman has a different duty to fulfil: to love and comfort those who are sacrificing themselves for the motherland' – he told her. Now he needed her, she was a joy and a comfort to him; but the time would come when she would be needed in the same way by her husband. He knew how to persuade her. He reminded her that he was lonely and unhappy, and kissed her. She pressed her face against him, hiding the tears, which nevertheless moistened

5 Victory to the Poles, destruction to the Muscovites! Hurrah!
6 A Polish man's hat with a square base and a tassel on top.

the sleeve of his dressing-gown, and promised him not to undertake anything without his agreement.

III

Only those who have experienced what the Poles experienced after the Partition of Poland and the subjection of one part of the country to the power of the hated Germans and another part to the power of the still more hated Muscovites, can understand the rapture which the Poles felt in the years 1830 and 1831 when, after their earlier unsuccessful attempts to liberate themselves, their new hope of liberation seemed about to be fulfilled. But this hope did not last long. The forces involved were too disproportionate and the attempted revolution was once again crushed. Once again tens of thousands of dumbly obedient Russians were herded into Poland, and at the command first of Dibich, then of Paskyevich, quite without knowing why they were doing it, proceeded to soak the earth with their own blood and that of their Polish brothers, to crush them, and once more to set in power weak and worthless men who desired neither the freedom of the Poles nor their suppression, but simply and solely the satisfaction of their own greed and their childish vanity.

Warsaw was taken and the independent Polish detachments utterly defeated. Hundreds, thousands of people were shot, beaten with rods, or sent into exile. Among those exiled was young Migurski. His estate was confiscated, and he himself assigned as a common soldier to a line battalion at Uralsk.

The Jaczewskis spent the winter of 1832 at Vilna for the sake of the old man's health: since 1831 he had been suffering from a heart ailment. Here a letter reached him from Migurski, written in the fortress where he was serving. He wrote that however hard were the experiences he had already gone through and which still awaited him, he rejoiced that it had been his destiny to suffer for his native land, that he did not despair of the sacred cause to which he had devoted part of his life and was ready to devote that which remained, and that if a new opportunity were to present itself tomorrow, then he would act again in precisely the same way. Reading the letter aloud, the old man burst into sobs when he reached this passage and for some time could not go on. In the final section of the letter, which Wanda read out, Migurski wrote that *whatever his hopes and longings might have been* at the time of his last visit to them, which would ever remain the brightest point of his whole life, now he could not and would not speak further about them.

Wanda and Albina each understood these words in her own way, but neither confided to anyone else exactly how she understood them. Migurski concluded his letter with greetings to all of them: among these he addressed Albina in the same playful tone he had adopted with her at the time of his visit, asking her whether she was still rushing about as she used to, running races with the greyhounds, and mimicking everyone so beautifully. To old Jaczewski he wished good health, to the mother success in household affairs, to Wanda that she should find a husband worthy of her, and to Albina that she should keep her *joie de vivre*.

IV

Old Jaczewski's health grew ever worse and in 1833 the whole family went abroad. In Baden Wanda met a wealthy Polish emigré and married him. The old man's condition rapidly declined, and at the beginning of 1833, while they were still abroad, he died. His wife he had not permitted to follow him, and to the very last he was unable to forgive her for the mistake he had made in marrying her. Pani Jaczewska returned to the country with Albina. The chief interest in Albina's life was Migurski. In her eyes he was the greatest of heroes and a martyr, to whose service she had resolved to dedicate her own life. Before going abroad she had already struck up a correspondence with him, at first on her father's behalf, then on her own. After her father's death she returned to Russia and went on writing to him; and once

her eighteenth birthday was past she declared to her stepmother that she had decided to travel to Uralsk to join
Migurski and there become his wife. Her stepmother at once
began accusing Migurski of selfishly wanting to relieve his
own difficult situation by captivating a rich young woman
and compelling her to share his misfortune. Albina grew
angry and informed her stepmother that no one but she
could think of imputing such base thoughts to a man who
had sacrificed everything for his own nation, that Migurski
had on the contrary refused the help she had offered him,
and that she had decided irrevocably to join him and become
his wife, if only he was prepared to grant her that happiness.
Albina was now of age and had some money – the thirty
thousand *zlotys* which her late uncle had left to each of his
two nieces. So that there was nothing to hold her back.

In November 1833 Albina, as if for the last time, said
farewell to the family who were tearfully seeing her off on
her journey to this distant, unknown realm of barbarous
Muscovy, took her seat alongside her devoted old nurse
Ludwika whom she was taking with her, in her father's old
covered sleigh, newly repaired for this long journey, and set
off on the highroad.

V

Migurski was living not in the barracks, but in separate
quarters of his own. Tsar Nicholas I required that Polish
officers who had been reduced to the ranks should not only
have to put up with the hardships of an austere military life,
but also suffer all the humiliations to which private soldiers
were subjected at that time. But the majority of the ordinary
men whose duty it was to carry out his orders were fully
aware of the harshness of treatment meted out to these
demoted officers, and without regard to the danger involved
in any failure to carry out the Tsar's will, deliberately failed
to carry it out whenever they could. The semi-literate commander of the battalion to which Migurski had been
assigned, a man who had been promoted from the ranks,

understood the situation of this once wealthy, well-educated young man who had now lost everything: he felt sorry for him, respected him, and made all kinds of concessions in his favour. And Migurski could not help appreciating the generous spirit of the lieutenant colonel with the white side-whiskers on his puffy military face, and to recompense him Migurski agreed to give lessons in mathematics and French to his sons, who were preparing for entry to the military academy.

Migurski's life at Uralsk, which had now been dragging on for some six months, was not only monotonous, dreary and dull, but very hard into the bargain. Apart from the battalion commander, from whom he attempted as far as possible to distance himself, his sole acquaintance was an exiled Pole, an uneducated and disagreeable man of a thrusting disposition who worked in the fishing trade. The principal hardship for Migurski lay in the difficulty he experienced in getting used to a life of poverty. Following the confiscation of his estate he had been left quite without financial means, and he was making ends meet by selling off whatever gold objects still remained to him.

The single great joy of his life in exile was his correspond-ence with Albina, and the charming, poetic image he had formed of her during his visit to Rozanka remained in his soul and now in his banishment grew ever more beautiful to him. In one of her first letters to him she asked him, among other things, about the meaning of his words in the earlier letter: 'whatever my dreams and longings might have been'. He replied that now he was able to confess to her that his dreams were connected with his desire to call her his wife. She wrote back that she loved him too. He responded that it would have been better if she had not written that, for it was dreadful for him to think about something which was now most likely an impossibility. She said in her reply that it was not only possible, but would most certainly come about. He wrote back that he could not accept her sacrifice, and that in his present circumstances it simply could not be. Shortly after writing this letter he received a package of

money to the value of two thousand *zlotys*. By the postmark
on the envelope and the handwriting he could see that it
had been sent by Albina, and recalled having jokingly
described in one of his earliest letters the satisfaction he felt
now at being able by the lessons he gave to earn enough to
pay for all the things he needed – tea, tobacco, even books.
He transferred the money to another envelope and returned
it to her with a letter begging her not to destroy the sacred
nature of their relationship by bringing money into it. He
had enough of everything he needed, he wrote, and he was
completely happy in the knowledge that he possessed such
a friend as she was. With that their correspondence came to
a stop.

One day in November Migurski was at the Lieutenant
Colonel's house giving his sons their lesson, when the
approaching sound of the post sleigh bell was heard, and the
runners of a sledge came crunching over the frozen snow
and stopped in front of the house entrance. The boys jumped
up from their seats to find out who had arrived. Migurski
stayed behind in the room, looking at the door and waiting
for the boys to return, but through the doorway came the
Lieutenant Colonel's wife in person. 'Some ladies have come
asking for you, Pan,' she said. 'They must be from your
country – they look like Polish ladies.'

If anyone had asked Migurski whether he thought it
possible that Albina might come to see him, he would have
said that it was unthinkable; yet in the depths of his soul he
was expecting her. The blood rushed to his heart and he ran
out gasping for breath, into the hall. In the hall a stout
woman with a pockmarked face was untying the shawl which
covered her head. A second woman was just going through
the doorway which led to the Lieutenant Colonel's quarters.
Hearing steps behind her she looked round. From beneath
her bonnet shone the joyful, widely-spaced radiant blue eyes
of Albina, their lashes covered with hoarfrost. Migurski stood
rooted to the spot, not knowing how he should greet her or
what to say. 'Juzio,' she cried, calling him by the name his
father had used, and she herself had used in the old days,

and she flung her arms round his neck, pressing her face, rosy with cold, against his, bursting into laughter and tears at one and the same time.

When she had found out who Albina was and why she had come, the Lieutenant Colonel's kind-hearted wife took her in and gave her lodging in her own house until it should be time for the wedding.

VI

The good-natured Lieutenant Colonel managed after considerable trouble to obtain an authorization from the high command. A Catholic priest was despatched from Orenburg to marry the Migurskis. The battalion commander's wife acted as proxy for the bride's mother, one of Migurski's pupils carried the ikon, and Brzozowksi, the Polish exile, was best man.

Albina, however strange it may appear, loved her husband passionately but did not know him at all. Only now was she really getting acquainted with him. It stands to reason that she discovered in this living man of flesh and blood a great many commonplace and unpoetic things which had not been part of the image of him which she had nurtured and carried in her imagination; yet on the other hand, precisely because he was a man of flesh and blood, she discovered in him much that was simple and good, which had also not been part of her abstract image of him.

She had heard from friends and acquaintances about his bravery in war and she knew for herself how courageously he had faced the loss of his status and his liberty, so that she imagined him in her own mind as a hero, invariably living a life of exalted heroism; whereas in reality, for all his exceptional physical strength and bravery, he turned out to be as gentle and mild as a lamb, the simplest of men, with his talent for genial jokes and the same childlike smile on his sensitive mouth with its small blond beard and moustache, the smile which had attracted her long ago at Rozanka – but also in his mouth the never-extinguished tobacco pipe which proved particularly trying for her during her pregnancy.

Migurski too was only now getting to know Albina, and getting to know the woman within her. From the women he had known in the period before his marriage he had never gained any understanding of woman herself. And what he discovered in Albina, as in woman in general, surprised him and might well have made him disillusioned with woman in general, had he not felt for Albina a special and grateful tenderness. For Albina and for woman in general he felt a tender, slightly ironic indulgence, but for Albina herself and for her alone he felt not only loving affection, but also an awareness of and an admiration for the unrepayable debt created by her sacrifice, which had given him such totally undeserved happiness.

The Migurskis were blessed in that, directing all the power of their love on one another, they felt amid so many alien people like two half-frozen wanderers who had lost the winter road, yet managed by their mutual contact to keep each other warm. The joyful life the Migurskis spent together was enhanced by the contribution of Albina's nurse Ludwika, who was utterly self-sacrificing, devoted as a slave to her mistress, full of good-natured grumbles, amusing, and ready to fall in love with any man whatever. The Migurskis were blessed too with the gift of children. At the end of a year a little boy was born; a year and a half later, a girl. The boy was the image of his mother: the same eyes, the same playfulness and grace. The little girl was a fine, healthy child, like a little wild thing.

Yet the Migurskis were still far from blest by their separation from their homeland, and most of all by the harshness of their unaccustomed humble situation. Albina in particular suffered from this humiliation. He, her own Juzio, a hero and a model of humanity, was obliged to stand to attention before any and every officer, to carry out rifle maintenance, to do guard duty and to obey every order without complaint.

On top of all that, the news they received from Poland continued to be extremely miserable. Virtually all their close relatives and friends had either been exiled or, having lost everything, had taken refuge abroad. For the Migurskis themselves there was no prospect of any end to this situation. All attempts to petition for a pardon or at least some improvement in their conditions, or for promotion to officer rank, failed to reach their destination. Tsar Nicholas conducted inspections, parades and exercises, attended masquerades and flirted under the cover of his masks, and galloped unnecessarily through Russia from Chuguyev to Novorossiisk, St Petersburg and Moscow, frightening ordinary people and riding his horses to exhaustion; and when a bold spirit plucked up the courage to ask for some alleviation of the lot of the exiled Decembrists or of the Poles who were now suffering precisely because of that patriotism which he himself extolled, he would stick out his chest, fix his pewter-coloured eyes on whatever happened to be in front of him, and say: 'Let them go on serving. It is too soon.' As if he knew when it would no longer be too soon, when it would be time to do something. And all the members of his entourage – the generals, the chamberlains and their wives, who were busy around him looking after their own interests, would feel moved at the extraordinary perspicacity and the wisdom of this great man.

All the same, there was on the whole more of happiness than of unhappiness in the lives of the Migurskis.

So they lived for a period of five years. But suddenly there came upon them an unexpected and terrible sorrow. First the little girl fell ill, then two days later the little boy: he had a high fever for three days, and in the absence of medical help (there was no doctor to be found) on the fourth day he died. Two days after him the little girl also died.

The only thing which stopped Albina from drowning herself in the River Ural was that she could not imagine without horror the state her husband would be in on receiving the news of her suicide. But it was hard for her to go on living. Hitherto always active and solicitous, she now handed over all her concerns to Ludwika and would sit for hours doing nothing, gazing mutely at whatever met her eyes, then suddenly jump up and run off to her tiny room and there, ignoring the consolations offered by her husband and Ludwika, she would weep silently, merely shaking her head and begging them to go away and leave her alone.

In the summer she would go to her children's grave and sit there, lacerating her heart with memories of what had been and of what might have been. She was particularly tormented by the thought that her children would still have been alive, had they all been living in a town where medical aid was to be had. 'Why? What for?' she thought. 'And Juzio and I, we want nothing from anybody, except for him to be able to live in the way he was born to live, as his grandparents and his forefathers lived, and all I want is to live with him and to love him, and to love my little ones and to bring them up.

'Yet suddenly they start tormenting him, and send him into exile, and they take away from me what is dearer to me than the whole world. Why? What for?' – she hurled this question at men and at God. And she could not conceive of the possibility of any kind of answer. Yet without an answer there was no life for her. And so her life came to a standstill. This wretched life of banishment, which she had previously managed to beautify by her feminine good taste and elegance, now became intolerable not only to her, but to Migurski, who suffered both on her account and because he did not know how to help her.

VII

At this most terrible time for the Migurskis there appeared in Uralsk a Pole by the name of Rosolowski who had been involved in a grandiose plan for a rebellion and escape, drawn up at that time in Siberia by the exiled Catholic priest Sirocinski.

Rosolowksi, like Migurski and thousands of others condemned to Siberian exile for having desired to live in the manner to which they were born, that is as Poles, had got involved in this cause and had been flogged with birch rods and assigned to serve as a soldier in the same battalion as Migurski. Rosolowksi, a former mathematics teacher, was a long, thin stooping man with sunken cheeks and a furrowed brow.

So it was that on the very first evening of his time in Uralsk Rosolowski, as he sat drinking tea in the Migurskis' quarters, inevitably began in his slow, calm bass voice to recount the circumstances which had led to his suffering so cruelly. It appeared that Sirocinski had been organizing a secret society with members all over Siberia whose aim was to incite a mutiny among the soldiers and convicts with the help of the Poles enlisted in the Cossack and line regiments, to rouse the deported settlers to revolt, seize the artillery at Omsk and set everyone free.

'But would that really have been possible?' enquired Migurski.

'Quite possible, everything had been prepared,' said Rosolowski frowning gloomily, and slowly and calmly he proceeded to tell them all about the plan of liberation and the measures which had been taken to assure the success of the enterprise and, in case it should fail, to ensure the safety of the conspirators. Their success would have been certain, but for the treachery of two villains. According to Rosolowski, Sirocinski had been a man of genius and of great spiritual power, and his death too had been that of a hero and a martyr. And Rosolowski began in his calm, deep, measured voice to recount the details of the execution at which, by the order of the authorities, he and all the others found guilty in the case were compelled to be present.

'Two battalions of soldiers stood in two ranks forming a long corridor, each man holding a pliant rod of such a thickness, defined by the Emperor himself, that no more than three of them could be inserted into a rifle muzzle. The first man to be brought out was Dr Szakalski. Two soldiers led him along and the men with the rods lashed him on his exposed back as he came level with them. I was only able to see what was happening when he came near to the spot where I was standing. At first I could hear only the beating of the drum, but then, when the swish of the rods and sound of the blows falling on his body began to be audible, I knew he was approaching. And I could see that the soldiers were pulling him along on their rifles, and so he came, shuddering and turning his head first to one side, then to the other. And once, as he was being led past us, I heard the Russian doctor telling the soldiers, "Don't hit him too hard, have pity on him." But they went on beating him just the same: when they led him past us for the second time he was no longer able to walk unaided, they had to drag him. His back was dreadful to behold. I screwed up my eyes. He collapsed, and they carried him away. Then a second man was brought out. Then a third, and a fourth. All of them eventually fell down and were carried away – some looked as if they were dead, others just about alive, and we all had to stand there and watch. It went on for six hours – from morning until two in the afternoon. Last of all they brought out Sirocinski himself. It was a long time since I had seen him and I would not have recognized him, so much older did he look. His clean-shaven face was full of wrinkles, and a pale greenish colour. His body where it was uncovered was thin and yellow and his ribs stuck out above his contracted stomach. He moved along as all the others had done, shuddering at each stroke and jerking his head, but he did not groan and kept repeating a prayer in a loud voice: '*Miserere mei Deus secundum magnam misericordiam tuam.*'[7]

'I myself could hear it,' said Rosolowski rapidly in a strangled voice, and he shut his mouth and breathed heavily through his nose.

Ludwika, sitting by the window, was sobbing and had covered her face with her shawl.

'And you had to describe it to us! They are beasts, nothing but savage beasts!' cried Migurski, and throwing down his pipe he jumped up from his chair and hurried out into the unlit bedroom. Albina sat there as if turned to stone, gazing into the dark corner of the room.

7 Have mercy upon me, O God, according to Thy great mercy.

VIII

The following day Migurski, on his way home from a lesson, was surprised to see his wife hurrying to meet him with light steps and a radiant face. When they got home she took him into their bedroom.

'Juzio, listen to me.'

'Listen? What do you mean?'

'I have been thinking all night about what Rosolowksi was telling us. And I have decided: I cannot go on living like this, in this place. I cannot. I may die, but I am not going to stay here.'

'But what can we possibly do?'

'Escape.'

'Escape? How?'

'I've thought it all through. Listen,' – and she told him the plan she had worked out during the night. Her plan was this: he, Migurski, would leave the house in the evening and leave his greatcoat on the bank of the Ural, and beside it a letter saying that he was going to take his own life. They would think he had drowned. They would hunt for his body and send in a report of what had occurred. Meanwhile he would be hiding – she would hide him so that he could not be found. They could go on like that for a month at least. And when all the fuss had died down, they would run away.

Migurski's first reaction was that her scheme was impracticable, but by the end of the day her passionate confidence in it had convinced him, and he began to be of the same mind. Apart from that, he was inclined to agree with her, for the very reason that the punishment for an attempted escape, the same punishment Rosolowski had described to them, would fall on him, Migurski, but if they succeeded she would be set free, and he saw that since the death of the two children life here had been bitterly hard for her.

Rosolowski and Ludwika were let into the scheme, and after lengthy discussions, modifications and adjustments the plan was complete. To begin with they arranged that

Migurski, once he had been presumed drowned, should run away alone on foot. Albina would then take the carriage and meet him at a prearranged place. This was the first plan. But later, when Rosolowski had told them of all the unsuccessful escape attempts which had been made in Siberia over the past five years (during which only one fortunate man had escaped to safety), Albina put forward a different plan – namely, that Juzio should be hidden in the carriage and travel with her and Ludwika to Saratov. At Saratov he would change his clothes and walk downstream along the bank of the Volga to an agreed spot where he would board a boat which she would have hired in Saratov and which would take the three of them down the Volga as far as Astrakhan and then across the Caspian Sea to Persia. This plan was approved by them all, as well as by its principal architect Rosolowski, but they were faced with the difficulty of fitting the carriage with a hiding-place big enough to take a man without attracting the attention of the authorities. And when Albina, having paid a visit to the children's grave, told Rosolowski that she felt bad about leaving her children's remains in an alien land, he thought for a moment, then said:

'Ask the authorities for permission to take the children's coffins away with you – they will grant it.'

'No, I can't do that, I don't want to!' said Albina.

'You must ask them. Everything depends on it. We shall not take the coffins, but we shall make a large box for them and into that box we shall put Josif.'

For a moment Albina wanted to reject this suggestion, so painful was it for her to associate any such deception with the memory of her children, but when Migurski cheerfully approved the project, she agreed.

The final version of the plan was thus as follows: Migurski would do everything to convince the authorities that he had been drowned. As soon as his death had been officially recognized she would apply for permission, following the death of her husband, to return to her native land, taking with her the mortal remains of her children. Once the permission had been granted everything would be done to give the impression that the graves had been opened and the coffins taken out, but the coffins would remain where they were and instead of the coffins it would be Migurski who would take their place in the specially constructed box. The box would be loaded on to the tarantass and so they would reach Saratov. At Saratov they would transfer to the boat. In the boat Juzio would emerge and they would sail down to the Caspian Sea. And there Persia or Turkey awaited them – and freedom.

IX

First of all the Migurskis purchased a tarantass on the pretext that Ludwika would soon be leaving to return to her homeland. Then began the construction of the box to allow Migurski to lie in it, if only in a contorted position, without suffocating, to emerge quickly and unobtrusively, and to crawl back into it when necessary. The designing and fitting out of the box was the work of all three of them together – Albina, Rosolowski, and Migurski himself. Rosolowski's help was particularly vital, since he was an accomplished carpenter. They made the box to be fixed against the front-to-back struts at the rear of the coach body and flush with it, and the wall of the box which lay against the bodywork could be slid out, allowing a person to lie partly in the box and partly in the bottom of the tarantass. In addition airholes were bored in the box, and the top and sides were to be covered with bast matting and tied up with cords. It was possible to get in and out of the box by way of the tarantass, which was fitted with a seat.

When tarantass and box were ready, and when her husband had yet to make his disappearance, Albina began to prepare the authorities by going to the Colonel and telling him that her husband had fallen into a state of melancholia and was threatening to kill himself, and that she feared for his life and begged that he might be released before it was too late. Her acting ability stood her in good stead. The fear and anxiety she expressed for her husband appeared so natural that the Colonel was touched and promised to do all he could. After that Migurski composed the letter which was to be discovered in the cuff of his overcoat left lying on the river bank, and on the evening they had chosen he went down to the Ural, waited until it was dark, laid the clothes and the coat containing the letter on the bank, and returned home. They had prepared him a hiding-place in the loft, secured by a padlock. That night Albina sent word to the Colonel by Ludwika to say that her husband had left the house some twenty hours earlier and had not returned. Next morning her husband's letter was brought to her, and she, with every appearance of deep despair, went off weeping to show it to the Colonel.

A week later Albina submitted her request to be allowed to leave for her own land. The grief displayed by Madame Migurski affected everyone who saw her: all were filled with pity for this unfortunate wife and mother. When permission had been granted for her departure, she made a second request – that she might be allowed to exhume the bodies of her children and take them with her.

The military authorities were astonished at such a display of sentimentality, but agreed to this as well.

On the evening of the day after this permission had been given, Rosolowski, Albina and Ludwika drove in a hired cart, containing the box, to the cemetery where the children were buried. Albina fell to her knees before the grave, said a prayer, then quickly got up, and turning to Rosolowski said:

'Do what must be done, but I cannot have any part in it,' and went off by herself.

Rosolowski and Ludwika moved the gravestone aside and turned over the whole of the top surface of the plot with a shovel so that the grave looked as though it had been opened. When all this was done they called to Albina and returned home taking the box, filled with earth.

The day fixed for their departure came at last. Rosolowski was rejoicing at the success of the enterprise which seemed almost complete, Ludwika had baked biscuits and pies for the journey, and repeating her favourite turn of phrase, '*jak mame kocham'*,[8] said that her heart was bursting with fear and joy at the same time. Migurski was filled with joy, both by his release from the loft where he had spent more than a month, and still more by the renewed vitality and *joie de vivre* of Albina. She seemed to have forgotten all her former grief and the dangers, and as she might have done in her girlhood, ran to see him in the loft, radiating rapture and delight.

At three in the morning their Cossack escort arrived, bringing with him the coachman and a team of three horses. Albina, Ludwika and the little dog took their seats on the cushions of the tarantass which were covered with matting. The Cossack and the driver got up on the box, and Migurski, wearing peasant clothes, was lying in the body of the tarantass.

They were soon out of the town, and the team of good horses pulled the tarantass along the beaten roadway, smooth as stone, through the endless unploughed steppe overgrown with the last season's silvery feather-grass.

X

Albina's heart had almost stopped beating from hope and delight. Wishing to share her feelings with someone else, she now and then, almost smiling, made a sign with her head to Ludwika, indicating now the broad back of the Cossack seated on the box, now the bottom of the tarantass. Ludwika stared motionlessly ahead with a meaningful expression, only slightly pursing her lips. The day was bright. On all sides stretched the limitless deserted steppe and the silvery feather-grass shining in the slanting rays of the morning sun. Occasionally, first on one side, then on the other side of the hard road on which the rapid, unshod hooves of the Bashkir horses rang out as if on asphalt, the little earth-covered mounds made by gophers came into view; one of the little creatures would be sitting up on sentry duty, and anticipating danger would give a piercing whistle and disappear into the

8 As I love my mother.

burrow beneath. On rare occasions they met with passers-by: a string of Cossack carts full of wheat, or some Bashkirs on horseback with whom their Cossack exchanged animated remarks in the Tatar tongue. At all the posting stations the horses were fresh and well-fed, and the half-roubles provided by Albina for vodka ensured that the drivers drove the horses, as they put it, *like Feldjägers,*[9] galloping all the way.

At the first posting station when the first driver had led away the horses and the new driver had not yet brought out the new ones and the Cossack had gone into the yard, Albina bent down and asked her husband how he was feeling and whether he needed anything.

'Excellent, don't worry. I don't need anything. I wouldn't mind lying here for two whole days.'

Towards evening they drew into a large village called Derchaga. To give her husband the chance to stretch his limbs and refresh himself Albina told the driver to stop not at the posting station but at a coaching inn, then immediately gave the Cossack some money and sent him off to buy milk and eggs. The tarantass was standing beneath a projecting roof. It was dark in the courtyard, and having stationed Ludwika to watch out for the Cossack, Albina released her husband and gave him food and drink, after which he crawled back into his hiding-place before the Cossack returned. They had a new team of horses brought round and continued on their way. Albina felt her spirits rising more and more and was unable to contain her cheerfulness and general delight. There was no one to talk to other than Ludwika, the Cossack and her little dog Trezorka, so she amused herself with them. Despite her plainness, at every contact with a man Ludwika would immediately detect him sending amorous glances in her direction, and she now suspected something of the sort in her relations with the burly and genial Ural Cossack with unusually bright and kind blue eyes who was escorting them and behaving most agreeably towards the two women,

9 Couriers or special messengers.

treating them with gentle and good-humoured kindness. Apart from Trezorka, whom Albina had to threaten to prevent him from sniffing about under the seat, she now found amusement in watching Ludwika's coquettish advances to the Cossack, who was quite unaware of the intentions being ascribed to him, and smiled agreeably at her every remark. Albina, stimulated by her sense of danger, by her growing conviction that their plan was succeeding, and by the splendid weather and the fresh air of the steppe, was enjoying the return of those youthful high spirits and merriment which she had not felt for such a long time. Migurski could hear her cheerful chatter and he too, despite the physical discomfort which he concealed from them (for he was extremely hot and tormented by thirst), forgot about himself and rejoiced in Albina's joy.

Towards evening on the second day something came into sight in distance through the mist. It was the town of Saratov and the Volga. The Cossack with his farsighted steppe-dweller's eyes could distinguish the Volga and the masts of the ships, and he pointed them out to Ludwika. Ludwika said that she could see them too. But Albina could make out nothing, and remarked loudly, for her husband to hear:

'Saratov, the Volga' – and as though she was talking to Trezorka, Albina described to her husband everything as it came into view.

XI

Albina did not let the carriage drive into Saratov but made the driver stop on the left bank of the river at the settlement of Pokrovskaya directly opposite the town itself. Here she hoped that in the course of the night she would be able to talk to her husband and even get him out of the box. But throughout the short spring night the Cossack did not go away from the tarantass but sat next to it in an empty cart which was standing beneath a projecting roof. Ludwika, on Albina's instructions, stayed in the tarantass and, convinced that it was on her account that the Cossack would not leave the tarantass, laughed and winked and hid her face in her shawl. But Albina could see nothing amusing in this and grew more and more worried, unable to understand why the Cossack was so doggedly attached to the vicinity of the tarantass.

Several times that short night in which dusk almost merged into morning twilight, Albina left her room in the coaching inn and walked along the stuffy verandah to the porch at the back of the building. The Cossack was still not asleep but was sitting on the empty cart, his legs dangling. Only just before dawn when the cocks were already awaking and calling from one farmyard to the next did Albina, going down to the yard, find an opportunity to exchange a few words with her husband. The Cossack was now snoring, sprawled in the cart. She cautiously approached the tarantass and knocked on the box.

'Juzio!' – No answer. 'Juzio, Juzio,' she repeated more loudly, now becoming alarmed.

'What is it my dear, what is the matter?' came Migurski's sleepy voice from inside the box.

'Why didn't you answer me?'

'I was asleep,' he replied, and from the sound of his voice she knew that he was smiling. 'Well, and can I come out?' he asked.

'No, you can't, the Cossack is here.' And as she spoke she glanced at the Cossack asleep in the cart.

And strange to say, although the Cossack was snoring, his eyes, his kindly blue eyes, were open. He looked at her, and only when his glance had lighted on her, closed his eyes.

'Did I just imagine it, or was he really not asleep?' Albina wondered. 'I expect I imagined it,' she thought, and turned back to her husband.

'Try to put up with it a little longer,' she said. 'Do you want anything to eat?'

'No. But I should like to smoke.'

Albina again turned to look at the Cossack. He was sleeping.

'Yes, I imagined it,' she thought.

'I am going to see the governor now.'

'Well, it is as good a time as any ...'

And Albina took a dress out of her trunk and went back to her room to change.

When she had changed into her best widow's dress Albina took a boat across the Volga. On the embankment she hired a cab-driver and drove to the governor's residence. The governor agreed to see her. This pretty little Polish widow with her sweet smile, speaking beautiful French, made a tremendous impression on the governor, an elderly man who liked to appear younger than his age. He granted all her requests and asked her to come to see him again the next day to receive a written order to the town governor of Tsaritsyn. Rejoicing in the success of her petition and the effect of her own attractiveness which she could see from the governor's manner, Albina, happy and full of hope, drove back in a carriage down the unmetalled street towards the jetty. The sun had already risen above the woods and its slanting beams were already playing on the rippling water of the mighty river. To right and left on the hillside she could see apple trees like white clouds, covered in fragrant blossom. A forest of masts came into view by the river bank and the sails of the boats showed white on the water lit up by the sun and rippling in a light breeze. At the landing-stage, having consulted the driver, Albina asked whether it was possible to engage a boat to take her to Astrakhan, and at once dozens of noisy, cheerful boatmen offered her their boats and their services. She came to an arrangement with one of the boatmen she particularly liked the look of and went to inspect his open-hulled barge which was lying amid a crowd of others at the wharf. The boat had a mast which could be stepped at will and a sail to allow it to use the power of the wind. In case there should be no wind there were oars provided, and two healthy, cheerful-looking barge-haulers-cum-oarsmen, who were sitting on the boat enjoying the sun. The jovial pilot advised her not to leave the tarantass behind but to remove the wheels and instal it in the boat. 'It'll go in just right, and you'll be more comfortable sitting in there. If God grants us a bit of good weather we shall make the run down to Astrakhan in five days clear.'

Albina bargained with the boatman and instructed him to come to the Logins' inn at the Pokrovskaya settlement so that he could have a look at the tarantass and collect a deposit. The whole thing worked out more easily than she had expected. In a state of rapturous happiness Albina crossed the Volga once more, and bidding farewell to the driver, made for the coaching inn.

XII

The Cossack Danilo Lifanov came from Strelyetski Outpost[10] in the highlands between the Volga and Ural rivers. He was thirty-four years old and he was just completing the final month of his term of Cossack service. His family consisted of an old grandfather of ninety who still remembered the time of Pugachov, two brothers, the daughter-in-law of the elder brother (sentenced to exile with hard labour in Siberia for being an Old Believer), Danilo's wife and his two daughters. His father had been killed in the war against the French. Danilo was the head of the household. On the farm they had sixteen horses, two ploughing teams of oxen, and fifteen hundred *sazhens* of private land, all ploughed and sown with their own wheat. He, Danilo, had done his military service in Orenburg and Kazan and was now getting to the end of his period of duty. He kept firmly to the Old Faith: he did not smoke or drink, did not use dishes in common with worldly people, and also kept strictly to his word. In all his undertakings he was slow, steady and reliable and he carried out everything his commander instructed him to do with his complete attention, not forgetting his purpose for a single moment until the job was properly finished. Now he was under orders to escort these two Polish women with the

---

10 A settlement inhabited by descendants of the Streltsy (archers), a state security force established by Ivan the Terrible and disbanded by Peter the Great (1708).

coffins to Saratov, to see that nothing bad befell them on the journey, to ensure that they travelled quietly and did not get up to any mischief, and on reaching Saratov to hand them over decently and in order to the authorities. So he had delivered them to Saratov with their little dog and their coffins and all. These women were charming and well-behaved despite being Polish and they had done nothing bad. But here at the Pokrovskaya settlement last evening he had seen how the little dog had jumped up into the tarantass and begun yelping and wagging his tail, and from under the seat in the tarantass he had heard somebody's voice. One of the Polish women – the older one – seeing the little dog in the tarantass had looked very scared for some reason, and grabbed hold of the dog and carried it away.

'There's something in there,' thought the Cossack, and he started to keep his eyes open. When the younger Polish woman had come out to the tarantass in the night he had pretended to be asleep, and he had distinctly heard a man's voice coming from the box. Early in the morning he had gone to the police station and reported that the Polish women such as were entrusted to him and not travelling of their own free will, instead of dead bodies were carrying some live man or other in their box.

When Albina, in her mood of jubilant happiness, convinced that now it was all over and that in a few days they would be free, approached the coaching inn she was surprised to see in the gateway a fashionable-looking carriage and pair with a third trace horse and two Cossacks. A crowd of people thronged round the gateway, staring into the yard.

She was so full of hope and vitality that it never entered her head that this carriage and pair and the people clustering round might have anything to do with her. She walked into the inn yard and at once, looking under the canopy where the tarantass was standing, saw that a crowd of people were gathered round it, and at the same moment heard the anguished barking of Trezorka. The most dreadful thing that could have happened had happened. In front of the tarantass, his spotless uniform with its bright buttons, shoulder-straps and lacquered boots shining in the sun, stood a portly man with black side-whiskers, saying something in a loud imperious voice. Before him, between two soldiers, in peasant clothes and with wisps of hay in his tousled hair, stood her Juzio, raising and lowering his powerful shoulders, as if perplexed by what was going on around him. Trezorka, unaware that he was the cause of the whole disaster, stood with bristling coat, barking with carefree dislike at the chief of police. On seeing Albina Migurski winced and made to go towards her, but the soldiers held him back.

'Never mind, Albina, never mind,' said Migurski, smiling at her with his gentle smile.

'And here is the little lady in person!' said the chief of police. 'Welcome to you, madam. And are these the coffins of your babies? Eh?' he said, pointing to Migurski.

Albina made no reply, but simply crossed her arms on her breast and gazed in open-mouthed horror at her husband.

As often happens in the very last moments of life and at other crucial points in human experience, she felt and foresaw in an instant a multitude of thoughts and feelings, while not yet grasping her misfortune or believing in it. Her first feeling was one long familiar to her – the feeling of wounded pride at the sight of her hero-husband, humiliated before these coarse, bestial men who now had him in their power. 'How dare they hold *him*, the very best of men, in their power!' Her second feeling, which swept over her almost at the same time as the first, was an awareness of the disaster which was now complete. And this consciousness of disaster revived in her the memory of the chief disaster of her life, the death of her children. And now once again the question came to her: what for? why had her children been taken away? The question 'Why have my children been taken away?' called forth a further question: Why was her beloved, the best of men, her husband, now in torment, now being destroyed? What for? And then she remembered that a shameful punishment awaited him, and that she, she alone, was to blame.

'What is your relation to this man? Is this man your husband?' repeated the chief of police.

'What for, what for?!' she screamed out, and bursting into hysterical laughter she collapsed on to the box, which had been removed from the tarantass and was standing on the ground nearby. Her whole body shaking with sobs and with tears streaming down her face, Ludwika went up to her.

'Panienka,[11] my dearest Panienka! *Jak Boga kokham*,[12] nothing will happen to you, nothing will happen!' she said, distractedly running her hands over her mistress.

Migurski was handcuffed and led out of the inn yard. Seeing what was happening, Albina ran after him.

'Forgive me, forgive me!' she cried. 'It is all my fault, I alone am to blame!'

'They'll sort out who is to blame in court. And I've no doubt the case will involve you,' said the chief of police, pushing her out of the way.

They led Migurski down to the river crossing and Albina, not knowing herself why she was doing so, followed him and refused to listen to Ludwika's advice.

All this time the Cossack Danilo Lifanov was standing leaning against a wheel of the tarantass and glaring angrily now at the chief of police, now at Albina, and now at his own feet.

When Migurski had been led away Trezorka, now left alone, wagged his tail and began to fawn on him. The Cossack had grown used to the dog during the journey. Suddenly he pulled himself upright, tore his cap from his head and hurled it with all his strength on to the ground, pushed Trezorka away from him with his foot, and went into the eating-house. Once inside he ordered vodka and drank solidly for a day and a night, drinking away all the money he had on him and everything he had with him, and only on the next night, when he woke up in a ditch, was he able to stop thinking about the question which had been tormenting him: why had he done it, informing the authorities about the little Polish woman's husband in the box?

11 Diminutive of 'pani' (mistress).
12 As I love God.

Migurski was tried and sentenced to run the gauntlet of a thousand rods. His relatives and Wanda, who had connections in St Petersburg, managed after much trouble to obtain a mitigation of the punishment, and instead he was sent into permanent exile in Siberia. Albina travelled after him.

And Tsar Nicholas Pavlovich rejoiced that he had crushed the hydra of revolution not only in Poland, but throughout Europe, and took pride in the fact that he had not betrayed the ordinances of the Russian autocracy, but for the good of the Russian people had kept Poland in Russia's power. And men wearing decorations and gilt uniforms lauded him for this to such an extent, that when he came to die he sincerely believed that he was a great man and that his life had been a great blessing for humanity in general and for Russians in particular, those Russians to whose corruption and stupefaction he had unwittingly directed all his powers.

ABOUT THE TRANSLATORS

LOUISE and AYLMER MAUDE spent much of their lives in Russia. Their Quaker background led them to share many of Tolstoy's views on spiritual life, moral obligation and passive resistance to violence, and they helped him to organize the Doukhobor migration to Canada in 1893. Aylmer Maude, whose business activities left him time to write a biography of his friend, also translated most of Tolstoy's major works in partnership with his wife. These translations, which were commended by the author himself, are still widely regarded as the best.

NIGEL J. COOPER read French and Russian at Christ Church, Oxford. He has recently retired from Middlesex University where he was a Principal Lecturer in Modern Languages.

ABOUT THE INTRODUCER

JOHN BAYLEY is former Thomas Warton Professor of English Literature at the University of Oxford. His many books include *Tolstoy and the Novel*; *Pushkin: A Comparative Commentary*; *The Short Story: Henry James to Elizabeth Bowen*; *An Essay on Hardy, Shakespeare and Tragedy* and a detailed study of A. E. Housman's poems. He has also written several novels.

This book is set in BEMBO which was cut
by the punch-cutter Francesco Griffo
for the Venetian printer-publisher
Aldus Manutius in early 1495
and first used in a pamphlet
by a young scholar
named Pietro
Bembo.